The Harsh Lands

The Complete Survival Trilogy

F. D. Brant

F. D. Brant

GRESHAM, OREGON

Copyright © 2016 by **F. D. Brant**

All rights reserved. No part of this publication may be reproduced, distributed or transmitted in any form or by any means, without prior written permission.

F. D. Brant
PO Box 522
Gresham, Oregon 97030
www.fdbrant.com

Publisher's Note: This is a work of fiction. Names, characters, places, and incidents are a product of the author's imagination. Locales and public names are sometimes used for atmospheric purposes. Any resemblance to actual people, living or dead, or to businesses, companies, events, institutions, or locales is completely coincidental.

Book Layout © 2014 BookDesignTemplates.com

The Harsh Lands/ F. D. Brant. -- 1st ed.
ISBN 978-1-946179-00-5

This work is dedicated to family. After all where would we be
without our families?

Let tomorrow bring what it may.

—THOUGHTS OF JEROD FROM, OF GODS STRANGERS
AND MESSENGERS

CONTENTS

TIME OF ISOLATION..7

DESPERATE TO SURVIVE...............................371

A TASTE OF HISTORY PAST............................803

C H A P T E R   O N E   O F

Time of Isolation

Sampson hurried along the thoroughfare trying to move as fast as his overweight body would allow. He needed to find his supervisor now. Unfortunately she was located completely on the opposite side of the communications complex. While he was in charge of his section, an underling, the news he had needed to be brought to Shana's attention personally and could not be sent over the circuits. So by avoiding eye contact with the many others he passed, and breathing quite hard from the exertions, he continued to move with strong determination. It had happened again. This was the fourth time in the past annuals, and he was shocked when it had happened on his shift, with his team. Just what was going on? Finally nearing his destination he found that he was raising a sweat. He just hated sweating, but this time he had to endure it as well as making this contact with his boss. He had never liked Shana, but knew that he could never become a supervisor of her level. First, he was not one born into the proper order, and second he knew that he could never match the intelligence necessary to oversee such an operation as this.

Finally reaching her entrance he stopped, caught his breath and tried to calm down. These meetings were rare, and he preferred it that way. Then gathering his courage he entered and encountered Susan, the one who ran interference for the boss. Again he had never liked her either, as it seemed that she always put on an air of superiority around any who were lower or worked under Shana. "Susan, I need to have a conversation with Supervisor Shana, and no before you ask, this cannot wait."

Looking down at him she said, "Who are you to just barge in here? You do not have any right to demand anything, ah . . . let's see . . . *underling* supervisor Sampson. Do I have it right?"

When she said these things it seemed as if she was attempting to get something out of her mouth such as a bad taste. Shaking his head he could tell that things were going from bad to worse. But what could he do? What he had was critical and they had been told that if another incident happened that he, or any of the under supervisors, had to go to their supervisors immediately and inform no one but them. He wasn't even supposed to inform the underworkers for the lead supervisors. It was to be for their eyes and ears only. Carefully holding his anger in control he gritted his teeth and said. "Yes, you have it right. I must see Lead Supervisor Shana now without delay."

"Without delay? What is it that could be so important from your *minor* position that could even require a minute of Supervisor Shana? Her time is always filled, so, if you please, make an appointment and come back later. You are interrupting my work and I for one will not allow you to interrupt hers. Now get out of here before I report you!"

About this time Lead Supervisor Shana hearing the loud conversation in the outer office went to investigate. Catching the ending conversation from her underworker, and seeing one of the under supervisors from the communications section, she became curious. Underworker Susan catching the gaze of Sampson turned and saw Shana there and started apologizing for interrupting her work and that she had everything in control and this minor supervisor was just leaving. *Why was he here?* Then she saw that under supervisor Sampson was looking intently at her. She also knew that he had never liked her, so again why was he here? Looking directly at him Shana asked. "Under supervisor Sampson may I inquire, why are you here?"

Again looking directly at her, he was at a loss for words. The directive had been explicit, nothing could be said to any others just his boss. "I have something that must be given to you, but only to you." He stammered.

"What's so important that it couldn't be communicated over the circuits?" Then she saw a troubled look on his face, and indecision there. Yet at the same time a look that said that he would not give up on this.

"Ma'am, this has to do with the most recent directives that said that if a specific circumstance or event happened that I or any of the other under supervisors must report in person, immediately without delay, and I for one am not going to violate such a mandate. I am here as it requests."

Shaking her head, she had really never liked this under supervisor. She had never liked people who had let themselves go like this. He seemed fat and lazy, and seemed to be the type that used the rules and regulations strictly as written — never bending or thinking outside what was there, one with little imagination, yet one who did what was necessary and kept his underworkers to task – one which caused as little friction as possible. "Which of the many mandates would this one be, under supervisor Sampson?" With so many coming out she never had time to read many of them anyway, depending on her staff to keep her informed.

Now what, Sampson thought, the mandate had been specific. No one but his supervisor could hear what he had to say. Then he remembered that if there was situations like this that he could specify a color to let her know. Now if only he could remember the color. Blue! Blue was that color. "Ma'am, ah color it blue", was all he said.

When he stated the color, she immediately paused. He had given her a code color that reflected an emergency of some kind and could be private and for her eyes and ears only. She then turned to her underworker and said, "Under Supervisor Sampson may enter." She then turned around and went back inside of her office wondering now what could be so important for him to have used that code. She didn't have to wait long as he entered her office right behind her. "I don't have much time, what is it that is so important?"

"Ma'am, do you have this room secured for silence? The directive said that before this information was to be given that all security features must be activated."

Sitting back down at her desk, she motioned him to a seat, and then pushed a few buttons. "Okay, I have activated the security. Again what is it that required you to use the code word?"

Not quite sure how to continue he hesitated and then said. "Ma'am we've lost communications with another city. It has gone silent without warning. We have tried for the required amount of time to reestablish contact, but like the others it is like it never was."

Silent and shocked at what had just been relayed to her, many questions went through her mind. *Was it just a temporary loss or is this going to be like the others? Which one this time and what truly is going on? If it is confirmed then this will be the fourth city lost.* She slumped her shoulders and then asked, "Which City have we lost contact with?"

"Terra ma'am. It is one of our larger cities and had many a backup, especially in communications. But without warning it went silent and we have been trying now for hours to reestablish contact, but all we get is silence and static."

After minor supervisor Sampson had left she sat for a short time defeated by the news. Something was happening to their cities, but with no information there were no answers. She knew that right now she would have to drop whatever had been planned for the day and head out and find the other department heads to see if the information that she had been given was confirmed there. If so then they would have to inform the council. *Four gone now, that's a frightening thought. Just what's happening to them? If they are being destroyed, why were there no refugees – again if a disaster had befallen them why no contact?* Yet, when one looked at the order of loss, it appeared that something else was going on.

* * *

When the information reached the council they immediately called an emergency session. When one city had disappeared off the grid it had been a major concern – but now with four gone it had become something unthinkable. They knew that they were vulnerable to the primitive tribes and clans that existed here. But so far they had just warred among themselves, more concerned with each other. As far as these tribes and clans knew, the cities did not exist, and if they thought that they might, it was more legend than reality. So what had changed? Why were their cities disappearing?

Because of the low populations, they knew that there was no way for them to fight or go to war against these people. So instead technology had been developed that blocked the cities from view. It required a lot of power to maintain the illusions that they created. So, most of the funds and work, went into maintaining and upgrading the power units. They even had created large backups just in case something happened to the main units. Over time they had been able to create both holographic images of the lands around them to give the illusion that where the cities were located was desolate useless lands – to further the chance that the primitives would not be interested in investigating the areas. Plus a minor force field that required a device worn by the citizens to be able to pass through. With all of the city's needs existing inside of these protections there was very little reason to leave. They also kept devices in the cities that allowed them to monitor the few entrances and exits into the cities.

They had depended on these protections for generations and it had always worked. So they had grown complacent. Because of this complacency they had few that could even fight, as it had never been necessary in the past. Yet something had changed, and now the cities were disappearing. With no hard evidence they did not even know why. So with the loss of this fourth city they, the council, had almost panicked. They spent half a day uselessly arguing back and forth coming up with no answers or solutions. Until finally the head of the council called a break realizing that until they had some answers there would be no solutions. Sione, the council head then summoned the *underworker to the council* Sayvon to his side and said, "Sayvon, I need you to get in contact with Shayne. Have him report immediately to my chamber. We need answers and we can sit here all day debating and still have nothing in the end. Do not waste any time, I am calling a recess when I go back into the council meeting area. If necessary give him the code color yellow. It will let him know that this is most serious."

"Where would I find this Shayne, sir? This is someone I am unfamiliar with. In fact I do not ever remember this person ever mentioned at all."

"Not surprising really. You see he is the leader of what we thought was a program that we would never use. He has been before us many times a long time ago, imploring us to keep what he works on . . . his life work really, alive. I must admit that there were a number of times we almost cancelled his section, but that is old history. You will find him and the ones who work for him at the edge of the city close to the wilderness that lies beyond. The compound is actually blocked off from the city and those who live within this compound are trained from their youth to be what they are. They usually work in teams of two, and if siblings so much the better. Here, if you look at this map of the city they are located there." Taking Sayvon to a picture on the wall he flipped a switch, which then revealed the map. He pointed to an area that seemed almost unused. There appeared to be no major structures, nothing to indicate industry or farming, just a few minor structures and that was all. It could have been one of the many parks, but was so far out of the way that it would be one that no one would ever have need of visiting.

Looking closely at the map Sayvon asked, "I don't really see how you even travel there. And why would anyone want to live and work there anyway?"

"Understand this, if anyone is going to solve this puzzle and what is happening to our sister cities then it is he or one of his teams. Remember we have become a people that have depended on our machines and as such probably could not survive on our own without them. Shayne is a throwback to an earlier time when we were just beginning to bring our machines on line. He and any of his many teams could survive out there in the wilderness and among the primitives. Something neither you nor I, and I suspect the rest of this city, or any of the other cities could do. You see we are the last city to even allow this program to continue. So he and his teams may be our last chance to keep what we have. Or become like those other disappearing cities leaving not a trace of whom we are or what we did behind. I suspect we are dealing with a change within the primitive world. And somewhere along that line they have learned of our existence and worse have found a way to penetrate our illusions and protections. We are not a warrior race, and I suspect that we are an easy people to conquer if an attacking army can get past our protections. So please hurry, and if you look closely you can see that you actually have to go this way, away from this compound before you can work back to it." Then pointing again at the map he traced out the route that Sayvon would have to take. "Now here you should find some signs that actually will direct you to the compound. The signs will simply say The Wilderness Space."

Sayvon shuddered at the thought of having to go into a space like the wilderness outside the city. He was a citizen of the city and had no wants or desires to be even close to a place that simulated the wilderness. But he had been given a directive and he would follow it to the best of his ability. What Sione had relayed to him worried him more than this trip he had to take. Now once he found it could he convince this Shayne to follow him back? He had never been given that code color before. The highest he had ever used was blue. He did not know that there was one higher than blue until now. Now he wondered if there was any that was higher than yellow? He did not know. While he looked at the map he also realized that it would take him the rest of this day to reach this compound. It would be dark and if this area simulated the wilderness what was in there? He never considered himself brave but now had no choice but to face this unknown.

CHAPTER TWO

Sayvon had gotten lost a couple of times, as this was part of the city that he had never been in before. It seemed to be much older than the portion he worked and lived in. In fact one of the major signs he had come across stated "Old City". It seemed to be poorer and more run down, but that could be an illusion since you could see the age in the buildings. The pathways and sidewalks were worn and narrow in comparison to the main city, and as dusk approached it appeared that even the lighting was dim and dungy making the area appear to be unsafe. Yet he knew that it was illusion since there was little crime. At times he would pass couples arm and arm paying him little or no attention. And then there seemed to be many children running around playing their many games. He with his nervousness just pushed on until he reached the edge and saw one of the signs pointing him in the proper direction. It was fully dark by the time he had reached the area and was immediately blocked by a wall that had to be twice his height.

Why the wall? Walking along the wall, it just seemed to go on forever.

Eventually he reached a small door that had a light above it, and what he guessed was a monitoring device. Looking closely he saw what appeared to be a summoning device. It showed little use and left him wondering if it actually worked. So he pressed the button and found that his initial assessment was accurate. The button had not been used in who knew how long, and was resisting his effort to push it in. Finally it seemed to loosen up enough and appeared to function. He waited what he considered was adequate time and with no response tried again and he decided to knock also. Again waiting for what seemed a long time and again without response he gave up and started to leave, then jumped when he heard the grating of the door sliding open. Turning around he saw a youth, but one who was dressed strangely. There seemed to be an air about him that made Sayvon really *look* at him. He couldn't place the difference but it was there. The youth stood there silently waiting for Sayvon to say something. "Ah, I'm Sayvon; I have been directed by the head of the council Sione to seek out Shayne. I have something for his eyes and ears only."

The youth only nodded, and then signaled Sayvon to follow, turning around and immediately headed back inside expecting Sayvon to follow him. Realizing that was what the youth wanted he finally got himself moving and as he entered the compound the door closed behind him with a heavy thump causing him to jump and cringe. It sounded so final. Then the sounds within the compound started to assail his ears. It was too dark to see, and he found himself stumbling as the youth, sure footed, continued and was actually outdistancing him.

The youth seemed to have an easy flow to his movements like he was a part of this world and not the one Sayvon had just come from. There seemed to be a confidence, a quiet confidence that spoke of tests and trials that had been overcome. *What is this place anyway? Who is this youth?* He had never said a word or offered him his name. Again why did this place even exist? From the signs he knew that the area was not a secret, yet in all of his life he had never heard of it or what its function was. One thing for sure he was learning quickly.

As his eyes adjusted to the darkness he could now see that they appeared to be walking on a dirt path that led up to some small structures just ahead. He then noticed that the youth leading him was barefoot. The structures in the distance seemed to be lit, but the light emanating from the windows were weak and seemed to flicker. Why was that so? He was so out of his element that he could not come up with any satisfactory answer at all. Eventually he was led to one of the units in the center. Here the youth that had brought him here pointed to this one building. On the door he could barely make out the name Shayne. That was all it said. There was nothing to identify that he was even the one in charge. Why was that so? It was something else that did not make sense. Turning around he saw that the youth was leaving and heading towards one of the other buildings leaving him alone. *Were they all this way here?* Shrugging, he went up to the door and started to knock only to have it open. A man stared at him seemingly sizing Sayvon up immediately. Sayvon saw someone who was only a little taller than him, but his skin appeared to be brown, and if he guessed right this man had to be lighter than he in weight. There seemed to be no fat on this man at all. *Didn't he eat?* The next thing that registered was this man was not young. There were streaks of gray in his dark brown hair, and he also had facial hair . . . something that was never seen within the city at all.

Smiling Shayne said in a soft voice. "Come in, come in! I don't get too many visitors from the city here at all. And to have one from the council is so rare that it has only happened once in my lifetime." He then signaled Sayvon up the short set of wooden steps and inside the small building. Once inside he saw why the lights seemed so dim and flickering. Instead of the lighting that was powered by the power units of the city, what was here appeared to be lamps and candles. The lamps had some type of clear oil inside of them with a wick and a chimney. Everything within glowed under the flickering yellow light. Nowhere that he looked could he find anything of the city. The furniture was rough and seemed to be made from natural things. Even the cooking appeared to have been accomplished over an open fire type conveyance. As his eyes continued to search the room he found nothing in it that was familiar. Then looking back at his host he realized that the clothes he was wearing also appeared to be made by hand. There absolutely was nothing of manufacture here. It appeared that someone's hands had made everything here. Then noticing the floor he saw what appeared to be an animal skin laid out like a rug. Stammering he asked, "Is . . . was that real?"

Smiling Shayne said, "Of course. It at one time was a living animal. By watching you, I believe that you have searched this whole area and, I assure you that you will not find anything that you commonly use in the city. Everything you see was either living or was constructed from natural materials. You see, here one must be able to live in the wilderness beyond. That means that what you take for granted does not exist here. So one must learn to use what is available. If you do not then you have *no* business here."

That last statement seemed to be directed at Sayvon. And in truth if it wasn't, it would have been easy to interpret it that way. This Shayne had a way of looking at a person that appeared to look to your very soul, judge you, and then if found wanting, ignore – or at least give no signs of trust. *Why had he agreed to come here?* He was so far out of his element that he was even at loss as what to say. He again stammered, "Sir, I have been sent by Sione to have you report to him immediately."

"Sione? I am afraid that name does not seem familiar. I assume he is of the council since I can see on your shirt the badge identifying you as the underworker to the council. Who is he anyway?"

Somewhat affronted by this revelation and question, he became indignant. "He, sir, is the head of the council!"

Laughing Shayne said, "Did I ruffle your feathers? You must remember that here you and your city do not exist. We do not keep up with the policies or politics, and who may be in charge at any certain time. As I said earlier it is rare that any city member visits here, and rarer still when someone from the council puts in an appearance. So why would it matter to us?"

Sputtering now with a deeper indignation Sayvon said. "Because it is the generosity of the council that has made sure that your section still exists. If it were not for them keeping it alive, then like in the other cities you would not have been able to continue!"

"Is that all? Gee, and to think that because of the council, which, by the way, this operation has cost them little to nothing, that I have a job. Gee, I just don't know what to say."

To Sayvon the sarcasm was so thick he could have cut it. "It . . . it's true! We are the only city left that still allows this to continue. With just a stroke of a pen you and your section could be gone like everywhere else."

"It's the other cities' loss. And if this council were stupid enough to eliminate the only section that could give them intelligence on what is happening outside of the cities then it, in the end, would be their loss. Oh, I'm sorry; I've not even offered you anything or a place to sit. Where are my manners? By the way, are you finished with your worthless threats? And can you tell me why you are here, especially since it is after dark. You have me curious, as no one comes here after dark."

One thing for sure this Shayne had continued to keep him off balance since he had arrived here. He thought that his political savvy and the ability to spar verbally were pretty good. But he was finding out that he was no match for this Shayne. There was nothing he could use as a weapon against him. It just seemed that he did not care, and it appeared that he was being toyed with. Not by some amateur, but someone who appeared to be more amused by his attempts. Something like a cat playing with a mouse, and he was that mouse. It made him more uncomfortable. To be out of his league here was an understatement. How did one attack someone that seemed not to care? "Look, I know it is unusual for someone from the city to come here. In fact I did not even know that this existed until today. As far as what you do here I don't know that either. But I was sent to get you. Sione, who is the council head, said that it is urgent, and to not wait until the morning when it would be daytime here. So I am here because of that request. At least you could honor it and come back with me and find out what it is he wants to discuss with you. I was told that this had to be a face to face meeting, and he directed me here."

Again laughing Shayne said, "You fool. Here, other than what you saw at the gate into this place, there is nothing of the city, which means that there are no devices or such that allows me to talk over the airwaves to anyone. If anyone wants to talk to me they have to talk to me in person. So you, thinking that it will show some importance, by showing up here to talk with me really means nothing or anything at all. Yes, there is a part of this facility that has those capabilities, but they are mobile units – off limits except during training . . . normally shut down and inoperative. Here, everyone learns that it is important to have direct contact. There is much that can be learned from another when you do that. For instance you are both extremely nervous and have a fear of this place. Plus I can read that you have an overblown view of yourself, where you work, and whom you work for. It is there for any to read." Then shaking his head he sat down in a chair that was next to a table. He signaled for Sayvon to do the same.

Now sitting across from Shayne again he asked himself, *who is this person? He surely did not have any proper respect for the city and its leadership. So why would Sione want to speak with him?* Personally it appeared to be a lost cause. Shrugging his shoulders he then said, "I see that I have wasted my time and yours. I will go back and report to Sione that you are not interested."

"Interested in what? You have yet to even present anything other than the leader of the council wants my presence. With so little presented you have yet to give me a reason. For all I know he wants to show me off to some of his political friends. I do not have time for such nonsense."

What Shayne said was true. He had only said that the leader of the council wanted to see him. But since being here he had been so out of his element that he had been completely off balance. He had never faced anyone like this – someone who could read him like an open book. After all he had prided himself in the ability to hide his true feelings and motives. Yet here before him was someone who had just proven that premise to be false. "Look, I was sent to get you. There is an emergency and he, Sione, felt that you and your teams were the only ones who could help."

"Ah, now that's better. Was that so hard? What kind of emergency are you talking about here anyway? I haven't sensed anything unusual happening within this city . . . not that I get into it very often."

"Nothing has happened to our city, but that does not mean that something isn't going to happen."

Curious now Shayne asked. "And what do you mean by that statement?"

"Look I am not at liberty to say, but I was told that if I was unsuccessful that I was to say yellow."

That stopped him. Yellow was the code for most serious. Once he heard that he did not say anything else. He stood up, grabbed a coat and headed for the door. "Aren't you coming? After all you needed to get me to come along. So I'm coming along. Lead away!"

Shocked and still off balance, this sudden change left him even more unsure. "Okay, you're not planning on doing something are you?"

Shaking his head Shayne said. "Now what would give you that idea? You gave a color code and it answered my most immediate questions. I will now go see your Sione. So lead away. And do not worry I'll protect you from the dark."

* * *

Back at his cabin now after being with the head council member all night, he remembered that as he had begun his walk to the council chambers if the quoting of such a high emergency color had been appropriate. After all, there was only one color higher and that was black. Between blue and yellow there were also two others with green being the one just above blue, and brown just below yellow. White was all clear, and red the first towards emergencies. So the order began with white, then red, blue, green, brown, yellow, and finally black. When Sione brought him up to date as to what had been happening he knew that it could have been very easy for this Sione to have used the final emergency color, yet, by not doing so showed him that maybe this councilperson might actually have some common smarts. Something that appeared to be lacking in most politicians and one of the many reasons he normally tried to avoid them.

Four cities gone! What had happened? At least this Sione knew who to turn to, to find out. He and his teams were the only ones equipped to live outside the cities, and having heard that his teams were the last to exist in any of the cities left him sad. Had the cities progressed so far in both their ego and ignorance to think that something like this could never happen? The answer was obvious to him, *yes*. Now it would fall on him and his teams to try and find out what was going on, and who was responsible. He suspected by the way they disappeared that it had something to do with the primitive tribes.

Somehow through a failure or something similar one of the cities became known, and once known was then destroyed. And if some of the tribes had united, these combined tribes would be a force to reckon with. Since they had to survive in the wilderness, and the many skirmishes that happened continually between them, they were a strong wily enemy, while the cities would be a weak easy target. Once a tribe got beyond the outer defenses then the rest would fall quick with barely a whimper. This enemy would barely raise a sweat. Then by seeing how the cities were hidden, these primitives would seek out other such areas. And each time one was found they would learn more and it would become easier. In truth the facts supported this. There had been a large amount of time between the disappearance of the first city and the second. But then the times became shorter and shorter as the third and fourth city vanished.

It was time to bring in his second and then get some sleep. He knew with the information that he had that there were to be many sleepless nights ahead of them. Time was short, and the longer it took to find out what was going on, the more chances other cities would fall. So heading back out to the middle of the compound he rang the bell with three short rings signaling assembly and waited. Within a few breaths the compound filled with the students and teachers of the wilderness. He waited until the restlessness left the crowd and silence followed. Looking around at his teams he felt proud to be a part of them. Now they would be tested to the fullest. Had there been enough done? Or would he find, like the cities disappearing, that they were lacking. Looking around at the gathering crowd he said. "After generations of work here where everything was just simulation and scouting, we now are to face a real test." He could see the smiles on their faces as they anticipated actually doing something. "I would like the leaders and trainers to remain here. The rest of you are dismissed, and shortly after I talk with this group they will pass on to you what we have discussed. Be prepared, our time is short, and our very existence may come down to what we learn and do. Other than that, it is all I can relay to you at this moment. This will involve everybody, so there is no need to fear that any of you will be left behind. Thank you." He turned and headed for the common eating area where the teams would meet as a group. As he left he saw that the trainers and leaders were following him and the rest heading back to whatever assignment they had before the call to assemble.

CHAPTER THREE

He had gone over in his mind, as he was walking back to the compound, what needed to be done. But fatigue had clouded his mind, and while he had some ideas it was important to use the whole team to lay out a plan of action. Once he entered the common eating area he signaled the leaders to sit at any of the many long tables. "I've just spent the night with the leader of the council. I can see from your questioning looks as to why I did such a thing, since you and I know that we rarely see anybody here let alone someone from the ruling class. In fact, as you know, I have only seen one here in my lifetime up until last night. I figured that most likely it would be bad news, something like, they had finally decided that we were to be closed down as the costs of running something like this, even though it's not much, was not worth keeping it in operation. In fact I had a confirmation that the other cities have already shut down this operation and we are the only one that is remaining." Letting that soak in for a moment before continuing he then said, "Fortunately for us that was not the reason for the visit or the request that I return to the chambers of the leader – I was given yellow." He could see the reaction from the group when he had given them the color. Watching them he could see them looking at each other and with concern in their very beings showing through he said. "Yeah my very reaction – I know that many of you have relatives, and loved ones living in the city as I.

They in the city do not understand what it is that we do here, and as you know I have a sister and her family there also. We, like you, and yours, are very close although we do not get to see each other very often. I find it necessary to live here to maintain the edge that we must have if we ever have to use these skills that are taught here. And now, I for one will be happy that I have done just that. Getting back to the color, when I was given that, I dropped everything, even the conversation that I was having with this official and immediately went to see this Sione. I did not know him, but for your information, he is the head of the council. He relayed to me that within the last couple of annuals that four of our sister cities have vanished, period." At this point he paused to see how that had affected them. He could see disbelief in their eyes and actions. Something like this had never happened. They couldn't even remember when one city had disappeared. Four was unthinkable, and to have them disappear in such a short time brought worry to all of them. "This information can be passed to everyone here with the admonishment that it must stay here. No one outside of this compound will be allowed to know this. So gather your teams and students and give them this information and start preparing for an exit from the city. We do not have much time, and we do not know which city may be next. I am not opening this for questions at this time. I want this information out to the teams as quickly as possible. I need feedback and ideas. That's all for now, Skylar, I need you to remain behind."

He watched them as they quietly left. It was obvious that they were in deep thought about what had been revealed. Looking back at the tables he saw Skylar waiting patiently to see what he wanted of him personally. He headed over to the table where Skylar sat and joined him by sitting across from him. "So what are your feelings on this?"

"Are you sure what you have presented us is accurate? No, if you went and were shown the information, and I think I know you well enough, then, it probably is correct as far as it goes. If what little we know is true, then I have to agree I think all of the cities are vulnerable." Looking down at the table and thinking a little before he continued Skylar said, "Okay I did not see the data as you, and I know that you gave us a very short version of what was found since as you say you were gone all last night. That must have been some session. Hmm, so what is the plan? I mean I have so many questions, and very few answers. I guess the important one is, are we ready to face what this threat represents? So what is it you want me to do?"

"As I said I need to get some sleep, but this will not wait so with you second-in-charge here, you need to get moving on some type of plan. I said this would involve everyone and that is the way it must be. I feel with this unknown threat that all of us will be needed to come up with some solution. I talked long with Sione and he said that they on their end would be attempting to find a way of changing and improving the defenses. We on our side must find out how they found out, and somehow neutralize the threat, and as I said we do not have much time. Of course we are assuming that the tribes are responsible, but it is the most logical conclusion. Plus without any additional assistance from the other cities, we overall, are a small group and there's a big world out there. Here let me give you this." He then handed Skylar a stack of papers and continued, "Normally they, the ones in the city, do not use paper. But Sione knew that we did not have the devices here to read the information that way and had this printed out for us. Read up on it, this is everything that I know at this point. I should be back at it around mid-day and at that time I'll join you. Once you read through this stuff I think you will agree that our time is very short."

With a troubled look Skylar asked, "How much of what is in here can I reveal?"

"Everything. We do not have time to play games here. And who knows any one of the members here may have something that we would not have thought about. Right now, as you will see, we are lacking any real hard facts. But the conclusions from what has been gathered are hard to dispute. Okay then, I'll catch you a little later or maybe sooner, if I am unable to sleep." He then bid Skylar a goodbye and headed off to his cabin to try and catch a few hours of sleep.

After Shayne had left Skylar remained sitting for a little while. He scanned the many pages, and as he did he became a little more alarmed. As Shayne had said the information was sketchy, but the conclusions made in the report appeared to be correct. Included with the papers was a map showing the cities and when he studied this he saw that the ones that had disappeared were north of them but on a direct line to their city, which had the name Sequoyah. Again if accurate, the times between the cities disappearing were shortening tremendously, and if the timeline shown here continued, it would not be long before another city vanished. Could they act in time to prevent it? When he truly thought about it the answer was probably not, as there just wasn't time. Smiling, although it was a grim smile he said softly. "Yeah, time was something that we had on our side. We wished for something to happen to go and try ourselves against the real world, and now with this crisis we have it." Shaking his head he continued, "So now what? Now that we have gotten what we wished for, now what?" He didn't have an answer for that one. So sighing he got up and headed out the door. There was a lot of information that needed to be passed around and sitting here thinking about it was not going to get it accomplished.

The next few hours he moved from group to group, passing on the information and stating that after the evening meal that there would be a gathering there in the eating hall to discuss further what their actions would be. And yes, what Shayne had stated was true. Absolutely everybody would be involved – from the rawest members up to and including Shayne who is their leader.

Then Skylar thinking about how the area was laid out began to go over in his mind the shortest route around the facility. Except for the mated couples, strict discipline and separation was maintained. There were barracks for the single males, and barracks for the single females, and these were located on opposite sides of the compound. Between these two locations sat the mated couples' cabins. During the days and of course during the night exercises they worked side by side, but the idea of cohabitation between unmated members were discouraged, as this could lead to problems at a critical time and put more than just the couple at risk. Many of the exercises they were involved with could cover many weeks at a time. One group would establish a village in their compound area within the wilderness that had been created within. They would try as best they could to appear to be no more than any other of the many tribes and villages that existed in this world. During the exercises a second group then would become a rival tribe and attack the first to see how well the first group had set up their camp, taking in the factors of location to the necessities, and defensibility, followed by how well they guarded their area, and then how well they would fight to protect their site from a rival village. The simulations were to be as close as to real as they could make them.

Some of the older teams of two had, carefully in the past, gone out into the real wilderness and observed tribes as they lived, fought, and died. Everything had been recorded so that not only would the observations made by the teams be known, but also there was a visual record that went with the narratives. These observations were something that periodically they would perform. So that any changes in the way the tribes interacted could be viewed and studied. Yet, again, something had changed, for the cities now seemed to be the targets, and very easy targets. Skylar hoped that other cities had picked up the alarm and were doing something to improve or change their defenses. The report overall had concluded that what had been working in the past was no longer. If rapid changes were not made, then there would be no cities left, and they and their way of life would be gone forever. What had happened to make that first city vulnerable? Then, what was it that revealed the others that had fallen? What was it that the primitives had learned that allowed them to penetrate the veil that had hidden them from their sight until now? As he thought about this the biggest question of all entered his mind.

How had they succeeded in bringing down the cities so that not a word could get out that they were under attack? These people were not technologically advanced so how would they know what to do to make sure that nothing ever got out of the city once they attacked?

Before he knew it Shayne was standing next to him appearing blurry eyed. "Shayne, you know after reading what you handed me, and then going around and bringing all up to date with this data, I've become more alarmed by the minute. There appears to be more going on than when you first start putting the pieces together. Oh and did I mention it, you look like hell."

"Thanks, I feel that way too . . . and yeah, you too. It's the same with me. I really am worried. From what I can see, it has become easier for these primitives to get inside our cities, and to keep anything from getting out to warn the other cities, they have to be well organized. I mean we know that they can organize for the hunts, and attacks on other tribes. But this is something far beyond such a thing as this. Our smallest cities are larger than five of the tribes combined. Of course if you were to look at only the fighting element of these tribes then it would increase to probably twice that many. We have seen over the years that a couple of tribes would get together to put down a particularly troublesome group, but rarely more than that. It's like they can only stay aligned a short time before they begin to fight each other. These actions show a change and one we know absolutely nothing about. Because of this, we now are paying the price of this ignorance. I had really thought that we really were keeping track of what the primitives were doing, but this has left me knowing that our intelligence gathering is truly lacking."

"Yes, that's obvious. But we were unaware that the program that we are under no longer exists in the other cities. There is no way that we could cover this whole world from here. It is, or was the responsibility of each city to provide intelligence from their local area. It now appears that as time went on that such a thing was no longer considered necessary, except here. So now we are paying the price of complacency and of dropping our vigilance."

"I couldn't have said it better. I never realized that we were it either. I've been sending out reports as required as long as I've been in charge. And I know my predecessor did the same. Who would have guessed that this information was going nowhere, and it had been a waste of time to submit these reports?" Shaking his head Shayne continued, "Now what? We are up against something unknown, and obviously quite dangerous. How are we with our small group going to be able to defeat what is causing this? If we had other teams from the other cities there would be a better chance of solving this. But it's just us." With that stated it shook him to his very core. He had always thought that there would be additional help from the other cities if some major crisis developed. Well, a major crisis had developed and there would be no help, absolutely none at all.

Now deep in thought the two walked the compound heading for commons to make contact with others. It would be a few hours yet before they met at the meeting after the evening meal. Looking around they could see the serious worried expressions on all that they passed. With the weight of decision lying upon them, the afternoon drug by slowly, but eventually it was time for the meeting. This was to be a fact-finding session, attempting to come up with some ideas as to how to tackle this with such a small group overall.

* * *

As he prepared for sleep, Shayne felt that after the meeting that they had made a good start, but knew that was all. There had been many a good idea thrown out. Now they had to find the best of them that fit the circumstances, as they knew them right now. But, be willing to make adjustments on the fly as new facts and situations became known. This was not going to be easy at all. Just what was it that had revealed that first city to the primitives? And then what had these primitives found that revealed the other cities to them? He had no answers at all and it worried him, and even the assumption that it was the primitives causing this was just a guess. Tomorrow they would be sending out an advanced scouting unit to see if anything could be learned. At least the way out of the area for him, and his teams, was well hidden.

There was a cave system that lay to the south edge of their manmade wilderness. It was well hidden with a door that appeared to be nothing more than any of the many boulders and rocks that covered the hillside. What had surprised the ones in the past who had discovered the cave complex was the sheer size. It appeared that the whole small mountain was hollowed out sometime in the distant past. It could have been the results of ice or maybe an extinct volcano. Whatever had caused it, it had left at least one large grotto somewhere towards the center. They had found three points that one could enter or exit and these had been disguised and hidden well. It was the way the teams who researched the wilds left and entered. They had explored the whole region to make sure that there was no place that someone on the outside could observe a team leaving one of the two exits that lay outside the city. At those two exit points there had been some observation ports cut in the past that allowed anyone from inside the caves to observe the outside areas.

The grotto area housed their special equipment and was large enough to hold the entire force. So if the unthinkable ever happened then they could hide until they could then leave safely. Speaking of the equipment, it was probably time to check the portable units completely. He thought that, most likely, they would be using everything that was stored there. This was to be an operation that involved all, and that had never been done before. How had they gone from being comfortable and secure to this state, and all in one day? And why had it taken so long for this information to get to him? He thought that if they had received this information after the second city had gone silent that there was a chance that they could have discovered what was going on, how they had been discovered, and then been working towards a solution – leaving the possibility that the last two cities would not have gone silent at all. Sighing, he knew he wasn't going to solve this tonight, and if he was to be coherent tomorrow he needed to get to sleep. So finally climbing into bed he tried to relax. But his mind just would not stop. So for what seemed to be an eternity he tossed and turned, and then somewhere during all of this mental turmoil finally fell asleep.

* * *

Something awoke him and he did not know what it might have been. It was still dark out but he could tell that dawn was just about to arrive. Questioning himself again, just what had awakened him? Then he realized that something just did not feel right, but he did not know what it was. Now alarmed he jumped out of bed, quickly dressed, and went out into the courtyard. When he arrived he found that he was not alone. He was not the only one who felt that something was amiss. Then it hit him. It was the silence. There was always a background hum coming from the city and now it was silent. Then it hit him hard. He suspected that this city was about to be attacked and somehow the enemy had shut down all the power to the city leaving it completely open and vulnerable. Now there would be no time for planning, and with his small force, he would not be able to help any in the city. He first thought of his sister and their close ties, and knew he could do nothing to help her or her family. Shaking his head he grabbed the nearest person standing there and told him to wake everyone and to head for the grotto. If they were going to help any of the citizens of this city or the other cities that had gone dark, they would need to survive. Now being a hero and charging into this city would only bring them death and expose the rest to capture.

He admonished the people he grabbed to keep it quiet and to get to the grotto as quickly as possible. He could see shadows as his teams began their near silent exodus out of the compound to the caves – his only hope that they would be there before they were found. As the sky grayed he then heard the attack begin and shuddered inside knowing that people were both dying and having worse things happen to them, and there was absolutely nothing he or any of this group could do to slow or even stop it from happening. Again he thought of his sister and her family and almost cried out in anguish over his helplessness. He knew that the same thing was probably going through the minds of most of the people here. They all had family or loved ones in that city and they could do nothing to save them. Why had this attack come so close on the heels of the fall of the other city? One thing for sure he had his answer. No longer would he have to speculate on what was happening. He now had direct proof.

He and the rest now had to close their ears to what they were hearing. They could hear the screams and cries of the residents of the city as the primitives began attacking the residences. Could they get to the caves before they were discovered? Shayne swept the compound to make sure it was clear, and he remained as the rear guard to insure that all were ahead of him and retreating to the grotto. Even with the chaos within the compound they continued to move quietly and quickly with purpose. For this he was proud of them. It would have been so easy to panic, and to add additional noise to their movement, increasing the chances of being discovered. As he entered the edge of their artificial wilderness he saw some of the primitives coming over the wall. They had gotten out just in time. He hid behind a tree and then sped down one of the many pathways that ran throughout the area. He then came up against the hill turned left, went through a number of heavy bushes, then around a boulder which had a tree next to it. Once around the tree he entered the cave complex and closed the door behind him, and locked it. He then headed down towards the grotto and the growing crowd around him. What had surprised him more than the attack was the number of primitives that were coming over the wall. It appeared to have been enough to equal at least two tribes. And this would have included all the women and children, and old people. Yet, these appeared to have been ones who were male and were of fighting age. Yes something had changed and it bode badly for them and the cities.

He could feel the fear, confusion, and suddenly a sense of anger running through the crowd. Then one of the young members yelled, "Why are we running? They are attacking our city! Are we cowards, just hiding while our families are being killed and who knows what? Come on we have been training for this."

Shaking his head he could understand the sentiment. But if they went back out to meet the primitives then all they would be doing was throwing their lives away and solving nothing. Now the best courses of action was to admit that they would fail here, but hopefully in the end, find a solution, and save others. There was absolutely nothing that could be done to save their loved ones at all. Turning towards the one who had voiced his concern Shayne said. "I understand exactly what your feelings are, but understand this, if we were to go out there, we would just be throwing our lives away accomplishing nothing. If you do not believe this I want you and someone else, someone of your choice, to climb up there and look out onto the grounds and tell the rest here what you see." Then seeing some reluctance on the part of the speaker he then said, "This is not a suggestion this is an order. You need to see for yourself what we are up against. Then with you and the other you can come back down and let the rest know what you have seen. Now go and be back down in no more than ten minutes." We do not know how long it may be before our escape may be discovered." He then watched as the individual with another of his choice headed up the pathway and then up the ladders to the observation point. Once there he watched them pull back the cover and saw both of them visibly flinch.

Then he saw their shoulders slump, and he knew that now they also knew that it was hopeless and if indeed had they returned to the compound then they would have either been captured or killed. He watched as the two slowly closed the port and made their way back to the waiting group. The one who had protested spoke in a subdued voice said. "You were right. If we had been waiting and tried to help we would now be either dead or captured. There is nothing we can do. I have never seen that many primitives. We barely would make a dent in the tide if we each had killed ten of them." Then with a look of desperation he asked, "What has happened, what has changed? I don't understand at all. How are we going to be able to do anything against that horde? How are we going to be able to prevent this from happening to the other cities? We are not a warlike people."

Shayne could see the hopelessness showing in the faces of his teams. Then again shaking his head he stated. "I wish I had an answer for you. But I had only learned of the threat yesterday. I have no answers, solutions, or even an understanding of what has changed. But know this, we are going to try and solve this. Solving this is for a future time, now we have to escape and survive. So we will be on the run for a while. This will be hard and dangerous, as we must find our way to one of the remaining sister cities if possible. I am sure the alarm is already been given out since our city has gone silent. We are the fifth. I just hope that we do not lose too many more before we are able to change the situation. It is now obvious that we have become complacent and have allowed something to change. By not being vigilant we have now paid the price. If we are to prevent the ending of our cities and us then we cannot go on as before. Understand this, we are going to escape, and we are going to survive. This road ahead of us will not be easy. But you have to understand this; we must stick together, fight together, and work together. I believe that we are the only chance that the remaining cities have. So we must survive. Now let's work towards the hidden exit . . . and yes we are going to take all of our equipment. I have a strong feeling that we will need it in the upcoming escape, followed by whatever plans we come up with, due to changes in the situation. We need to go with stealth. One last thing . . ." He paused then dropped his voice to almost a whisper before continuing. " . . . When we survive this and then find out what has led to this change, we are going to eliminate the cause, and then hopefully be able to rescue our families and friends that have survived this attack, and of course the members of the other four fallen cities. I am sure that they have been enslaved and their lives will be pure hell, not much different than ours from this point on. We will at least have our freedom, something that they will not. But if we are captured then everything we have worked for and now working towards will be in vain, and the hopelessness of our people will be complete. As long as we are out there they have something to hope for. Now let's move and get as far away from here as we can. Be prepared for anything. These primitives are not stupid, and they live in that world. It's a world that we have only played in. They have the advantage, and as such we must learn quickly or we ourselves will be no more." At this point he turned to his second and said, "Let's get moving. I really have no idea if the primitives will find a way in here or not. I don't want to be here if they do."

At the end of his statement, the teams began the hike through the caves to the hidden exit lying on the backside of the hillside. The exit was located in a dead end canyon where there was a large rock face. At the point of the exit, the canyon was choked with small trees and brush – giving the appearance that it was impenetrable, and nothing of value to make it a place to go and explore anyway. The one danger to this blind canyon lay with its opening. A small group could keep anyone in the canyon from escaping. But since there appeared to be nothing of value here, it had always been felt that no one would ever take the time to even explore it. Then, once beyond the canyon entrance there was at least three ways out, making it more difficult for any that would want to follow, to know the direction they would take. As they neared the exit from the caves they released the small drones that would appear to be nothing more than birds. So if any were actually there the watchers would not give these drones a second thought. As they monitored the drones they saw a single primitive watching up on the ridgeline. "Okay I need one of the better scout teams to go out there and take out that single observer. And be very quiet about it. We cannot afford an alarm to go out." There was a pause and then Shayne continued, "Saige, Shellian, you two are the best we have, I think you two will go out and take care of the primitive. Once you are in position we will send two more out to grab his attention to make it easier for you. Let's get this done."

The exit was opened just enough to allow Saige and Shellian out, then immediately closed. They slowly worked themselves up tight against the canyon wall that would hide them from the observer. Using hand signals they carefully worked their way down the length of the canyon and took the right branch, continuing to keep the primitive out of view. Of course by doing this it meant that they couldn't keep tabs on the observer, so they really had no idea if he was staying where he had been first observed. If he had moved then they could be walking right to where he was and be seen. Luck held with them, as at one point they were able to briefly view the primitive. Since they now were closer they could see that he appeared to be a youth, probably out on his first raid. If they had anything to say about it, it would be his last.

* * *

Kor had been disappointed. At first he was excited when he had been informed that he would join the raiding party. It would be his first, and to be able to join the warriors in battle had always been his dream, and now it appeared it was coming true. He also thought that he might have his first female then also. Yet when they approached the area he had been assigned this duty to be a watchman. A watchman . . . that is a child's job . . . not a warrior's. What made it worse lay in the fact that he was completely isolated, and knew that there would be nothing happening here at all. There was only a flier or two now and then. This place was desolate, nothing to interest one. Why had he been given this assignment when all the action was on the other side of these hills? The sun had been rising for quite a while and it was dead silent, nothing, just nothing was happening. So bored, he glanced around, picked up some pebbles and tossed them over the side to watch them as they cascaded down the side, creating small landslides with the loose soil that rained down to the canyon bottom. He was about to throw another over the side when some movement caught his attention. Unbelieving he saw two females coming down that dead end canyon. Where had they come from? He worked himself up to the edge so he could watch them. He wanted to see where they were going. Maybe he would have his first female anyway, and who knew maybe two. With a wicked smile on his face he concentrated on the pair as they stumbled down the canyon coming closer to his location. Deciding it was time to move he stood up to begin his approach only to hear something behind him. As he turned he felt himself being pushed. He fought hard to regain his balance since he was standing on the edge, but realized that there was no way he would be able to prevent the fall. Screaming once he fought hard to regain his balance, but then slipped over the side and then fell to his death.

* * *

Saige stood there with Shellian next to him and looked down and waved at the two women. He wouldn't have thought to do it that way. But now that he thought about it, it had made perfect sense to send out only women making it appear that they would be vulnerable easy targets, something that a young primitive would concentrate totally on, not thinking that it was an ambush. His estimation in the capabilities of Shayne just rose. By doing it this way they would be out of the area with none the wiser. And with the body of the primitive at the base of a cliff, it would appear to any that he had simply slipped and fallen. As long as they covered their tracks and left no evidence then there would be nothing to alert the attacking force. With a signaling wave the two women headed back to the cave exit and signaled the rest that it was now safe to exit. Fortunately the craft they had were partially hovercraft and as such, would not leave any tracks. Because of the noise they were only used in this mode when there was no other choice. The craft would normally navigate on six wheels. At the back of the group were the trackers with the responsibility of wiping out any sign that they had been here. Now it would become more difficult. Shayne signaled Saige and Shellian to join the teams and then sent out a scouting group ahead of them. He would also have teams of out runners and flankers to both sides and the trackers taking up the rear position. Now once they were in the canyon networks ahead there was a greater chance to escape. Yet, he knew that they were far from safe. After all if there had been a lookout posted here, there was a great chance that there would be others.

No one spoke, and any communications were completed strictly through hand signals. Silence now was their friend, and any noise could compromise their position. So quickly and with stealth they moved into the center canyon. From here this one branched in four different directions. Initially their direction would be west. This would lead them deeper into the wilds. Once there they would have time to set up camp look at their options and figure out which city to head towards. They had to survive, as now they knew what was happening and who generally was responsible for the disappearance of the cities. They were the only ones who truly knew. But were they good enough to avoid the primitives and get this important information where it needed to go? Shayne knew that the nearest city was many weeks away. But it may be that it would serve them better to head for one that was still further away. There had been such a short time between the fall of the previous city and theirs that by the time they could reach the next closest city it may have become a victim of the primitives and could easily have fallen also.

At least with the canyon complex they were working through, the further along they proceeded, with the many additional branching directions they took, the less of a chance they had of being discovered. Shayne, as did the rest of the team, knew it was a desperate time since the primitives could only continue to be successful if the remaining cities were kept ignorant as to what had been happening to the ones disappearing and going silent. While he had these thoughts running through his mind one of the forward scouts signaled back that there was a small force of primitives ahead of them and these appeared to be seasoned warriors, not the young one that had been watching the canyon they came out of. He signaled for one of the forward scouts to come in and let him know what they were facing. Turning to the rest of the team he signaled for complete silence and all of their equipment was shut down. Fortunately most of the craft they were bringing with them was still hidden. Everyone else faded into the surrounding sparse vegetation and waited for the signal to move. There was a heavy tension in the air as they all were aware that their lives were on the line, and they were far from successful in leaving the area unscathed. Shayne, waiting until the scout was close enough that the sign language they used would be easily recognizable, He then signed, "What are we facing, and can we get around them?"

The scout answering back said, "It appears to be twenty to twenty five warriors, and it appears that they were recently in a fight. They seem to be on alert, but presently are not moving."

"Can we move around them without being seen or heard?"

"I don't really think so. They are right in the middle of the main canyon floor where it splits in the four directions. I think we will have to wait until they move. Possibly, if they were not so alert and expecting anything . . . but I suspect they are there to cut off anyone who escapes from the city, you know like us."

Shaking his head Shayne then signed back, "Okay then keep us informed, stay out of sight, and if anything changes let me know. We cannot fight them as it would give us away, and by these primitives believing they have everyone, it is the only way we have a chance."

The scout signaled his affirmative, and then disappeared back the way he had come. Shayne coming back to the team then signed that they were stuck and would have to remain in the stealth mode for who knew how long. He knew that every second they stayed this close to the fallen city the greater chance of discovery. But what could they do, if they attacked the group, they would give themselves away, if they waited they could be discovered which would result in the same thing. So throughout the day they sat quietly, nervously, praying that no one would not come along and check on the one they had killed, and that this other group of warriors would move soon.

CHAPTER FOUR

Keenan was shocked. He was in charge of his section of the communications center that kept the many cities linked, and within two days two additional cities had gone silent. No explanation, no warning, nothing. While each city had their own individual communications, theirs was the hub where all the cities, that still existed, kept in contact with each other. He had his suspicions, but again had no proof. What exactly was going on? At this rate by the end of this annual all the cities could be gone. With no proof he couldn't even put forth his theories. He knew they would just laugh at him, saying something like, "Look at it. Almost all of the cities that have gone silent have been in one area of the continent. So some natural disaster must have befallen them. After all with our technology we are well hidden from the primitives, and there is no way it could be them anyway. We've been able to put the fear into them that we are from their primitive gods so are off limits."

He had to admit that their arguments were valid enough, but these arguments just didn't feel right, and they did not really fit in the pattern as he saw it. Well it was time to go over to the one above him and report the loss. Sighing, and then shaking his head he knew that it would be just filed and he would be told to forget about it. "Sometime soon a valid answer would be found, and please no more of your stupid theories." Had they as a people become so complacent that even with disaster looking them in the face they could not see it? For that he had no answer. He just hoped that what they were saying as the probable cause was correct, and what his theories were, was not. Yet, he had this nagging feeling that he was absolutely right . . . yet . . . with no proof he was just going in circles. "By the gods!" he yelled, "What is going on?" Looking around he saw the startled looks on the ones who worked under him. He then responded, "Sorry team. It's just something is happening to our people and the ones over us are going on as if nothing has changed and nothing has happened. It seems that they are denying all of this. I feel that they are going to do this even if it happens to us. And then wonder what happened?" Shaking his head again he headed out the door to report his findings knowing again that it was futile.

Kellen received the news from Keenan with little acknowledgement leaving Keenan frustrated with the response he received. But there was little he could do about it. With foreboding he then headed back to his section completely at loss as to what to do or where to go. This lack of concern on any of the leaders' part could lead them all to disaster. Kellen, immediately after Keenan left, could see the anger on his face, but he had been specifically told to make it appear to be something minor. Yet he was very worried, and once he knew that Keenan had left he went out with no explanation to his underworker and went to report to the next higher up.

Again what was causing their cities to disappear like this? They had been safe and hidden for generations, why now? What had changed? Why was there no communications or at least refugees from these silent cities? Of course the distances between them could be part of the answer, since the portable communications devices were of very short range. Only the major communications centers within the cities allowed direct contact between all of them. So there may not have been enough time for someone from one of the silent cities to get close enough to use the short-range devices or even reach one of the other cities as of yet.

Still it was a worrisome thing, and with little facts and no information what could their response be? And if it turned out to be war, well that would be a bad thing, since they did not even have an army to defend their way of life. There had been no need for such a thing. Their technology had kept them safe to pursue other endeavors. Now if it came down to fighting for their very lives could they do it? He knew that their city, Keahilani, had shut down their wilderness project, oh, at least 10 annuals ago. It seemed to be something they no longer had a need of. Were they wrong? He had to admit he had no answers for any of the many questions that this emergency brought forth, none at all.

* * *

Shayne signed back to the team what the forward scouts had passed on to him. "The scouts stated that a small group of what appears to be warriors just came into the area and appear to be hanging around. Fortunately it was after we had killed the one enemy so they are not alerted at the present to either our location or us. We do not know if they are here just by chance or are here to collect the one we killed. Every moment we have to stay here gives them a better chance of discovering either the entrance into the caverns or finding us. We cannot take them out, as it would then alert the primitives that someone has escaped. So we must just wait, and pray that they do not find us. Keep it silent and continue using sign language." He could feel as well as see the tension and fear in his team. Would they be successful in their escape or be caught?

Time continued to drag as they waited for the scouts to inform them that the war party had moved on, but none had been forthcoming so far. As the morning crept along and nothing seemed to be happening, Shayne could see that many were becoming restless and wanted to do something, anything. The waiting was becoming unbearable with discovery likely at any moment. Finally as they reached mid-morning the "all clear" sign was given. Shayne turned back to the group and signed to them to wait, as he would go forward to confirm. He then left, and again what seemed like an eternity he finally returned and signaled for the team to move out. The warriors had left the area, and apparently were not there to collect the one lookout from here. They then continued to push west through the major canyon complex. Every additional branch of these many canyons increased their chances. They knew by nightfall that they had to be completely out of the area. With heavy hearts and with some distance between them and their lost city they looked back and saw smoke rising. Some of their beloved city was burning, but from the amount of the smoke they could tell that it was not the whole city. Without power the fire extinguishing equipment would not work. It was a sign to them that they would never be able to return here and presently they were a people without a home. As far as they knew they were the last of their city.

They really did not know if any of their city had lived through the attack. They suspected that it was a possibility but there was no proof. These thoughts weighed heavily on them as they worked through the canyons further from their home that would be no more.

That night with the day full of avoiding roving groups of primitives they finally found shelter in a small copse of trees and within a small stream ran merrily on its way. But none of the team felt joy in the sounds of the stream as it bubbled over rocks on its way to who knew where. They were exhausted; beat, both physically and emotionally. Had it been only this morning when their city had fallen? It seemed like a lifetime, and that they had always been on the move, dodging and hiding. They ate a cold meal afraid to have a fire, or anything that would give them away. Shayne set up watches for the night wanting them changed every couple of hours. They had to be alert and any member on guard duty for longer than that could become careless. And carelessness was something they could not afford. There was little talk, as most seemed to be asleep on their feet. So after eating most fell into an exhausted sleep. At this point there had been no young ones to complicate their escape. Although a few of the women that were coupled were early in carrying their first child, and if they went full term before they were able to enter another city there could be problems. Walking among the sleeping team members Shayne was very worried. He knew that the next few weeks were going to be hell. They always had had the city to fall back on and now it was gone. Would they be good enough to be able to completely survive without its support? For this he had no answer, or was likely not to find an easy one. He missed a hot cup of shick. He liked it strong, bitter and very hot. It seemed to help him keep going. But he knew that they would be eating cold meals for many days to come and until they could build a fire he and all the rest would be without it.

Then it came to his mind that now they were going to find out rather quickly if they were good enough to avoid the roving patrols of the primitives. Whoever was presently in charge of these primitives seemed to have some military sense about him. Everything that he had witnessed showed discipline, organization, and precision in carrying out the attacks, the posting of watches, and the roving patrols. It had to be that way or else someone from the city could escape and alert others to what was happening, and thusly change things, making it harder for these attacking forces. *Just what is this unknown person offering the tribes that he seems to be uniting?* Then while on this track of thinking Shayne thought, *we have to find out who this one is the ones who directly support him, and then find a way to either eliminate him, or at least make the rest of the newly aligned tribes to become distrustful.* At this point his mind became too clouded with fatigue to continue so he found a place on the ground and like the rest fell into an exhausted sleep.

It seemed like only minutes when he was awakened, but it was just before dawn and they had to be up and moving out of the area. It was going to be difficult to eliminate any sign that they had been here. They were just too large of a group. While he had them spread out to take care of the morning nature call he knew that with the amount left behind that there would be a scent that could draw the primitives right to their campsite. With that in mind, he assigned a group to cover the wet spots with soil and leaves to help hide their passing of the area. Again with hand signals they headed out, with scouts out front and to the rear, and out-runners or flankers to both sides. It was a cool and very clear morning with a light haze in the distance. It was going to be a very long day. They would be moving from now, before the sunrise, to after the sunset. It presently was the late summer months, and the daylight period was much longer than the night.

* * *

After a week of dodging patrols and putting much distance between themselves and their starting point Shayne finally called a halt. They were presently in a small hidden valley that would provide them shelter for a few days before they continued. Looking around he could see the haunted expressions on many of the faces. There had been too many close calls in their escape. But so far their luck had held and as far as they knew they had been undiscovered. Shayne knew that their luck would fail at some point so immediately had the members practice their combat skills. Then Shayne and Skylar would call in the teams of two and start going over strategies to infiltrate the unknown leader's camp of the primitive alliance. Somehow they had to gather intelligence, and find ways to bring it down. Otherwise their way of life was complete, finis, over, done, or whatever other word came to mind. Plus, now that the escape had been successful, it was time to find an uninhabited area and set up their village. They had to blend in and appear to nothing other than one of the many primitive tribes. It would have to be their base of operation, and it needed to be somewhat close to the alliance but not so close as to make them a target since they were not to be a part of the alliance.

While this was happening they would send out two teams of two to head for different cities and hope that these teams reached the cities before the primitives did. Yet all of this was in the future. As of right now they hadn't completely escaped, close, but not yet. All he could hope for was that the equipment they used would remain undiscovered, and if found by the primitives, it would immediately give them away as being from the cities. Again, because of the short-range communications devices within these units, they needed to be much closer to one of their sister cities so that they could communicate over the airwaves.

This led him to thinking about the differences between the cities and the primitives. Why the two differences? If the history taught in their learning centers had been accurate, and who knew for sure, since history is rewritten over time to fit the present leaders, and the ones who did the writings – yet this written history said that at one time they were all one people. All advanced, with no primitives. There were factions within and eventually somewhere along the time line war had broken out involving the whole world. Some seeing the futility of such an action vowed to remove themselves from the fighting and try and preserve what they had. It is unknown how they accomplished it, but from their actions the cities came into existence and remained outside of the fighting and the death and destruction. Hidden in the desolate untraveled areas, it became *the time of isolation*. As the war raged outside of this isolation they continued to thrive and develop methods that would hide their cities. Then eventually the wars ended and the remnant of those who had fought in those many wars had reduced them back to a primitive way of life. And this way of life had remained as it was presently for hundreds of turns around their sun. It appeared that the primitives would always remain so, with no desire to rise above whom and what they were. So as time had continued, as it always does, the cities remained hidden – observing their once brothers and sisters and remaining unseen.

A commotion brought him out of his thoughts and he quickly looked around to see what was happening. They were under attack! Where had the attackers come from? No time for questions or answers now! It was time to fight or anything they had planned for the future would be naught, and if they did not get out of the area safely, then none of the other cities would ever be safe. As these thoughts ran through his mind he saw one of his team go down under a spear. That was the last direct image head had as it became complete chaos around him as they desperately fought. It seemed that an hour must have passed but he knew it could only be a few minutes in truth. Soon, their training paid off, and they were able to overcome the attacking primitives. He immediately sent out hand signals to search the area and to allow none of the primitives to escape. If they did then their own escape would end here, as the alliance would be alerted to their presence.

As he caught his breath he first wondered how they were found. He thought that they were well hidden. Looking around at the team he was proud of what he saw as without a word they were looking after any that had been wounded in the brief battle. He was glad that these primitives that had attacked them seemed to be a small group. Probably one of the many patrols that this new alliance had working the countryside, and eliminating any competition. What worried him lay in both the discovery of their location, and while yes they had succeeded in overcoming the small patrol, it had proved more difficult than it should have been. They had been lucky. In fact the only severe injury was the first one he had seen before the chaos. The one who had been speared had been lucky, as the spear had missed any vital organs and major blood vessels, but still he had lost a lot of blood, and seemed to be breathing rapidly and appeared to be somewhat pale. The rest of the injuries seemed to be flesh wounds, cuts and scrapes. Turning to the group once it had been confirmed that all the primitives were indeed dead he said. "Okay, I guess we've now had our first taste of battle. I myself did not care for it, but our training seems to have paid off. Still, we were lucky once again, as this was a small force. I believe that had it been a larger scouting party that we would be the dead ones." He let that comment soak into them before continuing. "How we were located I do not know, but it shows that we are not as good as we thought. So if we are to survive, we must get better. Now bury those primitives, take whatever we can from them, as we may need the items, and then prepare to leave. It is obvious we cannot stay here. If we did we would be very foolish indeed. I do not know how much time we have, but I can guarantee that once this group is missed they would be searched for."

"Shayne?"

"Yes Saige what is it that you want to ask?"

"How would the primitives leave their enemy's bodies? Would they bury them as you proposed, or would they strip them and mutilate the bodies? So in their afterlife they could not attack the other spirits."

"Ah I see your point. If we bury them we would be giving ourselves away that we are not a part of this world but of the cities. Okay let's follow what these primitives would do and get out of here."

* * *

The following days and weeks indeed turned into hell as the words he had spoken became true. They found themselves fighting for their very lives as they continued to be pushed further from their goal and deeper into the untamed wilds. Each fight, each ambush left them weaker as some fell to these attacks. In one of the last desperate fights they lost half of their remaining healthy members. Even the leader Shayne was severely wounded. The second in charge had been killed only the previous day. Shayne, before this fight, had then placed the sister and brother, Shellian and Saige as seconds. But if this continued then it would not matter as they would perish and any of the knowledge they had would perish with them.

That evening Shayne called the two to his side and stated that most likely he would not live out the night. He was very pale and his breathing ragged – they could see desperation in his eyes when he knew that he would not be able to continue to lead their small band of refugees. Shellian then said, "Shayne, I know that you have been hurt and your injuries are bad. But you must survive. Who else could lead us? I mean you have taught us how to survive and how to depend on each other. It is you who is the heart, strength and soul to us. You are our leader."

He could see the pleading in her eyes but he felt the truth deep down inside of him. He knew that even with what they had medically, that the wound he had received, in the end would be fatal. Without the access to one of the cities they did not have the means to stop the slow bleeding that was happening inside of him. And he could feel his strength leaving him as his blood loss continued. Smiling up at her, even though it was a weak smile at best, he said weakly, "I have always been a realist. I have been given no special protection or immunity from what has happened to our city and to us. So why should I be any different than the rest of you?"

"But Shayne!" she exclaimed, "You are our leader. If you die how will we continue? We all look up to you. You're the one who gives us confidence, the one we draw our strength from, and the one with the knowledge . . ."

Interrupting by laying his hand on her Shayne said. "Shellian, Shellian, there is nothing I can do to change what has happened." Then catching his breath he continued, "It will now fall to the two of you to take over for me. I do not know what lies on the other side of this physical death, but I do hope there is something. If so some day we will have a chance to meet again. But for whatever reason my time is coming to an end. I believe we are all here for some purpose. I never knew what mine was, and I guess now I will never know, but please . . ." His tone in his voice dropped as they could again see the desperation in his eyes. " . . . Please get any part of this team safely out of here. We are being forced into the mountains and away from any of our other sister cities. It may be that we . . . you will have to survive there for a long time . . ." He then drifted off to unconsciousness without completing his thought. Shellian and Saige looked at each other, Saige being too heavy of heart to say anything at all. This seemed like the end, and for Shayne it was as he quietly slipped from this world as they watched.

Sister and brother looked at each other and neither spoke, as they could not believe he was gone. Shayne had been their leader from the beginning – well at least as long as they had been around. His knowledge and strength seemed indomitable. How could it be that he was to be one of the ones killed as they ran their desperate escape from these primitives? What were they going to do? How were they going to survive? Just what was to be their fate? It seemed that a dark cloud now hung over everything. They had lost two thirds of their numbers on this escape, and had to abandon their mobile units – no longer having the number of members to be able to operate them. Plus it was slowing them down and now speed and stealth was of the essence.

Suddenly they both realized that someone had been speaking to them. Looking up from their overwhelming grief they realized that the woman who had been caring for Shayne and had witnessed his end was asking them something. "Again I ask, now what? What are we going to do?" Looking at her they both could see the pain in her eyes and they reflected that it was probably the same if they could look into a mirror and see their own. Neither had an answer but they both knew that whether wanted nor desired, Shayne's last request was for the two of them to lead the remaining members to safety if at all possible.

Saige then said. "First we must lay our leader to rest." Then breathing deeply and turning to his sister he continued. "Shellian, go inform the others of Shayne's passing. I fear we do not have much time to us and we are going to have to leave this place before the sunrise if we are to survive." Again pausing and then coming to a decision, he realized at that moment that all of the older generation was gone. It was difficult to realize that now they were the older generation here, but indecision here would and could finish them. "We must, as Shayne requested, head into the mountains. It will probably be our only salvation. For some reason that we have never been able to discover, these mountains are a sacred and a feared place with these primitives. They rarely venture into them. When they do, it is usually their holy men only. So it may be that these mountains can be our sanctuary."

Shellian stood there unable to move. It was obvious to Saige that she was on the verge of tears as was the other woman who had been caring for Shayne. He had to admit it himself that he too was emotionally drained. But if they did not get moving and soon it would not matter as they all would be joining Shayne much too soon, and if that happened then they would have failed completely. He walked over to his sister and gave her a hug. She clung to him with her head on his shoulder. She seemed to be shaking and he realized that indeed she was crying. He found that the other woman had joined them and she too had tears flowing. He thought he should say something but could come up with nothing to say that would comfort any of them. So they just hung together for what seemed like a long time. Finally pushing them gently away from him he said. "I'll go out and let the rest know. Please prepare our leader for burial and I will get the rest started in digging his grave. I truly fear that we do not have as much time to honor him, as we should. But in the end I think he will understand." He then turned and left the small shelter they were in leaving the two women alone.

* * *

Had it been just 14 days since they had lost Shayne? It seemed more like an eternity as they continued to be harassed by the primitives. At times it seemed that they had lost them only to be struck by a small patrol. Yet, now they were finally entering the foothills, and the patrols seemed to be less and of smaller parties. But that did not seem to lessen the danger. It appeared that many of these groups were much better prepared and wilderness wise than many that they had evaded when they were barely outside of the city. The city, now it was hard to even remember much about it, as the continual fear, fighting, running and hiding appeared to be their life now. It was as if the other life they had known was no more than a dream. And who knew – maybe it was. And what they were now involved with had been their true life. Saige, looking around to the remainder of the team thought that they had come so far. Although looking at them one would not have guessed such a thing. The clothes that they wore was ragged, torn, dirty and worn. And the bodies wearing the clothes looked no better. Eyes sunken from too little sleep and food, skin dirty from not being able to bath, and a fear that seemed to permeate the group, each wondering if they would be the next to fall. Still they had learned. And Saige thinking back thought that when they were still in their compound that they knew so much. Now he knew that what they knew there had been no more than child's games. So proud of their skills and abilities that they had looked down on the ones actually living in the cities. Shaking his head all he could say now was – "How ignorant we all were. How proud we were of the abilities. How much we believed that we could match the primitives and because of our superior society and equipment that there was no way that the primitives could beat us." Well it had all been proven false. So here they were running and fighting for their very lives.

Saige, crouching down behind a boulder that sat on top of a hill, looked out over the valley that they would have to traverse. Camping down by a stream that ran through the center of the valley was one of the numerous patrols. Shaking his head and pulling back away from the hilltop he signaled the team to head back to the copse of trees. He then joined them and said, "Okay we have a real problem. From what I can see there is only one way through this valley and they are camped right next to that route. I need a couple of you to monitor them, and for heaven's sake, do not be seen. I'm going to send a couple of others to scout to either side and see if there is another way through here. But unfortunately it seems that everything has pushed us here. I know from what we have seen that there is a good possibility that we once pass this point, will begin our trek into the mountains." Shaking his head and breathing deeply before continuing, "Maybe then we will finally be able to take a day or two and just camp and give everyone a time to rest." Looking down at the ground and then at each that was with him he then said, "Still I can hold no promises for any of us." Then pointing at two of the people with him he said. "Okay I want you two to have the first watch, and then I'll send a couple to relieve you. Unfortunately for all of us, we cannot chance a fire so we will all have travel rations. The one thing I know is that we cannot just stay here. So whether we find an alternate route or have to sneak by this group tonight we must continue to move." He then got up and the rest of the team that was with him headed back to the camp leaving the two to watch.

When they got far enough away from the camping enemy he had the remaining team that was with him spread out and recon the area where they were staying. He needed to be sure that they were hidden. This delay was dangerous. It was time they could ill afford. The mountains were so close now, but still completely out of reach. It would be tragic if they came so close to their goal only to fail. Yet there was very little they could do about it. If it came down to it, that the only way through was where the primitives were camping, then they would just have to figure out how to do it. As the day waned away and the scouting teams reported back it became obvious that this was the only way through the area. Thusly, why it was guarded as it presently seemed to be. So how were they going to be able to continue? One thing for sure they would not be able to backtrack and try and different direction. They had barely avoided a number of patrols and to expect their luck to continue was just too much to expect.

"Now what?" One of the members asked to no one in particular. He was answered with silence. Again this had been a question that had been asked over and over again. They were stuck and no obvious solution had been put forth. Then Steen said, "I don't know if this would work but what if one of us went down there dressed as a courier with a message that stated that it had appeared that we went a different direction and that they could move to a different location to try and intercept us. Then we could wait for them to pull out and go through safely." One of the others then said, "Right if we have time for them to pull out. You know how close we came to being caught just this morning. I really don't think we can wait that long." Silence fell over the group once again as it seemed like a good idea, but the weakness in it became obvious once it had been pointed out.

Saige asked, "Do any of you have any other suggestions? We need to come up with something quickly as has been stated we are out of time and out of chances."

Sahar followed up by saying, "I thought of one but immediately discarded it. Since the way these primitives are, our women would pay the price – and I for one am not willing for that to happen."

"And what was that Sahar?" Saige asked. "Right now we just don't have anything. So maybe putting it out there where we all can hear it might give someone else and idea." Saige then stood up and started pacing. He could feel the pressure building as each minute passing brought them closer to discovery. Their band was now down to 15 and with such a small force they were at a point that once discovered it probably was over.

Taking a deep breath Sahar paused and then said. "Okay, ahhh . . . I was thinking of guards and prisoners heading through to some unknown destination. But I realized that the women would have to pose as prisoners, which meant . . ." Here trailed off to silence. He did not need to finish, as they all knew what he meant. While like the other idea it initially seemed good until they realized the consequences. Their women would have to submit to the primitives since they were prisoners and be subject to the whims and needs of the primitives in the camp. And with the diminished size of their group there was no way they could prevent it from happening.

"Okay we have had two ideas put forth, and both have strong points and some very telling weaknesses. Let's see if we can strengthen either and try and eliminate the negatives."

About this time as the sun was setting the two who had been watching the camp reported in and stated that it appeared that there were only two guards placed out in a roving patrol. From what they could see they changed them every couple of hours to keep the guards fresh and alert. Otherwise it seemed that most of the remaining primitives remained in camp just lying around.

After they reported in and had given them what they had observed, Saige asked. "How can we put this to our advantage? I am surprised that they are not putting out at least four guards. But maybe it has been so quiet that their guard is down. So they are doing the minimal. Maybe, who knows, waiting to be relieved? This means they may indeed be waiting for a courier to give them new orders. Okay how can we take advantage of what we may be guessing is going on down there?"

Saar, who was their medical person suddenly, looked excited. "Saige what if we take that rotgut alcohol that we stole from one of their villages, spike it with our knockout drug that we extract from some of the native plants, and somehow get them to drink it? Of course the only ones that wouldn't be allowed to drink would be the two guards. But I think it would be easier to deal with just two than all of them down there, don't you think?"

"That's a great idea, and being that they are a patrol getting them to drink shouldn't be a problem. The problem is to keep them from being suspicious. Okay everybody we have many parts here, let's work something out quickly. We need to be moving as soon as we can."

* * *

Stone and Sahar approached the primitive camp with trepidation. Stone was elected as the one to pose as the courier and Sahar his guard. They had observed this enough over time to know the exact process. So that part should be easy. But putting oneself directly in contact with the enemy was not something either of them was truly interested in doing. Well, it was too late to back out now as the guard had spotted them. "Guard! Take me to the commander of your patrol. I have a message of importance that must be delivered – For His Eyes Only!" Sahar remained silent trying to look fierce and suspicious. He was to remain silent, as his grasp of the primitive's language was rudimentary at best. Stone could have easily passed as any of the primitives from his skin coloring to his build. So they hoped that it would not raise any questions as to where Sahar may have been from. Still he was a close second to Stone, but a poor second if one really was honest. Sahar carried the backpack that had the spiked booze in it. As of yet they did not know how they were going to pass it on, but hopefully something would be presented that would make it seem natural.

The guard looked them over, but did not say anything. He then gestured for them to follow him. Knowing now to be silent, they followed the guard to the center of the encampment where the guard then went up to one of the largest members who was sitting by the fire. The guard pointing at Stone and Sahar simply stated "courier", he turned and left and went back to his post. Stone waiting, since by the way it appeared to work from their previous studies he, as a courier, was superior to a simple patrol commander. Slowly the commander stood and both his girth and height made both of them feel as if they were children. It was difficult to keep from flinching, but somehow they hid their reaction. "I have a dispatch from the one in charge. Is there a place we can pass this on – as it is for your ears or eyes only! And yes, before you ask, I do know what is in this, since not all commanders can read." He said this last part in a way that made him appear superior to any who could not read: Again knowing that he needed to do this to play his role.

The commander looked at him suspiciously for a moment then shrugged. He then led them off to one side and said. "Okay, here is far enough. Reading is not important in leading a patrol or fighting." He then puffed out his chest and stated, "I have fought and won many a battle and have worked my way to becoming the leader here. For this I do not need to follow any scratches put upon a skin. What is it that you need to pass on? And since you are here you can take one back from me. I am tired of having to sit here and so is the rest of my clan. Nothing is happening here and I suspect it will remain so. Now what do you have?"

"The ones that we pursue have moved to the West and will not be coming through this area. You are to move your patrol to the West and join up with others to continue the pursuit. None must escape. By keeping our enemy ignorant, only then, can we conquer all. That's all it says." Stone then held his breath to see how the commander would respond worried that they had put something in the dispatch that would tip him off. But then he saw a big smile on the commander's face and knew that they may just be successful.

"I told them they wouldn't come this way, but no, they said that this was the only way through this area and needed to be guarded. We played a game of chance to see who would pull this duty and I lost. Now maybe we will see some action." Then shaking his head he continued. "Now if we only had something to drink and some females to celebrate this."

How had this worked out? The commander was practically begging for alcohol and he happened to have it. Smiling at the commander he said. "I cannot provide the females for your pleasure, but coming this way we . . ." He paused and put a look of conspiracy on his face before continuing. "Well let's say I felt that such a patrol as yours needed something to help celebrate this change of plans. And since no one will know exactly when I arrived to pass on your new orders, then there is no reason not to enjoy the night and leave in the morning."

"Am I to believe that you are going to provide us will something to drink? This is highly unusual."

Careful now, Stone quickly thought, and then said. "Ah yes, these are unusual times are they not? Who would of thought that the many tribes who have fought each other are now allied and working together?"

Shaking his head in agreement the commander asked. "True, true, so where is this *drink* that you are offering us?

Turning to Sahar he said, "Guard please pass on to the commander the supply that we requisitioned."

Bowing to Stone Sahar knelt down, removed his backpack and proceeded to empty it. Stone then said, "I am sorry that there is not as much here for all to get a complete enjoyment from it but it is war and many things are hard to find."

"As you said it is war and we had nothing. So now we have something. Are you going to stay with us since it is almost dark?"

"No, no, can't, as there is another patrol that is to the east of you that must be informed. So I must be on my way immediately – by your leave." Stone then did a short bow to the commander turned around and left the encampment. Trying to make it appear to be as one who needs to be somewhere else quickly, but not so quick to raise suspicions, after all having succeeded to this point and to be too much in a hurry could give the whole thing away. Once a little distance had been placed between the two of them and the encampment Stone stated softly so only Sahar could hear, "I, for one, am glad that we did not go with the other plan that had been put forth. We only have six surviving women with our group now and to have at least 30 in that camp that would want to use them is just too much to think about. I really doubt if they would have survived the ordeal."

"I can't disagree with that statement at all. I have to always remember that as far as these primitives go, women, or females as they call them, have no names, are property, and like the grazing animals are there to both be protected by the males and bred by them. And as far as they are concerned that is as far as it goes." Then shaking his head Sahar continued. "It is a point of view I just do not understand, and probably will never believe in. I mean our women contribute so much overall. To leave part of the race out because they happen to be able to produce offspring, and then figure that's all they are worth just doesn't make sense."

* * *

They continued to monitor the primitives' camp and could now hear boisterous voices, laughter, and see general horse-play emanating from the camp. Then somewhere half way through the night it grew strangely quiet. Even the fires that burned within the camp boundaries seemed to be dying down, as if no one was attending them. Saige then sent down a scouting team to see what had transpired. In too short of time the scouts returned and the leader of the 3-man team reported back. "Saige, they are all dead."

Turning around to their physician Saige asked. "How much stuff did you put in the alcohol anyway? Our goal was to knock them out not kill them, what happened?"

Saar, shrugging, had a perplexed look on his face said. "I really don't know. While I made it a little stronger since they usually are a bit larger than us, I did not put enough in there to kill anybody. Other than that, I cannot explain what happened."

"Nothing we can do about it now. Let's move and I want two of you to take up the rear and wipe out our tracks approaching and leaving the camp so that there will be no evidence that we were even here. Let's move! We've lost enough time and I for one am happy that the pursuers behind us have yet to catch up. Now be very quiet. If we are lucky it may be a few days before the bodies are discovered. Giving time for the wild animals to work over the camp, further confusing what happened here. If things go in our favor it may be that the deaths will be attributed to one of the tribes or clans that have not joined this leader, who, we do not even know anything about as of yet."

Shortly they were working their way through the camp as it had been set up right across the trail leading out of the foothills into the mountains. There was a temptation to search the very silent camp, but moving on was much more important at this moment. Then once through and across the small stream they hid while the final two wiped out their tracks as best they could. In what seemed like an eternity they finally joined them. The plan was a simple one. Now that they were past one of the final obstacles, to push through the remaining portion of the night, then continue through the next day and finally rest the following night. It would be rough but they needed to be at the base or in the mountains by then. Saige looking around in the rising moonlight and then at his small band realized that they all looked like hell. They were dirty – filthy really, and while so far they had gotten this far, there was a weariness that one could see in everyone's eyes. There appeared to be gauntness in all of them also. They had prided themselves on being self-sufficient and were proud of the fact that they could do this better than any in the city. But now he was beginning to wonder if they had been fooling themselves. Now without the city to at least allow some support they were finding it much more difficult.

Of course they had been on the run since they had to abandon the city. So finding the time to actually gather anything had been impossible. Once they had to abandon their machines then the ability to manufacture any food or medicines were lost. So, as they got closer to the mountains, their present goal – and this had become their goal when their way had been cut off from reaching any of the remaining cities – their supplies were almost gone. Now they moved as quickly as the darkness would allow them, with scouts out in front, runners to each side and a trailer to confuse their back trail as best that could be done in the darkness. Tonight it would only be the small moon that would give them light. But it would not be much as he would have liked. But better than the darkness they were now working their way through. He was snapped back from what he was thinking about when one of the scouts had stopped the group. "What's happening?" Saige asked.

"We are going through an area we know very little about – kind of blind here. There's either a camp up ahead of us or maybe a village. We need a couple more to come with us so we can scout out what we are dealing with here, and if there is a way to go around without arousing suspicions."

Signaling the rest to stop and rest for a moment and then looking down in thought before speaking Saige asked, "Tell me what you have seen? Was it a single fire or shelters or what? I'm just trying to get a size here. You know we are not in shape at all to fight. We have to run. But our food is all but gone and if there is an opportunity to add to our stores we may have to chance discovery."

"I don't think that's a good idea. From what we saw they seemed to be on alert. I don't know again if it is another patrol, part of this new alliance, or a clan that has not joined and is being harassed by the others. There is just no way to know."

Shaking his head and sighing Saige said. "We have to know one way or the other." Then pausing for a moment and thinking before speaking again he continued, "Okay, you're probably right. Let's scout it out and see what we face. But make it quick. We don't know how long it will be before the bodies of that main patrol are discovered. I am hoping that it is long enough to hide any evidence of our passing." Then signaling a couple of the other members of their group over to him he then said to them, "Join Staven and go scout out this camp and a safe way around. I need you all back in no more than 2 hours. That will put our time somewhere close to midnight. Again we need as much distance between them and us before sunrise. Now go and as always be very careful. Your discovery by this group could be the end of us all." He watched them leave until they disappeared into the darkness. Now came the waiting, which seemed to be the most difficult. He signaled to the remainder to join him for a moment. And waiting until he was sure they all were there, he brought them up to date as what had been passed on to him by the scout. "Okay, we need to spread out, but keep close enough so that each can see another, and try and get a few moments of rest. We may be here up to two hours, but right now it seems unavoidable." He watched them spread out among the underbrush, followed by small sounds of shuffling about, and then silence.

He must have fallen asleep – not a good thing, but the rest would help. It scared him that it had happened. It meant that he could have been taken and he would never have been the wiser. Yet something had awakened him. So carefully he looked around and shortly saw one of the scouts signaling him to come join him. Curious as to why the scout hadn't joined him he carefully worked his way over to him. He saw it was Staven, "What is it that you have found, and why not come directly to me?"

"No time, will explain it all later. But need a couple of others right now to assist. We've kind of found a windfall but will need help."

With a questioning look on his face Saige asked, "Windfall? What do you mean windfall?"

Quickly, Staven explained. "We've found a place where they have stashed some of their grains, and we need help to move a bit of it for our use. And don't worry we are being very careful and covering up what we take so that it will not be obvious that we are taking anything."

"Okay, but I think I am going to bring the whole group forward so that once we have what can be safely taken that we can immediately move on – just in case." Turning around he signaled the closest to him to round up everyone and meet with him. He waited and then took a head count. In the dark it would so easy to miss someone and leave them behind. "We are going to follow Staven and he will lead us to a place where we will refill our depleted food stores. Once that is accomplished we must immediately move on." Then turning back to Staven he said. "I guess this is some type of permanent settlement then."

"Yup, it appears to be so. In fact there appears to be only one night watchman out and about if you want to call it that. We spotted him right off, and he's staying pretty much in the light and actually looking into the fire that he is using to keep himself warm. It could be they aren't bothered too much as of yet, which is different than we first thought."

"Let's hope he stays that way, or that we are gone before he is replaced with someone who is more alert. We really do need something to break our way for once."

CHAPTER FIVE

Looking back as the morning started graying the skies, and the sudden coolness that seems to greet the dawn he realized that they had a lot of tension while they stole the grains that would hopefully sustain them as they finally made their way into the mountains. It had been a harrowing experience with two constantly watching the night watchman and two entering the small stone building and removing the grain and passing it on to the others. It seemed like an eternity with many stops and starts as at times it appeared the guard had been alerted to something. He really hated to steal, but at this time they had no choice. Once they had their supplies replenished they bid a hasty retreat and continued to move away from the area and towards the mountains. And now that the sunrise was just ahead they found themselves ready to find a way into those unknown mountains. Yet there seemed to be some kind of draw on him that he did not understand. It was like one of those itches that lay just below the surface. One of the types that you try and scratch and where you scratch is not where it truly itches.

As the suns came nearer to the time of showing and it became lighter with the mountains slowly being revealed to them in sharp detail, it was as if they had been here before. But that was all but impossible. As far as he knew there had never even been one of their cities located here. Of course he could never say for sure, but – well, something just seemed to be drawing him. Looking around he could see that it seemed to be affecting the others the same way. At the present they were taking a small meal break before they headed into those mountains. They had built a small smokeless fire to give all of them something hot before the day really began. Shellian, his sister, approached him and gave him something hot to drink. Looking questioningly at her he asked, "What's this? I thought we had run out of our teas and shick a long time ago."

Smiling back at him she said. "Ah that shows you don't know everything . . . actually one of the two who was inside that storehouse found a small stash of this stuff. While I am sure it is not as good as our own it will have to do."

Taking a deep breath and smelling the aroma from the tea he said. "I'm not going to complain. We haven't had anything at all for what seems forever. At this moment it is even hard to remember that we once lived in Sequoyah and had such a different life than the one we have now."

Sitting down beside him with her own cup she sighed and smiled a sad smile, "No truer words were ever spoken. Yet, here we are. I know at times it seems like our life, before the loss of the city, is more like a dream than real. We've lost so much since that day. Not just our way of life, but all those who started the journey with us, and now lie in graves behind us. All of our leaders, friends, and loved ones that are no longer here make it really hard. I mean at times it seems like it would be easier to just give up. There are now only fifteen of us, and only six being women. While I know that we can fight, we have a lesser chance of winning than the men. So really we have nine of you guys and six of us." Trailing off for a moment, letting the silence rise before she continued, "I know, as you do, that if we are caught again that we probably will die. And for us women it will be worse before death takes us. Is all this flight worth it? I know when we started we were to try for another city, but now we can only flee to the mountains as all of the other options have been taken from us. I'm tired and I can see that the rest of us are too. It's easy to understand – too little sleep, food, and constant vigilance, fighting and flight. Look while there is no defeat in our group, yet you can read the weariness in their very souls. I can see it in you and of course I worry. It is part of being a woman."

Thinking for a moment before answering, Saige replied, "Everything you have said is true. I have no answer as to the whys – yet . . ." He paused a moment turned and looked into those mountains as the gathering light revealed them to him. "Yet, for some reason I am finding myself drawn to these ancient mountains. Looking around at the rest who are here with us, I can sense it is the same with them." Then turning to her and looking deeply in her eyes, he said, "See it in you also. It is almost like there is a reason we are heading deep into this unknown. But I don't know why or even understand what is drawing us here. I know it seemed like we were being herded in this direction. And I suspect that camped patrol at the only path through that valley was to be our end. Still . . . still there is something here I don't understand. It seems to be just out of reach – just beyond understanding." Looking down he realized that without thinking about it he had emptied his cup.

Then looking up he could see that it was now time to move on. "I guess we will only know what it is when and if we get to wherever this is leading. It's time to move again. I for one will be glad for this night since it will mean we will be able to camp and catch up on some needed rest."

She couldn't disagree with him. She was exhausted and knew that they could not stop until this very night except for a possible cold meal at midday. Sighing and slowly getting up she said, "I wish that I could just wake up and find all of this had not been real. Then we would happily still be in the compound with the city still there and with nothing out of place. Instead we seem to be living this nightmare, where it is all gone, and we are refugees with no home, and no place to go."

He had no answers for her, and knew that really none were needed, as it was just a statement – one that had much truth to it. Standing he signaled the rest to assemble and to be prepared to move on. The Sun was now touching the tops of the hills to the east of them. It would be a couple of hours before the second much smaller sun would rise. Then picking what appeared to be an animal trail he led off. They needed to be away from any civilization by the end of this day. And the fact that the primitives considered these mountains a place of fear was their major hope and refuge, and that the only ones that they might encounter here would be the priests who would be asking of their gods whatever it was they needed, and to leave the tribes and clans behind, and to remain here isolated in these mountains. At this moment he did not send out scouts ahead, that would come later. Right now he needed trailers to watch their backs. Once it could be determined that they were safe from pursuit then he would put out scouts ahead. They just did not have enough surviving members to do both.

The trail they were on seemed to run parallel to the ridgeline, but below the top. It seemed impossible that such a trail should be here as the sides were steep and there was a long way to the bottom of the canyon. He suspected that if any fell that it would be to their death. There did not seem any way one could get up the sides. Yet he knew from experience that these trails, made by the animals, had to lead somewhere and usually did not just end. This he was counting on, as he wanted them to stay off of any of the trails that had been established by the priests and the few hunters that braved the hostile spirits that lived in these mountains, as primitives believed. Still as they worked their way along this small dangerous trail it was a slow and careful hike. By midmorning they were still over the same precipice. The canyon below had continued to deepen and they could hear the roar of flowing water and what they assumed was a waterfall. But none of it was visible to them. As the suns continued to rise in the sky they found that they were beginning to sweat heavily, and still this trail had continued; now slowly climbing towards the ridgeline. If it reached the top they would have to stop and make sure that it was safe to pass over and remain unseen.

From where they were, it appeared that the trail was approaching a large boulder which sat above them. At this moment it looked as if the trail would just end there. If so, they were in trouble, as there had been no place along the path that branched off or even gave them an opportunity to leave it. Once they reached the boulder, they found that again sometime in the ancient past, this monster had been up above them and had then fallen. It must have had a weak point within it.

When it had finally struck the ground from where it had originally been, it split in half with the lower portion sliding away and down, opening up an area between the two pieces, and it was here that the trail continued. It was a tight fit but with work they got through. Once through, the trail entered head high brush and then dropped down the other side into a small valley that was completely hidden. Here they found a small stream flowing, with a very small pond where out the backside the water continued to flow out of the valley. There was also a small pasture, so it was a good place for the grazers to come. Now, the question was, did it just end here? Even with no answer to that question, it was a good place to take their break before continuing. It was very quiet and peaceful. He looked at the area regretfully as it would have been a great place to stop and let everyone catch their breath and recover their strength. But it was just too close, and even here as remote as it appeared to be, they still could be found. Well, they would eat their cold meal here. He decided that probably they would now pull in the trailers and put out scouts ahead, returning to as close of a normal setup that they could make happen with their reduced numbers.

Yet, if the grazers came here, where were they? The trail looked used and there had been fresh droppings along the route. Looking around he could see some additional piles here. Yet at the moment there were none to be seen. Maybe they were here, but since it was still close to where the hunters came, they had learned to fear and were in hiding. If so this may not be as safe as he thought. In fact it may be a place those very hunters came to hunt the grazers. Alarmed now he signaled them to silence followed by the signal to carefully search for any sign of the primitives having been in the area.

And shortly a couple of the members signaled that they had found something. He went with stealth now and signaled the rest to remain hidden and joined the two. There before them was a fire pit. But fortunately it had not been used in quite some time. But now it was obvious, that as appealing as this place had been, they could not stop here and must immediately continue leaving no trace of their passing. Yet, was this a good or bad sign? It meant that the fire pit hadn't been used in a while, but did that reflect a change of location or just that it was one of the many visited areas the hunters traveled. With no idea of the history of the area they could not take that chance.

He turned to signal assembly and to move out when the two trailers came rapidly over the hill from where they had just come and signaled that a group was approaching. They hadn't had much time to even check the area out but now they had to get out quickly if they were to remain invisible. The valley that they were in was too small to have any hiding places. Flight out of the area was their only choice. So Saige signaled retreat and out of the area. This was going to take a few moments since they had been unpacking to eat a quick meal. One of the trailers finally approached Saige while the other kept a lookout just below the entrance. The lead trailer then said. "We are probably no more than 10 minutes ahead of them at the most. So far they have been making the journey in this direction at a leisure pace. If they pick it up it will be in shorter."

Shaking his head Saige said. "And I almost missed it. The signs were all here, but none of us saw it." Turning around he could see the rest were very busy putting things back together and coming rapidly to form around him. To the ones who had gathered he stated softly. "We have very little time so begin heading out to the upper side and away from where we entered. We need to stay hidden since a group of hunters are approaching. We'll take a head count once we are all outside of this area and away. Now let's go." Then staying with the trailers he began wiping out whatever sign they had left. He knew it would be a poor job, but these hunters were not tracking or looking for anything at this point. So maybe they would get lucky.

Taking a final quick look around, he trailed the others out of the valley hoping that they had done a good enough job. As he slipped through the brush and behind a boulder on the upper side the hunters came over the hill and into the small valley. How much time did they have before they started going after the grazers that had to be hiding in the area, he had no idea. But they needed to be as far away as they could be. The problem was these were hunters, so it had to be done carefully, so as to not alert them in pursing. But again, not knowing the area, they were not even sure what the easiest, safest, or fastest way out of the small valley could be. They, as a group, pulled back deeper into the brush where it was confirmed that everyone was there. Now once again they were on the run with an enemy close by. He had hoped that they had finally left that problem behind, but it was painfully clear that it wasn't that way at all.

* * *

Hours later they worked their way along the edge of a high mountain meadow. The air was cool, crisp, and very clear. From here they could see the valley below that they had escaped, and the one with the dead patrol located at the only path through the area. Yet its distance was great enough that the details of the area could not be discerned. They then hiked around a small outcropping and the view was gone. Here they found that once again they were dropping down into a large ravine, and once there they remained in it, as it appeared to be running in the general direction they wanted to go anyway. He finally pulled in the trailers and ran scouts out ahead, as he felt that they were probably far enough up into the mountains that finding a viable trail and a place to stay for this night was of greater importance. He could see the fatigue in each and every step all of them were taking. They needed a stopping place – one that would provide a respite for them. It would only be one night, but it would be something that none of them had had in a long, long time. As they continued to push his mind started drifting back on their history, as they knew it: They had been taught that they had become separated from the ones they now call the primitives at least a millennium if not many millenniums in the past. From what he could re-member there had been a great war and their people had found the desolate as rarely traveled areas and began the process of setting up their cities – using the technology to hide them from the rest of this crazy world. At the time they all had been on equal footing, but it could be seen by the ones who estab-lished the cities, that it would not be that way for long. The fighting was destroying everything and once it had finished its destructiveness then the survivors would be starting over. Yet, at this present time, it had appeared that these descendants had learned very little as they continued to fight among them-selves.

But something had changed, if only partially. They still fought, and they still killed each other. But now, somehow, they had become more organized, and he suspected it was under one charismatic leader. Then the primitives had discovered the cities and as each one was found it was conquered, destroyed, leaving ghosts and ruin in their wake. Coming back to their present situation, once they were able to establish a place where they could rest and be safe, then they would need to find out who this leader was, and how they could eliminate him. And do it before all of the cities were no more. It appeared that, more than likely, this time the destruction would be complete and all would be brought down to the level of the primitives. He suspected that once this new leader, who seemed to be bringing many if not all the tribes under his banner, died that no one left within the leadership would be strong enough to hold the alliances together, at least that was the hope. He knew that their long-term goal was to eliminate this unknown leader who had brought so much destruction down upon them. But obviously their short-term goal was to survive long enough to be able to get around to that other goal.

The ravine they were in took a sharp right turn then began a steep uphill climb. Here, there were exposed boulders that they had to work over and around. He began to wonder with the depth of the ravine why there was no water running in it. While it was late summer, almost fall, the area here showed signs of plenty of moisture, and this was a large ravine showing much water flow. Again, continuing the uphill trend it returned to its original direction. In the distance they could hear what sounded like a lot of water flowing. It was time to exit this place, so he signaled them to leave and with much exertion, as the sides were both soft and steep they finally stood above the ravine. Ahead of them and shadowed, it appeared that just around a bend in the distance there looked to be a hint of a waterfall. Then as they got closer it was now obvious why the ravine had been dry. The roar of the waterfall now was deafening, and the volume coming over it was surprising. But they could not get any closer, as there was a growing lake between them and the falls. There had been a landslide, which had blocked the flow of the water down the ravine. From what they could see it would be a while before the water level reached the top of the landslide. But it would and then go over the top and break the dam causing a flash-flood taking anything and everything that would be in its path. The sight was both breathtaking and very dangerous. They had been lucky that it was still holding. If it had released while they were traversing that ravine they would all have been killed.

The scouts reported in saying that the area around the falls was impassible, and that they would have to work more to the east and around this area. They said that there was another animal trail that was even more precarious than the last one they were on. But it was good enough to use and that it would take them to the top where they all could see the beginning of the falls. That there was another alpine meadow complex before it became a broken land once again and that there was a shallow cave where they probably could finally break. It was partially hidden by the vegetation and if one did not look directly at it, one could very easily miss it. With that information, they followed the scouts finding the description they had given about the animal trail was well understated. He wondered how the animals had even formed this. There was a number of times where in the past shale had slid off the mountainside above the trail and added to its precariousness. They used a rope and tied everyone together so that if one of them slipped and fell it would not be to their death. There was a couple of close moments when some of the shale that they were walking on slipped and fell down the mountainside over the edge and then it seemed like an eternity before they heard it hit the mountainside far below. No doubt about it, if one of them fell they would not survive. When they finally reached the meadow complex all were breathing very hard and were shaking from the ordeal. In fact as he wiped his forehead he found sweat. It surprised him since the area they presently were in was cool. He hoped that they could avoid having to hike that trail again. Going up was bad enough, but going down would be worse. This increased his respect for the two scouts, since not only did they climb up this trail twice, but had to descend to find them. He had to admit he for one was glad it hadn't been him.

Once everyone had caught their breath, the scouts led them across three large meadows then against a rise just before the rough country started. At first he did not see anything at all, but the scouts just kept going and suddenly what he thought was shadow became the entrance. Turning to one of the scouts Saige asked. "How'd you ever find this thing? I mean I was following you and you were making a direct line to the entrance, yet until just now I did not figure it out."

Smiling he said, "It wasn't me, it was your sister. She said that something just did not look right about that. I said, nah it's just shadows. Again she said no, not true. Look it is too dark to just be shadows. Come on, we need to investigate this. And so she dragged me up here to look, and as you can see she was right and I was wrong. We did a quick inspection to make sure nothing was using it for a home, and then once we confirmed that, came back to get you. Good timing too, since we are almost out of daylight. I checked and there is a good supply of dead wood and the cave's location is such that it will not be visible at all unless you walk right up to it. So while not perfect by any means, it is the best we have found. Also scouted for tracks of the primitives and no sign that they have been anywhere around this area. I think we are probably the first to be here. Water isn't real close but not so far away to be a burden. I think also from the reaction of the grazers that they don't see us as a threat – another sign that the hunters have not been here to lead them to fear us."

"I guess you've answered all of my questions even before I could ask them." Looking around he could see the rest of the team moving inside of the small cave and briefly disappearing from sight. Then shaking his head he continued. "I just wish that we had more time. We need a place that we can remain for longer than overnight. Much of our clothes and equipment are in need of repair or replacement. And I must admit like any other male around here seeing our women with less is always exciting, but at the same time it is not a good thing that our clothes have worn that thin. Without that equipment that we had to abandon, and I do hope we hid it well enough from discovery, there is no quick and easy way to do the work we need to accomplish, or repair or replace the items we need.

I guess it is time to chance it and take an extra day, if for no other reason than we need the recovery time. On top of it all we have been on the run and really have no idea of where to go from here. So we need to send out scouting parties and find the best way out of here. While I don't necessarily want to disturb the grazers, we need the meat and time to prepare it for the trail. The grains that we *borrowed* from that last settlement will only last so long and will not sustain us like meat will." Then pausing and looking around in the failing light he said, "Enough on this we need to get things moving before it becomes too dark to see. Besides I need to talk with Shellian and thank her for this discovery." He then turned and went up to their new temporary camp and joined the rest of the group.

* * *

They remained in this area for two days before continuing on to find a more permanent location. In that time they had killed one of the grazers at night so as to minimally disturb the rest. Then they jerked the meat over small fires, packed and divided it among the members, and attempted to hide any trace that they had been there. Still they knew that with the amount of time that they had spent here, that it would be nearly impossible to completely wipe out any sign. The scouting had produced a couple of promising possibilities, and they knew that they needed to go deeper and higher into these mountains. So the decision was made to take the rougher route they had discovered. Guessing that if the primitives found this camp that they would assume that the ones they were following would have taken the easier and more obvious route out of the area. To help further that impression, half of the remaining members worked up that trail leaving easily followed tracks, before backtracking, and heading down the actual trail, which first dropped down into a canyon with high narrow walls extending up and out of sight, immediately placing the entire team in deep shadows. From the narrowness of the gorge and steep sides it obviously was an area where the suns rarely reached with their warmth and light. The chill was immediate and penetrated the warmest of clothing that they were wearing. The time they had stopped had given them the respite to be able to make small repairs and get a little extra rest, something that had been rare, having to actually lift their spirits. Now instead of feeling dread, and impending doom, or death, there seemed to be an uplifting, and anticipation of what lay ahead of them. Now instead of being just one step ahead of the next fight, ambush, or accident, they had time to be careful and to plan. Yet with all that lay behind them, they had become much better at living in the wilds. Even though their numbers now were less than one third of the original group, in many ways they were stronger, more cunning, and with their abilities tested to the limit, their confidence in what they could do, became very strong. Now with the additional time, hiding their trail should overall be successful. They had to disappear, as if they had never existed. So now was the time to accomplish that. The previous campsite would be the last the primitives should find; it was time to become ghosts, spirits, and find that place to begin the offensive against their enemy. But that was still sometime in the future; right now they were very much on the run with no home or no real destination.

Eventually the canyon walls retreated, opening up to a broken land. It gave the appearance that sometime in the great past mythological giants had been angry and were throwing large boulders around. There was very little vegetation here, and ice was everywhere making footing extremely treacherous. If one did not consciously concentrate on his footing he found himself on his behind quicker than he could react, and it hurt. Yet the animal trail they were following continued to wind around and through both the ice and broken land. This trail had to be going somewhere, as there was absolutely nothing for grazers to eat here. Yet at this very moment it was not obvious. At midday they finally stopped and ate a cold meal.

And cold was an appropriate description, as their breath came out in great white clouds. Even though the suns shown down on them there appeared to be no warmth and the breeze that was blowing through this empty land cut right through them leaving them to find the lee of the boulders hoping to have them at least block some of the wind. Looking out across the landscape from their limited view, it appeared that this flat valley just went on forever. At this point they did not know if they would completely cross it before dark. But each knew that they did not want to spend the night here. As cold as it was now it would be deadly at night. That made this meal stop one that was very short and then they were on their way once more.

There was something about this area that felt haunted – as if they were continually under observation. But, it was a silent cold world. No sounds of birds, or the scurrying of the small animals or any movement other than they, giving the appearance that there were no others here but them. Yet as they worked their way deeper into this frozen land their alarm continued to rise. Saige could see it in all of them as each member continued to search the area with their eyes, trying to locate some unseen danger. He could feel the short hairs on the back of his neck rising up, yet like the rest he could find no source to this sense of being watched. He had to admit that this barren landscape, one totally lacking in any vegetation, still had too many places for a predator to hide, surrounded as they were with the piled ice and scattered boulders. If one were able to get up high enough this area overall would appear to be flat. What had happened here to cause this? Looking ahead the wild animal trail continued. Even the trail seemed to pass by areas that would have been easier, it was like the animals that traveled here were sensing and avoiding something threatening.

As the day progressed, and there was no letup in the tension, they found that their nerves were raw and all of them were on the verge of panic. The strength of the feeling could not be denied by any of them. But there was no source that any had found. Just what was going on, what was causing this sense of dread? Unconsciously they had picked up their pace just wanting to be away from this place. Finally needing to break they stopped to catch their breath. Seve standing next to one of the large boulders bent over to get something out of his backpack when something huge, white and extremely quick flashed through and missed grabbing Seve because the animal had expected him to remain standing. With a roar of frustration it was gone. All were standing where they were, frozen in position from the shock of the attack. No one had seen it, and only for a brief moment had it flashed by. Disbelief hit them at the speed of this predator – something that size shouldn't be able to move that fast. Then Saige yelled. "Grab you gear and run down the trail now! We have to get out of here; we have no defense against whatever that was. I don't want any of us here when it returns. And who knows if there is one, there may be others." Quickly they put their packs back together and started trotting out. Now they would again not be able to rest until they were completely away from here. It still was shocking as the speed of this predator. Guessing from the brief glimpse he figured that it was twice the size of any one of them.

"Anybody get a look at whatever it was or can identify it?" Saige asked. There was no answer, just the sound of heavy breathing and feet hitting the ground. He knew from the history of the cities that none of them were located in these mountains so this predator could be completely unknown to them. It may also be another reason why these mountains were off limits to the primitives, except their holy men. But there had to be more to it. Even a beast like whatever this one was could be hunted down with enough hunters. Still what if they had a tendency to run in packs? Now that would be scary. A herd of grazers could be wiped out in an instant of time. He hoped they were solitary. As the adrenaline burned away there came an awareness that once again with too little sleep and too little to eat their reserves were being used up and if there was no respite their bodies would finally just quit and refuse to move.

Looking ahead it appeared that they had much too far to go to get out of this haunted ice and boulder covered plain. Looking back he could not even see where they had entered the area. Then turning back around he saw the group stop and was standing and with the clouds of breath coming from the group as they caught their breath. Catching up he stopped quickly. Before them was a chasm cut by a fast flowing river. Here the trail just stopped. Looking desperately around he wondered if the game trail just ended. But that did not make any sense. Did they miss something in their desperate flight to this dead end? One thing for sure if the beast decided to attack again they had nowhere to go. "We must have missed something. There has to be branch off of this. We know that the grazers do not make these trails that lead to nowhere. With whatever that is behind us we have to search as a group. I do not want any of us separated or alone. We cannot lose anyone. We barely have enough members alive and healthy to be able to survive." They carefully backtracked for a distance, and then returned to the edge; finding nothing – yet there had to be something. What had they missed? "Anyone see anything?" Saige asked. All he could see was the shaking of their heads. Looking down at the ground and closing his eyes he thought hard. There just had to be something they had missed. He suspected that at one time that the trail probably had a passage over the river here and that it collapsed. But the trail still showed use so the grazers had to have found a way around which meant they had missed something. "Okay let's do this, let's split the team in half. No I do not want us to separate. We need all of us together if we have to face that thing again. I want one half to concentrate on one side of the trail and the other half to search the opposite side. Now let's do it."

It took a while, time they had not to waste, but eventually in an area where they least expected it they found where it branched. There was a place where one side dipped away and another split boulder sat in the middle of this dip. When one first glanced at the boulder the split did not appear to be large enough to allow passage between. But upon closer inspection they found tuffs of hair clinging to the sides showing that the grazers had gone this way. The soil here was too hard to leave any tracks or show any depression, but once through to the other side of the crack the trail became obvious. He wondered what had happened to the original pathway across the gorge and how the grazers had located this alternate route. The direction it ran did not seem to lead in the direction that they needed to go. In fact it appeared to head back from where they had started that day. But they stuck with it since there were no other options, and eventually as the level of the trail continued to fall it then made a sharp turn and dropped steeply down. They now could hear the rushing water in the distance and knew that now they were heading directly towards and probably at level with the river. Now the question was, did it end at the river, or was there a way across at this point? With a ridgeline blocking their view they could not see anything of the surrounding area at all. In fact as they had dropped down into this area they once again had walls rising up on both sides of them. If the primitives had been here they would have been trapped since there was no way up the sides and only back the way they had come or forward towards the unknown. Again it was deeply shadowed and quite cold so they continued to press forward towards the increasing sound of the flowing river.

Saige was working the rear guard when the leaders turned a corner and just stopped. And as others reached the same point their reaction was the same. Curious he pushed forward and found that his reaction was just as the rest. Before them the area opened up and there was a large open alpine meadow with numerous trees dotting the area. Off towards the area where they had been stopped by the chasm lay a huge water-fall that had not been visible from above. Sweet smells wafting off the grasses and alpine flowers were quite pleasant and for a short distance the river was wide and slow before narrowing again and heading off over another precipice. Here in the distance and across the river they saw grazers with their heads down and a few looking in their direction. They showed some curiosity but did not have the stance of ones ready to take flight. After seeing nothing threatening these few that had watched them returned to their grazing. Shellian commented, "I think this might be a good place to camp for the night. From the reaction of the grazers I don't think we have to wor-ry about whatever that was, that attacked us up there on that ice and boulder strewn flat land."

Still taking in the scenery Saige paused thinking that they really needed to continue, but there was very little daylight left and he had to admit that there was every sign that she was right. It very well could be that the predator that had attacked them only roamed the area that they had just left. There definitely was something about this particular area that lent itself to relaxing. He had to admit it was almost an idyllic scene. "You may be right. There's not much daylight left and we have no idea what's ahead of us. And I have to agree that we are probably not going to find anything better." Then coming to a decision he said. "Yes, let's do it – but first let's move to the other side of this river. The last thing I would want to happen is for us to get stuck on this side if the river suddenly increased because of some rain that we wouldn't be aware of. Shellian, once we are across, signal camp. Then once its set up we'll get together and see what the others feel and how we should continue."

* * *

It had been a peaceful and a quick night. While they posted guards and rotated them often, the rest slept hard and deep from exhaustion caused by the days of being continually on the run, having to be forever vigilant, fighting and trying to stay ahead of the enemy. The plan had been to be back on the trail by sunrise but it was midmorning before they were moving again. Now they hiked through knee high grasses that were curing in the late summer, early fall. They suspected that both fall and winter would come early to these higher mountain ranges. So they knew their time was short and they needed to find a place where they could winter. It needed to be found soon, because they would have to gather foods and such to carry them through winter, and right now they had little. While this place that they were leaving was nice, it was open and would probably be buried deep in the winter snows and would not be a good place to stay. So they moved on, both to put more distance between themselves and the primitives, and to find better shelter.

Once across the meadow the trail began its climb out and head deep into the mountains. As they continued to climb the trees began to thin out and eventually disappear altogether. Although higher up they could see scattered alpine trees. Looking back across the landscape they could no longer see anything but the mountains. The place they had left was as if it had never been. Now all that was visible was the surrounding rugged wild mountains that may have never seen anything like them. Saar commented to no one in particular. "This surely is beautiful, but I sense very dangerous. None of us have ever lived in such an area, and I being the doctor for this group am worried, as I have no access to anything I am familiar with. I know nothing of the plants, and our equipment that we had to abandon, had the facilities to allow me to manufacture medicines, as I needed. Now – now I don't have anything at all. It really is a worrisome thing."

Saige didn't say anything, as he had no answer. Instead he nodded in agreement. There were many things that they did not have, and would have a desperate need, before winter arrived. The major question running through his mind was, did they have enough time left before winter, and would they find the necessary shelter to get through what he suspected would be a harsh winter? With these thoughts weighing heavily on his mind he really did not see the beauty that now surrounded them. He had been pushed into this leadership role before he *might* have wanted it. He had known that Shayne was working with both he and his sister to be his replacements someday. But that was to be far in the future, not under the duress that had led to he and she, now leading this ragtag remainder of their civilization. He wondered idly if other cities had gone dark. He suspected that *possibly*, was the best answer.

Again remembering the history that had been taught, there had originally been eight families that established the first cities. In the intervening time the cities had expanded to the known thirty. But with at least five now gone that he knew of – which included theirs – that had reduced the number to twenty-five. At least the original city was well hidden and purposely never placed on any of their maps. While most of the maps that existed were kept in the ruling hall he was sure that one might have fallen into the primitives' hands, making it easier for them to locate the rest of the cities. But he really had no proof, since most of the cities existed in similar lands, this alone could be enough, giving the primitives a place to consistently search out for additional hidden cities. Yes it now was painfully obvious that they had become too complacent, too comfortable, and ended up with too much belief in their advantage of technology over the primitives. They were now paying a hard price for such stupidity. Should they have reached out a long time ago and tried to establish some type of relationship with the primitives? Well it hadn't been attempted, so maybe the result would have been the same. Now it appeared that the primitives were bent on destroying all that they could find. Why? Again he had no answers, just speculation, and with nothing to support that speculation he may as well be spitting into the wind for all the good it would do him.

Someone had just spoken to him and because he had been so deep in thought he did not hear at all. Looking to his side he saw Shellian looking at him questioningly. Smiling he said, "Sorry Shellian, but I was lost in thought. I for one was not expecting to take over the leadership so soon."

Nodding her head in agreement she said. "Yeah me neither. But I simply asked you about that plain area we had crossed yesterday. What do you think caused it to be that way? I mean if you look at either side it is heavily forested with many plants and meadows and such. But that area was bare of anything that was living, other than that predator that we really never saw."

"I really don't know. Maybe you should ask Stone since he is our geologist and plant specialist. But my guess would be that sometime in the past that there was a flood through that area. It's the only explanation I can come up with that could create such a place as that. But, I for one am glad that it was only one day's travel to get across. I really would not have wanted to spend the night there, as cold as it was during the day, and then give those predators another shot at us."

She shivered at the thought, "I have to agree with that. All I saw was a flash and in that brief flash the impression was that it was huge and extremely quick. It left me wondering why just the single attempt. I mean it appeared to be something that would have had no problem in coming back and attacking us again."

"I don't know, but my guess is that it had been following us for some time, waiting for the right moment to make its attack, and when it failed, and thanks to the stars that it did, it felt that we would be alerted. Since it did not know what we could or could not do, it may have decided to go after something else. Again not knowing what it even is, I know nothing about how it lives, hunts, or anything at all. So once again it's just a guess on my part."

"Thinking that it might have been following us for some time just sends chills through me." Pausing briefly before continuing, Shellian said, "I mean any one of us could have gone out to take care of nature's call, been alone and vulnerable and then could have been attacked and taken away and no one would have had any idea what had happened. I doubt that there would have even been any real sign left behind for even out best tracker to figure out what had happened."

"Very true, but at least now we know that they exist – even though I would guess that we would have little defense against them. Just not enough is known. So let's just hope that they roam and hunt in that plain and are nowhere else." He then looked at what they were hiking through at this moment and then said. "Not to change the subject but this area is absolutely beautiful. How long have we been climbing? Sorry I really haven't been paying attention, just too much on my mind."

"Really? I would never have guessed oh brother of mine." She answered sarcastically before continuing. "I could see that, but it probably isn't a good thing. I mean we all need to stay alert for dangers – after all this is all unknown to us."

There was no argument for that statement. Yet it had been very difficult not to become deep in thought. There was so much that was unknown behind them and definitely ahead of them. How could one plan at all when he did not even know what question to ask? Looking around the area they presently were hiking through, it was a mix of alpine plants and scattered trees. While the soils looked rich it was also quite rocky. Looking closer at some of the rocks, which were exposed he realized that they were volcanic in nature. His conclusion from that observation was that the mountains they presently were in probably were extinct volcanoes. There sure had been no signs of such activity in this direction as long as he could remember, and as far as their history books spoke. All they stated was quote, "There is a rugged mountain range to the north, which has been little explored." Well, these mountains were going to be explored now – not by choice but by necessity. The air was beginning to take on a chill as they continued along the trail. The breeze definitely had a bite to it. Looking up they could see that in the far distance that there still was snow and it was obvious to them that it probably never melted. Presently they had no clothing that would keep them warm in such an area so they would have to avoid it if at all possible. But the trail continued to wind through the sparse trees and continued its upward climb. Off to the west they could see where a cliff line developed and slowly the trail was working itself towards this cliff edge, eventually reaching and then paralleling it. Looking over it had to be at least 300 meters straight down. It was a dizzying height, and with nothing there to prevent one from falling, it had been difficult getting close enough to even peer over the edge. When they approached the edge they could hear the roaring of a great amount of water, and looking ahead they saw the beginnings of a waterfall dropping over into the abyss, crashing with a roar far below. The trail was heading directly towards it.

When they finally reached the top of the waterfall they could see that the amount of water going over the edge was tremendous. The river – and it had to be called a river – was at least 40 meters wide at this point and was moving rapidly. There was no safe way to cross it. Like the plain they had crossed the day before, the river was filled with boulders and the water crashed and bounced around these obstructions giving the appearance of anger from the water trying to move these obstructions out its way. There was a heavy mist coming off the water and it cooled the air to almost freezing. It sent a shiver and chill through them and they had to withdraw beyond the mist and find a place out of the wind and in the weak sunlight to warm themselves. Where the light touched the mists, rainbows formed throwing vibrant colors into the air. Here close to water they took their midday break. Saige called a brief meeting to find out how all was doing and what their next move should be. Up until now it had been flight, but with the final flight from the primitives behind them they now needed to find a semi-permanent camp area and the sooner the better. They were in trouble and he knew it. It was late in the season here and looking at that snow on the higher peaks let him know that once winter set in they were going nowhere until spring thaw. "Okay all, we have been doing nothing but running, fighting and reacting to what has been happening to us. There has been no time for planning except for what the situation dictated at the moment. Now that our first danger is finally behind us we now have a greater one ahead of us. We need to be looking for a place to wait out the winter. And while I am not an expert on the weather it is obvious to me that winter comes early here and probably stays late.

"If you look at our food supplies I doubt that we have enough to last out the next ten days let alone a winter. Plus we have no shelter or clothing or anything. What the primitives could not do to us down there, winter up here could. So in the next few days we need to be finding that shelter. I suspect that this mountain and maybe the whole range of mountains here were volcanic at one time. We do not have time to build any-thing even if we had the tools to do it. So we need to find one of the many caves that volcanoes create and then start work-ing hard on preparing it for a winter stay. That means building a wall at the front of the cave to help insulate it against the cold put together enough firewood to both keep us warm, and to cook by. I suspect that we will be having a fire going all the time. If that is the case think of how much wood that will re-quire. Then we have to face the real problem, even if we solve these first two – food. So we will have to be sending out hunt-ing parties to bring in meat. Then it will have to be smoked and cured so that it will last the winter. And again like the firewood we will need a lot of it since there are fifteen people here. At least with the skins, from the animals we bring in for food, we should not be lacking for materials to make clothes.

"Now when you think about it there are so many small de-tails that will be necessary to accomplish that I have only covered the big ones here and now. You have to think about sanitary requirements, utensils, sleeping areas, bedding, and on and on. We do not have a lot of time to do this so once we find our spot we will all be working from dawn to past dusk. Sleeping I do not think will be a problem." Looking over the group he could see that what he had just passed on to them had them worried. Like him up to this point it had been just survive another day, avoid the primitives and continue mov-ing. Now they had to change their mindset and begin to set up something more permanent.

CHAPTER SIX

As he feared, winter struck hard and with a fury in these mountains that they were unfamiliar with down in the lowlands. It had taken them five days to finally find something suitable to last out the winter that was approaching. Then the work really began and the small group worked from before sunrise to well after sunset. It was hard grueling work and while there were complaints, and many a sore muscle, they all knew that what they were trying to accomplish here would make the difference between survival and death. There would be no in-between here, and in this harsh world they were now living, there would be no forgiveness. There had been little time to really explore the cave they found that would meet most of their needs. Water was close, but not so close that it would draw unwanted animals or people their way. Plus it was partially up the side of a hill so that if the snow piled high they would remain above this snow. It faced at an angle to the prevailing winds so as to keep the winds from entering into the cave and chilling it further. When Stone looked at the cave when it was first found, he felt that it probably was a steam vent from the extinct volcano, and it had vented both vertically and horizontally with the vent hole out the roof being small. This provided a place for the smoke to escape when they built a fire or fires inside the cave. It appeared that in the distant past when this was forming that it blew out the side of this hill placing debris everywhere – giving them ample building materials to wall up the entrance. A few trees also were close further shielding the entrance from sight.

With their group being this small, they could only send out two hunting teams, with each team consisting of two individuals. They had to hunt well away from this area, so if it became necessary, that during the winter they would be able to hunt closer to their camp for additional food. They had completed the transformation before the first flakes of snow began falling. This spurred them on to even greater effort. And if one looked around at the team now they would have appeared to be even more primitive than the ones they had fought. Working the skins into leather for clothing had changed their appearance. Now everyone was in the leather from the game that was also their food supply. While the meat was the main subsistence they also collected nuts and plants to help round out their nutritional needs. This season they could not be selective. Later, if they survived, and with more time, there would be more variety in their foods. Saige, looking at the group working in the camp outside of the cave, as they prepared the meat for drying, reminded him of the holos they would watch in school showing how their ancient ancestors lived and interacted with each other and other tribes. At the time of youth he thought it was fun watching, but since it was all a reenactment anyway it probably was not like what they were being shown. Yet, now he had to admit that the scene he was seeing here was uncannily just like the ones in those holos.

While the opening into this particular cave wasn't very large – one still could walk into it while standing – it was large enough to admit two abreast. Once inside it opened up with the roof sitting approximately 6 meters above and side-to-side 20 to 30 meters. It appeared that as the original magma and water steam headed for the surface; they stopped here, expanded, before finally blowing out in the two places which became their entrance to the cave and exit for the smoke from the fires. Inside they built, using wood and stone, areas for privacy since they were a mixed group. There were a few off-shoots from the main tunnel and while not truly explored there were two on opposite sides and deeper inside that they turned into places to take care of their nature calls. And if someone in the group broke the rules they were placed on the duty of cleaning these areas and hauling the waste outside a safe dis-tance away. Not a job any wanted but still necessary. So if all stayed within their rules then all would rotate through the job with none excluded. In another offshoot they found a large bowl shaped by the flowing lava that they converted into a bath.

Close to the area of the cave, they found clay from which they then began to make pots. While they had no way of firing them to proper hardness what they did produce worked. Frag-ile yes, and because of this they made as many as time would allow. In some of the larger vessels they had created they heated water for the bath. After all with 15 people in an en-closed area for an extended period of time it could get very ripe. They rigged a couple of skins over the entrance to again allow for privacy and set the rule that if it was closed off then it was occupied and off limits until the entrance again was open. When one used the bath they were also responsible for emptying and cleaning it. They had found that one of the plants up in these highlands absorbed water and left a pleasant scent, so the women collected as much of this as they could find. Stating, "It's all right if you men don't mind coming out all wet, but we would prefer to be dry, and the scent from the plants are pleasant too." There had been plenty of dead wood in the area so they began by working the wood that was furthest out leaving the wood close in for later use if they had to add to their supply. So, while a long way from perfect, what they had created was very livable.

* * *

Pulling back the cover they had over the opening to help keep it warmer within the cave, Saige briefly stepped outside and immediately shivered. The temperatures between inside and outside were vastly different. There was a strong wind blowing, but fortunately he was out of it. It had been snowing now for many days and from the looks of the clouds, which were sullen, dark, and appeared to be heavily laden with moisture, there would be many more days of this storm before it broke. Not used to being inside as long as they had, he began to get what he had heard called cabin fever. While there was plenty of room even with the fifteen of them inside he never had to stay this long without going outside to at least see the sky. Once this storm broke they would have to go get more tar for their torches. They had gone through their supply much quicker than they had planned. He also knew that soon they would need to learn the area they were living in. While preparing for this winter there had been little time to actually explore and map the area. If for some reason the primitives were to come up here they would need a quick and safe way out of the area. There was much that needed to be done and it fell on his shoulders, he and his sister's shoulders, he corrected himself – since before Shayne had died he made it clear that the two of them were a team and were to lead as a team.

It still saddened him every time he thought back to that night when Shayne had died, and he was sure it was that way for all of them. He heard the cover being drawn back and turned to see Shellian coming out to stand next to him. Like when he first emerged, she shivered, crossed her arms and hunched against the cold. Wondering why she came out he asked. "So sis why leave the warmth of the cave?"

"Oh I guess like you the cave just seemed to be closing in on me and I needed to get out for even a couple of minutes. I saw you leave and thought this would be a good time to do it since you would be out here. I knew that at least with this storm blowing that you wouldn't be too far, so there would be two of us, *as you have requested,* and not just one."

Shrugging he said. "You got me there. But I was going nowhere except right here and to admit it; I was going stir crazy in there and just needed to step out for a short time. Besides it gave me a chance to see how deep this snow is getting. But I am sure that is not the only reason. I know that Shayne left both of us in charge and with such a small group of us remaining it is not necessarily a difficult task for the two of us. Keeping all of us alive might be though."

With a sheepish look on her face she paused then said, "Yup I guess that's true. Look with all of us so close in there – I know there's plenty of room, but you know what I mean. There are nine of you guys and only six of us. It would have been nice if it was a little more equal, but it isn't. While it hasn't happened yet, I think these inequalities in numbers are going to be a real problem. Now with winter here in full force we will be forced to be together and if things take their natural course we will be having issues with coupling. And for example take Sorrel, she's a big flirt and I don't think she would be interested in settling for any single man. And she is the type that would enjoy seeing jealousies arise over her. Then there is Sabryn, quiet, strong, and not interested at least outwardly in any man. At least outwardly . . . although I suspect she secretly has someone in mind. At this moment I really do not know. With me as one of the leaders I am not confided in as much as I would like. But also being female I know what I see and . . ." Shrugging again and looking into her brother's eyes. "And I could talk about the other three, but their stories would be similar."

"What about you? I noticed that you did not mention anything about your feelings or the direction they are taking? I know for a fact that you have been drawn towards Saar." Seeing the reaction of Shellian he said. "Now don't you deny it! So far he has been oblivious to any of your looks, but I haven't been your brother all this time without learning how to read you at least a little."

Looking down at the snow covered ground before answering Shellian then said. "Okay I am sweet on him, but that's all. Is it that obvious?"

"Probably only to me, since like I said, I know you. Otherwise it would appear to be just a leader's interest in someone under him or her. But you are right. I have only been thinking about surviving this winter, learning as much about this area as we can and trying to keep all of us safe. I hadn't even considered the coupling aspect, and, oh my, that would mean that you or I would have to perform the ceremony if two of them really wanted to become a couple." Now it was his turn to look down before continuing. "Hey sis, I had enough on my mind before you threw this one at me. Thanks a lot."

Smiling she said, "You are welcome of course. But again with so few women that will mean that some of the men will be without and that could further the problems. And no, I am not suggesting that we all start sleeping around and spread the wealth here. All I am saying is that eventually there will be coupling and that will lead to some uncomfortable moments. Oh, by the way, is there one you are especially sweet on? I mean, I usually catch that with you as much as you have with me, but so far I haven't."

"Are you kidding? I've been so involved in trying to keep us alive and together, such a thing hadn't even entered my mind. In fact it probably wouldn't have had at all if you hadn't brought it up. I guess I can see why Shayne wanted both of us to lead. Hey I don't know about you but I am starting to get very cold here and my feet are numb. Shall we go back inside before both of us become icicles?" He could see she was beginning to shiver.

"Of course, I am freezing, but I needed to bring this up because I could see what's coming, and saw that you did not. Now lead us back inside where it is warm. But remember, if you set a rule such as *always a team of two*, when any leave the cave, then it applies to you too."

As he pulled the material away from the entrance he whispered. "Yes mother." and with that they both laughed and returned to the warmth of the cave.

* * *

The storm continued to unleash its fury for another four days before it broke clear and cold. Still, all were eager to get outside and breathe air other than what existed inside the cave. The world they were now seeing had completely changed. With ice hanging from exposed overhangs and trees, the area was completely white. The trees held a heavy frosting of snow in their branches and the world around them, after the winds ended, was silent. It was not known who started it, but suddenly they were all involved in a huge snowball fight. Laughing and acting like children, this continued for a while. It was a sign that finally they could let down a little from the pressures of the recent past. Their breath was coming out in great clouds in the crisp air, and once the initial exuberance had been burned off, they relaxed for a short time. Then as they began to retire back into the cave, each person grabbing additional firewood, to restore their depleted supplies, heading back to the warmth that the cave provided. They smelled of smoke, and when first breathing the fresh air, realized that the cave itself had to smell that way. Having been in it continually they had become used to the odors and no longer even smelled them. Now returning from the outside, it was quite obvious. Storme then said to no one in particular, "Oh this place stinks. I think it would be a good idea to open our front entrance and air this place out!"

"What? And then lose all of our heat?" One of the guys yelled back. "After all it didn't bother you until now." That brought a laugh from everyone.

Saige thought that this was probably the first time in a long time that the spirits of the group were up. It was a good sign, but he knew as they all did that winter here was just beginning. This first storm had dropped enough snow that it was between their knees and the ground. He wondered just how much would fall, and with no experience he had no answer. One of the first things that struck him once the fun was over, was that footing had changed. How did one get around in this stuff? It was something he hadn't even considered, again not surprising since where they were from it never snowed. Then calling for attention he said, "Now that was fun, and it has been a very long time, too long really, since we've had much of that. But something came to me while we were out there. Since we all come from a place where we never see this stuff, especially this close and personal, how does one walk in it? I mean right now it is to our calves and we cannot see the ground underneath. Everything now is hidden under this white stuff, so again how does one hike in it without both hurting and tiring oneself? And this is only the first storm. I don't even know how deep it's going to get before winter is over. But if this first storm is any indication I suspect we will be digging out just to keep our entrance open." These questions quieted the group down and he could see it was something that had not occurred to them either.

Stone replied saying, "There must be a way, since we are not the first to ever live in this stuff. I mean there must be some way that we do not have to break trails through this stuff, you know stay on top of it, but I have no idea how."

"Okay people, I think this is the first real problem that we have to solve. We need to be out here and learning as much as we can about these mountains. We need to be able to locate other areas that we can go to if we need to leave here. We did not have time to find anything else, and if we were found now and had to leave, we have nowhere to go at all. We have left ourselves no safety net, no escape, and I know that we really had no choice given the time limits that we had, but now with winter upon us I do not think we will have any problems from the primitives. So as severe as this is it will be our chance to find those other places that we can retreat to if the need arise."

Then one of them stated, "Now Saige why did you have to go and ruin all the fun. We've been running, fighting, busting our butts to finally get where we are now – and we have lost many a good person along the way. Finally we've had a chance to let down just a little, and then you go and spoil it with what you just said." This brought a chuckle from the group as it was recognized for what it was. It summed up what had happened to them, and then for the first time they had taken a break, giving them all time to forget, even if just briefly. Now before they even had a chance to warm up, Saige was already hitting them with the new responsibilities.

Shaking his head and smiling Saige said, "You are so right, and I am sorry. But since Shayne has placed this position up-on both Shellian and I, I just do not want to fail in that trust – not only to him and his memory, but to all of you. If we all die out here, yeah I know we won't know anyway, if we all die out here then I have failed in that trust."

"That's all right." Another yelled. "If we all die out here we will kill you for failing," which brought another laugh.

Shaking his head again Saige continued. "Okay, point tak-en. We will just take this day off and tackle the problems tomorrow."

* * *

It then took them the better part of the major moon cycle to finally solve the problem of walking in the snow. They had tried a number of different methods, from breaking new trails in the snow, to trying to work a drag to break it up, and none of them worked. Then Stone suggested that they try to figure out how to walk on top of the snow, which brought a laugh since no one could see how it could be done, they were just too heavy. But that got them thinking and they realized that if there was a way to distribute their weight over a greater area then it could be possible. The first attempts were ugly, awkward, very difficult to use, broke often, but it proved the concept. In fact it was almost freeing to be able to move across the snow in this fashion. As time continued to pass, they made small improvements until it worked. They were finding muscles that they never used as working with these "shoes" required learning a new way to walk. Yet they found as the soreness worked out, they could cover a greater amount of territory not having to worry about obstructions as they had, when there was no snow on the ground.

Then one of the women turned up pregnant and neither she nor her lover would admit to anything. With everyone in so close proximity; it was surprising that any could find a place to get physical without being found out. Yet it now was obvious that was exactly what had happened. And it was the flirt Sorrel, so it could have been anyone. Looking at her he could see defiance and smug look on her face. Shellian had warned him and here was the proof that she had been completely truthful and right in her conclusions – now what? Then, in a short time came another shock. One of the two who were out on patrol, searching the areas and mapping it so that they could find a second location, came back into the camp winded and quite excited. Steen yelled. "I need help now! Stone fell through some of the snow that had hidden a crevasse and has fallen out of my reach. He doesn't appear to be hurt but, he appears to be on a narrow ledge and there isn't anywhere he can go but down and it is a long drop." It was midmorning and the two of them had been out since dawn, so there was a good possibility that where he had fallen was not close. No one said leadership was easy, and it just appeared that the problems and near disasters kept coming faster than he, Shellian and the rest could find answers.

Leaving the women in camp, Saige and the six other men followed Steen as he led the way back to where the fall had taken place. As they worked their way to the site, Saige saw that this was in an area that none of them had ever been. As he had feared it took them a few hours to reach the place of the accident. As they approached, he had them slow down and then use poles to check the depth of the snow. They did not need another to join Stone, complicating an already difficult situation. In the distance he could hear another one of the many waterfalls that they had encountered. At least, he mused, there was no lack of water. Now it was time to work out the rescue. Working slowly up to the edge, he looked down and saw Stone standing on a too narrow ledge that just looked like it could collapse at any moment. Then slowly withdrawing, they tied a rope that they had brought around one of the large trees that was close by, and with that anchor worked their way back to the ledge that had been revealed under the snow. But before the rope could be lowered, there came a sound of shifting snow, rock, and soil, and part of what they had just been standing on gave way and disappeared. Had they remained there even for a second more it would have caught all of them. They realized that they had been standing on top of one of the many lava tubes and this one had been thin. It had taken the additional weight of the snow and when they added their own body weight it became too much and collapsed.

Looking down at the fallen earth and snow they could see that the drop even to the piles that were just created was at least ten meters. What next? The collapse was between them and where Stone had fallen. "Now that complicates things." Saar stated. "And if it collapsed here where else does this tube run? And is it just as thin skinned as this portion just proved to be?"

"Hey doc, we have enough problems here without you coming up with questions that bring even more to our attention." Steen commented. "Okay Saige I'll add my own, now what?"

As he looked over the now very dangerous situation, he cautiously peered over into this newly opened area, he shook his head and stated, "I don't know, and I am obviously open for suggestions. This opened a pretty good section and looking at the edges of that lava that was revealed . . . well, it looks as if it would cut our rope to pieces let alone any one of us. And you are right, not only can we not be sure of our footing, but even looking inside this tube we cannot see its true direction and we will possibly see another collapse if we cross it, and it is between us and Stone." Then looking up because it suddenly became shadowed, he saw that clouds were starting to build which probably signaled the arrival of a new storm in the near future. "And if I am reading this sky right we will be having new snow soon. Come on everyone we need to get Stone and get back to the cave." Then yelling he said, "Stone! How are you faring so far?" He then listened hard and heard a distance voice say.

"Getting very cold and I think this may have been a place where that tube that I just heard collapse pushed out the side of the mountain. Maybe the collapse was a good thing, and one or two of you could carefully lower yourselves into it and see if you can find where it pushed out the side. It will be above me. When I fell through I found myself on a smooth slide and my momentum almost carried me completely over. The only way I was able to prevent it was by grabbing desperately at some vegetation that had been growing here. Thankfully it held, but there is no way I can climb out without help."

"You're the expert on this stuff. Okay maybe it's the best answer and right now I do not have any other ideas – okay we will try that." Then turning to the others he said. "Alright you heard him, I want you Seve and you Staven to be the ones to go down. We'll use the rope we have tied to the tree to get you down there and then you two can take one of the other ropes, then see if you can find the side tube that he fell through. We'll keep the rope off the tube's edge so as to not have it cut. But I have to admit that from what I can see, other than where we broke through, it's very dark down there. Did we bring anything that we can make a torch with?" Looking around he saw Seth reaching into the pack he had brought, bringing to light the materials to put together a torch. At least one of them had thought about the possibility of needing one. "Okay let's get moving on this we are running out of time once again, and why does it always seem to be that way?" He wasn't expecting an answer to his final question, but it did seem that every time they ran into some emergency or need that the time constraints would push them into the solution before they had time to truly work it out.

Now working carefully they lowered the two into the tube and watched as they lit the torch and then disappeared from sight. Now all they could do was wait. The rest could do nothing so they pulled back, dug down through the snow to the bare ground and with care built a small smoky fire. While dead wood was plentiful, it was full of moisture, which tended to hiss, pop, and spit as the moisture was forced out the wood as it burned. They could hear the voices of the three but could not make out their conversations. As they waited by the fire they would rotate one member to the tube edge to watch for the other three. Eventually the one who was watching signaled them, and they all then came over to the collapsed area. They could see that all three were now there and ready to be pulled out. Saige breathed a sigh of relief, and once they were out they headed back to the cave. The winds had picked up again and the sky was dark and ominous. Shortly it began to snow once again and by the time they had reached the cave it was snowing heavily. The temperatures had dropped considerably and they were chilled to the bone just wanting to stand around the fire until they felt comfortable again.

Going off by himself for a brief period of time Saige asked himself, "What's next?" He knew that they still had to get out and explore when the weather allowed. If they depended only on this one location they found, and if discovered they would be in real trouble, not that they weren't already. There needed to be at least one other location, and not close by, that was stocked and ready if the need arose. *So again, now what?* They were finding out that this mountain they presently were staying on was riddled with lava tubes and the incident today came close to taking them all out or at least severely injuring them, which was just as bad. Deep in thought he did not hear his sister approach and was surprised when he heard her speaking. "What's going on Saige?" She asked.

Looking up at her since he had been sitting and leaning back against one of the walls in the shadows he asked, "What do you mean? There's a lot happening as usual even for a place and time such as this."

Shaking her head she said. "You know what I mean. It sounded like this rescue could have been much worse than it turned out, and now we have one of the women carrying, and you know that with as much time that we will probably be in here that she may not end up being the only one. Nothing you or I could say will stop that from happening. It's cold and many are showing signs of being lonely. You and I are being kept quite busy trying to lead them, but there is not enough to do to keep all of them active. So they are drawn together for warmth and then it ends up going further than any had planned. But I suspect that there are no regrets. With all the hardships and losses that all of us have endured it is surprising to me that the reaching out to each other hasn't happened ear-lier. So I suspect even as small a group as we are we will see a rash of pregnancies soon. We have no birth control other than abstinence and that's not going to happen.

"Then once these women start birthing then what? Again we are not prepared to deal with new lives. We have nothing – nothing at all and with only Saar who never was one to take care of women . . . well, you can see where this is going."

Reaching up and pulling her down beside him he said. "I never thought that being a leader could be so hard. It is driv-ing me crazy. We need to establish a second camp yet from the incident today it is much more dangerous out there than I first thought. Yet, we cannot stop looking, but do I send someone out into this unknown knowing that they could fall to their death or injured and die in this weather? Yet, If I don't, then we risk discovery, and if found then there would be nowhere to go and with all of our supplies here . . . Well, you can see there is this problem and now this other one has been brought into the open by the pregnancy of Sorrel, and as you just now pointed out, you are sure it will not be the last. I guess I should have guessed that it was going to go that way, but was hoping it was something that wouldn't. I tell you this if there was some way I could just give this up and let someone else do this job I would. But Shayne put his trust in you and I, and I can see that the rest look to both of us for decisions. So I guess we are stuck." Then looking at her he shrugged.

"Now before you ask, no I am not sleeping with Saar – not that the temptation isn't there. After all, I get cold at night and the thought of a warm body next to me to keep me warm is a temptation – one that I have been able to ignore for now. Like you I'm trying to be an example, and while I know that I'm in charge of the women here, as you the men, and then the two of us together the whole group, it still is something that is hard to ignore. I was just hoping that this wouldn't begin until late into the winter. Then if we had some pregnancies at least when they came to term it would be good weather. Now with them starting this early there is a chance that we may be still fighting bad weather further complicating things. As you have pointed out we have no idea how long winters last up here."

Silent for a moment Saige contemplated what Shellian had just told him, he then said, "And you feel there's nothing we can do about it. So should we conveniently ignore it? Or is there another solution that you have in mind?"

Shaking her head she said. "No, I have no answers for you. Other than the two sexes living in two different locations and not in the same cave would there be a slight, and I mean slight possibility of preventing this. But we are all together in close contact and there is no any way to change that. So no I do not think we can ignore it but I don't know how to prevent or present it either."

Sighing he said. "Okay then, just another of the many problems to face. Not that an increase in our small population is a bad thing. But as you have stated, we are not prepared for the consequences that this will present. And maybe that is the way we need to present it to the rest. Especially now that it's out in the open with Sorrel being the first to prove that there has been coupling going on. After all she cannot deny it since it is the only way one can become as she is."

Laughing lightly even though the weight of leadership was upon her she said. "Oh I am sure she would try, but there is only one other way to get that way and we have no way of providing that service here."

"That's very true. I only hope when she reaches term that the birth is not complicated since we are in no shape to handle complications here. Since our annual is 540 days, and how long does a woman normally carry before she gives birth?"

"Roughly half of that time, give or take a few on either side. But there can be complications that could endanger both the mother and unborn child. That's the greater worry, since we are so unprepared to deal with this." Then shrugging she continued. "But I guess women have been doing this since the beginning so if it was successful, and since we are here, then I guess we can learn to survive – although I for one would not want to be birthing without the pain relief drugs that we use.

I've had it described to me by mothers who say it's like being ripped apart down there and that when the drugs hit that it is a welcome relief."

"So, why would one put herself through it more than once? I mean I understand the physical draw and need between the sexes, but to experience that kind of pain and then go back and do it again, that almost sounds masochistic to me."

"Again I have no personal experience yet. Although I know my time will come. But from what mothers have said that once the child is born then you forget all about that pain and are instantly in love with this new completely helpless person who must depend on you totally for everything."

"I guess that's as good as explanation as I'll ever get, and since it is something as a man that I will never face . . . I guess I will never really know. Oh well, I guess since we are once again snowed in for a while I might as well present our situation to the group. Maybe we should start calling ourselves a clan or something since our birthplace is now gone and in a sense we are starting over far away from our home. And maybe we can start venturing outside our naming and not stick with names beginning with "S" as our city did."

"Do you think that's a good idea? I mean there is a chance that we will be able to reestablish it sometime in the future and our society has always required that the members of any city be named with the primary letter being the same as the city."

"True, true, but we are now without and we have no guarantee that we will be able to rejoin our people and the city was destroyed. This new leader of the primitives has them organized well. I don't know how easy it will to bring him down, or if that does happen, if it will be enough to break the ties that exist right now between the tribes. I suspect that they will break up once he is gone, but I cannot say whether that's just speculation on my part or fact. Anyway that's in the future and this isn't passing on what we just discussed so I guess I better just get to it." He got up went over to the fire where the majority were located, signaled a gathering waited until all were there and then said to all.

"We came close to losing a few of us today. This area appears to have many hidden dangers. It still hasn't solved one of our main problems and that's being located in only one place. If we were found then we would lose completely. We have nothing, no caches no place to go, nothing. So if for some reason the primitives came looking and found us I suspect that we then would become no more just as our city has become. I, like you am hoping that the snows and storms we have been experiencing will keep them out of the mountains. Plus whatever superstitions that seems to make it an area they stay away from, but again at least in the lower areas it does appear that the hunters do come to hunt the grazers. So even with the danger we have to find a second place, stock it, and make sure all of us know its location. This search and subsequence supplying of the second camp will take much of our time during this winter. Yet when the weather is like this we will be doing very little, which brings me to my second concern . . ." Pausing a moment before continuing, he was still a little reluctant to broach the subject but it had to be done.

"Okay all, I know we are a mixed company here, and that all of us that have survived are fully grown and are quite aware of the biology of life." Taking a deep breath before continuing and also looking at each one of them he said. "We are to try and avoid coupling since we are in no way prepared to handle pregnancies, births or any of the many complications that can arise from them. But it has been happening, and I know that it is something that will naturally happen – especially this time of the year when not much can happen and the nights are very cold." He could see the reaction from them and some appeared to have a guilty expression on their faces. So if he needed proof it had been happening it now was proven. "One of our women is indeed pregnant." Waiting to see their reaction he glanced towards Sorrel and still saw that smug look on her face and defiance in her stance. Well he would see how well she handled birthing when it was her time. "No I am not going to put a name to the one, but shortly it will be obvious to all who it is. While it is something that is hard to do all I can do is ask all of you to try and avoid any more pregnancies. We have nothing here to make it easy and we men outnumber our women and we cannot afford to lose any of you women. As it is to *you* our future belongs, and without the proper care when you are carrying we could lose any of you. That's all I am going to say on that subject for now.

"We will be continuing our mapping and patrols once this storm subsides. We have to find another place and soon. While I know from what we are seeing that up here the winters are long and harsh, but if we have not established our second camp before spring then I really believe that we will be in deep trouble. Okay then let's keep the camp we have here well supplied and clean. Our doctor can only do so much and we are responsible for the hygiene of our living areas."

CHAPTER SEVEN

It now appeared to be mid-winter and so far the only known pregnancy was Sorrel's. But whether that was because the rest were being careful or just luck, he did not know. It was time, with the last storm they had just faced, to head back out and explore some more of the area. So far with the few forays into the wilderness beyond their cave that they had been able to do, no second site had been located. On this rotation it would be Saige and Shellian who would be out. When the rotation came around that partnered them Saar would be in charge while they were away. After all, no one wanted to make the doctor mad since he was the only one who could treat anything serious. "Okay Saar I guess that about covers it. As far as the plan goes we will be out at least to dark with a possibility of not returning until late tomorrow – so until sunset tomorrow there should be no reason to worry." Saige shrugged and then continued, "As you know our plan is to continue up from the point where the accident had taken place, go deeper into the mountains and see if there is another location for us."

"Yeah, it's all good . . . but why both of you at the same time? Again I know the answer, since we rotate so that way everyone has gone out with the other members of our group. But I hate it when it finally comes around to the two of you heading out."

Smiling a teasing smile Saige asked. "Is that the only reason doc?" He knew that Shellian was growing closer to Saar and it was obvious Saar had feelings for her.

Flushing a little from the obvious reference he asked. "Is it that obvious? I mean nothing has been said between us since both she and I have too much going on to have much time to even talk."

"Yes it's that obvious, but both of you are just too responsible to allow something like a relationship get in the way of your duty, at least for now. I just wish the rest would take the two of you as examples of how we need to be, but I guess I am asking too much. Anyway don't worry too much since we were trained as a team and we are close. If you remember – even though it is getting hard to do so – Shayne had continually placed the two of us as the top working team. I don't know, maybe it is because we are siblings, and have worked together for annuals, so I feel confident that we will be back." At this point he heard Shellian say something. He turned around to face the entrance where she was standing. "Yes Shellian?"

"Saige the sun is beginning to break so we need to be going."

"Well doc you heard the boss – see you when we get back." He then joined his sister and they headed outside to a crisp cold morning. Clouds formed each time they breathed out, and they could feel the bite through their clothes, which sent an involuntary shiver through them. "Boy its cold out here!" Saige said.

"You're not going to get me to disagree. I thought we dressed warm enough but now I am not so sure. I am glad we packed heavily though so if we need to add something it's in our packs. Now, since I haven't been where Stone fell to that ledge, why don't you lead on, *oh brother of mine*. I think once we get moving that we'll warm up. It's just the shock of leaving a warm place into this very cold one."

Nodding Saige led off heading deeper into the mountains remembering back to that day when they headed out to make that rescue and almost having to face a second more dangerous rescue. They had been lucky that there had been some warning. Now they were heading back into that area, an area that they had avoided, but since the other directions had produced nothing it was now the best unexplored area that could produce a second campsite. The snow crunched under their "shoes for walking in the snow". "You know we need a better name for these things."

"Name for these things? What are you talking about Saige?"

"Oh these inventions that we came up with, you know the shoes for the snow that allows us to walk on top of it instead of having to break a trail through it."

"Do they require a special name? I think 'shoes for walking in the snow' is just fine. After all it tells anyone just what they do and isn't that what a name is for?"

"Yeah I guess so, but it seems so awkward. Think about it. *I'm going outside, now I am going to put on my shoes for walking in the snow.* Now doesn't that sound funny?"

Laughing at his antics and the way he stated it she said. "I see what you mean. But does everything need some kind of name?"

"Now hold on sis. It seems to me that you women are guiltier of naming everything than we guys. You know assigning pet names to this or that."

"We don't do that . . . oh yeah; I guess we do don't we. Okay guilty as charged sir."

Laughing as they continued their hiking, he found that once they were moving that he was warming up. The views in the cold crisp clear air were spectacular. It was almost like they could see far enough to find their destroyed city – but he knew that was impossible. The landscape they were hiking through was pristine, with the trees having a heavy white layer on top of the green. And where the mists from the rivers drifted, there were sheets of ice reflecting the sunlight in an almost blinding array of color. And where the sun shone through the mists small rainbows formed drifting with them and then disappearing – an area that was just as dangerous as it was beautiful. They continued talking as they worked their way to where the lava tube was exposed. From there he hoped to find a way past and then head higher into the mountain. With the one collapse in that area, a quick survey had identified a large lava flow in the very distant past, and probably the reason for the one huge lava tube that they had almost fallen into.

Yet unlike the cave they were presently living in, there had been no sign of any cave of that size located. Yes there had been a number of smaller ones, but none were big enough to sustain a group their size. Nor were there a number of smaller ones close enough together to be used. It had been a frustrating experience. Once they had begun finding the smaller caves, before they located the one they were living in, it was assumed that it would be a simple thing. Yet it had proven to be anything but. So now deep into winter nothing had been located, although with the amount of snow that was on the ground that in itself was no surprise. At least they were learning the area, which was just as important as finding a second camp. So once they had worked their way past the lava tube they would be in unknown lands.

As it approached midmorning they finally reached the place of the collapse. Shellian said, "So this is it. Hmmm, I thought it was smaller from the description, and the area doesn't quite match the picture I had in my mind. In fact I would never have guessed that this was the area at all. The only real hint is that cliff off to our right. Did you have time to figure out which way the tube ran? I mean I would hate to fall through it again like you guys almost did."

"The best we could determine was that it continues north from here. Kind of in the direction we are going since we are heading higher up. Apparently when this thing was active, it was very active and hot. This would not been a place that I would wanted to be. So, I for one am glad that this one died thousands of annuals ago. And as you can see the trail that we have available to us is limited, so all we can hope is that the tube veers off in some other direction, and we are not hiking on top of it for very much longer. I do not want to tempt fate."

Nodding in agreement she said. "Me either really. So how do you want to do this? Other than *careful* of course."

"I really am not sure. But this was one of the reasons I brought the rope along. I think for a while we will tie it between us so that if the unthinkable happens then at least the one or the other of us can keep us from falling too far."

Pausing a moment before answering she then said. "Okay, sounds like a plan to me, since I cannot think of any other solution."

Looking at his sister in the morning light he thought. *She really is a beautiful woman. Tall, lithe in build. Her skin browned by being outside, green eyes and dark blonde hair that is now down to the middle of her back, but is being bleached by the sun to lighter tones. She moves with the grace of a hunter. You can read the confidence she has in herself and her abilities.* Shaking his head he thought that if the relationship between Saar and she continued he would have a wonderful mate. That was something that was difficult to comprehend as they had always been together and the thought of her leaving to join another man just hadn't entered his thoughts. But he knew that was the way of life and he would be happy for her when that time came – that's if they survived to allow such a thing to happen. Then to cover his thoughts he said, "Then let's be at it, and I don't have to remind either you or me to be careful, since we do not know what this snow is hiding underneath."

He removed the rope from the pack and they tied it between them. He led off using the walking stick he had to probe the snow ahead as they worked their way up a narrow V, which was the only way out from where they were. It was a rugged broken area and it must have been hell when this eruption had taken place. It literally appeared to have blown up. But again this had been a long time ago since trees and plants in the area had reclaimed the land and many showed age. As they worked their way through the V, the trail pushed ever higher and while they were breathing hard from the exertion when they came out of the V and found themselves on top and once again in the open. Once there they had to stop and catch their breath, finding another alpine meadow covering they suspected at least a kilometer. Partially covered in snow, but some areas were bare of snow and it led to questions as to why.

"So I see we have a small plateau here. But why snow, no snow?" He asked. Then before she could respond a heavy wind hit them almost knocking them off their feet and chilling them to the bone. "Well, I guess that explains it." He yelled over the wind. "Let's find us somewhere out of it. Damn that's cold!" Looking at his sister he could see her teeth chattering and knew that it was exactly the same for her. They headed towards an area that still had much of the snow on it assuming that it was protected from the wind and when they got there it was in fact calm.

"That wind just cut through everything", she said. "I was warm and fine until it hit me and then instantly I was freezing."

"Same for me, I think we will stop here and have our midday meal. At least here out of the wind – don't know how far this goes and what if any would be out of these winds. I'll look around and see if I can find us any wood, if you would, see if you could find a place that we can build a fire. He then untied the rope that was around his waist and she did the same, he coiled it and placed it back into the pack and headed off to find wood to build a fire. She went around a small curve in the protruding rock that jutted up out of the meadow, which protected them from the winds, and dug down a short way through the snow and found plenty of rocks to build a small fire ring. He, in the meantime, searched the woods near the open meadow looking for protected dead wood for the fire. They both carried materials to start a fire, but there was no way to carry more than that and still be able to carry their packs. Eventually he found where a couple of ancient trees had died and fallen sometime in the past. There he was able to find much dead wood that was away from the snow. With an effort that left him breathing hard he finally had a large stack and headed back to where they had planned on building the fire only to find that Shellian was nowhere around.

Thinking that maybe she needed to make a nature call, he decided that was not such a bad idea and went back to the tree line to relieve himself. He then returned and she still was missing. Now he began to worry a little. There were predators around, but they had rarely seen any of them. It appeared, like much of the animal life here, at least here in the higher elevations, some of the predators slept through the winter. There was still a little snow where they had decided to break and he then circled their temporary camp to find her trail, and shortly he picked up her tracks heading deeper into the meadow towards a rock face. She had taken her pack so he felt confident that she hadn't been attacked by an animal, but instead had seen something that had drawn her attention. With the air so clear it turned out to be further to the rock face than he expected. When he reached it he then saw Shellian emerging from what looked to be shadows. She turned and saw him and then waved. With concern on his face he finally reached where she was standing. "Don't ever do that again!" He admonished.

"Do what?" she asked perplexed.

"Leave like that. When I got back you were gone. I figured you went off to relieve yourself and thought that it was a good idea so I did the same. But when I got back a second time you still was not anywhere to be found."

"Sorry brother. I really had not meant to just disappear. And you are right that's exactly what I was originally doing. After setting up for the fire I realized that it would be a good time to do just that. So while you were gathering wood I headed off in this direction took care of the need, and then turned to come back when I saw this rock face and something just did not look right to me. So I decided to investigate."

"Investigate? Investigate what?"

Pointing she said. "This."

Looking hard in the direction she was pointing he at first saw nothing, but by looking to either side of where she pointed he found a darker area in the shadows that she had emerged from. "So what is it that you found or thought you saw?"

"Well, like when I found the cave we are presently in, the shadows here looked just wrong. So I thought it was best that I check it out. And since I was closer to this rock face than I was compared to where we were planning to camp I decided to investigate. Come brother I have something to show you." She began to walk back into the shadows, making a quick right, she disappeared.

Shrugging he followed and found that he had just entered another cave. But this one was different. There was a soft glow to the walls allowing him to see the interior with this dim soft light. "What is this place?" He asked knowing that she wouldn't have an answer.

"Don't know." She replied somewhat subdued. "I don't think this one is natural. But it isn't very large. Not large enough for a second location, but, well, it's just different."

That was an understatement. "Tell you what, I'll go back and get the wood that I brought to where we were going to build our fire. Why don't you set up a fire ring at the entrance to this and then after we eat we can really look this over. You are right about the size, but that doesn't mean that it can't be used for a supply location. What do you think . . . we are what, probably about ten kilometers from our winter camp?"

"Actually I think we are a bit farther than that. Remember it took to mid-morning to reach the area where the accident happened. And you had traveled there before so it would seem to be less distance to you than to me because you were familiar with it. So I would guess that it's probably closer to fifteen by the way we had to go. But by one who flies probably no more than five or six."

"Yeah you were always good at estimating distances and you are right the first part of our travels appearing to be short. I'll go get the wood now, see you back here shortly . . . and . . . this time don't wander off."

As he disappeared from sight she went to collect a new set of rocks to form the fire ring when a couple of things struck her about this strange cave. But until she finished constructing the fire ring she would have to wait to confirm what she thought she had observed. In a short time due to the amount of available stones she had a proper fire ring constructed. Saige had yet to return so she prepared to go back inside the small cave to confirm what her mind had shown her. Since she had more time inside, she felt that he would not have had a chance to make the same observations, so before pointing them out she needed to make sure. Leaving the bright sunlight, she reentered the cave and again was struck by the soft glow that the walls were emitting. It did not take long for her eyes to adjust to this softer light. She did a careful search of the cave finding the soils on the floor to be soft and powdery. While doing this she heard Saige approaching and then the pile of wood he was carrying hit the ground. Then she heard him call out for her. "Saige, I'm in the cave. Something struck me as strange about this and I am checking it out. Go ahead and get a fire going then come in here and join me. I think you will find this interesting." She then continued her investigation. Shortly she heard the crackle of a fire and then Saige was inside the cave with her.

"Okay sis, what have you found?" He asked

Signaling him to join her she pointed at the floor of the cave and said. "First there are no tracks of animals in here – small or large, just none. At first I thought that the ground here was hard, but as you can see it is anything but . . . so why no tracks? I thought well maybe a wind worked its way in here and wiped them out. But then I noticed that there are no droppings, no leaves, nothing at all. It's like someone had come in here and cleaned it out. That got me to worrying that maybe someone had and whoever it was, was not far away and would be returning. But the minute I thought that I dismissed it as this place seems to be quite undisturbed for a long time In fact the only tracks are ours."

Looking closely at what she pointed out to him he said. "Okay I see what you mean. I just realized something else. Does it seem to be warm in here or is it because I have been moving out there in the cold and wind and have stepped in and out of that weather."

Thinking about it again she said, "No. No I think you're right. And if you are right where is the heat coming from? Now this becomes stranger by the minute."

At this point both began to search the cave more closely and after a period of time came away with no easy answers. There appeared to be no reason for the light, the heat, and the absence of animal sign inside this cave. "Well this might not be large enough for a second living site, but I see a potential for storage. Since it seems that no animal can get inside here for whatever the reason is, then it would be a great place to store our food, and whatever other items that could be destroyed by animals. But who made this place, what for, and when?" He asked.

"You got me on that one." She replied. "Do you think we should return and report our discovery to the rest so that some of our supplies could be moved here as you suggested?"

"No. Again at first I thought so myself. But we need to finish our exploring. One day or two won't make that much of a difference. And we still need to locate a better place. Not that this is a bad one. But again it's just not big enough to be anything more than a storage area and we need another place to stay."

"Okay then I'll mark it on the map that we are making while we eat and then we can continue up the mountain."

He took off his heavy coat and found that indeed it was warm inside the cave. Warm enough that he could have left the coat off. He shrugged back into it and they went out to the fire with both lost in their thoughts as they ate their midday meal. Finding this particular cave left him feeling uneasy. Maybe whoever had built it was responsible for the primitives being afraid of the mountains and making it sacred and off limits to other than their priests and the occasional hunters. He suggested the same to Shellian, who was deep in thought herself. She was also putting the details on the map they were constructing as they explored. He wasn't even sure she had heard him, but what she was doing was critical anyway and what he had asked had no real answer.

"Saige I just don't have any idea at all. It truly is a mystery. It's obvious that whoever did this did not construct the cave with primitive tools. But to add the light, put up some type of barrier to the keep the animals out, and add heat also. It sounds like something we are capable of truthfully. But as far as I know from what history that was passed on to us in the learning centers we were never in these mountains."

"My conclusions also. But who knows, maybe this is old enough that it could relate to a time before the great wars that led these people becoming primitives. There is nothing in our history books to let us know the true level of technology from that period. But if that is true that means this cave is at least a few thousand years old." Thinking a moment before continuing he said, "I don't see how anything could continue to function for that long."

"I have to agree with you. Unless, like our people, there was a small part of them that survived and took refuge in these mountains – bringing their tech with them. And then over time they just disappeared for who knows what reason. So this may not be that old. Still it could be."

Suddenly alarmed, Saige said, "What if they did not die out or disappear and are still hidden in these mountains?"

Catching his drift she suddenly picked up the same sense of fear and said. "And if they are still around we may be under observation right this moment and never be the wiser."

"Yes, and the way we are dressed we would appear to them to be the primitives." Pausing a moment and thinking he said, "Now wait a minute here. Did you see any sign of anyone or anything at all when you found this?"

"No, but that doesn't mean anything at all. This cave may only be used as a forward point of observation so it would be one that would not be used very often." Still in her voice there appeared to be a small amount of doubt. After all, other than this small abandoned cave, there was no evidence of anybody around, still . . . still that did not prove that there wasn't either. "Okay brother what do you want to do?"

Looking down and taking a deep breath before answering he said, "I'm not really sure. So far there has been no proof of anyone here other than us. But again as big as these mountains are an army could be hidden away and never be found. And just as easily some other remnants from the same war our ancestors survived could have retreated into these mountains and then became completely hidden, or because of the harshness of living up here died out. I guess we will have to continue our exploring, but with the idea that we may be under observation. After all if these people we are imagining *are* real, then with the time that has passed they would be very good at concealment – probably much better than we are since they would live here."

"So you think then if they are here that there is a good chance we may not see them at all."

"That pretty much sizes it up, unless we accidentally stumble across one of their hidden cities, and if there are such things here, I have no idea what to look for, how they would have hidden them, or what they would look like."

"True", Shellian replied, "we've only been here a short time and really only because we were forced here. So we know so very little about this whole mountain range. After all, we both know that we, as a people, live in the valleys and flatlands and did not venture into these or any mountains that I know of. And, as you pointed out we wouldn't be here now if we were not forced to be here – although with as small of group that we have I think we have done quite well."

"Yeah, but remember we have been trained to survive. Had it been some of the regular members of the city and had they made it this far – which is doubtful – they would not have had the tools or knowledge to have lasted this long."

Shaking her head in agreement she said. "Yeah you're probably right. So that brings up the question, if a group from the wars came up here, could they survive if they had no training? I guess part of the answer is here with this cave. But that only proves that for a period of time someone survived, and does not mean that they still are around."

"Well as you said, this is all speculation. So unless we actually find some proof that is newer than this cave we can assume that we are alone up here. But at the same time keep it in our minds that we may not be and act accordingly." Sighing, he continued, "I guess we need to put this fire out and continue on. I think we will stay out overnight and then circle back to our camp. This discovery is such a surprise, and actually a little encouraging."

"Encouraging? Really? What do you mean by that?" She asked perplexed.

"Even with the equipment to construct this small cave it meant that whoever did this had to be up here for quite a while, which means that they survived and that is good news for us, giving us an example that it is possible to do so." Then waving his hand at her as he saw her reaction, he then continued. "Yeah I know we are surviving also. But so far we have luck on our side. There have been a couple of close calls, but no serious injuries, and best of all no deaths. Our party is so small that losing any would put the rest in jeopardy of failure and death. Again, as we both know we do not know how long this winter is going to last, and we have one woman who will be adding to our numbers soon. Who knows others may be joining her. After all, each of these pregnancies, while a good thing in the long run, actually increases the chance of loss – so even this is a very worrisome thing. And, as you also know, we have fewer women than men. So if we were to lose even one of you in childbirth, well it would be something else that could push us to the brink of dying out."

Silent for a moment she said. "Okay I'll concede what you stated, and everything you've just said has more or less been with me also. But there is something you did not think about here. Imagine this. Instead of living up here to build this cave, what if they lived down below and then during the warm season sent work crews up here to build this. I mean that could be a possibility also."

"You're right, but why? I mean this is or seems to be quite isolated. And it's a long way from the valley floor where the primitives presently live. But that doesn't mean it couldn't have been done that way. I just can't come up with a reason as to why – okay, I guess we're ready to continue. Which way would you like to tackle this, sis?"

"How do you mean that? Tackle what? The direction we are going, or to be careful and watchful, or be aware that we could be watched, or what?"

Grinning he said, "Oh all of the above or whichever one hits your fancy. Actually I just meant lead on as we head deeper and higher on this mountain. It does appear that you have an ability to pick these caves up, while the rest of us miss them. Why is it anyway?"

They began to work their way up and away from the discovered cave following a dim path that one could sense more than see. "I really don't know what it is. If I did then I could teach others to do it. But something just doesn't look right to me when I spot them." Shaking her head as she thought about it, "And really that's the best I can describe it. I don't know what the difference is or what is wrong, but to me there just is."

* * *

They covered another ten to twelve kilometers before stopping for the night. Again along the pathway they had decided to travel they did not find a second cave until just before dark. And this one like the last one had been constructed. It appeared, at least from the two that they had discovered, that they were built to cover a specific distance. So, if there had been travelers, sometime in the great past, then these would provide permanent shelters that would require no maintenance. It was a simple solution, but would have required an enormous amount of labor to construct. Again, like the first one they had found, this one was not large, and the floor was covered in loose powdery dirt with the walls having the soft glow and the area warm. Again no animals or animal sign was found within the cave. What was it that the builders had used that prevented wild animals from crossing the thresholds? It was an ability they did not possess even when they still were in the city. Now the question they faced was where did this pathway, one so unused that it was almost invisible to the eye, lead?

As they had continued their exploring that afternoon they finally had come to the conclusion that they were alone. The evidence, as they continued pointed to something or someone from the distant past. The path they were now on, the undisturbed nature of the two caves, the shear feeling of abandonment and disuse lay upon everything. Again, as they had searched the two caves, there was nothing within them either. Nothing had been stockpiled for travelers, such as firewood or even places to sit. It was like a decision had been reached and everything of value had been removed. Then, whomever it was that had built the caves, simply vanished. As they sat close to the small fire before retiring he said, "You know whoever these people were; they may be the reason for the fear and sacredness of these mountains to the primitives."

"Really? How so?" She asked.

"Okay now, let's, for an example, take these caves that we have discovered. For us it is a technology we can duplicate – well most of it anyway. But for the primitives it must have appeared to be magic. I am sure that with much labor they could dig a cave or pit, but to add the heat, lighting, and protection is so far beyond anything they could do that it would mean that maybe their gods had created them. And so far this is all we have found, these caves. I suspect that as we follow this path that we will be discovering much more. Again I think that whoever these people were, they wanted to be isolated. Otherwise why build your civilization in such a harsh and remote place? So if it was also part of their plan, then it is only logical to think that they would then put something in place to scare and keep the primitives away."

"I guess what you are saying makes sense. But what if, instead of wanting to be isolated like this, they had no choice. Now before you say anything let me finish. Look at our cities and us. We have kept ourselves isolated from the primitives for what . . . thousands of years. And part of that reason is we were afraid of what now is exactly happening to us. So what if these people faced the same issues and problems? So the isolation was not so much a choice as a necessity. And then to build in safeguards would only make sense. After all that's exactly what we did."

Thinking about what she said made sense. Yet he knew that either scenario was possible and that they were just guessing. Standing up and then pacing around he said, "I wonder if maybe in the end they suffered the same fate that we as a people are now facing with the primitives."

"No I don't think so. If that were true then these mountains wouldn't be off limits to the primitives. They would have conquered their demons and then they would have been free to travel here – although I wouldn't know why . . . anyway enough of the speculation. We still don't know enough to be able to come up with any real answer. At least with the cave we can sleep easier not having to worry about any wild animals disturbing us or needing to keep a fire going just to keep warm. So right now I am thankful for whomever it was that constructed these caves. And with that I am going to retire back into this one. We have much to do tomorrow so I want to get a good night sleep. There are some mysteries here and I for one would like some answers."

"Okay sis. I'm still too wound up but promise that I will be with you shortly. This surely is a puzzle that we have uncovered. And you're right we aren't going to solve it with the little we know right now." He remained by the fire for a while longer thinking about what they had uncovered and discussed. Now another issue came to mind. But it was too late to discuss it with his sister. That would have to wait until the morning now. This exploration that they were doing was to be only two days, which meant that they should begin their loop back in the morning. Yet, these first pieces of this new puzzle had him intrigued. As far as they knew they and their cities were the only ones to have broken away from the ancient wars and then hidden themselves from the world. So now it began to appear that maybe they were not the only ones to have done that. So they could return back as planned tomorrow or they could continue in their present direction and hope to discover more. One thing for sure, they couldn't split up, with one returning and one continuing. "Oh well . . ." He said softly. "I'm not going to answer this tonight. Better go in and get some sleep." He noticed that the fire had burned down to coals anyway and he did not want to add any more fuel. So with a sigh he got up and headed inside the cave where he heard the even soft breathing of his sister. It was obvious that she was asleep. Well he needed to be there himself. So he climbed into his sleeping sack and tried to find a comfortable position, turned over, and the next thing he remembered was the gray of dawn.

Stretching he looked over to where his sister had been sleeping and saw that she was already gone. Taking a deep breath he crawled out of the warm sack and then headed outside where the air was crisp and his breath came out in clouds. He saw Shellian next to the fire pit coaxing a new fire. "Chilly out here this morning," he commented, "I wonder what the builders used to power these caves. Yes I know that the earth is a natural insulator. But that still doesn't account for the difference."

Looking up from her 'fire starting' she said, "Just another piece of this puzzle. I'm sure that part of the solution has to be some type of a solar collector. But there isn't anything around that I have been able to observe that could be that kind of device. I know that in our cities that such a system got its power from the power unit – not solar. Out here there is no such luxury. So like you I don't know. Besides this wasn't our expertise anyway. If we had an engineer or someone like that then they might know immediately how it's done."

"True, ours is wildness survival, and right now I am glad that it is. If we had one of the city's jobs we probably would be dead right now. Hey I'm going out to make my morning nature call be right back." He then left to relieve himself, and when he returned she had a roaring warm fire going. "That feels great. It's funny how something as simple as a camp fire can make one feel comfortable and safe."

"True, it's really surprising how little it takes to make one feel comfortable. You know after I left you last night to lay down a thought entered my mind . . ."

"Only one? That's a surprise." He said laughing lightly.

Looking for something to throw at him and finding nothing she said. "You're lucky I couldn't find something. Cause I would have done it too."

Still laughing Saige said. "Yes you would have, and I would have had to run because you are very accurate when you throw something. Anyway like you, after you left, I had something come to mind also. Bet cha' we thought of the same thing."

"Okay smarty what was it that I was thinking?"

"First off as a woman most of what you think I haven't a clue. I think that most women are not able to figure out what another woman is thinking. So being a man my chances of even coming close are, oh I don't know . . . maybe a million to one, or maybe a billion to one. But on the serious side, I think that you came up with the same conclusion that we have to decide whether to continue with our discoveries or turn back, finish our loop, and be back to camp by tonight. Does that sound about right?"

"Oh aren't you the funny one this morning. But I cannot disagree with anything you have said. And yes that's exactly what struck me last night. But I did not want to come back out and talk about it then, as I have to admit that I was quite tired and ready for some sleep."

"I had the thought just after you left, and decided that I did not want to bother you with it since discussing it last night or this morning would change nothing, and, well I decided to wait until today to discuss it with you. Now that it seems we, once again, were on the same page, what are your thoughts? Do we finish it like originally planned or do we continue to explore and find answers to the questions this is presenting?"

Looking in her bag and inventorying it she then said. "Okay first of all, I personally would like to continue. While we do not have a lot of food here if we are careful we can probably extend it for a couple more days. I know that they are expecting us back tonight, and by not showing up we will cause undue worry, especially for Saar. But what we have found so far leads me to want to continue. I think if we are back within five days at the most it should be okay. But to be safe for both of us I suggest that we travel on until tonight and then return no matter what we find or don't find. Then we can plan a larger, time wise, exploration and be better prepared. How does that sound to you?"

CHAPTER EIGHT

Saar was worried. Shellian and Saige should have been back two days ago and had yet to make an appearance. He had reluctantly taken over the leadership while they were absent and really did not want to have this position permanently. He had observed both Shellian and Saige while they solved the day-to-day problems and thought for a short time it should be easy. Yet observing verses doing was vastly different. And when he found how petty some of their group was and the small problems that continued and were never solvable he really, really wanted nothing to do with this position ever again. *How do they do it?* He thought. *I just don't understand.* He was their doctor so he was very familiar with responsibility. But there, it was with each, as they had needed his services. So, while overall he was responsible for all of the members, it was only in the role of a doctor, not leader. He was finding that there was a vast difference between the two.

And now it was snowing again. It had started late on the third day and had yet to stop – the only advantage to this storm over others, there were no winds with it. It was dead calm. And when one walked outside in the snowfall it did not feel overly cold. But with the way snow fell and the patterns the mind formed with the falling snow it was easy to get disorientated. *So again where were they? Did something happen that has either injured or killed them?* Oh my how he hoped not. It was not only the fact that he and Shellian were becoming serious, but as small as their group was losing just one more was a bad thing. But two would be devastating. With confirmation now that four of the six women were pregnant, this factor alone would put a large burden on them, but to reduce their numbers by two could be fatal. He found that he continued to watch the opening to outside hoping that any moment they would come through and join them inside the cave.

Looking around to the rest he could sense that they were as uneasy about the situation as he. Again where were they? He saw Stone approaching took a deep breath and when he stood next to him asked. "What can I do for you Stone?"

"Not much doc. I can see that you are worried about our two leaders and I was going to ask yesterday to grab someone and go out and search for them. But first the clouds dropped down and formed a thick fog, and then when it lifted it began to snow. So I knew that you would say no. And while I might have disagreed with you I knew that you would be right. So what do you want to do?"

"To tell the truth I don't know. I would love to be out there trying to locate them, but as you have so well stated, the weather is once again against us. So I guess we just have to wait. Yeah I know waiting is a very hard thing to do, but it would be foolish to go out in this stuff. If something has happened to them then there's nothing we could do anyway. But as you and I know we are experts in living in the wilderness, and before you protest I know it was down where we came from. But much of what applied there applies here also. And because we know what to look for, anything that is different we learn quickly. Think about it Stone, just how much we've already learned up here? And we've been here such a short time overall. Again I know that at times when we are locked inside this cave that it seems to be an eternity. After all we are used to the open spaces and not spending all of our time inside a cave like this."

Sitting down and thinking about what Saar said, he realized why Saige and Shellian had left him in charge when it was their turn to explore. Yet he could see that Saar was nervous about it and really did not like being the leader. Still because of those reservations he probably was a good choice. He knew that a couple here really wanted to be in charge, and he thanked whoever was in charge of watching them from above that when Saige and Shellian left that they did not put one of those in charge – especially Schylar. He could see him pestering both Shellian and Saige all the time to take over while they were gone. It was obvious that he was power hungry. But while he had these ambitions he did not have the skills – not that any could tell him. He had an overblown view of himself and his abilities. If one was around him long enough he would tell you what the two in charge were doing wrong and how he could do it so much better. He had convinced at least one of the women in the group and she was now sleeping with him. And Storme was now pregnant with his child. So it went deeper than just believing what he spouted around the camp. At least that relationship was obvious. Stone then came back around from his thoughts and looked back at Saar and said, "I know what you mean. It is so tough to have to just wait – when it is easier to just go do . . . whether doing is right or wrong. So I commend you on not giving in and allowing any of us to go looking. You did good."

"Thank you for that Stone. Believe me it was one of the things I really wanted to do – you know go and find them. But I realized how stupid that was. Yes we know approximately where they were going. But again that's only an approximate. According to what they've found would then determine if they stayed on the planned route or went a different direction. Heck I know that even extending their time out was included and I am hoping that is exactly what this is. Oh while you are here, sorry different subject here, I am worried with only two of our women not carrying what this will do for the rest of us. I know that you are not involved with any of them so I am not accusing you of anything here at all. It's just as these women come to term it will be difficult for them as well as the rest of us. I think that we are pretty strained now. But when the babies arrive, and from what I can see other than Sorrel, the other three will be close together when their time comes, that these women will be incapacitated for a short time while they are healing and nursing their newborn. I am sure that the men that have fathered these children will be distracted also. It is only right that it should be this way. Of course with Sorrel no one knows who slept with her or who the father is. We may never know other than it has to be one of us. And I am not saying either you or I, since I am sure that neither of us joined her in her bed. But whoever it was, and again I am sure with her personality it was more than one of us she bedded, it will again be a distraction for those men. I know I'm a little long winded here but I see how you kind of observe what's happening so I thought it would be a good idea to bring you up to speed with my concerns. Anyway it means with at least half of our group either out or distracted it could lead to problems, accidents and not enough of us left to be able to provide what we need. Plus I do not have any of the necessary pain drugs to ease these births. I regret it, but we barely have anything at all that I had at my disposal back in the city. Now don't think that you are the only one I am telling this to. I've kept both of our leaders informed. Although I already know that Shellian is quite aware of all of this. I guess I could or maybe should say that it was she that brought it to my attention, even though I was kind of aware of it. Does this make sense to you?"

Sitting down next to Saar, Stone thought a moment before answering. "I know of only one other woman in our group that is pregnant, are you telling me that it's more than that?"

"Yes actually four are, and no, Shellian is not one of them. The only other woman who is not at this time is Seirra. And in her case I don't know if it is luck or if she has been avoiding becoming physical. But it would not surprise me if sometime in the near future that she joined the other four. As far as Shellian and me, we both know our feelings, but for now, we are not sleeping together, besides we are just too busy with what we have to do to find time for such a thing. And to be honest even with this long winter here in the mountains and being closed in like we are I am just too tired by the day's end to do anything but fall asleep when I lay down."

"I knew that doc. Hmmm, so Seirra is one of the only not carrying. In a way I am surprised. I mean she is a beautiful woman, and open, easy to talk to and friendly. With her natural beauty you would expect some of the other women to be jealous of her, but she has a natural way of deferring such things. And in truth I do not think she even sees herself that way. I am sure she has had many suitors here who would be more than happy to be chosen by her."

"I can't disagree with that assessment. I really think she has her eyes on just one male here, and he is completely unaware of it. After all he is so busy trying to keep everything from falling apart that he is blind that way for now."

"Ah I see. You mean Saige don't you. Well if you are right I am sure somewhere along the line she will make it clear to him that he is her choice. In a way I couldn't blame her. After all, our leader, with his sister of course, is a deep thinker, he tries to anticipate, plan, and really cares about what happens to us – just the kind of thing that a woman would really want in a mate. So what are the chances that he will ever notice doc?"

"Not my place to say, but what worries me is that this leaves a number of men on the outside, and that could have dire consequences." Then pausing for a moment, a smile came across his face he said somewhat softly. "Of course with the way Sorrel is offering her charms to any, maybe it won't be an issue. Oh by the way Stone it appears that with the present arrangements that you are left out in the cold. You aren't taking advantage of Sorrel's offers are you?"

Laughing softly and shaking his head Stone replied. "No doc, she holds no interest to me. And yes I know the situation but I am not alone in that area. But you must remember doc that I am a loner anyway, and an observer. That's why I know what I know. But who is actually taking Sorrel up on her favors I really don't know. Although it would not be too hard to narrow it down especially if the other three who are now carrying are in solid relationships. We know that you and

Shellian are getting serious even though the two of you try to avoid it openly. And that Saige is too busy and wouldn't take Sorrel up on her offer if she did offer. And I just confirmed to you that I am not involved with her. So let's see here whose left? There are only Sajan, Sojar, and Steen left. And from my observations she has approached all three of them at different times. Oh I know throughout a day she is around most of us, but she seems to linger around them more than the rest of us."

"Something to keep in mind that's for sure. Have you passed this knowledge on to our leaders yet? I'm worried that if she continues as she has, and truthfully I don't see her changing her ways anytime soon – although her up and coming child birthing might give her second thoughts, but I doubt it – that this could lead to open, or maybe not so open conflict between her lovers as they vie for her favors. And from what I have seen she would love it. I wouldn't be surprised if she has already started to hint to any or all of them to manipulate them into doing something stupid."

Both Saar and Stone jumped when another familiar voice answered. They thought they were alone and had been deep in their conversation. "Damn it Saige! Where or maybe I should say when did you get here?" Saar exclaimed.

Standing next to Saige was Shellian, and then smiling he said, "Oh long enough to get most of what this conversation was covering. Parts of it we were aware of but the two of you have confirmed some of what we were not sure of. Now before the two of you start asking questions of us we need to get a little food, and warm up a bit. This storm was a surprise, and while we had clothes enough, when that fog dropped on top of us it changed the look of everything. We had to be careful not to go in circles since all of our landmarks had been obscured.

This slowed us down somewhat. Anyway we will call a general meeting once we have had a chance to eat something and relax a little. Until then we will allow you to remain in charge. You can pass it on that we want to talk with everyone. On this trip, well let's say we found something interesting, kind of tantalizing, but for now that's all I'll say. See you shortly." And with that both of the leaders headed deeper into the cave to grab something to eat and to relax for a short time.

Looking over at Stone Saar said. "I almost jumped out of my skin there. I mean I thought we were alone and then to have them both there without either you or I sensing they were here, well you know what I mean."

"Yeah doc I do. But you got to remember that they were the best at stealth. So if any could sneak up on us and leave us unaware it would be them."

"I agree, but we were discussing some very sensitive information here, and had others come close enough to hear us then something might have gotten out to the rest that could be misconstrued, or changed to be damaging. I guess we will just have to be more careful when we discuss this kind of thing in the future. But I am glad that they are back, safe, and I for one will be glad to give them back the reins to this small group. I never wanted it in the first place, but know that I or maybe you will have to do it again once they have to go out again as a team."

"I know that both of us have their trust. And it is something that I don't take lightly, and both of us know that they would never put Schylar in charge, but that doesn't keep him from trying." Pausing for a moment Stone continued, "Again I know that neither you nor I ever want to be the leader here, and I think that is why we end up being in charge when they are gone."

* * *

"Okay all, since it is obvious that we were out a lot longer than the plan had called for there had to be a reason for us to extend out exploration." Looking around to make sure he had the entire group's attention Saige continued. "I think that I will allow Shellian to fill you in on the initial find since, as usual, she was the one who discovered it. I don't know why or how but she has a talent for finding caves – Shellian . . ."

"Okay Saige, simply stated we were taking our mid-day meal break when I noticed something amiss, kind of like when I found this cave, and then went to explore to answer my curiosity. At the time Saige was out in another direction gathering wood for our fire. He came back to the spot where we had set up and of course I wasn't there." She then went on to explain what she had found, and at that point turned it back over to Saige.

"Needless to say we were excited to have found this cave. But as she has stated it was much too small to act as a second camp area. But it's manmade, not natural. So that got us to wondering if maybe some other people had survived the great wars and had escaped to these very mountains. We then became worried that if that was fact they could still be here and we could be under observation. Yet, both the cave and the path showed no use in the recent past. In fact we felt that it hadn't been used in a very long time. The path was almost nonexistent, and we sensed more than saw it." He then went on to explain the finding of a second cave along the path. Here they had made the decision to continue up the path for another full day before returning, knowing that it would extend their time out to twice the planned time. But they had hoped to find an answer to this new riddle. "At least with the way they are protected, we can use them for caches of additional supplies and know that they will be safe. Unfortunately all we found on that additional day of travel were two more of the caves. Yet the pathway or trail continues deeper into the mountains. So as soon as this storm ends and we have some decent weather once again we will continue our search up that pathway. Plus while we are waiting, I want some of our supplies divided out so that we can begin using the closest as our first cache." He then concluded by saying. "I don't know who made those caves only that the technology is similar to ours, but with a couple of advancements I am unfamiliar with. So I am hopeful that at the end of this trail we will have our answer as to who is responsible for this cave system."

* * *

It took another seven days before the quiet storm finally broke. Anytime someone went outside they found a world shrouded in a heavy freezing fog and mist, but with no winds at all. It was a silent white world that completely changed the area from what they were familiar with. Even with the snow that had fallen before this storm, the changes it brought were great. Landmarks now were under a meter of new snow, which was powdery. If one ventured out into it without the shoes for snow they would find themselves up to their waists in the white stuff. Surprising to any who did venture out was that it did not feel cold even though it had to be close or below freezing. Finally on the eighth day the fog finally dissipated and a bright sunny day dawned. But with the fog gone it now became bitterly cold and winds began to blow and the powder drift with those winds changing, once again, the landscape.

Saige, staring out at the scene before him, was eager to get back out and to find where that trail would lead them. But now with this new snow he also knew that it would be almost impossible. So with impatience building that he had to fight down, he had to wait, and probably now with this last storm it might not happen until spring – whenever that would be. He sighed turned and went back inside. As he did he found his sister standing next to him. "Okay sis how long have you been standing there?"

"Oh long enough to see the frustration on your face. I know that you want to get back out there. Well, so do I. But nature decided that we must wait. I know that you have been tempted to go ahead and just do it, but I can also see that you haven't given in to those temptations. Anyway the reason I needed to talk to you wasn't this. Our food supplies are beginning to get a little thin. I suspect that we will probably have enough, but being unsure how long we are going to be stuck in winter I don't know. Stone also informed me that we should probably get a detail together and find some additional wood. Now I wish those caves that we found were larger since they self-heat. We then would only need the wood for the cooking fires. Also with so many pregnant women around I worry about their nutritional needs. We don't have everything we normally would. So I worry about the health of their unborn children. Plus if you haven't noticed they are eating more, which is digging deeper into our limited supplies. So we really need to be prepared to send out parties soon even if there are signs that this winter is over.

Oh by the way I've noticed how Seirra seems to only have eyes for you, and keeps being around you whenever it is possible. I think she really is trying to get your attention."

Looking down with a slight frown on his face he said, "Really? I've been so busy with, oh just about everything like you that I haven't even noticed."

"Yeah I know, and I can see that it has somewhat frustrated her. I think she really wants to be with you."

"Oh come on sis, she'd be better off with Stone instead of me. Even though you and I never thought we would be in charge of this group and Shayne would continue to lead, well here we are. And as such I barely have time to think let alone let another woman in my life."

"Another woman? Who's the first? You're not telling me that you are involved with Sorrel are you?"

Laughing he said, "No sis, she has tried but I have no interest that way. If you think about it then the answer is obvious. The first woman is you, of course."

"Oh. That's right. I mean I am a woman, it's just I wasn't looking at it in that way. After all I am your sister. But I have to admit that does make me a female. Okay that's a relief that it isn't Sorrel, but you had me worried there for a moment. But I still find some time for Saar. So there is no reason that you couldn't find time for Seirra."

"Easy for you to say . . . by the way did she put you up to this?"

Shaking her head while she smiled she said. "No dear brother, just an observation from that first female in your life that's all."

Raising his hands in surrender he said, "Okay, okay I get your point. But come on I barely have time to keep this group together . . . hmmm so how do you find time for Saar? I know that when we go out that both he and Stone are in charge so that means a little more contact, but at times I find it difficult to breath with all of this stuff. I now often wonder how Shayne did it. And as far as I know he had no woman in his life other than his family. And of course that means his sister, since from what little I knew of him their mother had passed a number of years before."

"So are you trying to emulate him Saige?"

Frowning he leaned forward and asked. "How so, Shell'?"

Exasperated she said. "Okay, *now* think about it. We both respected him. He did a great job of keeping our unit together, and of course our unit was much larger then. He seemed to be able to lead without effort, but I am sure that was just a front. Since we both now are in charge and I for one have found it much more difficult than I ever imagined. So now I have even more respect for what he accomplished. But if I am going to continue in this role I will not follow him down the path of being single. In fact right now it is probably more important than it was then. We cannot say what is happening with our people or the cities. We are completely isolated, without communication, and we have no way to make contact at all. For all we know we may be the last of our people. And that, dear brother, is a scary thought. So for you, even if it is an unconscious act, that you have decided to become even more like him and remain aloof from the rest and remain single, well I think you are wrong." She stood then and put her hands on her hips before continuing. "And as far as finding the time oh dear brother, it's all a matter of perspective."

Interrupting her he asked, "Perspective? How so?"

Shaking her head she thought. *Sometimes he can be so dense.* "Okay it's really simple and I know we all have our blind sides okay? If there is something that we really want to do or get involved with, then for some reason we find the time to do whatever it is. But if it is something that needs to be done and maybe, I don't know, maybe it's disagreeable, or not our favorite thing to do in the whole world, well then it just seems like the time is never available to get it accomplished." Then she said sarcastically, "Funny thing."

He was quiet for a moment. "Okay sis, point taken. But I worry about such a thing and it's another reason I did not want to start a relationship with any of the women."

"And what could that reason be, oh dear bro?"

Breathing out heavily he said. "Look neither you nor I wanted this job when it was given us. But we are stuck, and I know why it was both of us and not just either you or me, or someone else. By having two of us and of the opposite sexes he made sure that there would be a female leader to deal with the females, and a male leader to deal with the males. And that the two leaders would have to be close so that they could talk with each other and keep each other informed. So we were the logical choice. Not only because we are related but also because we have worked as a team for as long as we trained. So we know each other, and we have also garnered respect from the rest of the unit with our skills. And I am sure these were all factors in us getting us placed into this position of leadership."

"Words are all this is. What is it, don't you like her?"

Shaking his head as he tried to explain, and found himself doing it badly. "No, no that's not it. Don't you see that by becoming interested in one woman that I could alienate both other women who may have thought that it would be nice to be a mate of one of the leaders, and the men who cannot because of the number difference, have a mate. It would be like a power play, you know, using the power of the position to get what I want."

"Well guess what. They will just have to deal with it. Besides are you going to allow someone else to control you from afar? And there isn't even proof that any of what you stated is fact or would become fact. Yes I know that it's one of the many possibilities, but only one. So for me, if for nothing else, would you at least talk to her? I can see that by your obvious actions of ignoring her, you are affecting her and I am beginning to see doubts from her, and her confidence in herself is beginning to fail. She doesn't understand why."

"Why? Why what?" He asked perplexed.

Shaking her head she said. "Oh you men . . . What is it with you? At times I think you are just plain dumb. Whether we like it or not, let's be honest for a moment okay?" Not saying anything but shaking his head he signaled for her to continue. "In our society both sexes are treated as close to equal as they can be, but nature has made woman to be a little smaller than man. So she generally has to look up to her man. This immediately puts the man as the more important in the relationship, kind of the one in charge from her point of view. It kind of goes back to childhood when you always looked up to your parents, the ones with the authority. I'm sure it's not meant to be that way, but it is what it is. And I am sure that in many of the relationships that everything is as equal as it can be and others where one partner dominates the other. But generally it is you guys who are the ones in charge. Not that as women we don't run things. After all there must always be someone behind the scenes to keep everything working. And that's not to put, we women, in a subservient role here. Look Seirra is not the type of woman who is going to try and bowl you over with her charms or let you know what her feelings are until she knows what yours will be. So she is being herself and trying to get your attention the only way she knows how. And how have you reacted? By completely ignoring her as if she did not exist. That can't bode well for anyone be it man or woman. Since we all want to feel like we are needed. So when you completely ignore someone like her she begins to wonder if there is something wrong with her. And then that begins to cascade into the many insecurities we women seem to live with."

"Insecurities? You? I haven't seen any Shell'."

"Oh they are there dear brother, they are there. I don't understand why but can guess that it is probably tied to our hormones that seem to control our lives so much. But who knows the real reason, I don't."

"Okay sis, you've given much a lot to think about. And I promise to try and find time for Seirra. But I still worry about what the rest will think."

Glaring at him she said. "Who cares what the rest thinks. Let it take its course. If you two grow to be a couple so be it. If not . . ." She shrugged saying, "Well, so be it also. But at least both of you will know."

* * *

The respite was short and another storm closed down on them and lasted another seven days burying everything deeper in a blanket of white. When any would venture out they would have to clear the entrance. But finally it did break and the suns shone brightly, almost blinding any who ventured from the gloom of the cave. During the time of the storm Saige finally put forth the effort to at least talk with Seirra, finding that she was somewhat shy and insecure around him. He found that at least for the moment these attributes were drawing him towards her. But at least for the time being he kept her at a distance. He really needed to think this through. He still worried about how beginning this relationship could be seen by the others in their group, but shrugged when he realized that his sister had been right. In truth it was none of their business. As long as he was not using his power as a leader to force someone into coupling with him there was nothing any could say. And he was trying very hard to make sure that he avoided doing that.

With the storm over he organized a team to go with him to the first cave that they had located. It was now the plan to move some of their supplies to this location so that if something disastrous was to fall on them here at their primary location that they would have at least something to fall back on. After discussing what they had discovered some speculation had gone on about the possibility that there could be more of these caves closer to their present location. But with all the searching and exploring that had previously been accomplished in the area, and with none found, there was no ready answer. Other questions had come naturally to mind, such as who had built them, why half to a full day apart and why did they seem to either begin or end where they did? Again with so little known there were no ready answers yet. Of course they could be close by, but were hidden well enough that they had yet to be discovered. This first trip would have the purpose of pinning the location for the ones who had not been there. Then when he and Shellian headed out to continue their search Stone and Saar would organize the shifting of some of their supplies.

Saar remained at the cave while Stone was one of the party members with Seve, and Staven to round the group out to five, leaving ten back at camp to assist in the division of supplies. Eventually the group reached the meadow area where Shellian and he had taken their mid-day meal. Like before it was windy and quite cold. So they pushed through and then around to the lee side and immediately felt warmer once out of the harsh wind. Here he let Shellian lead the group to the cave. Like the one they presently were living in, this cave was almost invisible to any who did not know where it was. Stone shaking his head asked, "Shellian, how do you do it? I mean both caves, this one, and the one we live in, is almost impossible to locate, and see, unless you happen to be in the right place, you can't see it. And even when it is pointed out it takes one a little while to find it. Yet, you seem to just do it."

Smiling and shaking her head she said. "Stone I don't have an answer for you. All I know is that when I look at a hillside like this there is something about it that is wrong. I can't even tell you what that wrong is, but once I sense its wrongness then I start searching for the why. And so far it has revealed these caves. So when I figure it out I will definitely pass it on, and that's really the best I can do for now. But now you understand why I have to be on the team that is locating these things. I just seem to be able to find them while none of the rest of you can. And since my brother and I are a trained team, this is why we are the ones who will continue the exploration. We just work very well together. So while we are gone on this next leg of our search, both you and Saar will be in charge. Not that we haven't already explained that, but now that you and the rest of this team has seen this cave I believe it now is clear as to why it is us that must continue on."

Then Saige spoke. "I know that since Shayne made us the leaders that it may not seem smart for both of us to go out and do this and be away from the group for as long as this takes, but Shellian has stated it much better than I ever could. We, she and I, are a team, and as such know how each thinks and reacts which gives us an edge. But I do believe that you Stone, and Saar back at camp, are good seconds. So if the unthinkable did happen and we were lost then the two of you could carry on. I don't know how else to say it."

"Saige, I wasn't complaining about what the two of you are about to do. I just wish one of the other of us were going also. But I understand why. Our group is so small that losing you two would be a burden on our survival, but three could be enough loss especially with as many of our women who are with child now, that we could perish. It's a tough decision however one goes about it."

"True, Stone . . . And I know that you weren't complaining. It's just by you being on site where the first of these were found, you can now understand why we decided as we did. Believe me we do not like the idea of both of us out for the time we figure to be gone and leave the rest of you alone like that, but as you have stated there really is little choice. Shall we go up to the cave?" Seeing no objections he signaled Shellian to lead on.

She led them up to the entrance and then inside with the rest discovering what they had when it was first located. Soft powdery dirt floor, a soft glow coming from the walls, and warmth that was not overpowering but comfortable. A perfect place for any of the small wild beasts in the area, and yet there was no sign that any had ever been inside. "It sure would be nice to know what the builders of this cave used to keep the animals out." Seve said.

"Yeah, wouldn't it." Staven answered. "It sure would make it nice to have back in the cave where we are. We seem to be continually fighting those small creatures. Always into something and we can never find where they are coming from or where they go once we chase them away."

"Well, all of you, you now know where this thing is. Shall we eat before we head back?" Shellian asked. There were no arguments, so they sat in the cave and ate their travel rations before preparing for the return trip. "You know Shellian I surely would like to know how you do it. I know you've said that you don't know yourself . . . but what a talent. If it hadn't been for you and your talent how much longer would it have been before we would have found shelter, and then would we have had enough time to prepare for this winter? Although right now I am beginning to worry a little, since we have no idea how long it lasts up here in the mountains, are we going to have enough food to get us through the rest of the time?" Pausing a moment and organizing his thoughts, Seve continued, "If we were below where we came from I would say that winter was almost over, but up here I just don't have a clue." The rest had to agree. None of them had a clue. They had lived in the lower lands all their lives, and had never even ventured into these mountains. After all the cities were their sanctuaries and up until the primitives found a way into them, the same cities had been their protection.

Thinking back while the others discussed general issues, Saige let his mind drift to a future meeting with Seirra. He had to admit that he found her quite attractive. And again if he thought about it he probably would have been interested in her back when they still were in the city. But at that time their work and training had never brought them into contact with each other. So until this disaster struck the city she was an unknown. He realized that with so few women that it limited one's choices. He laughed inwardly as this sounded to him like he was out choosing some beast of burden, or maybe some type of material or other item he had planned on making his own. Not a real live person, who had their own ideas, rights, feelings, and views on things. Shaking his head he came back to it and realized that in some ways when one of the opposite sex did join with another they both gave up some things, compromised on many, and yet remained who they were essentially. So while there had been very little really said at this point – he really felt that he was walking on sharp stones here – he could see that she was attracted to him. It was something that he had not noticed until Shellian very pointedly stated that he had been blind and that by completely ignoring the situation was really making things worse.

So he began to watch her now and then and found that indeed just as Shellian had stated, Seirra continued to be in places that would keep him in her sight and to be in places where they would "accidentally be in contact". Yet as busy as he had been, and he had to admit to it, *blind*, he really never saw it. He guessed that part of the reason lay in the fact that they had more men than women and because of his position he considered himself outside of the right to couple with any of women. After all that would be an abuse of the power he had been entrusted. And presently while his contact with her had only been brief with conversations never getting past the polite stage such as "Have a nice day", and such he found that his thoughts continued to return to her. Again shaking his head he did not understand it at all. There just had not been enough of anything between them for him to begin to think about her this often. Then he worried that if they started getting serious how would the rest treat her. Since he could not be there all the time to protect her if things became ugly, well it just added another burden and complication to the "what ifs". Again going back to the conversation with Shellian, he knew that she was correct. But human nature being what it is this would not change the possibility that she would become a target, and someone to use against him, or as a tool to get he and Shellian to allow someone to get away with something. Shrugging inwardly, he found that he could come up with all sorts of problems that could happen because of this possible relationship with Seirra. He was then brought back to reality when Shellian asked. "So Saige are you ready to return with the rest of us to camp? Or are you just planning on staying here as a hermit?" That brought a laugh from the rest as he realized that everyone else was packed and ready to head back but he had done nothing.

Embarrassed a little he said, "Sorry. I was deep in thought there and hadn't realized that you all were ready to head back . . . just a sec here and I'll be ready."

Then Shellian hit the mark with the comment. "I am sure we all know where your thoughts were Saige, and I don't really think it was on what we were discussing here."

He smiled and said nothing, not wanting to dig a hole any deeper than it obviously already was. He grabbed his pack and then joined the other four and they headed back to the main camp. Shellian then came up beside him and whispered. "I haven't been your sister and partner all these years not to know how to read your sign." She then continued on ahead like nothing was said. He looked down briefly and smiled. If ever there was a truer statement he hadn't heard of it. He knew that he could do the same with her, so it was only right to know that she could do it also.

It was late in the day with the suns setting that the five made their way back into the camp. When they entered the cave Shellian and Saige found that the rest had been busy working on sorting, and separating their supplies. When the two of them looked at the supplies that were left it seemed like so little. Now alarmed Saige wondered, would there be enough to make this division, and worse, was there enough to get them through this winter. Fifteen people go through a lot of materials, and now with four carrying it increased the need. Looking over at Shellian he could see the concern in her eyes also. But what could they do? Was there someplace that they could find some of the grazers to increase their meat? Or because like them food was scarce during winter, would there even been enough meat on them to be able to provide meat for them? *Great!* He thought. *Now we will have to wait to continue our exploration, and now go and see if we can find additional food. When will this winter end?* He then said. "Saar I see you have been busy while we were gone. I guess the next question I have is, is this all that we have left?"

Shaking his head Saar said. "I'm afraid so. It's a lot less than I thought we had. As one pile it doesn't look too bad. But once you separate it down like this it becomes obvious how little we have left. It is a worrisome thing. I mean we have no idea how much longer until spring arrives. Looking at this I have calculated that if we kept everything here, and I suspect that is what we must do by the way, that we have about thirty to thirty five days' worth of food. And if we ration it a little, maybe extend it by ten to fifteen days, but that's all. And the women who are now with child we cannot reduce what they need or their unborn children and they themselves will suffer because of it – and that is the reality of it Saige. I'm sorry but there it is."

"Okay then, there it is and none of us can change it. So any additional exploring or discovering will have to wait. Does anyone here have some suggestions as to where we could find foods to supplement our dwindling supplies?" Saige thought that since each member had been out and had searched and opened other areas that were unknown to them that there was a possibility they had either seen something or remembered something that could help. But at this moment all he was met with was silence. Looking at each member before continuing he then stated. "We have no choice left to us. If the weather holds, and I cannot guarantee that one, then we are going out as teams of three as hunting parties or teams of two for searching. So that if something is found such as a grazer, then two can dress it out while the other returns to get others so that we can then haul the meat back. I only want two teams out at a time that way if something is located then there will be enough bodies to get the carcass. Any team that goes out must, and I emphasize must, be back by dark whether success-ful or not. And on that happy note let's just get to the evening. Tomorrow this all begins in earnest. Oh Saar, since you are our only medical help here you are stuck. So I guess I am go-ing to keep you assigned to rationing the food. With the women who are pregnant we need you here just in case some-thing happens with any one of them. Pick a second among our group to assist you. And if I smell things right it smells like food is ready to eat so shall we?"

While eating one of the men mentioned that as they had explored that they had heard a sound that kind of sounded like a whoosh, and had lasted for a little while before growing quiet again. But where the sound had been coming from appeared to be through a narrow deep ravine that dropped out of sight, allowing no view into the area where the sound had originated. He stated that they had stood there for a short while before continuing and had heard other sounds in that area there was similar, but seemed to be more distant. Stone then brought up that since this had been an active volcano sometime in the past that most likely what they were hearing were geysers, and there probably were a number of hot springs in the area also. According to the size of the canyon, it could have a number of protected meadows, which could be snow free due to the heat. Of course by not seeing what had been described he could not be really sure.

"So Staven, do you think you could find it again?" Stone asked.

Shaking his head Staven said, "I'm not really sure. You see that was back at the beginning of winter, one of the first ones I went out on." Turning to Seve he asked. "I think you were with me that time; do you remember where it was, at all?"

Thinking before answering he knew that he had always been one that could easily get lost. Directions such as north, south, east, west, meant nothing and he could get turned around easily. He found that he normally had to depend on the other member of the team to locate a specific direction. "Come on Staven you know I could get lost just heading outside of this cave. There is no way I could take anybody to where that location is. I probably wouldn't even recognize it if

I was standing in the very spot where we first heard that sound."

Sighing Staven said, "Okay, I'll have to think about it. But it may take a little time for me to remember. We've been all over these mountains; well at least all over them close to camp. And I have been out a number of times since then and haven't been back close to that area, so I will just have to work on recalling where we were. And before you say it's important, believe me I know. But I didn't consider it so at the time so I did not lock the location in my mind. So right now it could be any number of places. So let me think about it."

Shellian looking over the group asked. "Have any of you heard or found a similar thing such as these possible hot springs while you were out exploring?" Again no one answered. Shaking her head she said, "I guess I can take that as a no then."

Later that night before they retired to their separate sleeping areas, Shellian said, "Saige I really do hope that Staven remembers. You know what may be a good idea is to send Stone out with him. Geology is one of Stone's specialties and maybe between the two of them they can find those, what did he call them, oh yes, geysers. I've never seen one – I bet they are spectacular."

"What", Saige asked, "A bunch of hot water shooting out of a hole in the ground? You think something like that would be spectacular?"

"Oh come on Saige. Can't you see that something like that has to have beauty tied with it? I know that if one was to be foolish enough to be too close when it let loose that it could kill or at least severely injure you, but I really bet that they have their own beauty."

"Could be, but right now that's the last thing on my mind. I can only hope that Staven remembers and that it is as Stone hopes. But with no idea as to where, we'll keep our rotation, and without a location we may, once again be in serious trouble." Breathing out deeply he continued, "Anyway, I'm tired, and once again we have much too much going on even for winter time to find any real time to relax. See you in the morning Shell'." He then turned and went into his area and prepared to sleep. She watched him go shrugged and then retired herself. She thought as he left that he really seemed a bit down. Not surprising really, since it wasn't that long ago that indeed they were still just a brother and sister continuing their training just outside their city, with no thoughts beyond what the next day would bring. Now all of that appeared to be no more than a dream, and the reality they were stuck in now was, at times, crushing. It appeared that when one problem was solved, so many more appeared to take its place. "Oh well", she said to no one in particular since she was alone. She then sighed and lay down to go to sleep. While she had been with them when they went back to newly discovered cave, there had been much going on here also, and the day just flew for everyone, and once again she found herself almost asleep instantly.

* * *

Another storm had struck in the night, but this one appeared to lack the strength of the others that they had faced so far. And by late afternoon was gone. They hoped that it was a sign saying that winter could be close to an end. But when they stepped out after the storm left it was bitterly cold. It had to be well below freezing, and the breeze that was with it just cut right through whatever they were wearing. Exposed skin felt like it was freezing almost immediately, so after an initial foray out of the cave everyone stayed inside. How was it that it looked so inviting and warm outside but was just the opposite? Standing at the entrance and looking out through a small opening Saige wondered if they were going to make it. There had been so many friends lost during their flight to here, and while presently they were okay, there was no proof that it would continue that way. He could feel the pressure building inside of him, as decisions that needed to be made were not coming to him. Shaking his head he thought, once again that he really had no desire to be put in charge of anybody, let alone this group, but he knew that he could not forsake the trust that Shayne had put in him and Shellian. Shaking his head once again, he thought, *Four women pregnant and one at least halfway through her term. Don't these people realize what a complication this adds? Or do they not care and are looking for whatever comfort they can find?* Well he knew that it was cold here and it seemed that at night that the women were cold and to have a warm body next to them was a comfort. Unfortunately it never remained just a warm body next to them and now without the protection that was available in the cities they were paying the price for these indiscretions. Not that he could blame them. Even Shellian had mentioned that she was cold at night and the thought of having Saar next to her to help keep her warm was a temptation, which so far she had avoided . . . but for how long? He knew that both of them were right for each other, and again only because of the circumstances they remained separate.

That brought him full circle to his own situation and the fact that Seirra was still trying to get his attention. He really did not know what to do about it. So far he had kept his distance by using his position as leverage and what conversations they had were quite impersonal. But he knew that shortly he was going to have to make some kind of decision about her, and truth be told he really had no idea. Up until Shellian had pointed it out to him he had really never paid that close attention to Seirra. But since that time he had observed her, when he felt that he would not be intruding, or because he was one of the leaders that it would appear that he was marking out his territory, he could see her interest. So far he felt that he had been successful. Taking a deep breath he then thought about her. He had to admit that she definitely was attractive, and yet . . . and yet there was this subtle feeling that she did not see it herself – her natural beauty. Just a little shorter than Shellian, she had a lithe athletic build, and seemed to be able to move with a natural grace that most of the other women that had survived lacked. In fact the only other woman that moved that way was Shellian. It spoke of strength, intelligence, and an awareness of the physical world around them. When he thought about it, in many ways, the two of them were quite similar. He was surprised that he hadn't noticed it before. Yet when she was around him she seemed shy, almost withdrawn. It was something he really did not understand.

He realized suddenly that someone was just behind him. Thinking it was his sister he said without turning around. "Shell', what are we going to do?" Then realizing that it wasn't Shellian he turned and saw that the person standing behind and close to him was Seirra. He smiled even though it was a sad smile and said. "Sorry Seirra, I thought you were Shellian."

She was looking up into his eyes and he saw doubt and maybe a little lack of confidence there. "Saige, I saw you standing over here by the entrance and you just looked lonely and somewhat forlorn, and I thought I would come over and see if there was anything I could do to help."

Again with a sad smile he said, "Seirra, are you trying to mother me? I know it's a natural thing for women to want to do. But I do thank you for the offer." Then before he realized he put his arms around her and hugged her. For some reason it just felt natural and right. She had put her head on his chest and sighed softly as she clung to him. He then realized that he was beginning to have another physical reaction that was completely unexpected. And he knew that she could feel it also and at that point she clung tighter to him. At this point he knew that she knew, but before anything could be said they heard a heated argument between two of the women, he released her and left to see what was going on and if he or Shellian would have to intervene. Having four pregnant women around was not the easiest of situations to deal with. It appeared that their emotions were always on the raw edge, and anything would set one or another off on some tirade. While the cave system they were living in was not necessarily small, this constant chaffing from these imagined slights made it seem much too small. He arrived at about the same time as Shellian and they saw two of the women, Storme and Sabryn, ganging up on Sorrel. At the point where they had arrived, the argument or fight, had become quite loud, and anger had flared between the three of them.

It was obvious from the vindictiveness that was being thrown at Sorrel that they did not like her lifestyle and were letting her have it. He suspected that because Sorrel was free with her body that maybe she had coupled with their men. With no proof other than the fact that the two men in question had probably looked at Sorrel, it was still enough to make these women suspicious. He was pretty sure that nothing had gone on, and Shellian had been monitoring the situation closely. But Sorrel had one of those bodies that men just naturally looked at. And of course she knew that, and had taken full advantage of it. And because she liked an open free relationship she had not settled on any one man – making her the target of the three women who had. Plus it appeared that as the women got deeper in their pregnancies and their bodies changed to accommodate the growing fetuses so did their emotions, doubts, and it never took much to bring these doubts out. So looking over the scene he finally had to raise his voice to be heard. "Storme! Sabryn! Sorrel! Enough! Let's end this here and now. Listening to the two of you, Storme and Sabryn, I think that you are making accusations where you have no proof, and we, Shellian and I have been watching things." Storme interrupted and said. "Right, and if you have watched things as well as you say you have then who is the father of her child? For all I know it could be my man Schylar or hers", pointing at Sabryn. That way she throws her body around I wouldn't be surprised if she has coupled even with you Saige."

Before he could say anything Seirra said with much emotion. "No he has not coupled with Sorrel!"

Storme turned and faced Seirra and asked. "Why is that Seirra? Have you been warming his bed at night?" And with those questions asked Seirra's face flushed red. Then in triumph Storme said. "So that's the way it is."

"No Storme that is not the way it is." Saige answered. Although he knew that they would not believe him. But from Seirra's reaction he now knew that she had wanted to share his bed, and that Shellian had once again been correct. "In fact, it seems that you are accusing any man including yours, of sleeping with any of the women, so is it you who is cheating on Schylar? Since I have found that the ones who usually make such accusations are usually doing it themselves, and because they are, they suspect that all are guilty of doing the same thing. Is that what it is Storme?" After asking he could almost see the truth in what he had asked. But he suspected that while it may be something she may have contemplated, he felt that it was something that she probably could not be successful at doing. Since she had a tendency to want to do what Sorrel had done so successfully she then felt that all would be that way, and because she couldn't or wouldn't, it frustrated her more that some other woman could, and then have such a physical draw on her chosen man. "This ends now. We are not going to be throwing unproven accusations around just to heal our hurt pride. You two have no proof of anything you are accusing Sorrel of doing." Seeing the rebellion in both of their eyes, he continued. "No, it ends here and now. We have to live together and while I cannot keep you from disliking each other, these confrontations are to end now."

"So what are you going to do if we don't want them to stop?" Storme asked defiantly.

Smiling at her he said, "Very simple Storme. It really is. You see we have no choice here. So if one decides that they don't want to live with the rest then we simply will put you out. In this case it would include Schylar since the two of you have decided to couple. And with the discovery of these other caves there would be a place to send you. Does that answer your question Storme?"

Looking at his face and then at the faces of the rest that were now present she could see that he was quite serious but wanting to get the last word she said. "That may be so, but this isn't over, and there may come a time when you and Shellian are no longer the leaders. I think then Schylar will be, and we will see who is put out." And with that statement she turned and left, leaving Sabryn standing there by herself, with Sorrel still standing defiantly across from her. Saige had to admit even with her late in her second third she still was a beautiful woman, and would still turn the head of any man. Then gently he asked, "Sabryn, do you understand what was said here? Do you understand that with the way we have to live right now that it must be this way?"

With her shoulder slumping in defeat she just shook her head, sighed and then said. "Yes, Saige . . ." Then looking across at Sorrel she said with strong emotion. "But she!" Pointing her finger at Sorrel, "She had better stay away from my man!" Then a little more softly she asked. "You two aren't coupling are you?", as she pointed to Seirra, and he.

"No . . . no Sabryn, we are not coupling. Although from Seirra's reaction here I suspect that it is something that she would like to see happen eventually." Once again Seirra's face reddened. He took a deep breath and continued "I have not coupled with any as I have felt that it would look like I was using my position as one of the leaders, and to be truthful I have been just too busy to even consider a relationship at this time – *so even the accusation of me coupling with Sorrel is really a joke.* If any member of this group is under scrutiny it is Shellian and I. Since we are the leaders we are constantly in contact and observation by everyone. Don't you think that if something was going on that all would be aware of it in a short time? And as far as Seirra goes, at the present we have barely had a conversation, let alone discussed anything about coupling or becoming a couple, so put that out of your mind also."

At this point Sabryn just shook her head, and then like Storme turned and left the area where the confrontation had begun. Shellian looking around at the rest still standing there, with most looking down at the ground, she could tell that the rest were uncomfortable, she then said gently. "Okay, I think this is over for now. So let's get back to whatever we all were doing before this outburst." Then seeing little movement from the gathered group she said. "Let's move, unless one of you wants to discuss something here and now?" Then looking around and making brief eye contact each shook their heads and then slowly drifted off. Shellian looking at her brother said. "I was afraid that something like this was eventually going to happen. Something about 'we' women who are emotional anyway, it becomes much worse during pregnancy. So I would be surprised if this did not happen again in some form or another. *So dear brother be prepared.* I suspect it will be very tough a number of times between now and when we will have new lives joining us. And then it probably will get worse."

"Worse? I thought this was bad enough. How could it get worse?"

Smiling she said. "I can see you haven't been around too many babies. The ones who will have these new lives will have their lives run completely by them. There will be too little sleep, distraction when they are away from their children, tempers, arguments as they come to terms with their offspring."

Laughing he said. "You make it sound like it's the worst thing that one can do."

"Yeah I guess it does sound that way. But from what I have seen, well I know you have never been allowed around at birthing time. But all of us women share it. At that time there is much work, after all it isn't called labor just for fun, much pain, and they say it is like trying to eliminate a large rock, and actually some tearing of the tissues, so don't be surprised to hear screaming when it comes to that time. But after it is all over and the child is born then you can see that almost immediately that what the woman has just gone through is forgotten and all she can see is that child and the love for it just pours out of her very soul. I don't know if I can explain it better than that, and I haven't gone through this yet so I can only tell you from what I have observed."

Silent for a moment as he took in everything she had just told him, Saige said, "Ouch! I guess we men are just on the sidelines and, well how can you women want to go through such a thing? I mean I understand why coupling. It is the way of life. After all if it hadn't happened in the past we wouldn't be here now. But knowing that you are taking a great chance to be on the road that will lead to being uncomfortable for the time that you are carrying the child inside of you and then knowing that sometime in the future you cannot avoid all that pain and suffering . . ." Shaking his head he continued, "Well I just don't know if I could do it."

"It's all there, but there is also wonder . . . and I guess I really can't quite come up with the word for it. But from the beginning, when you have sickness in the mornings letting you know that you are pregnant, which fortunately goes away in the first third, then in wonder you watch your body begin to change. Of course we are not necessarily happy about that, but it is part of life. Then comes the time when you first feel the baby move inside of you. It is an unbelievable and happy time. You know that your baby is alive and now you actually can feel and see it move. But as you reach the end of your third-third, you are tired, you feel like a large fish, you cannot keep cool, and because the baby is taking so much of the inside of you, you find that nature calls are very frequent. At this time you are very ready for this to be over, but still fear that time. So I guess that's just about it. Well, then the labor starts, and you are scared, because you know it is time, and you cannot stop this until it's over, and you have your new child in your arms."

"Well for not finding the words I think you did a pretty good job. And you are looking forward to this sis? In a way it sounds like something that should be avoided."

Laughing at him she said, "I think when it finally happens to me, and of course to whomever you eventually couple with, that you will have a different view."

CHAPTER NINE

Seirra sighed as she looked across the cave to where Saige, Shellian, Stone, and Saar were in deep conversation. It was at least seven days ago when the two of them had finally made the first physical contact, and Saige had briefly let down his guard. Then came that fight and since then he had avoided her. When he had held her it just felt natural and good and when he had the physical reaction to her closeness it had surprised her. And when she looked up she could see the surprise in his face also. But even that felt right. Now he was cold and distant. She remembered what he had said and realized that it was something she hadn't considered – that any leader was under the watchful eye of the group more than any other individual. So somehow she needed to find a way to move this relationship further along. The one thing she knew for sure, that after her first real physical touching of him, and then the way he and Shellian handled the situation afterwards, made her more determined that he and she should be a couple. But now with what had been revealed could it ever happen? She took a deep breath and continued to work the skin into clothing and was at a loss as to what to do next. She had to find a way . . . she just had to.

But she now also knew that it was obvious what her feelings for him were. Shaking her head she thought. *If I could only have controlled my emotions and not have blushed like I did. And I know it had to be really bad since my face was hot both times. Now not only does he know but so does everybody.* And while it was true they were not a couple and they had not slept together, from her reaction, the rest, even with the denial, could easily assume that she had. Again what could she do?

Glancing over briefly from their meeting Saige knew that he wasn't being fair to Seirra, but he felt that right now he had to keep his distance to reinforce to the rest that there had been nothing going on between them. But the rumors of their relationship kept coming back. *If only she hadn't turned so red when the accusations were thrown out,* he thought. But at least he now knew what Shellian had told him was quite true. No doubt that Seirra wanted to be with him. But for now it just couldn't be. Turning back to the other three in the group he said. "Sorry, a little distracted, what was it that you asked?"

Shellian smiling back at him said, "Never mind dear brother. We can see that you are distracted, and you have been through much of what we have been discussing. So why don't you just go over there and talk with her. It's out in the open anyway. Not that anything has really happened between the two of you. But with the rumors and stories flying around here, the two of you have been coupling for quite a while. So why not just make those rumors come true? It was obvious to all that she really does have feelings for you. And your denial, while I know it is true, didn't fly with the rest. No, I'm not talking about Stone or Saar who are our seconds here, but the remaining ten, well I don't know if all of them do, but the majority appears to believe it. And Storme, with the encouragement of Schylar, is pushing it for all it's worth.

"It's obvious that Schylar is trying to drive a wedge between you and the rest. And while we all knew it, this is the first time he has come out in the open to push like this. If you think back to when the attack first came back at the city he was the one who was questioning Shayne. Of course Shayne had confronted him and made him go up and view that attack. But he has always been a pain, and he has always wanted to be the leader. Although I know that it would be a disaster if he led anyone."

"Yeah", Stone said, "he is the greatest of leaders in his own mind, that's for sure. But it would scare me to death to have him in charge of anything. Incompetent really is too weak of a word, but it's the one that comes to mind right now."

"Anyway this is off the subject. We need to get our teams back out and locate that possible geyser area. It quit snowing about two days ago and so far the suns have been shining. But there has been no heat in them up here. So I am hoping that shortly it will warm enough to allow the next team out. Hmmm . . ." She said as she was looking at her notes. "It appears that Sojar and Steen are due to be the next exploration team out. So where do we need to send them? I know the information that we got from . . . ahhh . . . you know who, was pretty vague. But at least we know the general direction they had traveled since it is written in our logs. Of course this trip out is to try and locate those possible hot springs. If found and the grazers are there, then we can send in a hunting team. Any that we have sent out so far have come back empty."

"I think we probably should have them go out in the morning. We can't wait very much longer. Food isn't an issue yet, but from what we have discovered it will be soon and I don't want us to reach that point. Do any of you have any better ideas?" Saige asked

Pausing a moment, Saar asked, "So how long should they be out before reporting back in?"

"Good question. It seems to me that we were running one-day explorations at the time, so I would guess two days only." Looking around at the others Saige asked, "Does that sound good?" He looked around at the other three once again and they nodded their heads in agreement. "Okay with that solved what do we do with this deteriorating situation here in the cave?"

* * *

With it announced at the supper meal, Sojar and Steen prepared their supplies to leave at first light. Looking around at the rest of the group Saige could see suspicion on many of the faces. Shaking his head, he really had no idea how to defuse the growing animosity against both he and Shellian. Yet somehow it had to be done if they were to stay together. Again shaking his head he wondered if maybe it would be easier to just let the team fall apart. But he immediately put that thought out of his mind. Shayne had trusted the two of them to keep them together, and no one said it would be easy. He knew that there was only so much one could do when trapped within a cave for this long winter. So it gave time for such rumors to fly, to build, and to be believed. It did not matter that there was no truth, if repeated often enough, they took on a life of their own and became the truth. So he knew that for the present that he could not, would not, make any move to reinforce these rumors. That left Seirra out in the cold so to speak, and he hoped that she understood why he had to do this for now. With the coming of spring and the work that spring would entail he felt that much of this would just flow away as the ice did when the spring rains hit – something about busy hands, if he remembered correctly. Tired he decided to go to sleep. While there may have been idle time for many there had been none for him and he had to admit he was tired. Tomorrow would bring a whole new set of problems, and they hadn't cleared the ones from today. *Oh well,* he thought, *tomorrow is another day.*

He was up before dawn to give last minute instructions to the outgoing two. Pointing out on their rough map he made sure that they knew to cover some of the earlier explored areas. They had to find where the grazers spent the winter. Standing outside the cave in the cold morning air with their breaths coming out like smoke, created by the crisp clear air, he watched them until they were out of sight. It would be two days before they returned. Then it would be time to put out the next team. So far they had been lucky. Other than the incident of falling into that old lava tube there had been no serious injuries. All he could do was hope that with winter nearing its end that it would remain that way. This first winter here in the mountains had been rough. They barely had time to prepare for it, and now with winter still upon them, they were beginning to pay the price of insufficient preparation. Even though it was very cold out, for the moment, it really felt great to be out and in the fresh air. It helped clear his mind, and since the cave had been closed up it had begun to take on an odor all its own. And it was not the best of smells, but he found that one got used to it. It was only when one came out into the fresh air did one really realize how bad it had gotten inside the cave. One thing for sure when spring came, there would have to be a major cleaning and airing out. Right now it stank of bodies not bathing enough, urine, dirty clothing, smoke, and who knew how many other things. So lingering outside to watch the suns rise over the horizon, he finally chilled enough that he needed to go back in to get warm.

* * *

The next two days flew by, and that truly was a surprise. But it had remained clear and cold, and from what they could see it might remain that way for at least a few more days allowing a couple of additional teams out. While not desperate he had the short supplies on his mind constantly trying to come up with some solution, and he knew that he was not the only one. It was to main topic of conversation anytime people got together to talk. They all realized their plight. He heard one of the women who was outside scream, and then heard her yell for Saar. The whole camp spilled outside to find out what had happened. Once outside they found Steen bloodied and broken, without Sojar. It was obvious from his condition that he barely made it back. Saar arrived and immediately took over the care and signaled for a few of the men to carry him in and place him by the fire. Steen's breathing was ragged, and there was a slight froth on his lips. He was immediately placed by the fire, and then Saar did a quick examination while he ordered some items, and then he shooed everybody away saying that until he had a chance to really check the injuries that it would do none of them and especially Steen, any good to hang around. Turning around to leave Saige spied Sorrel and she was white as a ghost. Looking over at Shellian he saw that she was looking with concern at Steen and was about to leave. Going over to her he said. "I think you need to go talk with Sorrel. She looks really bad right now and I think she's going to need some support."

"What do you mean? She's been really strong throughout this . . ." Turning and looking at Sorrel she said. "Oh . . . I see what you mean. Of course I'll go comfort her." She then left immediately and was at Sorrel's side with her arm around her shoulders. She led her away and then out of sight. He knew that when she found out what was going on with Sorrel she would pass it on to him. Right now he needed to know what had happened out there, but knew that it would be some time before any answers would be forthcoming. He glanced over where Saar was working on Steen and then at Steen and realized that he was out cold. Shaking his head, he needed answers and he needed to know where Sojar was.

* * *

It was hours later when Saar came to see Saige. Shaking his head Saar said. "I tried to save him, but without my equipment that I had available in the city there just was no way. He had internal bleeding, and I think a broken rib had punctured one of his lungs. All I really could do was comfort him while he slipped away from me. It's a miracle that he got back here at all."

"Did he tell you anything at all? I'd really like to know what happened."

"It was pretty garbled, but I think I got the jest of what he was trying to tell me. First off he said that it was their fault that it happened. Both of them got careless since they were getting close to the camp. I think that's why he made it back. They were only less than a half-day's hike and were eager to get back. He said that they didn't find what they were sent to locate, but that there had been a great number of tracks from the grazers, which in his mind meant that they were on the move. Plus while he had to admit that he had coupled with Sorrel it had become plain as time had continued that she was favoring Sojar, and he her. So he thought that soon Sorrel would not be offering her body to anyone but Sojar. He said that they had stopped and had not considered where they had stopped since they had felt safe. Then like down below when that predator attacked us and missed, another one or maybe the same one attacked them and had grabbed Sojar, and at the same time it's shoulder had hit him hard in the chest. He said all he got was a glimpse at the creature and it was huge. He said that it was gone and he heard Sojar screaming as the predator disappeared and suddenly the screams just stopped, and he knew that Sojar was dead. When he tried to get up he hurt everywhere, and he felt broken up inside. He knew that he was severely injured and was trying desperately to get back here to both get help, and to hopefully live. And that's about it. After that he sort of just went back to sleep, and never woke up."

Looking down at the small fire he had built, Saige thought. *We've been so careful. We made it this far without any serious injuries or death, and winter is almost over. Now in one incident we lose two. I wonder if that predator was following the herds and saw the two of them. Heck all of this winter we haven't even seen any sign of the beast. Other than the large tracks we found lower down we've never even seen one. Now what?* "Thank you Saar. I know that you did the best you could." Shaking his head he asked, "Why now? We have almost beaten our first winter here." Then more softly more to himself than Saar he again asked. "Why now?"

"I know that you really aren't asking me that, and even if you were I have no answers for you. I've been asking that question . . . what's that?" He asked when there appeared to be a sound of approaching people. Their tone was ugly.

Schylar came over from the far side of the cave with eight others of the group. There was triumph written all over his face, and with a sneer he said. "We've put up with you, your sister, and you Saar, and even though Stone isn't here he is included in this." He then pointed to Seirra and said. "You, since you have been sweet on him can join them," which she quietly did. Saige could see the fear in her eyes and realized what was coming down. Schylar had convinced the rest that it was time for a change in leadership and any who had been in the inner circle of the present leadership would have to go. "We've not liked the way you have been leading us for a long time. And now your leadership has caused the death of two of us, so we decided it was time for a change. In the morning the five of you will leave and never come back."

Softly Saige said. "Don't you mean that you've decided Schylar? It has been obvious all the way back when the city was first attacked that you did not like the way Shayne had done things. And he then proved to you that he was right. But even that did not sit right with you. It has been obvious from the beginning that you have wanted to be in charge. Isn't that it?" He then looked over the rest that stood with him, giving them a hard stare." He could tell they were uncomfortable with the action, but at the same time were unwilling to go against him. Then to the group he said. "So that's the way it is."

Schylar answered. "Yes Saige that's the way it is. If I had my choice I would have put you out tonight to fend for yourself, but they convinced me to wait until morning. So at first light you will leave, and from that point on you will not return under threat of death. It's just that simple."

Saige knew that they were outnumbered even if four of the group were women carrying. But it would do no good to start a fight since it was obvious that sometime earlier that they had taken all of their weapons so that they were now unarmed. It would serve no purpose since Schylar had somehow convinced the rest that he would be a much better leader. So taking him down now would not change the feelings that had grown against them. "To prevent any others from getting hurt we will do as you demand." Then turning to the rest again he said. "I really hope you know what you are doing. Because I think you are putting yourselves in a very bad situation." Then turning back to Schylar he asked. "Are at least going to allow us our share of the food, and some of the weapons, or is that going to be denied also?"

Sneering again he said. "Of course, and that has already been done, and as far as I am concerned you're getting more than you should. I would have put you out with nothing."

Looking at him in pity now Saige said softly, "I'm sure you would, I'm sure you would. Anything to cement your power, and it would be easier just to kill us off, wouldn't it?"

"Enough! Everything that needs to be said has been. We will see all of you out of the cave in the morning. Until then have a good night, your last in this cave." He with the group who followed him turned to leave when Saige interrupted them once again.

"Sorrel," He asked gently, "You can join us and leave in the morning. I believe you would do better this way – would you do that?" Looking closely at her he could see that she was still quite white. She didn't say anything, but the accusations that he was responsible for the deaths were in her eyes. She just turned and left. He knew that Storme had been working on the other women, and there would be no help or mercy there.

Shortly Schylar with the rest turned and left them alone, but they knew not totally alone. They were sure that there would be someone spying on them all night. "I hadn't realized that it had gone that far." Saige stated. "Did any of you sense it at all?" They all looked at him and just shook their heads. Taking a deep breath he continued, "I guess we have no choice. So gather your gear and join me back here. I do not think it is a good idea to be apart tonight. Just because we have been promised that no one will be hurt or killed we can-not be sure of it. So from this point on we need to stay together. And that is everywhere including nature calls."

When he had stated it, they realized that he was probably quite correct. That any one of them could become victims and their injuries or death could be chalked up as an accident. So quickly they went as a group to each of their sleeping areas, collecting Stone and then gathered their equipment and re-turned to the area where Saige and Shellian were. "This is such a big mistake." Saar said. "I am the only doctor. Don't they know what they are doing to themselves?"

"No doc, I don't think so." Stone answered. "But when someone like Schylar makes this type of move he believes he is so much better, but we know that they have just doomed themselves."

"I know . . . it's just that I took an oath to heal and protect life, and they have knowingly just thrown all that away. I worry about these women, but even more about their unborn children. Yet, they all have thrown in with him." Then shaking his head he continued, "I just don't understand . . . not at all." None of the others had any answers to give him.

* * *

The next morning at sunrise they were all outside the cave. Saige looking at the group could see no change in their expressions and knew that there would be no way to change their minds. Sighing softly, he shrugged and with the others headed away from what had become their home. They had been given only their knives; all other weapons had been kept. At least the five of them had a destination, the caves that they had located. But since the ones who had just thrown them out knew of the first, they would continue on to the second. Again he and Shellian felt that the ones who would remain here would not go far to find them, or spend the energy locating the almost invisible trail that they had followed to the other caves. Once again the weather appeared to be ready to change. It had been sunny now for a few days, but now it felt like snow. They needed to hurry if they were going to arrive at the first of those caves before the snow began to fall again.

They pushed through the morning and as midday approached it began to snow once again. Fortunately they now were just a short distance from the first cave. But if this storm turned out to be severe then it would delay their move to the ones further along. Plus new snow would make it easy for any to track them if they so desired, and it was something they did not want or need. Nobody spoke as they made their trek up and deeper into the mountains. They all knew that with what had happened that their chances of survival had dropped significantly. Thinking about what happened Saige felt that now he had failed Shayne. Had they been a little more alert to what had eventually happened, maybe, just maybe it could have been stopped. But as someone had once told him, "You can 'what if' yourself to death, and that doesn't change a thing. What is done is done and there is no way to go back and change it. So get over it and live with it, and do the best you can." He had to admit it was good advice, but it still was hard to live with this apparent failure.

* * *

Once inside the first cave they broke down what gear they had. Saar turned to them shaking his head saying. "I just don't like it. I know I am repeating what we talked about last night, and I am sure we all are thinking it right now. But I just don't." Pausing before continuing, "I know I know there's nothing we can do about it at all. But I am a doctor and all of my instincts say that I should be there if there are any complications with those women, and I won't be, can't be . . . oh I know it was their choice, their decision, but they are wrong, so very wrong." He could see that there was no disagreement from the rest of them and fell silent.

Saige signaled Stone to join him and then the two went back out into the snowstorm. "We need to gather some wood – at least enough to put a meal together. I still haven't figured out how this cave is heated, but at least we won't need to worry about a large supply to keep us warm. We need to be on our way to the next one as quickly as we can."

"Yeah I agree. I can't say that they will come after us, but I want to be sure that if they do decide to do that, that we are where they cannot find us. Darn! Now we have two enemies to worry about, and one of them are our own people. Saige, I wish I had seen it coming to this point also. I mean we had discussed the fact that there were some problems but how did he and Storme keep it such a tightly kept secret? Usually in such a small group nothing is kept hidden long."

Shrugging Saige said, "Wish I knew. Why he was one of the ones who had to survive all the way here I don't know. There are so many others who either died or were captured that deserved this." Shaking his head he continued, "I will never understand how this works. I mean we lost so many good people coming here, and somehow one of the worst ones survives and now have divided us further. I just hope we can survive now. I was worried about our chances when there were fifteen of us. Now it's just the five of us. I don't know, maybe it gives us a better chance. And now I wonder if we will be able to do anything at all for our people. That's if any of our cities have survived these attacks. I mean I hate just not knowing but again there is nothing I can do about that either." They continued through the wooded area picking up firewood where they could find it. Again much of it was buried in the snow. After finding a sufficient amount, the two of them returned to the cave, dropped their load outside and returned to the warmth within. While they had been gone the remaining three had made the area within the cave as comfortable as they could for the short time they were going to stay here.

Shellian said, "I know, before you say anything that our plan is to remain here as short as we can. But that doesn't mean we can't be comfortable while we wait. I, for one, do not want to tackle the next part of this journey with a storm blowing out there. And yes I know we will want to go before the storm blows over so that the snow will cover our tracks. But I think personally that we will be safe today, and should just spend the rest of today here, and then have all of tomorrow to reach the second cave. We discussed that while the two of you were out gathering wood and concluded that it would be a good idea. Well, Seirra listened more that said anything." Looking directly at her she asked, "Seirra you have been awfully quiet, is there something wrong?"

Still not saying anything, she just shook her head in the negative. But anyone looking at her could see that she was upset. Well, truth be told, that probably applied to all of them. "Anyway I think that Schylar and Storme will be too interested in making sure that they are in control than pursuing us." Silent for a moment she continued, "I do hope that they like their choice for a leader back there. But I think everything is just about to come unraveled. I really think that they are not going to survive. He has never been a leader no matter what he thinks of himself. And that is going to haunt them and I believe destroy them."

No body disagreed with her assessment. In fact if there was anything that they could agree upon it was that Schylar would destroy the ones who threw in with him.

* * *

The next seven days passed rapidly as they had continued up through the caves that Shellian and Saige had discovered. Until they had reached the final one that they had discovered, and here they had made their base camp. The storm had lasted three days, and had allowed them to leave no trail behind them. So if Schylar decided to pursue there would be no trail for him to follow. Here once again they needed to follow the almost invisible path to its source. Worry was with them since they had been given much too little food to be able to last more than fifteen days. They began to ration the food to extend their days, and they knew even then it would not be enough. They had to find something and very soon.

They continued their exploring deeper into the mountains, following the almost invisible path that had been placed who knew how far in the past. They discovered six additional caves, all constructed, and all with the same unknown heating system and dim lighting. But here they just ended, or begun, they did not know which. But as each new cave was discovered they would move their camp into it until now they were days away from their original camp. Saige, thinking out loud, said. "I just don't understand this. These caves have me stumped. I mean look they are at half-day intervals. The first one you found Shell' was where we made our first camp, and this one just seems to be either the last or first. Either way we should be within half a day of either the end of the trail or the source, I don't know which. It just seems weird to me that there should be nothing but these caves. Yet we have searched both sides, the first one that we found we searched for additional caves and there were none. Not to say that we could have missed them, but the faint trail that we followed to find all of them disappears beyond this one, and beyond the first one."

Listening as he talked it out Stone then said, "I agree. It is a puzzle that's for sure. The trail that we followed is very ancient and like you and Shellian stated you sense more than see it. But to have nothing at either end just doesn't make sense. And from looking at them they were never constructed to be more than a safe stopping point along this route. So where do these things lead us? Right now I have to admit the answer seems to be nowhere . . . but why nowhere? Why waste your time constructing these things? I just don't know or understand the logic of it all."

"The one thing I do know that if we do not find some additional food soon the rest is a moot point anyway. We are down to just a few more days, so either we find some of the grazers to provide meat or we find something else. Right now we cannot be particular in our choices", Saar added. "Yes I know that as we found these caves that we have been searching, but not the location of where the grazers, which stay in these high areas are hidden, and these mountains are huge so they could be anywhere."

It was dawn and all had eaten far too little, but had no choice. Breathing out heavily Saige said, "I guess today then we all should go out. I think our gear is safe here. I think that we will form two teams with Shell' and I on one and you three on the other. We'll work northwest, and I'd like the three of you to work northeast. We all need to be back here tonight, so keep that in mind – half day out and half day back, just that simple. And yes I know it's never that simple climbing around these mountains, but with our group now down to what it is we just cannot be out longer than that for now, at least until we have some additional food. Okay then, let's head out, and we will see you tonight." He shouldered his pack and headed outside of the cave and waited for Shellian to join him. They needed to find something before the food completely ran out and they became too weak to search.

As they explored the area that they had assigned themselves they found the going rough. The area was a broken land. Yet whatever had caused it was long in the past. Again because the area had been volcanic, they assumed it was the old volcano. Breathing hard as he pushed through another large crack in one of the many broken boulders he stopped to catch his breath. "Shellian this area is rough. I haven't even seen any sign of the animals that live up here. And there doesn't appear to be any game trails, paths or anything. Do you think that maybe we should abandon our search of this area and just move on to another one?"

Shrugging she said. "I don't know, I really don't know. But we are not far from mid-morning so let's push through to at least that. Boy is this land broken. I can't see very far in any direction and setting any landmarks are difficult. It had to be an explosion of some kind to fracture these boulders like they have been, and then this brush, tough with wicked thorns on them. The stuff doesn't even want to break. It's like it's made of iron or something similar. I have a feeling that we really haven't gotten very far from our cave. I hope the others are having a better time of it than we are. And I have to agree I've seen nothing to indicate anything as far as animal life goes. Okay, I've caught my breath shall we continue then?"

"Yeah, this brush is tough but did you notice that it seems to have a lot of spring in it also? This stuff, because of its strength, might make good bows. And we do need to make new ones since Schylar and his group confiscated the ones we had. But it's something we can check on later, if there is to be a later. Okay I guess I'm rested also." Then with a sigh he headed back out and pushed through another section of the brush. Here between the broken boulders the brush forced him to move to the right. As he stepped he found nothing under his feet, screamed a warning to Shellian, and felt himself falling.

There had been no warning of a drop off or cliff but it had been there, hidden. He felt that he had been falling for a while but suspected that it was just an illusion, but he could see trees rushing up at him and then he struck them near their tops, falling through them as the limbs broke his fall somewhat, but when he finally struck the ground he remembered nothing.

Shellian hearing her brother scream and warning her, crawled through the brush, up to the edge and caught a brief flash of him falling and then lost sight of him. Looking desperately for a way down to see if he was injured, or worse killed, she could find nothing. Now what to do? Now what *should* she do? There had to be another way down there. But did she chance it or should she go back for help? The problem with that was the other members would not be back until dark, and then they would have to wait until morning to get back here and that might be too late. She yelled down to Saige hoping that she would hear and answer from him but all there was, were silence and the sounds of the breeze blowing through the scrub trees and brush. Again she searched desperately for a way down and found none. Then making her decision she marked the location and began to head back to their present base camp. She needed help and knew that with a prearranged signal the other team would return, cutting their exploring short. It was something they had arranged just in case of an emergency. It was a last resort as it would identify their location and it was something they had wanted to avoid if at all possible. But now there was no choice.

It would be after midday when she got back to their camp and lit the signal fire and then throw on it some green boughs to produce smoke. Once there all she could do was wait for the other team. But in the mean time she could put together some items that she thought they could use.

* * *

He returned to consciousness and just lay there for a moment trying to get himself together. He remembered falling and desperately trying to grab anything to break his fall, and then hitting those trees and falling through the boughs. He remembered the sound of breaking branches and then he had hit the ground and had passed out. *I guess I should try to move.* But again he just stayed there and didn't, afraid that he may have broken something. Glancing up he saw his path through the trees, and then looking around he saw that he had landed in a deep bed of needles that had fallen over time from the trees in the area. He now knew that through a combination of luck and this deep soft surface that he had landed on was the only reason he was alive. It must have been close to a thirty-meter drop, and the trees he'd fallen through had to be close to twenty meters tall. Finally taking a deep breath he slowly sat up and inspected his body. He found that he hurt just about everywhere and that he was bleeding in a number of places from the cuts and scrapes he received from the branches as he went through them. With a careful check of his body he found that there was nothing broken. He just could not believe his luck. That fall should have killed him, but here he was alive if not hurting, but alive. *Now where is here anyway?*

Finally, gingerly he stood and found that he was favoring one of his legs. Pulling up the pants leg he saw a large ugly bruise that covered most of his thigh. He must have struck one of the larger branches with this leg and again if that is what happened he was fortunate he did not break it. Looking up as he hobbled around he saw where he had fallen and now could see the trap he had stepped into. From above, this small valley wasn't visible and where he stepped off was a rounded end that appeared to sit just a little higher on the side he had stepped off. Searching carefully he could find no way back up, at least at this point. *So how long was I out?* He had to admit he had no idea, and with much of this small valley in the shadows at this point he had no way to judge. Then he remembered that he was with Shellian at the moment of the fall. He then yelled to see if she was still around, but there was no response. He had to assume that she went back to get help. Looking around he found a dead branch that he could fashion into a walking stick. He was finding it difficult to walk with that bruise. It must be very deep with the amount of pain he experienced every time he put weight on that leg. *Guess I better look around . . . if she went back to get help it will be a while before anyone could get back here anyway.* Then he realized that something here did not feel right. At the moment he could not place what it was.

It was silent. Other than the breeze that was very gentle here at the moment, there were no sounds of birds or the scurrying of the small animals, just the wind. At least it felt somewhat warm here even with the heavy shade. Then he realized that there was very little snow on the ground. It was winter and late into winter besides. There should be a lot of the white stuff but there was just a dusting. Again looking up he could find no reason for the lack of snow. There was nothing above to block it from here. He realized this as he looked around, while he had been standing and leaning on his walking stick, he then began to explore this strange place. As he limped away from the point where he fell, he worked towards what he hoped would be an opening into this valley and a way of escape. But in a short time he had reached the other side and found a pond with a waterfall providing the water for the pond. But there seemed to be no exit from the pond, and while the waterfall was not large it was large enough to require the water to exceed what this pond could hold. So where was the excess water going?

Once again he realized that something wasn't right about this pond also. But what was it that was wrong? Then two things struck him at once. First while the pond was not huge the edges were far enough away from the disturbance caused by the waterfall that it should be frozen, but was not. And secondly the pond did not look natural. There was something about it that said that it had been constructed. But what that was he could not say at the moment. He bent down and put his fingers into the water finding it quite cold, in fact cold enough to numb his fingers. Looking into the water he found it crystal clear and he could see all the way to the bottom. While not especially deep he could see that as he looked further from the edges that it continued to drop in depth. And he thought that he could see fish there also, but with the shadows could not be sure. *At least I won't lack for water, and if I have to remain here for a while probably won't lack for food either.* As he continued to work his way around the valley he was beginning to believe that it would turn out to be completely surrounded by cliffs – making it a trap for anything that fell into it and maybe the reason for no animal sign.

Working his way to the side with the deeper shadows he stopped and stared, then looked hard once again. Then shaking his head he thought. *No that can't be what it looks to be.* But it did. From where he was standing it looked to be the edge of a building – one built out of the native stone but looking so old that it almost looked to have been here since the beginning of time. Shaking his head again, he thought. *This has to be an illusion. After all why would there be such a thing in the valley? And if indeed it is a building how was it built and by whom?* He slowly worked his way towards what he thought could be a building and as he got closer he could see it begin to take shape. There was no doubt now, his eyes had not deceived him, it indeed was a building. Now excited he limped up to the corner that he had seen and stood and looked at it. Indeed it could have been here since the beginning it looked that old. But at the same time there should have been signs of decay, of it returning to where it came from. Yet it did not. How was that possible? If there were no one here to maintain it how could it continue to exist?

* * *

With no answer from Saige she made her way back down the mountain towards the cave they had made their base camp. With the other members of their now reduced group also out exploring she would have to use the signal fire to call them back. From her initial scanning of the small valley she could see no way down. Her impression was that it probably was an area that collapsed when the volcano was still active. Then over the years after the volcano died it become a small hidden valley with no way to get to the floor except by using ropes. She could see a point opposite where a small waterfall cascaded over the edge and entered a small lake below, but with the amount of trees she could not see much more. She knew that it would be hours now before she could make it back. But she worried that with the troubles that they had with the rest of the group that by sending up the smoke signals that she would be giving away their location. So that meant that once they had determined what had happened to Saige they would have to move. There just was no choice. With their location compromised they would be open to attack if Schylar decided that he would want to just eliminate them completely. She did not feel that he would since they were pretty even, with very little chance of surprising her and the others with her, plus there had been time for them to replace the weapons that they had lost, but one could just not be sure.

It was between midday and dusk when she finally reached the camp and had to stop and catch her breath as she had almost run the last portion. Sitting on a large rock just outside of the cave she contemplated lighting the fire or not lighting it. Was she ready to let the world know where they were? She knew that they had arranged the fire as a last resort and had discussed it for size and visibility. They had felt confident that no one in the valleys below would be able to see the smoke, and if so that it would be so faint that it should raise no suspicions from any there, just their local group would be affected. Knowing in her heart that this could be the only chance that Saige could have she took a deep breath and then went ahead and lit the fire. Once it was burning well she added a couple of green boughs. These immediately began to steam and smoke changing the almost invisible smoke to white as the moisture burned out of the boughs. It then briefly turned dark as they were consumed. Once the boughs were consumed, the smoke cleared once again and was a very light blue, almost invisible. She waited for a short time and then repeated it, and once again for a third time. Once the final boughs had burned she extinguished the fire. Now all she could do was wait and hope that they had seen the signal.

She knew that it probably would be a few hours before they returned so she began to go through what they had. Yes they did have rope, but would it be enough? And if not what did they have that could be used? Stretching out the rope she thought that maybe it would be long enough for them to be able to reach one of the trees, and then climb down that way. She could tell now that it would be the only way they would be able to descend into that hidden valley. Time dragged as she waited for the rest to return and she continued to pace, looking out in the distance a number of times thinking she had heard them approaching only to be disappointed. She also looked back down the mountain to see if maybe Schylar and his group were heading their way, but she knew that was foolish since it was at least a four day hike to here from that original cave. But she couldn't stop herself from checking now and then. After all she had just compromised their location so she worried that the others would show up immediately. Eventually she heard crunching on the gravel that was surrounding the cave. They had suspected that it was material taken from the hillside to create the cave. And shortly Stone, Saar and Seirra arrived. They were breathing hard and had a worried expression on their faces. When they had set this signaling system up they really thought it would never be used. "What's going on?" Stone asked, as the other two caught their breath.

He had pushed them hard to get back and had actually made great time. But now she could see that the other two were quite winded and it would take a little while for them to be ready to travel again. Quickly she outlined what had happened and that they would need to move out immediately if they were going to get back to the area before dark. It also meant that there would be a good chance that they would need to spend the night close by the valley since the area they had been searching was treacherous. There were many places one could get hurt.

"We need to hide anything we don't take with us. If all of us are going to be gone then it would be easy for the others", Saar said, "now that they should know approximately where we are, to come here and destroy what little we have left."

"True, very true. I didn't think about that. What if we just take all of it?" Shellian asked. "After all we carried it here and since we would only be going a shorter distance it should not be too much of an issue." She could see a little rebellion in Seirra's eyes but she didn't say anything. Once she had found out that it was Saige that had fallen she wanted to go there as quickly as they could, but now with what had been said Seirra knew that it would delay their departure.

"Saige could be seriously hurt. Do you think it's a good idea that we take this additional time to get our stuff when he could be dying?" Seirra asked.

"It's been hours Seirra, and it will not be easy to get down to where he is. When I sent those signals out to get you back here it probably alerted the others to where we are. We can't afford to lose what little we have so we really don't have a choice. We must take everything or risk losing everything including our lives. It really is that serious. If it means we end up losing one of us then there is very little we can do about it, but by not covering ourselves here we could find ourselves at the end also. Yes I do know you care for him, we all do, but we can do him no good if we do something stupid that will end up destroying all of us. After all he is my brother and we have been close all of our lives. I hate the idea of delaying but

Saar has made a very valid point, and once he did, I happen to agree with him. So let's see how fast we can get this stuff together and then I'll lead us back to that hidden valley."

Looking at the positions of the suns they realized that by the time that they reached the valley once again that it would be close to dark. But it was something they would have to face once they arrived. After a day of exploring, returning to their camp and then once again heading out they found that they were tired, which meant that they would have to be doubly careful. It would be much easier to make a mistake and not recognize it until it was too late, when one was exhausted, and the snow that was on the ground did not make it any easier. Even though the trail that she had taken was plain to see, it was obviously not an easy path. As they struggled their breath came out in great clouds of steam. It was also cooling rapidly as the suns began to set, and the sunset that was displayed as they continued the climb, was spectacular. It was absolutely clear with no sign of any approaching storms. Probably a good thing, but it provided another problem. Clear skies at night meant extreme cold, and they would not have the heated cave this night. As they continued their trek Shellian began to wonder if they should have waited until morning, but immediately put that thought out of her mind. That could be too much time and might ensure that her brother would die. So what if they were a little uncomfortable tonight if it meant that Saige would survive.

It wouldn't be the first time since this whole mess began, and she suspected that it would not be the last. And if they were unable to stop the primitives then there would be other refugees heading to these mountains. But with the failures that they had faced she wondered if they could have any impact at all, or even if they would be around to try. Considering the size of their group originally and what it was now it did seem impossible. Feeling the cold beginning to penetrate and the shadows lengthening she picked up her pace once more. Once again time seemed to be against them. She slowed as they got close to the area. She did not want to repeat what had happened to Saige, but was stopped in her tracks as standing before her was Saige. At loss for words she just stood there and stared.

Smiling although it hurt Saige said, "Now don't just stand there with your mouth open say something."

"Sorry. Ah, but, I saw you fall and from what I could see that valley was completely walled – especially on this side. There was no way out of there. So how'd . . .

"How did I get out sis? Is that what you are asking?" He then turned slowly around and said to all of them. "Just follow me and all will become clear." He then began to limp off in another direction beckoning them to follow. Shocked by seeing him it took a moment for the rest to react and begin to follow. Since he was moving slowly because of his injuries he was not that far ahead of them. Saar looked at Shellian and said. "He obviously has some injuries, but for someone who fell as far as you said he did, he seems to be in remarkable health." Saige appeared to be heading straight for a rock wall. There appeared to be no reason for this action as there was no trail, and the area was somewhat exposed. Shrugging they tried to catch up only to watch him walk right up to the wall and then disappear from sight. It surprised them enough that they stopped in their tracks once again, and again stared. What was it that Saige had discovered? They quickened their pace and then when they approached the same area Saige made an appearance as if he had walked through solid rock and then asked. "Does something about this appear to be familiar?"

"Yes." Saar stated. "Yes this appears to be something similar to what we are using in the cities to hide entrances. But why would such a thing be here?"

"A very good question and one I think will need some time to confirm. But my initial impression is that this, although obviously much older, is of the same technology that we use in the cities."

"No. No can't be. There's no record of any of this here in these mountains. Yes I know I'm the doctor, but I always enjoyed history and it has been my hobby. Well, at least until our world fell apart."

"Understood Saar, but before we really get cold let's all step inside. I think that there are many surprises awaiting all of us." He then turned and once again disappeared. This time they followed and found that they were standing on a large platform sitting above a large open cavern, and it was warm. When the warmth hit them they shivered a moment as the heat penetrated. "I haven't had much time to do any real exploring here. And I know it is almost a miracle that I am even walking let alone standing before you. And I'll explain my side of this adventure, but let's take the ladder down to the floor. I can see by the size of your packs that you've brought everything with you. Would that be because someone lit the signal fire?" He saw them nod their heads. He then gingerly climbed down the ladder to another platform, and then continued the process through two other platforms before finally standing on the ground. Even though the light was dim, the whole cavern was bathed in the soft light. It was huge, and looking around there appeared to be many areas that had been modified for storage.

One thing about it, whatever this was, it was not a small operation. It would have been easy to put their whole compound in here and still have room. Then it came to them that the volume of this area was enormous and yet the whole area was warm. That took some power and yet there was no sign of any. Looking down they could see Saige's tracks from his earlier walk across the dirt floor. These tracks led away into the distance towards what they suspected were the valley that he had fallen into.

"Okay some explanations are necessary." He said as he led them across the floor in the opposite direction of his previous tracks. "When I fell I thought I was dead. But after falling for about ten meters I was fortunate enough to fall into one of the many trees. The boughs of the tree broke my fall, and I broke many of the branches on the way to the ground. Then when I hit the ground it knocked me out. I don't know how much time passed before I was conscious. But the first thing I noticed was the tree I had fallen through above me, and then realized that I had also fallen into a deep pile of needles which further broke my fall. No, as you can tell I did not come off unscathed. I have many cuts and contusions, with some of them deep, but at least none of them were close to a main artery so they scabbed over pretty quick. I have a large deep bruise on this leg and it's why I am limping, and to be honest I hurt just about everywhere. Later Doc you can check me out to be sure nothing is worse, but overall I feel very lucky. I then searched this small valley for a way out. Found some things that just did not look quite natural and then found the corner of an ancient building, which led me to this huge cavern and then hearing all of you. I wasn't sure of the way out so I climbed up and saw that there was an entrance there at the top. And for now you know the rest."

They stopped briefly looking around the enormous cavern. Its height disappeared above them and it seemed that it went on forever around them although they knew it was an illusion. Near some of the walls there appeared to be small structures. Guessing, they felt that at one time these structures were probably a place where supplies had been stored. Again looking at them from a distance one had the impression that the owners had just temporarily stepped out and would be returning at any moment. Yet at the same time the place had the feel of age laying on it. "What is this place?" Saar asked to no one in particular. "And who used it and built those structures?"

"You got me Saar", Saige replied. "As you know I have been here just a little longer than you, by no choice of my own I might add, so I truly know no more than you at this point."

"Really just thinking out loud Saige," Saar replied, "I'm sure that all of us are wondering the same thing. This building that you found, where is it from here?"

"Well before we stopped to admire the sheer size of this place I was heading to it. Very little of it shows in the valley and I was surprised when I found the entrance to it. I expected it to be just a home, a place for a small group to live, but . . . well instead of just telling you, follow me and you can see for yourselves." He then led them across the floor of the cavern to another wall that again appeared to be solid. Yet looking down they could see his tracks disappearing through the seemingly solid wall. Again another barrier like they were familiar with – identical in fact to the ones used in their cities.

Contemplating what little had been revealed so far Stone said. "I wonder . . ."

"Wonder what Stone?" Shellian asked.

"I know we have seen very little yet, but what we have appears to be very familiar. I don't know or understand how all of this could still be functioning after all of this time, but it is. So there has to be some type of auto maintenance going on here. Otherwise it would have quit a long time ago. Still . . . still this feels like we are home, in one of our cities that are down below."

"Yes, I think you are right Stone." Shellian said. "It is, well it was like the moment we came inside that we immediately felt comfortable, safe, and yes like we were back in one of our cities."

"That's quite a conclusion being that we have seen so little of this place", Saar replied. "But yes I can understand it and really have to agree. And truthfully, I cannot even tell you why."

"Ready?" Saige asked. He could see that they were and so he went through the illusion and they then followed him. Before them was a set of double doors, which they went through. Once through they stopped again in awe with what was before them. Here they found a large area that could easily have been an administrative section. There were places to handle whatever supplies that would arrive in that cavern, and a section with cubicles for whatever business needed to be carried out. Behind the cubicles were a few rooms with standard doors identifying ones who were probably in charge of the operation. All of it laid out neatly making the different areas easily accessible for any that required the services provided.

"What is this place?" Seirra asked, "This is just huge. Why here in the mountains? There's nothing here for something this size?"

"I can't disagree. When I came into the building it stopped me in my tracks. I've really had very little time to explore it, but from what I have seen we are just touching the very beginnings of this place. Before coming into the building I realized that there was another problem and it was the trees. There was something very wrong with them. I don't mean that they were damaged or dying or anything like that – well, other than the damage I did falling through one of them. But they are subtly different than any I remember seeing and are living around these mountains. That's not to say that that they don't belong here since plants and trees are not my specialty. Well, as we finally get back outside, inside that valley you'll see what I mean." He then led them down a hallway, which had a number of closed doors on either side. Finally ending at a set of double doors, which he opened, and walked into what looked to be a large dining area, and off to one side, an area that appeared to be a large kitchen. Then on the opposite wall a couple of doors that looked to be entrances into public bathrooms.

"You know what; I think I could use that." Shellian said, pointing to the door for the woman's restroom. "I wonder if it is still functional after all this time. And if it is it sure will beat using the bushes for our nature calls." then turning to Seirra she said. "Shall we go find out?" They both left and entered the restroom leaving the men standing there.

Shaking his head Saar said. "Now that is something I will never understand."

"What's that Saar?" Stone asked.

"Why is it that any time a woman wants to use a public restroom that they always must go in packs, or at least two of them? After all when we use them we just go. Sometimes it's with another guy, but most of the time it's just us, one at a time. But if there are at least two women, then they always tag team it."

"I've never thought about it", Stone replied. "But you're right. I've never seen any of them go to one of these things alone."

They sat at one of the tables that were anchored to the floor waiting until the women made an appearance from their trip. With no one speaking initially and all just looking around. "I would say that this place could seat maybe fifty or sixty easily", Saar said. "And I suspect that whoever was here probably worked in shifts, so that means that this place could have had at least one hundred to one hundred and fifty people, if not more. What's off in the other direction from that administration area Saige?"

"Don't know really, didn't have time to explore it yet. But my guess is, that's it is the main way through. It wouldn't make sense for the main thoroughfare to go through a place where people eat. But to have a place to eat close to the working areas makes total sense."

"True, but working areas for what?" Stone asked. "While I know that we more or less just walked through that cavern I didn't see anything that would constitute work."

About this time Shellian came out of the restroom and quickly joined them at the table. "Hey! Guess what we found?"

"I hope an operating restroom." Saar answered

Laughing she said. "Yes, and so much more. Care to guess?"

"Well a working restroom is plenty for me." Turning to the others he asked. "I wonder how they did it. This place hasn't been used in what seems forever. Yet so much of it appears to be in working order."

Placing her hands on her hips and shaking her head she said. "You men always are looking at how things work, instead of just appreciating that it just does. Okay since none of you want to guess I'll tell you. These restrooms are equipped with showers. The real thing and like everything else they appear to work and there's hot water also. So I don't know about you but I am tired of smelling like smoke and I for one am tired of smelling dirty bodies. So I suggest that the three of you go check it out and if yours are so equipped go clean up. Oh by the way there seems to be supplies of towels and believe it or not some type of clothing that whoever worked here used. So we can also get out of these skins and into something a little more comfortable." She then turned around and headed back into the restroom.

Looking at each other for a moment they then got up from the table and headed into their public restroom. Pushing through the door they found a large area with the standard urinals, toilets, and sinks. But further in there was a section that held supplies of toweling and clothing, and just beyond that there were showers. Not waiting they stripped down, looking in one of the cabinets they found something that could pass as soap and went into the open shower area. Later, with the clothes provided in the restrooms they emerged feeling clean for the first time in what seemed like forever. But even though they had started their showers later than the women, the ladies had yet to emerge. "Wonder what this material is?" Saar asked idly, as they waited for the women to make their appearance. "You know I've forgotten how good a shower feels." The rest had to agree, and to be out of those skins, which had needed cleaning for a while, but with nothing to change in to, they had to make do. Looking at the clothes that they were in, they found that it changed their looks, now not appearing to be a part of the primitives. The items were one-piece coverall style – making it easy to get in and out of. The material could have been paper, so they were a one-time use and then probably recycled. In the supply lockers all of this clothing was a simple light blue. It appeared to use some type of magnetic closure so there were no buttons or other type of fasteners. "I don't know about you . . ." Stone said. "But I think I want to go check out the kitchen area. If this place is similar to the cities then they probably have food processors in there. I really don't think that this would be an easy place to grow food. Although I bet with something this size they probably have hydroponics somewhere." Looking around they saw that the women still had not emerged and so agreed with Stone. They all got up and headed into the kitchen area. The first thing that hit them was that everything was spotless, and no dust lay anywhere. It was obvious that it had been shut down with the idea that it could be a long time before anybody returned. "This will take some time to figure out." Saige said. "This was a careful shutdown and it appears that the equipment has been mothballed, but with the idea that it can be brought back quickly if needed – which makes sense, as this would be one of the first places I would reactivate after returning."

Shellian and Seirra finally emerged from the restroom and saw that the men were not around. "Now we couldn't have beaten them out", Shellian said. "After all I've never seen a man take a shower that he wasn't out way before any of us. So I wonder where they went?"

"I think I hear voices over there towards the kitchen." Seirra said as she pointed in the direction.

"I do think you're right. Shall we go and join them?" They headed into the kitchen and found the men once again in deep discussion about something. "Okay guys what's going on?" Shellian asked.

"Wow! Look at you two." Stone exclaimed. "Oh while we were waiting it was decided that we'd come in and check out the kitchen. After all we are just about out of what we brought with us. So it was a good time to check it out since we really didn't know how long the two of you would be. But personally I can say the wait was worth it."

Looking at Stone with askance Shellian asked. "Now what is that supposed to mean?"

Laughing at her look he said. "Now Shellian you have to admit that with the way we have had to live that none of us looked the best that we could. I am just saying that I appreciate the change. Besides it appears that you and Seirra had more choices in the one-piece outfits than we did. We had the choice of, oh let me see, one color, while I can tell there was a much greater selection for you – and I have to admit that they fit rather well also."

Shellian had picked an outfit that was pale yellow and with her tanned skin it worked very well for her, while Seirra had found one that was a darker shade of green and again had done her justice. Stone continuing said. "It's nice to be really clean again, and if I cannot appreciate what it does then . . ." He shrugged looking to the two other men for support.

Laughing Saige said. "Don't look at us Stone. It looks like you're doing a great job of digging your own grave right now, and besides I've never succeeded in winning when sparing with words with either Shellian or Seirra. So leave me out of it."

Saar looking around at everyone just shook his head. "Okay guys not to change the subject, but to change the subject, we do need to figure out how to get this back on line so that we can use the facilities here."

"Breathing out deeply Stone said, "Thank you Saar, and you're right. But I think that Saige should continue to show us what he has found so far. Then we can come back and try and get this and anything else we need back on line. So Saige, if you would?" Stone then stepped back and gestured for Saige to continue.

Looking around at the other four Saige said. "Okay? If you are ready, let's do this. Like I said before we were interrupted . . . not that it was a bad interruption." He added hastily as he headed through them and led them out of the eating area through a set of double swinging doors and into a hallway. Looking down the hallway there were a number of closed doors on both sides. He turned left where there was only one door at the end. And like the one they had just gone through it was double swinging doors. Once through the door they found themselves in a large room with a single table and many chairs around it. There were some small cabinets around the perimeter and on the walls that the doors attached to. But the opposite side was all windows. But at the moment, with the soft light that was in the room, they could not see through them. It was now nighttime and completely dark out. So the only things visible were their reflections on the glass, or whatever the windows were constructed from. Glass first came to mind, but then they realized that unless it was tempered that regular glass would probably been destroyed by now. "Well I was going to show you the outside portion, but that looks like it will have to wait until the morning. I guess we should explore in the other direction from the cafeteria, dining area or whatever you want to call it, and see what exists in that direction. So far I haven't found any living areas, but I suspect with the size of this place, there has to be."

No one said anything other than nodding in agreement. So they turned around and headed back through the areas they had just left, then through the administrative work area and then once again through double swinging doors. Immediately the atmosphere changed. It was obvious that this was the area where the living area had been built. The first doors they saw were marked for single men on one side and single women on the other. As a group they went inside of both finding that the side for the men was generally open with cabinets that divided the areas from each bed and chair arrangement. The cabinets were spacious and allowed each one who lived here their own space. On the far side was the common bathroom with the normal items including the open showers. Seeing the arrangements Seirra then said. "I just don't understand this, and I never will. I could no more shower in such a place, then run around without my clothes. How do you guys do it?"

It was a question none of them had ever thought about. As a group the three of them shrugged. "I have no answer for that as this is the way it has always been and it doesn't bother us at all. Why would it bother you?" Saar asked.

Shaking her head Seirra replied saying, "I don't know it just does. Shall we go look at the other one, you know the single woman area?"

"Why not" Stone replied. "I've never really been in one of those as such places were always off limits to us. So lead on if you would Seirra."

"Okay I will. And I think you will see that it is quite different. Oh by the way, I think I am beginning to believe that our ancestors built this place. There are just too many things that are the same. If the other side turns out to be like I suspect it will only strengthen my beliefs." She then led them out and then across the hallway and into the single women facility. Immediately it was obvious that it was set up completely different. Each area where the single women would live had "L" shaped walls blocking any view from the next area, giving each woman almost complete privacy. If there had been doors on the front then it would be so. But instead there were curtains hung in the openings. Once inside the cubicle they found dressers mirrors and cabinets that would hold infinitely more than any they had seen on the men's side.

"Wow! Is this the way it was in our compound back at the city?" Stone asked.

"Pretty much so", Shellian said, "But I am sure there are some differences, but I think I have to agree with Seirra now. This could be close to what we are used to. But until I look at the bathroom here I'll hold my judgment."

"Okay then, why don't we?" Saige asked. They made their way into the bathroom and were immediately met with the differences between the two. All toilets had stalls, and each shower was also enclosed. Everything based on privacy and just the opposite of the men's unit. "This is so different. I didn't realize that you women took your privacy that seriously."

"Well, we do Saige", Seirra said. They as a group then left the area and then continued down the hall. Here they began finding what could only be called apartments. These obviously were for the coupled members. While not large they at least were comfortable.

After some additional time had passed Saige said, "I think I would like to continue this, but I don't know about you but I haven't eaten for a while and my stomach is complaining so let's go back to the cafeteria and eat. We can discuss what we have found so far and then actually retire to a real bed. I know what a concept. But I suspect that we won't sleep too well on them anyway. You know strange bed, strange environment, and strange noises, all leading to poor sleep. Tomorrow we can do a better search and maybe get the kitchen operating again. I suspect that there may be some emergency supplies around somewhere. So if we can find those it will at least give us something until we have this facility up and running again." Then with a sweep of his hand he asked. "Shall we?"

Laughing Stone said. "Call me anything but late to a meal."

* * *

It was entering the middle of the night and like a prophet, he found that indeed he could not sleep. So Saige headed out of the large room past the silently working bots that appeared only at night to clean. He suspected that there were similar bots that did the repairs. Breathing deeply, and with eyes that were burning, he headed off through what they had believed was the admin area, then through the lunch room, out the other side and into the large glassed room that he suspected was used for executive meetings. Pulling one of the chairs back he sat down staring at the opaque windows seeing only a reflection of the interior from the soft glow of the lighting. He did not know how much time had passed but he suddenly realized that someone else was entering the room. Looking back at the entrance he saw Shellian coming in. She, seeing him smiled, but it was a sad one. "I see you couldn't sleep either. Seirra was out cold so instead of staying there and maybe waking her I decided to go and walk. I really needed some time to think, and you?"

"I don't know, maybe it was the sound of those bots going about their business. You know a different sound. And since it has been very necessary for us to always be on the alert for danger . . . well it's a different sound. Then knowing I wasn't going to be able to sleep both for that reason and the fact that I hurt just about everywhere I decided to come here. Don't ask me why it just seemed like a quiet area that one could look out from. But of course I forgot that these windows are built somehow to prevent any light from the inside to be seen from the outside. So all I could see was a reflection of this space."

Coming over and then sitting across from him Shellian said. "I wonder if Seirra is right." Then shaking her head she continued. "I know right now there is no way of knowing. We've seen so little of this place. I guess it's just idle speculation on my part. But . . . but it just feels right. I don't know how else to explain it, it just feels like us."

Sighing and then shaking his head Saige said. "I just don't know. I have so many questions. Like why is this place abandoned? Obviously from what little we know right now, this place was shut down with the idea of returning someday. Yet no one ever did. And yet the bots have continued their work, again for how long is anyone's guess. It is the only reason that I can see that this place is in the condition it is. It looks like whoever was here just stepped out yesterday. Yet there is a feel of age on this place – a feel of real age, like it has been here for thousands of annuals. And if that is so can we solve the puzzle as to why someone left a perfectly good facility and never returned? I don't know." For a short period of time both were lost in their thoughts as these puzzles lay before them. Finally restless once again Saige said. "I have to get up and move, I just can't explain it but something about this place really bothers me. So I'm going to walk a little and probably try to get back to sleep. I think that tomorrow some of our questions will be answered as we search this place. I guess then I'll see you in the morning sis." He got up and left the room leaving Shellian alone with her thoughts.

I can understand it. She thought. Then looking down at the huge oblong table she got up and idly walked around the room opening the cabinets that lined the walls – finding pitchers and glasses in some and pads of paper and writing implements in others. It established for her that this was a place for meetings . . . but what kind of meetings? There was nothing left to give her any hints at all. Finally weariness began to overcome her once more and she got up to head back and try and get some additional sleep. She sighed, shrugged, and then left the room leaving it vacant and silent once more.

C H A P T E R   T E N

The next several days they explored the facility finding many important areas including the nursery, learning center, hydroponics, and security. With the location of the nursery and learning center found, just down from the apartments, this confirmed that there had been children of different ages here. This only deepened the mystery as to why the abandonment. With families now confirmed, and from personal experience of what lay outside of this facility in these mountains, why place themselves in this environment and the hardships that existed? Something really terrible must have happened . . . yet . . . yet there was nothing to indicate a problem or disaster – nothing at all. The discovery of the security office excited them all. Since there they would be able to find information on the facility. But the greatest find within the unit was the monitors. Once again they still functioned and through the rotating images they got a view of the whole facility. And then to their surprise, each of the caves along the pathway came into view. So somehow even these were under constant surveillance. It took about half a day for them to figure out the basic system, although manipulating those images was well beyond them. And now armed with maps of the facility and images generated by the security system they began to get a real feel for the layout. Surprising to them was the similarity to the layout of their city. But all could easily be racked up as coincidence. It was decided that one of them would stay in the security office and monitor the rest as they worked their way around. Again like before they worked in teams of two. Then by accident they found that there was two-way communications with the security section and anywhere they were within the facility.

That got them to wondering if it was the same throughout the network of caves that had been located. There apparently were thirty of these caves, allowing these people to travel far down the mountainsides in just about any direction. By having the caves monitored these people would know if it was safe, which led them to believe that like the facility, that there had to be voice communications within the caves. After all it made sense so that if there was danger detected, then the travelers could be warned. Of course it could also be that the travelers carried some type of device that allowed them to communicate, but if it was anything like they had presently it would have been short ranged. Not allowing for the great distances and line of sight problems that they had to deal with.

On this day Saar drew duty in the security office while the two women worked their way through the school to see if they could find out what was being taught there and to compare it to what they had learned in their own educational system. Nothing had been located as of yet to identify the people who had built this place. And while the clues stacking up still pointed to their own ancestors, they had no proof. The two men were working the large cavern where they had first entered. Since that time they had located three other entrances or exits from this hidden facility, but still used the one Saige had found when he first left. "Everyone!" Saar stated. "I need you all to report back to the security office now. Something is developing and we need to be together on this."

The two women looked at each other and Shellian asked as she looked up into the area where the camera was located. "What's going on Saar?" But he just repeated that they needed to come to him directly.

Hearing the request as it echoed in the large cavern, it took a moment before they understood what had been asked. They stopped immediately and at a fast pace headed back. In a short time they had joined the other three there since the two men had the furthest distance to travel. They saw the others looking at a couple of the screens intently and began to ask what they were looking at when a movement caught their eyes. "What the heck is that?" Saige asked.

Saar not taking his eyes off the screen said. "This is the view in the area of the third cave. And I do believe that what we are seeing here is Sorrel."

"Sorrel?" Stone asked. "What the heck is she doing out there, and from what I can see alone?"

"How can you tell doc? The image is still distant from the camera location. I can tell that whoever it is that this person is definitely female, and pregnant – quite pregnant, but other than that I don't recognize her." Saige said.

"Give it a couple and I think you will. Being that I am the doctor for this group I've become pretty familiar with all of you."

Laughing and lightening the moment, Saige asked. "How do you mean that doc?" This immediately brought a chuckle out of the rest while Saar's face reddened a little.

"Now hold on there! You know what I mean."

Patting his shoulder Saige said. "You're the one who said it not me." Then pausing briefly he continued. "Yes we do know what you meant, but it was the way you said it that made me think that way. Anyway I'll take your word for it. I know that from a distance I can recognize Shellian from the way she walks and her movements, and I know it is the same for her since we have worked and trained together for most of our lives. It can mean the difference between living and dying. So I trust your judgment. If this person keeps on heading in her current direction then she'll be very close to the camera shortly and we'll have it confirmed. Have you seen anybody else out there, or any who may be following her. You know something to lure us out in a trap of some kind?"

"No. Once I saw her I began looking at the other cameras that are behind or in the direction we originally came from. And then looked ahead just in case they would be ahead of her, but she appears to be quite alone."

They all watched fascinated with the image as it approached the camera's location. Shaking her head Shellian said. "She looks like hell. I wonder what happened." Then pointing at the screen she said. "Look how dirty she appears, and the clothing looks damaged." Then Sorrel passed the camera's location close to the cave. There she stopped and looked desperately around. They could tell from both her body language and her haggard look that she was near to the end of her endurance, and that she had lost all hope. Then Shellian asked, "What has happened back there? I mean this woman we are watching is in her early third-third, and yet she is risking everything to be away from shelter. With the amount of snow on the ground and the way she is dressed she has to be cold, and she'll find no sign of us either. I'm surprised that she's gotten this far. So what do we do about it, and is this some kind of trap? I know Saar, you've been making sure that it isn't, but that doesn't keep me from worrying about it."

"Look", Saige said, "if she continues as she is, she will almost naturally be heading in the right direction for the next cave. It doesn't look like she's carrying a pack or anything extra. This looks like a decision that she made quickly, and did not have time to prepare."

"You're right." Stone answered. "And that's not a good thing. I mean when one has the equipment with them to make such a journey and not be carrying then it's not too much of an issue. But here with this she is in very real danger. Not only to herself but also to that child she is carrying. I say let's go get her before she gets into any more serious trouble." Looking around he could only see agreement on the rest.

Saige seeing the response of the others said, "Okay, I have to agree and I can tell the rest of you feel much the same way. Shell, you come with me and we will go and meet her. I would like the three of you to continue to monitor the situation from here. Run it in shifts. I know at this time we have yet to figure out the voice communications for the caves, but keep working on that. There has to be something here that allows it. After all whoever built this place has the devices all over the facility and also visuals. And since we have visuals at all the caves it is only reasonable to assume that there is voice also." Then turning to Shellian he asked. "Shell', shall we go?" And then turning back to the Saar he said. "Yes I know you being the doctor would love to be one of the ones to go. But if this turns out to be a trap we cannot afford to lose you. Just be prepared to take care of her if it isn't." Then looking one last time at the screen he shook his head and said. "She really does look like hell." And with that statement, turned and left the security office with Shellian close behind. "Shell' grab those communicators so that we can hopefully be in range and keep in contact with whoever is in the security office. I'll grab some of the food, and weapons. We'll meet at the ladder in that large cavern." If she was at the third cavern from the original direction that they had come from then it would take them over a day to reach her, unless they pushed hard.

* * *

The two of them had pushed hard to get down to Sorrel. At the same time they continued to test their portable communication devices to be sure that contact could be kept. Sorrel had shown up on the screens about mid-morning and it had taken another thirty minutes to get everything together. They fairly trotted to the first cave covering the distance in only a couple of hours, but the day was advancing, and they wanted to find her before night where it would be much too easy to miss her. Again, what had happened back there to make Sorrel take off with nothing but what she was wearing? And how had she been able to follow the almost invisible trail that had originally led them to the hidden facility? However she had done it, could she continue to do it? So far the information they had received back from Saar, who remained on duty back there, stated that she had found the cave and was presently inside of it. He then reported that the other two were attempting to figure out if there were listening devices set up inside these caves and tied into the security system, but so far they had been unsuccessful. So there was no way to really know what Sorrel's condition truly was. But the images they were receiving did not give him much confidence. Sorrel looked pale and drawn, and from the images her breathing was heavy and ragged.

Saige and Shellian continued to push as the day rapidly flowed past them. Then Saar contacted them. "I think she has passed out. She hasn't moved from that cave and she appears to have slumped over. You need to hurry! I really don't know how long she has. I'm also giving this over to Stone so he will be your contact. I need to take a break and then go to the infirmary and prepare for your arrival. If it was only she to worry about it would be bad enough, but she is carrying a child, and with the stress she's putting on herself right now, there is a good chance that she'll lose it. I want to do all I can to prevent that from happening. Stone will keep me informed of your progress, and Seirra is preparing some meals while we are busy here."

"Okay, this is Stone so I have it now. So how far are you from reaching the second cave?"

"I don't know for sure", Shellian replied between the breaths as she tried to catch her breath. "But I would guess that we are between the first and second from this direction, which would put us between the third and fourth from the other direction. We are still a few hours out, and with us trotting we are covering a lot of distance, with a lot to go, but we think that we will be there just before dark. I really hope she can hold on. What really sucks here is that we haven't found any way to let her know that help is on the way. Yes, and I know right now she is unconscious so it wouldn't matter any-way. But it's just that if you know that someone is coming for you it gives you hope where there may have been none be-fore." Turning and looking at Saige she could read the determination in his face. She figured that hers looked much the same. "Well brother shall we pick it up again? At least there has been no new snow so that it won't be hiding any new traps for us."

"True, but I just thought of something that worries me. Like you, I have really enjoyed this nice weather, and am hop-ing that spring is just around the corner. But Sorrel is leaving tracks that will be easy to follow. And we are now doing the same thing, which means we will be leaving an easy trail for any to follow right back to the facility. And with this situation being desperate, we will not be able to cover any of our tracks. So we will be giving away our location."

"Yeah, but what can we do, leave her to die out here?"

"No, you know me better than that. But this is putting us back at risk. It's just another one of those things that makes it so much more complicated. I almost wish for a storm now to cover both her tracks and ours, but what will be, will be right now. She is more important anyway. Okay, done with our brief break let's push on through this time. I think if we con-tinue alternately walk and run that we should just about make it before dark. Darn!" Saige exclaimed, "I wish we had fig-ured out if there is a way to communicate with the caves, it would make it so much easier."

As they trotted there they received no new updates and hoped that no news was good news. Finally as the suns began to set and the shadows overtook them they could see the loca-tion of the cave in the distance. At this point the portable communications devices were becoming inconsistent. But at least they were able to make one final contact so that the ones at the facility would be aware of their approach. Of course they knew that shortly they would be visible on the screens as they came into the hidden camera's range. And then finally, they saw the mouth of the cave. The communications from the security center now was almost unintelligible, but they could at least tell that they now were visible to them. Taking a deep breath they walked into the cave and found Sorrel half lying on the floor unconscious. She looked worse than the images had shown them back at the facility. Looking at each other Shellian said, "Now what? We won't be able to move until the morning. Look I'll set up a bed for her. Why don't you go out and gather some wood and start a fire. I think we are going to have to nurse her back a little before the morning, and from what I am seeing here we will probably have to watch her closely tonight."

"You'll get no arguments from me Shell'. From what I see here if we are able to move tomorrow I suspect that it's going to take us all day just to move up one cave instead of all the way back." He began his way outside stopped, turned and then asked in a tone that showed he really wasn't expecting an answer. "Shell', I wonder what happened back there after we left? It had to be something really serious for Sorrel to take off like this with no preparation." He then left to gather some firewood and to light a fire.

Once he had left, and under her breath more to herself she said, "Yes, Saige, I do wonder."

It was a sleepless night for both of them, as Sorrel remained unconscious and continued to look pale and drawn. They had tried to get some broth down her but were unsuccessful. This was a very serious situation and now once again they were too far out to be able to communicate. If indeed they were able to move tomorrow then once they came back into range they would have to let them know of the seriousness of the condition. "Saige, do you have anything that we can write on? I know with our need to leave it was something I did not even consider."

"Why sis?" Then he just said, "Oh." He thought a moment and then shook his head. "No I don't remember seeing anything like that. Maybe we could take one of the burned sticks and use the charcoal on the end to write on something. Then we could at least let them know what we need."

"My thoughts exactly. Now, we need something to be able to write on, any suggestions?"

Looking around inside the cave neither could see anything that would work. Knowing from the view of the cave on the security screens they looked at the wall across from its probable location.

Studying it for a moment Saige said. "I wonder . . . be right back." He then headed outside where the fire was burning grabbed a burned stick or two then returned inside. "Now let's see if this can be seen." He then tried marking the cave wall and with the soft glow and some experimentation he found the size of letters needed to be visible. It was going to take a few more sticks, and he knew that the message would have to be very short and to the point. Turning around he could see Shellian studying both him and what he was trying to do. "What do you think?" He asked.

"Well it's a little hard to read but I guess it will have to do. What do you want to say?"

"This is a little more serious than what we first thought. So I was thinking that we need Saar to meet us at the next cave. It's not something I really want to do, but neither you nor I are doctors and her condition is beyond us. I just hope that we can move on in the morning. I really have no idea if any of the others are following her or not. I just don't like this."

"You want to say all of that?" She said as she interrupted him.

"No just thinking out loud here, sorry, just these few words. 'Need Saar at first cave tomorrow', I hope that's enough."

"Me too." Then turning back to her patient, when Sorrel moaned softly, she said again with a slight edge of desperation in her voice. "Yeah, me too."

* * *

The twin suns were rising in the sky and Sorrel had yet to wake. Her breathing had eased and she appeared to be resting now, but sometime soon they would have to try and wake her and move on to the next cave. They had no way to know if the message they had put on the wall was received at all. So once they began the journey back they would continue to try to make voice contact once again. The problem with these devices was that they were line of sight only. And in these mountains there were few places where it was line of sight. Both of them standing by the entrance looking outside were deep in conversation when Sorrel said in a very weak and surprised voice asked. "Where . . . where did you come from? When I found this cave I thought that it was the end. I was scared to death, but I had nothing left – just nothing left at all." She then began crying softly which shook through her whole being.

Shellian immediately went to her side, put her arms around her shoulders and said, "It's not important Sorrel, not important at all. We are here and we are going to do all we can to get you through this." Turning to Saige who was still standing at the entrance she said. "Well, just don't stand there Saige, get us something to eat. See if that broth we had prepared for her is still hot from our morning fire, we need to get some food into her now, and then move."

"Sorry sis, I was just surprised that she was awake. Be right back!"

* * *

It was mid-morning before they could begin their return trip. Both Saige and Shellian took turns in supporting Sorrel. There was no doubt that the trip just to the next cave would take them all day. Sorrel had no strength at all, and leaned heavily on the two of them as they continued their trek. It was a miracle that Sorrel had made it as far as she had, let alone finding the path that led by the caves. The trip back to the next cave was an ordeal. Sorrel was now running a fever and ranged from semi-consciousness to short periods of ramblings about nothing at all. They half carried and half supported her the whole distance. It was now obvious to them that if they had not come to rescue her she would probably have died in that cave. It saddened both of them with that thought. There had already been way too much tragedy and death in their group, and to be close to that once again was something they did not even want to consider. Eventually close to dusk they saw the location of the cave in the distance.

As they got closer they saw two emerge and come towards them. As they got closer they relaxed recognizing Stone and Saar. Not that it was likely, but there had been a slight possibility that it may have been someone from the other group. Stone arrived first and said. "Here let me take over. I'll carry her and Saar will monitor as we move." Then looking close at Sorrel he continued saying, "She really looks bad. I hope we've gotten to her in time. I wonder what happened?" Then Saar joined them with deep concern on his face he studied Sorrel for a moment.

"Let's get her inside. She really is much worse. We really need to get her back to the facility, but it is almost dark and we haven't located any of the lights that we could use to see our way. So I guess we are stuck here for this night." Then looking at Saige and Shellian he said. "You two look like your all done in. Look we have a fire going and food already hot. Why don't the two of you go get something, we can handle this for now. I think we will be carrying her on a stretcher to-morrow." Shaking his head he said. "I really did not think she was this bad. The screens surely did not do her justice that's for sure."

That night she never regained consciousness, and the next day they carried her on a stretcher, for which again, she was totally unaware of anything. Eventually, with all four of them rotating the job of carrying her, they finally reached the facili-ty early in the afternoon. There they took her to the infirmary and Saar began to work on her. Seirra stopped by briefly be-fore returning to the security office. Since she had been the only one left at the facility, she had locked herself inside the security office while they had been gone. Once the chaos was over they would again work it in shifts. Now Sorrel's survival was in the hands of Saar, and in the inner strength of Sorrel. Saige, Stone, and Shellian headed for the cafeteria area to get a meal and to relax for a short time. "I really wonder what has happened to force her out like this." Shellian asked.

Shaking his head Saige said, "I know you did not expect an answer, but I have no idea. Something must have gotten pretty desperate down there to make her leave."

"You mean she didn't tell the two of you anything at all?" Stone asked

"She was only coherent once and since then has either been unconscious or delirious. When we showed up she was out cold, and it wasn't until later that she opened her eyes and asked how we had gotten there. But that was just about all. We all but carried her all the way to the cave where we met you and Saar. And from there she never regained consciousness. So in reality you know just about as much as we do." Shellian said quietly. They all were silent for a while, and then Saige got up and started pacing. It was obvious that there was restlessness there, but the other two remained silent.

"I wish we could have seen it coming." Saige said.

"See what coming Saige?" Shellian asked.

Waving his hands in the general direction from where they had come from, he said. "Oh that conspiracy that split us up. If we had then there is a good chance that we all would be here, and all the women who are carrying now would be better for it since there is better food and actually a place to take care of them. Instead we have what we have now – no idea what's going on down there, one of the women running away from it and endangering her life . . ."

Shrugging she said, "Well we didn't. And unlike some of the exercises we did back in the compound, we can't go back and try again to get it right. We've been over this again and again, and we probably should have seen the signs, but we didn't or if we did we ignored them with too many other things demanding our attention – so, quit putting yourself down for it. We have to live with what we have now and we cannot change a thing."

"You're quite right. I keep seeing Shayne lying there on his deathbed staring up at us, pleading that we take care of what was left of our small band, and then to have it end up like it has. I just feel like we have failed him, and ourselves."

"I can understand that. But remember we are not the mother and father of the ones who are not here with us. So they had a right, at least as far as they were concerned, to do what they did. If they felt that our leadership was so poor, then they should have made it known. But as you know they didn't. Instead they chose to do it the way they did, and any bashing you do of yourself is not going to change that at all. I know it's a difficult thing, but we need to move on. We still haven't been able to find out what caused the primitives to do what they are doing, and that was originally what we were to do. Instead we have been fighting just to stay alive. We've now been here almost through this long winter, and being isolated as we are, I have no idea what has happened down below. As far as I know all of the cities may have fallen by now or maybe only a few more. I think . . ."

Saar entered as she was finishing her statement and interrupted. "Shellian I need you now, and I've already grabbed Seirra. I think that Sorrel is going to lose the baby, and there's nothing I can do to stop it. I need both you and Seirra's help now if I'm to save her life. Hurry!" He then turned and left leaving silence and concern behind him. Shellian got up quickly and headed out of the cafeteria to head for the infirmary, leaving Stone and Saige alone. Saige, shaking his head, said, "I don't understand it, I just don't. We were doing okay and had made it through most of the winter when the breakup happened. While things were not the best, we were doing okay. Now there's a possibility that we will lose another one, and from the worry on his face I'd say it's a guarantee that she'll lose the baby." Then taking a deep breath he continued. "Well Stone, I guess it leaves you and me to keep the watch in security, so why don't you go and take the first watch, and then later I'll relieve you. I'm sure whatever the outcome from the infirmary we'll know as soon as they know."

Stone rose from one of the tables, and nodded in agreement, but did not say anything, heading out and towards the security office, leaving Saige completely alone. Once again taking a deep breath he thought. *What's going on? Is everything going to continue to unravel? Or will there eventually be some good news out of all of this?* Looking around, his thoughts continued to flow. *Well, I guess I have to admit that by finding this place that this is something in the right direction. But even finding this place was a complete accident.* Then laughing and shaking his head as his train of thoughts continued, *Yeah, an accident caused by an accident. Enough on this I've got to figure out what we need to do from here. I mean we really know very little about this place as of yet.* He got up, and with no clear destination in mind, walked out of the cafeteria, and then found himself in what they were calling the executive meeting room. Sitting there at the large table he stared out through the windows to the outside world, finding that he couldn't sit, got up and went outside to walk the small hidden valley to try and gather his thoughts.

Stone reached the security office and found the door wide open and the room vacant. He had expected that, and so entered and began to monitor the area. He saw Saige leave and then followed him as he entered the meeting room, and watched him as he exited that room to go outside. He hadn't said much, but it worried him that Saige had felt so personally responsible for what had happened. He could tell that it weighed heavily upon him. Shaking his head, he knew that he had no answers and from what was happening in the infirmary, the tragedies were still coming. While he knew from observation that Sorrel appeared to be a strong woman, he did not know what the loss of her child, following the loss of the one she apparently loved, would do to her. While, from what Saar had said, she would lose her child, would they then lose her too? He looked back up at the numerous screens and then consternation furrowed his brow. Could it be? Turning to the intercom system he paged Saige to come to the security office, and continued to monitor the screens while he waited.

In a very short period of time Saige arrived breathing hard. "What's up Stone?" He asked.

Pointing to the monitor that had rotating images from the cave system on it Stone just said, "Watch. It will take a moment for it to come around again but I need you to confirm what I thought I saw. I think this is the first cave past the one we wintered in." They both waited while the images of the other caves flowed past and finally the one he was waiting for flashed on the screen. "See!" But then the images moved on. "Darn! I haven't figured out how to lock this on the images I want. Do you know anything about it?"

Shrugging Saige said. "No, not yet, but remember we've not been here very long and really haven't had much time to figure anything out yet. But I think I saw what you did. We'll wait until it comes around again and see if they are still there."

"Do you think that they could be looking for Sorrel?"

"I don't know . . . just not enough information here – but from the brief look I think there are only four of them and two of them are women. Again because it was so brief I cannot even tell you who they are. Wait . . . it's coming around again." They both concentrated on the monitor as it once again flashed briefly on the cave before moving on to the other cameras. "Yes definitely four of them. Darn! Wish I knew how to stop this so we could really look."

"Know what you mean Saige. Now what? I mean we don't know if they are out just to hunt for more food, or are they trailing Sorrel, or what their intentions are at all."

Shaking his head before saying anything, he stated, "Okay Stone, I guess all we can do is continue to monitor their progress and see if they head our way. The only good thing we have right now is that we are equal in numbers with that group, and they have no idea that we can watch them or that this facility even exists."

"That's true, but it hasn't snowed and I'm sure the trail that Sorrel left will be plain as day, and then when our tracks show up, they will know that we are out here and that we came and picked up Sorrel . . ."

". . . Which means that they would be able to follow our tracks right back to here, great! Another problem while we are dealing with this serious health issue." Shaking his head Saige continued. "Okay, point taken, but for the life of me I don't know what to do about it right now. At least the way into this place isn't obvious. I'll go up and brush away any of our tracks leading to the entrance up top, and I guess all you can do is keep monitoring them. They are a couple of days away yet, and there's still a chance they will just turn around and head back. At least we can hope."

"Do you think we should inform the rest of them?"

Thinking for a moment, Saige shook his head. "No . . . no, they have enough going on right now, and really do not need anything distracting them. I know that Saar has turned off the camera and mic in the infirmary so I would have to go in person. I suspect that what is happening there does not need to be observed. And it is why he asked for Shellian and Seirra to assist him. No unless they appear to be a threat, we will just keep it to ourselves for now . . . Ah, anything else before I see what I can do to wipe out our tracks?" Stone just shook his head no. "Okay then, I'm on my way to clean up the tracks. Don't know how long I'll be gone, so I guess you have it here until I get back." Saige left and headed out through the large cavern – a cavern they had yet to discover its true purpose – up the ladders and then out through the hologram.

He returned several hours later glad to enter the facility. The air still had a bite to it and to be back inside where it was warm felt wonderful. He immediately headed down to the security office to be updated by Stone. Walking into the office he found Stone waiting for him. "Saige glad you're back!" As he continued to monitor the screens, Saige looked and was surprised. "How'd you do that?" He asked.

"This time, with the amount of time I would be spending in here, and knowing that there had to be a way to set this monitor to watching a particular cave, I just started checking things out. Actually found a manual buried deep in one of the cabinets over there. Fortunately it was a training manual that somehow had been left when they abandoned this place. Anyway the way this system is built, it's set up to be able to stop at any particular cave you want, and when you do that, one of the other monitors takes over the role of scanning the rest." Then pointing to the screens to make his point he then continued. "I've been watching the next one in the series that leads up here once they went out of sight from where I first saw them. Interesting stuff in this manual, I think we all need to read it. And I mean we *can* read it. This is another confirmation that we are dealing with our own ancestors here. Unless there was another common language on this world then this is just too much of a coincidence."

"Yeah I know. I've kept trying to resist it and be skeptical, but there is just too much evidence that this place was built by our ancestors. But as to why I just don't know. And was it built before the war or after . . . And why in the Sacred Mountains? There are just so many unanswered questions. So I guess the real question now, since I've been gone long enough, is . . . have they shown up at the next cave yet?"

"No, but it could be any time. I've been going between the two of them – the first one where I saw them and then the next one in line. Oh, it says in the manual, that at one time there were more monitors set up to watch the trails, but eventually they were removed since the primitives appeared to avoid the mountains except for an isolated hunting party now and then."

"Okay, any word from the infirmary yet?"

"No, and no one has left it either. The monitoring system is active in the hall and has shown nothing at all. So I guess whatever is happening in there has to be very serious."

"Okay Stone, I'm going to get something to eat and then come in and relieve you so that you can get a break. When I come back you can show me what you have learned. I'll be in the cafeteria or lunchroom or whatever we are going to call it.

If anything new shows up or the infirmary contacts you let me know." He then turned and headed out. He hoped that the work he had performed outside would be enough. He almost turned around and headed back to the security office when he realized that he should have asked if the caves were wired for sound, but thought better of it and went to get something to eat.

Sitting alone there, all he could do was shake his head. *Don't things ever get easier, and why does it seem that the problems just continue to pile up?* Well he had no answers for that. So with the meal finished he headed back to the security office. Stone hadn't contacted him, and with silence from the infirmary he could only hope that it meant that it was still good news. As he entered the office he saw Stone staring intently at the one screen that had the cave system on it. "What are you seeing Stone?"

"I'm not sure as of yet, since the camera angle isn't the best. But I thought a caught a flash of something . . . there! It happened again." Looking harder and closer at the screen and with Saige joining him Saige asked. "Can you bring this up on one of the other monitors?"

"Yes, yes I can. Give me a sec here." Stone then fiddled with some of the controls that were part of a pullout shelf and then on the far side one of the monitors that showed the valley changed to reflect the same image that Stone had. "There, now you can see if you can catch whatever it was I saw."

"A pullout", shaking his head and smiling, "Something I wouldn't have even considered. Well, I guess it makes sense considering how tiny this place really is." He then took the seat on the opposite side of Stone and began staring at the screen. Presently nothing was happening and then like Stone he caught a flash. Glancing over he could see that Stone had seen it also. Then before their eyes the four came into view. The two of them looked at each other and Saige said. "Well I guess we can now say that they are definitely coming our way. Okay for now I have it, so go get something to eat. Then when you are finished come back and show me how to make all of this work."

"Ah, Saige I don't know how to work all of it yet. In fact I've barely figured out what I have so far. But I must admit that getting some food would be nice. But this is becoming serious. I'll go get something and bring it back here then I can show you what I have learned, and you can at least read some of the manual also." He handed it to Saige. "See you shortly and no not a word from the infirmary." Stone left and headed for the cafeteria to put together a small meal and when he arrived he saw Seirra sitting there. She appeared to be beat and down a little. She hadn't seen him enter as her back was to him, so not to startle her he made some noise. She then turned and faced him. Yes, no doubt about it, she had a defeated look on her face, with puffy eyes showing that she had been crying. "Seirra, can you fill me in, or has Saar decided to wait before passing on anything?"

Shaking her head as she sighed, she then took a deep breath. "Stone, this is so tough – probably more for a woman than a man, since we carry the lives inside of us." She began crying softly again just for a moment and then got her emotions back in control. "She's definitely going to lose the baby. She's still unconscious and not doing very well and she has gone into labor. I think it's a situation where it will be either her or the baby and her body has made the decision that it will be the baby. But from what she looks like I can't say that we are going to save her either."

Coming over to her he offered her his arms, which she gladly accepted. Then once again while in his arms she began to cry all over again. They stood there silently while the tears flowed, and finally when they stopped she said. "Thank you, thank you Stone. I really did need a shoulder and someone to hold me. And Saige wasn't here." Then taking a deep breath she said. "Look, if Sorrel survives this she's going to need some serious support. I know that both Shellian and I will be there, but I suspect that someone like you would be a good thing also. Now don't give me that look that you don't think so, I know better than that. It will be a shock to her when she learns of her loss, and it is something that could cause her to give up completely. We . . . we can't have that. There are so few of us now and to lose any more of us would be so devastating."

Silent as Seirra talked, his first thought was, the last thing he needed was to become involved, but as she talked he realized what she said was very true. He also suspected that when she finally met with Saige that she would say much the same thing to him, if Shellian didn't beat her to it. So taking a deep breath he said. "You're right, and I, we, can't afford any more losses. I'm sure the reason you are here is to take a break and get something to eat. Well, so am I. I'll go get something from the kitchen for both of us. Once I get back I need to tell you something also which is not going to improve your mood." Seeing her about to ask he held up his hand telling her to wait, and then headed off to the kitchen to get something for them. *It just goes from bad to worse. But there is nothing we can do but see this through. Oh well, Saige was right in worrying about the others trying to find us and now with a pathway almost to our door, and with everything that's been happening – well I don't know if we will survive this. Enough!* Shaking his head he needed to keep his thoughts more positive. From one individual set of skills and as a group they had survived and would continue. Grabbing the disposable plates he brought out the food to the two of them. "Seirra here you are, and I'll grab a couple of glasses of water. Look, the situation may be getting worse. We, Saige and I, are tracking four of the group who threw us out. And with the trail that Sorrel left and then when we went and rescued her . . ." Shaking his head before he continued. "A baby could follow the trail that we left. So it will be no problem for them. Saige went out earlier and tried to confuse the trail up to the entrance on the top, but how successful it will be I just don't know. So when you go back into the infirmary pass it on. I'm sure that the three of you are taking breaks one at a time. And from what you have told me this appears to be something that will involve all of you for quite a while. So Saige and I will continue to monitor the situation, and if it gets serious, not that what's happening now isn't, then we will come in and inform all of you or at least put it over the system. But until then just pass this on and worry about what the three of you are trying to do." She picked at the food, eating a little of it, but he could see that everything that was happening was bothering her. "Look you need to eat, just as I do. If you don't then you'll start to weaken and then you may find yourself in the same situation as Sorrel. No not pregnant and about to lose your child, but if she wasn't as ill as she is then there could be a great possibility that she wouldn't – lose her child that is. So if you don't eat you could become just as ill. Besides if you don't I'll sic Saige on you." He finished the statement with a smile. He had just finished his meal himself. "Okay, I've got to go back to the security office. We both are there, so if something comes up, you or any of the others can find us there." He left and entered the security office and then related that he had met Seirra in the eating area taking a break and that he had passed on to her what they knew at this moment. "Anything new since I was gone?"

Shaking his head he said, "No, nothing. I've not learned to read lips and they are only facing the camera now and then anyway. Plus I haven't taken much time to scan this manual yet. It's quite thick, really thick. Anyway the four of them appear to be arguing about something. You can tell from the animated movements and the facial expressions. I don't know if it has to do with staying there before continuing or something else. It really sucks not having any voice. It sure would make this easier and either increase our tension or make it go away. We really have no idea of what their intent really is, and that is a real bother. I guess at least at the moment with them still at this cave we know that they are still far away from us. So again, what did Seirra relate to you?"

"First let me say that she was depressed, and it's understandable. Sorrel is deathly ill, and right now it is touch and go. She stated that Sorrel has gone into labor and it's much too early, so she will definitely lose her child. But as bad as that is, Saar is worried that she may not make it either. So from what I could gather, the three of them will be in there with one taking a break now and then, until she either dies or the crisis is over. So we will be on our own – I know great timing. So once again because of the pending situation we are once again outnumbered by our opponents."

"I know I said it earlier, but does it ever get any easier? Here we find this facility and I feel that finally something has broken our way only to see that once again we are facing unknown dangers and unpredictable problems. I just don't know why, and I just do not understand any of this. Okay Stone, I guess enough on this, look I'll continue to cover this for a little while longer. Head out and get yourself some air, and maybe relax for a while. Come back in four hours and then with that change we'll continue to switch off every four hours. That way at least we will be more alert. Does that work for you?"

"You're the boss, and I think it will work out fine. Maybe in that time you might find out more about this security system."

Smiling and shaking his head once again Saige said, "One can only hope . . . yes, one can only hope." Then taking a deep breath he said, "Now go and get away from here for a while. See you back in about four hours then." Stone nodded in agreement turned and left the office and was gone. Saige then turned back to the monitors and saw that the four, who they had been monitoring, seemed to reach some type of agreement. From what he could see it appeared they were going to stay there. It made sense really — as the day was close to over and there was no need to be traveling in the dark. But not knowing what had been said or why they were there he had no idea what their need or agenda really was.

* * *

For the next two night and day cycles the ones in the infirmary continued to minister to Sorrel. While Stone and Saige continued to monitor the group heading their way. At this point they had traveled to the last cave. From there they were less than half a day away from the facility. As he suspected, the tracks that had been left in the snow made it easy for them to follow. And it would have been obvious to the group that at some point that Sorrel would have picked up some help. At the time that the two had rescued her, there had been no thought of or way for them to cover their trail, and now it was coming back to haunt them. He knew that once they had reached the final two caves those additional tracks would reveal more of them. So with Sorrel at this point, there would have been at the least, five sets of tracks. He had back-tracked to the first or last cave earlier and tried to hide the trail that he and Shellian had taken on that fateful day of discovery, and later that same day the rest of them, to this hidden valley. He tried to make the path that Saar, Seirra, and Stone had taken to be the one they all had taken. But with some work it would not take the four of them long to figure out that, that was a false trail. All it really was more of a delaying tactic. And once they figured out the correct direction both he and Stone would need to be in the better position offensively.

Still no final word from the infirmary, and the brief contacts they had still placed Sorrel on the edge of death. She had finally aborted and her stillborn child had been a girl. He could see with the brief meetings with the two women that it had affected them deeply. Both were crying at the loss, but really couldn't say much – *From such a good beginning another tragedy.* Just when would they end? Maybe with the death of all of them, and then the silence of this facility would return, quietly waiting until it once again was rediscovered. Watching the monitors both Stone and Saige could now see that the ones they were monitoring had met once again back at the cave after following the false trail and were now heading in their direction. All the delaying actions were now over. At least the trails leading into the facility had cameras covering the whole distance. They would know when to be ready to face them, and it would be today and towards evening. Saige sent a voice message to the infirmary to bring them up to date, and then a tired Saar answered voice only. "I think we are close to a resolution here. There have been some subtle changes that could mean that she is going to recover. But it is still very much in doubt. I wish I could send you some help, but this still requires all three of us. And to be honest one of the girls is asleep right now, and the other is quite exhausted. There has been absolutely no chance to be away from Sorrel. It's just that close. If we were not here, then she would have died, not that that outcome couldn't still happen, because it could. But at least she has a chance now. But I just don't know how she will be mentally when she finds out all that has happened. I know, but we've got to get her body healed and then face that later. Good luck and I mean that. All of us in here are counting on what the two of you do. And when this is over I think I'll sleep for at least a day myself." He then signed off and it was quiet once more.

The two of them looked at each other for a moment. Stone had to agree it would be nice to have all this nastiness over with but it continued to be with them. "That's good news, I think. I mean at least there is a slight sign that she's made the turn to recovering. Okay Saige how do you want to handle this?"

"I really have no idea. I think taking *a wait and see* position for now is the best. If they come up and do not find the side trail that leads through the hologram, and just head up to the edge of the cliffs, then they will probably just head back thinking we had to have gone in a different direction, no matter what the tracks show. Since the other side was a false trail, they might come to the same conclusion. After all we were exploring in many directions when this place was located by accident. Whoever placed it here knew how to hide things. I did notice that there are a couple of places built into this facility that allows defenders to be above any hostiles. So if it looks like they are coming this way I guess you and I will have to go there. Until then . . ." He trailed off and shrugged. So far the four that were approaching had only been seen from a distance, so no real intent could be assessed. Why only four instead of the full seven? Again, no answers. "Stone, I'll cover here for the next couple. Head out, relax, get something to eat, or whatever. Then come back and I'll take a break. Once they get close we'll both be here and monitor the situation, and if it appears they will be heading for the facility then we will go and meet them."

* * *

Evening was approaching and after monitoring the group up close and personal, Saige felt that they were not looking to attack anybody. In fact they looked tired – whipped actually. There was a sense of depression that lay on the four. Their body language seemed to say, we give up. What had happened back there since they had been kicked out? Whatever it was couldn't have been good. Since right here in this facility they had Sorrel and she was in serious condition, and now these four, while healthier than Sorrel, did not look much better. Turning to Stone he said. "I don't know about you but I don't think they are here to attack us. They look like hell, defeated, and at the end. Go up to one of those points for defense. I think I am going out to meet them and see what I can find out.

No I'm not going out into the open where I can become a target, but something is just not right here. I mean look at them."

"Yeah they look pretty bad. But it could be a ruse."

"And that's why I need you to be where you can watch the whole thing and defend both me and the facility if need be. If one of us doesn't make contact and they continue to work the area, then they may discover this place when we are not quite as prepared as we are now. Yeah I know, just two of us is really some preparation."

"Got a suggestion Saige, let's send the image to the infirmary since both of us will be away from the security office, and that way they will know what's happening."

"You can do that? I didn't realize that these images could be transferred."

Shaking his head and smiling Stone said. "Yes, it's in the manual, although it wasn't easy to find. I think whoever worked here in the past probably was trained for it, so some of what is in the manual is not explained, but assumes that whoever is reading it is familiar with the subject."

"Saar, this is Saige. The ones outside are close. We are leaving the security office now, and Stone will transfer the images from here to the monitor there in the infirmary so that you can watch from there. Hope to be back shortly." Stone and Saige then left the security office not awaiting a response from Saar, and headed for their different positions. Saige would wait until he got a signal from Stone saying he was in position before heading out. And then carefully make the approach to the ones outside. At no point did the group of four approach close enough to a hidden camera to be recognized. Both Stone and Saige thought they knew who the four were, but until Saige was close enough to positively identify them they would wait. Saige waited at the top of the platform until he got the signal from Stone that he was in position, and then waited for the signal that he could see the approaching group. He knew that they were getting close, but not so close that they would be there immediately. So the waiting dragged on for what seemed like forever. Then he got the signal from Stone and left the facility through the hologram and carefully worked his way towards the main trail, if it could be called such, which he and Shellian had followed in what seemed so long ago.

With the countryside being as broken as it was here, there was no problem finding a place to remain out of sight and to be able to observe the trail. Shortly he heard a conversation and knew that they were now approaching his position. He continued to observe as they came in sight, hiked even to where he was, and then continued on apparently completely unaware that he was there. What he saw disturbed him. They, on closer inspection did look like hell. He recognized them immediately. Although he had to be sure he was right. As they were quite dirty, appeared to have not eaten well, and the two women in the group both pregnant looked drawn and tired. This definitely was not a war party. Taking a deep breath Saige asked." What are the four of you doing here? And do not turn around as we are watching and have you covered with weapons."

He could see their reaction in the scrunching of their shoulders, but then when they recognized the voice their shoulders slumped. "Saige? Saige is that you?" Starr asked. There was a trembling in her voice and he could tell that she was close to tears.

Then in a softer, gentler voice Saige answered. "Yes, yes Starr it's me."

"Thank the stars and heavens!" She exclaimed. "We have been desperately looking for you or Saar or any of you. Can we turn around?"

Looking them over, he could see that none of them had their weapons even out of the sheaths. And from his observation there did not appear to be any interest in bringing their weapons to bear. "Yes, but just be careful. I don't want something to happen to all of you because one of you got careless."

"No problem Saige . . . and we understand." Seve responded. The four then slowly turned around and faced Saige and he immediately saw their surprised reaction when they saw him. After all, he was no longer in the animal skins but the disposable clothing from the facility. He obviously was well fed, and clean. Silence reigned for a short time while both sides sized each other up. Once again Saige could see the poor condition that they were in. "Okay would one of you please explain why you are here?" Sabryn stepped forward and before any of the others could say anything she signaled them to be quiet.

She then said, "Saige, first off let me say personally I am sorry for what transpired back in the cave. Storme and Schylar convinced us that they would be the better leaders. Every time any of you would do anything he or Storme would show us how it could have been done so much better if only they were in charge. Eventually they convinced us and then the five of you were ejected. Now looking back I can see it was a mistake. From that moment on the two of them did nothing but demand that we wait on them hand and foot, and continually remind us that they were in charge. They started to be more demanding and put more pressure on Sorrel and were demanding that she and Sajan live together. Sorrel wanted nothing to do with it. It was then, as retaliation, they began to hold food from her. So in desperation she left, snuck out. We wanted to go and get her, but now the three of them demanded that we stay. Somewhere and somehow once again they ended up with most of the weapons and we were at their mercy. Then once again they started rationing out the food with the three of them getting the greater amount, while the rest of us got next to nothing. No matter how we reasoned or pleaded it was to deaf ears. So the four of us got together when we could, and decided that like Sorrel we had to get out of there. So, on some excuse each of us went outside of the cave at different times on different errands and then never returned. As far as I know the three of them are still there in their kingdom with no one to rule. I, for one, am glad to be away from them.

"Then once away we could only go in the direction that the five of you, and we suspected that Sorrel went. But all we ever found were tracks in the snow. Some of them newer, which we assumed were Sorrel's, and others that were much older which we guessed, were you and the others. We were afraid that we would come upon Sorrel's body because at the time she left she was in pretty bad shape. Her tracks confirmed that also, since they weaved a lot. And we just followed the tracks and here we are now facing you."

At no point during the story, as it was passed on to him, did Saige interrupt. Then shaking his head he asked. "So what is it that the four of you are wanting of us? After all you were part of the group responsible for kicking us out. Why should any of us care what happens to any of you now?" He was asking hard questions, and he knew it but he needed to know if they could be trusted enough to be able to bring them inside the facility, or just to leave them to themselves and the elements. There was silence and a look of defeat on their faces. He waited and still silence. Then taking a deep breath with his hands on his hips he asked. "Well, is anyone going to answer me or are we going to just stand out here and enjoy the sunshine?"

"What is it that you want us to say Saige?" Seve asked. "We all have paid a heavy price for our belief in Storme and Schylar."

This angered Saige. "No, not close to the price that Sorrel has paid. All of you have cost her, her child and maybe her very life. Right now she is fighting for that . . . and how she will be after this ordeal is anybody's guess. So, not one of you have come close to paying the debt that you now owe at least to her." He was mad, and wanted them to know it. So as he had stated the facts he put as much of his feelings into the statement as he dared. He could see them flinch under his hard questions and statements. "Again why should we bring you back into our group? What is to prevent you from doing what you did again once you have recovered?" Again he could see the complete slumping of their shoulders as his hard words and questions struck them. If they had appeared defeated before, it was nothing to how they looked now. They looked at each other and without a word turned to leave, with no obvious place to go. It struck him to his very soul to see it. Should he invite them in or just let them go to what he knew would be their deaths. He watched them as they began walking away with indecision riding him. Did he just let them go, or what? He had no answers. And because of this indecision riding him and the war within himself as how to solve this dilemma, he was frozen to inaction. After all they had come close to killing them, and now if he let them go he would be putting the sentence of death on them. *Damn, what I am supposed to do? I really don't want them to die out here. We were put in charge of these people, but they rebelled. But if I bring them in they could again.* They were almost out of sight as they headed back towards the cave again with complete defeat in every step they took. Not once did they look back. For them it was over, finished, and they could not change anything. This warring going on inside of him continued to freeze him into inaction. One side saying, that they were only getting what they deserved, and the other saying, that they had learned their lesson – why let them die?

Stone, from his position inside the facility, could only see the interchange between Saige and the group. From the animated movements the conversations had to be somewhat heated, but suddenly he could see complete defeat in the four, and defiance in Saige, and then something else. He could see the four leaving and from a brief view of one of the women he thought he could detect a tear running down her cheek. Just what had happened out there? Saige appeared to be frozen where he was standing with his arms crossed. Once they were out of sight he quickly got down from his position and headed outside to find out what happened. As he approached Saige he saw that Saige was just staring. There was an obvious battle going on inside of him, and Stone was not sure that interrupting him right now would be a good thing. But he needed to know – what happened out here? Standing there he could see that Saige was not even aware that he was there, what to do? "Saige," he spoke softly, "Saige what happened? I could see all of you but could hear nothing. Why are they leaving and having the look of death on them?" Expecting an answer all he got was silence. And still Saige stood there silent and far away.

So are you going to lower yourself and become what Schylar and Storme did to you and the rest that are with you? Saige thought. *Or are you going to admit that you are wrong here and go get them. You do know that you just sentenced them to death. It was obvious that they had nothing, no food, no additional clothing, and no real weapons, almost like you did when you were thrown out. Does this revenge really make you feel good? After all that's all it is. And if it does what does that make you?* He was so deep in the internal fight that he did not even see or hear Stone approach. Finally through the fog of the inner struggle he heard Stone ask him something. Seeing him stand there made him jump slightly. "When did you show up? He asked in a distant voice.

Not quite sure as to how to respond Stone paused before answering. "Saige, I've been here for a little while. Just what is going on here? I mean I could see all of you but heard nothing and now they are gone looking like death warmed over and you are like this."

Sighing Saige said softly, "I sent them away.", as he stared once again off into the distance. *Why are these decisions so hard and why am I having this internal fight? It really sucks to be in charge, and have to make the tough decisions. It would be so much easier to just follow. But I wasn't given that option. And I guess the real question is was I in the right to do what I just did?* "I just sentenced them to death . . . they have nothing at all and winter is not over . . ." Was he really seeking revenge, or maybe retribution for what had happened to Sorrel? But the longer he thought the more he felt that the decision that he had made was wrong. These people had once looked up to him for their direction, but with what he just did he was no better than the leaders who led the conspiracy. Shaking his head he said. "Stone, I just don't know. When I sent them away it seemed right at that moment, but now . . ." He trailed off once again.

Helpless and not sure what to do Stone stood there and waited. He knew that if they did not go after them shortly that there would be a good chance that they couldn't catch them, and with night approaching they would be easy to miss. None of them knew the area that well, and the cameras were not set up for night vision. So once the suns set and darkness arrived, then there would be no tracking or viewing. He knew that they would probably try and push through to the cave but again he knew that it really was too far to go. Especially in the condition the four of them appeared to be in when they slowly passed by his hidden position. "Saige, we need to go get them before they completely disappear. We need them as much as they need us. Just what did they tell you anyway that led you to send them away?" Looking at Saige he could see that he wasn't going to get an immediate answer since that faraway look was still in his eyes. Stone could tell that he was fighting something deep inside of him.

Saige looked up and then at Stone and asked. "What did you ask? Sorry Stone but I am trying to make this right in my mind – to understand what happened here and to come to a right decision."

"That's all well and good. But if we wait too much longer then we will have lost the opportunity of going after them and bringing them back. And losing that opportunity in the end may weigh heavier on you, then you standing here frozen out of any action at all. Come on! Let's go get them, unless there is a specific reason or danger from them that you haven't told me. Is there?"

Shaking his head he said. "No."

Grabbing Saige by the arm he said. "Okay then, let's go and prevent another tragedy here, and one that we would in the end regret." He needed to get moving as too much time had passed and with each passing moment the four were getting further away and increasing the odds that they would miss each other. Then Saige seemed to have come to a decision, looking into the eyes of Stone and said. "Okay, Stone, you're right. Let's go find them and bring them inside."

* * *

When Saige had refused them it was a complete shock, although not completely unexpected. In silence the four of them, feeling death upon them, left. Not one of them turned around to see what Saige might be doing. Now time was against them. While winter would be over soon, it wasn't now and they needed to find shelter for the night. They were too far from the cave to be able to get there and traveling at night in this unfamiliar broken land was not an option. So they began to search for a place off the trail where they could get out of the cold winds that were beginning to blow. The two women had quietly been crying the whole distance, and there was little the two men could do to comfort them. It was over – finished, and who would have thought that it would have ended this way? Shortly they found a likely place to pull off the trail that was surrounded by boulders that at least broke the wind. Plus here they were almost invisible to any of the night predators that roamed these mountains. Seve and Staven left their temporary shelter to get firewood, while Starr and Sabryn stayed. The two women went through their meager supplies, and knew that they barely had enough for this night, let alone the time that was left until the end of winter.

Eventually they had a small fire, and by choosing this location they and their fire would be invisible unless someone was very close. With a voice filled with failure and dread Sabryn said. "I was hoping . . ." Then taking a deep sobbing breath she said, "I was hoping that they would take us back. It really was our last chance." It was silent for a while as no one wanted to speak, and what she had stated summed it up quite well.

"Yeah, I know. But what did we expect? I mean we threw them out, so why should they care about us? Are we not getting exactly what we deserve?" Staven asked, not expecting any answer. Again it was quiet. Now what could they do? There was no food, and no place to go. No time to find their way back down the mountains where they were sure it was now spring, it appeared to be completely hopeless, and thusly the deep silence each with their own thoughts. Again with the silence both Starr and Sabryn began to softly cry. With all the strife, and difficulties that they had endured up until now they had been ecstatic when they found they were carrying new lives inside of them, but now it wouldn't matter. Whoever these new individuals were, they would never become, live, or have a chance in this world, and these thoughts were tearing the two of them apart. Staven and Seve could only watch helplessly as their women cried. And to know why, and to be able to do nothing to change it, ripped them apart inside. It was as if a dark fog had settled over them and even the light from the fire could not penetrate the despair that the four of them felt. Let it end, and let it end quickly, but even here they knew better. They were not the type to take their own lives, but ones to fight on to the very end. What truly was to become of them?

It was now fully dark and the cold closed in on them. With inadequate clothing and bedding they got as close to the fire as they could, but the fire did not appear to be putting out much heat as they shivered with the increasing cold. The wind had increased and every time a gust would find them they would try to huddle even closer together. It was going to be a miserable night and none of them were going to get much sleep. They felt that if they tried that there was a good possibility that they could die from exposure anyway. Maybe that would be the easy way out. Just let the cold take them, but once again they knew that they would fight – fight for life. But why . . . why not just let it end here? There had been so many more when they had started on this journey, it would be easy now to just join the many who were no longer with them, the ones who had perished along the way. They had thought that they knew so much, and would be able to go through anything and come out alive, but now they knew better, so why not let the cold take them? It was during these thoughts that they suddenly realized that they were no longer alone. Turning around they found on either side of them Stone and Saige. But even seeing them stand there initially did not register. They were too deep in their misery and self-pity to realize what they were seeing. "Are the two of you real?" Starr asked incredulously.

Stone and Saige looked at each other and then at the four and then Stone said softly. "Yes we are real. Now gather what you have and follow us. It is much too cold for any of us to be out here tonight. We have better shelter not too far away. Would have gotten to you there earlier, but we could not find the place where you had left the main trail up here. In the failing light of dusk we missed your point of leaving so had to carefully backtrack once we realized that you had."

Still not believing what they had both seen and heard Sabryn asked. "Are you sure? Are you sure you want us to come with you, and that both of you are nothing more than a wish for something different and that I'll wake up and find it all a dream?"

"No Sabryn", Saige said softly, "this is not a dream, although it would be nice to find out that this whole adventure that we are living was no more than a dream, and I would awake back in the compound thinking – wow it seemed so real. But it is real and so are we. Now let's get moving before it gets any colder."

CHAPTER ELEVEN

Summer began with the temperatures rising, but remaining cooler than the lands that they had left. There were two new lives in the group now – a boy from the union of Starr and Staven, and a girl from the union of Sabryn and Seve. Sorrel had recovered, and with the loss of her child, had clung to Stone as he tried to comfort her. As time healed the wounds she and Stone grew closer together. And it was obvious that now she looked to his strength to help her through. She was no longer the open and defiant one, but quiet and almost afraid to do anything. With her confidence completely shattered by the ordeal that she had lived through, she looked completely to Stone for approval. Stone took the role of protector and healer seriously and slowly there could be seen a change in her as the past was slowly slipping away from Sorrel. For the longest time she isolated herself from the rest, but eventually with a lot of work from both Saar and Stone they were able to get her involved once again. And if truth were told, it was probably the arrival of the two new lives that was the deciding factor. Yet even here, you could see the yearning, and the hidden tears, from her personal loss. For the rest it was a time of discovery and understanding. This facility was indeed a place of their ancestors, and they were learning more with each new discovery or reactivation of the equipment, machinery, or computer systems within the structure.

"Okay all." Saige said, as they sat in what they still called the meeting room. Everyone was there today including the two babies which were contentedly asleep on their mothers' laps. So as not to wake them, the conversations were kept low and soft. "What have we found out so far? First off, I'll start by saying that I have now investigated the waterfall and the system that brings the water into the facility, and have to say that it is completely manmade. I know that it looks natural and I think that was the plan, just in case any of the primitives got past their fears of these Sacred Mountains and investigated. It's a masterful job and only because we are from the same society and level of technology I found it. So Staven, have you been able to get the main computing system up yet?"

Shaking his head he said, "No. No not yet. It is still password protected and I have yet to figure out what it is or how to find it. We have much of the system that is automatic and accessible, but where the important records are, is still inaccessible. I'm sure that from the way this place was still operating when you and Shellian found it that there probably had been a plan to return here, if not permanently, at least periodically to check up on things. So I suspect that there is something that is kept within this place that has that record. But so far we haven't found it. But on the positive side, we were able to get the educational programs running and they seem to address children from just about toddler to young adult. While we haven't observed much of the data yet, there are some things we have seen that we feel just can't be right.

But there was also a large library of digital readings, so we feel that maybe what we are observing is a fictional story or something like that."

With a look of questioning on his face Saige asked, "How so?"

Taking a deep breath trying to get his thoughts together before continuing Staven said. "Well, if we look at what we have been taught in our educational system we have been in our cities since the Great War a few thousand annuals in the past. And it was that Great War that caused the ones we now call primitives to abandon the technology that we use and become what they are presently." Looking around he could see the rest of the group agreeing with him. "Okay, from what I get from the teaching computers they completely contradict that. So that is why I question it."

"Contradicts what part?" Shellian asked.

Pausing for a moment before continuing Staven said, "Pretty much all of it, and that's why I question it." He could see with that statement that all of them were looking closely at him.

"Are you sure?" Sabryn who just looked up from watching her sleeping daughter, asked.

Again taking a deep breath and pausing before answering Staven said, "As sure as I can be right now. But until we can access more than what we can right now I can only question it."

"Okay then, I guess all we can do is continue to get more of this facility operational and then some of these new questions might get answered." Then turning to Stone, Saige asked. "Have you and Sorrel learned any more about that large cavern, where we first entered this facility, was used for?"

"First off," Stone began, "It is much larger than we first thought. And if you go back to the distant end of it you can see where it has been sealed. We haven't been able to discover if this sealing is because of danger beyond that point or whether it was just a good place to seal it off, or whether there is really anything of importance beyond it. There doesn't appear to be any doors, holograms or hidden entrances beyond that point, and the lighting just sucks by being almost absent. Plus back there the cavern curves around into a little cul-de-sac. Here we found large, well, what I could only describe as tanks and equipment to operate them. From the little investigation we have done they appear to be empty at this time, and no these tanks did not hold water or anything like that. In fact they have the markings that show that whatever the contents had been that it was poisonous. From what we have observed so far, it appears that our ancestors took advantage of one of the extinct volcanoes to build this facility, thusly shortening the time necessary to build this place. But we've only explored in the one direction, and there's so much more. And that's just about all we can say right now. Again we have more questions than answers, Saige."

"Okay, how about the hydroponics Starr?"

"Again, just like everyone else, the system is automatic with little need of us doing anything. We haven't figured out much, but really don't want to tinker with it since it is our food supply. But we can see that it actually sits lower than the pond so it just uses gravity to feed the water through the system, and the lighting that is used is both natural and artificial, with the lighting being directed by skylights, and where it doesn't provide enough then the artificial lighting takes over."

"I guess that just about covers it then. While we have found out some things there is still much we do not know at all. I feel right now that we are more visitors here on a tour than actual guests who are part of this place. There is still so much we don't know, and until we do there is very little at this point that we can do to help our cities. We can only hope that the primitives do not know the location of all of them and that ours falling so quickly after the one before was just coincidence. So keep working on this and we'll meet again in a couple of days. And if my stomach is telling me anything I think it's time for lunch. So let's go eat and then get back at it. Thanks for the updates, and now we all know everything that is known." Saige then pushed back his chair and headed for the cafeteria. He had to admit he was hungry. Still it was frustrating to have been here to the end of winter and through spring, to now at the beginning of summer and still know little more than they did when they first entered here. Yet, at the same time to be in the best shape physically and mentally that they had been since the fall of their city and the harrowing flight so long ago. Now if they could only learn why this was here and if it predated the existing cities or was just a part of the network.

After lunch Saige headed for the security office, as it was his shift to monitor the cave system and approaches. But with the arrival of the four other members there had been nothing but the local animals that would periodically show up. The three who were behind the conspiracy were never seen again. Either they stayed at that first site or returned to the valleys. Stone, who had a knack of discovering how much of the equipment worked in the security office, would be there with him as they continued to research this hidden place. As he watched the many screens Stone asked more to himself than to Saige. "What's this? Hmmm, now that's interesting."

Half listening and half watching the monitors Saige asked. "What's interesting Stone?" As he looked down on Stone, who was under the consoles and built-ins, which housed the equipment and was generally out of sight except for his legs sticking out.

Stone backed out and sat on the floor looking up at Saige and said. "I think there is a hidden door down here. Probably requires a key or something to open it – not very large, but in a place where one would normally not look for anything. Do you remember that set of keys that we found here, and do you remember where we put them? There's a possibility that one of them might unlock this thing." Again more to himself than to Saige he said. "I wonder why one would put something like this here? It's not easy to get to, or find, and there is very little space to work down here. There isn't any access to the equipment from here and it just looks like a place to put one's legs and feet while working here." Then shaking his head he continued, "Just doesn't make sense to me."

Getting up from the chair he was sitting in, Saige went over to the cabinets where they had first found the key rings. There had been many and they were both color coded and identified for the different sections of the facility. Opening the large cabinet that was attached to the wall he looked over the keys and asked. "Okay Stone, we have, oh I don't know how many keys here, which one do you want to try?"

Getting up off the floor Stone came over and joined Saige as they looked over the vast array of keys there. "I keep forgetting that this facility is large and there are a lot of doors, and all of them have locks. Which makes me wonder, why so many locks? I mean we are guessing that there probably were roughly 100 or more people here, and there appears to be just as many keys. Were they that untrustworthy, or was it to keep the others from getting into anything if they found a way into the facility?"

Shaking his head as he smiled, Saige said. "You got me Stone. I know that in the compound where we trained and worked there were few locks. But I know that in the city itself that all the residences and places of business had locks. So maybe it's just something that is common with us. By the way, how are you and Sorrel getting along? I know that at first she just needed to support and someone to help her rebuild her confidence in who she was, but I think that it's much more now."

"Yeah, it's much more now. At first I was reluctant to be the one to help her, but it has worked out well for both of us. Hmmm, now if I was one to want to lock something up, and yet have a key available in the security office to be able to open it in an emergency how would I place it?"

"Hey, isn't there a second set that wasn't in here", Saige said. "In fact I think that we had to use them to open this key cabinet. Now where are they now?" Both of them started searching the small room, since the keys in question hadn't been touched since they had first opened the locked cabinets within the security office, and after about an hour of fruitless searching Saige said. "Ah, here they are."

"Where? I don't see anything?"

"Well, believe it or not, since we haven't used them, and all of us have used this office as we each shared monitoring, somehow they got knocked to the floor and . . ." He laughed and then smiled, "They ended up on the floor under these consoles and in one of the corners where they probably were kicked – right next to where you found that hidden door." Then pointing to the very corner he said, "See . . . right there."

"Okay I can see them now. Okay, keep your monitoring up and I'll retrieve them and then try the different keys to see if any of them work." Then grabbing the ring he said, "Even with this office being small there are a lot of keys on this thing. They can't all be for here. Okay this is going to take some time since the keys are all similar and only the color coding identifies different areas." Sitting on the floor once again Stone began to study the ring of keys. He leaned back and placed his back against one of the walls as he looked at each key. "I would suspect that it would be one that is used rarely, but that is only a guess." Again saying this more to himself than Saige, "I wonder . . ." Then deep in thought he quietly said, "I wonder if this hidden locked door is for emergencies only. If that's so, then using our color scheme I should try the ones that are for the highest danger." Looking closer he found three keys marked that way. Then crawling back under the unit he grunted as he shifted to get into position to be able to try the keys. After a couple of attempts he said triumphantly. "Got it!" Saige could hear the turning of the lock and the squeaking of the door as it complained from being opened. "There appears to be a few manuals and stacks of papers in here. It's too dark to make anything out. Here I'll hand them up to you." He then handed Saige a large stack of paper, and a few thin books and then crawled back out from underneath and joined Saige. "So what do we have here?"

In his hand Saige saw that there were complete schematics of the facility, and then to his surprise on this was a statement identifying the large cavern as a spaceport. He looked at it questioningly, a spaceport? But as far as he knew they never had been in space. And there had been nothing ever taught to reflect that possibility, yet what else could this mean? Meanwhile Stone was going through another stack and then said, "Jackpot!" Saige asked, "Jackpot? What do you mean?"

"Saige look at this! This booklet here has the emergency override codes for everything here including the main computing system. With this we should be able to finally get into it and find out what this place is all about."

"This is great news, but I have something here also that needs some understanding. Look here, this map or schematic of this place lists the large cavern as a spaceport. My first thought was outer space with space ships landing here, but we never achieved space flight, right?"

Stone thought a minute and said, "I don't think so. As far as I know we have always been here on this planet. We know that most likely there are other intelligences out there, but from the observations that have been made; the distances are so great that it would be almost impossible to travel them and survive. And that doesn't include the deadly stuff out there that our planet protects us from. Yeah, now what did they mean by that? I mean as large as that cavern is I guess you could have a space ship land there – a space ship, wow. Are you sure you are reading that right?"

Handing it over to Stone, Saige said. "Here you look at it. See, plain as day it says spaceport."

Stone couldn't deny it. But did it mean something else. "I wonder if we will find the answer once we get into the main computing system."

"Good chance. I think I'm going to call another meeting since this is important, and all of us need to get right on it – Especially if the overrides that you found work."

* * *

Indeed! The emergency override codes allowed access to the mainframe and they were finally able to learn much about not only the facility, its beginnings, purpose, and why it was located where it was, but it was the part about themselves, and this was the most revealing and shocking revelation. They learned that unlike what they had been taught, that this facility had only been in existence for somewhere between two to three thousand annuals around the binary suns. It was the first on this planet. Its location had been carefully planned and located, to make it easier, both to hide, and to provide access to most of the species of this planet. And they were not from this world at all, but their ancestors had come to study these primitives and remain completely unknown to them. Their ancestors were anthropologists, sociologists, scientists, and such. Their ancestors were from a distant world called Earth, and the war they spoke of in the histories of the cities had nothing to do with this place at all, but one that involved their home world. Whenever it happened, the ships no longer came to this place to bring supplies, and other vital equipment. The war had been a surprise and there had been no time to leave. They had become isolated and had no way to return to their home world, thusly beginning a *time of isolation*. Eventually even the communications network went silent and they knew not of what had happened.

Over the next, what they called a year around the twin suns, they worked on trying to reestablish any communications with their roots, but all they got was static and silence. So it was decided that they would need to move from these mountains and establish a number of hidden cities using the technology that they possessed to keep these cities invisible to the primitives and to continue to study the people. Once they left this hidden facility it would be powered down to the minimum, and all of the automatic equipment placed in the maintenance phase and set an automatic signal to alert any from their own home world that they were here. As this history became available to them, they continued to look at each other as one surprise after another was revealed. Everything they had been taught, everything that they had believed, was a lie. While they were similar to the primitives, that was as far as they could go with it. Nothing else was compatible. There could be no children from the union of the two different species no matter how similar they appeared. From the surveys that had been performed, at least the fruits produced by the vegetation and the meat from the animals, were edible and would sustain them. But even here they relied more on their hydroponics than on what the world could provide.

Here they learned that part of the plan had been the signal, one that continually pulsed out to space – an SOS for any who might travel close by. Then if they responded to that signal it would set in motion another signal and operational plans for the cities to return here. But either the signal failed or no one passed by this remote region of space – because, as far as they knew, the signal was never answered. And so the cities grew and the truth disappeared over time. The histories changed to reflect only this place, and the true origins were forgotten.

Stunned to silence they could only look at each other as the information continued to scroll across the monitors. And while it explained much, it still left much too much out. And still the information continued, and when it finally reached a breaking point Stone paused it. Taking a deep breath and looking around he said, "We started reading this in the morning. I think if you all look around you will see that it is now dark. We have been here all day, with brief stints to the restrooms and taking care of the children, but other than that this day has flown. I think we need to break, eat something, and then absorb what we have learned here today. I have to admit that what this has revealed makes me wonder if any of it can really be true – or is this some type of cover story if the primitives ever found this place. Yet, I feel that what we have just witnessed is true, so very true. I am worried about what it hasn't said." Silence followed.

Shellian then said. "I have to agree Stone. This is almost too much to take in, let alone accept. So let's all go eat something in the cafeteria, and decide while we are there, if we want to continue this tonight or wait until tomorrow. This changes things."

With his brow furrowed Saige asked. "Changes things? How so, Shellian?"

"Well, think about it Saige. If what we just sat through is true, then we are the interlopers here, not the primitives. And while our people had done a good job of staying out of the way of the primitives, and not interfering with their way of life, other than to observe and record, which is what we in the scouting unit did, and is what our ancestors were doing anyway, then do we have the right to interfere, even if it means the destruction of our cities?"

"Good point and that really causes a dilemma. Okay we aren't going to answer any of this right now, let's go eat as Stone as suggested. I really had not realized that this much time had gone by." They got up as a group and left the meeting area and headed to the cafeteria much subdued, and silent. Shellian had made a valid point, did they have the right, or should they try to just let the cities die and bring as many as they could back to this hidden facility?

It was decided while they were eating, that since the information was going to be still available later that all would take the rest of the night off, and come back after the morning meal to continue to see what else this facility and computing system had to tell them.

* * *

"I've had all us of gather once again this morning, not that we weren't going to do this anyway. Last night I couldn't sleep for the longest time and so not to bother Seirra, I got up and went to the terminal that we had, and read some additional stuff on what our ancestors faced. So I have marked it on all of your monitors to read as I read it to you. But before I do that I need to bring all of you up to date on what they were thinking." Pausing a moment before continuing, he stood up leaned forward to make his point before continuing. "With the news of the war, and unfortunately they never learned with whom, they knew from the received communications that there would be no one coming to get them. And what made it worse lay in the fact that a supply ship had only been there a short time before the announcement of the war, and would have been ample in size for all of them to leave and go home. It wouldn't have been a comfortable trip, but quite workable.

Then for the longest time they were in a quandary as to what they should do. You know should they stay here in this facility, should they try and make real contact with the primitives that they had been studying, should they leave? But as each question was answered the only real answer was to build the cities in the valleys, and lowlands, in places that the primitives would not normally want anything to do with. And that was how and why our cities came to be. So with the decision finally made they planned to make the move at a time when the primitives would be staying within their villages and camps, and to assist each one of the new sites until they were up and running, and all the security measures could be put into place. Even with the equipment they had it took about five annuals around the suns to accomplish. They established twenty-six cities, which eventually expanded to thirty, each with a name that attached to the letter of the alphabet that they and we use, with the names coming from our home world. That's why they are so different from the names that the primitives have attached to places, lands, mountains, and such – different culture, different beginnings, and truthfully a different world. Some of the cities were empty, but they knew that eventually that there would be enough population to begin to fill them. The other decision lay in how people in each of those cities would be named. By doing it this way they would know immediately which city one came from and its location. At least that was how it was planned. Thusly that is why all of our names begin with an "S". Of course, the first people in our city had names that started with any number of letters. But, I guess at the time of the decision it made sense to them. Anyway that kind of brings us up to date with our beginning history. I've skipped over a lot here and tried to just cover the highlights. Now here is what the leaders said at the time they prepared to leave, and I quote."

"After much thought, discussions, and deliberations we have decided that it is necessary for us to leave our hidden facility in the mountains and establish cities below. Since we are not of this planet, and had only originally come here to study the people it has been decided that we must keep ourselves separate from the true owners of this planet and let them advance as they naturally will. With that isolation each city will become one onto itself. While communication between cities will exist, there will be minimal travel so as to avoid alerting the primitives of this world of our existence. While we plan for the long term, it is hoped that whatever this war is, that for us it is short, and not terribly destructive, and that in the near future we will have a ship arrive to rescue us and then at that time be able to return to the Earth our true home. Until then we will live, and remain isolated from this world and its peoples using the technology we have to essentially become invisible. We have set a beacon, a signal to any passing ship that we are here, and where we presently are located on this planet. We have planned for the long term and truly hope for the short. Below is a map and marked locations of all of our newly established cities. So that if any do arrive here and find the facility empty they will know that we are here, alive, and well. This will be the last communicate that I have placed in the system as my last act as administrator of this facility. It has been a great assignment and we have learned much from our studies, but all may be for naught since in the end we ourselves may become natives of this world with no knowledge of our true past."

When he finished reading Saige remained silent for a short time to let the words of the last administrator of the facility sink in. "Okay all, there you have it. If any of you doubted it at all, here is the final proof that originally we were from somewhere else, a place called Earth. It's obvious that he and the people who were here were looking forward to returning, but whatever this war was, it ended any such hope, and we are here because of their work and planning. Now what do we do? As you can see the original plan was to remain isolated from the primitives and allow them to continue on their own path. But now we have been discovered. Do we just let this continue and save a few by bringing them to this hidden facility or do we somehow bring an end to this sudden gathering of the tribes by bringing down their leadership? These are tough questions and we need to answer them quickly. We are few and so we will not be able to bring an end to this by any direct means. And we really have yet to even establish where this leadership is located. So for now I leave you with this and later today we will get back together and discuss it. Thank you all for being here this morning and now let's get to whatever we were to do before I called this, and yes I know that originally we were going to continue here. But for now we need to continue to learn all we can about this facility."

Before any could get up to leave Sabryn interrupted and said. "Before we go, a couple of things hit me when we both read and heard what the administrator said. So if you will wait I would like to see if any of you see what I just saw."

Saige looking over at Sabryn said. "Hey if anybody has any additional input I'm all for hearing it. What do you have for us?"

"Well, in truth I'm still thinking this out. But what he left here explains a lot." Then taking a deep breath before continuing she said. "Look, if we really compare this place with our cities there really isn't much difference. I mean we were able to come into this place and everything about it was somewhat familiar, you know just like in the cities. Does it strike anybody that there have been no improvements or inventions in the cities to help?"

"What are you getting at?" Saar asked as leaned forward placing his arms on the table.

Clearing her throat she said, "I think it explains why that was so. Our ancestors were waiting for someone to come and return them to our home world, this place they called Earth. So there never was a time where they had planned on staying here. The cities were just a temporary refuge while they waited out whatever this war was. And as far as we know right now, no one has ever arrived to pick up any of our people. So that brings up a more worrisome thing, and it's this. While we have no proof one way or the other, we could be the last of our species. We could be the last that ever could have called this Earth home, the place where we came from, our mother world." As she finished it brought another silence to the meeting as each contemplated what she had just stated.

Shellian, looking down at the table, thinking for a moment and then looked up at the rest at the table said. "I guess that's a valid assessment, and I did not even think about it that way. So from what you just said, and again we have no way of proving it one way or the other, we could be it – we and our cities that is. We have no idea what the war was about as the details are basically nonexistent. We don't know if maybe another spacefaring race found the Earth and started a war or whether it was our own people. Either way I guess it really doesn't matter, since no one showed up to collect the scientists and their support staffs. So it would be easy to then conclude that we are it, we are the last. So with those thoughts it now strengthens our need to find a way to break this alliance, or alliances, and have things return to like they were before. But I have to admit that this discovery we have made will make it impossible to return to anything close to the way things were before the primitives began destroying our cities. So I guess this makes it more imperative that we find a way, not that it wasn't before. At least it reinforces the need to interfere instead of just letting the primitives have their way with the cities." Then taking a deep breath she asked, "There's much to think about here, is there anything else that any of you want to bring to our attention?" She looked around the table and saw that none did. "Okay then as my brother said earlier, let's get about our day's work and we will meet back here again with the evening meal."

They broke up at this point and headed out in different directions. Except that Seve approached Saige and asked. "I know whatever we decide we will have to do it indirectly, since we are so few, but something came to mind while we were in here. If our ancestors were anthropologists I'm sure at some point that they had to contact the primitives to get closer, which means somewhere they would have to had pack animals. But so far there is no sign of any such thing here at all. And all the maps have shown just the facility and this valley. So where would they be? I feel that they would have kept and bred their own so that they would know them. Plus it would be something to use for trading. After all to be a real observer, and still remain apart from these people the perfect role would be a traveling merchant. So where is anything on this?"

Shaking his head, Saige had no idea at all. "You've raised some valuable questions, Seve. See if you can follow up on those if you can. There has to be something in the system on the methods they used to study the primitives, and there you might get a hint to where these animals might have been kept. Personally I would say that it would have to be close by – again, someplace hidden, but not so far a way that it would provide undue danger to either the animals or the people either tending them or picking them up for an assignment. Since Sabryn, your significant other, brought out those other points, the two of you can research it together. I guess you probably could leave your daughter with Starr since she's got the duty today of searching the schooling records. Since she will be in the playroom area anyway with her son, then adding your daughter should both help as the two infants could be watched at the same time. Plus I think it only fair if Sabryn periodically checks in on them and assists anyway. I know she will anyway since both she and Starr breast-feed their babies. I've pulled the security detail today so if anything comes up that is where I'll be. And good luck, I think that you're right. It makes sense to do it that way. Now all we have to do is find the proof, and then hopefully the location of where these animals were kept. Although I doubt that any of them could still be around after all of this time. Yet, this facility is fully operational, maybe the place where these animals are kept is also under computer control."

"So you think that maybe there would be a chance that there would still be some of the animals around today? It has been an awful lot of time that has passed since they abandoned this facility. And we are truly just guessing that it is one of the methods they used to contact and study the population."

"True, but once you mentioned it, it makes perfect sense. That way they would not have to be from or live in any one tribe. They simply could say that they were beyond the mountains and that they are trying to open new trade sources. And by studying them like we did from a distance, they would have had a pretty good sense of what would have worked and what would not have – not that it didn't have its own share of risk, but I think it would be less than if they had joined a tribe. Then there could have been problems when one tribe attacked another, which as we know is quite common – at least until recently."

"Yeah, I guess so. Okay we'll get right on it and be back here with anything we find with this evening meeting." Seve turned and left to take this new assignment. Saige then headed off to the security office to monitor the facility and the surrounding area.

As the day progressed and with nothing showing on the screens Saige was becoming bored, but knew the importance of continued diligence, and then thought. *I wonder . . . If these screens are covering the facility, the surrounding areas, is there a way to see if the system checks other areas also? If an animal husbandry area does exist one would think that it's under the same system.* Standing up and pacing, he knew that Stone had become the expert, and while the rest of them could operate the equipment, it was not to the expertise Stone had demonstrated. Well, all he could do was try. Turning to the now much used manual, he began to leaf through it to find out if there was a way to view alternate locations that may have been on the system, but did not require full time monitoring. But after a couple of hours of frustration he was no closer to finding out if there was a secondary, lower priority monitoring system in place. If there had been it could have been general knowledge, and something that the security personnel were trained for, and thusly it had no need to be included or required to be in that manual. After all, the manual was more of an instruction manual on the operation and repair of the equipment, and probably was a standard manual for any security facility wherever it might be. Not something that covered the different possible circuits unique to each facility that as they could exist.

He knew that Stone was out in the hidden valley, searching for alternate accesses and also working in the hydroponics section. While yes much had been automated, there were some areas they found that required their assistance. In fact some of this portion had shut down and was awaiting a human hand before continuing operation. So he and Sorrel was there, with her being exclusively in the hydroponics. "Sorrel, are you there?" Saige asked. He had the one of the monitors covering the hydroponics and at this moment no one was in view. Not surprising really, considering all that was in there, and with only one security camera there were many blind spots. After a short time period he asked again. Then he heard some light laughter, and then he saw Sorrel come into the view of the monitor.

With a smile on her face she asked. "What do you need Saige?"

Smiling back, he thought. *It's good to see her smile again. Stone has been good for her.* Instead he said. "I'm looking for Stone, is he with you right now or is he out in the valley?"

With a look of devilment on her face she said. "Oh he's here. Do you want to talk with him?"

Then it hit him what had been going on, and quickly said. "No, no that's not necessary. But when he can I would like to have him come to the security office. I need his expertise, and he may be able to help me solve a possible problem." Then smiling he said. "The two of you can go back to what you were doing." He then cut the connection. He had to admit that it really was good to see her smile again, and to have those looks that could just drive a man crazy. And he knew once he saw it that she and Stone were involved physically at the moment he had tried to find him. He then laughed quietly thinking. *Isn't that the way of it? You decide it would be nice to get as close as the two of you can, only to be interrupted. And it's something you really don't do a lot when comparing it to a full day. But for some reason when you do there always seems to be something to interrupt it.*

* * *

"That is a problem Saige. It's something I didn't think about. But you're right, there's a good chance that there is a secondary non-critical section that the security office here could switch to just to make sure everything was okay." Glancing at the panel Stone just shook his head. "I'm going to have to think about it. You said that you looked through the manual right?" At which Saige nodded his head. "I guess I wouldn't expect it to be there, but one could hope. Hmm . . . I think I've tried most, if not all of these different switches at one time or another . . . but, haven't gotten around to labeling them yet. Well at this moment you got me." He got up and took a deep breath, leaned on the ledge that served as a desk staring at the monitors thinking.

Saige leaning back in one of the chairs looking up at Stone asked. "Do you think that what I am suggesting could exist?"

"Yes, once you suggested it, it makes perfect sense. I know that it's important to be able to have the priority areas always monitored, but there has to be secondary areas that just did not require constant surveillance, so either they are on passive systems, and if a sensor went off alerting the security office, or there is a way for them to check into those areas now and then. You've definitely given me a problem here Saige, not that there aren't constant ones anyway."

"Yeah, ain't it true – and so many discoveries about our past and us. I really wonder what this Earth looks like, or maybe looked like. I mean, after these people being informed that there was a war on, and since then, there has been no communication, no contact, no nothing and that isn't good in my way of thinking. And only a couple of things come to mind when I think about it. Either the Earth was destroyed, or the records that we are here were lost. And after seeing how this place operates, in my mind it would be the former before the latter. But again with so little to go on who can really say what happened."

Shaking his head Stone said, "Not me, I mean just a short time ago I was happy and dumb in my ignorance. You know, working in the compound and thinking just about learning what I could. And now that life seems like a dream, unreal, like it never happened, and now this present life being the real one. Oh just an FYI here, while I have been exploring this place I can see where the first section was built, and then over

time others added to it. Most of it looks like a common plan —
prefab would be my guess. In fact I would say that if our people were on other planets in other solar systems then these are
probably what they lived and worked in."

"Makes sense I guess. It would make it easier to transport,
or build, or however they did it, if all the pieces were made to
fit together with minimal effort. I mean, could you imagine
having to build here in this hidden valley by scratch?"

"Not really", Stone responded. "But some of the stuff outside is actually native. So I guess that they were here a long
time. I mean think of the work that went into redirecting that
small river into this valley. Hey I have a question. Have any
of us figured out where it goes once it leaves the facility? I
mean it falls over the cliffs into that large pond where it is
used. But there is no way that we could be using all of that
water coming into this valley, and during the spring melt there
probably is much more and yet the level on that pond never
changes."

"No, never really thought about it, but it's a very good
question. So what does that panel over there do?" Saige asked
as he pointed to a small panel that sat by itself in one of the
corners of the room. "By the way the reason I'm trying to figure this out is because of something Seve said to me. I have
him researching it right now, but your question makes me
wonder if this is where that water might be going after leaving
the main facility."

"What the heck are you talking about Saige?"

"Sorry, Seve suggested that one of the ways that our ancestors probably contacted the primitives, to get up close and
personal, was to become traders, which meant that they would
have to have pack animals somewhere, and thusly where the

water is going. So I figured that if they did, these animals would have to be close by, and probably were taken care of by the automated equipment or systems. So I thought that these animals would be on a lower priority circuit, thusly why I had you come here to help and see if we could find one."

"You don't think that they would just have haggled for them do you? It would be easier than trying to keep your own herd."

"True . . . but there are some other considerations that would make sense in keeping their own herd. For example, they could, as we did before we found this place, use the hides to make clothing that would match what the primitives wear, they could provide meat to supplement the vegetables that the hydroponics section produces. From what I have seen so far there are no replicators for foodstuff. Just those large ones we found in the maintenance section."

"True," Stone responded, "but while all of that could be a fact, we really have no proof yet."

"I know, but we really haven't been here long enough to even do a cursory search of the records, let alone a complete one. I just think, from my own point of view, and I realize that we are talking about a great distance of time between when they were in this facility, and now, that it really is the easiest way."

Stone had moved over to the questioned panel and studied it for a moment. "I don't know. There really is very little here – nothing labeled, of course that's not a surprise since most of the stuff in here wasn't labeled, and really only this dial." Looking closer at it he could see that it had different graduations marked outside of the dial itself. A closer inspection revealed a white mark on the dial nob, which corresponded to one on the markings outside of the dial. "I wonder . . ." Stone reached down and turned it to the next mark on the panel, and turned to Saige and asked. "Did that do anything?"

Saige had been watching Stone and quickly turned back to the monitors and was silent for a moment. "Stone come here and look. I think you found it, but look at what's on the monitors right now."

Stone came over and was surprised to find that now they were watching the base of the mountains and all of the approaches. Again like the other view that showed the direct approach to the facility where there were more cameras than monitors, two of them rotated images. On one of the areas they could see hunters working the herds. "Let me try a different setting and see what we get", he said excitedly. But before they could, the monitors changed their views. "Wait . . . what's happening here?" They both watched as the monitors shifted their views with one automatically taking over the views of the priority circuit and then another taking over the views of the secondary circuit they had just opened. The rest of the monitors went blank as if waiting for something. Both Stone and Saige looked at each other surprised by what had just happened.

"Stone, let's put it back in the first position and see if things go back to the way they were. I'd hate to lose this because of something we did."

Nodding, Stone had to agree. He then turned the nob back, and in a short time all the monitors were back to the way they were before. "That's a relief. So it looks like, at least from the first experiment here that each position changes how the monitors work and what they then receive. Okay, do you want to try the other positions on this switch to see what is here?"

"I guess, now that we have confirmed that once we reset it back to the original position that it works like it did when we got here – yeah go ahead." Stone switched back to the previous setting that they had just tried, waiting, while the monitors adjusted once again, to the new command. Once there, he moved it to the third position. Here the two monitors that sat in front of the chairs showed signs of picking up something, and what they presented was a complete and unexpected surprise. "Can this be real?"

"You're asking me? Come on here, how would I know?" Stone responded. They both stared at the two monitors as the images changed. "It surely does look like it's coming from above our world, but look at the quality of those images, and look there; you can actually see a really large herd on the move. This has to be real."

In awe Saige just stared at the images. There was no doubt that they had to be coming from above their world. It meant that their ancestors had placed these cameras in orbit, and from the views they were seeing it had to be an orbit that kept them in the same location monitoring a large swath of the planet's surface. To see their world from space made them appreciate the beauty of their world, well, their world now, since they knew that they originally were from somewhere else. "I wonder what our home world looked like from this type of a view." Saige asked. "I've never really seen anything like this and it really is beautiful."

When Stone had placed the switch in the third position another panel lit up that sat between the two monitors. They both looked at this panel that until now had never been active, and saw that there were twelve active switches, and on either side was a small stick like device that they all had played with but until now, seemed to serve no function. Again looking at each other both seeing the same questioning look, Stone asked. "Okay, now what?" He could see Saige just shaking his head and shrugging.

"I guess we should try one of the buttons that just lit up on this panel, and since you've been the one to discover this, I'll let you do the honors, Stone."

Not sure it was such an honor since they were treading unknown territory here he hesitated, then reaching a decision shrugged, and pushed the first button and immediately both monitors settled on only one image from above. Saige then reached for that stick that had been standing next to the panel, and there were two, one on each side, and moved it. Immediately the image moved in closer to the surface, and as he continued to move it, it continued to get closer. It almost felt like they were falling towards the ground from a great height. He quickly let loose thinking that he might be bringing something down on them since the image they ended up with was of the mountains where this facility was located. But once he released it the image returned to its original view. "What the heck was that? I mean, you did see that didn't you, Stone?"

"Yeah I saw it, and like you I thought, what did we just do? Did we bring something out of the skies that was going to fall on us? But when you released it everything returned so I'm thinking that somehow it, whatever it is, doesn't move, but enlarges the area its viewing so that one can get a closer look at something that it can see. Let me try the one I have on this side and see what it does." Stone pushed a different button then moved his stick and the image changed location. This apparently let the operator shift views, and so between the two sticks they could bring an image in closer and then look around. "Why not use your stick again and I'll see if this one can change the angle of our view." So Saige pushed the stick again and brought the image in closer to the surface. Then Stone moved his and indeed it changed the perspective. It allowed them the freedom of searching a complete area that was under the view of this camera, wherever it was located. Again once they released the sticks the image returned to the original position. Now both were excited with the prospect of what these images could do for them. They looked at each other and both began to speak, stopped, and then laughed. "Go ahead Saige, I think we just came to the same conclusion."

Smiling Saige said, "Probably. But before we jump to any conclusions let's try some of the other buttons." Which is exactly what they did, and each provided a different view of their world. "This is great! I think we can use these to find out where this alliance is, and it will provide a great way to monitor any of us once we really learn how to use this tool. Is there any more settings on that nob?"

Stone turned back to the original nob and then said. "Only one more, but I really don't know what would be left since what we just viewed kind of covers everything."

"True, but try it anyway." Stone set it to the last position, and immediately images of areas around the facility that normally didn't show up on the priority channel came into view. As they watched the images flow by one of them showed a meadow with a herd in it. "I wonder . . ."

"Wonder what Saige?" As the new images continued to flash by on the monitors seeing areas they had never witnessed before.

"I bet you that scene we just saw is the herd we have been looking for . . . Now if we can only figure out where it is."

"I don't know if there is a way to lock on just one image yet, when they just rotate like they are now. There, it came around again. Nothing about it looks familiar to me, not that I know whole heck of a lot about these mountains yet. This range is huge and I can see why our ancestors would have picked it. It's a place where it would be easy to hide something so it never could be found, and with all the natural caves, caverns and such, it's an ideal place to use for exactly what they used it for, hiding this facility."

As they watched, the images continued to rotate, Saige said, "It really cannot be too far away. They'd need access to it from here, and we really don't have any idea yet how many teams they would have sent out. But again looking at the size of this facility, and the number of different tribes or clans that are out there I bet there would have to be many teams. And I would guess that a team was a minimum of two – one that would go in, and then one would monitor the situation from a safe distance. You know kind of like how we were doing it before the city fell. And since we now know that there never had been plans on staying here, I suspect that very little has changed. And the way we have been doing it probably came from our ancestors originally."

* * *

That night at the group gathering and meeting both Stone and Saige went over what they had discovered, with Seve and Sabryn adding to what they had researched and discovered. But the discovery of being able to see their world from space excited most of the team and they wanted to see it for themselves. So after they finished with the meeting they all filed into the small security office where with all of them there, there was barely standing room. Then Stone and Saige demonstrated what they had found and how it all worked. He had Stone also go to the last position so that the other members could see the secondary areas that could be monitored from the security office, and had asked the rest if they had recognized the area where the herd animals appeared to be. Unfortunately no one did, so the location was still a mystery. Then each member wanted to try the new settings and as the night continued to advance, eventually one by one they left until only the one who had the duty there tonight remained, and for the first shift that would be Staven.

Saige now undressed and ready for bed talked with Seirra who was already in bed. Breathing out heavily he asked. "What do you think about what was located today?"

She was silent for a moment and then said, "I think we have much to learn about whom we really are, and that goes double for who our ancestors were. Now come to bed, I need you close to me tonight. It has been a surprising day."

"Surprising? How so?" He asked as he continued to sit on the edge of the bed.

Shaking her head she said tiredly. "Oh come on Saige. It made sense that they had security set up to monitor everything close to this facility. But to have set up everything else that we've seen took some time and effort, let alone the cost. And then to do whatever they did to be able to see the world from space. All these things were unknown to us, and in my mind unexpected. Think about it Saige, if we knew that we could see any part of this world from space, don't you think we could have had a better warning that our cities were going to be attacked like they were? I mean we're beginning to have a larger mystery here as to why none of this was known by the cities or the ones in charge. You'd of thought that this information would've been there somewhere in all of them . . . Yet, not a word, not a hint, just nothing. Now enough of this, come to me now would you?"

Her questions were thought provoking, but those would have to wait, as he then climbed into bed and got really close to Seirra.

* * *

After a communal breakfast the orders of the day were quite simple. Find out where this other area could be. The research that Seve and Sabryn had performed the day before had really turned up nothing new as far as the location of the husbandry area. They were able to read many of the field notes left by the researchers, and the mention of going and picking up an animal as they prepared for the next portion of their research. But for the ones who had written these notes the area was a known. And from the tone of the notes the area wasn't too far away. With time moving much too fast, and not really knowing how many other cities had been located by the primitives, and then attacked, they needed to move. There, of course, was still much that needed to be done. They really wanted to find a way they could return the favor to the alliance that had formed. It now was obvious, either they survive, or perish as a people. And they wanted the former not the latter. Yes, if all the cities were lost then their small group might, and that was a slight chance, survive and be able to begin to build again. But with only ten of them would it be enough variety in the gene pool to avoid genetic problems? As this was not their field of expertise, none of them could truly say.

Staven, Starr, Seve, and Sabryn would search the main facility to cover areas they had not searched before. With Saar and Seirra working the Security office, at least through the morning to early afternoon, Stone and Sorrel would continue their search of the large cavern, which they now knew as the spaceport, where the shuttles would bring in supplies and take out the research data and whatever other items that were slated to be returned. Saige and Shellian, because they had been trained as a team, would work the valley itself. This was to be the most thorough search of the facility they had made to date. And yes, while there were both maps and schematics of the facility, not every area was properly represented. The maps were more a fire or emergency evacuation plan, than a detailed layout. Again, they suspected that, somewhere within the computers that information existed, but so far none of them could find it. They also suspected that the layout was something that was commonly used throughout any of the areas where their people needed to set up both a working and living area. It only made sense to do it this way. By using a modular system, then all that would have to be done beyond this would be the standard stuff like water, waste disposal, and foundation, and there was even a possibility that only leveling of the ground may have been required. Yet from what they had seen so far, these units were also built to last. Of course the maintenance bots could have something to do with that. Yet they also sensed that once a project had been completed that these units could then be pulled out, serviced, and placed in storage or sent out for use somewhere else.

As Saige and Shellian worked the valley Saige asked, "Shell', how's it going with you and doc? I mean with it as busy as it is we haven't had much of a chance to just talk, other than business I mean."

"It has been crazy hasn't it? And here we are now in summer, although I have to admit that summer here in the mountains is more like a cool spring day down below – and it rains a lot too. I think even with the heat I prefer the lowlands where we came from. But to answer your question we are quite happy. Of course it would be a better situation if we didn't have to deal with the possible extinction of us."

Stopping by the man-made pond, and picking up a small flat stone Saige skipped across the water until it sank out of sight. Then taking a deep breath he said. "Yeah, there's always that. We have Saar and Seirra trying to locate the base where the alliance is working. And if they don't find it, then the rest of us will continue to use the surveillance system until we do. But right now I still haven't a real idea how we are going to be able to stop or break up this alliance with so few of us. I know that everyone is trying to come up with something that will work. I suspect that we will only get one chance at this. So whatever it is that we do it has to work the first time and be totally successful."

"Gee, you don't want much," she said as she laughed, "but you are right. We are not going to get a second chance." Then smiling Shellian said. "No pressure here. We must pass this class with a perfect score, and tell me Saige, how many classes that we have taken over time have we've passed with a perfect score? I was good in some of them – actually great in one or two, but perfect, never happened." *But what choice do we have? Our people are out there dying, and they really don't have a clue. This alliance has been successful because they haven't let anybody escape.* She thought. *Well until we did, and right now we are almost useless anyway.* After this brief stop, both left the pond to continue their search of the valley floor for something that may have been overlooked or missed.

* * *

"This cavern is really big," Sorrel said, "and there just has to be better lighting somewhere."

"Probably, but I suspect that there is really only lighting in the work areas. As you said this place is huge. And if they only used a portion of it why light the whole thing? I know that they had portable lights, but none of them work now, and none of us are really good at working those industrial replicators, so we haven't figured out how to make new ones. So I guess we just will have to search in this gloom. At least there is some lighting; otherwise I suspect that it would be pitch dark in here."

"Yeah that's probably true, but wouldn't you think that there would be some type of emergency lighting just in case they had to come here? I mean even though there's a little light here; it's so dim that one could easily get hurt by stumbling over, or into something that can't be seen." *Yeah I know you mentioned the portable lights they could carry, but there has to be something better than that.* "I guess all we can be is careful. I don't need something else to happen to me. That last time I was close to death, and I for one do not want to repeat it."

"How much do you remember of that anyway? I've meant to ask but, something always came up or I would forget. But if you don't want to talk about it that's okay too."

"I really haven't thought about it a whole lot. I remember leaving our first cave, sneaking out without anything. I felt that it would be too dangerous to try and steal something to help. I knew where the next cave was and headed for that one.

But by the time I reached it I was weak and I could feel a fever coming on. I had no choice once I got there but to continue. I was desperate. I couldn't go back and I didn't know where you guys had gone. Sometime after I left that cave the fever hit and really don't remember much of anything – just waking up in the infirmary, and being informed that I had lost my baby, and that I was lucky to even be there at all. When I found that I had lost the baby I was devastated and really didn't want to live. Well, from there you know the rest." She shrugged before continuing. "I don't know, maybe not remembering is the mind's way of protecting us. But that's the best I can do, and who knows, maybe later more of it will come back. But at the same time, it may never."

Looking down at the dirt floor he thought once again. *She's really is a strong woman. And maybe it is good that she doesn't remember. I know from what Saar stated, she had almost died at least three times, but something in her, some hidden strength kept her going, and now I find that I have grown close to her. So I for one am glad she is alive.* "You're right it's probably a good thing, a way for someone to protect themselves. After all if you don't recall anything, it can't come back to haunt you and give you trouble later on." They continued on quiet both in their own thoughts walking carefully through the twilight that the cave provided. As they proceeded the cave began to narrow, and they finally located the far wall. From there they moved along it briefly in both directions finding nothing to tell them that it went any further, they turned around and began to retreat back but then stopped. Out of the corner of their eyes they caught what looked to be another dim light in the distance off to their right. It was so dim that at first they were not sure if they had indeed seen anything. It might even be a crack admitting sunlight from the outside. Turning to Sorrel, Stone asked, "Well, what do you think? Should we try and find the source of that light I think we are seeing, or just head back?"

"We were sent out to try and find out more, so I guess we should just go ahead and look. I suspect that all we will find is a crack and its light from outside. But if we don't check it then I guess we really haven't done our job," She looked down in that direction, "I must admit that it's pretty dark in that direction and it would be easy just to skip it."

"My thoughts also – okay then we'll go do it, but very carefully." With hands on the wall they headed in the direction of the dim distant light. Shortly the wall on their left closed in and they found themselves in a narrow passageway that if arm in arm they could reach out and touch both walls. Still it was close to pitch black as it could be with only the dim light ahead of them in the distance. At first it appeared to be receding from them, but that was impossible so it had to be an illusion, a trick of the eye. Finally it appeared to brighten a little, but not enough to light their way, so they continued their careful approach. Then her hand brushed against something and instantly the area they were in lit up, temporarily blinding them. "Ouch! That's really bright! What did you do Sorrel?"

With her eyes screwed tightly closed and watering from the change in light, she whispered. "I really don't know. But I can't open my eyes yet, it's just too bright."

"Know what you mean." He then found that he could slowly open his eyes without it hurting too much, and finally they adjusted to the brightness, and he breathed out a sigh of relief. "That's better. Now let's see what happened." Turning around and looking back from the direction they had just traveled he could see that the passageway they had just entered in the twilight was now lit. "I wonder where the switch is on the other side, since it only makes sense that there would be more than one. It would suck to have to come all the way here in the dark just to turn on the lighting."

"True. Look there it is, a panel built into the wall here. It's what I must have put my hand on. And look ahead of us, doesn't that look like a door?"

Before going to that closed door, Stone retreated to where they left the cavern and had entered the passage, he then said. "Sorrel come here, you've got to see this." She had briefly remained behind as he had retraced his steps not knowing exactly what he was trying to do. She then joined him and then shook her head. If they could have found the companion switch to the one she had accidentally found, then coming to this side passage would have been a breeze. On the floor of the cavern was a double row of lights shining up from the ground towards the hidden ceiling above. The lights formed a path that led directly across the cavern floor to where the bright lights in the passageway were presently shining. As she looked closer she could see that some of them were partially buried under the loose soil that made up the cavern's floor. "That would have been nice if we had found the other switch that's for sure. But now I am wondering where that door leads?"

Shrugging and smiling he said, "You women, always curious. I guess we should go and find out, now that we can see everything. Lead on, oh lady of mine." He then bowed to her and motioned with his hands for her to lead. She giggled slightly and took the lead back into the passage, with a stately walk. They both arrived at the door at the same time, as there was room enough for two to walk abreast and still be comfortable. Looking at the walls as they proceeded towards the closed door Stone said. "You know this looks like it was widened. I suspect that the original passage was a steam vent from this old volcano, but there definitely are signs of additional work here and see as we approach the door the area has been enclosed and constructed so that this ending wall and door would fit." Shaking his head he thought. *This really is fantastic work. And considering how old it is, it really was built to last. If I didn't know it's age I would have thought that it truly was not that old. Hmmm, I really wonder what other secrets this place holds.* They stood there staring at the door not sure if they really wanted to open it or not, but finally Stone reached out, turned the handle and opened the door.

* * *

"You know Seirra, I can't get used to this feeling that I'm falling every time we adjust our views from wherever these things are located. It almost makes me ill with; I guess you could call it motion sickness. And I swear whatever this is, that it is falling out of the sky – yet . . . We've done this a lot and they're still there. So logically I know that they remain wherever they are. And this still makes me wonder what happened in the cities so that they forgot about this. I mean we all have seen the records here and now know the truth. But it has been so skewed in the cities and the way it is taught in the learning centers, that none of the truth is known." Saar complained.

Smiling at him for his minor complaints, she really couldn't blame him for his thoughts. And she had to agree that when they used these small sticks to adjust their view, it really did feel like she was falling. But what a tool, what a view, and it really showed her the beauty that this world had, albeit somewhere above this world. She'd been dazzled by the shear variety that she'd been shown. And also the sheer size of their world – well not their world even though they had lived here for a few generations – really was a surprise. It was not surprising then that they had yet to find out where the alliance was headquartered. She felt that they could probably be here for days upon days and do nothing but search and barely touch all that was being revealed to them. "Well Saar, I know what you mean. It does take some getting used to that's for sure. Hey, it surely is a great view. This world is just gorgeous, I never realized that at all, and so large. I haven't even begun to recognize everything we've spotted so far. There has to be a better way of doing this. Not that I'm complaining, but we cannot even be sure at this point where we are looking. And I am worried about our people who still are living in whatever cities that haven't been located by the primitives, and of course for the ones who have been captured, and probably been made slaves or worse."

"Yeah, I know, but there's really little we can do. After all, considering what this alliance has accomplished so far, well whoever is in charge has successfully gathered many of the tribes and so far has been able to hold them together, has accomplished. We, who now know, what's going on, well, you can count on the fingers of your two hands of those who know, and we are supposed to defeat that? I think the odds here are a little one sided, don't you think?"

Looking down at the floor and then at him Seirra said. "Yeah, I know all of that. But what can we do? I mean, somewhere here we have to find an answer. We don't know what happened to our own people. I am meaning the ones from our own home world, and it they were annihilated, wiped out, then, as far as we know, we are all that's left. So somehow we've got to find a way to break this alliance, and finding it is the first step. So I guess instead of talking about it we should be a little more diligent and at least locate the area they are working from. Then we can decide what to do from there. I wonder if any of the other teams have found anything as of yet?" She glanced once again at the screen that was in front of her and noticed the small letters and numbers that were displayed at the bottom of the screen. "Saar?"

"Yes Seirra, what is it?" He asked quietly as he studied the images on his screen. He had to admit that she had been right. This world was much larger and varied than he ever imagined. When this search had started he thought it would be a simple thing. Since they could see from the sky it should be a snap to just see the gathered tribes. But he had been proven wrong. And all of them had been going over and over the images produced so far with no apparent success.

"Has anyone figured out what these letters and numbers mean yet?" She asked.

"Not that I have heard of. In fact someone guessed that it might just be a way to tell you, you were looking at a different image from wherever they are coming from – in space I guess. Why? Is there something about them that seems important? Or are they in your way, because if they are, I've been shown a way that you can remove them, or make them larger or smaller."

Shaking her head she said. "No, no that's not it. They are not causing me any issue at all. It's just that there has to be a reason that our ancestors put them here, and I feel it's not something to do with which view we are seeing. Look, if I shift the view to a different portion of this world from the area I am looking, then numbers change. So it has to be something more than just a way to identify the view we are seeing."

"Ah, I see what you mean. But what it means I really have no idea. Maybe it's something you can bring up tonight when we get together. It could be that one of the others has some idea, and right now I think I'm going to get us something to eat. Be right back, we can eat here while we continue our search." He then pushed back his chair got up and headed out the door. On his way out he asked. "Is there anything special you would like me to bring back?"

Without turning around and continuing her search she said absently. "No, no not really . . . surprise me."

* * *

Sabryn and Star, because of their children, worked the facility around the areas of family living and schooling, while Staven and Seve concentrated on the areas that dealt with maintenance, and operation. Not that there would be a true chance of finding the area where the pack animals were kept, but there could easily be a reference to, or an alternate way, that could be located somewhere within the facility. Part of the reason for the search in these areas was to be able to say that they would have searched everything and covered every corner once they finished. And if in the end they came up empty, then there was a good chance that this idea of an alternate entrance was incorrect. "Whew! I think you just loaded your pants little one." Star stated. "I guess we need to take a break here and change your pants." Fortunately at the time they were close to what they had determined was the daycare area, and immediately headed that way. While there, Sabryn decided she would check her daughter's diaper also. It probably would be a good time to feed them and put both down for a nap anyway. One of them would remain with the children and the other would move over to the terminals in the schoolroom and at least continue to search the files. "So Star, is everything going okay with you and Staven?"

"Yeah, no complaints. He helps where he can, but is a bit clumsy around the baby. But he'll get better. Like all things it just takes practice – After all these things do not come with instructions. So it's an on-the-job training type of thing. And as you know if you get it wrong, the boss here will let you know in no uncertain terms."

Laughing she had to agree. If her child did not like what was going on she would let them know her displeasure immediately. "It's funny how that works. You would think that because we are the parents that we would be the ones in charge. And that's so far from the truth. Okay that's done. I guess I'll feed her now and then put her down, stay long enough to see her asleep, and then go do the searching – actually if both of them go to sleep, then we could prop this door open and both of us could work. How does that sound?"

"Like a good idea to me. But we'll see if he will go down. At times it just seems like all he wants to do is go." Starr responded, "But it doesn't allow me to do much when he's like that."

* * *

Staven was covered in the grime from the pump house. Shaking his head he found that after complete search, he determined there was just the one door and that was it. After crawling through the numerous pipes, pumps, unknown equipment and searching all of the hidden areas, he had come up empty – other than the fact that he had skinned a knuckle or two from slipping and falling. He hoped that Seve had better luck, and he thought that he had better join him since the area he was searching was both the electric and steam room, separate of course since electricity and water did not mix. One thing for sure it was easy to tell that the whole thing was modular in design. It would have made it very easy to set up, and to repair if it needed to be. And he was sure that this probably had been repaired a number of times over the thousands of annuals that it sat here empty. He knew that after the two of them finished here, they would move on to the maintenance section, but between the two areas they would head back in for a bite to eat, before continuing. So far nothing had been found to indicate a way to the pack animals, if there were any at all.

Seve, once he had entered the electric room, just shook his head. This place was huge, and while the task was daunting, it wouldn't get done if he just stood there looking at it. He knew that as soon as Staven finished in the smaller pump house that he would join him. With that in mind, he thought that probably the best thing for him to do was to either work the steam room, which provided heat and air conditioning to the whole facility, and provided the push for the turbines, or to concentrate on the electrical. Obviously for safety's sake the two were separated, but since the steam room required a substantial power source it was only smart to locate it close to the generators. He knew that the generators used a number of sources including solar, water, and yes even the steam that was generated in the next room. It also used materials that could not be recycled, and vented any of the smoke, which was almost invisible, out through one of the many chimneys that the extinct volcanoes had created in the distant past, effectively hiding its location. In his hand he had a schematic of the room, and there were numerous doors marked, but not all of them were identified as to what they were or where they led. Which probably meant that whoever worked here was familiar with this standard layout and did not require a full labeling.

Thinking about it he decided that he would work the steam room because it was smaller. He headed off that way, with his reasoning being that it was much smaller of an area, not really much larger than the pump house – he should be finished in about the same time as Staven. Then when Staven showed up from his search of the pump house they could both work the electrical room and all of the doors. He opened the door into the steam room and immediately felt a blast of hot damp air. Shaking his head he thought. *It surely is named right. I really would not want to be assigned this section if I had been here back then.* He thought that most likely the bots handled most of the work anyway, yet moisture was the enemy of the bots, so he couldn't be sure. But at the same time, felt that it had to be inspected and confirmed that there were no problems. So even if the previous owners had to come here only once a day to confirm things were okay, it would still have been a miserable visit. Looking through a small steam cloud that appeared to be venting, he saw the entrance to the small operations center. It sat higher up and had what appeared to be windows that overlooked the entire facility. He worked his way there, climbed the metal ladder to a small platform that led to the door. Opening the door and entering into the control room he saw a panel that allowed the operators to manually override any portion, and to completely shut it down if some emergency required it. There he found on the back wall a drawing that showed the emergency evacuation routes out of the facility with this area highlighted. It was really hot and humid here and he wondered how and why this equipment didn't rust. After all, with the constant attack of heat and high moisture, it should show signs of rust and damage. Yet from the condition of everything there, it could have been placed there yesterday, and not the thousands of years in the past that he knew was fact. *What did they construct this stuff out of? While I know that something like this isn't my specialty back in the city, I don't think our stuff held up nearly as well as this.* Shaking his head at these thoughts he continued to look around the small room. *I guess even though we thought we were advanced, what this place has shown me so far, is that we have lost some of that knowledge that this place has demonstrated so competently, and it has been shown by the way we have found things. So much of what we don't understand our ancestors took for granted . . . and how do I know that? Because they did not label something, because it was common knowledge, so it did not require labeling, that's how.* "This isn't getting this place searched. I guess I should just use this evacuation sheet and check it against the doors it has people leaving by." He said quietly to himself.

He took out a small notebook and drew a rough copy of the emergency evacuation plan and then headed back off the ledge to the floor and in among the pipes, heat, humidity, and steam and then looked at the floor. He, to his surprise, found that the floor had large markings on them. He followed one around the corner and found a large arrow painted on the floor with the words emergency evacuation written within the arrow. Shrugging he thought, *why not*, and headed in the direction the arrow pointed.

* * *

Later with an unsuccessful search of the steam room, he met up with Seve and they first went to the showers to clean up, and then headed to the cafeteria to grab a bite to eat before both of them searched the electric room. When they entered the cafeteria by chance they found Starr and Sabryn had arrived just ahead of them. "What a surprise." Seve said, and Staven couldn't agree more. So far the day for them had been unsuccessful, but not completely, since they now knew more about the facility, its layout, and construction. It once again, gave them insight into their distant ancestors and how they thought, lived and worked.

* * *

"So Stone, what do you think? Do we continue, or do we take a break and get some food?" Both of them were standing in front of the closed door. Neither had ventured, as of yet, to open it and see what lay on the other side.

Taking a deep breath, Stone had to admit that he was getting hungry, but at the same time curiosity was driving him forward. "I guess what we can do is open it and see what's there, then before we go past this point, go back and get something to eat. That will leave most of the afternoon for us to continue our exploring. And I think that we need to locate the switch on the other side so that we aren't stumbling around in this semi-darkness. There has to be one. Now I wonder if they are timed or motion sensitive – which could be the case also, since that way, once a master switch was thrown, anybody walking in this direction would turn the lighting on. And since this cavern is part of the natural landscape here, it would have been something that would have been added at a later time – I'm speaking of the work on this steam vent or lava tube, and possibly what's on the other side of these doors." He paused knowing that he was delaying, as he shook his head. "Let's just do it." He reached for the handle and gave it a twist. At first nothing happened, and then he realized that he had been pushing on the door, so he then pulled and it opened. Looking through the now open door they could see what looked to be a small lighted room. They entered looking around. On the right wall they found another door and this one had a small glass insert which allowed one to look inside. Peering through, they could see steps heading up and out of sight.

The wall opposite of the door they had entered through was solid. But the left wall had two double doors, which had no handles. Between them was a small panel, which had two buttons on it, the top with an arrow pointing up and the bottom, which just said basement. But that bottom button also required some type of key for access. "I wonder what's down there, if anything." Sorrel said, then continued, "Probably not important anyway, but what does this other one do?" As she asked she reached out and pressed it with her finger. Both of them jumped as both sets of the closed doors opened revealing another small room in each. Again both were frozen in position with indecision as to what they should do. In that time of delay both doors closed again. They both looked at each other and Stone asked. "Now what was that all about?" In the cities that they had grown up in, all the buildings were single story, and the ones that had basements used stairs to access those areas. This was something they had yet to encounter. "Tell you what, before we go any further let's get some food in our bellies, and think about this."

"Works for me," Sorrel said. She was no more eager to go into a small room that had no apparent exit than Stone was. And once the doors closed and they were inside could they then get out, or was it a trap of some kind? They turned back to the door they had entered this room through, opened it, and saw that once again it was dark. "I guess that confirms that these lights are at least on a timer. Do you remember where that switch that you hit was located Sorrel?"

She nodded her head and then stepped out into the passage. As soon as she did the lights came back on. "Looks to be motion sensitive. So I guess the switch I accidentally found was a master switch. Still like you, I think there has to be one on the other side somewhere. But maybe it isn't important now. Shall we go eat something then?"

As they entered the cafeteria they ran into the four who were searching the facility directly. They were well on the way to devouring their meal when Seve looked up as they entered and asked. "How's your search going so far? We've been unsuccessful overall."

"Let us grab something then we'll fill you in to what we've found so far, and maybe it's something that will help – don't know really at this time, but ran into something strange, or at least different." He paused there and then went and grabbed a plate of food for both himself and Sorrel. She had gone to get them drinks, and then joined the others at one of the larger tables. Once they sat down Stone then continued, "First off let me say that that cavern is really huge. From what I can determine it's mostly natural. I really wouldn't have wanted to be here when this volcano let loose. It's no surprise the primitives fear these mountains. Anything close would have been wiped out, and the amount of smoke and ash this thing had to put into the air would have put the fear of the gods' anger in such a people. And with no lights, other than a few to keep it from being totally dark, it was difficult just to walk across the floor, let alone see anything. But when we got to the other side" . . . he then went on to explain what they had found and that before continuing they needed to eat.

"Wow, that's more than any of us has been able to find so far." Staven said. "Are you planning on going into one of those small rooms, or what?"

"No don't think so right now. I think instead we'll just climb those stairs. I suspect like the ladders we used to first enter here, that it is another way in and out of this place. Once we check it out, then tonight like the rest of you we will fill everyone in. Then with more of us we can figure out what those two small rooms are all about."

* * *

"So what do you think Sorrel? Should we see what those small rooms are all about – you know if one of us stays on the outside and one of going inside, or should we just take the stairs?"

"Well, I don't know about you, but the stairs are something I know about. This other thing I don't. So until I know more I think I'll stick with the stairs, thank you."

Laughing lightly Stone said. "You know what; I have to agree with you. Maybe later." He then bowed and swept his arms in the direction of the door that led to the stairs and asked. "Shall we?" Smiling she curtsied and together they entered the stairway. "I think we'll take it to the top to see where these things end, and then explore the different exits as we come back down. How does that sound to you?"

"Works for me," Sorrel responded. They looked up and could see that it appeared that the stairs went quite a ways up. So they began the ascent. It appeared that at each level the stairs would switch back and make the rise and that it took one switch back to make what they guessed was a floor. After ten such switchbacks they came to a platform and another closed door. On the way up they had really only passed two others and they guessed that some of the area was no more than the walls of the natural cave. Catching their breath before opening the one at the top they reached and opened the door, stepped out, and then caught their breath once again. Before them was a panorama of both the mountains and views that appeared to just go on forever. Here, the area had been worked and some type of material laid that was impervious to destruction by nature. They saw tables, chairs, and some additional sealed cabinets similar to the ones they had found in the facility. Plus there appeared to be facilities for cooking meals, a small stage, and other items that they did not immediately recognize at the moment. The next thing they noticed was that there was a wall around this area that probably kept anyone, such as the primitives, seeing into this place. "Wow, this is beautiful!" Sorrel exclaimed. "And chilly after the cavern!"

Shaking his head and smiling Stone said. "If you want me to disagree with you it's not going to happen. And this place is huge. It looks like most of everyone who worked and lived here could be up here at the same time and it's invisible to the rest of the world. And it would give the support staff some place to go to get outside for a while. I bet now that we've found this place that there are others. Some place where the children could run around and play that let them burn off all that excess energy they all seem to have." They walked around quietly and inspected things as they went. Close to where they had emerged they found a double set of double doors built into the side of the rock face that was similar to the ones with the two rooms at the bottom. And here between them was a single button with an arrow pointing down. With a look of curiosity on his face Stone speaking low said. "I wonder . . ."

Looking up at him she asked. "Wonder what?"

At this point he reached out and pressed the button, which immediately lit up, and then both of them felt and heard a slight rumbling which slowly got louder. It stopped suddenly and there was a loud ding, followed briefly by a second one, both unexpected sounds making them jump because of the silence that had surrounded them. Looking up above the closed doors a light showed and suddenly the doors opened which made them jump again. And before them were the same two rooms they had witnessed at the ground floor. Frozen for a moment, Stone then started to enter one of the rooms, and as he did the door began to close on him. Instinctively he reached out to block it and found that as soon as he put pressure on it the door reopened. After a few seconds with him standing partly inside the door attempted to close again and once again it reopened when he pressed on it. "I guess we can say that whatever these things are, you can't accidentally get crushed by them. And I guess that would make sense by what we have found so far. Hey let's have you stand here and you can block the door and I'll check it out." And while they had been involved with the one side, the other set of double doors had closed.

Shaking her head, she said, "You're not going to get me to do that. Besides I'm smaller, let me get by you and I'll check it out." And without waiting for him to answer or argue she pushed past him and entered the room. First thing she noticed were the handrails, which were located on three of the walls, and then she turned to face Stone and then a panel caught her eye. "What's this?" With the way that Stone had been blocking the door his back had been to that side and he leaned around to see what she was looking at, lost his balance and fell inside the room with her. The doors immediately closed behind him and both of them were now inside the closed room. For a moment they looked at each other and then fought a little bit of panic and then she said. "Now you've done it, we are both inside of this thing, and now what?"

"I don't know, but at least it's lit. Well now that we are in here, let's look at this panel that you were pointing out to me. She reached down and helped him off the floor where he had landed when he fell inside. "Look this has buttons similar to the one we saw outside, and look there are two more one stating doors open, and the other doors closed." He pressed the one for opening the doors and they miraculously opened. He then followed it by pressing the other and the doors closed. Looking at her he said, "At least we aren't trapped in here. And I guess we don't need to panic either." Breathing heavily out and giving his head a slight shake he continued. "Okay then, let's see what this thing is all about now that we have, well, fallen into it."

She laughed and said. "Don't look at me. I wasn't the one who *fell* into it, as you just said. I was just standing here minding my own business when you stumbled in here and the doors closed." They looked around the inside once again and she continued. "I guess you probably could fit oh around twenty to twenty five people in here at a time. And if I remember right the other side was larger. Now why would you want to do that?"

He studied the panel and noticed that the bottom button stated "Ground Floor". So he reached out and pressed it. A number of things happened at the same time – first the button lit up, followed by a small clunking sound and then they could feel themselves descending, as the floor seemed to drop. She screamed in surprise as both of them reached out for the rails. For a moment it appeared that they were falling faster then suddenly it slowed down and came to a stop. As it stopped they looked at each other and she had that look that a mother gives her child when he did something he wasn't supposed to do. Then the doors opened once again and they found themselves in the area where they had first entered. "Wow, it just took us from the top to the bottom and no stairs to climb. Does it work the other way also?" She asked

"It must, as there are only three buttons here, and the one on top just states "View Deck". But the middle just has a number two. So I wonder if that is where that other door that we passed as we climbed the stairs on the way to the top. Well I guess we aren't going to find out unless we try it." He then looked at her and asked. "Would you prefer that we go back to the top, or do you want to see what this other area is like?"

Looking down at the floor for a moment she said. "We do know what the upper area is, and we are here trying to find out all that we can about this place, so I guess we should go there. Not that I haven't had enough surprises for one day." She reached across and pushed the middle button. The doors closed once again. They, at first felt nothing, and then they could tell that this room was ascending back up the way they had just come. But this time the ride was much shorter, they heard that chime again and the doors opened into a room similar to the bottom floor. They quickly stepped out and noticed that again, like the bottom or ground floor, the doorway to the stairs was located directly across from the doors that they had just exited. "At least that's consistent," he said. Looking to the right all he saw was a solid wall, but looking to the left he saw double doors, and then looking back as Sorrel he asked. "Shall we?" She nodded in agreement and both of them headed for the double doors.

* * *

"This electric room is huge, and I think I've confirmed that it uses steam from the steam room to drive these turbines here." Seve, looking around at the sheer size of the room they were in, shook his head. "I bet this is the largest of the modules that they had to bring in. In fact, I'll bet this consists of at least two of the buildings that they used. Then these generators – all four of them, would have been individually delivered. And that steam has to be geothermal. I know that back in the cities they used more solar and wind than what we are seeing here. But it must be based on what is available in the areas where they set up. In fact, now that I think of it, I can see similarities in the structures in the old section of our city, to what I am seeing here. So most likely, they used some of the modules to initially set up the cities. It would make it quick an' dirty."

"That could be true." Staven replied, "But if they had done just that, then why is it that this place appears to be complete and still working? I would have thought that they would have cannibalized this place to build the initial cities, but here it stands."

Again looking around at the large space, Seve shook his head. "I don't know, maybe they used those industrial replicators to produce them. But who knows, maybe it was important that this place continue to operate. After all, it was here that this research team had been placed, so by leaving it here, then if anybody did finally return, they would know that there were survivors, I think."

"I don't know about that." Staven responded. "I mean if I returned here and found it empty then after doing a planetary search I would conclude that the primitives had wiped out everyone."

"That does pose a dilemma doesn't it? How would you let any rescuers know that you were still here, when you knew that it would be necessary to abandon this place? As you just stated, leaving it empty and running would not prove anything one way or the other . . . unless . . ."

Looking closely at Seve, Staven asked, "Unless what? What have you come up with here?" He could see now that something was beginning to excite Seve.

"Look, and I think it's something that we have completely overlooked – if you were going to abandon this place and still at some time in the future hope for rescue, then you would have put something in place that would allow the rescuers to know that you were still here and alive. And not only that, but you also would have put something into place that would allow you to communicate to them from your cities. So I think that this is something we've completely overlooked, which means if I'm right, we can contact the cities from here and warn them. Let's go and find Saige, I think right now this is more important than finding what's here. After all, the remaining cities need to be warned, and as quickly as we can do it.

CHAPTER TWELVE

Eight cities had gone dark. Rumors flew, but there were no hard facts. And while the city of Keahilani was considered the pivot city, the one all communications passed through, the knowledge they presently had wouldn't fill a thimble. One would have thought that by now something would be known, and they could begin to solve the puzzle that had been presented. And while it was not his place of expertise, Keenan knew that somewhere there had to be a reason for this to be happening. Especially since all of the cities that went dark, did so, in the exact same way, and approximately at the same time of day. These facts alone spoke strongly of a correlation, something in common, but for the life of him, he couldn't figure it out. There was just too little known. The one thing that he could lay his finger on was the overall nervousness the permeated the air here. He suspected that it was the same for the rest of the cities. Well, his shift was almost over and soon it would be time to return to his residence. As usual, except when the cities disappeared, all the communications traffic was normal, routine, almost boring in fact. Standing at the railing that overlooked the floor he saw his people preparing to leave their shifts and the replacements waiting quietly to replace them. Sighing deeply he thought, *Yep, another normal day . . . Not that one cannot see the tension that is flowing through everyone, but, other than that, a very normal day.*

* * *

Seve and Staven headed back to the security office. At the moment they couldn't remember which section of the compound that Saige and Shellian were searching. Once there, Seve asked. "Saar, where is Saige right now?"

Looking up from their search he turned around and was silent for a moment. "Has something come up? Have you finished the area you were searching or what?"

Shaking his head no, Seve said, "No. No, but something occurred to us while we were working our area and we need to run it past Saige and Shellian. We feel that it's important enough that we run it past them right now."

Turning back to the equipment, he first looked at Seirra and said. "Seirra continue if you would. I'm going to switch this so that I can locate Saige and Shellian. If they are close enough to one of the speakers then I'll contact them." Then turning back to Seve and Staven he said. "They are searching the grounds, and that would mean that the meeting area would be closest. So why don't the two of you head there, and when we get their attention we will, or I will, send them there." At this point Seve and Staven nodded and headed back out of the security office. "I do hope they find them quickly. And yes I know it can wait, but we really need to be pursuing this, as well as everything else we are doing, and I have a feeling that the place to set such a thing up would be the security office, or the office of the one who had been in charge here. But it just seems like the security office would be the most logical place." Staven commented, as they reached the meeting room and waited the arrival of their leaders.

* * *

"You know Shellian, we've been over the grounds a whole number of times and so far we haven't really found anything new. I mean other than the fact that some of these trees are different, and that small area, where it appears that they used some type of climate control to allow the residents here to cultivate plants that wouldn't normally grow in this climate. I'm sure there are a few things like that that we have over-looked, but nothing on the scale that we are trying to find." They continued their search of the grounds and were heading back towards the main building that Saige had first found when he had fallen into the hidden valley. Shellian couldn't disagree with him. Everything he had said was true, and she was beginning to wonder if what they were trying to locate really existed. *It seemed so plausible at the time. After all, it would have been an easy way to make contact and observe, without raising any suspicions on the part of the primitives.* Shaking her head slightly she continued her thought process. *I would have sworn that our ancestors would have done this. But so far we have no proof at all, other than a brief statement or two saying that it was a viable option.*

"Saige, Shellian, this is Saar. Can you report to the meeting room? Seve and Staven want to discuss something with you, and they felt that it was something that needed to be brought to your attention immediately." Snapped out of her thoughts she asked, "Now what could that be about?" Not re-alizing she had said it she turned to her brother who just shrugged before answering her. "There's no way I'm going to know sis." They picked up the pace since they were heading back in that direction anyway, and in a short time entered the room from the same entrance where he had the first time. Once their eyes adjusted to the dim interior lighting they saw Seve partially sitting on the edge of the table and Staven looking out through the windows. Both turned towards them as they entered the room.

"Okay you two, what's so important that you needed to see us immediately? By some chance did the two of you find something?" Saige asked.

Seve and Staven looked at each other and the Staven said, "Well Seve, it was your idea, go ahead and tell them."

With a slight pause Seve got up off the table edge and said, "Yes, and no. No in the sense that so far in our search we have come up empty. But as we searched the two of us were discussing some things and then from that we realized something."

"Okay, you realized something and what would that something be? I mean we were not privy to your conversation so we really have no idea."

Smiling, and shaking his head Seve said. "Sorry Saige, it's just I was trying to set it up so you could see how we came by this. Anyway, we began to ask ourselves that if our ancestors had to abandon this place, like they did, and then set up the cities, like they did, then they had to have put in place a way for any rescuers to contact them. I mean, think about it. If rescuers found this place abandoned, would they just leave, or would there be something in place that would allow them to know what happened, and then have a way to contact our ancestors from here."

Quiet for a moment as the implications of what Seve just said really sank in, he sat down and put his arms on the table and then leaned forward. "That's an interesting thought Seve. And it makes total sense. But what would they have done? I mean . . . I'm sure that it is something that was standard, but standard for them not for us. Now all we have to do is figure out what that was." He laughed bitterly before continuing. "And since we are far removed from that time, and from what we have discovered here, we know that we have adjusted facts and our societies have changed, and with no known information left, I haven't a clue." Then turning to the others in the room he asked. "Any of you have an idea what they would have set up?" Once again there was silence and he could see that the rest were just as much in the dark as he was. "So in your thinking Seve, did you have some ideas as to where the rescuers might first go if they found this place empty?"

"Yes, that was the easy part. At least once we found out how this place was laid out and how it worked . . ."

"Let's keep the explanation short if you would. After all you've already convinced both of us, and I have to admit that I can kick myself for not thinking about it."

"Sorry Saige, I think either the administrator's office or the security office, and of the two I believe that the security office would be my first choice."

"Again I have to agree with you. So I guess we need to head there, and I know that all of us can't fit in there very well, but we can get a feed from there into this meeting room which allows communications in both directions, so Seve, you and I will go, Shell', you and Staven can monitor from here and give us any ideas and suggestions that need to be addressed." Saige then signaled Seve to precede him out the door and both of them headed directly to the security office. Once there, Saige said, "Saar can you set up a complete feed

to the meeting room? Seve has come up with something critical and we are going to need all of us to figure out the
solution. By the way has anybody had contact with Stone and
Sorrel?"

"Yes." Seve replied, "We met them while eating the midday meal. And they may be on to something. Anyway, they
had found another way, which they thought would lead out of
here, but hadn't had time to explore it yet. I suspect that we
will know much more tonight when they come back. As far as
the rest of us, we've come up empty."

"That may be true, but what you've come up with here,
Seve, may be the most important thing so far. I mean once
you presented it, then it was just obvious. Is that feed set up
yet Saar? Oh, and add the area where Starr and Sabryn are
working, if you please."

"Yup." Then pointing to one of the larger monitors he said.
"See, there they are." And as he said that the ones in the meeting room nodded their heads in response. He pointed to
another one and they could see the women.

"Okay, can all of you hear us in there?" Saige asked.
Again they nodded yes. Smiling for a moment before continuing he said. "Now come on, would one of you please speak so
we can adjust the volume in here."

Laughing, Shellian approached the monitor and said. "No
Saige we figured we would pantomime the whole thing and
make you figure it out. So how's this sound?"

At about the same time Starr whispered. "Sommer is
asleep, so we are going to remain quiet."

Nodding he said, "Fine." Turning back to Saar and Seirra
he said, "I'm going to have Seve repeat to you what he told us,
and I should have thought about it at the time he presented it

to us, and then all of you could have heard. But then again, I had no idea. Seve, if you will?" Then Seve gave a much shortened version of what they had covered in the meeting room.

Seirra then asked. "I wonder if these letters and numbers that keep coming up at the bottom of the screen when we are searching from the sky mean anything."

Looking over her shoulder Saige asked. "What are you talking about Seirra?" She then pointed at the screen she had been studying and said. "Right here, Saige."

He then looked closer and saw what she was pointing at and asked. "Do they stay the same?"

"No silly, if they did that I wouldn't have thought anything about it. If they had never changed, I would have assumed that it was probably some serial number or such that had to do with what we were using, but it changes according to what I am viewing. Now watch and I'll show you." He watched as she changed the view and as she had stated the numbers changed but the letters did not. Seve came over to join him and paused a moment. He had the look of concentration on his face as if he was trying to recall something. "I think we need Sabryn to come in here. She commented that she had found both in the computers and in the administrator's office in hard copy, something similar to this."

Looking up at the other monitor Saige asked, "Sabryn, can you come here now?"

She nodded and tiptoed out of the room and away from the camera, obviously heading to the security office, leaving Starr to watch Sommer.

* * *

"These double doors are really large." Stone commented. "Hmmm, did you look at that other room that moves and see if it might have been the same size or maybe larger than the one we rode?"

"Why do you think that something like that would be important Stone?"

Gesturing with his hands he said. "Look at the size of these doors. I mean there has to be a reason for them to be this big, and the moving room that we just left isn't big enough to require doors this size. So I'm wondering if the other one is larger that's all."

She turned around and pushed the button on the wall that activated the moving rooms and waited until both the sound of the ding and the panel above the doors lit. She stood in front of the one that was to the right of the button and waited while the doors opened. She then peered inside and said. "Yup, this is at least twice the size of the one we were in, and if I am honest, these doors are larger also. So what do you think it means, Stone?"

"My guess is that it's a way to move large things, maybe supplies, or whatever, out through those double doors. So, it could be that where this leads, is a storage area and that would explain the size. But until we actually go through them it's all conjecture – shall we?" He pushed through the doors and found that they were in a small room with a second set of doors similar to the first. But unlike the first set these were not manually operated. Try as they may, the doors would not push open. Looking around Sorrel saw a square silver plate on the wall closest to her. She reached out and pushed it and then the doors swung outward allowing them to pass. Stepping through the doors they found themselves in another tunnel, again, he suspected that originally it had been a steam vent caused by the extinct volcano. Still, he could see that it had been modified to accommodate whatever their ancestors had used this area for. Along the floor and ceiling there was recessed lighting which turned on as they approached, and on one of the walls, an identical panel to the one Sorrel had pushed to open the doors. "Must have some type of motion sensor for these lights – good way to conserve energy, to only have them light when they are needed. And doing it this way means that someone cannot accidentally leave them turned on."

The tunnel changed in direction bending to the right in a gentle curve and then coming back to the original direction. Up ahead, in the distance, they could see what appeared to be another set of doors. Once there, like the first of the double set, they were able to push through them, only to find once again a set that required pushing a plate. When the doors opened they were hit with a blast of fresh cool air, but from what they could see, they were not yet truly outside. Walking through the doors they found themselves in some type of building. Yet the floor was a mix of dirt and straw, and looking around they could see some the areas had concrete floors. Just past the entrance, and looking up, they saw a pulley system set up that could hoist items and move them around this building. Above they could also see shelving and platforms for storage, and presently most were vacant. There was a musty smell and they could hear the bleating of animals somewhere in the distance. After leaving the warmth of the compound it felt almost cold and both shivered in response to the change in temperature. Both looked at each other and then Sorrel said. "I think this place is probably where they take care of the animals, and obviously they used it for some type of storage. But since this seems to be open to the weather, I don't know what that might be?"

"I don't know either; shall we explore this before we go outside? You know it really doesn't feel like this place stays open all the time. I bet you that when the suns set those large doors close down for the night. I suspect that like the sensors that turned on the lights as we approached, that there is something similar set up to close the doors when night falls or the weather gets really nasty." Stone stated as he looked around. They slowly walked around the interior of the building and found many stations positioned at different locations, most they had no idea what they were used for. "Well, I am really starting to develop an inferiority complex here. I mean, the ones who built this place were our ancestors, and obviously they knew what all of this was for, and I haven't a clue."

Nodding in agreement, she looked down for a moment and said. "Enough of this, let's go outside and see what other wonders our ancestors left us." They headed out through a huge opening, stopping briefly; Stone noticed the opening had a huge door, which was on rollers, which would allow it to slide to cover the opening. Studying it closely he could see that that the rails that the rollers tracked in showed signs of usage. He commented. "See, the tracks show signs of usage which means that they probably do close and open." Looking up, he saw that he was alone and that he had been talking just to himself. *Now where did Sorrel run off to?* He raised his voice and yelled, "Sorrel? Sorrel where are you?" Looking around the area he presently was in, he noticed that there were at least two more buildings to his left and on the right arose a volcanic wall that he suspected was another cone from one of the extinct volcanoes. Not getting an answer, he headed towards one of the other buildings that were a little distance from where he was. As he walked he could hear his footsteps crunching on the gravel. He looked down and realized that this whole area had been covered in gravel, and it extended around the other buildings as well. With no response he was getting worried that something may have happened, but realized that there was little chance of that actually happening, and got his emotions back in control. He went around to the right of the furthest building and stopped and caught his breath. Before him lay a large meadowland and surrounding it completely, rising to a great height, was the volcanic walls. Again he marveled at the sheer size. And again was thankful he hadn't been here when these mountains had exploded with volcanic fury.

As he surveyed the beauty before him, off in the distance he could see Sorrel standing and staring at something. He then made his way to where she was standing, and was about to admonish her for getting separated, when he, following the direction she was looking, became distracted himself. Out in the distance was a large herd of what he knew was the herd animals that the primitives used for their milk, their skins, meat, and for transport of materials. He saw that like the two of them, these animals, well at least a number of them were watching them also. "Well", he said softly, "I guess this answers the question, as to whether our ancestors had their own herd or not." He was then silent as the quiet beauty of the place settled in on him.

She turned to him with a sad smile on her face and said. "Yes, I guess so." *It's just so sad to realize that sometime a long time ago our ancestors worked and lived here. Had created all of this, and then because of something we really do not understand, had to abandon it. And then it lay sleeping, awaiting the day when someone would rediscover it.* She gave herself a mental shake and continued saying, "Let's go out there and see what there is to see. One thing for sure, with the natural walls around this place, these animals can't leave, and it protects them from their natural predators also. There has to be some type of a water source out there, and from looking at how green everything is, I bet that this place has either a high water table, or our ancestors set up some type of irrigation system to keep it this way."

"You're probably right, and I'd guess that it's sub-irrigated. But seeing what we have found so far, it would not surprise me to find that they artificially irrigated this place. And I agree with you, we need to walk this out and explore it. One of the main reasons we need to do this, is because, they had to get these animals in here in the first place, and I guarantee it wasn't the way we came. So there has to be another outlet where they could take them out of here. Plus, I feel that it needs to be far enough away from the main facility that there is no hint of where the facility is located. And again you are so right; this place is just so beautiful. Who would have guessed that such an area as this existed here?"

Looking at him she said, "Well then, the day's flying by, let's do it." They headed off towards the wall on the right figuring to follow it around, since it would logically be somewhere along one the walls that the exit from this place should be. Looking up at the sky he saw that they really did not have much time. While summer days were longer, they had entered this area late after lunch, so the day had been more than half over when they discovered the meadows. Unconsciously he picked up the pace. She found that he was starting to pull ahead of her slightly and said. "Hey, this isn't a race."

Smiling slightly he said. "Sorry Sorrel. Didn't mean to do that, but we're running out of daylight, and I guess I just unconsciously picked it up to try and get around this place before darkness fell. I mean, look at this place. It's huge! I'd guess we are looking at a circumference of oh, I'd guess around ten kilometers, and I suspect that it will be pushing dark thirty by the time we head back to those buildings."

* * *

"Can you watch Sommer for me?" Sabryn asked. "I don't know if I can help, but it sounded urgent."

"No problem, after all, there seems to be an excitement in Saige's voice. I wonder what's come up. I know that we haven't found anything that we didn't expect here where we are in the facility. Maybe one of the other teams found something."

"You know that could be it. Anyway I just fed her and put her down for a nap and she fell right to sleep, so if you just look in on her a couple of times it would be appreciated."

"Oh you know I will. We do this all the time for both of our children, and I'm not too far from doing the same with my son – feeding and putting him down for his nap. And I think that like your Sommer, Shayne will be down for at least a couple of hours. That will allow me, and maybe you, if they let you go, to continue to search the records."

Smiling as she went out the door Starr heard her whisper, "Thank You", as she disappeared from sight. Sabryn hurried down the hallway, at the moment she was almost on the opposite side of the compound, and it would take her a little time to get there. As she hurried along her way, a smile came to her as she thought about her sleeping daughter, and wondered what the future would hold for her. *One thing for sure it will be different in so many ways. Even if we are able to break up the alliance, we now know that the past, as it has been taught, is completely wrong. I really wonder when it got changed to what we were taught. And where is our home world? There's absolutely nothing in any of the records even identifying its location. But I guess I can kind of understand it. That means that if something happened to one of the outposts, that the information on its location could not be compromised. Still, I would really like to see it if it still exists, and there is just no way to know, is there?* She reached the security entrance and found that other than Starr, who she had left with the children, Stone and Sorrel, everybody was here at the security office. "This is a surprise." She said, as she saw all of them there. "Are we having a party or something?" This brought a chuckle out of the group. "Would you like me to come in, or just wait out here? It's getting a little tight in there, and I don't know if I could fit comfortably with all of you in there."

"No, we do need you in here. Seirra wants to show you something, and see if it looks familiar to you. Seve thought that you had either seen, or mentioned that you had seen something similar, and that it might hold the key to solving another of the many puzzles we've found since this place was discovered. And while it's a little crowded, it's really not that crowded since I believe that if we needed to, we probably could put everybody in here. But instead it's just a few and I know you were just jesting anyway. The rest of the team will head back to the meeting room where they can continue to monitor us." They began filing out and headed back leaving plenty of room for Sabryn to enter the security room. She watched as they left and stood silently for a moment before entering the security office. She looked around briefly and then at Seirra, who was looking back at her.

"Okay, I'm here. What's so important that you pulled me away from our search? Not that anything new has been found, but I really did not figure that we would be looking at anything else until we had finished the searching."

"Seirra showed me something and again, as I said, Seve thought that you had seen something like it, so if you would?" Saige then gestured for her to come forward and look at the screen.

She came forward and looked over Seirra's shoulder and asked. "What is it that you want me to see?"

Seirra pointed to the bottom of the monitor and said. "It's these letters and numbers that change when I or any of us change the view." She then demonstrated. "See what I mean."

"Yes and no. The letters stay the same; it's just the numbers that change. Hmmm, let me think." She was silent for a moment and thought. *They are right. I've seen something similar to this. But what is it and where?* Shaking her head as she continued to think, *I've been through so much stuff lately just where is it that I saw this?* She could feel the pressure mounting as the silence in the room grew, but at the moment she didn't have a ready answer. "He's right, I did mention something about letters and numbers, but I'm drawing a blank right this moment. Just let me think about it, okay?"

Saige shrugged and said. "At least it was worth a shot. So you do remember something, but not much more at this moment. Okay keep thinking about it. Tonight I want all of us back together to go over what we have learned, or not, and maybe by that time you will have come up with something."

Again shaking her head, Sabryn said. "I'm so sorry. It's just we have been researching so much stuff lately that it just escapes me for now." She saw that Saige was nodding his head, and signaled her that she could return to what she had been doing.

"At least we may have an answer soon." Then looking up at the camera he continued. "Remember we all need to be in the meeting room after dinner so that we can compare notes, and has anyone heard anything from either Stone or Sorrel since the midday meal?" All he got was silence. Breathing out heavily, he finished by saying. "Maybe they had better luck, so I guess everyone can go back to doing what they were before this interruption. We will look at what Seve suggested, and hope that Sabryn can remember. I think somehow it is all tied together. See you all later."

* * *

The suns were dropping down behind the horizon by the time Stone and Sorrel reached the buildings once again. They had at one point cut across the meadowland to at least check part of it out. But to do a thorough search would require another day, if not two. The first thing that they noticed was that the pack animals were heading towards the buildings also. "Maybe they spend the nights inside one of the buildings." Sorrel suggested.

"Yeah probably", Stone responded. "It probably provides not only protection from the weather, but from the predators also, even though there has been no sign of any. I bet that these doors on the large building close at night also."

"Really? Why would you think that?" She asked.

"Well think about it. If you remember what the entrance looked like, there was no soil buildup or signs of disuse on the rollers and channels. To me, that speaks of constant use. That way, in the cold of winters it would provide protection for the beasts of burden. And I suspect that once they are here that there are bots that monitor them and probably are also responsible for thinning of the herds so that they do not outgrow their food."

"And that's probably where the meat is coming from." She was silent for a minute before continuing, "I think we need to hurry back. We've still got a ways to go, and I'm finding that I am actually hungry – haven't done this kind of exercise since we've been here. And we can truthfully say we found where the beasts are kept. I know, it still doesn't explain a lot, but it surely is one step closer, don't you think?"

He had to agree, and he reached out and took her hand, and then hand in hand they retraced their steps from earlier in the day, as they headed back into the facility.

* * *

"Has anyone seen either Stone or Sorrel?" Saige asked as they began sitting in the meeting room. Looking around, he saw that overall that no one had. He wondered what had delayed them. He knew that from what had been relayed to him, that they had found stairs that climbed out of sight, and a couple of enclosed rooms. From the brief description that he had received, the area was a place that he did want to visit, and the feeling he got was that most of the others here were of like mind. "I guess they will show up when they get back from whatever they have found. So let's open this up with each of us passing on what we have found, or not found today, and I'll start it. Shellian and I searched the grounds completely, and overall nothing has changed. We found a small greenhouse sitting back in a hidden corner that we felt was there for the use of the staff. You know, for things like growing flowers, or plants, and I think that it was also used for school projects, as there was a section that was separate that had a sign stating *education* – other than that, nothing at all new. Seve, Staven, your turn." He sat down and Staven got up.

"Both the steam room and the electric room were completely searched, and other than learning that most of our system is based on geothermal and solar, we have nothing to report. Everything there was as expected. While there, of course, Seve came up with his ideas that were then presented, and I think Sabryn now has the answer to the question that was asked of her after lunch." At this point Staven sat back down, and turned it over to Sabryn.

"Once Seirra had shown me those letters and numbers I knew that I had seen something similar, but where and what I couldn't remember. But before I get to that, I need to say that our primary assignment was to search out the immediate facility, and nothing new was found, and the maps and schematics of the place are accurate. Now, onto the other, I now remember that there are three places that I remember coming across those combinations of letters and numbers. In the system it describes these as longitude and latitude. It is a way to locate something anywhere on this world. So when they were looking at a certain place on this world from those views it was automatically providing the longitude and latitude. The measurements that are used are degrees, minutes, and seconds. And don't ask me why, I'm not the one who developed the system. Longitude measures through the poles and latitude measures from the equator. With these two, and the breakdown, any place on this planet can be located. Once you realize that, then it would make sense for someone to leave information on the locations of the planned cities. So once I understood that, I went back through the records that existed in the computer, and found a reference to a source in the administrator's office, and a second tied directly to the security office. It required one to go to the admin office, to get first, the list of the cities, their names, and such. Plus there was a password there to use in the security office that would then release not only the locations by this system of longitude, and latitude, but emergency frequencies to contact them."

"You mean that there might be a way that we can contact each of them directly? Wow this is great news." Saige stated excitedly. He turned to Seve stating, "I guess you're right, and when you presented it, it made sense." About this time the doors opened with Stone and Sorrel arriving.

"Sorry about being late." Stone said, "But we have some very important news to pass on, and while on that subject, did we miss anything?"

"Only the fact that we may now be able to contact the cities, and let them know what is happening, that's all . . . Anyway Sabryn, are you finished with your report?" She nodded and sat down. "Okay then Stone, since you are standing, go ahead and let us know what you have found, other than the area that you had talked about over lunch of course."

"Simply put, we found it. Well at least part of the puzzle anyway. As you know, the stairs led up, and we climbed them to the top. We discovered, albeit accidentally, what those rooms were also. Since we never had a need of them in our cities, it would never have occurred to us that it was a way to move between floors, without walking. They transport one from one floor to another. It is a different feeling when they begin to move. If they go up at first you feel heavier, and quite the opposite when you go down in them." Catching his breath for a moment, he leaned forward supporting his weight on his hands that he had placed on the table. "While that is a nice discovery, the question is why would they need such a thing? It turns out that there are just three stops that we could get to. There is at least another, but that one requires a key, which we did not have. But I would guess that it is another supply area. The ground floor is at the level of the cavern, and the top floor exits to an open lunch slash meeting area, beautiful really. But the one in the middle empties into a room that has large swinging doors, big enough to move large crates through. So initially we thought it could be just another supply area, and when we went through it, there was a worked steam vent and . . ." He went on to describe all that they had found, and apologizing at the end, since they had been unable to do a complete search. "My feelings are that there has to be an exit on the far side, somewhere that would not compromise this compound, and besides I can't really see anyone bringing those animals through the area where we entered. And for now that's all we have."

Smiling Saige said. "With the way things have been going I was getting very frustrated on the lack of progress, and now all in the same day things have moved so quickly that we will be working hard on solving the problems that have now been presented. Oh, one more thing Sabryn, did any of that information include locations for the primitives?"

Shaking her head she said, "No, the notation stated that since many of the primitives were nomadic, and had no real permanent location, that only full descriptions of their lives were included."

"I guess we can't have everything, but that sure would have been nice. Okay, it looks like we have a lot of work ahead of us, so in the morning, normally Seve and Sabryn would have manned the security office, but I am adding both of you, Seirra and Saar back there. There's room for that many in there. We need to get that information and figure out how to contact the remaining cities, and of course the first one we need to contact would be Keahilani, since it is the pivot city, the one that maintains all communications traffic between the cities. They could get the word out quicker than we could. The rest of us will head out to this place that Stone and Sorrel located, and see if we can find that exit. Truly we are running out of time, and so far we haven't been able to locate the alliance headquarters. But we do have, or will have shortly, the coordinates of all the cities, so we can narrow the search area down a bit by comparing the times when the cities we know were taken by the primitives, and by looking at the differences, come up with a much smaller area to search. If there isn't anything else, I for one have to admit that it has been a full day." He looked around and saw that the rest agreed with him. "Okay then, we is done here. Let's all meet for breakfast in the cafeteria and then we can go as a group to our different areas. And I'm going to take a chance and not have anyone monitoring the security office tonight. So far, we haven't seen a primitive within kilometers of this place. We need everyone for what is happening tomorrow, and all to have a full night's sleep. So, good night all, and thank you for all of the effort that has gotten us to this point." He watched as the members filtered out of the meeting room. He saw that Seirra waited until all the rest had left and then came over and joined him.

"I agree I'm really tired tonight. Do you really think that we will be able to contact the cities?" *I really do hope so, there has already been too much loss here, and if there is a slight chance that we can alert the rest to what's happening, then maybe they can come up with some way of keeping the primitives out.* "I know there is no way you can answer that right now, but I had to ask."

He reached out and hugged her and then took her hand and said. "I really never, well Shellian and I really never wanted this job, and to answer your question, I don't know. After all, all of our training was to spy on the primitives, and not repair the equipment. That was for other members, and none of them survived our flight to here – so all of us are flying quite blind here. And while everything seems to be working because of the bots and replicators, I just don't know." Taking a deep breath and shrugging he said. "I really wish I did, but I have to be honest, I just don't. Enough on this, I'm tired, lets head back to the apartment and call it. I have a feeling that the next few days are going to be extremely busy, not that most of them haven't been, but we now know so much more, and I do hope we can use what we learned to stop the slaughter and slavery of our people."

"I do love you, you know that?" She asked as she looked up into his eyes and smiled.

Smiling back at her, she could see softness in his eyes as he said. "Yes, I do, and I knew that for a long time. It was just that back in the cave I couldn't show any favoritism towards anybody, and especially you, but I have to admit that I am in love with you also. You have become very important to me in so many ways."

Then smiling mischievously she said. "Well, let me show you tonight how much I appreciate you." And then she laughed as they headed for their apartment.

* * *

Keenan stayed long enough to make sure that the shift change went smoothly, and then headed out to grab something to eat before he went home. He was in a dark mood, and really did not want any company tonight. The word coming back from the council was nothing but political mumbo jumbo saying absolutely nothing, and the information being passed down by the over-bosses was just as bad. In other words, nothing was known, and nothing was being done. Was this paralysis to continue, until, for whatever reason, the light would be turned off here? Again he had no answers. He wanted to do something, anything, but again by not knowing what had happened he was frustrated, and had no real direction to go. He was a man of action, one who wanted to delve deeply into the problem and get it solved. And this was the reason for his dark mood. *Yeah, it's obvious that nobody knows anything, and is just saying what sounds good. Why isn't someone out there trying to find out? Instead all we get is talk, talk, talk!* Breathing deeply and shaking his head slightly his thoughts continued unbidden. *I just don't get it. Why haven't they sent someone out to at least check on one of the cities that have gone dark? Yeah, I know, not one of the cities is that close to each other, but if I remember correctly, there was supposed to be some type of special team to do just that.* Now with a bit of sarcasm his thoughts continued. *Oh that's right. Budget cuts, since we never had any need or use for that department it was eliminated as waste.* Chuckling inwardly he just stared out at nothing in particular as he headed for his favorite restaurant. *I guess tomorrow will be another day, and maybe, just maybe, someone will do something – yeah like that's going to happen.*

* * *

Morning came too quickly, and all of them filtered out to the cafeteria for breakfast. Looking around, Saige could see that most looked blurry eyed and somewhat drug out. *At least*

I'm not the only one that looks that way right now. But it was little consolation, since they needed to be fresh and alert today. He really wanted to be able to make contact today, and to completely explore the meadowlands that had been discovered yesterday. Looking around he noticed that the women were missing at this moment and realized that it was their day for kitchen duty at the meals, and as he realized that, the women began to bring in the food and as the smells reached him he realized that he was quite hungry. Smiling at them as they piled the plates of food in the middle of the table he could hear his stomach rumble in complaint and anticipation. The women then went back briefly to the kitchen and brought out steaming pots of coffee. It had been something they had discovered here, and all of them had found, that like their ancestors, they were living on the stuff. It was different than the *shick* they drank back in the city, and he had to admit, better. Once the coffee had arrived they sat down and Shellian said. "Well, dig in everyone while it's hot. I do not like cold food." Someone replied. "My parents raised no fools; you don't have to tell me twice." This brought out a general chuckle from everyone there. Then all that anyone heard was the moving of plates, silverware, and cups as everyone concentrated on the food and drink.

* * *

It had been a restless night and Keenan was short tempered and in no mood for the normal political crap today. So he knew that he had to keep his mouth shut, and to be careful, so that he did not say something that would put him on report. Things had been building for quite a while now, and if something did not happen soon, it would not matter, he would blow up anyway. It seemed that all of the ones above were avoiding any mention of the problems that were now confronting the cities. *As if ignoring them would make them go away.* Yet, as he looked around on his way to work, everything was just too normal. Shaking himself inwardly he thought once again. *Eight cities gone, and still no one to explain why, and no one who will take responsibility for trying to discover the reasons why they have gone silent.* He knew that right now he was too old, and had too many minor health problems, to be one who could do the discovering. It was another point of frustration for him. Back in his youth, he had almost joined the ones who were active in keeping an eye on the primitives, the research, and advancements that they made. And yes, even the fighting between the clans and tribes. All of this was important, but before he could join, the council disbanded it as unnecessary. So here he was all this time later close to the age of no longer working, to have this crisis show its face, and no one willing to do anything about it.

He knew that the city of Sequoyah had been the last to maintain the unit that worked out in the field, who had trained continually to be able to work among the primitives, if it came down to the need, but Sequoyah was one of the cities that had gone dark, and so any chance of discovery went out the window with them. He looked up and realized that he had reached the central communications center, and wondered how he had gotten here so fast. It appeared to him that he had just left his apartment. At least if something happened to this city there would be no family for him to lose, he mused. He had been coupled twice, but it had never worked out. And in those short unions no children and his parents had died a long time ago, as had his one brother and sister. Oh if he searched he probably had a couple of nieces and nephews but he truly did not know. Looking up at the large clock he found that he had time to get something hot to drink before beginning his shift and headed for one of the machines before relieving the last shift.

* * *

As they walked the large cavern towards the entrance to the stairs and moving rooms, the lights turned on automatically, as they came into the range of the hidden sensors. Before them, lay a pathway of lights, shining up from the ground towards the ceiling that was high above them. This area had to have been a large pocket of magma, that had disappeared, leaving this cavern here a very long time ago, and it was huge. Sorrel and Stone led the way, and they shortly arrived at what Stone felt was originally a steam vent. Making the turn, the passageway lit up as the floor had, and before them they could see the closed doors leading into the room where the stairway and moving rooms were located. "The stairs are on the right through a door, and on the left is the other rooms, and straight ahead is a wall," Stone commented as they reached the door. As they prepared to enter, the rest could see that there was wired glass to allow them to look into the room. Sorrel then held open the door and with a flourish, waved them through. As all of them entered, the room was exactly as they had described. Stone then went over to the doors on the left and pushed a button that was between them. The doors opened immediately causing Saige, Shellian, Staven, and Starr to jump. Laughing softly Stone said. "Sorry about that, I didn't think they were going to open that quickly. But hurry everyone inside. These doors only stay open for a short time and they will close again." Hesitantly the four of them joined Stone and Sorrel inside. And as he had stated the doors did close. Stone then turned towards the panel and pressed the button for the top. He could feel the tension in the air, since the other four did not know what to expect. There was a soft whirring sound and suddenly the room was moving upwards and they briefly felt heavier, then just the opposite as it slowed and then came to a stop. The doors opened and they now were outside of the facility. "Quickly now – these doors will close again. It really isn't a problem, as you can keep them open by blocking them." Stone then demonstrated, as the doors had begun to close and he blocked them and they opened again. "The other moving room is much larger, and I suspect that it is the one the used to move freight up and down."

They took a quick tour around the area and had to agree with the assessment that they had been given the night before. Again, it was obvious, that from the trails on the mountains that this area would be invisible. And the views from here, as described, were spectacular. "I can see that this would give any of the support people a place to go that would be safe and still be outside. Yes, I know that they probably walked the small valley, but this area gives you vistas to stare at, and one does not feel closed in at all. It is just beautiful." Saige said.

Stone then led them to the stairs, and they descended to the middle area and the large swinging doors that marked the passage into another worked steam vent, and out into the buildings that led into the meadowlands beyond. Once there, after a brief stop in the buildings Starr exclaimed as she saw the area. "This is so big, quiet, peaceful, and really, really beautiful too." Then turning around and looking at the rest of them, she could see that all of the rest were in agreement with what she had said.

Sorrel then stated as she pointed out into the distance. "We ran out of daylight, and unlike the buildings which seem to have a dusk-to-dawn lighting system, there are none out here at all. We were only able to get less than half way out there and had to return. Stone figures that this place has to be around ten kilometers around." Then she pointed towards a different area and said. "Over there is a small lake. We didn't have time to figure out whether it was natural, or something that our ancestors had built. But we were able to confirm that this volcanic wall goes completely around it, protecting the animals that are in here."

"Were either of you able to get close to the pack beasts at all?" Shellian asked

Shaking her head Sorrel said, "No, they were still out towards the other end of this giant bowl, but as night approached they were beginning to head back to those buildings. But we were out of time and needed to get back. Yet, from a distance, they showed more curiosity than fear. But whether that's because there is nothing for them to fear here, or because the bots have worked with them, I really don't know."

Turning around and facing the group Saige said, "I guess even with your description I didn't think this would be as large as it is. Okay, here is what I would like to happen. Staven, you and Starr take the left wall and follow it out. Stone, you and Sorrel, since you have been here, work up through the middle of the meadows, and then Shellian and I will work the right wall. We should be able to see at least some of the others as we work our way around. Then we will meet on the other side, and see what we find. We can then break for lunch and continue. You all know what we need to do, so let's get to it."

* * *

"You all know what we are here for today. Seve, you and Sabryn search that manual and database and see if there is any mention on how we tie what you Sabryn found to anything here in the security office." Turning around and facing Seirra, Saar continued, "Since you were the one who actually discovered the locations being placed at the bottom of the screen, maybe you can find out which of these, I guess you can call them, eyes-in-the-skies that will get us closest to Keahilani. And since part of our job is to keep us safe, for the first part of the day here I will monitor the area. We'll all switch jobs later. And as Saige said, we are in a critical situation, and time is, as usual, running out on us and our people."

Seve turning to his mate said, "You've been great on searching the database, and if Shayne becomes fussy or needs to be fed, you can slip out to the nursery and take care of his needs and probably be able to continue the research."

Smiling and shaking her head she said. "I have no problem with that, but we created this child and we *will* share in everything. Of course, since I am breast-feeding him you cannot take part in that, but I expect you to go with me with everything else, and that includes helping me put him down for his nap or change his messy pants. That's the way it was in my parents' house and that's the way it will be in ours." She looked over lovingly to the sleeping baby that was lying in a small portable bed, oblivious to what was going on around him. "It appears that Staven is totally into fatherhood, and he is carrying Sommer on his back, as they are exploring that meadow."

"Yeah I know. It's just something I have to grow into. In the house I grew up in, mom and dad stayed within their roles.

Mom took care of us and dad did the rest. I think probably it had to do with the fact that they worked closely with the primitives and that's how the primitives that we observed sort of lived." Then putting his hands out in front of him in defense he continued. "So it was the way I thought it was supposed to be, but I can see that it is so much better to share in everything. But it is going to take me some time to change the way I was raised."

Saar then interrupted saying, "Now that we have had our family discussion, can we get on with this?"

Both turned around and realized that was exactly what they were doing, and apologized profusely. When Saar turned around he saw Seirra smiling. "So what are you smiling at?"

"Oh them. The one thing everyone forgets when they get into a relationship is that both are coming from different places, have different views, and have different experiences. So, there is much the two of you have to overcome, and it's really surprising that anybody actually stays together. But I guess we all learn to adjust if we really care."

As he thought about it he had to agree. Even he and Shellian had had some growing pains, but both of them were willing to work on it. Shellian was a very strong willed woman and one who had confidence in her abilities. And he had to admit that she had earned that right. "I guess that's very true. Oh well, I guess the show's over, so to all of us, let's get to it."

* * *

Keenan, looking over his workers knew that they had sensed his mood, and were being very careful to stay out of his way. They all had been, at one time or another, on the receiving end of his displeasure, and it was not pleasant. So they all walked on eggshells and avoided direct eye contact. Yet, all of them had to admit that they would not want to work with anybody else, as their boss even when he was in a foul mood, made sure that all were treated fairly. They knew that as much as he would not put up with anything from them, he was the same way with his own over-bosses. So they, in some ways, were able to do more and have a little more freedom than the other shifts. Still, they could sense the electricity in the air, and now was just waiting for it to discharge, and hope everything would return back to normal. But this had been something that had been building for a while, they knew it had to do with the cities that had gone dark, and the weak excuses his over-bosses were passing on to him.

Shaking his head as he paced back and forth on the raised area in the back of the center, he felt as if something was about to happen, and he hoped that it was not another city going dark. But the morning passed quietly, and all appeared to be much too normal for him. And even with this semblance of normalcy, he still sensed that something was very wrong. So with a deep sigh, he headed for the midday meal, and looked for a table that would isolate him from the rest of his peers. He was in no mood for company. As he sat down with his food, he looked across the cafeteria and saw Kiley approaching his table, and he looked up at him and glared, and almost laughed as Kiley stopped dead in his tracks, changed direction, and headed for another table.

Later, back on shift, he thought that other than supporting his body, that the midday meal was worthless. He couldn't even remember finishing it and leaving, let alone tasting anything. Looking over the workers again, everything appeared to just be as it should be, and yet, he felt that it was just wrong. How it was wrong, he had no idea, but he just could not put down the feeling that it was. He turned his back and stared at the wall deep in thought, trying to come to terms with this foreboding that appeared to penetrate his very soul. There was a crisis, but looking around one would never have guessed. Maybe that was why he was feeling this way. Everything appeared to be very normal, and it was anything but. "Sir?" He barely heard it and then thought. *Sir is it? How I hate to be called that.* Then shaking his head inwardly, *Yeah, I know it's a sign of respect, but I always figured that it belonged to my parents or someone older than I am. Okay, who asked?* Turning around he saw Kacey standing below him. She had worked here for about eight annuals and was very good at what she did. She monitored the little used channels, and he had tried to get her not to use *sir*, but she had insisted. With a mental shrug he asked, keeping the tension he was feeling out of his voice. "Yes Kacey, what is it?"

She paused for a moment not sure how to continue, and the indecision was plain on her face. She looked down at the floor for a moment and then said, "I'm not sure what to make of it sir . . ." She immediately paused again when she saw him glare at her for using *sir*. "I'm sorry, but I just can't change the way I was raised."

Looking at her, he could see a nice looking woman, not pretty by any means, but one who could be attractive if she dressed a little differently and wore her hair in a different way, but she preferred to keep things as plain as she could, while working. As far as he knew she was still single, and he tried to stay out of his workers personal lives, unless it had an effect on their work. "Yes, yes, I know, but as you know, I've never cared for it." Sighing, he continued, "This is getting away from why you are here, now please continue."

She nodded her head and he could see that she almost said it again but paused. "Okay, I just received a communications from a channel that has never been active."

"You mean active while you've worked here, right?"

Shaking her head she said. No, no as far as I can see, and I've checked the logs as far back as I could, it has never been used. And this channel has our highest priority color attached to it. And the signal is weak and scratchy, but I think I can actually hear someone trying to communicate with us."

"Are you sure?" Then shaking his head he said. "Of course you are, sorry about that, but it is a surprise that's all. What does the monitor tell you?"

"That's the really weird part; it's saying that it is originating from point Alpha."

He looked perplexed for a moment and then glanced over at his monitoring panel and saw that one light was flashing, and like at her station this light had never flashed in his twenty-five years of working here. "What the heck is going on?" He thought a moment before continuing. "Okay Kacey transfer it to my station and I'll take it from here, and please set up for record, we want an accurate recording of this, and if it turns out to be some type of hoax, then we'll have it all down. And please monitor it with me so that if something comes to mind that you want to either ask or add you can." He glanced up at the clock and it said 1433.

* * *

"Look, when we pushed this button that is marked with the highest priority color, then this happened." The other two stared at the center panel than now was lit up. A message appeared on the monitor that sat above this panel and stated, "Ready to Transmit". "Who'd of thought it would be that easy?" Saar asked. He looked around at the rest and he could see the surprise in their eyes also. "Okay now what?"

"Now what, what?" Sabryn asked.

"Well, as far as I know, we were just supposed to figure this out, and then report back to Saige and Shellian on our research, not actually make a connection." Saar responded.

"I guess it's too late for that now." Seirra replied. "It looks like it has sent out a carrier wave, and set itself up, and connected to Keahilani."

"Which means", Seve said, "that some type of confirmation would have happened there, so they would know that someone would be trying to contact them." They could now feel the excitement building inside of them, as well as nervousness, as they realized what was happening. After all this *time of isolation* they were finally going to be able to talk to a city.

Saar, looking around at the rest asked, "What should we say?" He could feel the tension in the room as the other three shrugged. "Take me to your leader, doesn't work here," he said, trying to ease the atmosphere. And it had its effect by a series of small nervous chuckles that the statement evoked. They all jumped when a scratchy but understandable voice came out of the panel.

"Who is on this priority channel?" The voice asked before continuing. "If this is some kind of joke or prank we are not laughing here. And if it is, then there are serious consequences for operating on this channel." The voice said with strong authority.

They looked at each other for a moment and then Seve said. "You'd better respond, or I guess the better question is, have you figured out how to respond?"

"Ah, this is Saar."

"Saar? Who the heck is Saar, and since you are connecting through point Alpha why is your name beginning with an "S"?" Keenan asked.

"Point Alpha? Look, whoever you are, since you haven't identified yourself, if you happen to really look, you will know that on any of the circuits or maps for that matter, there is never a mention of this place, point Alpha as you called it." And it was true, this location had never been on any map and the list of cities never had one that began with "A". And because it had never been there, there never had been a question as to why. Now their little band knew why, but nobody in the rest of the world did.

"True." The voice agreed. "But for some reason it is on my panel, although I've never seen it activate or become active in any way. And I am Keenan, the leader of this shift." Again he couldn't keep the suspicion out of his voice.

"Keenan is it? Okay then, there is a reason for that, and if what happened to our city had not have happened, then all of this would not have happened, or had become known. Anyway, I am a doctor, and as you have guessed, we are not from here or there. Our city *was* Sequoyah." That brought silence for a moment, as if the speaker on the other end was trying to assimilate what he had just been told.

Then in a softer tone Keenan said, "Sequoyah is one of the cities that went dark." Then with the realization of what had been just relayed to him he continued. "You aren't trying to pull some type of prank here are you? Because if you are, then I personally will be sure to see you pay for it."

Saar looked around at the rest of them that were in the security office and just shook his head. He then took a deep breath before speaking again. "No, Keenan. In a way I wish it were so and our city still existed. But it is gone as are the others, which have gone dark. And on that subject just how many have gone dark now?"

"Have you been out of the loop or something? Everybody knows that we've had eight cities go dark. How is it that you don't know that?"

"I guess you can say that we have been in isolation for somewhere close to or more than a full annual. And let me say that we know why it is happening, and that every city that still exists needs to know this information, and all of you need to figure how to fix it now."

"Okay, right now all you are doing is talking in circles. You've given me no proof of who you are, and how you got on this channel, or even what this channel is for. I don't think I've even heard anything about it at all, and I don't remember any mention about it in the archives."

"Okay, okay then, what is it that you need from us to prove that we are legitimate and not someone who is trying to pull off some big publicity stunt?"

"Good question, give me a moment and I'll get back to you. I've got to find some info on your supposed city, and then I'll ask the questions, you then can give me the answers, and confirm that what you are telling me is true. Be right back." The mic then went dead.

Saar, looking around at the rest shrugged. He had to admit that he thought it wasn't going to be that hard to get things moving once they made contact. But it was turning out to be much more complicated. Turning around he asked to no one in particular. "I wonder what that is all about? After all it's not like we are all jokesters here, and just love to put something over on any who are gullible. So what's the problem here? Is there something I did or said to make this guy suspicious?" He could see that everyone in the room had no answers for him, so all of them just waited until this Keenan made contact with them again. Yet, at the same time, there was an excitement building. Now they knew for sure that other cities had not received the same fate that theirs had, and there were still ones of their own species around. Saar, thinking, *I need Saige and Shellian here, but there is no way. As far as I know they are half way across that large meadow by now and we will have no contact with them until they return tomorrow. They have planned on camping if necessary so that they could do a thorough job of exploring, and possibly finding the exit that they are sure has to be there. So I guess, since I've been in charge in the past it is all on me.* "What do you think he needs to know?" Saar asked the group. Again shrugging, as he turned back to the console, when he heard the crackling as someone on the other end was picking up a headset.

"Are still there?" The female voice on the other end asked. This is Kacey; I'm the one who monitors the less used channels. Keenan said that he would be with you in a moment. And since I do monitor these channels I heard the conversation between you and Keenan. Is it true that you are from one of the cities that went dark?"

Smiling, as Saar could hear the barely concealed excitement in her voice, said. "Yes, it is quite true. But I am sad to say at the same time that we are very few."

"Oh, here he is, and to let you know everything that is happening on this channel is automatically recorded."

"Thank you, that's good to know." Saar replied. He waited as the mic went dead once again, and then heard a different one being moved. He turned around placed his hand over his mic since it was voice activated, and said. "I may need help with whatever questions this person has, so listen well."

"Okay, Saar is it? Right. Saar, you say that you were originally from the city of Sequoyah. If this is so, who was your present head of the council at the time your city went dark?"

At least that was an easy question. But if he really admitted it, most likely, he would not have known, since they had more or less isolated themselves from the city to be able to work and live closer to the way the primitives did. And he had to admit that was probably why any of them were still alive. When the crisis had arisen it had been the leader who had contacted Shayne and then everyone in the compound knew. "His name was Sione. And I say was because I do not know of his true status, but from what we observed, there is little chance for any to have survived."

"Survived?" Keenan asked. "What do you mean survived?"

"Look, we can go into all of this later, have I not answered correctly? And if you have any additional questions please ask. Time is short and what needs to happen needs to happen yesterday, especially if you don't want to lose another city. And it's really that simple."

"Okay, you did, and I did have others but I'll accept what you have told me, but just one more thing, where did you and your over-bosses work?"

Laughing a bitter laugh Saar said. "We were the last of the scouting units. We had learned that all the other cities had dropped the units. We feel that if that hadn't happened then what has transpired may never have occurred. Look, I was told that our conversation is being recorded, and if that is so, you need to transmit a copy of what I am about to tell you not only to your council, but to every city that still survives. Our very existence depends on it, and it is that serious, do you understand?"

Still with suspicion in his voice Keenan said. "Oh come on, you're telling me this and expect me to just jump and do? Get real here."

Saar then interrupted Keenan and said. "Look we can argue this all day, and still not solve anything. When this was first brought to Shayne he was given the color yellow."

Then interrupting Saar, Keenan asked, "Shayne? Who is this Shayne that you are talking about?"

"He was our leader, but was killed during our escape. But that is old history now, and I am giving you a color that is rarely given as I feel it is that critical. And that color is *Black*." Now there was only silence on the other end for the longest of times. Then he heard a deep sigh.

"Okay Saar. You do know that using that color has, as far as I know, been used only once in our entire history. Are you sure you want to invoke black?"

Then in a quiet voice Saar said. "Yes." Then he let a few seconds of silence go by before continuing. "If there was something higher than black I would use it. This is that serious."

"Okay then, as you know we are recording this."

"I was told, but now I have a question for you. Can this be put to your council live? And if so, how long before they can be gathered?"

"I don't have that kind of authority!" Keenan responded.

"Then run the color black against whoever you need and let's move on this."

"Okay, I'll see what I can get done. In the meantime work with Kacey, and let her know the details so that there will be a small part that can be presented while the council is getting together."

* * *

The information passed through the cities like a wild fire. Now the cities that remained were on full alert, knowing what had happened to their sister cities. But no one had any answers as of yet, as to what they could do to stop the primitives. Saar was thankful that their *time of isolation* was over, that they had found that many of the cities had survived. But there still was a long and twisted road ahead of them as they came to grip with this alliance. But with knowledge, many times a solution could be found. And with point Alpha rediscovered, their true history would be known throughout the cities. And Saar for one would be glad to let Saige, Shellian and the rest of the crew know that contact had been made and plans were progressing. Still he knew that this was only the beginning, and there was much work ahead of all of them. Including the search for their home world, and whatever it was that had left them isolated here, on this distant world.

To be continued in the novel Desperate to Survive

F. D. Brant

P R O L O G U E to

Desperate To Survive

"Leader, I really do not understand this at all." He paused for effect before continuing, "These new females that we have added to our herd, a good portion of them have been with us now for one cycle of the seasons, and not one is carrying off-spring."

Looking down before answering K'jor said, "I know, but you must remember that it hasn't been for lack of trying. I know that most of the warriors have tried to breed with them, and once these new females realized that there would be no choice, they submitted. Of course there are a few that will fight it, but once these were made an example of, the rest allowed it. But you must remember that they are magicians. They have been able to hide unseen for who knows how long – I suspect generations if we really want to admit it. And I was hopeful that once we broke through and destroyed their magician lairs and ways that we would be able to reap riches that these must have had, and with the increase to our female herds it would mean that we would also have an increase in warriors to help us later to become the ones who would rule. And we surely ended up with enough females, even though most of the males are worthless as slaves. Once taken from those lairs of theirs, to work our fields and other places where we have need of their labor, they have died off quickly, and the ones that remain are almost not worth the effort or food to keep them around.

"Since the new females now understand has there been any further resistance from them when one of the males signals them for breeding?"

The second shook his head and said, "No, when any of our males gives the signal, then the female will stop what she is doing, undress and present herself, so that in itself is not an issue at all – especially when they have witnessed what happens when one of them refuses."

Nodding his head in agreement the leader said, "Yes, yes, that does usually bring the rest around. Once they realize that refusal will change nothing, and that it will lead to punishment. Well, all we can do is continue to try, but since they are of a magic race, maybe these females are able to prevent the carrying. And on that subject, have they gotten over the idea that they are allowed names? It is something that I really do not understand. They are just one of the herd, and as such they are not allowed that kind of individuality. I just don't know, and truthfully this whole thing has been much more complicated than I ever thought it would be. Just keeping the tribes and clans united for this fight, to locate, capture these magicians, and destroy their hidden lairs, has proven to be almost impossible. Especially since what we have found, in their *cities,* as they call them, there hasn't been the bounty we expected or had promised. And now it has been a while since our last successful campaign, and I can see that the tribes and clans in the alliance are starting to become quite restless, and might even want to bring up the old scars, hatreds, and such, and begin to fight among themselves again. We need to find another one of those hidden *cities*, again as the magicians' call them, or this may come apart."

"It's not for lack of trying, as in our attempt of successful breeding. We have patrols and scouting parties out, and now it appears that something has changed." He paused again, not quite sure how to state it. S'lon took a deep breath and then said, "Okay, look, something has changed. I don't know what. But somehow it appears that maybe they learned what's happening. It's the only explanation that I have."

Looking up from his working area K'jor asked, "Changed? How so? Did we not plan these attacks down to almost perfection, and yes, I know plans fail once one goes into battle. But from the ones we conquered I do not believe that any escaped. So there is no way that word could have reached the other hidden lairs as to what has transpired. We have completely eliminated anybody who could have possibly carried the alarm. Even that one group that had escaped was destroyed in the Sacred Mountains. So what could have changed?"

At loss as how to explain, S'lon shrugged, "Everything you have just stated is true. But I do not have any other way to explain it." He took a deep breath and let it out slowly before continuing, "These lairs that we've conquered were not close to each other, and while the population in any one of them was greater than any one of our clans, or tribes, it still wasn't large. So maybe there are only the few that we found." Shaking his head he continued. "I mean how do we know just how many of these lairs are out there? And maybe, just maybe we have cleaned them out, and there are no more."

Breathing deeply and loudly the leader said, "That is a possibility, but I have a gut feeling that there are more of these magicians out there, and until I have proof otherwise, we will continue to go after them." With that he waved his hand at his second to leave. He had much to think about, and needed to come up with something to keep this alliance together.

Seeing the dismissal he turned and left, frustrated, as he really got no satisfactory answers to his many questions. But K'jor was very busy, and while it had been pleasurable to breed with the new stock, it was also very frustrating to see that none of these females were now carrying. *Just what magic do they possess that they can prevent such a thing from happening anyway?*

F. D. Brant

Saige looked across the hidden meadowlands as the morning light crested the extinct volcanic walls that surrounded
them. With the clouds that hung in the sky and the suns rising,
the clouds took on many colors, from a deep gray, and as it
lightened, to a brilliant orange. If the situation wasn't as desperate as it was, such a sight would be worth stopping and
enjoying. But fall would be here and in the lowlands soon,
and that would mean that the primitives once again should be
looking towards winter and a possible break in the attacks on
the cities. With the destruction of who knew how many cities
since their desperate flight, when theirs had been one of cities
lost to the primitives, they had been cut off, isolated ever
since. And he knew that none of the surviving cities had any
idea as to why the ones that had been attacked had gone dark
– silent as if they had never been. Whoever this leader of the
united force was, he had been smart enough to make sure that
no one left the attacked cities to warn the others – except their
scouting unit, of course. And as far as the primitives knew

they had been destroyed on their desperate flight, and the few that may have escaped had died here in the Sacred Mountains.

He hoped that the team that he had left back at Point Alpha, the Alpha, or Alpha compound, complex, facility, or however else they had identified this place, had figured out enough so that when he and this group returned that they would finally be able to make contact with any of the surviving cities – if there were any. It was hell not knowing. Yet at the same time he did not know what his small group could do anyway. Sighing and taking one more look around he could see that the rest were beginning to stir. It was time to get moving, to find where their ancestors had left this meadow to do their research among these primitives. Looking at the size of this bowl he shuddered with the thought of how it must have been in this area when this volcano had been active. It was only one of many, and it explained why the primitives had considered these mountains sacred, a place of their gods. It had to have been a spectacular and awe inspiring sight when they had erupted. He was quite thankful that all signs pointed to these as being extinct. He walked away from camp and relieved himself, and then on the way back in smelled the smoke of their cooking fire. He realized that he was quite hungry and his stomach growled in agreement. *It needs to be today that we find the way in and out of this place. I truly did not realize the size of this hidden valley. Probably would have been smarter to have had everyone out here looking. But Stone and Sorrel had stated that it was huge, in fact around 10 kilometers around the perimeter from their estimation. Still until one actually sees it – well I just didn't realize it, that's all. It really makes it a very large area to explore and find that elusive point where one can leave this place, and find that other exit out of these mountains.*

On the previous day as they had worked their way across they had searched a number of likely places. But so far nothing had been found. There were a number of smaller cinder cones and many ridges and rises. With one area looking like a small town with the spires and blocks of broken lava, and another looked to be a small army in the distance. He had pictured in his mind a rolling meadow, not this broken rough land that surrounded them. Yet, he had to admit that what they were seeing made more sense than the images he had created in his mind. The history that they had been taught in their education centers had turned out to be false. It had been the discovery of this Alpha compound hidden deeply within the Sacred Mountains that had shattered that false history. Here they had learned that one of the strongest held beliefs that they were from this world dissolved away. This facility proved, for anyone who would doubt, that they were descendants of anthropologists, sociologists, scientists, geologists, the support staff, and the researchers – ones who had come here to study primitives, their societies, their interaction with one another, the planet, plant and animal life, and geology – they were from another world. But something had happened and they had become isolated. Their ancestors had decided to remain separate of the native population, and to *hide* from their sight, using the technology that they had to make their cities invisible, and to build them in inhospitable areas to make it even less likely that they would be discovered. It had worked for a few thousand annuals, but now something had changed and the cities were falling to these primitives.

Winter was a time, from their personal experience and study that the primitives stayed within their camps and shelters. But late spring was a time to search and prepare for battle and with it, he knew, this alliance would search for more of their cities. Yet looking at this camp he would never have guessed that all this had transpired, or was pending. Here, right now, everything looked so peaceful, so normal. "Hey Saige, how'd you sleep last night? Stone asked. "It was much colder than I expected. But I guess I can blame it on the fact that we have been sleeping indoors for quite a while."

He's right. Even though we spent half of the past winter in the caves on these mountains, the last portion, through late summer, had been spent in the Alpha so all of us have gotten used to being inside. "Okay, I guess, Stone." Then changing the subject, Saige said, "That food smells great. What is it about food cooked over an open fire that makes it seem that much more appetizing, anyway? Did you see that sunrise this morning, spectacular if you ask me? Look, once after everyone has gone off and taken care of nature and eaten, we'll get together and look at how we want to approach this day. We flat are running out of time, and I just did not expect that there would be so many places that could be an exit out of here. One thing for sure, we cannot allow the primitives to discover the Alpha compound. We do not have the strength to defend it. And I know from what we have deduced there is another way out of these mountains giving us other ways to protect these secrets."

"Yeah, it only makes sense. Compound Alpha's best security is for it to remain unknown, and hidden. Not that our ancestors didn't do a wonderful job of hiding it. After all if you hadn't literally stumbled upon it we wouldn't have found it."

Laughing at the comment Saige said, "Now that's an understatement, if I've ever heard of it, and thanks for being kind about that incident." Thinking back on what Stone had just mentioned he knew that he had been lucky that he hadn't been killed. He had literally stepped off a cliff and had fallen into the compound. So, "stumbled upon" was being kind. Looking around he could see most of the rest of the team were returning from taking care of the morning nature call, and gathering around the fire. They shared the cooking duties and this morning Staven and Starr were preparing the food. He could hear the friendly verbal sparring between the members of the team, which sent him back to where it had not been so friendly, and their group had literally fallen apart. Saige had to admit that much had happened in such a short time, and knew that so much more had to happen in even less time. But he did not even try to guess what the future might hold at this moment, and having any ideas on how to break the alliance, well, none at this moment. All he could do was shake his head, as what lay ahead appeared to be quite overwhelming, if not impossible for such a small group of people that they had. It saddened him to realize that in that desperate flight that they had lost almost all of their members, and the ten that were left were so small, so how could one then defeat the primitives?

* * *

It had been difficult to make this Keenan understand the severity of the situation and that they were the real thing, and not some prankster who was trying to pull something over on them. After all, the Alpha compound had been forgotten in time, like their true history. So it was of no surprise that there were problems. Saar with the help of Seirra, Sabryn and Seve were able to finally get the critical information that needed to be passed on to the remaining cities, about what had transpired with the ones that had gone silent, had gone dark, and why. After all, whoever led these primitives had made sure that the attacks would be, first, a complete surprise and there would be no alarms to alert not only the occupants of the city under siege, and second that none would ever escape to alert the other hidden cities. These primitives had complete success until their attack on Sequoyah, it was the only city that still maintained a trained group of individuals who could live in the wild, and possibly meet the primitives on their own terms, giving them the tools to survive. The rest of the cities had eliminated these elite teams, saying that it was too expensive, and "besides they were safe within their hidden cities so such a force was no longer necessary or needed". Out of the approximate 100 members that escaped from the city of Sequoyah only ten now remained. They had to fight for every foot of their flight, and the cost had been high.

It wasn't that Keenan was one who did not care, or just went through the motions; no he was just the opposite. In fact he had been questioning why, when the last city had gone dark, silent, and that the reaction from the ones in charge appeared to be much too nonchalant, and that it was "business as usual". It was because of his strength of character that it had been so difficult. He was not going to move anything further along until he knew that what he was receiving was authentic – yet, now that the word had gone out, now what? The small team at the Alpha facility felt their elation slowly diminish.

Now what? Saar knew that they were supposed to be getting ready to make this attempt at contact, then wait until Saige and that group returned, and once back then the contact attempt was to be made. But once they had put the coordinates into the system, the system had taken over and automatically began transmitting. There was nothing they could do but to continue at that point, which they did. And now that the cities were aware of what had transpired, again now what? It was not known how the primitives found them, or how they penetrated the veil that had hidden the cities from sight. Nor was it understood how someone had gotten this many of the tribes and clans together to form an alliance. Yet from the evidence that they now had this is exactly what had happened – *Again, now what?* How were the remaining cities going to be able to keep the primitives from attacking their individual cities, and to defend them? And how did the primitives know where to look? Yes each city had a map and location of all, but these maps were not easy to find, as they were hidden to prevent someone who had no need of that knowledge from accessing them, plus it required power to reveal the maps, and power was the first thing to go when the primitives attacked.

So while there was an initial exaltation from making contact, there was also consternation from not having a solution available to prevent further attacks. Saar looking back at the other three standing in the security office just shrugged. "I guess there's really not much we can do right now. I'll hang here so why not the three of you set up some shifts while all of you go and eat something. Then one of you can come back and take over so I can go and eat. I think that we will be very busy here for quite a while. I also suspect that we are going to get very tired of having to explain over and over again where we are and why we are here." So shooing them out he said, "Now go. I know that you Sabryn probably need to look in on Shayne anyway to be sure he's okay." He watched them as they reluctantly left the office and he took a deep breath. After all the silence that they had endured, they knew that soon they would be looking forward to, yearning really, just for that — silence once again.

CHAPTER TWO

K'jor sighed deeply as he got up from his working area. *It seemed so easy once we had discovered these magicians. To be able to get the tribes and clans aligned, with promises of wealth, prestige, and increases. And yes while we have in-creased both in slaves and females, it hasn't been nearly as successful as either I or the alliance has expected.* Shaking his head as he paced the bare room, he had no answers. The alli-ance was very fragile, and as his second had just stated, things just were not going well. *Yes, we increased our herd with many additional females, and even though there have been problems, most of them now understand what their roles are. Yes it had taken a few examples, which isn't something that I wanted, but it was necessary. After all, our roles as males are to protect the herd, to protect the females. And from this pro-tection these females are to allow breeding by any of the warrior males. Why do these new females demand names?*
It really made no sense to him at all. They were just that − females, and part of the herd. Yet these new ones to the herd had brought a restlessness to it, demanding things, that again,

the ones most outspoken had been made examples, to show the rest what they were and what their true roles are. Yet with some of them being in the herd for at least a full cycle of seasons none of these were carrying – and he had to admit that it wasn't for the lack of trying. He knew that these females had bled in their cycles which spoke that they were fertile. So why were none of them carrying? Shaking his head once again, all he could attribute it to was some magic that they possessed that allowed them to keep it from happening. He thought that maybe if they made examples of a couple of the stronger ones that just maybe it could be made to happen. But, then again, it went against their ways. Yes, if there was an obvious problem, a series of obvious refusals to submit, then the punishment was proper, but this – this was something different, something that they never had faced before. These females, being in their obvious prime time for breeding, but nothing coming out of it, other than he and the warrior males leaving their seed inside of them.

Enough on this! He had other issues now. The restlessness of the tribes, and the tension that was almost permutable, could almost be tasted, as it arose around him. They had been successful through this season of heat, and the past couple of seasons, finding and destroying eight of these magicians' lairs. But with season of falling, and season of cold approaching, and no others located, and again, with much in these lairs that were untouchable, because it had the magicians taint and thusly dangerous, the promised loot and rewards had not materialized. And, while the capture of these lairs had been easy, and they had been very successful, with little loss of warriors, the results were underwhelming, leading to this in-fighting and this alliance on the verge of tearing itself apart. But at this moment what could he do?

So far all of these hidden lairs had been located by how they were hidden. It was the one consistent thing they could find. Always in desolate out of the way places, areas where no one should have been able to live, and yet, these magicians did. Then there was that shimmering *veil*, more like heat waves, that hid the lairs from sight. And when one attempted to go through this *veil*, there would be both pain, and illusions of the mind, bringing terror and unconsciousness to any who attempted it. It brought back tribal memories that were told in stories of such things happening deep in their past. And of ones who had been severely injured awaking in, what only could be described as a very strange place, to be healed, and then once again find themselves close to their tribe with no explanation of how they arrived there, let alone why they were healthy once more.

This whole thing, the destruction of the magician lairs, wouldn't have even happened if not for an accident. Smiling as he shook his head, his introspection continued. Yes, if not for that accident, then this alliance, fragile as it is, would not exist, and these lairs would still be hidden from us and un-known. He remembered he was in camp, when one of the hunting parties returned with much needed meat. This party had been led by his second, and this hunting party rarely failed. But this time he brought back much more than meat for their clan – a tale, and strange clothing. Taking him aside S'lon stated that he had something important to discuss with him and at this time for him alone. So they went back to his portable shelter at the summer camp and S'lon sat down and waved for K'jor to sit across from him.

Then S'lon began, "We were following one of the herd beasts that we had wounded, and it ran far ahead of us. There was an argument about how much of an injury it had since it was out-distancing us, and appeared to be only slightly injured. But I prevailed and we followed it deep into the wastes, a place of little value, no water, much dust, and very little vegetation, you know the areas we know as the desolation. The only thing we could figure is that with its panic the beast just ran in whatever convenient direction it saw, and this direction was deep into the desolation.

Eventually we could see faltering and spots of blood showing us that it was finally reaching the end, and then we could fin-ish it, dress it out, and bring the meat back to our camp. Except when we arrived where the beast had fallen there were two strangers that were dressed in these clothes inspecting the downed beast – both young – one male and one female. This seemed strange to us, since females never accompany a male unless it is for breeding. They know their place, and it is with the other females of the herd, not like this. And if she was there for breeding purposes, then she should have been with-out clothes. We knew that the beast was going nowhere so we briefly studied these two from hiding in case this was a trap of some kind. But they seemed totally unaware that we were even close. It became even stranger, as it appeared that this female had a name – a name, can you believe it? We could see that she was well past the time of first bleeding, so she was easily in her time for breeding. As you know if she was not then she would not be touched – so are our laws.

Since these two were not of our clan, then we felt that we could consider them enemies, and as such, one of the many things we do with enemies is breed with their females who are of age, since if we can have her carry one of our offspring then it is a victory for us to have one of our own in their camp. So once we determined that it was only they we attacked them, tied up the male so he could observe how we had conquered both he and the female. As we began he fought his bindings screaming at us, until finally we just killed him. To our surprise this female had never been bred and she fought us as we became the first in her life. She ended up bleeding a lot from where we entered into her, and her screams were worse than the male had been, and she, as all of us bred with her, continued to fight until one of us hit her too hard and she succumbed.

If she had been one of our females then she would have ended on the rack for punishment, but here had given up her life instead." Then shaking his head S'lon continued. "It was a surprise to all of us that this female at a prime breeding age had never been touched. It is something unheard of, yet it was so. The only thing I regret out of this is that she succumbed. We do not kill females unless they break the laws, and even then rarely. So as proof we stripped both bodies, took the beast, dressed it out, and then returned. And I am filled with many questions, such as why only the two of them? And where were they from? We found no evidence of either a camp or clan home close by – and if there was one, why so deep into the desolation? There is nothing there to keep one alive, let alone a clan home. And if there was no clan home or camp close, then the logical conclusion is that they were lost. Yet they showed no sign of being lost. It was as if they belonged there, and it is a mystery."

"Listening until the tale was complete K'jor thought for a while and was silent. Looking at nothing he leaned forward from his sitting position and finally said, as he handled the bloodied clothing. "You are right, this clothing is strange. I have never seen anything so finely woven. We surely do not have the capability." Then pausing again, he came to a decision. "Can you take me to where you found these two strangers? I want to look at the bodies, and especially this female who had never been touched. She must have been ugly to have been shunned."

"That's the strange part about this; she was neither ugly or had anything physically wrong with her, so it is a mystery as to why she had never been touched."

Standing up and signaling S'lon to do the same K'jor said, "It is too late today to go, but early in the morning when the suns first touch the sky you will lead me back to this place so I can see for myself." And with that the two left the portable shelter and continued with the work the season of heat camp always required.

* * *

The suns were just touching the hills surrounding the camp when the two of them left. It would take half of the day to reach the hunting area, and from there S'lon would then lead K'jor through the chase of the wounded beast to the area where the strange ones were found, and subsequently killed. "The bodies should be undisturbed so that you can observe the remoteness of this place, and the very dryness. Nothing should be able to survive there. We saw no predator sign at all. In fact other than the beast that we tracked, there was nothing but the dust. It was a quiet desolate area with only the wind as company." Shaking his head S'lon continued. "That is why it was such a surprise to find these two here."

"Did they have anything such as travel packs and such things to survive in such an area as this?" K'jor asked.

Shaking his head as the continued their careful trek through the wilderness, and while they did not expect to be attacked by a rival clan or tribe, it was always a possibility. "No nothing at all. Just those clothes I showed you, and that was another part of this strangeness. This desolation covers days of travel, and while we were on the edge there were no other tracks. The way we entered is the only way from this side of this vast area. It made no sense." Then for a while both were silent lost in their own thoughts, studying the countryside, and moving with stealth through the land.

Looking up at the suns K'jor said, "I believe we will stop here as it is close to high point with the suns. There is water and shade here, and it is a place where we can stay out of sight of any who might approach." They ate a cold meal made of travel rations, relaxing and apart. By keeping distance, which was as natural as sleeping and waking, they could not be surprised or both taken if one of the enemies appeared. Then after a short period of time K'jor signaled that it was time to continue and for S'lon to lead. They were on the edge of the great herds, and it was here this very season that they would return to get the great supplies of meat to last out the long seasons of cold.

The area here was of mixed grasses and trees with the trees being sparse, and many small streams and one major river flowing through this vast plain. From the direction they had come from, it was heavily forested in areas and they lived hidden in the hills inside a natural rock fortress that their clan had captured and occupied for many generations. So many generations in fact, that the original owners were unknown and the mighty battle to take this fortress was more myth than fact. These mountains, which they lived within, were just foothills when comparing them to the sacred range that only the priests and a few brave hunters entered. Yet their seasons of cold were cold, bleak, and long. So it was necessary to store vast amounts of food for this. The season of greening was also short, the grains produced helped, and while they had tamed some of the wild beasts, there were too few to provide all the necessities from them – thusly the season of heat camp and the hunting of the wild herds.

The two continued their hike, both remaining silent using only hand signals, and the surrounding terrain to keep from sight. Again they kept distance between them, and hiked far apart creating more than one almost invisible trail. Stealth was critical since they were not the only ones who hunted the great herds. Yet these herds were so huge and covered such a great area, that very rarely did two tribes or clans ever meet. When this rarity happened it was more of high tension, and wariness as one group watching the other would back away, and then disappear. They were here for meat, not war, so during the hunting season there hung an uneasy truce between the hunters. That did not mean that if an individual could be isolated that a rival tribe would not either capture or kill that individual, as it was the way of things. To make one's enemies weaker if at all possible was the way of the world. It was also why any of the females who were brought along to take care of the meat were never allowed to leave the camp where they were always protected. Since the law that this clan lived by was as the world. If any of their females had strayed and been found by an enemy then like them, they would all have a turn at breeding her so that if by some chance it might lead to the carrying of one of their own. The females knew this, and as such had no desire to leave the camp to the point that a place within the camp had to be set so that they could take care of their natural needs.

S'lon signaled K'jor to join him and waited until he approached. Then pointing at the ground he said. "If you look here, you can see the spots of dried blood from the wounded beast, and the tracks are easy to follow as it bounded away. We were cursing at that moment, since it moved just as we had let the arrow fly just wounding it, we now knew that we had to track it down and finish it." He pointed in the direction the wounded beast ran, at which point both separated once again. Now until they reached to point where the beast finally dropped, and then the discovery of these strange ones, both would track separately with a great distance between them, again so that if one was found, the other could assist, or escape.

Soon they reached the edge of the desolation and here the tracks of the panicked and wounded beast was plain, as were the tracks of the hunting party as they followed it. It was obvious from the tracks of the wounded beast that it had nothing but flight in its mind, otherwise it would not have gone the way it did. For whatever the reason, at this moment, the winds were calm not stirring up the powdery dust that dominated the desolation. Once deep into this area and with no food or water available, the wounded beast would expire without any additional attacks from the hunters. K'jor was amazed at the stamina of the beast. From the signs, the amount of blood he was seeing, and the slight faltering of steps that the trail plainly showed him, it should have collapsed long before it got very deep into the desolation. He could see that even now one day later that the tracks were beginning to vanish as the winds stirred the powdery dust into small whirlwinds, with shifting and blowing dust clouds which abounded. This was a place utterly without life, and a place to stay away. So what were two young strangers doing in such a place? It truly was a mystery, and one that gnawed on his mind. Something just did not make sense. All these thoughts were in the background as to let one's mind wander here could easily lead to death.

He saw S'lon signal him that they were nearing the area where it all had taken place, and he looked around and only saw desolation. He, for one, would be glad when they left this place of dryness and death, a place of the spirit world and returned to a green place. Again he marveled at the strength of this herd beast. They now were deep inside the desolation, and as he joined S'lon he found ahead of him a large flat area surrounded by what he could only subscribe as something at one time that had to have been mud hills, but moisture had left them long ago. There were a number of small openings and a very small cave or two off the edge of this open area. The two of them were utterly alone, with only the sounds of the slight wind, and the beating down of the heat from both the suns, which were well on their way towards setting, and the ground, which radiated the suns heat back to them. They could feel the dust sticking to their damp sweaty skin; K'jor could see both a look of surprise, and consternation on the face of S'lon. "What is the problem?" K'jor asked.

Turning around and facing the leader directly S'lon stated. "I am sure that this is the area where it all happened. The tracks lead right here and the lay of the land is correct, but . . ." As he trailed off he shrugged before continuing, "This just doesn't make sense."

"What doesn't make sense?" K'jor asked.

"Look around, and what do you see? Nothing . . . Nothing at all. That is what doesn't make sense. Even though the tracks lead right up to this place, once we are inside of it here everything is gone, wiped out, as if it never happened – and we were here yesterday, that I am sure of." He then began to walk the area mumbling to himself, and pointing out things as if to get it straight in his own mind. Shaking his head and placing his hands on his hips S'lon said once again, "This just doesn't make any sense at all."

Walking up to him K'jor said, "Now look, from what I can see there must be at least six of these areas that look identical, so it could be just a mistake here, and you just came to the wrong one. We are running out of time and will need to be gone soon. I do not want to remain here overnight, even with the evidence of no predators. Let's take a quick look at a couple of others, and then wrap up here. You do not need to worry about your tale as false. You brought back the strange clothing from the two so you have your proof. So if you miss where it happened here in this desolation, well so be it. You are a great tracker, and I am fair at it also, and I have to agree that the tracks do lead here, and just end. That is not to say that these devil winds have not wiped out anything beyond this point, and that we have just stopped short of where it actually had taken place."

"No! No, I am sure it was here. But it is very strange. Without known predators or even tracks of such, the bodies, and the entrails from the herd beast all should be here – and if not that, at least the dried blood upon the ground, not only from the beast but from the two strangers that we killed. It is like someone came here after we had left the desolation and then returned to our camp, wiping out all traces. But then again, there is no evidence that anything like that, or what we were involved in, ever happened. How can that be?"

Shaking his head was all that K'jor could do as he said, "I don't have any answers, and I believe you. But then again, other than the missing bodies for which we cannot account for, it could have been these winds that wiped out any sign leaving it as if nothing happened. And who knows, since we shun these areas, there might be a predator or scavenger we know nothing about that prowls these areas, and if so they could be responsible for the missing evidence, or maybe it could have been the spirits of the ones who have passed over." Sighing he continued, "We've run out of time, and need to head back. But you've given me much to think about." Then looking over the area carefully once more, they headed back.

* * *

He had to admit it that even after returning to camp, it continued to worry his mind. He did not like this kind of puzzle. And it wasn't until that season of cold, back within the fortress with time to really think that the idea began to form that maybe it wasn't some unknown predator or such, but maybe a hidden people, magicians that could hide from sight, and chose to live in the areas of desolation. After all they would have to be magicians to be able to live in such areas. Again he had no proof, but promised himself that with the next season of heat camp that he would go back and do a much more thorough search.

CHAPTER THREE

Sighing, Saige was becoming a little frustrated. The six of them had just finished the circuit around the inside bowl, along the walls of the ancient extinct volcano, and while he had been confident that they would find the exit point that their ancestors had used, it hadn't happened. *I was so sure that it had to be along walls, but we did a thorough search, and nothing.* Turning to the rest that was with him he asked again. "Yes, I know, but are all of you sure? From the way we entered into this area, there is no way that these pack animals could be taken out of here. So what are we missing?"

Shaking her head Shellian said, "I don't think we really missed anything. With two of us going down the walls on opposite sides of this crater and two searching through the middle area, well admit it, we did a thorough search. We took it slow and studied every centimeter of this place, and we came up empty." Shrugging before continuing she said. "You've got to remember, not that you don't, that when our ancestors put this facility here, it was well planned, and well hidden. If you hadn't literally fallen into it I don't think we would've found it. So if the main facility is that well-hidden, it only makes sense that the exit or exits out of this large meadowland would be just as well."

Stone, picking up on the thread continued, "We all know that the primitives are much better at this than we are." Pausing as he saw the reactions from the rest, "I know, before all of this happened, we thought we were as good. But, I for one, have to admit that we were proved wrong, and it was just through luck and good leadership that we survived at all."

Both Saige and Shellian looked at each other, and then at the other four members who were with them and Saige said, "Yes, Shayne was a great leader, I cannot say that either Shell' or myself have been equal to his high standards."

"What?" Sorrel exclaimed, "What do you mean by that? I would not be here and alive if it wasn't for the leadership the two of you have provided. Yes, I know that I lost my daughter, and it still tears me up inside, and brings almost instant tears to my eyes every time I think of my unborn daughter that I'll never see, who will never have a chance at life. And before you two protest, remember it was Shayne who told the two of you to take over the leadership just before he died. And I trust his judgment, and especially one he made on his deathbed. And as far as I am concerned . . ." Pausing for a moment and sweeping her arms around to include the rest that was there before continuing. ". . . His choice was proper and right. Do you not remember all the fighting and skirmishes that we dealt with, and the only passage that led into these mountains that had been blocked by that large patrol of primitives? Who by the way, had been placed there to prevent our passage into these Sacred Mountains? And yet here we are, now knowing our true history, alive, healthy, and trying to come up with some type of solution to break this alliance that the primitives have forged – all because of the leadership from the two of you. Yes, looking back I'm sure that I could find some way to do something you did better, but isn't the final result all that is important anyway?"

"But Sorrel . . ." Shellian responded gently, ". . . at the end just before we found this place, we had lost our leadership to the conspiracy, and from that your very life had almost become forfeit, and not counting the loss of your unborn daughter, we lost five, count them, five members before it was finally over, taking our, oh around a hundred members down to just the ten we have now. Of course I'm not including the two new lives that have joined us now. So as far as we are concerned, that's my brother and I, we failed, and failed miserably. We should have seen it coming, and prevented it from happening. Then instead of just the ten we have now, at least it would have been five more, and maybe like the other two women here, you would be with your daughter now, *instead of having to lament over your loss*."

"Now hold on one minute Shellian." Staven stated, "I was one of the ones who were in the middle of that conspiracy. And other than the ones we sent away, it was our fault not yours. With everything you had to do just to keep us alive it's no surprise that you didn't see it coming. And had the rest of us been honest we should have recognized that both Schylar and Storme were eager to take over the leadership, but really had no skills to do it. So if any fault or blame needs to be placed it should be on us. And when we realized the very big mistake that we made, and was able to leave, we held out little to no hope that firstly we would find you, and secondly that you would accept us. After all if you had rejected us, like you first did, then we would have gotten what we deserved, what any traitor would deserve, but you and Stone came back for us, and now we have a child that like Sorrel's could be dead right now, along with us. And since bringing us into the facility we have been thankful every day that the two of you are leading us." Then waving them off when he saw them about to protest, he continued, "Look we had a rare opportunity to have been led by one of the best in Shayne, and then one of the worst in Schylar. So don't you think that we would know when the right ones are in charge? And I am glad it is not me. I am sorry that it took so long for us, all of us to realize it. Had we, then we probably would have put Schylar and Storme in their place. But instead we listened and believed them. So if any blame needs to be given, then it should be on us, the ones involved, not the two of you."

Silence reigned as both Saige and Shellian absorbed the words Staven and Sorrel had spoken. This leadership position had never been something that they had aspired to attain, and had reluctantly taken when there had been no other choice. They felt, as the rest, that there would be no way Shayne would die and he would lead them through all their present troubles. But it just wasn't to be that way and they had been placed in charge. Both felt that they had made mistakes, and blunders. "I don't know how to respond to that, Staven." Saige replied. "I . . . we, have tried to do the best we can, but know that we, well that I'm still learning, and that many times, just like this search we are involved with today, I fail in my guesses and assumptions." Looking to his sister for support, he paused not knowing how to continue.

"Look." Shellian said, "It was a real surprise to us when Shayne called us in and passed on the leadership to us. We never saw it coming at all. Both of us as a team are good at what we had been trained for, but never realized until it happened that Shayne had seen us, and our skills, as a team for scouting, to take over the leadership. Believe me, it was the last thing on my mind, and I am sure it was the same with my brother. Yet, it was Shayne's dying order, or wish, however you want to look at it. It still brings tears to my eyes as I see Shayne lying there with desperation in his eyes as he realized that he was dying and that there was nothing to change it." Choking a moment on the words as she recalled that moment, and almost bringing the tears back, she took a deep breath, shook it off and then continued. "This road to here hasn't been easy on any of us, and all of us have lost too many friends and comrades. We are barely a tenth of what we were when this all began, and with all that we need to do, and all that needs to happen I feel very inadequate. So all I, and I am sure Saige can do, is take it one day at a time. And any time we have a failure like this one, well I'll let my brother continue." Then looking at him, she shrugged and was silent.

"I guess what she's trying to say is that any failure against the time that we have means that we may have had another one of our cities fall, with any of the remaining cities, still none the wiser, as to why. So an assumption like I had here, and I know I wasn't the only one, but it cost us two days of fruitless searching, obviously we are looking in the wrong places. I guess we just haven't learned how to think like our ancient ancestors. Somewhere we have missed the obvious, and none of us have come up with anything that we can use against this alliance, let alone where it might be headquartered. So when we miss, make mistakes like this, it feels like a failure. And when it feels like that, then we feel – her and me – that we have failed as your leaders, and it hurts." Pausing once again and looking over the group before continuing. "Okay we've had our say, and now does anybody have any thoughts or ideas of where to look next?" Again there was silence as each considered the question asked.

"I guess", Stone said, "that like you, I thought it would be off one of the walls. But now it is obvious that it's not the place or if it is, then it's well hidden. So, I guess, even though Sorrel and I searched the meadowlands, as large as it is, it's the only place left. As it was stated earlier, there is no way that the exit is where we entered into this place. And not to change the subject but, I wonder if Seve, Sabryn, Seirra, and Saar has had better luck than we have? It would be nice to have at least one success out of this."

Smiling, Saige said. "I can't disagree with that. I would love to at least get some good news, and that would be the best. Especially if their research shows that we will be able to make contact. Then we can only hope that we can – well, the day is getting late let's head back to the facility, get cleaned up, find out what's been happening since we've been gone, and sleep in a real bed tonight. How's that sound?" He got the response he had been expecting as they all began to head towards the buildings that led back into the facility.

* * *

As they entered into the facility through the cavern, they began to smell food being prepared, and it made their stomachs rumble. The thought of a hot meal not prepared over an open fire really appealed to them now. And with the public showers just off the cafeteria they could clean up before eating, and that appealed very much to all of them – something about a shower that made one feel great. They, as a group, entered the cafeteria through the double swinging doors only to find three of the four members left at the facility busy putting the food together. "What's this?" Stone asked.

Smiling at him, Seirra said. "Well, we just couldn't have all of you return from your little foray out into the meadows, and then come back late on this second day without having something ready for all of you."

"Besides," Saar said, "we continued to monitor the meadow area so we would know when you would be heading back here. And we decided that it would be a great way to welcome all of you back."

"So why don't all of you head for those showers. I can tell by your odor that you've been out and about this last two days, and I'm sure that you have already discussed it anyway."

Laughing Saige asked, "Now Seirra, are you telling us in a nice way that we stink?"

Smiling, she said. "Saige, you can take it any way you like. But we won't be finished with the food until all of you are out anyway. And before you ask, Sabryn is working the security office." She made a shooing motion and said. "Now off with you, and we'll see all of you back here shortly."

* * *

After the meal Saar stood up and said. "Since I have been in charge of the facility, and haven't officially handed it back to Saige and Shellian as of yet, I'm calling a meeting. And yes even Sabryn will be in on it since we discovered how to use the intercom system. Bring your drinks with you, and if any has to make use of the restrooms do it now. There is much that I need to discuss with all of you, and I am sure that it will be the same with you to us who remained here. Now go and we will start just as soon as everyone is there."

Shortly, once everyone had sat down, with Saar still standing he said. "I'll open this up and bring everyone up to date as to what has been happening while all of you were tramping across the wilderness." This brought slight laughter from the rest.

"You seem to be in a great mood, Saar." Sorrel said. "Why is that so? Then pausing a moment before continuing, she smiled a devilish smile and said. "I've figured it out. Shellian is back." Then looking over at Shellian she saw her turn red briefly. She laughed and said. "I thought so."

"Now Sorrel, I have to admit to have Shellian back here safe and sound is something for me to be very happy about, since we have been apart for the last two days. But while that is very important to me, and I am sure to her, that is not the only reason I am very happy right now." Then turning to Seirra he said. "I'll let you break the news to them." Immediately everyone at the table other than the ones who had remained at the facility looked both at Saige and then Seirra – which caused Seirra to blush bright red. Laughing once again Saar said. "No, no it's nothing like that. I know that I'm the doctor around here and am usually the second to know if any of the women here are carrying, and at this moment unless one of you women have been hiding something like that, none of you are. No, this has to do with what transpired while all of you were out and about trying to find the exit from what I was going to call the hidden valley, but realized that where this facility is located is known to us as the hidden valley, so maybe we can . . . ah . . . call it the hidden meadowlands? Anyway now that we've finished embarrassing each other, I turn the floor over to Seirra." He sat down and then Seirra stood, still feeling her face a little warm from the flush.

"At least I can see that we all seem to be in a good mood. And on the subject we just touched, I honestly would like to add a new life to our small group, but it hasn't happened yet . . . which is fine." She added hastily. "That's getting off the subject anyway, and before I both dig a deeper hole that I can't climb out of, and embarrass myself further let's just move on."

"If you say so Seirra," Staven said lightly.

Taking a deep breath before starting she said. "As you know our assignment was to research the emergency plans, and communications circuits so that once everyone was back together that we could then put them to use and communicate with the cities. Well, what happened was more than we planned, and our *time of isolation* is at an end. When we activated the emergency circuits with plans of making sure that after all this time that they still worked, well, it or they just automatically connected." While the rest listened, she then explained all that had transpired since they had been gone. Yes it had only been two days ago that first afternoon when they made contact. And yes the information had been received, first with doubt, and then, when everything was confirmed, the information had been distributed to the remaining cities. They had learned that three additional cities had gone dark, making the total eight. At this point she sat down, and for the team that had explored the meadow area, there was a quiet silence as they absorbed the good news along with the bad.

Saar then stood up once again, and said. "The communications traffic that we are receiving now is driving us crazy. That's why Sabryn hasn't said anything from the security office as the voice from there is turned off." Turning and facing the monitor he said. "She can hear us," at which point she waved, "but if we had the sound on from there we wouldn't be able to concentrate. So, this brings us and you all up to date. Will you now let us know how it went on your exploration?" He then sat down turning it over to the other team.

Saige stood briefly and said. "I'm going to allow Stone to bring the four of you up to date, since it was Sorrel and he that found it in the first place. But before I turn it over to Stone, I – we have to say it really is great news that contact has been made, and at least the other surviving cities now know what they are facing. I just hope that we can break up this alliance before it is too late for us. The only thing we have in our favor right now is this hidden compound. And since it is in their Sacred Mountains it has a good chance of staying that way. With what we have learned here, I really cannot say how much will be believed back in the cities, but what can we say but the truth. I know that until it was shoved in our faces by being here, that I would have held incredulous anything that came out of this place. But as we who are here know, the proof is overwhelming. Still for many, even when the truth is such they will not believe. Such is life, I guess. Yet, even with the knowledge out there we have no guarantees that we will prevent the fall of our remaining cities. The only factor we have had in our favor is the distance between our cities, how they are hidden, and the fact that once winter arrives that the searches and attacks will end until late spring. We are heading into fall very shortly, which has traditionally, for the primitives, been a time of gathering for the winter time. So both searches and the attacks should diminish. That means that we will have a very short respite before the searches and attacks once again intensify. Again we need to be ready.

"Did anybody that you talked to offer any help for us? You know with the size of this place ten of us are too little. And the winter time would be a time to get additional bodies here to help. Although for the life of me I don't know how to get them here. It was only because of the desperation of the flight that we ended here in these mountains, and it is not close to any of our remaining cities."

Saar thought a moment before answering and then said, "In truth we've only been in contact for less than the two days you were gone, and I guess you could say that we spent a good portion of the first convincing them that we were real, and not someone just trying to screw with their minds. So I guess there's a lot of work ahead of us, both on the circuits and as well as solving this. And I guess to answer you, no; there just hasn't been the time."

Nodding Saige replied. "I guess that makes perfect sense. Like when this place was discovered it took a while before we really knew and understood it. Okay Stone, bring them up to date if you would." Saige then sat down.

Stone got up and cleared his throat before speaking. "Well, this is the last thing I really expected, but here goes. The feeling from all of us was to concentrate the searching along the walls with only two of us going down through the meadows and eventually we would find where our ancestors left the meadowlands. After all it was something that made the most sense, at least to us. Sorrel and I, when we first found it, had hiked some of the middle area, but only found some outcroppings, a large lake and the huge meadow area. So when Saige and Shellian suggested that four of us search the rim, with only two going through the meadows and it made sense. But, I am sad to say that the search was unsuccessful. We did a thorough search in both directions, with teams switching sides to make sure we had done a complete search with different eyes." Shrugging before continuing, he said, "It was a surprise, we really expected to just walk up and find it, but we were wrong." Looking around before asking, "Does anybody want to add anything else?" Getting no response he sat back down. It was silent for a short while then Shellian stood.

"It is getting late, we all need to add notes to the files, and I mean all of us. We, each of us have their own perspective on everything that has happened in the last couple of days, and it's important that we get those views entered. Then we can, at our leisure, if we can find such a thing, go back over all the data, and maybe something that someone observed might help. Plus with all of us back here, we need to share the duties in the security room. From what I am seeing I believe that we will need two of us in there at all times now." Then looking over at both her brother and Saar she asked. "Do both of you concur?"

Saar just nodded his head. Saige spoke saying, "That makes sense. I'm sure that Sabryn is going crazy in there right now with all the traffic that must be coming over the circuits." He looked up at the monitor and saw her smile and nod confirming his statement. "So I think it is a reasonable request. But, we still need to go out into that large caldron and locate the exit. All of this is important. Plus we need to start working with the pack animals so that they are comfortable with us, and be patient with us, since none of us has ever seriously packed an animal before. Yes I know, that in some of the training sessions that we did back in the compound we tried it, but to be honest we never seriously thought we would even need to do it." This brought a laugh from all of them as they visualized any of them trying to be successful. It looked easy, but they knew from personal experience that "looks" can and are deceiving. Turning towards Saar, Saige said, "Since you've been kind of in charge of the security room while we were gone, I'll let you set up a schedule, which once completed, you can post on all of the terminals. We are in desperate times here, and while it has been busy around here since we found this place, I have the feeling that this time that has passed by us will seem like time off in comparison to what we will be facing from here on out." Looking around the room he finished, stating, "That's all I have to say, does anybody want to add anything?" Again with no response he continued, "Okay then, until tomorrow morning – have a good night." Standing where he was until everyone had filed out he signaled Shellian to remain behind.

"Shell', what is your thoughts on how you want to attack that caldron?"

Shrugging and shaking her head she said, "I really don't know. Like you and I, and I think the rest that were there, we thought that the exit had to be along one of the walls. So with the training and practice that we all need to do with those pack animals, maybe just like the security office we should send out teams of two to continue the search. Even doing it this way will reduce the size of our people to only six working in the facility. We really could use additional people. I wonder if some of the cities may have only recently ended the program that we were a part of. If so, maybe we could find some way of getting them here to help – the ex-scouts. With the winter approaching, and the reduction in the patrols of the primitives in that alliance it just might be possible to get some of them here unseen. And with their skills to live in the wilderness have a real chance to get to the mountains, where we could have someone from here meet them and lead them back here." Then taking a deep breath before continuing she said, "The only worry is that one of the ones who would join us here may decide that because they were in charge down there, that they believe that they should be up here, and that will cause unending grief for us, and might make it difficult to accomplish anything." Shaking her head, she continued, "I don't know Saige. This whole situation just seems to get more complicated, what are your thoughts?"

"We truly could use more help, but you could be absolutely correct when someone from below got here, that they would want to be in charge. And if there were more members that had worked under whoever it is, then they would have the strength behind them to enforce it. That would be a mistake. Well, if nothing else, you've given me a lot to think about. Let's call it a night. We can tackle this in the morning when we are fresh. Today has been both frustrating and exhilarating, but I have to admit that I'm tired and ready for some down time. See you at breakfast tomorrow in the cafeteria, and then we can see if anything might have come to us over night." At this point both then left the meeting room, and headed for their own apartments.

As Saige headed down the hallway to the apartment, deep in thought by what some of the worries were, he unconsciously reached the door and entered. *Shell' has made a valid point. What if we did bring others in, and then because of their greater numbers they would decide that it was only right that they run everything from here, leaving us out in the cold so to speak. This is a big problem. Right now because of the work we've done, the exploring, and the uncovering of our past, I feel that now we have intimate knowledge and of course, experience on this facility. So, do we continue to work here as understaffed as we are, do we invite additional workers in, or do we not and continue to work this place as if it is our own? It would be easy to consider this place as home, with the loss of our city, and I can see why we could easily consider it so. But, do we have the right? Or better yet have we earned the right to claim it as ours?*

He found that he was sitting on a couch, and presently was alone. Seirra had yet to enter, and he had to admit he was looking forward to some close work with her tonight. But these thoughts kept nagging at him. *Eight cities lost. That means that if we can recover any of those people that have been captured by the primitives that we would be easily able to fill any of the empty spots here. Actually if we were able to recover ten percent it would be way too many just for here. This place was never meant to have much more than a couple of hundred. And I suspect that we are looking at maybe a few thousand that are probably being used as slaves, and worse.* He shuddered when he realized what was probably happening to the women. From observations that they had made, most of the primitives had taken the view and lifestyle of the herds that they hunted. He guessed it made sense, because the herd animals dominated so much of their lives. But that meant that any of the women who were captured would then become part of their female herds, and have to submit to any male. *At least, now with the information we have, no pregnancies could come out of those unions. But even the thought of having the women forced into such a thing hurts. Yet, maybe, while very unpleasant, and undesirable, still it might be better than torture, and death. At least while still alive, they have hope.* He just did not know how much damage to these women mentally, let alone physically, would result from their captivity and abuse.

With his eyes closed he thought, as he mentally shook his head, *too much to think about, too much happening and no answers for any of it yet.* He had been looking down, and suddenly realized that he wasn't alone. Looking up he saw Seirra standing in front of him with a look of mischief, and nothing else. He smiled as he thought. *It's amazing the difference between a loving relationship and one that is forced.* Very surprised to see her standing in front of him naked, he first wondered when did she get here, and then since the obvious invitation was before him he no longer cared.

* * *

At the cafeteria the next morning, a place that had become an informal meeting area, he and Shellian picked up from where they had left it the previous night. With a steaming cup of coffee in his hand he sipped and enjoyed the warmth and taste. "So Shell', any thoughts about what we left it at last night? Or like me were you too distracted to think about it." He laughed lightly remembering back to last night. He suspected that there was a similar reunion with his sister and Saar.

Catching his drift, she just smiled and said nothing for a few moments as she savored her coffee. It was amazing how much better coffee was than *shick*, and they always considered it a great hot drink to keep things going. Well, she knew that she would not ever be going back to *shick* if there was coffee available. "Yes, oh brother of mine we had a wonderful evening catching up on things. But even though that was so, I still feel, as we discussed, that it would be better if, at least for now, we keep it as it is. We've worked together, not just you and me, but the others who are here, for many annuals. And yes with all the trouble, and the losses we are few, but now we work very well together. And bringing in anybody would immediately cause friction and trouble, which, I have to say, is not a good thing while we are trying to solve this other life threatening thing."

"Yeah, I thought about it and have to agree. But here's a thought . . . what if instead of inviting any from the cities that are still hidden and alive, that as we start recovering our people we bring a few on board here. After all, like our city, theirs is forever gone, and if it has to be reestablished, then it will be as a new city somewhere else. And starting a new city may be very difficult, since the primitives are now aware that we exist. So while it may have been easy in the beginning when they first established these cities, now it shall not be so. I really think in the end, that the remaining cities will have to absorb the refugees, overtaxing probably most of them, but at this time it is the best answer I can come up with." He had been concentrating so much on Shellian that it surprised him when another voice entered into the conversation.

"Not a bad suggestion, Saige." Stone replied. "But we have yet to locate this alliance and where it is staying."

Turning around he saw that the rest of the group was here minus the two who were manning the security office. "So how long", he asked, "have all of you been listening?"

"Oh long enough to get the gist of both sides and the conclusions", Starr said. "I know that we would normally discuss things like this in a formal meeting, but I have to agree with what was being said here also." Then turning to the rest of them Starr asked. "Don't you agree? I mean it sounds almost territorial when you just think about it; we not wanting any others here and we surely could use the help. But I think that your conclusions are right. What do you think Staven?"

"Yeah, at first I thought the idea of getting more people in here to help us was a great idea, but when it has been presented this way, I cannot help but to agree. But how are we going to keep this from coming up as we deal with the cities? I mean, well, I think that they will be asking, don't you think?"

Saar, standing behind Shellian said. "Okay, all of you, I know that this conversation is important. But Saige, Stone, and you Staven have the breakfast duty, and while coffee is great, it won't sustain us. So go fix the meal, and then while all of us are eating it, we can continue the conversation."

Laughing as he got up from the table, Saige said. "Okay boss, right away boss", which brought immediate laughter from all of them.

* * *

It had been decided by Saar, that the couples would man the security office. He reasoned that because of the growing strength in their relationships with one another, that they would just work together better as a team. Of course there had been the joking about each distracting the other, which had brought laughter. Yet all had to admit it was a great idea. So after breakfast Starr and Staven relieved Seve and Sabryn.

Sabryn then collected her son Shayne who looked up at her through sleepy eyes. She knew that the babies complicated things, but would not have traded it for the world. She listened as Starr gave her last minute instructions on her daughter Sommer. Of course with both Shellian, and Seirra available, there never was a shortage of someone to watch the babies. Shaking her head she thought. *There's just something about women and babies. Always wanting to be around the babies, and always wanting to hold them.* Looking down into those loving, trusting eyes she would just melt. He yawned and stretched, then rolled over in his portable bed, and fell back into a contented sleep. She knew that shortly he would be waking and wanting to eat, so she and Seve grabbed some breakfast before retiring back to their apartment, where they would try to get some rest between the waking times of Shayne.

Fortunately it had been a quiet shift in the security office, but as day approached, it had begun to get much busier. And by the time the two of them were relieved there was much traffic on the circuits. Fortunately most of it was between the cities and not directed their way, and it was good to hear. It was a confirmation that many of the cities still existed. It made it feel like it was almost normal instead of what was really happening.

CHAPTER FOUR

It was late into the season of heat before K'jor had another opportunity to pursue his thoughts he had gathered from the previous winter. He told the clan to continue the necessary work, and that he would be gone several days. He told them that he needed to head into the desolation to talk with their gods, and he needed to do this alone. Yes he would take part of the hunters with him for protection against attack from a rival tribe or clan, but once the area of desolation had been reached he would go ahead on his own. He stressed that the same group should be back to the edge of the desolation on the morning of the fourth day. He would return then, meet the hunters, head back to camp and continue with the work to prepare for the coming of the season of cold and the returning to their hidden fortress.

That had been one day past and he was on his own, and while his memory of any area he had visited was good, it appeared that the winds, and what little moisture fell in these desolate areas had changed the land. At times he felt that he was headed in the right direction, expecting to see something familiar that he had locked into his mind, only to find the expected feature either wasn't there, or appeared to have moved. He knew that was impossible, after all only the gods or . . . That got him to thinking once again that maybe if indeed there was a hidden clan, that they had to be magicians, as magicians could cloud one's mind, make one believe one thing, and even change the lands. Stopping for a brief period of time, he looked around and once again saw nothing that was familiar. It was getting late on this first day, and he needed to find a place to camp, a place that would hide his presence. Yet, hide his presence from what? There had been only the dust and the winds. Not one flying creature, not any scurrying on the ground, no predator, or prey, just he, and the silence in what he could only call a dead world.

As he searched he knew that there wasn't even a dead bush or tree to get fuel for a fire, and he had hauled everything with him. As the suns began to set on this first day he finally found a small depression in one of the small hills, which he had to admit, to call them small hills was exaggerating greatly. Mounds would probably be more accurate. Still the selected camp would be out of sight, and protect him from the cool night breezes. He knew that there wasn't any water, so like his food, he brought it with him. The pack had started out quite heavy, but by the time he met up with the clan once again it would be empty. He built a small fire, just enough to heat some water. In this he added some herbs, and roots with a couple of pieces of fresh meat. This would be the only meal with the fresh meat, as it would become bad beyond this time. So the rest would consist of the dried and jerked meat that they would take back to the fortress.

As it became dark his doubts began to rise, putting down the strength of his conclusions that he had arrived at the winter before. *Why would any choose to live in such a place?* He began to feel foolish, yet he would stay to his plan. *Who knew, just maybe I'm right and somehow there is a people or clan hidden here. After all what better place to remain hidden; a place that all shun, as lifeless, without anything to draw one here, in other words, a perfect hiding place.* While this made sense, why hide in the first place? This did not make any sense. Yes all of the tribes and clans had a tendency to fight each other, but other than the skirmishes, no tribe or clan had completely wiped out another, at least to his knowledge. Yes, camps had been destroyed and the prisoners from these destroyed camps became either slaves or were added to the herds, but it rarely was the whole tribe. So maybe in the end this would lead to nothing but being alone. *Enough of this for now, my food is ready, and it's time to extinguish this fire.* Yet, he was reluctant to do so. This was a strange land, and who knew what gods, or spirits roamed it in the darkness. Still he was resolute, and he would need to stay at least for this night as this would be a moonless night.

* * *

As he continued to look back into the past at that first night he had to admit that he came close to just giving up. The destruction of the lairs, now in the present, had been successful, and he felt that there were more hidden deep within the desolation. Shaking his head and sighing, he knew that the combined tribes and clans of the alliance would be breaking up and heading back to their individual camps. It was time to prepare for the season of cold, and while it had been quite a sight to see the alliance attacking as one, he wondered if he would continue to have their support in the late season of greening when again he wanted to attack another lair of these magicians. Yet, after the eight they had been unsuccessful in locating any more. So maybe his second was right, right that they had wiped them out. Unable to keep sitting he began pacing, and even this was not enough. So he left the room and went outside to the fresh air and looked over what he now controlled and the many slaves and females that had been added not only to his clan but to all of the tribes and clans in the alliance.

In the next few days he would see less as the different groups headed back, until it would only be this one. He knew that they still needed to assist the hunters to finish the gathering for the season of cold. And now with additional mouths to feed it would require more. Again shaking his head, he just did not understand why these new females that had been added were not carrying. *Their magic must be powerful.* He knew that many of the females from his clan were carrying, so there had to be very powerful magic that protected these others. It surely couldn't be the males that they captured and used as slaves. They were next to worthless, and they did not appear to be much of magicians at all. He had asked them to perform some of their magic, but none could. Maybe the priests were right. The lairs themselves were responsible for their strength and skills in these arts – the reason that much of what lay in the lairs were declared untouchable. And once these were taken away from those lairs, their power was gone. Still . . . still, if that was how it was, why were none of the females from those lairs carrying? He had bred with all who were of age, as had all of the warriors, so again it was not from lack of trying.

Taking a deep breath and again shaking his head, his thoughts drifted once again back to those four days in the desolation. Deep in thought he went back inside to continue to review those first days there and once again, to see if he had overlooked anything at all. He leaned against one of the walls as he slid down to the dirt floor. That first night he spent in the desolate area had been a restless sleepless night. And then when he realized that he was thinking of that first night he remembered that one of the newer females would be leaving with one of the tribes in the morning. Yes he had bred with her soon after her capture from one of the lairs, but he had considered her a very healthy female and one who should produce many strong warriors. So he decided that he would have her report to him for one last chance to have her carry his child.

Getting up from the floor he went back out, signaled one of the members of his own clan and told him to have that female report to him as is proper for breeding, turned around and went back inside. As he waited he went back to the first night. He couldn't explain why, but it was as if the ghosts of, who knew of what, were haunting his dreams, and while he could not place any particular sound, maybe it was just the silence. A silence he was uncomfortable with, as the night usually had its own sounds. The sound of winds blowing gently through the trees, the scurrying of the small beasts, the sounds of the Loki that the flying ones fed upon, none of that here with the stillness that just continued to feed on his soul. It was a lifeless place, and again he wondered why he was here.

His thoughts were interrupted when as ordered, the female arrived. As was required she arrived naked, but also subdued, with a look of total subjection in her very soul. One who understood that she had no choice, and would submit as required. Shaking his head as looked at her, he could see the healthy body and as such he felt that there was no reason that she could not produce strong healthy warriors. Smiling at her he signaled her to his sleeping mat, his loins aching for her. Yes, one last time to breed with this one before she was gone.

* * *

The morning came much too quick, and K'jor heard the sounds of breaking camp. He knew that all the tribes and clans would be heading out today including his. They needed to prepare for the season of cold and that meant heading to the migrating herds, and then back to their main camps wherever they might be. He packed his equipment, rolled his bedding, tying it to his pack, went outside and joined his second. There was much dust in the air as the different tribes and clans completed their preparations for departure. Then silent for a brief time K'jor spoke as they assembled before him. "We have had a successful season. We have increased our slaves, and our female herds. While we did these things, I know for many it did not produce everything one wanted. But for good reason, the priests have put off limits much of what these magicians own, but we are destroying them one lair at a time. I feel that our gods are pleased. So, all who want to join me . . . us . . . this alliance, for next season's campaign will meet here again mid-way after the first signs of green. I feel that there are many more lairs out there and we need to destroy all of them."

Then looking around silent for a moment before continuing, he said. "With the knowledge that we have gained this season we should be more successful with the next one. With time comes experience, and with experience comes knowledge, and so what was unknown is now known, and because it is known we will defeat this hidden enemy. Now go your ways and we will meet in the near future." At that last statement he signaled break camp, and all returned and began the long trek to what still lay ahead of them.

Thinking back to late yesterday afternoon he had the female lay on his mat for which he then bred with her. She had her face turned from him and did nothing to prevent it, and remained silent as was required. When he had finished breeding with her she got up without cleaning herself, which again was required. It was a sign to all of the warriors that she had performed her duty, and could not be touched again for another full day and night. It was their way. Without a female there could be no new warriors, so while the females were required to submit, they were also not abused, thusly the limitation on how often a female must submit for breeding. The laws governing breeding were absolute and would not be bent or broken. All females who had bled were of breeding age, and must submit. Any female who was before the time of first bleeding was untouchable. The females were to arrive naked, silent, and ready to receive the male. The warrior, since this was a requirement to be able to breed, would then treat the female right. There could be no violence, and no abuse. If such were learned, then the warrior or whoever would be turned over to the female herd to be treated as they pleased. Once the breeding session was finished, then she would leave without cleaning up. This way it was obvious that first she had bred as required, and second that the proof was there for all to see, making her off limits until the required time had passed before she would have to submit once again. There were only a couple of situations where a female could refuse a request for breeding, and one was her time of bleeding, which cycled regularly, she was ill to the point of being restricted to her sleeping mat, or she was late in the carrying, where breeding could threaten her and the child she was carrying. She was unavailable after she dropped the child, and until the child was weaned, she was to remain outside of the breeding herd.

Punishment for failure to submit had to be substantiated by three males. This was to prevent false witness against a female by a male who did not like her. If substantiated, then she would be confronted with these facts, and allowed to defend herself. So if any of the above circumstances existed then it was within her right to refuse. But, if not then she would have to submit to the one who had requested it. Again with refusal she would then be found to have refused, which was considered a crime again the clan, she would then be placed on the rack. The rack was designed to strap a female into it in such a way that she would not be harmed, but at the same time could not prevent any male from breeding with her. Her offenses were the determining factor as to how long she remained strapped on the rack. When a female was placed on the rack, then she was available to any male at any time and the required time between breeding was waved. A mark then would be branded on her neck signifying refusal. If she ended up with two marks, and then refused to submit after that, then she would be ejected from the clan, with nothing – no clothing, no tools, no food, and no protection from the clan. It was as if she was no more.

There were laws that applied to the male also. First to have the right to breed with a female a male must be a warrior or a priest of their gods. This way the resulting offspring would have the strength of the two. As a warrior he must spread his seed among the females. If a female from a rival tribe or clan is found alone then she must be bred by as many males that are in the group that has captured her, before releasing her back. This purpose is to lead the enemy female to carry one of their own and from this begin to weaken their enemies, by having one of their own within the enemy's camp. There will be no breeding or an attempt at breeding a female before the first bleeding. If one has been found to have attempted or performed such an act then there are no second or third opportunities to correct. The one who has violated this is immediately expelled from the clan in like manner as a female who has refused. And lastly, any female of the clan will not be physically abused. No violence is allowed as it is the female that adds to the tribe. As in refusal, any who are caught doing such against a female has three opportunities in which to correct his behavior. If the male refuses, or at a later time returns to his old ways he is sent away unarmed and naked again never allowed to return under threat of death. A female from an enemy who has been caught and is away from their tribe or clan can either submit, or if she fights have a physical response in cuffing her into submission, and this is the one and only exception.

The females of all the tribes and clans were aware of this, and rarely ventured away from the "season of heat" camps, when the hunting and stocking of meat for the winter time was upon them. As the law was for their clan, it was the same for most. These things he contemplated as he watched the many tribes and clans leaving. This was the first time, as far as he knew, that there had been this great of gathering of what normally would be rival tribes and clans, ones that would be fighting each other. And because of this unique situation, it made some of the absolute laws change with additions. In no time in the known history had there been so many females captured, or slaves added. It was a new thing and required new thinking. He had gotten together with the priests and not only the priests of his clan, but the head priests of the other clans to help him work out a solution to this dilemma. With the destruction of the magicians' lairs, these females would not be returning to their places, so the rules of encounter with an enemy female would have to be changed – changed, specifically, to deal with these magicians, and the destruction of their lairs, and to make it very clear that this was an exception, and the only exception that would be accepted, by all who were in the alliance.

After much thought, arguments, and discussions it was decided that in view of the change the alliance brought and the fact that these females would not be returning, that they, after the alliance broke for the time between the season of falling and of cold, that these females would be divided among them and would then become part of the tribe or clan to strengthen them each in their own way. But, until the division at the time of leaving, they would be placed in a central location, be treated as females of the tribes and clans, and as such have the same treatment, being under the same laws – thusly providing some protection that an enemy female would not receive. And it was because of this he was able to breed with this particular female who now was leaving with one of the smaller tribes as a member of their female herd. Until the moment of the breaking of camp, she and all the other captured females, were available for breeding by the alliance warriors. Once the breaking of camp, then these females was officially members of the tribes and clans that claimed them by right of capture or conquest. He turned, and went back inside, sighed, picked up his travel pack, and then left joining his clan as they headed for the herds to catch up with the few from their clan who were working them. It was going to be a very tough season of falling with time shorter than normal to get the meat they needed. Plus the new slaves and females would have to be taken to their clan home as they would be useless during the hunt. And with the increase in size of their clan because of the captured magicians they were going to need so much more than they had in the past. Shaking his head he knew that the detour that they had to take to deliver these new females and slaves to the fortress was going to add time before they could hunt, making it even more difficult. But he could see no way around it. These new females were next to useless, and had much learning to do to be able to contribute to the clan. So it would be a burden to have them in, what would normally have been, the season of falling, camp. Yes it was pleasant to have them around for breeding, but without any experience in preparing the hides and meat for winter they would simply be taking up space, and the additional warriors that would have to protect them.

* * *

Sara, taking a deep breath looked out over the scene that was before her. She had now been a captive for close to an annual, and it had not gotten any easier. In her sleep she still relived in her nightmares of when the city was attacked, with the primitives breaking down the door to her home, her mate fighting desperately to keep them away and who then was killed right before her eyes. Then her own desperate fight to keep them off of her, and the rape that followed by the four of them. And then with little clothes on her body to be tied and led out to be put with so many of the other women, girls, and children before being untied. She felt dirty, helpless, and beat down. She could see that of the men who had survived had just as shocked of looks on their faces that she suspected that she did, and all the females that were in the same holding area as she. From the condition of the women, it appeared that all of them had met the same fate as she. There were tears and crying coming from most and of the ones who were not, some appeared to be far away as if what was happening no longer concerned them.

So many had broken distant stares that told her that they had been destroyed by what had happened to them, and only their bodies were still here, with their minds gone. She knew that most likely that these who maybe mercifully had escaped this way would probably be dead soon. She had searched desperately for her two children, again mercifully both were boys, but she could find neither. Then she saw the size of the force of primitives that had attacked their city and was shocked at the number. She knew that had they been prepared, that the city would have still fallen. She wished that she could at least go back and get some clothes and clean up as she, and looking at the rest of the women, shivered in the cool morning air. Looking around at the primitives she could tell that even if any asked for such a thing that it would be denied. It was a surreal scene before her with most of the women half naked, trying to hide their nakedness, and across the square their men being heavily guarded, with failure in their posture being able to do nothing for their women. What was going to happen to them? Since it had been morning, before any were normally up and about, most had not had the opportunity to relieve themselves and so with the women surrounding them, each woman took care of the need hiding behind the circle of standing women who watched outward to keep prying eyes from watching – there was blood left in many of those puddles. What else could they do?

She wondered if her brother Shayne, the one who was in charge of the scouting teams had escaped. But she doubted it. This attack had been too well organized to allow any to escape. She suspected that he was dead. Growing up together they both had worked as scouts. She had learned the language of the primitives as part of that training. Eventually she decided not to continue, had coupled and with her mate they had two sons who now were in their very early teens – one looking much like Shayne when he had been a teenager. Now all she could do is try to survive, and hope, even if that hope was slight, that somehow they would either escape, or be rescued. Again what was to happen with them?

That answer had come shortly. They all were herded out of the city, through the desolation that had helped hide their city, and then out into the grasslands, followed by entering a narrow canyon that opened up into a valley with meadows, trees and a number of small streams. In any other circumstance the setting would have been beautiful. But they really had no time to appreciate the views. Once they had left the city they never saw the men again. So their fate was unknown. Here they were put with other women, separate from the women of the tribes and clans. Just before being herded into a large enclosure they saw a number of racks that had women strapped in them. It was shocking in that all were naked, and unable to protect themselves. As they passed them they could see that the primitive men had sex with them a number of times and while these racks were shaded, and the design was such that a woman strapped in it would not be hurt, she could do nothing to prevent any male from taking advantage of her. They also noticed a small mark branded on their necks. Shocked from such abuse, all they could do was turn their heads away from the scene. There was absolutely nothing they could do about it. It made them wonder if they too would find themselves in the same situation very soon. The women who were in those devices had come from another city, and like them had been captured. The future surely did not favor them at this moment.

All of this had transpired a long time ago, but both with those nightmares and memories it was like it happened yesterday. Of course they had learned why the racks and why the punishment. From the primitives' point of view, refusal was against the whole tribe or clan. Back when she had been part of the scouting teams, she had observed some of the tribes. She hadn't understood their social order, there did not appear to be any method to how they lived. Now she knew, and unfortunately she knew personally. The times that she had to submit to them had been too numerous to count. They were uncouth, they stank, and their breath was even worse. And they hurt, since they never considered what was necessary to help, as they called them, a female to make it work right. It literally was wham, bam, and no thank you ma'am included. Then not being allowed to clean up afterwards was even worse. Yet again now she understood why.

In many ways, she guessed, that while the way they went about procreation was similar to the way of the herds, that there were laws in place to protect the female. And one of those had to do with no cleaning up after the act. It showed the rest of the males that she had performed her duty, and now was untouchable for a period of time. She was fortunate in one sense, by being older; she had not been forced into having sex with as many as the younger women. She had learned about those racks also, and had passed on this information to all of the women who had been part of the group that had been from their city. That time, until they were split up and the tribes and clans returned to their own permanent or semi-permanent settlements, was literal hell. All of them were raped at least a dozen times. After all what else could you call it? If one did not submit, even if submitting was against your will, you had that rack staring you in the face, where it was much worse.

Some of the most difficult members to deal with were the women of the clans and tribes. They only considered themselves females, and were proud of the times they mated with the warriors. And if the warrior was one of high prestige, they proudly showed off the proof to the rest of the females that they had mated with him. They were tougher to deal with than the men, since the men left the female herd to its own means unless they were, as they stated it, looking to breed with one of the females. Of course with new stock, so to speak, these became popular with the males, and built restiveness against them from the primitive women. It was never open, but things would happen to let the women from the cities know who was in charge in these female herds. It was back to the pecking order, and because she was one of the older women this leadership role fell to her for her people. But that still meant that as far as the primitives were concerned that the least among the tribe or clan females were still greater than the highest among the females from the lairs. She never understood why they were continually called magicians, or why their city was called a lair.

It hurt her to her very soul as everyday she could see the graves of the women who did not survive the ordeal, and what all of them from the cities considered continuing abuse. Many had given into the hopelessness that such thoughts generated, and the ones with broken minds had eventually perished. Since they had looked to her, even though she had not asked for it, she felt responsible for their deaths. But there was nothing she could have done to change it, or the outcome. With all the copulation happening with the women, she wondered why nobody had turned up pregnant. It just did not make sense. But she was quite happy that it hadn't happened. She knew that none of these women wanted a child from these males. From overhearing conversations, she knew that it had been a topic of discussion between the warriors and even the leader. From what little she could discern they thought that because they considered their city a lair of magicians, that they, the women, had power to prevent the carrying, as they called it. All she could do was shake her head at such ignorance, but something was going on. You just couldn't submit as often as they had to and not have someone get pregnant – mathematically and biologically it was impossible. Yet their fertile cycle continued, showing that both they were fertile, and that they were not pregnant. The other thing she learned was that the young girls were protected at least until they reached the age where, again as they called it, her first bleeding. At that point then she was fair game. And unfortunately a number of the girls that had been captured with them had reached that time and were unceremoniously introduced to the adult world, and not gently. Some of the graves she saw each day belonged to some of these young ones.

When the division came, once again there were hysterical crying, clinging and tears; all knew that they probably would never see each other again. And with the split they became weaker, not that they together had been a strong force. She found herself with the group that became part of the leader's clan, and they headed deep into hills. Where she hoped that at least for the time on the trail that the attempts at making them pregnant would stop, but such were wishes and not reality. Again, if the circumstances had been different then the area they were traversing would be considered beautiful. Eventually they reached their destination ten days later. Now within the fortress there could be no escape, and now with even more males and females around them, things for a while would become even more difficult.

* * *

Time had passed and now she was entering her second fall with winter just ahead. She truthfully could say that things hadn't gotten any easier, but at least there seemed to be an uneasy truce between her women and the primitive women. All that had come with her and the ones who had survived had learned the skills that were required of them. They assisted the mothers with their toddlers, knowing that once these children reached a certain age that they would be taken from them, especially if male. Males had to be raised as warriors and were taught by males only. She never saw her sons again. Every time she thought about them or her mate it tore her up inside, sometimes enough that she thought that just dying and joining them would be the way to go. She found that she would wake up in the middle of the night crying hysterically with deep soul wrenching sobs that were uncontrollable, and eventually she would fall back into an exhausted, troubled sleep. She lamented for her lost mate, she cried for the unknown fate of her children, and knew that she probably would never know what happened to them and that like those graves of other women, that this would, in the end, probably be her fate – a fate that never allowed her, or any of them for that matter, to return home.

She continued to submit, as did the others who had survived, again what else could they do? She looked out each morning on twenty-six graves, a reminder of those who hadn't survived the ordeals. But even after all this time, routine, and understanding of what they were up against, it hadn't gotten any easier. In fact at times it had been much worse as one or another woman would crack and become hysterical, requiring all of them to help the woman get back in control. While the loss of their names by the primitive culture hurt, they kept them among themselves. It was almost the only part of who they were that allowed them to keep their sanity. Still they only whispered them to each other. If the primitive women heard them they would be cuffed for such stupidity. Was there even a slight chance for rescue, and again why were none of them pregnant?

CHAPTER FIVE

"Look here!" Seirra exclaimed. "Something's happening, and I can't quite figure it out." She had been monitoring the feeds from space, and one of them had shown a great movement of something – animal or tribes she couldn't tell yet. With quick deft movements from long practice, she zoomed closer to what she had witnessed. "Saige, it's the tribes and clans, and I suspect that finally all this searching may be paying off. This has got to be where they're gathering to plan, and then attack the cities." She turned around and wrote down the coordinates that the view had given her so that she could come back later and study the area. Looking up she saw that Saige was standing over her studying the screen with her.

"Finally! We need to get Stone and Saar in here now. Can you set up the other monitors to show this? We need to start following some of the tribes as they leave. We'll worry about the clans later. We can probably pick them up at the hunting grounds and follow them back to their permanent settlements. The tribes are nomadic and we need to follow their range of travel. And I think that one of the smaller tribes will have to be our first target. We are just not a big enough group to go after anything larger. Although we have yet to figure out how we are going to do this. Yet, somehow we must. And each time that we are successful, it will increase our size, and maybe make it easier to accomplish what is before us." He turned and over the PA system asked for the two to come and join them as quickly as they could. He wanted Saar to contact the pivot city and let the information go out that the primitives were on the move, and then the three of them Seirra, Saige, and Stone, would try and monitor the tribes as they left and spread out in all of the directions of the compass. This was not going to be easy.

He turned and faced the door as Stone arrived and then shortly thereafter Saar. "What's happening?" Stone asked.

Pointing at Seirra, Saige said, "She's pinpointed the location of the alliance's main camp. They're breaking up into their individual groups and heading away to wherever, to prepare for winter. Saar, call the pivot city and let them know what is happening, we'll update you as we can. Stone, take one of the other monitors, we need to follow the tribes, and by their dress we should be able to tell the difference between them and the clans – they will be smaller and mobile, and it is one of these that we need to attack and recover any of our people that they may have. I'll put out a general statement over the speakers shortly as this will take priority over anything we may have discussed or decided to do. Once we figure out which one of the tribes will be our target, we will have to continue to monitor them so that we know exactly their range and what their habits are. Saar, I hope you caught that." He turned back around and faced one of the monitors and continued. "Stone, take this one – this is one of the smaller tribes, I'll take a different tribe from that one over there, and Seirra will use the one she is using to follow a third tribe. "Somehow this winter we need someone to go to this location where they've met so that we can study it. Again I don't know how, but it is something that needs to be done." Shrugging and shaking his head he said, "We just don't have enough of anybody to do any of this."

"Very true," Saar responded, "And even with this crisis, the cities that are still standing are very slow in recovering the scouting programs. Yeah, I know, some of them have had them closed down for quite a few annuals, and this isn't something that can just be rebuilt in a day. But, this needed to be accomplished yesterday, and even yesterday is much too late. Okay I'm contacting Keahilani now."

* * *

For the next several days the team followed the three smallest tribes out from the alliance headquarters and began to track their home range. As luck would have it, two of the three moved further away from their location in the Sacred Mountains, and the third, while not directly in their direction, did not head away from them, but even though they more or less approached them, the angle they took kept the distance between the Alpha compound and the tribe from getting any closer. It was decided that this would be the one that they would concentrate on. They passed on to the existing cities that they needed to monitor the other two tribes since both were close to a couple of the hidden cities and it would be so much easier for them, even with the scouting program having to be restarted from scratch, and that these reconstituted scouting teams needed be careful. It was imperative that these tribes be monitored.

During this time Starr and Sabryn had been preparing the computer system to send the data from the educational center out over the network so that the cities could have the true facts. They hoped that the ones presently in charge of those cities would allow the information contained to be passed on-to the citizens. It was not a time to suppress, yet government being what government is, it probably would try. Everybody needed to know, so that they realized what they were really fighting for. And while the information would be a shock to all, as it was to them when they learned of it, it would provide for them in the cities the impetus to push forward and try and protect what little they had. Again, while they could not prove it, they, their people, could easily be the last of their species – one born on another world, and not of this world. And even though the tribes and clans that surrounded them appeared to be similar, built similar, procreated in the same way, these were the only common factors. It had been determined that a similar environment had been responsible for the species, and why the Alpha Compound had been set up originally. One, to study and watch the development of this species, figuring that there could be some parallels to their own distant past, and to allow the sociologists, anthropologists, and other scientific fields to study what could have been early earth – but, at the same time, to stay out of sight, and just remain observers. And within the facility to have researchers and a large support staff, with all of this happening a couple of thousand annuals in the past.

"Doc, do you think that you could make up some more of that extract that we accidentally discovered would kill the primitives? And if so, is there a way to weaken it so that it either just makes them ill, or incapacitates them?" Pausing for a moment as Saige watched the monitors while Saar continued to monitor the audio channels. "I'm beginning to believe that this stuff may be our only way of at least incapacitating our first group – that small tribe that is southeast of us."

"I really haven't thought about it. I was shocked that, that was the outcome, since we have used it for as long as I can remember. Once processed its colorless, odorless, and has very little taste – as close as one can get to being tasteless. It has proven to be a great pain reliever in smaller doses, and in larger doses, to be able to knock someone out." Shaking his head before continuing Saar said, "I mean it was a shock to me, after all, my job is to save lives, and not take them."

Smiling Saige said, "And that's just what you did. You saved our lives. If the stuff had worked as you thought, we still would have escaped. And yes I know that this has bothered you. Shell' has told me a number of times." Laughing from the look on Saar's face he continued. "Now remember she is my sister, and one of the one's in charge here. We share all information that is necessary to keep us alive and healthy, and if you think about it, the health of our one and only doctor is kind of critical, don't you think?"

Nodding his head in agreement Saar said. "Yeah, I guess so. But I hope that's as far as it goes. There are many things between couples that should remain only between them."

Seeing the direction that Saar's thoughts were heading he laughed even harder. "Do you think that we share bedtime stories?"

Seirra who had been listening in on the conversation and saying nothing stated, "I hope not! After all that's not something that needs to be said publicly at all." Then looking directly at Saige, who was her mate, she asked. "The two of you aren't sharing stories are you?"

This brought even more laughter out of Saige who once he was able to stop asked, "Now are we starting rumors here? Do you really think that we share that kind of personal information, especially about our bedroom behavior? Now that's funny." Then turning back to Saar he continued. "Now wasn't it you and Stone that were discussing just that kind of thing back in the cave last winter?"

Saar flushed red briefly. "Ah, well, yes, but we weren't getting into any specifics. It was just conclusions from what we had observed, and knew that at the time that Sorrel had been sleeping around, and we did not know who the father of her child was." Pausing and shaking his head sadly before continuing he said. "And that became a tragedy in itself. But I guess it all worked out."

"True." Saige responded. "But were you not discussing, somewhat indirectly the very question you just asked me?" After asking he turned and faced Seirra also, showing that he was including her with the question. And as you and Stone discussed that situation in generalities, do you think it would be any different with Shellian and me?" He could see both of the nodding their heads. "Yes, we may discuss things on how the relationships are holding up. After all if we end up with couples fighting, and arguing, and with as small of a group as we are, such a thing could and would have an effect on everyone here.

"We've been together long enough now to know pretty much how all of us work. No I'm not speaking down deep on a personal level. Only each one and their mates can see that, but how we work together, and apart, and how we generally think and act. It's what makes things work well. As long as all of us stay within what we've become comfortable with, and no one steps outside of that, we function well. After all, all of us had been trained to work that way anyway. Shayne had always pushed the importance of that."

Smiling Saar said, "Well, that's a relief." And then glancing over at Seirra he continued. "And I'm sure that she feels the same way." He got a smile from Seirra who continued to study the monitors, showing that she was listening.

Then with a look of devilment Saige continued. "So you must be having some wild nights if that is a worry you have." Pausing with a large smile before speaking again, "I can always ask Shell' to confirm it. After all we have been a team since we were children, and as such we don't need anyone to say anything to know the answer." Getting the reaction he expected he again paused. "Okay, I know that works both ways, so enough of the teasing, and besides this getting off the subject."

"Subject? What were we talking about anyway? Oh yeah, the plant extract. What's going on in that mind of yours anyway?"

"Well, Shell' and I have been trying to come up with some way to be able to recover our people without killing off the tribes and clans that have taken them. You have to admit that we are terribly understaffed to do anything directly. In fact right now it looks like only four of us will go on this mission when we decide to move. That leaves six back here to monitor it. And no women will be going. I don't want to risk the few we have to be captured by the primitives. We already know what is happening to the ones who were captured, and I am not going to be responsible for sending another woman into the clutches of the primitives to abuse. So shortly Shell and I will be presenting our rough plan and we will need everybody to give us input to polish this thing. As you know, we cannot attack even the smallest tribe out there directly, so anything we do must be by stealth and misdirection. And at this moment that's all I am going to say. Other than I need you to start working on huge batches of that drug. And of course we now know why it killed that patrol, while the same doses would have only knocked us out. I know that you do not have any of the primitives to test, but we are probably going to have to test the only way we can and that is by using it in a real and dangerous situation. Until we can release some of our people and find out what is going on, then in many ways we are still in the dark. Of course any we can free will add to our numbers here, and maybe a few after a time of healing and recovery will be able to join us as we continue to go after, first the tribes in this alliance, and then, because they are much larger, the clans." Waving his hands when he saw that Saar was going to protest, "Yes, yes, I know that's all conjecture on my part and way into the future. But you may be surprised that it really isn't that far into the future. We have to at least raid one of these tribes this winter, and hopefully, more before spring. Remember eight of our cities are gone, and with them all of our people that lived in them."

* * *

They continued to monitor the tribes over the next several days with again the two larger heading directly away from the central command area of the alliance, and their location at the

Alpha in the Sacred Mountains. There were others, but again because of their limitations, they decided to only monitor the three. If the two that were heading directly away camped close to one of the still operating and hidden cities, then this information would be updated and passed on so that the closest city could watch them. This, of course, forced all the remaining cities to reinstate their scouting units. Some have been gone long enough that there were none around who had worked and trained for this difficult job. And to find the hardy individuals necessary, let alone train them in the short time that was now available to them, seemed to be impossible.

During this time as the rotations continued through the security office, and the two women with children continued to work with the educational computers, the rest of the team, other than Saar, who was busy with the equipment, producing the drug they would need, was out working the meadows trying to find the hidden exit and entrance. So far with a very thorough search, a number of times over, they had come up empty. Then came the day when they discovered it, and it was completely by accident. All of them had walked by the entrance at least ten times and had not seen it. Between the plant growth that was thick at this point and the illusion that the wall was solid, it had been easy to overlook. By only being there at the right time of day for the shadows to reveal an anomaly did it finally show. When they walked through the small opening, and it was again Stone and Sorrel who found it, it took their collective breath away. It took a few minutes to walk down the narrow passage which took a sharp right near the end. In fact at first it looked as if this passage was just going to end against a solid wall, and disappoint them once

again, but once there and the turn made, they found themselves in an area with many trees blocking their view.

Looking further to the right they could see the wall of the
extinct volcano continue to form what they were beginning to
assume was another natural and hidden valley, but until they
pulled out of the trees there would be no way to confirm this.
In the distance it sounded like there could be another of the
many waterfalls that were everywhere in these mountains.
Pushing forward, since the trees were thick enough to prevent
penetration, they finally edged around them. And as all the
indications showed, they found themselves in another valley
and meadow complex similar to the one that they had just left,
only this one being much smaller. "Wow!" Sorrel exclaimed.
"This is beautiful. How could we have missed this?" Turning
towards Stone she said. "I was guessing, when you and I first
found the meadows out there that, that was all there was. I
would never have guessed there could be a whole number of
them."

"I agree with you, but I should have known better. After all
geology is one of my specialties, and it is not unusual in an
area where a volcano has been active to have many islands of
untouched land, but it just did not occur to me that it would
apply here." Then shaking his head he said. "Don't ask me
why, 'cause I don't have an answer for you. I just assumed we
were dealing with only one." Looking across this smaller area,
he could see where the small falls were cascading over the
side, across a number of outcroppings that broke it into many
smaller falls and rivulets throwing small rainbows from the
mists created by the water striking the rocks on its way down
to a small lake. As captivated as he was with the sights around
him, it took a second to realize that Sorrel was trying to get

his attention. "Sorry, this just grabbed me." He stated as he turned to face her.

Smiling at him she said. "I can understand that, but look over there, isn't that a building?" Then getting a look of devilment in her eyes she asked mischievously. "Wouldn't this be a great place to couple?" Then she laughed as she began to disrobe. He couldn't disagree, and he had to admit having a hot woman as a mate had its benefits, shaking his head inwardly and smiling as he joined her.

* * *

Later after the passion had faded, they worked their way over to the building that was constructed out of the native rock. Once inside, it took a few moments for their eyes to adjust to the dim light. Here there appeared to be no artificial light, and looking up they could see what they assumed was sky lighting. But through the annuals of abandonment these were covered in layers of grime, and he suspected that there probably was a growth of moss also. "I think I'll climb up on the roof and see if I can clear the sky lights. You hang by this entrance and let me know how it works. Might have to figure out how to get some water up there and clean them further, but won't know until I get that growth off." He then turned and headed back outside and had to stop once again as the bright light temporarily blinded him, causing his eyes to water for a moment. Walking around the building, which was built against one of the canyon walls, he found handholds that had been carved into the rock, and he slowly, testing each foot and hand hold, worked his way up and onto the roof. Then gingerly, he walked across, not knowing how solid the surface was.

But found that he didn't need to worry as it appeared to be solid. The whole roof area was covered in growth, and he only located the sky lights by guessing and doing a preliminary scrapping with one of the long knives that they carried with them. As he cleared the material he could hear Sorrel moving below him. After a few minutes he asked. "Is this improving the light?"

Even though the reply was muffled by the thickness of the walls and roof he heard her say, "Yes." There was a pause and she replied. "Yes, it's working really well. There's still a lot of shadow in here, but I'm being able to actually see things in here now. And I think that there is no power here at all. But I guess that makes sense, after all this pretty far away from the compound, and this building is all by itself, so why?"

"Just wanted to make sure that what I was doing was working. This stuff has been on here from the looks of it for a long time, and the material that the light is supposed to shine through is pretty cloudy. So I was guessing that one of us would have to go over to the small lake and get some water and wipe this down. But if this works well enough, I guess we can wait on the final cleaning."

"Well, I can't say it's perfect, but I'm beginning to see things well enough to recognize the layout now. I think that once you get a couple of them scraped . . . look I'll come up and help. That way it will be done faster and then we can look over the inside of the place together." Then laughing she said, with a bit of humor. "After all, it is always nicer when we do things together."

Shaking his head and smiling he thought. *Back when we were in the cave I would never have thought of loving this woman. In fact back there she was so much trouble that we were constantly figuring out how we could control the situation. She was the first of the women who was with child, and she would not identify who the father was. We suspected that she probably didn't know, because at the time she was sleeping around. But so much had happened since those desperate times, and she lost her child and almost lost her life.* Now he couldn't see his life without her, and he knew that she felt the same way about him. He continued to scrape away and heard her coming up to join him.

"Okay, now that I'm up here which one would you like me to work on?" She was standing up close to where the handholds were carved in the rock wall.

Smiling and looking down at his handiwork for a moment, he didn't say anything. *She is such a beautiful woman, healthy, and so full of life and joy. I really thought that she would have permanent scars from her experience. But if she does, she hides them so very well.*

Smiling at him, and with a questioning look she asked. "What?"

Again shaking his head, he said, "Oh just you. That's all." Then sighing he continued. "You know you're so beautiful to me that it hurts, but to answer your first question. I think I counted five panels for the sky lights, so if we clear three of them that should be plenty. So work the one that's closest to you and then we both can work the center one." Pausing for a moment before continuing he said, "To the second, well let's just say that I love you and leave it at that." He sat back down and began to scrape at the vegetative covering on the sky lights once again. Concentrating on clearing the stuff off, he heard her sit down and soon could hear the sounds of Sorrel scraping. A little time later something struck him, and he looked up and over to Sorrel, but she appeared to be working away, and not paying attention to him at all. *Must have been my imagination or something fell I guess.* He turned back and continued his work, only to be struck again. This time he heard a giggle, and knew that she had thrown something at him again. She surely knew how to distract him, and he had to admit it was working.

Looking at him with a large grin on her face, she said. "You looked so serious over there. And so *tempting* of a target – I just couldn't let a moment like that pass." She then laughed.

Since he had a greater pile of debris he grabbed a handful and chucked it her way, which she easily dodged. She once again laughed and then stuck out her tongue at him. "You missed, and you're supposed to be a warrior. Some warrior you are – can't even hit a helpless woman."

Standing up once again he said. "Helpless? You? Somehow I don't think so. You seem to control the situation pretty well if you ask me, and I know that you aren't – helpless that is – but I'll say it anyway." He grabbed another handful and this time spread it as he threw it, making sure that she would not be able to dodge all of it. This started a free for all, and led to another physical session on the roof and in the warm sun. Breathing hard, all he could say was, "You sure make it hard for a man to ignore what you have."

Laughing once again, she said. "And that's the way I like it."

"Like what?"

"Why, I like it hard. After all it works better that way." Again she laughed. "But I think that both of us had better take a dip in that lake so we don't smell like, you know what, when we head back with the news that we probably found the exit out of the meadows. That's, of course, after we confirm that there is a way through the wall where this building is constructed.

"Good suggestion. I suspect that we reek a little, or maybe a lot. But do you think that this is the place? It could be that this is just an offshoot and that's all."

"No, I think this is probably it. As the light increased, before I came up here to help, I could see stalls, and storage areas. Then against the wall there looked like another one of those sliding doors, again not as large as the ones that are on those really big buildings just outside of the compound, but large enough for one of the pack animals to easily fit through with it packed. So I think that this was a staging area where they could do what was necessary before leaving, and be out of the weather if they needed."

"Sounds good to me. Let's get this scraping done, and then check it out. Once we confirm it we'll take that quick dip, and say we had to because of all the crap we got on us from cleaning off the sky lights." At this point, he turned back to continue when he heard her laugh softly. "What?"

Shaking her head the only thing she said was, "Oh you, that's all," and turned back to continue her scraping.

* * *

Sara sat working a hide to help cure it for later use when one of the older warriors signaled her that she was to breed with him. She sighed, shuddered a little, and with the rack always in the back of her mind went to him, undressed, and looked away. She had to concentrate on not making a sound.

Because when they performed the act they hurt. She couldn't flinch, or groan, or show any sign of the pain it caused her, having to lay there until he was finished. This one had never been gentle, and this time was no different. She suspected that there would be blood afterwards. When he was finished she got up carefully as it really had hurt, and now she was very tender. As was required she dressed, returned to the skin she had been working and said nothing. She hated them, she hated the mess that she was not allowed to touch, but knew that this still was better than the rack and the punishment it represented. Looking down, as she suspected, she saw blood mingled with everything else that was on her legs. Taking a deep breath she thought. *It would be so easy to join the ones who are in those graves, and leave all this behind. There were now forty of them, and it would be so easy to become forty one.* Yet in her heart she knew that she could not take her own life. So she continued to endure the pain and humiliation. There was such a difference between this and the loving relationship that she and her mate had. But he was gone, as were her children. With these thoughts she began to weep silently once again. *Oh to wake up and to find this was only a nightmare and not reality.* It was a hope, but that was all, since she knew that what was happening was quite real, real for her and all of the other women who had been captured.

Some of the women that had most recently perished had perished because of infection. From the rough treatment they were receiving none had time to heal, and since there appeared to be a desire to see any if not all of them carrying offspring, the pressure to breed by the primitives had increased. And these injuries caused by this, with no time to heal had become infected, and with nothing to fight the infections, with poor health, poor nutrition, and worse conditions, these infections increased in strength killing many. Again there was very little sympathy, let alone help from the primitive women. After all, these upstarts were taking the males away from them, and they did not like it. And so an uneasy and uncomfortable truce existed between the two groups, with the primitive women retaliating any time they felt they could get away with it. Sara was sure that some of the deaths of the city women were at the hands of the primitive women, especially when they were very ill. But she could never prove it. This meant that all of them were very alone, very scared, and depression ruled their lives.

* * *

"Look all; we are dealing with a very tough situation here." Saige said as he opened the meeting. "Not that any of us are unaware of that. Somehow we have to get something started that will start developing doubt with the primitives. So far they've had it their way, and I'm sure their confidence is riding very high. It was only through diligence that we've been able, finally, to locate their gathering place before heading out and attacking our cities. And we've been able to track one of the smaller tribes to just southeast of us here. Now we have to start changing the direction, and tide and make it begin to work for us." He turned to Shellian and said, "She's going to bring us up to date to what we know and what we face. Then I'll put out to you our basic plan for our first offensive." Stopping for a moment and looking at all of them, especially the women, he said. "None of you, and I am specifically speaking to the women here, but including all of us, will like what we are going to propose, but hear us out. And if any, and I mean any of you have something better we want to hear it, and hear it here in this meeting." He sat down and turned over the meeting at this point to Shellian.

"Now most of the history we are familiar with so I am not going to bore you with those facts. But what I need all of you to remember that we were a very active scouting unit until our city fell. And it is this I want to talk to you about. We all need to remember the ways of the primitives. It is so important that as we plan this offensive, at least initially, that we do not allow any of the tribes either within this alliance, or outside of it to realize that there is another player in this game. So I need all of you to remember your history of how the primitives act, how they fight, how they scout, and how they live. Because for us, with this small force we cannot let them know about us at all. When we are finished with an attack and withdraw it must appear to be a rival tribe or clan that is responsible, not us. That means when we do this that we *must*, and I mean there can be no variance here, we must act completely within character of the primitives. I'll let you think about that for a moment, and while I don't like it either, being a woman, I see no other way of doing this, at least until we know more, and we have more people to work with. Our goal on this foray is to rescue some of our people. And initially they must feel that we are a rival tribe attacking and taking bounty from the attacked tribe." She leaned on the table and again looked at each one that was seated before continuing. "I can see that some of you are beginning to realize what this will entail. So now we will take a brief break to give everyone time to think about what we've said so far and then Saige will give you the hard facts." Taking a deep breath she said. "Okay, see all of you back here in about fifteen minutes."

She looked across to her brother and asked. "Do you think that they will have figured out what the four of you are going to have to do?"

Shaking his head he said, "I don't know, but once I begin to cover what it is and what we need to act like, well, I know the women, the mates to us are not going to like it at all." Taking a deep breath before continuing he said. "Heck, I'm a guy, and I don't like it. But if we don't then there would be an immediate red flag raised saying something here is just not right, and we cannot have any hint left behind that says we are not the primitives." He then asked, "Like to get a snack and maybe a cup of coffee before we continue?"

"Sure, probably should bring back a couple of, what did they call them, oh yeah, carafes. That way we can have some of it sitting here to use during this next portion. I suspect we are going to be here for quite a while, and I can already see the protests. I mean, I'll be the fortunate woman here as my mate Saar will not be involved with this, so it will affect me the least. But we cannot put our one doctor in a dangerous situation. Otherwise he would be part of this team. I can only hope he understands that."

* * *

Standing again at the head of the table he waited until all of them had quieted down and was looking at him. "Now I am sure that we all discussed what has been said when we took the break, and tried to understand why it was important to bring up the primitives and their way of life." Stopping for a moment and looking over the gathering he continued, "Okay first off we have been studying the tribe we plan to attack, and looked around the area where they are staying to see what other tribes may be in the area. We found two, so from our aerial view we have determined these rival tribes' totems. So when we go in for this attack we will become one of these tribes. That way, quite naturally as far as this tribe goes, they will assume that the attack was from one of these and not us. And this is critical. It must appear to be one of them."

Again pausing he said. "Now before I continue on this, I want to point out that we cannot afford any losses. And we've found another way down through the mountains so that we will be just south of their camp. We will be using tactical headsets so that we can keep in contact with each other. These are so small that they are virtually invisible." Again he stopped, and looked at each one of them. "This will involve just four of us with Saar and all of the women remaining here. And before you object Saar, remember you are our only doctor, and as such irreplaceable, so you and the women will be monitoring the situation from here. I know that we have not figured out long distance communication between a ground force and here, and I don't know if our ancestors had such a thing – but if they did, and if it is still here and operational, we have yet to figure it out. So all this will do for all of you who are here is to know the situation, and give you time to prepare for our return, whether it is successful or not. So that means that I, Seve, Stone, and Staven are elected. It means that we have to get into those skins that we made when we were still in that cave, and it means that we will have to go out to the meadow area here and begin to practice for this task. It truly has to go as close to perfect as we can make it."

Again looking around the room before continuing he took a deep breath, letting it out slowly. "Okay, our plan is not to wipe out this tribe. With that drug that Saar has been producing we could just do that. But it again would look suspicious for such a small force to wipe out an entire camp. We will take out the guards, and with the dart guns and packets we can throw into the fires put the rest into what I hope is a drugged sleep." Pausing for effect he then asked, "With what we know of these people, what happens next?" There was silence, and then he could see the realization hit home. Smiling even though it was a bitter one he said. "That's right. We have to have sex with at least one of the primitive women in that camp. Otherwise something would be very out of place. At least we know that there would be no offspring created from the union. But honestly from what I have seen of these women, I really have no desire to copulate with one. And if any of you have any idea how we can avoid it I am all for it." The reaction was just about what he expected, but he had no other answers, and they needed to save both the men and women that were being held there." Again taking some time to let it soak in he said. "We begin our training this afternoon. We are to be a scouting team from one of those rival tribes who stumbled upon their camp and attack it, performing what they would do, and take captives back with us. That is how it must look. Okay now that you know what we've come up with we now have an open session to either accept what Shell' and I propose, or come up with something else that will work."

C H A P T E R S I X

K'jor stood at the entrance to the clan home and thought. *It's good to be back. And while we did okay with this period of rooting out the magicians, and we've increased our female herd, and slaves to work, it isn't quite what I had hoped or planned.* Turning around he said. "We're here, let's get the captives inside and explain to them where they will live and what will be required of them." The laughing he continued. "Not that the females don't already understand what their role is." This brought general laughter from his warriors. Since they had demonstrated what was required. And even though a couple had been placed in the racks to reinforce their role, overall these new females had bowed to the demands of the clans and tribes in the alliance. After all they had no choice.

* * *

The season of falling was here in earnest and the need to work the herds were strong. Otherwise there would be no meat to get them through the tough season of cold ahead. Where they were located, in the foothills, was such, that snow was common. And while not deep as the Sacred Mountains, it at least prevented travel, and at times even one from leaving their abode. Whether this shelter was a warrior's space, a common area like the female herd, slaves, or the place where the offspring grew. This latter area had to be kept warm since all offspring to the age of two and finally at a point of controlling their body functions wore no clothing. Once that time had been reached then the males would be removed from the care of the female herd and begin their training to become a warrior or a contributing member of the clan or tribe. No additional contact was allowed by any male offspring after the separation until they had proven themselves a warrior or priest – then, and only then, would they have a right to breed with the female herd, and add their seed and strength to the clan or tribe. This had been the way for as long as any could remember, and that included the story tellers, the true keepers of their past.

This was also a time of deep thought and preparing for the season of green, and a time for the female herd to begin carrying the next generation. When it was cold, it was nice to have one of the herd to warm one's sleeping mat, even if it was only for a brief period of time.

The female herd was responsible for the care of those underage, until the separation, and the young females would then begin their learning in the ways of preparing the hides, and the making of garments that all wore. They also learned the way of preparing food, and the preservation of meat. Here they learned their place and the importance of submitting only to the warriors, and only after their first bleeding. It was then that they would pass into full fertility and be able to honor the clan or tribe by being available and to produce healthy strong offspring. In the herd they would learn their place, and whatever special skills they showed would be encouraged and strengthened – bringing honor to the herd, and to the clan or tribe. And most of the teaching, most of the real work, for the herd was performed during the harshness of the season of cold.

So with the season of cold approaching and with this late start, the warriors left to hunt the herd beasts that provided for their long term needs. K'jor led, as he led the alliance. A few of the females would accompany them to work the meat into something that would be safe and transportable, followed by doing an initial preparation of the hides. They would be gone one full moon cycle, and two minor moons cycle. This would bring them to the brink of the season of cold, and the hunting party would need to be back inside the safety of their walls by then. Sara, watching the preparation, was quite thrilled when she found that none of the women, that the hunting party chose to join them, were from the cities. She realized that this made sense, as the city women were not very good at preparation yet, and with this late start efficiency was the key. So she, like the rest, that were to remain behind, watched as the hunting party left. This meant that with fewer males around that that should reduce the pressure on all of them to have to submit. Maybe, just maybe, there would be enough time between so that many of them could heal, including she. She turned to leave only to see that older warrior, the one who seemed bent on getting her pregnant signal. Looking down and shaking her head slightly she went to him, and prepared to submit. Now if she could just prevent herself from flinching. After this she hoped that he would leave her alone long enough to heal. With as dirty as these people were, it would be so easy to catch something from them and then die from it. It had already happened to far too many of captive women. To be injured down there from the rough treatment, and then not given the time to heal, followed by an infection that entered the woman's body through the injury, and eventually she would succumb – not having the strength to fight off the infection.

* * *

As they worked the herds for their needs K'jor again would return back to that incident that had eventually brought the alliance together. That first night in the wastelands had been hell. He had sworn that the spirits of the dead warriors were haunting him. He had thought he heard voices a number of times, but was never able to locate the source. When the suns arose the next day he was beat, on edge, impatient, and short tempered – lack of sleep did that to him. So instead of building a fire, which would be difficult with his limited supply of fuel, and he did not feel like trying to locate any additional wood to make it work, he ate his travel rations. His original time table was to be up to four days away here in the desolation, but he could see that water would be an issue, or at least he thought it would be, so he would use as little as he could to extend his time. The mystery of those two strangers worked on him. There just wasn't any explanation as to why they were here, let alone where their bodies had disappeared to. Were they of a magic race, a race that once killed, that they would just evaporate? He didn't know, and he had no way of understanding – to figure it out. So the mystery just deepened.

Those voices in the quiet of the night seemed so real, so close, but he had seen nothing. So once he finished his small meal he began to search the area where he had slept to see if he could find anything to explain last night. And as the suns climbed in the sky, the area began to heat and the winds pick up. Spirit spirals danced across the barren wastes. And other than the winds it was a silent dead world. Shaking his head he thought. *What was I thinking? Nothing can live here. It is a place of ghosts and spirits, a place of death not life. Even the very grasses that cover the plains cannot survive here, and the grasses usually survive in the worst of areas. But, I will give it through today, and if I find nothing, I will just have to assume that it is one of the many unsolvable mysteries. Mysteries that may have been created by our gods to lead fools like me to their deaths in these wastes . . . Chasing wisps of nothing, nothing but the ghosts and spirits who protect this desolation, and lead the foolhardy into folly and death. And even with the proof that there were two here, they too may have been part of the illusion to draw us back here. Back here yes, and for what purpose?* Again, for what unknown purpose could there be? The only thing that came to his mind, since he was a warrior, was a trap, and a very subtle one that would eventually kill him or any who would follow him here. And that immediately made him feel that he should run from this place.

He, as the leader of his clan, was a very good tactician, and from what his thoughts had brought to the forefront, he knew that if his conclusions were correct that he was no more than a child in comparison. This was subtle, so much so that even the most experienced would not see this trap. He began to look around expecting at any moment to be attacked, to be consumed. But the silence, dust, and heat were all that met him.

Eventually, he calmed down a little bit, but then another thought entered his mind. *What if it is the spirits of the dead warriors that roam this desolation? If so then by our mutilation of their dead bodies, they cannot attack, but only watch and wait. Watch and wait until I succumb to this place. Maybe to have my mind wonder and leave me, and then my body perish allowing my spirit to face them in their realm.* But even if this was so, he had no proof. As the day continued to pass and it became drier and hotter, with the breezes pushing the hot air and dust around, the silence remained. There just was nothing here, nothing at all here.

* * *

It was a time of hard work, and short days, and with the hunting and then dressing out of the beasts, and the few females that took care of the preparation, all by the end of the day were too tired to do more than sleep. Here, at these times, and while most of the tribes and clans were involved in the same thing, there were a few that used this time to attack. Feeling that with either, much of the warriors were involved with the hunt leaving the places where the clans and tribes lived vulnerable with a much smaller force to protect it, or because of the fatigue that the camps themselves would be easy targets. So guarding their camps and the places where they lived was paramount. Still they all knew that with their forces divided, it would be an easier task to destroy a rival, and since this was something that was required of all of them every late season of heat to the season of falling, it would be easy for a rival to know, to spy, to plan, and then successfully attack either the camps or the places where they lived. So as tired as they were, guards were always patrolling both the camps, and their home ground. Yet, what could they do, but what they were presently doing? If they did not hunt the herds then there would be starvation and death at home. If they were successful in the hunt, then they would be able to survive the season of cold's harshness, but at this time be a possible target for a successful attack.

So with each trip out to hunt the vast herds, each warrior knew that not only to be alert for the beasts they would bring down, but to be alert for the dangers others could provide. Most of the hunts, because of the vast herds kept all of them away from each other, and it was rare for one to be attacked. Rare yes, but not unheard of, and many of the ones that had been surprised were no longer around. So with the required alertness, the hunting and preparing of the beasts, the guarding of their camps, there was very little time for breeding, and little energy left. That time where the breeding would increase in intensity, would be the cold time ahead, where there was little to do other than repair or replace equipment that had fallen victim to the storms, winds, time, and usage. It was during this time that many of the females began their carrying. And with it, a hope for an increase to their clan, and as always, a hope for the increase in males to be raised as warriors, all to increase their size and importance in this world of theirs, yet many never survived the time of carrying. But that time was still ahead of them. Right now they were behind on the needs of the clan. With the late start on working the herds, they had to be a little more careless than he liked. That meant putting more of the hunters out to hunt and leaving the camp with too little protection. But he had no choice. With the increase, through capture, of their clan they had more that would need food, clothing and shelter. So with too little time, and with the increase, calculated risks had to be taken.

Back where the clan settlement was located, he knew that with the additional slaves, they were adding shelters for the increase. These new shelters would be very rough, but at least it would keep out the winds and snow. As time continued, then there could be some improvements made, but since these were for the slaves anyway, it did not really matter. Still not only would there need to be an increase in shelters, the amount of wood necessary, for both cooking and to keep one warm, would greatly increase. This meant, that this would, once again, reduce the amount of warriors that would be with the clan, and to protect it and the wood gatherers, while they were out gathering the wood and fuels for the season of cold. With a small guarding force he had the young females, who were learning, out collecting the dried dung of the herd beasts. These young females were before their first bleeding so were untouchable anyway. And while not a pleasant task, this dung was a great fire starter, and would reduce the need somewhat for tender. He felt good to know that where their clan was located, that it lay hidden from most, and so had a far less of a chance of being attacked. Less of a chance was great, but not perfect. It could still happen, and if it did, it would happen at such at time as this, where they were so spread out, and at their most vulnerable. After all they now had more of everything that some unknown rival would covet, and want for themselves. He hoped that the ones who had become part of the alliance would refrain from such a tradition, but he felt that once the alliance went it separate ways to prepare for the season of cold that all bets were off, and if they had felt slighted while working with the alliance, that once this break came that they would then take it out on another tribe or clan.

* * *

She lay on her sleeping mat racked with fever, and at the same time shaking from the chills. She drifted in and out of consciousness, never sure where she was. Sara felt weak and could keep nothing down. All she wanted to do was to roll up in a little ball and forget everything. What she saw, when she saw anything at all, was worried expressions on the women from the captured cities. The primitive females avoided her with a fear on their faces; saying that they worried that whatever she had could take them too. Even though it was difficult, this realization made her smile, even if this smile was inward. She just hurt too much to really care about anything. She could hear voices around her, but couldn't understand any of them at all. Every once in a while something cool would be placed on her forehead, and while this felt good, at the same time it chaffed her skin which was tender to the touch. Her teeth chattered from being so cold, and yet the fever burned deep in her soul.

When she dreamed it was a nightmare that continually repeated of the fall of the city, and the days of hell, and loss, her time since that fall, her life here at this clan's home, and the continued daily abuse. Even here in the fevered dreams she could not escape it. In some of the dreams she was fighting an unknown monster that was intent on consuming her very body and soul. She tried to push it away, tried to fight, but the monster's strength was too great. She felt herself pinned and then hard physical contact with every inch of her body. Again she fought but it was relentless. Finally the monster worked its way down to her private area and she screamed as the pain washed over her in great waves. Was this beast going to consume her from the inside? The scenes continued to replay any time she fell into a fevered sleep, and even during the brief times she had returned to the waking world, it was only for very brief periods of time, being more in the twilight than the real world. Maybe, just maybe, she was going to join her ancestors, and in many ways that would be a relief. Just to give up, to give in to the infection that was attacking her body. Yet, something deep within would not let her give up, give in, to leave. And while she bordered on the edge of death for many days, eventually the ones caring for her could see a change. Finally at some point, and they knew not when that point was reached, they could see that she was finally resting. And though the fever had yet to break, it was becoming obvious that the crisis was over for now, and even if it was slow, her recovery would be soon, but soon could mean months. Unless she relapsed, and without their medicines to help her fight, they knew that the infection could, and most likely would return.

She awoke coherent for the first time in sixteen days. She felt weak, shaky, and completely drawn out. There wasn't enough strength to even turn over to find a comfortable position. "Water." Was all she could croak, her voice barely audible and barely recognizable. One of the women, who had been keeping watch, helped her sit up, and Sara drank thirstily as the cool water penetrated her dry parched body. Then too weak she fell back to sleep and it was another two days before she again awakened. Breathing out heavily, she blinked several times and found as she continued to wake that she hurt just about everywhere, and in the darkness of the primitive shelter and with the light from the flickering fire she realized that it was night. Even though it was difficult to do she looked at her arms and the parts of her body that was uncovered, and was shocked. She looked more dead than alive, her skin pulled tight against her bones. She stank, and so did the sleeping mat and coverings she laid on and under. She was so weak that it scared her. Carefully and with difficulty she pulled back the covers and she was naked, and seeing the rest of her body scared her even more. She must have been close to death to look this bad. How long had the infection raged in her body? She had no answers, and no real memory of what she had just endured.

Turning carefully, she saw one of the young city women close to her. She could tell that it wasn't that long ago that she had submitted for *breeding* as the primitives called it. She could see both the tears and the pain on her face and longed to reach out and comfort her, but had no strength. She tried to speak but found it almost impossible. Trying to clear her throat she finally croaked out just above a whisper "Can I get some water please, and maybe, something to eat"?

The young girl jumped from the voice, as she was lost in her own misery, and world. And even though it was her time to watch over Sara, the abuse that she had just received tore her up. After all this was not the way it was supposed to be. But she had no power to change what was happening to her as any of the other captives. With their known world crushed and destroyed, and this new one harsh and unfriendly she did not know how she would be able to keep going. She had only been here a short time, and wondered how the other women who had been captured a long time in the past had survived as long as they had. Although looking at this Sara, she really did not look to be around much longer. She called out to the others softly, as it was nighttime, and many were asleep. But all knew that if Sara came around that the rest would be awakened so they could attend to her. After all she was their unofficial leader, the one that helped them through this hell they were living with and in.

* * *

Dusk had settled in a few hours ago, and the smaller moon would not be adding any light for a couple of hours. The four of them continued to monitor the tribe's hidden camp. They had been here in the area hidden for the last couple of days, waiting for the hunting party to leave and make it easier to get done what they needed to do. That had finally happened earlier today, and if everything held up, the hunting party would be gone two days and this one night, returning tomorrow at dusk. So it had to be tonight. As to hang around longer, waiting for the next chance risked discovery, and if discovered they were too small of a group to do anything but retreat, and disappear – losing their one and only chance at this. Once they were discovered the tribe would be on even a higher alert making it impossible, and all the planning and practice would be for naught. Because of the reduction in warriors and because of the hunt, there would only be two guards.

Back in the meadows outside of the Alpha complex Saige had worked and trained them relentlessly. They tried and worked a number of different scenarios trying to cover everything that might come up. Yet they all knew that when they finally arrived at the real camp that what training and practice they did would make them a better team, but not necessarily mean that what they were planning would be a success. After all battle plans only held up until first contact, and then were generally worthless. From the observations that they made with the eye-in-the-sky, as they were calling them now, they had figured out that there were eight captives from the cities. And that initially, if they pulled this off, these captives would think that things had just gotten worse, since it would appear that a rival tribe had just attacked this one, and took them as captives to who knew where. It would not be until later, once Saige knew that they were safely away, that the truth would be revealed. If the primitive encampment came out from under the effects of the drug too soon, then, if they had to abandon the captives, the illusion that it was a rival tribe would stand up. If they had revealed themselves too early, and the captives were recaptured by the tribe, then it would be known that there were others out here who were of the lairs, and that, under no circumstances, could be known.

Saar had come through with the darts that they would use to knock out the rest of the camp. But the ones who were on guard would have to be killed. Again everything had to be true to the methods used by an attacking scouting force. Nothing could be out of character, nothing at all. Saar also had come up with an innovation, so now they had two options to knock out the rest of the camp. He had developed a gas bomb. To use it, one only had to toss it into a fire or the burning coals of a fire. It would then release the gas, and the container would be consumed leaving no evidence behind. They had tested these a number of times, and with some small improvements got them to the point that even a fire that was down to its last few embers would be enough to set them off.

So with these as an addition to their arsenal, it became the preferred method of knocking out the primitives. With the darts, which they would have to recover so as to leave nothing behind, and it being dark, it would just be too easy to miss during the recovery and exit portion of the plan.

Now all of them were keyed up as shortly it would all become a reality, and either in about twenty minutes it would be successful, or they would have failed and would be running for their very lives. Saige wished he could communicate with the facility, as last minute intel would have been nice. But one worked with what they had. He signaled the "move" sign. From this point everything would be silent until the final check before the coordinated attack. And these communications would be very brief, just enough to confirm, and then either get the "go or abort" signal. They had finally decided that even with just four of them that they would continue as they did back in the compound, working in teams of two. Fortunately with only two guards out and patrolling, this would work. The camp was settling down and getting quiet as the tribe went to sleep. They would give it another thirty minutes, move into position and then make their move.

* * *

With help Sara was able to sit up. She was close to the fire, but with no clothes, and just getting over the infection, she was cold. Two of the women from one of the cities brought her something she could put on, and then brought her some broth, and water. While over the infection, her system still rebelled to the food, which she threw up immediately. So for the moment she drank the water, and let that settle on an uneasy stomach before trying to get something down again. Finally with care she was able to hold it down, but found that the effort had completely drained her and she was falling asleep once again. The next thing she saw was the sun shining through the open doorway as the building was airing out. She still felt very weak but better than last night. Right now she was alone. Looking around she saw that water and what was probably more broth sitting close to her. With care, because of her weakness, she reached for the water and drank deeply, feeling the coolness enter her body. Anything she did was difficult and took a lot of effort to perform. She knew that soon, someone would have to help her to the trench where they took care of their nature calls. She just did not have the strength to do it on her own. With her own reserves used up to fight the infection she had no endurance at all, and she found once again that after drinking the water and eating some of the broth she was tired. She lay back down, covered up, and once again remembered nothing.

When she awoke again it was early evening and there was the chatter of the primitive women, and some quiet talk from the captured women. Looking over she asked in a weak voice, "Can one of you help me to the trench; I really do have to go." Immediately two of the women came over, smiled briefly at her, even though she could tell that the smiles were forced, they carefully helped her up, and with her leaning heavily on both went to take care of nature. This was something that at one time was a very private thing, but privacy did not exist in the primitive world, so again with them supporting her because of her lack of strength, she took care of her need, and once finished the two helped her back towards the shelter. One had glanced over her shoulder, and then whispered to the other two saying, "That older warrior is following us. I hope he's not looking to have sex with one of us. He scares me, not that rest doesn't." Sara did not have the strength to even turn around and look, and the trip had just about exhausted her once again. It was going to be quite a while before she would be able to do anything on her own.

Before reaching the shelter she let the two that were helping her that she needed to sit for a moment as she just did not have enough left to make it all the way back. So they stopped and found a tree that she could sit and lean against to get some of her strength back. At this moment the older warrior caught up to them and signaled the two who were assisting to stand away from Sara. Sara looking at the two could see concern and fear. She had to admit that she had fear also. If he wanted to breed with her right now it probably would kill her. So she just waited, not knowing what her future would be.

He crouched in front of her and then began to speak. "I'm the one in charge of making sure all tasks are handled within the clan's home. I organize and put into action what the leader wants done. With age I can no longer join the other warriors in battles and skirmishes. So it is to me that the training of the new warriors falls. I know that you speak our words so that you understand what I am saying, while the rest from your lairs do not, as I do not understand them. It is obvious that the world you come from and ours is different, and the ones who passed into the spirit world since you have been brought here have weighed heavily. We do not take the loss of a female lightly. We know that it they and only they that bring new life and a new generation to our clan.

"There is much we do not understand, and part of this is why none of you are carrying. The only answer we have is that you have strong magic, or that the totem of your people is strong. So strong that we are not strong enough as warriors to overcome this protection and it protects you from carrying our offspring. It speaks that in some ways we must be weak. Our own females are carrying, showing us that we are strong, fertile, as is the land. But any who have bred with you and yours disprove this. We feel that we will continue to breed with, you and yours, until our totem is strong enough to overcome yours. Then when this happens, the warriors that will come from this breeding will be stronger than the rest. Yet it is very puzzling, very puzzling to us. We conquered you and your males with ease. And your males are no warriors, and are making poor slaves. So the strength cannot be with your males, but you and the other females are not warriors either."

He paused as if thinking and then changed the subject. "You almost left us for the spirit world. It is obvious to any that you are weak; still have much time until you have recovered. Because of this, and because we value our females, you and two of yours will remain outside of the herd for the next large moon cycle to give you time to heal. At that time we will see where you are, and then determine if you can be returned to the herd." When he finished what he wanted to say, he got up, went inside the female shelter and then left with one of the younger female primitives.

* * *

All of them were in position; they were giving it just a little more time. But they wanted to be done with this before the moon rise. Staven and Stone were on the far side of the encampment lying in a ravine that ran parallel to the camp. The guard on their side walked the edge of the same just outside of the camp. Where Saige and Seve was located had much more cover. The camp was placed against the hillside on the north with it facing the open range where Staven and Stone were. The placement of the camp was such that it could be easily defended, yet at the same time provided easy access to the grasslands where the wild herd beasts roamed. This area had been used by this tribe for many seasons of hunting. It was an area they knew well, and were comfortable with. If an overwhelming force were to attack, there were many exits to make pursuit more difficult. Other than the night fliers screeching their calls, it was quiet. Stone, looking over and getting Staven's attention, signaled that the guard was moving towards him, and be prepared to move away, if necessary. The guard moved past him stopped, spread his legs and began to relieve himself. Stone, shaking his head, gave the signal to move, and the two of them easily took out the guard who was in a very vulnerable position at that moment and unable to react to prevent his own death. Breathing hard, from the quick strike, both returned to the ravine to await the response from the team leader to move on to the next phase.

Shortly they heard a brief struggle and the silence, followed by Saige and Seve joining them. Saige signaled them to begin the next phase, and they silently spread through the camp, quietly opening the flaps and tossing the gas bombs into the fires that were in each one. They avoided both the slave and female tents. At this point, no more than four minutes had passed since they first attacked the guards. Within the female tent were the offspring of the tribe, and they had no desire to do any harm to them. But, to carry this off successfully, they would have to enter that tent, subdue all who were in there, perform the act, take their prizes, both the slaves and females, and leave.

Giving the gas time to work before moving on to the next portion of the mission, they planted the evidence that would be found in the morning when the tribe awoke and found that they were attacked. Once they had performed all that they had planned then the females would be drugged so as not to raise the alarm. But they still needed witnesses to this next portion, so this drugging of the female tent could not happen until afterwards. Taking a deep breath, Saige asked. "Are you ready for this?" He knew that for all of them that sex were a wonderful physical act between their mates and themselves, and that it could easily be a driving force for a guy. But none of them was looking forward to this encounter. Where they were crouched giving time to make sure that all of the camp was out, the odors drifting out from that tent were overpowering. The smell emanating was somewhere between too much sex, dirty bodies, and a heavy musk. It was so overpowering that it almost made them ill.

Gritting his teeth, Stone said. "I know that we have to go through with this, but that smell almost turns my stomach. How are we going to do this again?"

"I know that we need witnesses to the fact that we did, as they call it, breed with one of their females, so maybe if we open the flap and hold it in the open position, we can take one of them out in front into the better air, take our turns as they would and then get what we came for and just get out of here. I almost feel like after this that I'm going to want to avoid sex for a long time."

"Know what you mean Seve. But we have to do this, and that's a great suggestion." Saige responded, "So I guess let's get this over with, get our people and get out of here. Remember that until we are safely away we have to maintain the illusion that we are a rival tribe stealing prizes from our enemy. Only when we are sure that we are safe can we reveal to our people that they are in good hands. Okay let's get this done so we can get out of here. And if these females have anything we could catch, let's again hope that the concoction of drugs that Saar gave us takes care of it."

* * *

Even after the older warrior had departed with the female he probably was going to breed with today, she had to remain at the tree trunk that she was leaning against. She just did not believe that she was so weak. She had much to think about, but now would not be the time, exhausted as she was from this little excursion she had the two women help her back up and by the time she was back to her sleeping mat she was almost asleep. When she woke up much later that night she found the same two women still with her. By whatever luck of the draw, these two would be able to remain outside of the breeding herd because they happened to assist her at that moment. She was at least thankful for that.

After drinking more water, and eating more broth, and feeling a little better she could see that one of the women wanted to talk to her, but was afraid to do so. Nodding in this one's direction, she asked. "Is there something you want to say?" She had to admit that at this moment she could not recall her name, and again in the end it wouldn't matter, since here, they had no names.

Nodding her head the young woman said. "Yes, but I wanted to be sure that you wanted to hear what happened to you while you were very sick."

With a perplexed look, Sara asked. "Happened to me, what do you mean?"

With a quick look out the open doorway she then looked back at her and said. "It's just that, that old warrior is probably the reason you are still alive.

"Look when you fell ill, none of us knew what to do, other than to try and keep you warm and comfortable. We could see that you had a high fever, and at the same time chills were racking your body. We thought that most likely you had an infection, but we had nothing to fight it here. Everything we knew was lost back in the city. The older warrior came in during the early part of your illness. I guess to confirm that you were sick and not faking it to avoid all this unpleasantness." Here she stopped for a short time.

"He came in to check on me?" Sara asked. She knew that he was generally in charge of making this clan home, work, so she suspected that he considered it his duty to make sure all was running as it should.

Nodding this woman continued, "Yes. He had us uncover you so that he could look at your body. He signaled us to cover you back up, and left. You were naked because of all the sweating you did; we couldn't leave anything on you. You looked terrible. I didn't know if you would live or die then. But you got worse and we all felt helpless. We knew that the infection was winning, and you are the only one that speaks their language, and while I know you never wanted it, you are kind of our unofficial leader. You helped us through this hell, and if you had died, then we, all of us, would have felt totally lost and without any hope." She paused again, and then taking a deep breath said, "You have helped all of us survive this, and we have so little hope of ever leaving here other than the way it appeared that you were heading."

"You don't know how many times I had wished for that very thing. I've seen too many of us die at the hands of these primitives. I shudder to think what happened to our elderly. If you didn't notice, there were none of them in any of the camps." She could see the shock at the faces of the other women as they realized what she had said was true. While it was still an effort to talk, let alone concentrate Sara asked for her to continue.

"A couple of days later he showed up again. I can't tell you how much we fear him. He signaled for us to uncover you again, and at this point you really looked bad, real bad. He got down on his knees and began to run his hands over your bare body. You began to fight him in your delirium. You could tell that it irritated him, because such a thing is not allowed. He signaled us to hold you down, and we thought he was going to rape you right here and we were going to be party to it. But we had no choice, so we held your arms down. Even when pinned like you were, you continued to fight. I really don't know where you got the strength to do it, but we had a very hard time keeping you down. He started at your head and with a thoroughness I haven't seen, completely worked over your upper body; it was almost gross, the way he did it.

Once satisfied that whatever he was looking for wasn't there, he then straddled you with his back towards your head. He then did the same with both of your legs. It was like he was searching for something. Again you were desperately fighting him, and he signaled for two others to come over and hold down your legs and to spread them. We really thought that he was just about to begin the rape – especially when he started working your private areas. He did a very close inspection, and started touching you there, and you screamed. His searches became more intense until he found the spot that made you writhe in pain. At this point he had us turn you so that light from the outside would fall on you there. Again he kept at it until he found whatever it was that he wanted. Then he drew out this small knife. We were all very scared at that moment, because we now thought he was going to kill you. We were all shaking in fear.

"He then bent over resting his arms on your legs so that with his weight you couldn't move. He got real close so he could see whatever it was and then pricked something with the point which brought another scream from you. He repeated this a couple of times, and the ones who had been holding your legs could see what he had done, and appeared to be a little sick themselves. At this point he got up quickly and left. We all looked at what he did, and there between your legs from your private area was a growing pool of pus, and a sickly yellowish liquid that was oozing out from the wound he had created. Before we could do anything, he returned. He had someone else with him, who then looked at the wound. He left, and the older warrior pan mimed to us to clean you up. Then the other returned with some type of rough cloth that had crushed leaves of some type wrapped in it. The whole thing was wet. After we had cleaned you up, he went to work with this compress, and again signed us to repeat this and keep the wound open and draining until it no longer flowed, and to use this compress to keep it clean. And that's what we did. Both of the primitives continued to check in on you, and once that poison was out of your system, it became the turning point to your recovery."

With the story before her, at first she felt violated, once again, and then began to wonder why the primitive males had done this. With all the abuse that the women had suffered it just seemed so out of character to what they had experienced. Then she remembered what the old warrior had stated to her after her first trip to relieve herself after coming back to the world of the living. With the way they were being treated, and his statement to her, it just did not make any sense at all. *But how did he know? Or did he? Was he just guessing? Was he what they called a doctor? No, he's a warrior, so the one he brought had to be their doctor. So, again how'd he know what to do?* Then it came to her. In battle there would always be wounds, and she was sure that many over time would become infected, so he only was doing what they would have done when treating an infected battle wound – thusly the reason for the very intimate search of her body. He was attempting to find just that, an infection. Then looking up, after thinking all of this through, she asked, "Where exactly was this infection?" She could see the women who had assisted him turn red.

Quietly, the one who had relayed the story said, "Right where a man would enter you," and said nothing more.

It had been one of the worries, and with the conditions and requirements put on them, she really was not surprised. She knew that she had been injured there a number of times since the capture, and she was sure that when she was put back into the breeding herd that it could happen once again. That got her thinking about what he had related to her just a short time in the past, and while in their own way they cared for, again as they called them, the females, it still was a rough and painful way of life.

* * *

They entered the tent hoping that they looked fierce. With the strength of the stench inside it was difficult to do. The odor itself could have been a weapon. They threw some additional wood on a fire that was in the middle of the tent. This put additional light inside so that they could see what they were facing. In the far corner furthest away from the single exit huddled four women who were obviously from one of their cities. They were still somewhat dressed in the clothes of their culture, but most were no more than rags at this point and time and the condition of the clothes were so poor that it barely covered anything at all. The team knew that these women had been raped a number of times, and it explained the shocked distant expressions with hopelessness showing strongly in their bodies. Turning and facing the tribe females they chose a younger less filthy one and signaled the breeding sign. This consisted of partially closing the left hand and then taking the right thumb and placing it inside the left with a single motion. This represented penetration and breeding.

Two of them took her just outside of the tent, and while she put up a token fight, that was all it was. There just had been too many annuals of submitting for one of them to outright refuse. And they knew that if they fought too hard they would be cuffed into submission anyway. The other two guarded the tent and kept the rest under a watchful eye, and as each had their turn at the female they would rotate this guarding. Once finished they roughly grabbed the female and returned her to the tent and then signaled the four in the corner to come to them. They could see the fear in their eyes, and it hurt them that they could not reveal who they really were, but right now they were in the middle of an enemy's camp and had to maintain the illusion.

The women were slow to respond, and two of them had to go get them and encourage compliance. They could see the fear growing as they expected to have the same thing happen to them that they had just witnessed. Once outside and before leaving, Saige re-entered the tent and acted like he was building up the fire once again, at the same time giving the females a very stern stare, he placed another of the gas bombs in the fire and knew that shortly they would all be unconscious and would not be able to raise the alarm. When he saw the gas bomb about to release the gas he left. Then the four of them led the women into the ravine just outside of camp and Staven stayed with them and with weapons drawn and hand signals to let them know what would happen if they tried to escape. The other three returned to the camp and brought out the four men from the city that were in the slave tent. Then when they had all of them they laid a false trail leading away from the camp and deeper into the grasslands towards the camps of the rival tribe that they had left false evidence within the attacked camp identifying that tribe as the culprit.

CHAPTER SEVEN

For the first half of the night they pushed deeper into the grasslands. The direction was generally away from the Sacred Mountains and towards the rival tribe. Saige knew that the travel would be slower than they liked, but the eight prisoners that they had with them had been through hell before getting to the camp they had just been removed from, and now supposedly captured once again as prizes by another tribe. He knew that their spirits had to be close to rock bottom. Eventually they reached the stream that he had planned on using, and they, using the shallow stream as a way to hide their tracks, hiked in the cool water back and then into the Sacred Mountains where the stream flowed from. The four of them needed to push the eight hard, as the trek they had ahead of them would be all night, and then go until the zenith of the next day. They had to reach a hidden camp that they had set up. Once there he felt that they would be far enough away that they could take a couple of hours before moving on to the second camp. Once this second camp was reached they would be deep enough into the sacred mountains that they could reveal the truth. But until then they had to maintain the fear and the fatigue level to make sure these refugees from one of their cities did not try and escape.

* * *

It had been a tough trip with the exhausted members of the captured city. But Saige could see where the second camp was. It still would be a little while before the reached it, and with all of them taking turns watching their back trail they finally took a very brief break. Looking at the eight of them, he could see fear, almost panic in them, but he also could tell that they were so tired that they did not even have the energy to speak to each other. When they stopped, they just dropped and did not move. He was sorry for having to do this, but unfortunately it was necessary, and while they were scared to death, this would change shortly. He left Stone watching over them and went back to Seve and Staven and asked, "Anything at all?"

Both just shook their heads no. "I was able to look back at the camp, and there wasn't even any movement that first day until late in the morning, so by then we were already here in the mountains, and they were tracking our false trail out in the grasslands. But nobody has come this way. Staven, did you see anything different?"

Staven shaking his head said, "No, not at all. I think we were successful with our false evidence we left, and with our trail leading away from their camp. Saw no one at all coming this way."

Turning around and looking at Stone and the ones he was guarding Saige stated. "I'd like to tell them now, but I think we'll stay to our plan. We are just about to the second camp where we have all of our supplies and changes of clothes for them as well as us. I truly am quite ready to get out of this stuff." That brought a bit of laughter from the other two. They nodded their heads and agreed with him. "Okay let's get this last part done so we can quit scaring them and give them something positive since their city fell. By the way have any of you heard anybody mention a name of either the city or themselves?" None had so at this point they just did not know.

The three joined Stone and then with spear points they prodded the captives into moving. There was no fight in them at all, and it took all their energy just to get moving once again. Saige thought. *Oh boy, this is going to take a little longer than I thought. At least there's no fight in them to make this more difficult. In another day we'll be at the first of the caves and within a couple of more back at the Alpha complex. So far, so good, and may it continue that way. It looks like we convinced that tribe that it was one of their enemies that did this, and that is great news.*

By pushing and prodding the "prizes", as the captured ones would have been considered, they finally came around a rock face into a hidden bowl that had running water and a small natural cave. They led them to the cave, and then inside where they had their supplies hidden. Then Saige breathed out a large sigh and said, "Finally!" Looking at the shocked faces of the eight he smiled and paused before continuing. "Okay, all of you sit and relax. We will be spending the rest of this day here to give you a chance to recover at least a little before we have to continue. We'll get a fire going, and over there in those supplies are changes of clothes for all of you. And for you women, there's an area at the back that you can have a bit of privacy as you change out of those rags. Guys, we don't have that option, so we will just step outside to change while the women are in the back doing the same thing."

"Who are you?" Asked one of the women, who had just sat down and appeared to be on the verge of tears. "You're not any of those primitives that captured us?"

Quietly he answered, "No, our city was Sequoyah, and it was attacked and destroyed over an annual in the past. Of that city there were only ten of us who escaped. We are part of that ten."

One of the men then said, "But, but we thought, we thought that things had gone from bad to worse. We've seen what they had done to our women, and we could do nothing, and we were then forced to work for them, and when you raided their camp we thought, oh no not again. Why did you do it this way?"

Before any could speak another of the women asked, "And all of you raped that primitive woman, just as we had been, why would you do something like that? Are you no different than they?"

Shaking his head and again pausing before answering, Saige stated, "Look, we will try and explain everything. But I, and I know the rest of my team, want to get out of these skins and into something a little more comfortable. Then we will bring up some water from the stream, heat it and we all can clean up a little bit and feel better about it. We can eat a hot meal, and then we will introduce ourselves and you can do the same – you, not knowing who we are, and vice versa, makes this a little uncomfortable. Just know that for now you are safe, and tomorrow we will be heading out and getting closer to safety." Turning around he saw that the rest of the team had the change of clothes for them and the other men. "Okay all, let's get out of this stuff and into something that is in better shape and is clean." He signaled the men to follow them outside and pointed the women to the back of the cave.

A short time later when the men had all changed Stone yelled into the cave, "Hey all you women decent?" The heard a muffled voice saying to give them a few more minutes, and Stone shrugged, "It's something I'll never understand. It never takes us guys long to change but always seems to take twice as long for a woman. While we're waiting let's go get some of that water so we can heat it. We know that we could use some cleaning up, and know that all of you are worse off, so I guess we will need quite a bit of the stuff. Sorry no soap, but warm water and a couple of the rags we brought will get the worst of it."

Next to the cave entrance behind some of the brush that was there he grabbed a number of collapsible buckets and all of them went down to the stream and filled them, returned to the entrance where this time the women were standing. "You look much better now," Staven stated, "How are you feeling?" There were a few smiles, but they were more tentative than genuine. They could understand that, since the rescued really did not know if it was over or not. After all they were still in the wilderness with four men who still could be enemies and this was just an elaborate trap.

"I know that everything that has happened to you appears to be a horrible nightmare that you can't leave. With our fleeing from our city it was the same. We started out with a much larger force, and it was whittled down as we were harassed and attacked by the primitives almost the full distance we traveled." Stopping a moment before continuing, Saige looked them over and could see that they were almost afraid to believe that it was over for them, but at the same time if they could believe that they felt guilty because they were safe. Pointing to himself he said, "I'm Saige, and this is Stone, Seve, and Staven. When we get back to where we are taking you, you can meet the rest of us. Like I said earlier, our city was Sequoyah, and we learned that our city was the last city to have a scouting unit, and we are the remnants of the same. It is probably the only reason we survived. Now before I ask you your names I need to explain why we did what we did back in that camp." At this point he covered the why, and what they had to do to keep the suspicion from them and on the primitives themselves. He also stated that their mates did not like the idea any better, but there had been no other way to accomplish this misdirection. Once finished with the explanation he asked, "First any questions, and if not please give us your names?"

With no questions from them, he looked at the women first and they began to give them their names. Joci was the first, and seemed to be the youngest – pretty, but not beautiful, and probably in her late teens. Jas sat next to her and looked like a mother, probably somewhere in her thirties, if not pushing forty. Jeanna was the beautiful one of the group. Her looks naturally brought men's eyes to her. She appeared to be in her mid-twenties and the dirt that covered could not conceal her beauty. They all knew that once she was back to herself that she would outshine all of the other women. Yet, she did not appear to put on an air of superiority, but more towards just a normal everyday woman. Jessi from her build was more athletic. She could have easily been a member of one of the scouting teams, and she appeared to be in her early twenties.

The men as they went around and giving them their names were as follows; Jaiden who had to be in his forties looked more like a librarian than anything else. Jed was in his thirties and worked the hydroponics, a farmer at heart. In size his was close to Stone and had a similar build and complexion. Jarid, in his late twenties was the one that women probably would have naturally been drawn to. His looks were rugged and handsome with a natural body frame to compliment his looks. And the fourth of the men was Judd. From the looks of him they would have guessed he was in his early forties, but were surprised to learn he actually was in his early fifties. He ran his own business, and had helped many others get started in their own. After introductions were over, all of them now had names; the team began to prepare food for all, and to set up the sleeping arrangements.

"I'm sorry, but we aren't set up with places to take care of your nature calls, so we've kind of decided that when you exit the cave to take care of your needs that you women go down and to the right, as you leave the cave, and there's a copse of trees that will provide the privacy you need. We guys will go to the left and stay parallel to the rock wall. A little ways out there's a pile of rocks that will provide all the privacy that we need. As far as sleeping arrangements all eight of you will have the back of the cave with the women sleeping in the area that again provides them their privacy behind that hanging curtain where the supplies are stored." Saige looking at them could still see the trauma that they had endured. All he could do was shake his head. Thinking back, he suspected that before they found the complex, they probably would have looked much the same. "I suspect that all of you are quite tired, and once you eat we suspect that all of you will be falling asleep. Please do that. We have far to go and will be trying to push through, based on how well the eight of you do. The four of us will continue to guard and watch our back trail. We know that we can hide our trail, but the eight of you do not have the experience or skill to do that, so I know that there is sign out there that the primitives could easily locate and follow.

"And on that note, if we find that they are trailing us, *then,* be prepared to move, be quiet, and do as we say. It could save your life. Be prepared for a real surprise once we reach our destination. And just a warning, be prepared to unlearn all we have been taught about our history. It was a shock to us what we learned, but for now that's all I'm going to say. From the smells I think the food is ready, and from the sounds of the complaints from my stomach it thinks so too, so let's eat."

* * *

"This waiting is killing me," Seirra said. Looking around at the others she could see that she had already said this too many times, and she suspected that the others had felt this way. "Yeah I know, I keep repeating myself, but I can't help it if it is true. I know from the imagery that it appears to have been successful, but we really won't know until they're back, or, at least, to the cave system that our ancestors built. And it should be today sometime when they hit the first one. And until they are leaving the last one, and before they arrive, will be the first time that we will be able to talk with them, but this doesn't make the waiting any easier."

Nodding her head in agreement Sorrel said, "Very true. I think that we got lucky on this first attempt. Saige and Shell', with our input of course, put together a great plan, and it worked. I'm sure there were a few problems, there always is, but like you said, from what we could see they rescued all of our people from that tribe." Sighing Sorrel continued. "I just hate this inability to be able to talk to them, and to find out which city these people came from. To find out if it is one of the most recent to fall, or whether our people have been captives much longer." Then she laughed and starting teasing the other women when she asked, "You aren't jealous are you, because they had to get physical with one of the primitive women?"

That got the others to look at each other, and actually from the guilty looks on their faces Sorrel could see that she had hit the nail right on the head. She had to admit that it did bother her that Stone was one of the ones who were involved, but again it had to be done to keep it true. It didn't make it any easier when, in a way, your man was going to cheat on you, and it was being done in the open, but from what they knew of the primitives, if they hadn't then it would have led the attacked tribe to know something wasn't right, and probably look elsewhere for the attackers.

At the present Saar, the only man left at the facility, was in the security office monitoring everything. Soon Starr would join him to assist. Actually she would relieve him so he could come get something to eat, before rejoining her. The shifts were being split a little differently with four of the team gone. To keep it fresh they rotated a single member through on staggered shifts to keep at least one of them somewhat fresh. Any and all other work and research had stopped until the team returned, successful or not. So the four women sat around the table in the cafeteria, Starr with Sommer who was content and asleep, and Sabryn holding Shayne, who just seemed content to let his mother hold him. It was truly rare that the four of them ever had a chance to get together this way. With so few of them it usually was no more than one or two of them and most of the time the men would also be around. Not that this was a problem, but the women would have liked to have more just "girl time", where they could talk freely, or complain about their men and not be interrupted or have one of the opposite sex close by to overhear what they had to say.

It was quiet for the moment and Starr looking over lovingly at her sleeping daughter sighed and said. "I've got to go, if she wakes and wants to eat bring her to me and I'll get her fed." She got up and quietly left heading for the security office and part of her shift. Starr had to admit that she almost longed for the quieter days before they made contact with the cities. Since then the circuits between the cities and the Alpha complex, compound or whatever you wanted to call it was busy all the time.

* * *

Saige, looking over the newly released captives smiled inwardly. To him, it had almost seemed a lifetime that they were at this Alpha facility. With everything that was going on, it was difficult at times, to remember how he had found this place. It definitely had been the hard way, that's for sure. Turning around he said to the eight, "We are just about there now. And you will immediately recognize aspects of this place, and immediately see the similarities between our cities and here." The suns were setting and there were long shadows being cast by the mountains, and trees, lying across the valleys and depressions, allowing one to see the true scope of the broken lands. He had to admit that if it had been his choice this would have been the last place to put such a place, but it made total sense. As they climbed the path that he and Shell' had when they were exploring this area, all of what had happened, the history, the discovery, the confrontation, and the reuniting of the remnant of the scout team, all happened here.

He stood in front of the hidden entrance letting everybody catch their breath. "Okay all, we are here."

"Here?" Jaiden asked, "This doesn't look any different than any other place we've seen in these mountains. Are you joking with us? Because if you are, it's not very funny."

Smiling, although it was a sad smile, Saige replied. "No, Jaiden, I'm not, not at all. You see it is important that you see this as it is. Before us appears to be a solid rock face . . ." He reached out and his hand disappeared through that rock face, and then he withdrew it. "As you can see it is an illusion: An illusion just as our cities use to hide the entrances to our hidden cities." Again he stopped for a moment, looking them over, shrugged and asked. "Shall we?" He then disappeared from their sight as he entered into the facility, or to be more exact the entrance to the large cavern.

In a few moments the rest joined him on the platform that sat above the cavern floor, which was bathed in a dim soft light. He could see that it had the effect on the new members that he expected. They were quiet, and he could see the tension begin to flow out of them, when they realized that for them the nightmare was over. Saige sent Stone, Seve, and

Staven on ahead at this point. He wanted to be sure that everything was prepared for their arrival. And knowing the women who were here, he suspected that they would be impatient to both see their men, and to help the new arrivals. As he watched the three of them cross the dirt floor of the cavern he pointed out to the eight what they were seeing from where they stood. "For the next few days we will want you to recover. Saar will give each of you a physical, and whatever medicines you need to help your bodies heal, and to help clear any infections that you may have gotten during your long captivity. Then, and only when the doc gives you a clean bill of health and all of you feel up to it, it will be time to learn the truth about us." Turning towards the women he said. "I know what you had to face. You were required to join their breeding herds and submit to their males. Your names were taken from you, and then all of you were raped over and over again by the warriors. While they do not see it that way, it is the truth as far as our society sees it. And I know that the question would have come up as to why none of you ever became pregnant. Yet, as often as you submitted none of you did. I need all of you here to remember this. It will be one of the critical pieces that will help you understand what will be presented later, and will help you come to terms with what we have learned since rediscovering this place." Again looking at them he said, "Enough for now, let's go join the rest. I'm sure that a hot shower will feel great, and a change of clothes, followed by a hot meal. Then after that we will show you where the rooms for single members are so you can claim a space of your own. There tomorrow Saar will come for each of you and get you checked out, and other than that you will have free reign of this place. The rest of us have assignments that we must get to. So until the time you are cleared and then integrated into our teams, the time will be your own." They climbed down the ladders to the two lower platforms before reaching the floor, and headed through the double swinging doors into the facility.

* * *

Jed, looking around the meadows, was in awe to what he had learned so far. They had only been here fourteen days so far, and while it had been very difficult to accept, what he and the rest of the group that Saige and his had rescued, the evidence was overwhelming. He remembered the statement about the women not becoming pregnant, and he had to admit that they should have with as often as they had to submit. Yet, even now, living in the very facility where their ancestors had worked and studied the races of this planet and similarities to their own city Jade, well, it just couldn't be denied. As he walked this enclosed meadowland and the animals that lazily gazed at him when he came too close, he could almost feel safe. But the time of being a slave under these tribes and clans had left its mark. At least he had work here to help him forget. After all he was a farmer, so to speak. He looked the part and had worked the hydroponics, and had studied husbandry – although there had been very few animals in the cities. So studying them was just about all it could have been. But now here they were, and thusly why he was out in this place.

Jas, looking over at Saar felt somewhat out of place. Heck he could almost be her son if she really thought about it, but instead he was the doctor, and she was now his nurse. Her specialty had been pediatrics, and with few children there was not a great need for her services. Smiling she thought. *Ah, but it won't be that way for long. I am surrounded by young people who have coupled, and that leads to new lives.* She loved babies, and with Shayne and Sommer, she had two to help her pass the time. She had to admit that Saar was competent. She suspected that the fighting and running that they had to do probably had honed his skills and built his confidence. And with her arrival he now had someone to help. When the information about their true origins was presented she at first was in shock. It was counter to everything she had learned, but again she had to admit that the evidence was overwhelming. She knew now why Saige had made that statement when they were outside before entering this place for the very first time. She had to admit at that moment when he had stated that they were here, and all she could see was just a rock face, she felt at that very moment that some cruel joke had been laid at their feet. And then he demonstrated that they were facing the same illusions that the cities used, she then understood.

Jaiden, looking at the mainframe shook his head. *Yes, in many ways it looks archaic, but for as old as it is it functions quite well.* He had been a computer tech when Jade had fallen to the primitives. He had to admit that the physical labor that he had been made to do as a slave almost killed him. He never had been one to enjoy outdoor activities, and loved reading and computers. Like the rest, when the data was presented, at first he wanted to deny it. But, he asked himself why would they lie? And while Saige, Shellian, and the rest had been here for an annual, they did not have the skills to make this kind of change. Plus he knew that out in this world somewhere was an Alpha City or station. But its location was unknown. Who would have thought that it would have been hidden in the Sacred Mountains? Not he, that's for sure.

Joci didn't know what to think. She was young and had very little confidence in herself. She had dreamed, as all teenage girls, of meeting the right guy and then somewhere later becoming a couple and then having children. *After all, isn't that the way it's supposed to be?* She had never been physical with anybody, and when she had been captured, like all the women in the city; she was raped by five of the primitives. It had hurt, and she had bled quite a bit. In shock, she never, in her worst nightmares, imagined it would be like this. Then she was placed in the breeding herd and the abuse continued. It had torn her both physically and mentally. Now learning that at least she wouldn't carry any of the offspring of the primitives was a relief. But she hadn't reached the age where she knew what she really had wanted to do. So for now she just assisted all of them where she could. She had lost her family, and desperately wanted to fit in here – feeling that if she wasn't accepted that she would just die. So much had happened to her in such a short time, and none of it pleasant.

Judd was quite happy to be free of the primitives. At least he had been in some type of physical shape, so the work he had to perform did not kill him. He was sore for a while from muscles he hadn't used in a while, but at least he, even at his age, had fared better than many of the others. Quite a few were no longer around, having died or been killed for not doing what was demanded. And when the camp had been attacked, he was worried that he would have to learn all over again with new masters. This primitive world was definitely tough. And after being taken by the four, who he thought was from another tribe, and under threat of death and with weapons drawn, his thought of escape left. Besides he had nowhere to go, and really did not even know where they were at the time of the attack. He had heard from the women, that one of the primitive women had been raped by these four, which bothered him, but he was helpless at the time to do anything, as were the rest. Then, when they were safely away, to learn that it all had been a ruse, to place the blame on another tribe, and to learn that these four were their own people brought release that said, maybe this hell was finally over.

He had been in construction in one form or another all of his life. So he took over the industrial replicators, and the maintenance of this facility, although the auto systems had maintained the compound quite well. Still, as time continued to pass, and more were possibly rescued and brought here, space would have to be ready. So there was much to be done. Right now the dorms, as they began to call them, were very empty. Each probably could hold fifty people, and with only four in each it could easily feel that there was a lot of privacy. Like the others, he had lost his family. He did not know if any had even survived. Fortunately his mate had passed away earlier, and for this he was thankful, he knew the hell she would have been going through. But he had no way of knowing about any other members of his family, and because of this, it was something that continued to work on his mind. Yet, at this moment, there just wasn't anything he or anyone here could do.

Jeanna had been a teacher of the young. And history had been her major. So at first she had strong arguments against what was presented. Again she had to admit, that what Saige had stated before they entered the facility had hit home. As often as she had to submit to the males, she should have been carrying. And if not she, at least any of the other captured women from the cities. Yet, as far as she knew, not one had become pregnant from any of the too many unions they were required to perform. So after the facts were shown to her and the rest, she went back and studied the archives, and in the end, had to admit that everything was consistent and out in the open. Nothing was hidden, it was all there. Then, during her recovery, she had walked the cavern, saw the meeting area at the top of the stairs, she hadn't quite gotten brave enough to ride the moving room yet, and everywhere she went spoke of her city, and her people. Nothing was out of place, or jarring in a way that spoke of misdirection or lies.

With her skills she assisted Starr and Sabryn on gathering the information for dissemination to the remaining cities, and like them, hoped that the governments within those cities let the information out to all so that they could learn the truth about themselves. She really wondered what had transpired that left them stranded here on this world, a world that for quite some time they had been claiming as their own. Again she had to admit that it was a shock to learn that they had come from a different world and one that was hidden from them. Yes, as she worked the education computers, she had found images of that world, and had found it beautiful. But it was out of reach somewhere in the vastness of space.

Jarid had worked the public communications circuits — both the visual and audio. In the audio he had a popular DJ program that he worked every day, and once every five days a popular music program that went out over the visuals. Much of what was needed here at the Alpha was skills he did not have. But at least he could help man the communications in the security office, to take the load off of the others. With his verbal skills he could deal with the individual cities as they contacted "Point Alpha", as it was known in each of the cities. And of course he could and would assist anywhere else that they needed a warm body. It had been a shock to him when the city fell. It was early morning, and he had been at the studio preparing his audio program when the power failed. It shocked him at that point, since this had never happened before. Of course he didn't realize that it was the primitives that had shut it down, and that they were attacking their city at that very moment. By the time he had figured it out he was a prisoner and on his way to becoming a slave. And again he had no skills for the hard dirty work that he was *persuaded* to do. He had been threatened with death a number of times, but eventually had figured out what they wanted and after a very tough period of strengthening his muscles he had been able to maintain, but just barely. Food was poor, conditions worse, and like the rest he had little hope of surviving this, let alone be rescued.

When the camp, where he was a slave, was attacked his hopelessness rose. He had barely figured out how to survive here, and now, could he learn what his new masters wanted of him? It had been a good question. With the time he and the women had been with the tribe, they had picked up a word or two and learned what they could from observation. With the women placed with the other, as they were called – females, and he a slave, no contact was allowed. He and the other three rarely saw the four women from the city. And somehow, by luck he guessed, all of them were from the same city. Their annual had eighteen months, and without a way to track them, he had lost track. But he knew that it had to have been at least four or five. It seemed like it was summer when the city fell, and sometime in fall when the rival tribe's scouting force attacked the camp. Fear had invaded his soul once again when they were led out of their tent and he saw the bodies on the ground. The other tribe members looked fierce and looking around at the damage just these four had inflicted made him decide not to try and escape. He wanted to stay alive, desperately. Then came that trek into the Sacred Mountains and the revelation that they had been rescued.

"We would like everybody to report to the meeting area. There is much that we need to discuss, and we need to learn what we can from the eight of you who were captives so that we can plan on our next move", the voice over the PA system stated. "This meeting will be after the mid-day meal." He hadn't been here long enough to recognize voices yet, but that was coming along.

CHAPTER EIGHT

K'jor, with the others, was once again hunting the vast herds, and the campsite that they had chosen was the same. It lay untouched, with the ashes from the previous times cold, dead and spread out. It was here that he had first been introduced to the mystery. And as the preparations continued for the hunts, his mind went back once again to those moments he had spent in the desolation. He had become seriously concerned that the spirits were observing him. He could sense that he was being watched, but everywhere he had looked there was nothing – nothing but the swirling dust, hot winds, and the dry lands. Yet it seemed as if there were distant voices on the wind. Voices that was unrecognizable, almost just beyond hearing. He sensing them more than hearing, and when he tried to discern a direction there was none. It was as if these voices were coming from everywhere, and at the same time nowhere. He tried to go in the direction of them, but every time came away with nothing. *I don't understand this.* Looking up he could see that the suns were heading to late day, and soon it would be dusk, and at that time it would be worse. It was the time of day where the gods fought to keep the spirits at bay. And he was here in this desolation alone. Alone! It was a time when a warrior would be required to be his best, lest a spirit would inhabit him and take his body over for his own purposes. He knew that this would be his last night here and tomorrow he would return to join his warriors, and to return to camp.

All the areas he had been searching were completely devoid of life, and as the time continued to flow by him, he found that the areas all began to look alike. More proof that the spirit world had control of this area. *After all every place has its own look, its own feel. I know that there are always landmarks to identify, and special features that allow one to know a certain place is that place. But here all is the same. It confuses the mind. The heat cooks the body, and fogs the mind. The waves emanating from the ground obscure the true world, and allow the spirits to roam freely. It is a place of the dead. Again, why am I here?* Again he felt that now it had been for a foolish reason. But when one faces these lands of gods, he would always seem foolish. This was so opposite of the Sacred Mountains, and he guessed that it made sense. But he left this to the priests to figure out. He was a warrior and had enough to deal with in the real world. Once he left this place of death, and they returned to the clan's home he would discuss this with the priests – that's if he survived to do so.

He felt as if he was going crazy. What else could one call it? Something was here, just out of reach, just out of view, just beyond his understanding, but as to what it was he did not know. He could feel something vibrate, but heard nothing. It was as if the earth itself was about to open and swallow him whole. And why not, after all, all of his conclusions said that this belonged to the gods, to the spirits of those who have passed. So why not be swallowed. *Ah, I did not think of that. Maybe, just maybe this is exactly what happened here. It is so obvious to me now. When my warriors conquered the two, and the beast in this land the gods considered it a sacrifice to them and the very ground opened and swallowed the offerings – even though this was not our intent, or desire. We were only following the laws . . .* This gave him pause as he stood there thinking. *Maybe that's the answer. Yes the warriors were following the laws. So to the spirits and the gods of this land this was a proper tribute, and they then took this tribute.* With this line of reasoning he began to feel better. And right now the facts seemed to support his line of thought. *Well, I think that I am now satisfied, and I know what happened here. But it is too late to leave. So in the morning I will leave these lands to the spirits and the gods and know that we have upheld the laws, and our gods are pleased.*

He turned around and found that the winds had wiped out his tracks, and again where he was appeared to be no different than any other place he had explored in this desolation. Glancing once again at the suns he realized that more time had passed than he thought and dusk would be on him shortly. He needed to find a place for the night and have his fire going to be protected by the light from the fire. Without the fire, he could be attacked by the spirits he was sure that inhabited this desolate world.

* * *

He was snapped back from his thoughts as a courier from the alliance came into the camp escorted by some of K'jor's warriors. It had taken some time to arrange a method of moving messages within the alliance – then additional time to develop a method that would allow someone to approach a camp without being killed as an enemy. After much argument between the many tribes and clans he had melded together, it was decided that a spear with its point turned upside down and a piece of cloth attached just below this turned point would signal all that this individual was a courier moving messages from one tribe or clan to another. At this time the color of the cloth did not matter it was just a way to confirm to any that this one had safe passage and could go and see the leader of the individual clans or tribes. With a courier there could be one more warrior since the dangers of this world went beyond just the warring people.

Still he was curious as to why now. This method was generally used only during the times when the alliance had regathered, and was preparing for the next battle. Now with the season of falling, all were preparing for the long season of cold and had gone their separate ways. He could see that this courier was waiting patiently for some response from him to approach. He let him wait as he studied the individual. After a few moments he came to the conclusion that he was from one of the smaller tribes that roamed close to the Sacred Mountains, which was about as far as the wild herds traveled. He personally had never been very close to those mountains, or to the far south to see where the lands became perpetual white. He suspected that if one traveled beyond the Sacred Mountains, eventually the lands of perpetual white would be there also. But with so much required to keep one alive right here, he felt that to travel just to see these wonders were foolish. Life was too short.

Looking into the eyes of the courier he could see a bit of nervousness, and at the same time, an attempt to hide it. To show any weakness before any enemy was not good. Taking a deep breath he then signaled the courier to approach him, which the courier did. Written language was just being developed, and only a few of the clans had it. So he listened as the information was passed to him. The courier stated that, as he surmised, that he came from one of the smaller tribes, and that they had been attacked by a rival tribe, and their prizes, and reward for service to the alliance had been stolen. They had lost warriors to the fight, and the increase to their female herd had been taken along with the slaves. They had tracked the enemy deep into the grasslands, but the trail vanished and they were unable to locate where they had gone. Would there be anything that the leader of the great alliance could do to help?

He signaled the courier away and to wait. Shaking his head inwardly he thought. *When I first thought about trying to bring us together against these sorcerers and magicians, I thought this was going to be so easy. And as time continues to flow past me as the rivers, it just gets more and more difficult. If I felt in my soul that we have wiped out all the nests of these vermin then I would allow us to go back to the way we were. I have had enough of trying to keep these squabbling children from fighting each other, stealing from each other, and killing each other.* Shrugging, he came to a decision and signaled the courier to approach. When he arrived K'jor stated. "I can do nothing about your past, and the loss that you claim. The fighting between you and your rival is between the two of you, as well as the outcome from those fights. So if you lost your prizes from this season's campaigns, they are lost and we cannot, and will not, recover them for you. It is the season of final food gathering for the upcoming cold time. All of us of the alliance are pressed because of the late start to get enough food. So there are no free warriors to help you avenge your loss. While I cannot promise how next season's fighting will go with the alliance, I will offer you and your tribe first choice of the prizes we take, and that is the best that any of us can do. Now return and tell your tribe leader of this decision."

He could see that the hope had been for instant retribution on the tribe that dared attack one from the alliance, and the disappointment was obvious on the face of the courier. But he knew that his decision was the correct one. None of them had the time to go chasing a tribe at this time. And if they were stupid enough to have allowed themselves to be attacked, well, they got what they deserved. When the courier had left, with his second waiting outside of camp, and with the clan's warriors escorting them away, all he could do was shake his head. As he had stated to this courier, there was just too much to be done and too little time.

And it was these thoughts that brought back another curious incident that had taken place, after what had happened in the desolation. One of the warriors, who had been guarding the camp, said he had seen an apparition – a stranger, who was tall and in strange clothing, standing at the edge of their camp and staring. The warrior said he had to look twice to be sure. Yet this stranger *was* taller and did seem to be dressed strangely. He said that he stared at the stranger, and before he could approach the stranger faded away like the dust. And since this was soon after the death of the two in the desolation the warrior thought it had to have been the male they had killed who then crossed over into the spirit world.

* * *

It was great to see the gates once again. The time of hunting was over and the days of cold were close. As they had entered lands familiar to them they could feel their muscles beginning to relax, as well as their spirits soar. Still they had to remain alert for an attack, but did it ever feel good to be here. The hunting, as usual was successful, but brutal. They had to push harder than they ever remembered. K'jor thought that in the next cycle of seasons that he would end the campaigns earlier. This had been almost impossible this time to get the necessary meat, and skins, and to still be able to get all of that back home. And with the increase from their raids it had required more of everything. He had sent a runner ahead to let the clan know that they were arriving and it would be just before the setting of the suns – although the skies were becoming overcast with a promise of rain. Well, rain was important as it fed the rivers and streams, and allowed the grains they grew to reach to the skies. And it wouldn't be long until what they had would be stored for this time of the seasons. With the young ones and the slaves, the grains should have been cut, and now with the arrival of the warriors, the grains would be separated from the stalks, and then stored.

He knew that this was one of the major differences between the clans with their semi-permanent settlements, and the tribes. What grains the tribes gathered were wild and in the vast grasslands. Mostly they followed the migrations of the herd beasts, with most of what they needed coming from the same. And while part of the clothing of the clans was made from the same skins as the tribes, they had learned how to make clothing from other substances, including some of the hair of the beasts. The tribes overall were smaller than the clans. Although the fierceness of some of the tribes made them appear to be much larger. Their warriors were unmatched in battle, and most left them alone, including him. He had not approached any of these to join the alliance. Maybe if this alliance held that someday they, as the alliance, could go against these tribes and eliminate them. But who knew? There was a great chance that within a couple of full seasons the alliance would have become broken and no more. He found that with less than the promised loot, that many within the loose alliance were quite restless. He had to hold this thing together somehow, at least, until he felt that they had eliminated these magicians and their hidden lairs.

He didn't understand why he felt so strongly about destroying them, but he did. After all these magicians had remained hidden for again who knew how long. It seemed that they kept to themselves, choosing only the most desolate areas to maintain their lairs. They did not meddle in the affairs of any of the tribes and clans, and anything that he could surmise said that if one was lost and injured, that they may have actually healed and returned the lost ones. Yet, he just did not trust any of them or their hidden motives. And they had to have hidden motives to be living the way they were. Maybe they had some influence on their own gods, and maybe it could be that this influence could spill into the world of the living. He had to remember to have some discussions this season of cold with T'som. He was their head priest, and between the two of them they could come up with some answers to the many questions he had. While the males from these lairs appeared to be weak, the females, even though many had passed into the spirit world, were not. Their magic and totems were very strong. So much so that not one warrior had been successful when breeding with them to have these females carry. Their own females, many of them carrying, proved that the warrior's seed was strong, but not strong enough to be successful with the females from the lairs. What power they must wield to prevent such a thing.

Still it was a strange thing. Like their males, they did not appear strong. Maybe it was the lairs that gave them their strength. But they had destroyed their lairs as the found them, leaving them silent and dead as the areas of desolation they existed in. It was the continued failure of the warriors to bring these females to carrying that strengthened his belief that there were other lairs out there. These additional hidden lairs, still giving power to these females and giving them the ability to prevent the carrying, were proving that they and their totem were much stronger than any tribe or clan. With the cold time approaching there would be more time to try and change this. Yes, they would remain within the laws, but there would be an increase in the attempts, so that maybe soon they could overcome this strong totem that protected the magicians, making them stronger, and like the fierce tribes unconquerable. What warriors could be produced once they overcame the totem of the magicians? They could become the greatest of their clan, and of the surrounding clans. Still he knew that it was the thoughts of any that had been part of the alliance, since they all had their share of slaves and females. Whoever was the first to be successful in overcoming the totem would be unstoppable. The horns blew announcing their arrival, which brought him out of his revere, and at the same time in the distance the skies rumbled a deep rolling sound. He smiled accepting this as a good sign that their gods approved. After all it seemed that the gods were also announcing their arrival home. What could be better than that?

* * *

"So, R'san, how'd it go while we were away? I know between the raids on the lairs, and then the gathering of meat for the cold time, we have been gone a long time. It placed a larger burden on you, not that you couldn't handle it, but you had much less to work with, with most of the warriors gone." K'jor had to admit that even after all this time he still respected the old warrior. This one had even trained him, and had told him that he, because of his natural skills and abilities, would probably become clan leader. He hadn't believed it at the time. Since this warrior who trained him, did everything with no effort at all, while, at the same time, he struggled through his lessons on combat, tactics and such. But here he was many seasons later the leader, just as R'san had predicted. Still, smiling inwardly, he had to admit the he had even exceeded the old warrior's expectations by creating and leading this alliance.

In his usual way R'san paused before commenting. It had always been his way, and K'jor knew not to become impatient. R'san hadn't stayed alive through all those battles and skirmishes by being slow. He had always been second, never wanting to lead the clan. It was something that K'jor never understood. He had always felt that the clan would have prospered under R'san's leadership. "It has taken longer to accomplish what was needed without the necessary bodies to work. The slaves, we have lost many to the spirit world, cannot produce as well as our own. Yet, the tasks that you left for me are accomplished, if only barely. And no, before you ask, none of the females from the lairs are carrying. While there has been less to be able to breed with the females, some of our own are carrying."

"I noticed that the older female from the lair was not around, has she passed into the spirit world also?" K'jor asked.

Shaking his head he said, "No."

"Maybe I just overlooked her, but it does seem that there is less."

"That is true there have been many of the males and females of the lairs that have passed on to the spirit world. And she almost did the same. She became very ill, and I looked in on her a couple of times, and each time she was worse. So I inspected her for a wound and found one that was very bad. I opened it and let out the poisons and had our healer continue to tend to her. She and two of the females are in the healing area for the females and are out of the breeding herd until the next large moon cycle to heal." He paused as in deep thought, and seeing this K'jor waited knowing not to interrupt. "As you know, the ones from the lairs do not speak our tongue. They possibly speak the tongues of the gods, but this I do not know. Only T'som would know if that is the way, but this older female, who I have bred with a number of times trying to break the totem, knows our tongue. When I spoke I could see that she understood me perfectly. It is a bothersome thing. If these magicians are part of our gods, then it may be that she is a priest, one of high power. And if that is so, then I or any here will not be successful on making her carry. Yet, she almost succumbed, and entered the spirit world. I have to admit it is beyond my understanding. I understand why it is important to destroy the magicians and their lairs, yet at the same time if they are representatives of our gods, we could be dooming ourselves to oblivion, and find our spirits walking forever in the places of desolation. Again, this is something only a priest can answer, and yes I know we do not allow any females to be priests, but their strength, their totem appears to be very powerful, and when we captured them, they were not in herds like our females. They lived with individual males and only carried with these special males. I have to admit this is something well beyond my understanding, and I always thought I understood most."

These points that R'san were making, well what could he say? It was something he hadn't thought about, at least in the direction R'san had just led him. *What if that rolling thunder they had heard on their arrival was not a sign of approval, but of just the opposite?* He definitely would have to talk long and hard with T'som. "You've left me with much to think about. Do we have the necessary wood and grains stored for the cold time, not that I need to ask – since I know you well enough that if that had not been the case you would have confronted me right after we returned. This older female, while it is unusual that we even converse with females, do you think it wise that we actually talk with her?"

Shocked by the question from K'jor, he hesitated before answering. "Why would we do that? If we speak to a female it is for them to do as we tell them. We do not discuss anything with them. After all their purpose is to bring us a new generation of warriors and females, and to help strengthen the clan, to work where they are skilled, and that is all."

"Yes, all that you stated is true. But you have to admit that we have never been in this situation before. When we have added females in the past, eventually they carried our off-spring. Our tongue is the same throughout this land, and the only right a female has is to remain with her tribe or clan, or accept the attacking clan or tribe as her new home. If a tribe or clan had been wiped out in battle it was only right to add the females to one's own breeding herd. And we have wiped out these lairs so that they may not return, and we have added the females to our herds, but none of them spoke our tongue, none of them understood the consequences for refusal, and thusly why the racks – something that we have rarely needed. In fact I do not remember ever seeing one used in my lifetime, until now.

"All what you say is true." Again R'san paused, "But this is unprecedented! Are we going to weaken ourselves by submitting ourselves to the females? I cannot believe you are even thinking this way?"

Shaking his head, K'jor said. "No, no I'm not thinking that way at all. But if this one does understand our tongue, well, who knows she may be able to give us answers as to why."

R'san shaking his head said, "If she is indeed a priest or I guess priestess, since she is female, then how could we go against her power, or even believe what she would tell us? No, I do not think this is a good idea or direction. It will make us appear weak."

Smiling at the statement K'jor continued, "Appear weak. What does it look like to you when we, we as warriors cannot make any one of them carry? Does that not make us appear to be weak? That our seed cannot conquer them? Where have you ever seen it so? Yet, here it is right before us. So what would you have us do? After all you have much more experi-ence in life than I do, but I can see that you don't have an answer either. Okay, I will go see our priest and talk with him, and when I have I will have you join us, and see what we all feel about this. I guess at this point, as far as these new females are concerned, we will keep trying. Somewhere one will have to weaken and begin the carrying."

* * *

The cold time struck early, and while snow was something they dealt with, it usually did not hang around more than a day or two after the storm had left. But this season was different. And if it was beginning this way, would it be that way throughout the cold time? While they had always planned their supplies for the harshest of times, with the additional bodies to feed and keep warm, K'jor was already worried that it would not be enough. This time the snows did not leave but began to pile as the winds tossed it around like a child's toy. Looking into the great fireplace and the roaring fire within its confines, K'jor wondered how it could still feel so cold. If one got just a short distance from that fire one could begin to feel the chill that seemed impenetrable, refusing to leave, or be overpowered by the flame.

It was the kind of day that it would have been wonderful to have a female here to help warm his sleeping mat and his spirits, but that was not to be. Shortly the priest T'som would arrive and later R'san would join them. While all that was happening was unprecedented, they had to decide whether these females and the males that they had made slaves were actually servants of their gods, and what was happening, and not happening was because of that. After all if these magicians and sorcerers were servants of their gods, then by attacking and destroying their lairs, they were attacking the gods themselves. And he truly did not want to bring down their wrath on his clan or any of the others within the alliance. He paced the room like a trapped beast, he hated being stuck inside. It was confining and at times seemed to close in on him. Better to be out in the grasslands where one could see and sense all. Not here where everything was hidden.

He heard the stomping of the feet just outside of the entrance and knew that T'som had arrived. So standing his ground and waiting, he watched as the flap opened and the priest entered. "Good day T'som, priestly leader of our clan, please enter and sit." He stated by rote, the standard phrase when a priest entered one's place of living.

"May our gods favor you and yours." T'som responded back with his required reply. He stood a moment and then said, "It is not a good day out. I do not remember it ever being this cold." Looking longingly at the fire, and then next to it, he saw that the chairs had been placed close so that they would at least be warm while they talked. He also saw the large container that held the warm drink made from the grains they gathered. It was just slightly alcoholic, just enough to warm the insides. Smiling and looking at K'jor he said, "Ah, I see that at least we will be warm." He immediately headed for the chair he normally sat in when the two of them were discussing anything, and shortly K'jor joined him sitting down across from him. Between sat a small table which had the large container, and the mugs.

"We will have some time to cover much before R'san will join us. I want him here because he has been around much longer, and yes while set in his ways, and the ways of the clan, I value his insights. And what we are facing now requires as much insight as I can get. It has been a while since I have been even able to talk with you T'som. I never realized that when I began this that it would involve so much of my time. In many ways I miss the old days when it was just our clan and the problems and issues I had to face were small in comparison to what I am seeing with this alliance. Although without this alliance we would not have been successful in bringing to an end many of the lairs. And this is why I wanted to talk, discuss these issues with you. Some thoughts have been entering my mind and I felt that it was a subject that you could probably have better answers to, than I."

"Since a few of these new females have become part of the breeding herd for the priests, as well as the males as slaves, I think I can understand the issues and the questions that have arisen. Do these magicians or sorcerers have a power we are unfamiliar with? Why is it that none of the females are carrying? What is their strength that they can prevent the carrying? Why are the words they speak not understandable? Are they servants of our gods? And if so, is this why they are hidden from us? And is this weather at the start of the season of cold, a retaliation against us for attacking their servants? Why are there no breeding herds in those lairs and the females appear to have power and live with a single male? Do I have it about right?"

"Yes, and I know you probably have more that you could have added to the list of questions, but what you have said is very much the gist of it. So what are your thoughts on all of this?"

"To be truthful, I don't know all of the answers, or even pretend to know even close to all of the answers. Our gods can be subtle and quiet making it difficult to determine what their feelings are. And right now it is that way. Many times I can easily discern what it is that they want from us, and other times, like now, it is almost impossible. Like you, when you first discovered their lairs, I thought it was a sign from our gods giving us permission to destroy them, and to take our bounty from them. Then we walked through the fallen lair and we realized that much of what was there we could not touch. It had to be of our gods, or if not our gods, then the gods of these magicians and sorcerers. That meant that our bounty would be much less than promised. So much less that the only thing of value that we could safely take was the females and males. And since we destroyed their lair, it gave us the right to add the females to our herds and the males as slaves. Up to that point it all seemed quite normal, exactly what we expected, minus other bounties. But who was I to complain? We found and destroyed a hidden enemy, and increased our future strength by adding their females to our own herds. We increased our workers by the adding of these slaves. At this point all I could see, as you, was the increase in size and strength of our clan. And with these females carrying our offspring to weaken any of the other hidden, what was the word you used, ah *cities*, or lairs as we know them. After all, with each new female taken from those hidden lairs that is carrying our own, takes away the strength of the enemy that these females were a part of."

"Everything you have said is true, and up until that point it was as it should be. Then it all changed. Do you think, first that they get their strength to prevent the carrying from other hidden lairs that we have yet to find, or second that they may actually be servants of the gods, and it is they who prevent this, or maybe it is their personal totem that we must over-come, and be stronger than theirs – what are your thoughts?"

Quiet for a short time T'som stared into the fire before looking back at K'jor. "You've asked some very hard ques-tions, and at this moment I do not have a satisfactory answer for either you or me. But we, my priests and I, will talk with our gods and see what they tell us. But they can be fickle and not tell us anything, making us figure out what they want us to do. Yet, just maybe this stronger than normal season of cold is a sign from them that they are not happy with us or what we are doing. I cannot say. After all if they are not, is it because we've not done enough, or is it because we've done the wrong thing, or maybe we've been doing the right thing but we did not take out the specific lair that they wanted to see gone? Ah, this drink always hits the spot, especially when it is cold like now!"

Watching K'jor he could see the intensity in this leader. Thinking back, since he was a bit older than K'jor he remem-bered watching him work with R'san, and really couldn't see this one leading them some day. He knew that his path was different, and he was to be a priest. Yet his aspirations had never been to be the head priest, and yet here he was. As time had continued to pass by them he watched a change come over K'jor, and there he could see a sense of purpose and an intensity that no other in the clan had ever presented. Those doubts about this one leading the clan, and that is what had taken place quite some time ago, vanished. He was sure that the female, who was well beyond the age of breeding by now, if she was even alive, would have been proud that not only did she produce a great warrior, but a great leader. Of course with the way new lives were created within the structure no male could claim to be the one who fathered him, since all females of breeding age were bred by all of the warriors. Well except a small group who were part of the priests' breeding herd. But this was getting off the subject. Who would have thought that K'jor would have become greater than any and all previous leaders of the clan, and actually unite many of the warring tribes and clans? Not he for sure. And now K'jor was asking hard questions, and asking them of him, and he knew that at the moment he had no answers. And with R'san joining them shortly that it would become more difficult.

Yes, R'san, the mentor, to K'jor, the keeper of the old ways, and in a way the advisor also. Because, this old warrior was set in the old ways, he had originally advised against forming this alliance. And he was sure there were other things R'san had advised against that K'jor had over ruled to the benefit of all within the alliance that he had created. He also knew that there had been a meeting between R'san and K'jor before this one that would include the three of them. Inwardly and shrugging he could only advise and pass on what the gods had told him, and right now they were strangely silent. So all he could do is look at the very subtle signs and hope that he understood what was being shown to him and the rest of the priests. "This older female, the one that almost passed into the spirit world, one of the ones from the lairs, who is barely within the breeding time, it is rumored that you and R'san may have considered her of priestly caste, do I have it right?"

How is it that this stuff gets around? K'jor thought. *As far as I know only R'san and myself had discussed this, and I know that R'san wouldn't have said anything. And being I am the only other, and I know I didn't* . . . "Why are you bringing this up? It was only speculation on our part. Speculation because of the way the females live in those lairs."

Smiling inwardly T'som thought. *Ah confirmed! I wasn't sure that what had been passed to me was accurate, but now I know it is.* "Speculation or not, if she is, do you think it wise that she is kept with the regular breeding herd? Do you not think that she should be with her own kind? And where you would never discuss anything with her because she is a female, we could possibly discuss, from a position of power of course, this with her. And if you only wanted to make it temporary with her returning to the regular herd, that would be okay. It just may be a way of learning about their power and finding a way to overcome and defeat it."

"You've left me something to think about. But for now she is out of the breeding herd because she almost passed into the spirit world. So it will be a while before she is allowed to be bred once again. But R'san has made her his special project to attempt to overcome her strength, her magic, her totem and have her carry. And before you ask, no he like the rest of the warriors is spreading his seed among the herd. His thoughts on this have to do with his time that he has been alive. Figuring that his greater experience and cunning will be able to get past the defenses she has placed upon herself. And if he is successful, and again no, she, like the rest, is available to any of the warriors, so there is no special treatment. She like the rest must be available once a day if signaled. Look shortly R'san will be with us, very shortly really, then you can bring this up with him also. If he agrees, then I have no problem with a temporary assignment. And maybe you can learn what it is they are doing to prevent the carrying. I know that it is not us, or any of the warriors, as many of our own females are carrying right now, and I know by the end of the cold season most will be. Not that all of the offspring or females survive when they drop the offspring. We are not allowed to be around them at those times, but from the screams of pain and the length of time that passes before it is over, it is not an easy thing. But it is the way of life, pain that is, and so we enter this world from pain, and many times we leave the very same way."

"Those last few statements make you sound more like a priest than a warrior – so why that direction in your thoughts?"

But before any answer could be formulated, R'san entered, grabbed the only other chair in the room and sat down, at the same time grabbing a mug and filling it, and taking a large swig, sighing said, "Now that hits the spot. K'jor, I don't know how you end up with the best of this stuff since I know it all comes from the same place, but you do. Okay, I'm here, now what is it that you want to cover with me? While the season of cold is upon us, unfortunately there is always something that breaks, or happens that requires my time."

His entry and energy broke their train of thought and it was silent for a short period of time. All they could hear was the howling winds, and the snow as it struck the sides of the building as the winds tossed it about. "T'som has come up with a suggestion, but being that you have made this older female from the lairs your personal project, we need to ask you what your thoughts are." K'jor then related to R'san what the two of the had been discussing, and then fell silent to let him have time to absorb what he had been told."

Taking his time before answering R'san said, "It is something I have not even considered. But it does have some merit.

Although I do not like the idea of taking her to the priest's herd. As you know I have concentrated on trying to overcome her totem, and while this poison had almost sent her to the spirit world, she or any of the females from the lairs aren't carrying." Pausing and thinking a moment, he continued, "Although because of that poison and how weak she is, for her own health she is outside of the breeding herd, and will be for a while yet." Sighing and looking down at the dirt floor before looking at the two of them, he said. "I can understand why you would want your chance at this female. After all if she is as we suspect then you as our head priest would want to learn what you could. But I have a problem, a real problem with relinquishing her to your custody."

Smiling at him K'jor stated, "If I didn't know you better, I'd think that you have feelings for this female."

Guffawing at the statement, he asked, "Me? You've got to be kidding. She's a female and her place in the clan is where she is; to be available to all warriors, and to be proud to carry, to help the clan to grow stronger. Why would I have feelings other than that?"

"Then to temporarily move her to the priest's herd should not be a problem then, right?"

"I'll tell you what. I'll allow it for the time of healing only. After all she is my special project. I feel that it will be my experience that will finally get past whatever barriers she has placed there. Looking at her, we all know that soon she will be past the age of breeding, and I do not want to waste what little time is left with this one to beat her at her own game. I guess then very soon you will make the transfer, but she must be back here by the rising of major moon, so our healer can determine if it is safe for her to return to the breeding herd.

Now I have assigned two others from the lairs to help her healing, and they are also outside of the breeding herd. I will send them along with her under the same protection until they return. Then once the older female is cleared all of them will return to our breeding herd."

F. D. Brant

"Okay all," Shellian said, "I guess it's time to get moving here." Looking around the table, she had to admit that with eight new people the table where they were sitting did not appear to be as empty. It had been at least fifteen days since the rescue, and briefly looking out of the window she could see that winter had arrived. Now, like the primitives there would be little movement, especially here in the mountains. But that did not mean that preparations and such would stop. This next spring she as the rest were sure, the primitives would be gathering to continue to find, attack, and destroy their cities and their way of life. This was to be the second winter they had spent here in these Sacred Mountains, and remembering back to the first and those desperate times, she felt that even with the threats that lay before them they were much better off. "What this meeting is all about, not that you were not informed, is to gather what information that we can about the primitives, and do this while it is still fresh in your minds." Again she stopped and looked at the newest members to the Alpha complex before continuing. "The eight of you are the ones who will have to help here. And yes we know that the language of the primitives is very different than ours, but I suspect for the length of time that you were captives that you picked up a word or two, and if nothing else from what you have seen, have some ideas as to what changed. We know that your city, Jade, fell after ours – sometime late spring in this annual. So that means that you have been under the control of the primitives for close to half an annual. Now we know that it has only been a short time since you arrived here, and the scars that you have, visible and invisible, will make some of this difficult. But please understand that anything, anything at all; that you can remember will make the difference in our ability to end this alliance. I'm sure that you were as shocked as we were when you learned about this place, and what it originally represented to our ancestors. And for you women who had to endure the hell and worry of becoming pregnant under those really horrible circumstances, I know it is a relief to know that the primitives could not make that happen. Biologically it is impossible. This is not to minimize the abuse that you lived through, the worry, the pain, the not knowing, the overall brutal treatment that all of you received." She stopped here and Saige stood up.

"What Shellian spoke of is very true. She wanted to address you women to know that while we did not have to suffer like you did, we did suffer at the hands of the primitives. Our scouting unit was decimated by them as we tried to escape, and to eventually find this place, which was more by luck than skill. We thought that we were good at what we did, proud to be truthful. But we learned that our skills were no more than a child's when comparing ourselves to the primitives. I guess you could say we played at something that was serious, life and death serious, to the primitives." He looked at the men that they had rescued before continuing. "I know that what you had to witness, and the helplessness as you watched your women being raped is something that will always be with you. Then, going from free people able to do what you wanted, in your own cities, to slaves with no control over anything in your lives. Again watching from a distance as your women had to submit would have made it easy to give up, and fall into the depths of depression and hopelessness. Especially since the odds of rescue was virtually zero. All the cities were independent, and we have no armies, and no way to go and find our fallen.

The primitives did such a great job of bringing down our cities that not a word ever got out as to what was going on. In fact until we escaped, no one had. And from what little we can gather, the primitives have confidence that this is still the way it is. And until we found this place, and then again through more accidental discoveries, made contact with the hub city no one really did know what had happened to the cities that had gone silent. In a moment we are going to ask for as much information as you can recall. What we want to know, more than your life in the tribe that we rescued from, has to do with this alliance. We realize that, that time was nothing but shock, chaos, and disbelief, followed by much pain and suffering. You see, we need to bring down the alliance and have things go back to the way it was, or as close as possible, before it existed – where the primitives are more interested in each other than some hidden cities that do not bother them at all. Now in front of all of you are pads of paper and something to write with. We're going to ask a number of questions, and want you to both write your answers, and speak to us. Because something you say may trigger other questions that will help us solve this, and solve this we must. Yours was the luck of the draw, so to speak, as the tribe that you had become a part of ranged closest to these mountains. Had they gone a different way, you would still be with them, having to do whatever they would have demanded of you. So let's help those who are still captives, those who still have to submit, those whose freedom have been destroyed, and are completely hopeless, and probably feel as you did, that this would be how their lives will end." Once again looking over the table Saige asked, "When was your city attacked? Here I am referring to the time of day, not time of the annual."

Jarid stood up and said, "I don't know if you want us to stand and speak, but I thought I would. I was working before dawn on my program for later in the day. I guess it was probably around dawn, maybe sunrise; I'm not sure, since I was inside. But I know it had to be close to that time since suddenly the power quit. It was a shock! Never had that ever happened before." He then sat down, and began to write it down.

Jas then spoke up, and said, "It must have been somewhere close to that time of day because I was still in bed, and I'm an early riser." The rest nodded their heads in agreement.

"Just to let you know, it was the same with Sequoyah. And now that you've confirmed that the attack was pretty much the same, it makes me wonder how they figured out that the power systems were the key to letting everybody in to do their dirty work? And I think that as we rescue others from some of the other cities we are probably going to find it consistent. I guess until it doesn't work, they'll continue. So while they are showing some innovations in their attacks, it overall, isn't that imaginative. And I guess why change when it has been completely successful. That is, until we escaped. And our feelings at this point since there have been no additional pursuit, that they believe they killed all of us and their secret is still safe."

Giving them time to write before continuing with the questions, Saige drank some of the coffee that remained in his cup. He knew that after finding out about coffee he could have never gone back to shick – just something about the taste that just seemed to appeal to all of them. Maybe it had to do with the fact that more generations than he could possibly count had been drinking this stuff and it had become part of their physical makeup. He liked his strong, black and bitter, while he noticed that the women liked to add different things to the coffee, experimenting with the flavors, and passing on to the other women what they thought of the concoctions. He reached for a carafe and refilled his cup grabbing a snack that also sat on the table. So far these eight new members hadn't asked why the two of them were in charge, and seemed to accept their leadership. As they became more successful in rescuing their people he hoped that it would remain so. But knew that there were always others who thought they would be better at leading. It brought a shudder to him since he, and the rest of the original team, here at the Alpha had direct experience.

"Okay, I'm guessing that your city fell sometime this annual, and the condition all of you were in suggests that it could have been late spring to early summer, so this may have given you some time to at least learn a word or two of their language. We are fortunate that it is the same, at least for now, for all the tribes and clans out there. There is some variance, but not much yet. I guess that comes from there only being this one large land mass. From our views from above this world we know that there are many small islands, but none seem to be populated. What I, we, are trying to figure out here is this, how are we being viewed? And here I mean other than slaves and baby makers. There must be some feeling that anyone or all of you got about how they are seeing us. I know that when we were taught our history lessons in our learning centers that we were all one people. But now, and I hope you've had a chance to confirm and believe it in your own minds, we know we are not even originally from here. And ladies, that are why, thankfully, you never got pregnant from all the attempts to make you that way. It is impossible. I'm not a doctor or a scientist, so the data that is in this system goes way above me in that respect. But it is obvious that our original ancestors who were scientists were comparing the differences in our genetic structure. From what I can gather there are similarities, but nothing that is compatible with either race. So their females cannot become pregnant by us as much as you cannot become pregnant by them.

I am sure that this has made it more difficult for all of our women who are still captives. Since, as the four of you know yourselves, the frequency of having to submit is such that all of you should have become pregnant, but by not, you would be both relieved, but not understanding why you weren't, and at the same time with both the primitive women not happy with you, and the increase in the attempts to make you pregnant, it could not have been anything but hell. And I know that this would be something that would become a very big deal to the primitives. The best I can compare their life style to is the herds they depend on for food, tools, clothing, and so on. Only in their case instead of one dominant male breeding the females, in their society it is the warriors and only they who have the right to pass on their genes. Although they probably do not know that is what they are doing. Their societies are very warrior, and male centered. Women have no say, no rights, and must obey a lawful order from a male. While she has some protection under their system, she still is subservient to the males. While I knew some of this from observing, the meat of this information exists right here. So as time continues to flow past us, please study it. We need to know all we can. Now after this long winded introduction and a general overview of the primitives, I am sure that they have a different view of us now that they have destroyed many of our cities, captured many of our women and men, and other than the destruction of the cities and the increase in slaves, the other . . ." He stopped briefly and looked at the four women to emphasize what he was about to say, "aspect of increasing their stature, the size of their clans and tribes, and their strength through increasing, as they call it, their breeding herds has not materialized. Yes their herds have increased from our women, but nothing will come from the unions, anything other than the pain and suffering that you have experienced.

"This has to have shocked them to their very core, and I am sure it is a major subject anywhere you go in their world. After all they are warriors, and as such they feel that their 'seed' is also of warrior caliber. So for a mere female to be able to defeat them and their seed, has to leave them wondering what is going on. Again with this background and what the eight of you observed what are you sensing?"

It was very quiet as the newest members absorbed all of what Saige had just passed on to them. By living in this hell day to day, they hadn't thought about anything but surviving.

There originally have been twenty of them that had been turned over to the tribe as part of their reward. At the time of rescue they were down to eight, and felt that within an annual or so that the rest of them probably would perish as the other twelve had.

Saige looked around and could see at this moment that they did not have any answer for him. "I can see that you are going to need to think about this, and I can totally understand that, so we'll break at this point to give all of you some time to think about it, get together and talk about it, and then come up with some ideas of what you've observed. We have other questions, but for now I think they can wait. Getting an answer to this one I just presented to you is probably the most important one anyway. We'll meet here tomorrow morning after we eat so that will give all of you the rest of the day. Before breaking this up, do any of you have questions for us?" Seeing a negative response Saige said, "We are done here for today. Keep those pads with you and jot down anything that you think might help us. You eight are the first of what we hope is the beginning of rescuing more survivors from these raids. I know that we cannot save everyone, but we will try to get as many of our people as we can. And you can rest assured that you will be involved every step of the way." And with that he waved them out of the meeting room and waited until it cleared. Sitting back down and deep in thought he turned and faced his sister and asked, "What do you think? Will they be able to tell us anything? I know that when you are in the middle of surviving there is little time to see anything else."

Shaking her head, she said. "I really don't know. It's a tough call any way you look at it. I mean we can guess from what our ancestors have gathered over the time they were researching, and we can add what we personally have learned, but it also means by not actually being inside of that society we could guess wrong. And, dear brother, that is something we cannot afford to do. We've been successful this one time, but as you well know, it may be the only success for a long time. So we have to be so careful not to jump to or cling to half-truths and make them real. We really have to be sure, and in war, who can really be sure? I thought that you did a great job of presenting that information to them, and I could see that it did have an effect on them. I know that with all we have been taught, that to flip a hundred and eighty degrees is very difficult. Although once again I could see relief in the women's eyes, now knowing for sure that they will not be carrying any child from the primitives. I think that it would have been a reminder to them of these really horrible times that they went through. And I'm sure they are having enough nightmares as it is. I know for a fact that I would be. After all it's one thing to have a loving relationship and enjoy the physical side of that relationship, and the children that may come from it. While it is another to be raped all the time with no hope of escaping from it and then producing children that you really do not want, knowing that once you've done that, that it will continue that way through the rest of your life." She shuddered from both the comments she had made and the images that it had created in her mind. Taking a deep breath, she said. "And it is this, along with every other reason I can come up with that we have to end this, and end this once and for all."

* * *

It was early afternoon and all of them were in the enclosed meadowlands that were part of the complex, where Stone and Sorrel would be leading them to the passage that would take them to the building that they had discovered. This was a work party to clear off all of the moss and such that had grown over time, so that with the skylights cleared they would have better lighting inside, and be able to inspect the interior. With lighting existing almost virtually everywhere with in the facility, it just seemed odd that this place did not have lighting also. And this inspection, cleaning and exploring was to learn anything they could about it. Again the passage into this section of the meadowlands was wide enough to pass any of the pack animals through, but was so well hidden that they had missed it. After studying the entrance it became obvious that their ancestors had worked it to make it almost invisible, and when one actually looked at the entrance it just appeared to be shadow and a solid wall. No different than thousands of other places along the inner wall of the extinct volcano.

This location enclosed another smaller meadow area, and a spectacular waterfall and small lake. Again the lake had no apparent exit so the waters were probably exiting through some underground river. The beauty was enough to take one's breath away. And looking around they could see that there had been some tables and benches set up, along with what looked like a play area for children. So it was obvious that their ancestors saw it in much the same way as they. Pausing for a moment and just enjoying the serene images before them, they turned and headed for one of the far walls and the building they were to clean up. "How'd you find this place?" Jessi asked.

Turning around and smiling Sorrel said, "More luck than skill really. You had to be here at just the right time of the day to make the shadows dance in such a way that it made it look like something was wrong with what you were seeing, and then when Stone and I found it, and entered here for the first time it really caused us to stop and enjoy what we were seeing" At this point she stopped and smiled, since this only told part of the story. Since she knew that she and Stone had *really* enjoyed the view. "Then as we explored . . ." And then again thinking back, *Yes, we enjoyed and explored each other's bodies as much as what we were seeing here.* ". . . this whole area and found the building back against the wall. But even though it was there, since it had been built from the rock that is here it was hard to see." She pointed at it as they headed in that direction. "See, even though we know where it is you have to really stare at it to see that it is really there and not just another of the many rock formations that are around."

Looking hard in the direction that Sorrel had pointed, she couldn't pick it up yet. Some of the others from her city had been to this area and had described to the rest of them. But their descriptions fell short of the true beauty of the place, and it had sent chills down her spine. And she knew it wasn't because of the cold. There lay a thin covering of snow on the ground, with a promise of more to come. But today the suns were shining and it would be a rare day that they could get outside and do anything. And to speed things up Saige and Shellian had requested that everybody but the ones working the security office would join the work party. As they approached Jessi eventually began to discern the shape of the building, but it was difficult, due to the age and mosses that had become part of the structure. Again like the entrance to this place, this had been built to hide as much as to provide whatever service it was meant for.

Even with the suns shining they all could see their breath as it was cold. There was a soft breeze blowing and it had a bite to it that immediately made on catch their breath. Eventually they reached the building and where Stone and Sorrel led them around to the back side and then using the handholds climbed up on the roof. Followed by leaning over and grabbing the tools they had brought, with the rest of the team following them up. For the next several hours they cut, scraped, scrubbed, and removed the years of growth. Occasionally stopping to stomp their feet and rub their hands to help keep warm. Finally, with the roof cleared, they descended and entered the building. "Wow, what a difference." Stone exclaimed. "Everything was just shadow and darkness when Sorrel and I last visited this place. Now you can see everything."

The eight new arrivals were still coming to terms with all they had learned since being rescued. But as each new aspect was being revealed to them, the facts and the truth could not be denied. This place was the hidden, unknown city that all were taught about in the learning centers. But the reality was much different from what they had learned. And here nothing had been hidden from them. It was as their ancestors had left it – left it, with the hope that someday they would be rescued and returned to their home world, ending their *time of isolation*. And none of that had happened, and now if it did, would they be able to accept the changes that they themselves had made verses what their true home would be? Would they even be able to relate to their own people? Or because of this *time of isolation*, had they changed to the point that they would appear to be no different than the natives of this world? What they had learned and were still learning was almost as much of a shock as the falling of their city and then becoming captives, followed by the rescue and coming here. One thing for sure, nothing would ever be the same.

When Sorrel and Stone had reported finding this area and the building, the two had completed a brief survey of the interior. The sliding door would not budge so they were not able to confirm that this was indeed the exit from the meadowlands that the researchers used to interact with the primitives. Yet everything about this place said it was so. With all five skylights cleared, and even with the day waning, it was now a brightly lit interior. Gone were the shadows and darkness that had greeted the two. And now they could see why it had been impossible for them to slide the door open. It had the obvious latch that Stone and Sorrel had released, but on the back end was another that had been completely hidden in the shadows. And once this one was released, even though it complained at the treatment, the door slid easily on its tracks, which considering its age and lack of use was a surprise. Expecting it to be dark just beyond the building within the cave that they had exposed they were surprised by the bright light. Stone could see that like so many of the others that they had located since being here, that this was originally a lava tube or steam vent. But this showed extensive rework. There had been a lot of effort expended by their ancestors, and it was obvious that the plans had been for a long term study. Of course little did they know how *long term* it would be. "Stone," Saige said, "since you are our rock expert lead us on, if you would."

"Sure, no problem," then laughing he said, "Now you are sure you want me to do this. Because, if I remember right, it was me who fell through and into one of these vents sometime in the past – and truthfully, I don't want to repeat it." This brought a laugh from the original group leaving the newcomers wondering what that had been all about. Sorrel seeing the confusion on their faces pulled them aside and explained what had happened to Stone before they had discovered this place. Taking a deep breath and looking around at the rest Stone entered the tunnel. Looking down he could see that the floor had been smoothed and where the walls were narrowing down there had been work to keep the width consistent. "I think that we can only go a little ways down this right now. Once again time is against us and it won't be long before the suns set, and like this building there appears to be only skylights to light our way." He headed deeper into the tunnel where it took a sharp right and immediately opened into a large hidden room, again carved out of the living stone.

Here they found much of the gear that the teams would use when they posed as primitives. All covered with dust of the passing centuries, undisturbed, untouched, and unknown until now. Seeing all of this continued to confirm the original role their ancestors had performed, and in awe, silence, and reverence they quietly walked and stared at what was before them. Looking around there appeared to be no exit from this space which did not make sense. "Did anybody see a way out of here, other than the way we came in?" Shellian asked. She could see all of them looking around but also could see that once the question had been asked, followed by all of them searching, there just did not appear to be an exit.

"Okay," Stone said, "I'll backtrack a little and see what we missed. Go ahead and see what's here, this is really a very large room, something I wouldn't have expected at all. Anyway, be right back." He backtracked from the room to where the tunnel had made the sharp right, stopped, and studied the wall and like the entrance into the smaller meadow area there was a turn to the left that when one first looked it appeared to be a solid wall. Shaking his head at the illusion, he was beginning to appreciate his ancestors even more. Somehow they had figured out how to place things in such a way, that unless one really searched these openings, they would remain hidden. He marveled at the design. By placing the skylight where they had, the eyes were naturally drawn to the light and away from the shadows. And where the tunnel continued it was in the deeper shadows, almost invisible. As he walked into the shadowed entrance he was surprised at the very size of the opening. A pack animal could easily pass through this. Again shaking his head, he just could not believe they had missed it. He could tell that dusk was on its way and it was time for all of them to head back and follow these tunnels out to where they left the mountains. It was critical that they know all of these passages which lay before them. Still it seemed to him and he suspected the rest that what they were trying to accomplish was impossible, but what could they do? Just let it go? No, he already knew the answer to that. Too many innocent lives would be destroyed if this was allowed to continue. He could hear the voices of the rest as they approached his location. He remained where he was and watched as they passed his location unaware of this hidden entrance. The entrance seemed hidden no matter which direction one was going. Shrugging he fell in behind the last of them and left the tunnel system, joined Sorrel, reaching for her hand and together with the group headed back to the warmth of the facility.

* * *

Judd, had been elected, to speak, to pass on what they had gathered – information wise – from their meetings together from the previous day. As the eight sat around the table, with Saige and Shellian presiding, he stood up, clearing his throat he said, "I don't know how I ended up with this duty, but here goes. One of the things that we men have learned, and it doesn't make it any easier, since we were helpless to be able to help in any way, is that the women had it much tougher than we first imagined, at least for us, maybe not you and your scouting unit. Not only did they have to deal with the males, but there was almost as much abuse coming from the females. I guess these females were jealous that our women would be usurping them in their roles, since interest seemed to have increased towards our women by the males of the tribe. From where we were we could not see much of this. Yeah, we could see them having to submit, but not too often. We now know that it was very often, and now we know why pregnancy would have been a very real worry. With the conditions being as bad as they were, there was a good chance that if they had, and carried to full term that they would have died in child birth.

'For us, the men, we were beaten often and directed to whatever work they wanted us to do. While not fun by any means, when compared to what our women faced, while not easy, still did not compare. So now I, if not the other men who were captives, understand why we lost so many of our women. There had been twice as many captive women as men, and as you know from your rescue there was an equal number.

While we lost close to half of the men, it was probably closer to three-quarters of the women. I suspect that if we could visit the other tribes and clans that have taken our people that the attrition rate would be much the same." Stopping for a moment and catching his breath, Judd leaned on the table, and then grabbed some water before continuing. "All of us were so busy trying to survive that all we can come up for you is just impressions, and by not really knowing their language, again what little of it we learned really doesn't help a lot.

"As expected, there seemed to be a flurry of interest in the women, fresh meat, I think the term is, while we were cuffed, not only by the men, but by the women. Any time we were slow to do what they wanted, we paid a price. When we were first gathered and placed in the large enclosures we were separated, men and boys in one, and the women and girls in the other. And the distance between the pens, I don't know what else you could've called them, were on opposite sides of their compound. We were surrounded by huge amounts of these primitives, and there was no way, and I mean, no way to escape. In the distance towards where the women were being held there seemed to be some type of contraption. In it, well, it looked like a couple of our women were in it." He pointed to the four around the table and said, "They confirmed it. While I know very little about it, it seems that it is a punishment device that they use for women who will not submit to their will. And that is all I'm going to say about that, other than the obvious that our women were continually raped, and that didn't change, even after we were separated and given to the different clans and tribes. I, for one, have to say that it really sucked not being able to help and comfort our women. All we could do was watch and pray that something would come along and get all of us out of that living nightmare, which, thankfully, you and your team did.

"Although I have to admit once again, that when you attacked their camp, and from what the women passed on to us, since we weren't there, had sex with that primitive, we thought and they too, that things had just gone from very bad, to much worse. To us it did look like we were prizes being stolen from the tribe that had become our lives. So we did not know what to expect. We now know why you had to do all of it, including maintaining the illusion until you knew that there was no pursuit, and that we would be free of them. Although how just four of you pulled this off we really don't know, but are quite happy that you did. Again I have to admit that as we were being led away as captives again, that our mood was very dark, and we thought about trying to escape. But again had to admit, we were lost, we had no idea even what direction to go, and we probably would have just been captured once again making things worse. We all witnessed at least one of our own beaten to death, and it was not pretty." He again paused, "Again at this moment it's the best we can do. I know that this isn't much help."

"Survival was paramount to all of you, so it is no surprise that you weren't looking at other things. Possibly, if you had survived long enough and had remained a captive long enough, any of you could have begun to see the subtleties of how they were reacting to you and begin to understand how they were seeing the cities other than a place to destroy." Shellian, looking over the eight continued, "We hoped for more, but even what you have passed on to us can help. Not one of us in the scouting units have ever lived with the primitives, and to have something, anything, about how it is inside of their world is important. We need all of you to keep thinking about this. Not necessarily the abuse, but we do understand that it is difficult to separate one from the other. We have to build as much information on the primitives as we can. As someone said, knowledge is power. And right now even with what is in these computers, the primitives seem to know more about us than we do them." Again looking around the table before continuing she said, "Okay, I guess that will cover it for now. Just keep what we need in the back of your minds, and maybe something will click and what you remember can help."

After the eight had left Saige turned to Shellian and said, "I surely was hoping for more. But I'm not really surprised. Somewhere along the line we are going to have to get lucky and recover one of our own. And what I mean by that is a captive that was part of one of the scouting units. All of us speak the primitive language."

* * *

Staven, Seve, and Stone had been assigned the duty of exploring the tunnel system and to determine where it came out lower on the mountainsides. They had planned on a couple of days of being away and had packed to be sure that they had enough to go beyond that time if necessary. "Wonder if they'll learn anything in that meeting today?" Seve asked.

"Probably not," Staven answered. "Simply because when one is trying to survive, you are just looking at ways to make it happen, and not looking at other things. Still anything they can give us will help, eventually." Turning to Stone he asked, "Why are you so quiet?"

Smiling and with a faraway look he said, "Sorrel informed me this morning that she's carrying, pregnant. It has been such a worry for her that she wouldn't be able to after almost losing her life, and losing her first child."

The other two were silent, as they knew that they had been partially responsible for her loss, but could see from Stone's reaction that he wasn't even thinking in that direction. "I guess that is great news." Seve said.

Again smiling, Stone nodded his head and said, "Yes, it really is, a surprise, not that we haven't been physical, but with a chance that she could never be a mother, I know it was something that had been weighing heavily on her. Now we have to worry and see if she can go full term. And it is a big concern, worry if you may, to her and of course, to me."

"That's quite understandable really. But I've heard that a woman can miss her cycle every once in a while and still not be carrying . . ." Staven stated, as he stopped and faced Stone, "and it would just crush her if this turned out to be the way."

Stone thought a moment, back to when she had announced it to him, and he had, had the same concerns. He remembered back to when she has lost her child, and almost lost her life. The many days of being with her to help her through it, and the resulting strong relationship that had developed. Shaking his head he knew deep down that he did not want to go through that again, and he was sure that she did not. "She's taken that into consideration, and actually waited ten days before going to the doc, and Jas, who now assists him. I guess in a way it is nice to have a woman who can work with the other women. After all I know that most women would prefer a female doctor or nurse. Anyway, that's getting off the subject; both of them ran separate tests, and confirmed that indeed she is pregnant. You know that term wasn't used a lot, I mean we generally used 'carrying' for a woman with child, but it is one that our ancestors used, and we've sort of just picked it up."

"Well, if she went to all that trouble to make sure it wasn't the other way then its wonderful news. I know from talking with Sabryn, that she and the other women were really worried that after her near death, and loss of her unborn daughter, that she would never be able to carry after that. So this will be great news to them." Pausing for a moment before continuing, Seve said, "But I suspect that they already know. It's something that seems to get around without anyone saying anything. Fatherhood is interesting. I mean you are seeing things very differently as you watch your child grow, try things, and see things for the first time. It brings the wonder back into your own life with each new discovery and milestone reached. And it is work – all day and all night work. But I wouldn't trade it for the world, this one or the one we came from."

"Truer words were never spoken," Staven replied, "Sommer is a handful, but ever since she came into this world she has me wrapped around her little finger." Shaking his head with a smile he said, "I don't know how she did it but she did, and I have known that I'm in trouble with that one. It makes it difficult to set the boundaries that are needed, but, oh well."

"Guess we should get to searching out this tunnel system. There's enough adventure right here, but from what you are telling me, it sounds like the real challenges in life are still ahead of me, when our child enters this world." Sweeping his arms out in the direction they needed to go, Stone asked, "Shall we?"

"Sounds great, but I will just pass on one other thing, and I know that Seve knows what I am speaking about, and the feeling of total love and devotion that you feel when you have your sleeping child in your arms. It's an unbelievable feeling."

They reached the split where if they went right they would enter the room, but followed the subtle shift to the left. Again the distance between the walls would allow a pack animal ease in passing along the corridors. It was obvious that there had been much work on both the walls and the floor to keep the floors somewhat even and the distances between the walls consistent. Periodically there had been skylights cut into the roof, so while in the areas where there were no skylights, it never was darker than dusk. The grade here was always downward, and again the drop was not so major to make it difficult for any of the animals or people who would use these passageways. Eventually at what they considered a reasonable time, they were about to stop and take a break when just ahead in the distance the tunnel appeared to be much brighter. So curious, they continued a little further and were rewarded with the tunnel opening up into a small room that had benches carved out of the native stone, and some troughs for watering the animals.

Shaking his head once again in awe, Stone said, "You know, our ancestors seem to have thought about everything. I mean, look at this." He swept the area with his arms, pointing out the work and effort that went into creating this. "It's very obvious to me that our ancestors were here for the long haul. Everything I see that they did speaks of permanence, planning, and hard work. I would never have thought to create a break room like this. But now that I see it, it absolutely makes sense."

The other two couldn't argue. This had been as much of a surprise to them as it had been to Stone. "You're right, Stone. But you have to admit it is consistent to what we've learned." Staven thought a moment before continuing, "Now if you think about those caves that are strategically placed going away from the facility, basically in all directions, then what we are seeing here is consistent, and very much so. I guess we haven't really begun to think like our ancestors yet, and that is no surprise. Too much time separates us from them. And in that separation we have changed, which I guess makes sense. I just hope the change has been good."

"Amen brother," Seve replied.

CHAPTER TEN

Two of the primitives showed up at the door of the shelter where she, and the two who were helping her, were living, and demanded that all of them follow them. Very weak and a long way from recovery, Sara still required the assistance of the other two women to move any distance at all. At least it appeared that these primitives were taking that in consideration as they slowly headed off in a different direction, towards part of the clan's home that she had never visited. Right now any curiosity that she might have had, took a backseat to the effort of just moving. This weakness scared her. She had always been strong, even through the hell of child birthing. And right now she knew that she still was very close to death. If she caught anything, as weak as she was, she felt that there would not be enough strength left in her body to fight it.

* * *

The winds were picking up and as they gusted, shaking the shelter he was in, with forces that spoke of wanting to destroy. All K'jor could do was again wonder if maybe he had read things wrong, and now the gods were letting him know in no uncertain terms that he had been wrong. With these thoughts his mind drifted back once again to the beginning of all of this. He was spending his last night in the desolation, with nothing to show for it, other than, a growing belief that these areas were where the spirits lived. It looked, and felt that way. And he had seen nothing to change that opinion. It was full on dark, and even the fire he had burning in front of him appeared to give out a very dim light, with no warmth, and no protection. He could feel the spirits closing in on him, but other than the fire he had no defense. He could see that there would be little to no sleep tonight. He thought that if he did try to sleep that the ones of this spirit world would take him. And if a living person was taken by the spirit world his body would never have rest – living, but not living existing between the two worlds forever. To be tortured by the knowledge that one could not be a part of the living, and at the same time, not a part of the dead, forever roaming alone and apart from everything and everyone. He thought he had remembered a couple of people who had been touched this way. In his youth he watched as one of their very own become that way. And then he just disappeared, and no one knew when or how it had happened.

He remembered these thoughts weaving strongly through his mind as he got up and began to pace. The day had physically, mentally, and spiritually worn him down to where it took movement, any movement to remain awake. His imagination began to create beasts and spirits beyond the fire, and he did not know if they were real or just a creation of his mind. He was glad that he had at least the dried mud hill protecting his back, and so his vulnerability was only to the front.

Picking another point on this hillside, he sat down, figuring from this place he could see and react faster if something out of the dark attacked him. He leaned back to allow the hill to support him, but to his surprise there was nothing there! Off balance he fell backwards, received a large shock, and lost consciousness. As consciousness faded his thoughts said that he had failed, and the spirits with their traps had caught another.

* * *

Sara looked out the door and shivered. With the infection mostly gone her body was completely wrung out, and the thought of going out in this weather scared her. But in this world she had no choice, none at all. Either she did as she was ordered or pay with some kind of punishment. Steeling herself for the ordeal, she nodded to the two other women, and followed the two primitives that had demanded that she and the others follow them. Even though these two had slowed their pace they still were outdistancing the three women, since the two had to heavily support Sara. There just was nothing she could do to help. In her present condition she couldn't even make the trips outside to take care of nature calls. She was as close as anyone could be to be totally bed bound and death. She found that she was shaking not just from the cold and the cutting winds, but from weakness. It winded her to just walk at all. This scared her even more. This weakness was a sure sign that she was in very serious trouble, but again what could she do? She was at the mercy of this clan and its laws and rules. So with determination, and a lot of help, they followed, with her head bowed both because of the winds, and her weakness.

Eventually they got on the lee of some of the buildings, and with the winds blocked, it actually felt warmer. Looking ahead she could see the impatience in the ones that they followed, but there was no way she could pick up the pace. In fact, she had to stop, and with help lean against one of the buildings to get enough strength to be able to continue. Finally she nodded to the two and they continued up to a wall within the clan grounds, through a gate, and inside a smaller compound. She, with the other two, were led to a small building and the hanging skins that acted as the covering for the door were pulled aside and she was directed inside with the two women. *First impressions – warm, cozy, and dark.* Once her eyes adjusted to the gloom, she could see three sleeping mats, a place to both cook and serve food, and in the far corner away from the entrance a few chairs and utensils. Then she realized that someone was sitting in one of those chairs, but at the moment could really care less. She needed to lay down now. Whatever strength she had was gone and if she did not lie down she would fall down, support or not.

She signaled the two to put her down on one of the mats. With this male inside this place she knew better than to speak. After all it was not allowed when a male was present. She was half expecting to see the sign for breeding and waited for the inevitable, but it was not forthcoming. At least it appeared that they were going to abide by what that older warrior had said. Once on the mat, she found that she could barely stay awake, but tried. There had to be a reason for this one to be in here. Eventually her ragged breathing became closer to normal, and still this one did not speak. She then wondered if he was some guard or something, but again that did not make sense, but again she, from her exhaustion, clearly couldn't think straight, so reasoning out this puzzle was well beyond her.

He stood and approached them and then spoke. "I am T'som." When he spoke this it was as one who was used to wielding authority. "I am the head priest, and you three have been placed in my care for the duration of your recovery. For now, that is all I will say, since it is quite obvious that you are still very close to the spirit world. I will be checking in every day." At that point he turned and left leaving the three alone. Sara wondered what this was all about, but not for long as she drifted into a deep and exhausted sleep. The two that helped Sara reach this new place, and had been ordered to care for her, looked at each other, and then down at Sara. She normally translated what had been spoken by the primitives, but they could see that there would be no translations today. Sara was already deep in an exhausted sleep. The only thing they could discern, from the tone of voice, was that this one was another leader of some kind. It was obvious from both his body language and his overall aura that he had power here. But at this moment what that power was and if he was the overall leader they did not know.

T'som, upon leaving the shelter, could see that this female was very close to the spirit world. The distance hadn't been that great from where she had been living to this shelter, and she had barely made that distance. From listening to her breathing when she had arrived, with major assistance from the other two females, he could tell that it had all but done her in. He made a decision, and instead of heading back inside his own shelter, he turned and went back outside their area and proceeded to the shelter of the leader K'jor. This was an unplanned visit, so when he reached the flap that covered the doorway, he waited a moment, and then announced his arrival. As he was about to enter a female pulled the flap back and exited. He at once entered and found K'jor dressing. "What brings you back here in this storm?" K'jor asked.

"It is that female that has been assigned to me to learn what we can." He replied.

After dressing, he came over and sat in one of the chairs and with a questioning look asked, "Have you already learned something about these? And if so that was really fast."

Shaking his head in response, T'som said, "No, nothing like that. But from my experience, this one is very ill. She will not recover by the next full major moon cycle, and I suspect that it will be more towards three. Even with the assistance of the other two females, the short walk to where she is now almost sent her to the spirit world."

Quiet for a moment K'jor asked, "Is there maybe another reason that you might want to keep this one there longer?" He paused pointedly, "Maybe some ulterior motive to this request?"

"And why would that be, or what would it be? She's just arrived, and other than informing her and the two that this would be where they would stay until they were returned to the herd, I only know of her condition, which is very poor indeed. If I had known that she was this bad, I would have waited for this storm to abate, and then have made the move. Just this short time out in this weather and the short distance she had to travel completely wiped her out. When I spoke, she barely acknowledged that I was there, and I could see that it was a struggle for her just to stay awake long enough for her to listen to what I had to say. And besides, why would I care?

I know the importance of the females to our clan, even better than you, but she is only one of the many. But, as we discussed, if I am to learn anything from her, and hers, then she must be healthy. I will continue to check in on the three of the females every day, and you can send both R'san and your healer any time you want, and if it is every day, it is your right. If you want to check, again just do it. I will be having our healer look in on this one also, so if the two healers want to get together and discuss this, I have no problem." Inwardly he thought. *What is this about? He has his place and I have mine. Yet, it is like he is seeing something that is not there. This I do not understand. Maybe because I interrupted him with a female, that this has set his mind in this direction, and he is angry about such a thing. Who really knows? But if we are to learn anything, anything at all about these females that we have added, then I will need the time to find the answers. And with this one so close to the spirit world there is no way to get any of the answers until she is healed, the gods willing.*

"Sorry, T'som. I'm not, well, I'm not mad at you. But this storm seems so fierce for this early in the season of cold. It has me worried that maybe I did error, and misread what the gods wanted. I know that you told me that you have received nothing from them, back at the time R'san was with us. Has that changed now that we are alone? All of this has been weighing heavily on my mind. I expected this storm to have already broken, but there seems to be no end in sight, and it feels colder than I can ever remember. Are you sure that this is not a sign from them?"

"I truly wish I could tell you. But as I said when R'san was here, they have been strangely silent. But maybe this isn't caused by our gods at all. Have you thought about that?"

With another questioning look K'jor asked, "What do you mean by that?"

"These magicians or sorcerers and their lairs are both hidden and strange to us. So maybe we have been looking at this wrong. What if, instead of being servants of our gods, they serve different gods? And if they serve different gods, who's to say that, this . . ." Stopping briefly and sweeping his arms around, he continued, "this storm that we are facing now is from their gods, rivals to our own. And the reason why I, or any of the other priests, cannot get anything from our gods could simply be that they have their hands full dealing with this threat in their spiritual realm. So while we fight the battles here in the physical world, they are fighting these rival gods in the spiritual world. I don't know if this is what's happening, but this is a possibility. I have no proof, but thought that maybe it would be something I would pass on to you."

Again silent as he thought about what the head priest had said, he had to admit it was something he had not even considered. After all, what did he or any of them know about their gods. Other than trying to keep them happy and on their side, what could any of them know about their spiritual world? Any who had passed over could never return to tell them what it was like serving the gods. So, why wouldn't there be rival gods who grow jealous, and have their own worshipers, ones like they found in those hidden lairs. "I must admit, this is something I never even considered. And if this storm is a response from different gods, where does that place ours? Are these other gods stronger, so much so that they can warn us in this way to leave their people alone?"

"Don't take this for fact. I have no proof. But I think it is important that you consider it a possibility. Again what is happening could be from our own gods, and these are the only gods that exist. But just a short time ago we thought that we were the only people that existed, the clans and tribes. And then you found these hidden lairs with strange people, strange clothes, and strange ways of existing – picking only the harshest of lands to live, places that will send any of us to the spirit world – a place of strange artifacts that could only be of the gods. So would it seem strange that they would worship different gods? And with us now attacking these lairs, would not also seem logical that their gods would retaliate?"

"I have to admit that you've given me plenty to think about. All of this I haven't considered, haven't thought about, or even put it as a reality. Yet, everything that you've said makes absolute sense. I'm surprised that I just did not see it, let alone consider it. Okay, with the season of cold upon us I will have much time to think and consider what you've left me with. And I, and I'm sure R'san with our healer, will check in on this female often, and if what you say is true, there will be no issue with her remaining there until she is healthy enough to be returned with the other two, to the breeding herd. After all, we still must defeat their individual as well as collective totems if we are to become stronger. And if R'san is correct, by defeating the totem of this older female, the rest should follow shortly."

* * *

How long had she been between living and dying? While she had known that the infection that had almost killed her had left her weak, she did not realize how weak until being moved during that storm. As in a dream, she barely remembered the comments made by that priest. She had learned that he, two healers, and that older warrior had been here every day checking on her condition. She remembered none of their visits, if she had even been conscious. After being close to death before the discovery of the infection, she had hovered there once again after the move. She had been shocked to learn that she had been this way for close to twenty days. Now she was happy she didn't have a mirror because she suspected that she would be quite pale, and quite drawn. Even with consciousness returning, to just sit up had led her to shaking from the lack of strength. She could see the worry in the eyes of the two women who had been with her, but did not have the strength to even speak.

To feel this way scared her to her very core – never had she ever been this frail, this weak, and having to totally depend on someone else. She had always been strong, prided herself in her strength, both mental and physical. After all those many annuals of training in the scouting unit had developed a deep disciplined core, a ruggedness of spirit and strength that at this moment were as if they never existed. At the present she was propped up against one of the walls as she once again received some thin broth to eat. Even though it was warm in this shelter she was shaking from being cold. Just the effort of eating this small amount drained what little strength that she had, and she knew that shortly that she would be asleep once again. And in one sense, she did not want to, as she was continually facing demons in her dreams. Seeing her dead mate just out of reach, and her missing children, continually reliving the moments after their door was broken down, and the hell that followed. At least awake she could avoid them, but once asleep they were always there. She wondered why they had been moved, but at this moment in time could care less. And as these thoughts crossed her mind, once again, she faded from consciousness, into the oblivion and the nightmares in her sleep.

* * *

"You're right T'som, this female is very sick. I have seen very little signs so far that even indicate that she will recover from this. Yet, there seems to be a fighting spirit within her, and I see little signs that she is slowly returning. And I now understand why, back when you approached me with your concerns, that you felt that it had been unwise to move her, even though we did. That move definitely set back her time of returning. And when you first said that you felt that three cycles of our major moon would be more realistic, I did not believe it. But now I am of the opinion, that three may not be enough. And while I am not a healer, my opinion now says that it will be after the end of the season of cold before she will have recovered, if the gods allow. Each day that passes I still see the opportunity for her to pass into the spirit world. And if she does that, we may never know, never have the answers we are looking for. And she could defeat us by doing just that. If she was to pass into the spirit world before her totem was broken, defeated, then we may never be able to do just that."

K'jor got up and started pacing the room, unable to remain sitting for long. Another storm had descended upon them and was now dumping its fury around them. This season of cold was absolutely the worst he could ever remember. Turning and facing T'som he continued, "I've come to no conclusions as of yet, even about this female. It may be this sickness that she has could be a result of her gods defending her, and our gods attacking her. And with her in the middle not having the strength to either defend or attack. She is mortal like all of us and the gods are always immortal. It seems that we are no more than playthings. But like you said, all of this may not be the way of it either, and it simply could be that whatever it is that attacked her body left her in such bad shape that it will take a very long time until she has recovered. At times I wish that you hadn't brought up these other possibilities, as it surely complicates things, and I've had enough of that with the alliance."

Keeping silent and listening to K'jor, T'som truly could not add anything to what was being said. Sometimes silence was the best response anyway. There was so much he just did not understand, and he fully understood the quandary that K'jor was in. Heck, he faced that as the head priest almost every day of his life. Things were so much more complicated when one dealt with the spirit world, and gods. After all how could a mere mortal understand, let alone carry out, what the gods, who lived forever, wanted of their subjects? With an inward smile he thought that finally K'jor had to face some of what he did, and maybe it was a good thing. After all, K'jor had always been direct; let's get this done, and who cares about what the complications might be. Those could be sorted out afterwards. And now he seemed to be second guessing himself all the time. Yet, even here it was from a position of strength, as one in command. T'som had to admit that he felt lucky to have such for a clan leader. *May it continue to be so.* "Now you enter my world, where nothing is simple, nothing is as you see it, nothing is as you expect. It is not an easy place to be."

"No truer words have been spoken. I grow restless to return to battle. At least there, while the situation can turn complicated, it is there in front of you and you can adjust. This, this is beyond that. You cannot see your enemy, you cannot predict his direction, and you do not know the battlefield on which you are fighting. No, this is not my kind of fight! Give long knives, bows, and such. These I understand! But this other, this other is so far beyond me, so I am glad that I have you to cover our flank. Although at times with what you leave with me, it makes me wonder if you are not just attacking also." Smiling before continuing, K'jor said, "Now don't take that wrong. You are one of my most trusted, and we've been friends long before either of us rose to our places among our people, and I want our friendship to always be there. Again, at the beginning, which now seems more unreal, than real, I never saw or understood the consequences or directions this would take. It appeared to be so simple then. Destroy an enemy, grow in strength and stature from our successes, increase our herds, and our clan, and become strong enough that none of the others out there would want to attack us.

"Yet, while much of that has happened, I guess most of it really, we, well I expected to see an increase through our breeding with the new females that have been added to the herds. But while the increase in the size of that herd has been realized, none of those that have been added are adding to our clan. And it is because of this we are now here trying to learn why this is so, and of all things, having to depend on one of these females to enlighten us. Who would have ever thought that? Not me, never in my lifetime would I have thought that we as warriors, would be unable to make a female carry our offspring. Yet, that's the very truth that is staring right back at us. We consider ourselves strong warriors, yet these females, yes; these females are showing us that we are not that strong. After all they are defeating us. And if females can do this, how long will it be before we are defeated in battle?"

CHAPTER ELEVEN

Looking out the windows from the meeting area Saige smiled. With both his mate Seirra, and his sister Shellian carrying their first child he knew that with what had happened with Sorrel, that it would be something that would have weighed heavily on her mind. After all she had been the first to become pregnant so very long ago. But fate had intervened and she had lost her daughter, while the other two who had become pregnant later now had children. There had been a worry, because of the way she had lost her unborn daughter; that there was a great possibility that she would never be able to have children of her own. So when Saar had informed he and Shellian, that Sorrel was pregnant, and just glowing, it was a relief – showing that even she had been worrying about this. So if all the women who were now with child could go full term that would mean that all of the women who had survived the falling of their city and the desperate run to the Sacred Mountains would bring new lives into this world – *so many changes, so much still to do, and still no answers.* Yet, he had to admit, even in these rough times, life continued to flourish, continued to grow, and refused to go quietly.

And with the two children now both walking, well running probably would be more accurate, they seemed to be everywhere. And who would have thought that they could create so much chaos, so much noise, and disappear in an instant on those short legs of theirs. Shayne and Sommer definitely kept their parents fully occupied with just trying to keep up with them. So he knew that in one sense he was seeing his future. Yet, he had to admit it; he looked forward to the time when he and Seirra would be taking care of their own child. Although the thought of seeing her go through the pain of childbirth, after Shell' had described it to him, was something he did not want to happen, still, it is the way of life. And to him, with Seirra in the middle of her second third, she was more beautiful than ever.

And while it was nice to let his mind drift in this direction, it truly was not the reason he had come in here. With winter upon them, they needed to rescue more of their people. But at the moment he had no idea how to do it. The distances were just too great, and if the tribe that they had rescued the eight from had not been close, it would have been impossible. He knew from the records that when it had been originally decided to establish the cities that their ancestors did this during the winter time to minimize the possibility of being discovered by the primitives, who pretty much just remained in their camps and clan homes. And that they used a kind of shuttle that flew through the air, and was large enough to move not only the people, but the equipment to build the cities. But while there had been a description of these shuttles, no one had found anything on how they looked, how they worked, how big they were, what they used for energy, and besides even if they did know, no one here could operate one. So presently they were on foot. Even the machinery that they used when monitoring the primitives was slow, and housed the equipment they used to record, track, and keep in contact with the forward scouts. These machines had never been meant for fast or long distance travel.

* * *

"Well, Stone what do you think? After all you're the rock specialist." Seve asked.

"All I can say is from the amount of work that has been done on these tunnels that we are working our way through, our ancestors had planned on being here a long time. While I can see that they used some of the original steam vents and lava tubes, there are places where they have just worked through the solid rock to enter into another series of tubes. Look there and you can see where this tube turned away from the direction they wanted to go. The debris that is partially blocking it is from the waste when they added to the tunnel. And to keep opening up the roof often enough to let light in and keep the air fresh. This was well planned and executed." As they turned a slight curve they found another room like the one close to the beginning and entered into it. Looking around they could see that it was set up very much like the other one. This was the third, and they seemed to be spaced to give any who would be using the system an easy half day distance between. From the shadows they could see that this must have been one for overnight stays. Built into the rock walls were bunks that folded up and out of the way when not inuse. Again supply cabinets, and fodder for any of the animals, and a section built off to one side for taking care of one's bodily needs. Towards one side and away from where the animals would have been kept was a raised stone platform that had a fire pit and next to the pit a generous supply of wood.

"They must have used these pack animals to haul this stuff in here, unless they had another way of doing it." Staven commented, as he looked around the room, and as it continued to darken, and like the caves that they found before discovering the Alpha, the walls began to glow that same soft light. "I really wish I knew how they did that. It's been a mystery since Saige and Shellian found that first cave. And I'm noticing that like those it's warm here also – subtle, very subtle, so much so that it would be easy to not even realize it."

"I guess we've lost part of what we once knew," Seve said. "After all we know that these people were our people, which mean that when the cities were established, this again was common knowledge. Or at least the engineers knew how to do it. And from what we've observed, they used it everywhere. So why'd we lose it?"

"Don't have an answer for you." Stone responded, "But if we've lost the knowledge to build this, how much have we forgotten over time, just waiting for a rescue that has never arrived. Even the Alpha's location had been lost, although that may have been on purpose, since it was important to keep the knowledge away from the primitives. Still, its location had to be written somewhere in the cities, otherwise no one could ever return, and you know as I, that it was abandoned with the thought of returning someday. Everything had been mothballed, and all the maintenance bots functioning to maintain the place in working order – all speaking of us returning here someday. And yet, even our history changed from the true beginnings to the mythology that then became the truth.

We've learned a lot since finding this place, but I really feel like there is much it isn't telling us, because it was common everyday stuff. So instead of trying to advance ourselves, we've stagnated, playing a waiting game, and probably have actually lost a great deal in the process." Looking at the other two, and around the room Stone yawned, and said, "I don't know about you two, but once we eat, I for one will be ready to call it a day, and get some sleep. Who knows how far we still have to go?"

* * *

"Can any of you tell me where either Saige or Shellian is?" Judd asked, as he entered the cafeteria.

Starr looking up from breast feeding Sommer thought. *It won't be long before this will be a thing of the past. But it just seems so right, so natural. But Sommer is now preferring solid foods, and wanting the breast milk less and less.* "I think that Shellian is in the medical section. She mentioned that she was due for a checkup, and Saige, I think he has the security office duty right now, why?"

"I've just learned something that I feel is very important, actually probably critical for all of us to do what we need to do. Guess I'll head for the security office then, thanks." He headed out the opposite double doors and was gone.

Looking down at Sommer Starr asked, "Now what was that all about?" Then quietly laughing she could see that her daughter could care less, and was on the verge of falling asleep, with a very contented look on her face, then she said softly, "My how I love you my little one."

* * *

"What do you think, Stone? Where do we go from here?" Staven was looking around at the huge meadow that lay before them. They had just emerged from the tunnel through another one of those sliding doors into a meadow similar to the one close to the complex.

"Very good question," Stone replied. He was a surprised as the other two when they came back into the open. He had figured that their ancient ancestors had used these natural tubes all the way down the mountainside, exiting who knew where somewhere at the base. Instead they found themselves here, and while not as large as the one on top, this one was not small. *I can only hope that the exit out of this place isn't as hard to find as the one by the complex.* Taking a deep breath he said, "Okay, with the time that has passed since anybody has used this system we're not going to find a ready trail leading us to the exit. So, like our searches up in that meadow let's spread out and see what we can find. Seve, you take the left side, Staven the right and I'll go up through the center. That way we all should be able to keep in sight of at least one of us. Hey it looks like there are some of the same types of animals grazing in this one." He said as he pointed into the distance where these animals were barely visible. "Now I wonder how wild these are or if they've been worked by bots like the other ones?" Then turning to the other two he said, "Be careful, we don't know if they've even seen anything like us, and may decide that we are a threat. Let's take our time and do a thorough search, meet both of you on the other side of this thing." And with that began to head out into the large open area. Looking around and breathing deeply the cold fresh air, it smelled and tasted great after the tunnels. But there was a thin blanket of snow, not deep enough to bury the dead grasses, but it was obvious that as winter deepened that this area would be buried in the white stuff.

He could see the other two heading for the walls, and again all he could do was shake his head. This area had been another large caldron, and when these giants had been active this would not have been a very nice place to be. Everything that he had viewed said that these mountains had been completely built from ancient volcanoes. Evidence also pointed to them being extinct for a very long time. He knew from a few minor discoveries since living on these mountains, that there were a few hot springs and geysers, giving testament to the violent past. But the results from this mountain building were rich volcanic soils, and lush growth of the grasses, plants, and trees. Now if it wasn't so cold in the winter it would be a great place to live, not that the fresh air and views weren't worth a little discomfort. This brought a smile as he thought that with cold nights it was always nice to get warm with one's mate.

He stopped a moment, looked to see if he could still see the other two, and found that he could, but again this one area was turning out wider than he thought. Then he realized that something had penetrated his subconscious, as he had been thinking, something that seemed out of place, not natural. Looking back he saw a pile of rocks, not much different than any of the many that lay on the ground here. But there was something different about this one, and he turned around and went back to it. Then he realized that even though it was faint and almost worn away, there was a splash of paint on the pile. *A marker of some kind? Maybe, just maybe they did mark a trail across this meadow.* Now with something to look for he slowed his pace down and studied the many piles that crossed his path. After some distance and not finding another, he ranged back and forth to see if maybe he had overlooked one because it did not lie in the direction he had been searching. On one of the swings to the right he found another one, stopped, and tried to get the attention of the two searching the walls. Because he had slowed down, both were now well ahead of him and all he could see was their backs as they searched. Whistling he caught the attention of Staven, and once he did he signaled for him to join him. Turning in the other direction he attempted to get Seve's attention. But the winds were blowing away from Seve's location so he probably hadn't heard the whistling. So all he could do was wait until Seve turned to make sure he could see him, and then catch his attention.

He could hear Staven approach and then ask, "What's going on?"

"Right now I'm trying to get Seve's attention. With the winds sounds are being taken away from him, so he didn't hear my whistling. Watch with me and one of us should be able to get him to see us. If not, then either you or I must go get him, while one of us stays right here. I think that I've found what our ancestors did to make it easy to cross this area and know where you need . . . look I think he's turned around." Both of them began waving to get Seve's attention. Eventually they received the acknowledgement signal, and at that point Stone signaled assembly. While waiting Stone continued, "I think I've found what they used to keep anyone on track if they were coming across this area alone. As usual it's an accidental discovery, and because of the amount of time that has passed I almost missed it because the markings are almost completely worn away." Turning around and leading Staven to the stone pile he pointed and said. "Here, look closely and you can see what looks like paint. I found another one just a short time ago, but had to range a bit to find this one. So now with three of us to look we should be able to find others."

"Yeah, I guess that would make sense to do something like this. So how far apart are these things anyway?"

"I'd guess at least a hundred paces, maybe more. After all I've only found two of them, and did not take a direct route between them. They probably did this on purpose just in case the primitives came this far into the mountains to hunt. You know the fewer markers the less of a chance for them to be discovered."

"What's going on guys?" Seve asked.

"Stone may have found the path through this place." Staven replied. "Well, sort of, anyway. It appears our ancestors marked piles of rocks to keep anyone on track, but there aren't a lot of them. Stone feels it would be that way to keep the primitives ignorant."

"Makes sense to me." Seve replied.

* * *

"This meeting has been called this morning because of what Judd related to me last night while I was in the security office. We've been trying to figure out how we could cover the vast distances that we need to, and he may have found the answer. I don't know quite how we'll be able to use this yet, but can make a difference." At this point Saige sat down and turned the meeting over to Judd saying, "All yours."

"As all of you know, I've been a private contractor within Jade for just about as long as I can remember. Much of the work I did involve keeping things working, and using and maintaining the replicators was a major part of that. Without them we wouldn't have been able to survive where our cities were built. What most of you do not realize is that the computing system that operates these units is not part of the network. I don't know why, but it has always been that way. Still the computing power it takes to make these things work is tremendous, and maybe that is why they have always been isolated. Now why am I introducing it this way? Simple really. By these systems being separate there would be no way that anyone who did not have access or understand the replicating computers would know what is on them, what they can produce, or what their true capabilities are. So it would be no one's fault if this information would have been missed. To be honest, until I ended up in this situation, I missed it myself.

"Look, like you when I saw our true past, and realized that we all originated here from this place, and before that some other planet in the vast universe, it was a shock. That got me to thinking that while there has been little advancements, and now I know why, there had to be more than what we are using. And one of the mandates had been no traveling between cities once they were established. Yet, there had to be more than just these flying shuttles to move equipment and people around. And it was this and the machines that the scouting units used that got me looking through the catalogs within the system. For the longest time I was frustrated, because I couldn't even locate the plans on those units. And from the descriptions you gave me, I knew that they were not very new, and probably after they had been created, the information was buried deeper within the systems or maybe even wiped, to keep it out of the hands of people like me. So, most likely in the cities, this information doesn't exist anymore. But this is the original system, and one that has lain untouched for a very long time. And I was seeing much here that did not exist in those other systems. It confirmed that indeed either the information was never included or somewhere in the past it was wiped."

Saar asked, "Are you telling us that there was a conscious effort to remove something that could be important, critical to our survival? And if that is the true facts here, what else has our city governments done, that could jeopardize our survival?"

"A good question, Saar," Saige answered, "and it leads one in many directions, including the changing of our true origins. And it always brings up the question as to why the emergency signal from this place failed to continue to transmit. From what can be discovered at this point, much of this happened in the past, and I know that, that is an obvious statement." Pausing for effect Saige then continued, "Unfortunately we have no way of proving it was deliberate, or because it was deemed important to keep travel, and I suspect communication between cities to the minimum, that this information was left out intentionally – there's just no way to know." Turning back to Judd, he said. "Continue, if you please."

"Well, let's just say that what I was looking for was buried very deep. In fact none of this was in the catalogs at all. There was a section dealing with maintenance of the shuttles, and here listed under a subcategory were the units you, as scouts, used. And a whole subcategory of transportation vehicles that worked on the same principles as your hovercraft. Some could haul up to fifty people all at once, others were small and fast, called skimmers, and some had the ability to transport large amounts of material, including animals, in an attachment called trailers. The small skimmers could reach speeds of a hundred kilometers an hour, although I wouldn't recommend it. But even the heavier units could cover at least fifty kilometers in the same time if needed. And the good news is that these replicators here in this complex can construct them. The bad news is that there is no way to get one of those units off these mountains. If we could discover a way of moving them down the mountains in parts and put them together once we reached the grasslands, then we would have the freedom to move great distances rather quick, and be in many places that would be beyond the primitives understanding.

I do believe that somehow our ancestors used these things to move between the tribes and clans. I know from the data here, that we've been here a long time, but to gather as much as they have would have meant that almost everybody that was here would have to be in the field. And that ladies and gentlemen is impossible. So the only explanation is that they were using this equipment a lot to move from place to place. Then when the lifeline was cut to our own world, this information was buried, and with the establishment of the cities, possibly eliminated. From the dimensions, schematics, if you will, they are much too large to fit into the tunnels, which are being explored right now. And the terrain is much too rough for them to travel here in these mountains. Yet all the evidence points to their use. So somewhere there is an answer, and I am sure if it is here that we will find it. I'll continue to work the replicator system, but now by knowing what to look for, the rest can look in the networked system here in the compound. And this is just about all I have for you right now." Judd then sat back down.

Shellian slowly got up, being quite uncomfortable this late into her pregnancy. She had to admit she felt like a big ball, and felt warm most of the time, and with this out in front of her she could no longer sleep like she wanted, and all those trips to the restroom, but still had to smile to herself. It was such a wonder to feel that new life move inside her. "With what Judd has given us, we, not that we didn't before, have much work ahead of us. We really do need to move, this winter, to rescuing others while the primitives are not moving because of the, as they call it, the season of cold. So shortly we will assign different schedules for all of us to search the records." She looked around the table before continuing, "That's all we have for you now, but this is very important. While we may not be officially at war, we might as well be, so anything and I mean anything that seems like it could help bring this conflict to an end, we need to know. Have a good day all."

* * *

The three continued across this meadowland following the almost invisible markers left by their ancestors. Again it led to a passage within the huge crater and again like the entrance above, this path let to a smaller meadow and another building built from native stone, a duplicate really. So it was easy to find the sliding door, even with the skylights covered. Once inside the next tunnel system, they slid the door shut and continued on down the mountains. This time the tunnel was short and they came back out into the sunlight which blinded them briefly. Around them was a broken landscape with no sign of the continuing tunnel system that they had just traversed. Instead they found themselves back into the trees with a barely visible trail going down the mountainside, and as the suns approached the zenith they found another one of those caves that their ancestors had built. Turning to the other two Stone said, "This is just unbelievable. There was so much work and effort that went into this whole project. And we still don't know how they were able to both heat and keep out animals. Guess we'll take a break. If everything holds to what we learned, about dark we'll find the next one."

"I wonder," Seve mused, "yeah, I really wonder if these are monitored just like the ones close to the Alpha, or because these are so far away they didn't worry about it."

"That's a good question," Staven said. "There's just so much we don't know, or have lost since we moved to the cities, and maybe because these are so far from the complex they felt it was unnecessary. After all, there has never been anything in them, so if the primitives just happened upon them, they might think they were strange, maybe even something their gods created, but other than that what could they conclude? As we've learned, these mountains are pockmarked with caves created by these extinct volcanoes, and while a little different; I doubt this would generate much curiosity anyway. Besides, only the priests would possibly be up this far and only on rare occasions, some brave hunter."

Stone got up and headed out, saying, "I'm going to gather some wood. A hot meal before we continue would be nice. I'd guess with our progress, that tomorrow morning we should be back into the grasslands. We all need to look the area over so that we can add to our knowledge, as so far nobody has found anything in the system back at Alpha marking out these trails. So we are rediscovering all of this."

* * *

That night they were at the second of the caves, and while the trail had been almost invisible, they congratulated themselves on being able to stick to it. In some places trees had grown over the trail, and they had to work their way around obstacles that time and nature had put there. Yet they could see that if they had a pack animal there still would be no problem. None of these obstacles were such to block the surefooted animals. "I wonder where this eventually comes out?" Staven asked.

Shaking his head, because not one of them really knew, Stone said. "Don't know. But we've been heading down one of the gentler slopes, and there have been less rockslides and such here. Suspect that's why it goes this way. But I know that what you meant is where in those vast grasslands does this come out? Guess tomorrow we'll learn that one. Now that we are this far down it's really hard to see where this is leading. And I'm glad that the snow here has been light, and there's just a thin layer. I really wouldn't want to have to find my way with heavy snows on the ground."

"Agreed!" Seve responded, "Very much so. We've had enough issues with that when we spent our first winter in that cave. With us presently being in month D, and still looking at about six until the end of this annual, I'm glad we are doing this exploring now instead of maybe month sixteen or seventeen, when it would really be cold and miserable."

They knew that the primitives looked at their annual more as what season they were in, but with the annual being 540 days, and having learned that the world that they had come from ran to about 365 days, a similar monthly system was adopted. But with quite a few more days it was decided to make the months thirty days long with five six-day weeks giving them eighteen months. The system their ancestors adopted turned out to be simplicity in itself. With twelve months being the norm from their home world, they adopted a system of using the first letter of the months, and if there were more than one that had the same letter, then a number was assigned. Thusly the first month of the new annual would be J1, and the last month of the annual would be 18. Seasons were much longer leaning towards five to six months in length. And this cold season appeared to be one of the fiercer that they could remember. All of them were quite happy that it was this annual and not the last when they were trying to survive in the cave. Snows had been deep enough then. From the views from the "eyes in the sky", the lowlands, foothills, and grasslands were faring no better. It would be miserable no matter where one lived.

* * *

The three who had been exploring the tunnel system and pathway out of the mountains, arrived back at the complex six days after leaving, but before they could even relax, compare notes, and put together a report to present to everyone, news spread throughout the complex like a wildfire. Shellian's water had broken! A new life was just about to enter the world, and everything now became secondary as the women gathered to help with the birthing. With the father being the doctor, he would be closely involved. While not a requirement, all fathers were encouraged to be there and help their mates through this tough and difficult time. After all it wasn't called labor for fun. It was a long, tiring and painful road that would only end when the child and afterbirth had entered the world. And it wasn't uncommon for the first birth to take a full day and night, leaving the mother completely exhausted.

And while the men attempted to put on an air of normality, it was obvious that each one would be seen listening for some message from the infirmary, and something to come over the monitors to let them know that it was all right. They all knew that they had an important part in creating a new life, but it is the woman who really touches eternity. She is the one who must allow the new life to grow inside of her body, and then endure the pain of childbirth, feeling like you were being torn in half, when it was time for that new life to begin on their own. Saige, remembering back to the conversation he and Shellian had about this, wondered how she was doing. He could almost remember a wistfulness in her voice as she recalled other births from the past, and that someday it would be her turn. Again, all he could do was shake his head. He knew that in a few months Seirra would be in that same room bringing forth another new life that the two of them created. At this moment, he wasn't sure he wanted to be there to see her helpless against the contractions and helpless against the pain. But at the same time, wanted to be with her, supporting however he could. But what could he do, but watch helplessly?

It was evening meal time, and all of the women had taken shifts to eat, and would only pass on that everything was fine and normal, but that these things just take time. Then once finished with their meals, would immediately head back. Saige, turning towards Stone asked. "I know that with what's happening right now that it is hard to concentrate on anything else, but how'd it go?"

"Interesting, very interesting overall. I first thought that we'd be in those tunnels until we came out down in the grasslands, but if I'd really thought about it, that just wouldn't have made sense. I think why so much of the tunnels to start with, were to keep this place hidden. After all, except for the way we entered originally, there is no other way into this place. And the entrance that you found is in such a place that no one would expect it to be there. And there is no way anybody can observe someone going through that supposedly solid rock wall. So I give it to our ancestors, they were very careful to keep this place well hidden. Once you call a meeting, then we can go over it in more detail. Still, the whole way is easily traveled, and I know that's still very important. Besides, the three of us haven't had much of a chance to really finalize anything yet. I don't know, maybe because something has been distracting us all."

The last comment brought a smile to Saige, but he knew that at the moment that his sister probably wasn't in the smiling mood. It was something that he or any of the rest of the males for that matter would never experience, but he knew that if one cared deeply for his mate, then it was tough in its own way. "Yeah, that's true, and I guess I'll be the next in that room with Seirra since she is the next one who will be delivering soon. Even though Sorrel has had one child, she was unconscious throughout the whole ordeal, so I suspect that when it is hers and your turn, that like the rest of us it will be like the first time. Anyway thanks for the information. I want a meeting after the morning meal in two days to cover what you found. Of course neither Saar nor Shellian will be there, as there will be something else occupying their time. And I'm sure Shell' will need the recovery time, oh look it's time, got to report to the security office. At times, I almost yearn for the time before we contacted the cities. It was so much quieter then, but now we always need to have someone to man the communications system, and someone else to run down the answers to the too many questions we are getting." Getting up to leave he turned and said, "Go spend some time with Sorrel. She's missed you. And before you ask, no she did not make it known, but to any who knows her, and the rest of us do, then it was very obvious that she missed her man."

Stone had to admit that he really missed her also. They really had only been apart for six days, but it seemed so much longer. *How'd this attachment happen anyway?* He had to shrug, because it did not matter how, but now he couldn't see his life without her.

* * *

Sometime between the dark of the night and dawn the word came from the infirmary that the baby had arrived, and she was quite healthy, and looked much like her mother, which was appreciated. Not that Saar was a bad looker for a guy, but Shellian was truly a beautiful woman, in an athletic way. The daughter's name was Samantha, named after Shellian's, and Saige's mother. One who had passed away in their youth, and with a father that could not raise two children when they reminded him so much of his lost mate, they had become part of the scouting unit, and now here in charge at the alpha complex so many annuals later.

* * *

"I'm sure that all of us have looked in, on the new mother and daughter, and have personally seen that both are healthy, and all of you women ogling over that new one, wanting to hold her, and giving all of those suggestions to the new mother. And of course, she isn't here, and will be off any assignment for a while to give them time. Unfortunately for Saar he isn't quite so lucky, although he isn't here, since he is our only doctor. He has gone to an on call status so that he can help Shell' wherever he can." Smiling before continuing Saige said, "And the miracle of life continues. Not that the intimacy that led to this moment wasn't very enjoyable, the results still leave me in awe as to the creation of a new life. I know that for now, of the original group who was first here that Seirra and I will be almost the last, not quite, but almost the last to join the families that are being created here. But this is getting away from the reason for this gathering and that is for Stone to pass on to us what they have discovered." Saige sat down at this point and signaled for Stone to continue.

Standing up and looking over the group Stone began. "Now Seve and Staven, if I forget or leave something out then let me know." At this point he covered in a little more detail what he had related to Saige two nights ago. Then he began to describe what they found at the base. "What is interesting is where this came out, and what we found there. What I mean is this, the trail came into a hidden valley, and when I mean hidden I mean hidden. It's not large, but could sustain a few of the animals for a few days. There's water there with a small stream running through it. It took us a better part of half a day to find the exit out into the grasslands. It is surprisingly wide, but is such that it just doesn't appear to be anything but a dead end canyon. I don't know if it is natural or our ancestors constructed it, but however it is it works. Now all of this is interesting, but we found in one of the constructed caves, a large one by the way, a facility that again is well hidden, that can be powered by, well my guess would be solar. We didn't do a thorough search, but there seems to be no reason to need this capability, so it is a question as to why our ancestors built it. But there appears to be many small rooms, and areas to both bunk, and put supplies. So maybe it is a place where they could operate and be right at the edge of the grasslands. There is equipment there, mothballed like here when we arrived, and all of it appears to be maintained by the same type of bots. So as far as we could see, like here, once one pulls it out of the shutdown mode that it presently is in, everything should work."

"Did you get a chance to see what type of equipment was there?" Judd asked.

"Not really, we just did a quick explore, and confirmed that what we saw was in working order. After all, this entire trip was to learn about the route down from here, and finding this was a bonus, but we needed to return. So I am sure, now that we know about this, that we'll be heading back to do a more thorough inventory of what's there." Turning to Saige he asked, "Am I right?"

Nodding his head, Saige said, "Absolutely. Judd has discovered some interesting things while you are away, and I'm sure his question had to do with those discoveries. With the excitement that has been going around here in the last few days, I'm sure that no one has brought you up to speed on that. Let's just say he's made some discoveries that will definitely help, and later you can ask him. Now with this discovery, I'm also sure that he'll want to make the trip down and inspect that place, and if he discovers what I think he'll discover, then we will be moving our timetable ahead to possibly try and rescue more of our people this winter."

CHAPTER TWELVE

"Well Judd, your rescue seems to have been exactly what we needed to make much of what we have to do to go forward." They were standing in the meadows outside of the complex, before them sat one of the skimmers, a three passenger unit. And while snow had been building now for days, it had been sunny for the last couple giving time for the solar system in the skimmer to charge. "While we've all had training on our units that we used in the scouting section, this . . ." Saige paused as he pointed at the skimmer and smiled, "This is very different, and looks to steer differently also. Who'd of thought a round wheel to turn by? The support units that we would use, used levers and pedals to turn and stop." Then looking into the open cockpit he shook his head. "This is very different – two pedals and one lever. What did you say this lever was for anyway?"

"The best I could determine from the arrangement of the system is that the lever is attached to a device that is called a transmission. Even your support units had one. But it only provided one gear forward and one backwards. Because of the speeds this can obtain it changes the ratio to the drive system.

And the one button on the dash switches it between the air and wheeled drive system. But again unlike your units, these only have four instead of six. And because of the surface that these can travel, when in wheeled mode, they are not very fast. Although looking at some of the training videos that were on the system suggests that there are roads similar to what we have in our cities that travel across the countryside both in our homeworld and here, these skimmers or whatever it is they use, seems to use the wheeled system more – meaning more speed. Of course it is on those roads and not the open countryside like we face here."

Turning to the entire group that was standing out here, freezing, while waiting, for what was to be a demonstration, Judd shrugged. He had to admit that even with the suns shining as they were there seemed to be very little heat. Maybe it was because they were in the winter months, or maybe it was because of the height of this facility, he didn't know. But it was time to climb in and see if he could actually make this thing move. He motioned for Saige to climb into the passenger side and he got behind the wheel. He turned the switch which activated the motors, and the familiar sound of a hovercraft rose and the skimmer lifted slightly off the ground. Stepping on the break, he eased it into gear, released both the hand break and the foot break and slowly pressed the accelerator down and the skimmer moved easily forward. Smiling to himself, Judd hadn't been sure that it was going to work, but it was obvious now that it would. "Better put on that seatbelt." He admonished Saige, as he did the same. "I don't know how this is going to respond once we get up some speed."

Since he had never seen, let alone operated anything like this, Judd tentatively pressed the accelerator, and the skimmer responded immediately moving with a nimbleness that had been unexpected. This brought a large grin to his face. He picked up speed and while the winds that were striking them were quite chilly, the exhilaration from the speed they were traveling felt great. "How fast are we going, Judd?" He looked down and saw that they were moving, according to the dial at about twenty-five KPH. He never had been in something that moved that fast! Glancing over at Saige he responded saying, "Twenty-five, I'm going to go a little faster and see what it will do. We have pretty much a straight shot for quite a distance. But I do not want to turn it at these speeds – afraid I might upset the apple cart."

"Apple cart?" Saige asked.

"Sorry, an old phrase, that's been in my family for who knows how long." That stopped him for a moment, since at this time he could easily be the last member of his family. Taking a deep breath before continuing he said, "I really don't even know what that is, but saw some minor drawings in children's books a long time ago that supposedly was one of those things. Okay hold on, here we go!" He pressed down a little harder than he had planned and the skimmer literally leaped ahead gathering speed rapidly. And now with tears streaming down his face from the stinging cold air he glanced at the dial and saw they were now doing twice what they had been. It was unbelievable that something could move this fast across the ground like this. Looking over at Saige he could see a huge smile as well as tears from the cold on his face. He backed off and the skimmer slowed to a stop. Judd could feel his heart beating rapidly, and felt completely exhilarated from the experience. Turning towards Saige, he asked, "Well, what do you think?" He could tell that Saige was breathing hard, but the smile had yet to leave his face.

"And to think that we were traveling that fast!" Saige, looking back over his shoulder could see in the distance and almost out of their sight, the team still standing. "Wow, this thing is fantastic! I never in my wildest imagination thought one could travel this fast. And you are saying that we only were at about half of what this is capable of?"

"Actually once I looked over the specs on this thing I found that what I had stated in the meeting wasn't quite accurate. The hundred KPH that I gave you there was a suggested *safe* maximum speed for traveling in uneven terrain like this. They have the capability to go much faster, somewhere between hundred and fifty, to two hundred KPH. Although the higher speeds shorten the distance one can travel before having to recharge the batteries that this thing operates off of."

There was a brief period of silence, other than the sounds of the hover motors. "I did not think that there was any way that one could move that fast on the ground. This explains a lot, and surely will make moving around easier. Okay turn this thing around and take us back. I'm sure that the rest want their time riding along in this thing before the batteries die. How long will a charge last, and how long to recharge?"

"I can only go by what it says, since we have nothing to base it on, but with reasonable speeds it can go all day on a charge. And if it remains sunny, as you are traveling, then it continually recharges, plus it recovers some of the energy from the breaking system. There also seems to be some type of turbine that recaptures some of the air movement off the hover section to put energy back to use. And that's all I know, and as far as recharge, I guess that would be variable to how much sunlight there is at any given time."

* * *

"While I know that it is winter, we do not have time to sit and just wait it out as our people are suffering at the hands of the primitives." Saige looked over all of them as they sat around the meeting table. Looking at his sister he couldn't help but smile as she held her sleeping daughter. *It wouldn't be long before Seirra would be doing the same with their child.* He thought. "Judd has confirmed that there is a smaller version of the replicators down at the base of the mountains, and it was specifically placed there to produce and maintain the field operations of our ancestors. With this knowledge, he's been working overtime, with help of course, to get the equipment we need produced, and we've all been training in the skimmer up here in the meadows. Fortunately all of them work similarly so there will be no issue moving from one type to another. Sabryn, can you bring us up to date on that research project that you've been in charge of?"

Standing and facing the group Sabryn cleared her throat, and glanced briefly at the new life that was at the table with them and smiled briefly. "Since many of you have been helping me on this you know what it generally is all about, but with only pieces and not the whole thing. We really needed to know how our ancestors presented themselves to the primitives so that they could get up close and personal. They needed a way to establish a relationship with the primitives that would allow them to contact any and all of the tribes and clans. So they created the traveling merchants. Their front stated that their clan was from far beyond the Sacred Mountains, and that this was the first opportunity that they had to come this far south. Their goods were implements that were just a little better than the ones that the clans and tribes could create on their own. Plus they healed the very sick. By doing this they built a reputation that protected them from attack – so much so that they were almost given the status of traveling priests. And any who would attack them would be distained by all others."

She reached down and took a swallow of water before continuing. "Okay, that was all well and good, but once we spread out to the cities this practice was stopped, and unfortunately, to our loss. Had we continued this practice, then we would have had the necessary warnings to maybe prevent what has happened, and is continuing to happen." She could see the reaction through the small group as they understood that once again there had been a failure in the system that their ancestors had established. She could see this in their eyes, but like them, did not know if this had been caused by a decision at the time they broke up to move into the cities, or it was something that was decided later, like the elimination of the scouting units.

"I can't lay the blame for any of this on the present leadership, except maybe the closing of the scouting units. We have no way of knowing if any of our leaders in the cities were even aware that this existed. All of us knew that a city known as Alpha existed, but it was a hidden one, and that was all. Now all of us know the truth about it, and so many other things." Again pausing, she looked around the table once more and saw Saige nod to her to continue. "What I want to cover now but briefly, is how they set themselves up, and then

Judd has something else that he's discovered that will make all of our lives in the field much easier."

With that statement the rest turned and looked at Judd who was leaning back in his chair. He smiled and signaled Sabryn to continue. "We found a whole section dealing with the role of the ones who play the part of the traveling merchants. After I go through this and after Judd have said his part, Saige will give you the cover story that we will use. Initially we will be putting out two teams, and now we will be able to monitor them individually, which is very important. Anyway, we've been working on the clothing that the ones who will be the traveling merchants must wear. Fortunately there were still some of those things existing in that room that was discovered, plus a data terminal set up specifically to keep track of the needs of the field researchers. From that we have all that we know. Besides the goods that we will carry, and in these initial forays it will be knives and bow strings, there is a frame that mounts on top of the packs that has bells attached to let all know that we are the merchants and we are neutral, and we are off limits to attack. I know that it's been a long time since the merchants traveled, but we need to reestablish them, and learn whatever we can – for now that's all I have, and with that I'll give it to Judd."

She sat down and waited as Judd stood up. One thing for sure, it had been fortuitous for them when Judd had been part of the first group they had rescued. So much had been learned since his arrival, and they were so much further ahead in their planning because of this. "My part in this meeting will be short. When I learned about the "eyes in the sky", first off I really wondered what they were. So curious I did some research and found that they really are known as satellites, but we've called them the other for so long it probably will just stick. That's neither here or there, but I found that any time that our people would prepare to explore a new world they would ring it with these things. They have much that they can do besides just giving us great images and these satellites are even better than the first ones they setup here. They have the ability to be linked, to be used for communications – I suspect that's how the cities keep in contact with each other, which means that with the proper equipment any, and I mean any, in the field can talk, update, and have a two-way conversation with us here at Alpha. I'm still learning about the rest, and there is so much more they can do, but for now this new knowledge is critical for our needs. I'm in the process of fabricating the necessary equipment for the two teams, and we'll do some testing soon. That's all for now, so I'll give it back to Saige." He then sat down and once again leaned back in his chair and turned and faced Saige.

Saige again stood up, took a deep breath and said, "With the traveling merchants being out of circulation for as long as they have, we have to be sure that when we reappear that we are consistent with what both their oral and in some cases written history will say about us. So before we actually go to the field we, the two teams and the rest who will support us, will learn this inside and out, we cannot afford to make a mistake here. And with the support staff having to be immediately available to access something from the records that the ones in the field may need to keep things in control. For example, say we contact a clan, and the clan leader asks us who the last clan leader we talked with was. Now something like that would exist in either their verbal records, or written records, so it is something that we must know."

Leaning on the table and looking hard at all of them before continuing he said, "We cannot screw any of this up. The cover story is simple. The history that has been established by our ancestors stated that we are a clan from the far north, well beyond the Sacred Mountains. Our story is this: Sometime in the great past a landslide blocked the only route around the mountains and we, even with our minor priestly status do not travel through the Sacred Mountains. It has taken us all this time to discover a new route and to be able to return to the south. And with our return, we are only sending two teams out, since we've no idea what has changed since we last visited this area. But with these two we are trying to establish what used to be, by our own records and traditions. With contact established, and our ability to keep in contact here at Alpha, any of the cases that require our "doctor skills", will be immediately referred back to Saar." Turning towards him Saige said, "Sorry about that Saar, but you and now Jas who assists will be on call for this. I can only hope that eventually we rescue another doctor to help relieve the burden. As we are able to recover more of our people, your job will only get harder." Then turning back to the rest he continued," We will be starting out for our first attempt in less than a month, so everything will be very intense around here. That's all I have for you now, do any of you have anything they want to add before we break up and get to it?" Looking around he saw most shaking their heads and the others remaining silent. "Okay then, we're done here."

* * *

"Problems, Judd?" Seve asked, as the small team worked at the field unit at the base of the mountains. Everything at this location was very minimal. Even the system to keep power to the equipment was barely enough to allow it to run for any length of time.

Shaking his head Judd said, "No, I guess not. I'm just used to working with the stuff from the cities, or now from Alpha, but I guess our ancestors had to cut somewhere, and again with as little space as there is here, you can see that they had to cut corners. And unfortunately it seems that they did, just about everywhere." Again pausing as he looked around he said, "Well, I guess I can understand it. This was never to be used other than to build and maintain the equipment they used during their research. So there was, in a sense, more leisure time to get things done. Time to let the solar system recharge, and time to make repairs – all the things that we don't have the luxury of, especially time. So it's frustrating when you're in the middle of something just to have it shut down because of the lack of power, or because that particular component wasn't included here. Truthfully, I was beginning to feel really good about our ancestors, as everything I had seen and worked appeared to be over engineered, and robust. So finally, I'm seeing the other side where things were skimped upon, and things barely operate." Shrugging he said, "But what can we do? All we can do is take the time to get these things built and tested, but know that it's going to take much more time than I would like to invest, that we can afford to invest really. I know that Saige is impatient to get moving on this, and I can't blame him. Every day that we delay there's another chance that we've lost another of our people to the primitives. And from personal experience, I don't want our people in the hands of the primitives any longer than necessary. So here we are against the clock so to speak, against this equipment, and against the limited time our people have to survive."

"Yeah, believe me we do know the feeling. When our city was attacked, and we were able to escape, the original plan was to work our way back to one of the other cities. But we were never allowed. And from the original size of our scouting team, in the end we ended with just the ten of us, and the frustration that we had the knowledge of what had happened but no way to let anybody know. And knowing that we couldn't and that other cities were falling in the very same way just tore at our very souls." Taking a deep breath before continuing Staven said, "But it really was worse than that. We lost our leader in one of the many skirmishes, and he put Saige and Shellian in charge and through their leadership they got us into these Sacred Mountains. Got us safely to a place where we could possibly survive the harsh winter, and then we rebelled, and kicked them out. So at that point we almost destroyed any chance for any of us to help. You don't hear either of them talking about it, and you won't. Yet in the end of all of this they took us back without reservations. And I, for one, am quite grateful that they did. We were very close to death at that point, and if they had sent us away, as they had the right to do, I or the rest of us who were involved wouldn't be here, and I suspect that you and the ones with you would still be with the primitive tribe since they wouldn't have had enough people to go and rescue you. I guess Shayne, he was our leader, was right in who he chose to lead us. And I know now that they never wanted it, and because of this none of us will ever go against them."

Thinking a moment, Judd said, "I know when we finally learned the truth, I at first thought that those two were pretty young to be in charge like this. But as I've watched them, they appear to have a maturity well beyond their years."

"Living through what we did can do that to a person." Looking over at the panel Staven said, "Oh well, looks like the light's gone green again, so I guess we can move on to the next step."

"Yes it has. At least the time between the recharge is somewhat quick, but it sure seems to drain faster. Too bad we couldn't do some of this back at Alpha, but it surely would be a bear to transport anything down here, and time consuming, and probably in the end, not much savings of time even with these quick cycles. Okay let's get that next piece replicated and move on. We have too much still to accomplish."

* * *

"From the 'eye-in-the-sky', imagery I think we're about to be hit with a strong storm. It looks like it has been pounding the grasslands, and as it is approaching these mountains seems to be getting stronger. I know it's frustrating right now, but we're not going to be able to do anything until after this one blows through. Guess everybody can continue to practice, and continue to work on learning the language of the primitives. I know that as we enter these different villages – especially the clans' home turf – and such that we'll be planting bugs to begin a serious monitoring of the tribes and clans. So knowing the language will be critical." Turning around to Jed, who was in the security office with Saige, Saige asked. "How's the manufacture of the trading goods going? Are we going to have enough to do this job?"

"From what I can gather, yes, it should be enough. But you know this is just a guess. We've never done this, and either you'll end up with too much or too little. It's just how things usually work out."

* * *

K'jor remained within his shelter as the storm raged. This season of cold definitely was the worst. Even the elders of the clan were commenting that they could never remember one so bad. The sounds of the winds descending on them were deafening, tearing loose anything not tied down, and propelling it with crashes across open spaces. The shelters shook under the force and threatened to come apart, but somehow remained standing. What heat they had from the roaring fires seemed to be sucked out, leaving the only places within that were warm was when one stood very close to these fires. This was the second day, and if anything was true of this storm it appeared to be stronger today than yesterday. If it continued or became even stronger there'd not be a shelter left standing when it finally moved on. While briefly looking into the fire, with this storm raging in the background, his thoughts drifted back once again.

He didn't know how long he had been unconscious, but when he awoke it was still dark. When he sat up he first wondered if somehow the spirits had found a way to get past the protection of the fire and the light it produced. After all he had leaned back against a solid, well what he thought was a solid hillside, but had instantly fallen through and into unconsciousness. Before him he still could see his fire, although now it was dying down because no additional fuel was being added. Why could he still see it? If indeed he was now in the spirit world, was the normal world, even in this place of desolation that visible? If so, then it explained why the spirits could do so much harm. After all, if they could see his world this easily, and he knew that the spirit world was a place that could not be seen by him or anybody else, how simple it would be to attack and destroy. But if he were in the world of the spirits, where were they? Like it was when he was by his fire, he was alone. He knew that he was supposed to meet his clan in the morning, but he wasn't sure that he could return, cross over to the world of the living. He thought that there was a good chance that he would roam these wastes in the realm of the spirits until they released him, returning him back as one neither dead nor alive forever to haunt the living.

He sat watching his fire die, unsure as to what he should do. If indeed he had somehow accidentally entered their realm, maybe they had not realized that this was so. It would behoove him to watch and wait. He did not want to give away his position. With the light of day things might give him some ideas, so he sat cross-legged, not moving, reaching out with all of his skills to remain hidden. Somewhere along the time that flowed past him, he fell asleep, and awoke with a sudden start to the full suns rising. As he tried to move he found his joints stiff from remaining in one position too long. He felt like an old one, and panicked briefly when he thought that this could be the results of being in the realm of the spirits, draining his strength and youth, leaving him a shadow of who he was. Still it was morning and he needed to relieve himself, so got up, albeit slow, and carefully, and after looking around took care of business.

At least his weapons and water skin had come with him when he had fallen. There was a gentle morning breeze blowing that presently was cool, but held a promise of heat later in the day. Turning away from where the ashes of his fire lay, he saw that there was a narrow ravine with high sides that twisted away into the distance. He decided that since he had yet to be discovered that he would explore this, and since this appeared to be the only way to go; he felt that it would be simple to return to this spot. *How would spirits look in their own realm?* He had to admit that he didn't know. Again so far as he could see, he was the only living thing around. That brought a rough laugh from him as he thought about it. *Yep, if this is indeed the spirit world, I would be the only living thing here. All others would be spirit.* With all the stealth he could muster he worked his way down this ravine, and wondered if this was necessary? After all if the spirits who lived here were unseen, they could be watching him right this moment, and laughing at his antics of trying to stay hidden. It left him undecided as to whether to continue in this way or just give up and hike it. In the end he decided to continue as he started. He had no idea if any of what he had been thinking was true or not, so he'd rather be safe and continue this way until something proved he should change his tactics.

Stopping briefly and taking a large swig from his water skin, he could neither sense nor see much change as this ravine wound and twisted through an unknown section of the desolation only giving him a close view of the trail, the sky, and the hillsides that bordered this wash. He found that slowly the wash was opening up, and the mud hills were slowly getting smaller. He made a sharp left jog followed by an immediate right. He stopped immediately and his jaw dropped, this had to be a mirage.

* * *

"K'jor! K'jor, this is T'som, just a word if you please."

It took a moment for K'jor to understand that someone was at his entryway. With the winds howling as they were, it was almost impossible to hear anyone speaking or yelling. "Come in! Come in; get out of that nasty weather. What brings you out in this?"

Looking down and shaking his head, he said, "I wish I didn't. The trip from where I live to here was just bad. Look, with the weather turning so bad, I checked in on that female that we have placed in the care of us priests. She's still hanging on, but barely. Whatever she had gained, she has now lost and is almost at the door of the spirit world right now. It almost makes me wish that those travelers would show once again."

"Travelers?" K'jor asked with a look of consternation on his face.

"Well, I've never seen one of them, but they are mentioned a number of times in our archives. A number of generations ago they were regular visitors to all of the tribes and clans. They took no sides, and always said that they lived far to the north of the Sacred Mountains – saying, that there was only one very torturous and very dangerous way through to us in the south. They said that they took no sides in whatever conflicts we had, and would trade freely with all, offering the same to all so that none would gain an advantage from their wares. But one of the services they offered was healing. The records speak of many who were very close to the spirit world only to recover after these travelers treated them."

"Why have I never heard of them, and better yet why haven't we seen them?"

Shaking his head T'som was silent for a moment, and then shrugged, "I have no answers for you. If the truth be told, I wouldn't have known anything about them either, except when this female took a turn for the worst, I felt that maybe somewhere in our written text there would be something that would help, and then came across this information. These travelers used pack beasts but on the back of them had bells that would ring as they moved, proclaiming who they were, and they were enemies to no one."

"I'm sure somewhere along the times that they were here that someone must have attacked them. I can't see it not happening." K'jor replied.

"That could very well be true, and maybe that is why they stopped coming, but there is nothing saying that this ever happened, and that any remains of such an attack were ever discovered. Whatever their gift, if we are to learn anything at all from this female, then we need whatever these travelers did or used. After reading and rereading everything I could find on them, I suspect that their way may have become blocked. The one consistent comment made was how dangerous the journey to our side was and that this path could disappear in a moment of time, isolating them once again from our side of the Sacred Mountains."

"This female is that weak? She is really losing the battle?"

Sighing, T'som said, "Yes." He then sat down heavily before continuing, "And I fear that if she does pass through to the spirit world our one chance to understand will be lost.

Let's pray to our gods that maybe soon that these travelers do return, although I could see from our writings that, that wish had been put forth a large number of times. Did you know that there was a time in our past where our clan was almost wiped out? And it was not from attacks from others. It was as if an evil spirit had moved in and was sweeping through our people, killing them one at a time, and sometimes many would fall in a day. There was much prayer going out to our gods to purge whatever evil was causing this, and to grant the return of the travelers. But either the gods heard and gave us pity, because the travelers did not come, but eventually the deaths stopped, and for a very long time we were weak, and would have been easily conquered. Yet, somehow we survived. So while the chances of seeing one or two of the travelers are very slight, it would be a good time for them to show again. For this is beyond your or my healers."

"Are you sure that these travelers as you called them, are not myth? I remember nothing ever being mentioned about them at all, nothing."

"At first I would have thought that also. But, there's just too much confirming that they were real. There is even a discussion that some of our warriors, at the time the travelers had visited, decided that they would follow them back to their homes, their clan, and discover 'their secrets'. From the narration the best the clan had in trailing and hiding attempted, and that it was it, emphasis, *attempted*. The results were embarrassing to say the least. It was as if children were trying to track and follow these. Our people would keep a great distance, track them, and then feel that they were succeeding only to find the travelers turning the tables upon them and walking into their hidden camps, smiling, and with the gentleness of speech warn them that if they persisted in these attempts that they, the travelers, would no longer visit the clan, offer their wares, or provide help with the sick. Then as easily as they appeared to the ones who were following, they would disappear." T'som paused for a moment, deep in thought, "You don't think that these stories of them being from beyond the Sacred Mountains was just a misdirection and that these strange ones that we are calling sorcerers and magicians may be the descendants of the travelers?"

Silence followed as the questions that T'som had just presented left him without words. Shaking his head, K'jor had no idea how to answer. This was becoming more complicated by the moment, and he was learning more about their past and incidents that until a short time ago did not exist as far as he knew. Shaking his head in disbelief K'jor replied, "I don't know what it is about you T'som, but it seems like every time that you show up here that you pass on more information that continues to make everything more complicated, and more difficult for one to come up with some type of decision. It was so much simpler when I was ignorant of all of this. And misdirection would be something that any of us would do. But there is a problem with tying these travelers into the sorcerers and their lairs that we are attacking, and that is this, if these travelers were from these lairs, why did they stop? After all with them being so close it would have been easy to continue to do what they were doing. And from what you've just told me about these travelers, my guess from our attacks and observations on these lairs, I see no sign that they are even close to being as skilled as your research suggests. In fact I would say that very young here within the clan's walls are more skilled than any of them. So my first thoughts are no, these cannot be of the same as your travelers, but I know that time changes things. Still if they are one in the same, what was it that made them quit?"

"You know I have no answers to any of that, and you also know that it is my job to bring you anything that can affect us. And this turning for the worse by this female is, as I said at the beginning, the reason for turning to the old words. And the possible conclusion that these lairs and the travelers could be one in the same just came out of what little evidence I could find. And maybe there is no connection at all and what the travelers said was true. That they do truly come from beyond the Sacred Mountains, and that the one and only way to our side was destroyed and prevented them from returning. I don't know – it's all just speculation. The records just say that there was no tapering off of the visits, they just stopped suddenly, and no one heard or saw them anymore."

* * *

"Okay all; once again we're here in another meeting. I would never have thought so many of these would be necessary. After all when we were just a scouting unit, we'd be lucky if we met formally once a month, but now these things at times seem to be almost daily. I have to apologize for that, but as we get closer to the time of heading out into the field once again, we continue to have to work together and discuss as a group how we are going to accomplish all of this." Saige paused for a moment, looked around the table and then said, "We've established the camp at the base of the mountains, and using the historical data that was in the systems here, we've duplicated not only the setup, but the camp location. It seems that to be consistent our ancestors established a base camp that would be visible to all of the tribes and clans, but at the same time off limits. In that cave at the base of the mountains was much of the equipment they used. And with Judd there we were able to duplicate most of it. I suspect that soon it will be known that the, oh by the way, I learned that we have been calling them the traveling merchants, but to the primitives we will be known as the travelers. Right now we of the scouting unit are doing most of this work, but later as the rest learn you will be involved. Unfortunately because of the ways that the primitive societies are constructed you women will not be involved with the field work at all. Instead all of you will be here working the support side. There's absolutely nothing we can do about that. After all you women are very important, and we cannot afford to lose any of you. Starr will be presenting some important facts that have come out of the research that our ancestors did, and then we need to figure out how to perform the same things ourselves. They obviously were concerned with the safety of their people in the field, and had developed methods to watch and protect them, and this is one of the things we all need to concentrate on. Now we are not nearly the size of that staff so we've got to figure out ways that will work for us." He turned to Starr and said. "It's all yours.", and then sat down.

* * *

Sara knew that she was in trouble. She could feel herself getting weaker, and her times of being conscious of her surroundings were getting less and less. When she could see the two who were trying to nurse her back, all she could see on

their faces was worry and fear. She could feel the fever returning, and chills were once again racking her body, while at the
same time she burned deep inside. With all that had transpired
she really did not know if she had enough inner strength to
survive this bout. She had been wasted from the last episode
and she had barely survived, she just did not know, but as
these thoughts poured through her mind she felt herself drifting off once again, and then remembered nothing.

The two women watching over Sara looked at each other
in silence. The fear was deepening for them. If she did not
survive, they would be sent back and would have to submit
once again, and without Sara there to help them through these
horrible times, they were once again without hope. After all
what could they do, and what could they hope for? With the
direction things had progressed, all that they could see was
their own graves sometime in the near future, and no comfort
between now and when their time arrived.

* * *

Starr stood up and looked over the group. Sommer was
sleeping, so for now there would be no interruptions, which
was critical, as they were just about to embark for the first
time something that their ancestors did routinely. "We're at
the end of this work and the beginning as we try and emulate
our ancestors' research, even with the storm as it is, we will be
fielding only two teams and with the setting up of the base
camp at the base of the mountains we've begun to establish
our story. Thanks to Judd we now know much more of how
our ancestors operated and protected the teams." Everyone at
the meeting briefly glanced Judd's way, which he

acknowledge with a curt nod. "Simply stated, these 'eyes-in-the-sky' have much more capability than we ever imagined. They even can peer through a storm and see the ground, and also with something else built into them one can actually remove the vegetation and see the bare earth – and darkness is not an issue either. Before you, in the paperwork that has been passed around, are the assignments, and these take priority over anything that we may have had going on. The two teams will need all day and all night monitoring and support. And while from here we can do little to actually protect them, we can keep them apprised of what is happening around them. You will see in narrations that are included, that our ancestors faced problems all the time when dealing with the primitives. We can expect no less. Also in this packet is very explicit instructions on operating the different aspects of these, well, I guess the proper name is satellites. All of us who are in the support role back here, and that will be we women, must become familiar with their operation. And now once again because of Judd, we can communicate to our field teams anywhere on this world. No more issues with only visuals, no more seeing something and panicking because we can't talk to the ones we are watching. And with this discovery we now know why there was nothing set up at the caves approaching this place for talking back and forth. As usual the solution was right in front of us, and we didn't see or know it. So study this packet and learn what is there. It could easily mean the difference between life and death to our field teams." She sat back down, and Saige stood up once again.

Leaning on the table and looking at each of them, it was coming down to the time of the beginning of this operation, and weather good or bad, would not, could not delay its start.

"All of us are critical, very critical to the success of this, so let's make sure that the teams are as much protected as they can be, and with that, we are done here. This whole operation kicks off before the rise of the suns, even though with this storm we won't be able to see them, tomorrow. According to what this storm is doing will determine whether we leave the base camp or not, but the hope is that we can. Our people are suffering and we need to learn as much as we can, in the shortest amount of time."

* * *

"Why bring this up anyway?" K'jor asked. "If these travelers haven't been seen in many generations, why would you think that they would suddenly show now?" Looking hard at T'som, he could see that something was up, but knew that the priest would answer him in his own way and his own time. Sighing he asked, "You know something don't you?"

"Funny you should ask." T'som got up from the chair he had been sitting in, and headed over to the fire to warm his hands. Even with the roaring fire going this shelter was anything but warm. He turned and grabbed the chair he had been sitting in and dragged it closer to the fire. Shaking his head he said, "I'll never understand this, with a fire going like this one, that a shelter can be so cold." He sat back down and signaled for K'jor to do the same. "Look, I was out and about, checking in on the young ones, and the females who are responsible for them. After all for many of these young ones, this is their first season of cold, and you know that we do lose a few to the cold, and whatever weakness that seems to attack during this time. Did you know that we had a courier, a runner, stop here very briefly?"

"A runner, with the storm tearing through the grasslands like this? Why wasn't I informed, and at least have this one report to me? He is from the alliance, right?"

Smiling, T'som waved his hands, palms out saying, "Now one of the reasons I am here is to inform you that indeed we had a runner stop by. But since it was not an emergency or something that required it to be immediately brought to your attention, I told that gate guards that I will pass on the information to you. The runner did not even enter the compound, but was immediately away. As to why this couldn't wait until the storms were over I don't know. Because, you see, what he had to say would and could wait. So while, as I said earlier, that I have been researching our past in our writings, I did not know what to look for, at least until that runner showed up. He was announcing that the travelers had been seen at the base of the Sacred Mountains in a camp waiting out this storm. He was sure that they had to be the travelers as they were exactly as described, down to the pack beasts, and the bells to let all know that they were not enemies. So now after all this time they've returned."

"Don't you find it convenient that with everything that has been going on that they suddenly show up?"

Smiling T'som said, "No, not really. I suspect that any time that they would have shown up would bring questions. From what I could gather we are only looking at a very small group of travelers. It could be that they are here to be sure that they will be welcomed as they had been in the past. After all if we had become hostile to them, then the loss of just a small group in the overall scheme would be tolerable. I suspect that if they find that they will be welcomed that we will again begin to see more of the travelers. I don't even know if this first group will even look in on us. I surely hope so. I'm really curious as to why it ended, and now why they are back."

Smiling himself, but in K'jor's case it wasn't a pleasant smile. "Me too, I'm really curious as to why now? I guess once this storm leaves we can send out our own runner, and see if we can entice these travelers to come here. After all, as you've said, we can use their healing abilities. And I'm really curious as to the whys. You know – why they stopped, and why at this particular time they are back."

CHAPTER THIRTEEN

"Remember that now you must go by the name that you've been assigned, since our way of naming is so vastly different." He looked at the five who were in the camp with him before continuing. "Jed, you and Jarid will have to remain out of sight here, as well as the points where we disembark from the haulers. We have a lot of ground to cover and not enough of us to do it. So this is our first attempt at this, and we only plan on hitting about two groups of the primitives a piece. Then when that is accomplished, to return here and wait until both teams have returned, compare notes, and see if we need to modify anything we are doing." The winds were still howling and the tent that they were in at the base camp rocked danger-ously in the winds, threatening to both lay flat on top of them and to fly away and join the winds. "Judd you will be respon-sible for Stone who we will know as L'sum, and Seve who is known as K'fah. Jarid you have me and I'm J'far, and Staven who is T'soh. From this point on that is who we are, and we cannot afford any slip ups, slips of the tongue, on any of this. We've been studying these primitives most of our lives, and now we get to see if what we've learned will pay off." Saige began pacing the tent. He had to admit that he was nervous as hell. All their work had always been from a distance, but now, like their distant ancestors, they were going to get up close and personal. And he hoped that they were ready. Their group was still too small to be able to afford any losses.

Looking outside, they could see that it was still quite dark, but in a short time the gray of dawn would be touching the horizon. It was hoped that the storm would abate today, or at least reduce in the intensity and fury that it was demonstrating right now. With the new equipment that Judd had provided, they felt that there was no way they could get lost, and one of the devices would lead them right back here. It was disguised as a heavy necklace, and the communications devices were placed in the ear, which transmitted back to the haulers, which had stronger equipment. The haulers then would relay the signal to the "eyes-in-the-skies", and then to the Alpha complex. Built into those necklaces were cameras so that both the visual and verbal could be recorded, and studied later. The clothing that they wore was actually modern materials, but appearing to be identical to the standard dress of the primitives. The advantage being that the modern materials would keep them both warm and cool no matter the variances in the temperatures. Because of this it gave the illusion that they, as the travelers, did not have issues or were affected by the weather.

In the bags that they carried were the almost microscopic bugs that they would leave behind to continue monitoring the primitives. They would last up to half an annual before running out of power, or breaking down and if in the sunlight would recharge. It was hoped that this would be enough, and by then they would no longer need them. But that was in the future, and the present was almost an unknown. On the pack animals in the many packs were their wares of bow strings, and knives, and the antibiotics that they would be using to help cure any that they were asked to see in the capacity of healers. Of course with the ability to communicate directly to Saar, it would greatly simplify their tasks. Here, again because of the differences between them and the primitives, they were depending on the formulas that their ancestors found successful. From what Saar said, there really was only a slight difference between what they themselves would use, and what appeared to work for the primitives. So it had been easy to get enough of the medicines made that both teams would have plenty, if in the end, all they did was play the role of healers, and not merchants. And while they appeared to be unarmed, other than one long knife that they carried sheathed and attached to the belt, there was a device that threw out in a circle radiating from them a shock field that would stun anyone, or any group that became hostile and tried to attack. They had to depend on the ones monitoring their progress to be informed of any of the primitives who might be either trailing them or setting up an ambush.

All of them had to smile, when they realized that it was this method that their ancestors had used, to foil many attempts by the primitives to learn more about the travelers. With the information and technology that they had available, their ancestors could see and hear a great distance from wherever they were and from the haulers could follow them and see vast areas around the ones actually doing the ground work. Yet from the reports that all of them had read, they knew both from personal observation and these reports, that even with the technology, it had been difficult to outwit the primitives. And that made perfect sense. After all they lived and fought most of their lives, surviving not only the environment, but the struggles with each other. It was a difficult existence, and it tended to winnow out the weak, leaving only the strong, and cunning to continue. "Ready Jarid, Ready T'soh", Saige, as J'far asked. Taking a deep breath while looking out, he could see the beginnings of gray in the east. It was time, and from this moment on they were travelers, not ones from the cities, not the ones from a different world. All they could hope is that all of the training, and preparation would be enough.

* * *

R'san, sitting in the shelter of K'jor stated, "Even I cannot remember such a severe season of cold, and I've lived through a few more than you." At this point he laughed. It wasn't like he could definitively say that there never had been any like this. After all he could only look back over his own life. And he knew that there could have been such a season of cold when he was young, but would have forgotten it over time.

Smiling K'jor looked at both R'san, and T'som, as the three of them sat close to the large fire. "I don't know about all of that, but T'som has pointed out that somewhere in those old words that there have been such seasons of cold in the past — although I don't know whether he's just saying that or whether it is actually true." It was a slight dig aimed at the head priest, since there were two warriors in the space, and only the one priest. But K'jor knew that T'som would take it as it was meant. K'jor knew that it took both of them to insure the security and wellbeing of the clan. And after all, T'som had gotten his shots in himself. There really was a strong friendship between the two, and this one-upmanship that both of them did was all in fun, and he had to admit that T'som got the best of him many times.

Smiling at the two of them, T'som replied, "Ganging up on me are you? And me just a lowly priest, how could you think that I would do such a thing? After all I have to face the gods every day, and I obviously cannot physically fight you, because you are both warriors. What chance would I have?" Not being able to hide it, he finally burst out laughing. "Sorry I couldn't carry it off this time. But back on the original subject here, it's really hard to determine if what I've read can be translated to what we are facing this season of cold. But a couple of the past priests actually took records of how deep that white stuff got, measuring it against a body. You know, to the ankles, to the knees, and so on. And it is the ones who did that that has showed me we've faced something similar in our past – although we are still early in this season. So, I don't know if, in the end, that this one will be the worst we've ever faced."

"I truly hope not." R'san stated, "Because with the increase, I do not know if what we have put away will be enough. The wood that we burn to both keep us warm and cook our food is being used at an alarming rate. And no, before you ask, we are not running short already. But if we get a few good days, I will be forming a few work parties to try and find additional supplies. Not to change the subject, but to change the subject, have either of you heard any more about the travelers?"

It was not a surprise question; it was something that had been on all of their minds. After the first report, no additional runners had stopped by to bring them up to date. But again, that was really not a surprise as the storm still raged, and gave no sign of breaking. And K'jor wasn't going to send a runner out in this weather to confirm what had been passed on to them. Both T'som and K'jor just shook their heads in the negative. "Being the leader of this clan, and of course the alliance, I would like to know if what we were told is true, but I'm still responsible enough that I'm not going to send anyone out in this storm to confirm the story. If they have returned, then they aren't going anywhere anyway. After all, if our old words are correct, then they are here to trade, and to offer their services, and again with the old words telling us where their base camp is located, we can send one to check when the weather or gods wants to cooperate." At that moment a particularly strong gust of wind struck the shelter, shaking it with a fury that said that it wanted to tear it down, and spread the shattered pieces across the lands. There was a deep roar in the wind, and while it was at its fury, the three inside were silent, listening to the wind, and hearing the creaking and groaning of the shelter as it withstood the onslaught. Shaking his head, K'jor asked, "Are you sure that somewhere along the way to now, that I haven't made our gods angry? I felt like the timing of that wind was such that they could have been giving us their opinion."

* * *

When the four of them exited the tent, and the two who would operate the haulers remained inside and out of sight, the winds hit them full force. It instantly took their breath away, and chilled them to the bone, even with the modern materials and insulation. Moving to the lee side of the tent to get out of the winds J'far yelled so that he could be heard, "Wow, this is nasty! We may have to wait until this thing breaks. At least by staying here and working on the routines that our ancestors established we can get more into these roles. And we know that the word is out that we are back. So maybe losing a day or two isn't going to change things too much. Let's walk the camp, check in on the animals, sorry, I meant beasts, look in on our supply shelter and get back to where it is warm. It's much too dangerous to be out in this for any length of time."

"I can't disagree with that at all!" L'sum replied. The other two just nodded their heads in agreement. It was obvious that they were cold and miserable, with their heads scrunched down, and their hands inside of the clothing. They quickly made the rounds to confirm that all was well, and returned to the warmth of the portable shelter.

"I really didn't expect it to be that cold out there. I don't know about the rest of you, but this appears to be colder than that winter we spent, ah, there I go again, season of cold we spent in that cave. Got to quit that! None of us can slip up on this, it would give us away. I know that with where we are supposed to be from, that there could be a little difference in words and accents, but it cannot be something that we would say, and not the primitives." Looking around at the two drivers he knew that they had a limited understanding of the primitive's language and of what had just been spoken. All of the field team was now using the language of the primitives. And while the two who would move them about had begun to pick up the language, they were a long way from being fluent. Seeing that, Saige as J'far, said, "Sorry about that, but we've got to stay within character, so most of the time we'll only be speaking the primitive tongue. While this time out will be a short one, keep practicing. It would be better if all of us could remain in character, and while you may never be located while we are out, we cannot guarantee that fully. The four of us will only be speaking it, and if you need to understand something we've been saying let us know. Again like when we came and rescued all of you, we cannot afford any mistakes, or any losses. So work hard on this. We're going to stay a little longer, it's dangerously cold out there, and if we end up dying from exposure, we would have failed. So now we wait once again."

* * *

It was another two days before the storm blew itself out, giving the drivers plenty of time to immerse themselves in the language of the primitives. The four who were to carry out the roles of the travelers, worked continually with them to sharpen and improve their understanding, and it had helped all of them. Before the sunrise on the third day they were heading out to their appointed locations, with a tentative plan to be back at the base camp in two days. There was some flexibility built into the schedule since there would be no way to know how the contacts were going to work out. And again, since they had never done any of this before, all they had to go on was what had been written by their ancestors. And Stone as L'sum, with Seve as K'fah returned on schedule, but as the second day waned and darkness approached and the other team hadn't reported in, they were becoming worried. Yet there was nothing from the Alpha that spoke of trouble. Not that they could go charging in and rescue them if they were in trouble. So they had to sit and wait, and count on the support team to do their job. And once they had started this operation, they had to continue it for the duration that they had set, before returning. "This is always a worry, when we run separate operations like this," L'sum said. "And with the variability that is always there, it changes things constantly." He was pacing the tent area out of sight of any of the primitives who may have been watching the camp. Once outside of the tent they had to immediately resume their roles of the peaceful travelers who appeared to have a strong confidence in their abilities, and had no fear or worry of the tribes and clans south of the sacred mountains.

K'fah, sitting cross legged and leaning forward just shook his head. "Look, we've been on similar operations, even though we never made contact with the primitives during those times. Heck, we didn't even know that it was something that our ancestors did routinely. And in our scouting and spying operations, very few stayed within the original times that had been set up. There was always something that came along and altered it, and I suspect that this is the same. So all this pacing that you're doing won't change a darn thing. So just relax, and if you can't do that, go out and check on the pack beasts and make sure they are okay. It's something we'd do anyway, and it would give you a chance to burn off some of that worry."

Shaking his head and waving him off L'sum said. "No, not now, maybe a little later, I think that I'm just a little too wound up right now to pull it off." Looking over at Jarid he could see that he, at least, understood a little of the conversation between the two. Taking a deep cleansing breath he asked. "So Jarid, first off have you really been able to follow our conversation, or should we be translating?"

"Most of it, although with the speed that the two of you are talking, I'm missing a lot simply because I have to translate each word, and try and then put it together. Then by the time I do that you both are somewhere else in what you're talking about. I kind of figured both from the way you are pacing this place that you are worried about the other team, and that Seve, excuse me, K'fah reminded you that the schedules are a loose affair, and with no alarm coming from the team responsible for monitoring us, then we really shouldn't be worrying either. Is that just about right?"

"Yeah. Not bad, guess you're getting it then. At least for us it turned out to be easy, since we made contact with those two tribes, both small, and only one had any of our people, and fortunately not many. I know that all of what we are doing will eventually allow most of the ones who survive their captivity a chance to return to us. But it is so frustrating to see them suffer like they are, and appear to be completely unconcerned, as if they are nothing. It really tears at the soul."

* * *

J'far and T'soh followed the runner as he led them back to the clan's location. "This is highly unusual; we have our own plans and direction, so I hope your clan realizes how much we are sacrificing by this change. There were no plans this time to go this deep into the grasslands and foothills. This first journey since the rediscovery of a way past the Sacred Mountains, was to only confirm that first, we were still welcome, and second that as we last had been here, if trading was something that all of you here would still be interested in doing, Thirdly was to insure that the trails found would remain open throughout the season of cold, and thusly why we are here now."

The runner listened, shrugged and continued on his way. "I don't know of your plans, all I can do is as my leader asks. It is said that one of the skills that you and the rest of the travelers possess is of healing. And right now there is one of importance that is close to the spirit world that could use that skill. That is all I am allowed to say at this point. You will be meeting with both our leader, K'jor, and the head priest T'som. They've both had their healers taking care of the one who is close to the spirit world."

"And that is why, and the only reason that we agreed to come with you. By doing this we will have left the others who are at the camp worried, and if a certain period of time passes without our appearance, they will assume that we were attacked, and are no more. At this point we will leave the grasslands, head north and never return." Saige knew that he needed to keep the pressure on, to include this runner. Fortunately they were being monitored and all of this was being recorded. They had been heading for one of the tribes when the team that was monitoring him informed him that they were going to be approached shortly. It helped him feel a little safer than even back when they scouted the primitives. So with the pack beast, bells ringing with every step, they proceeded to follow the scout.

* * *

"Your runner informed us that you had need of our healing methods, and that one of your clan who is important is close to passing into the spirit world. Maybe it was fortuitous for us to have arrived here at this time. There has been much discussion, once a way was found around the Sacred Mountains, as to when we should attempt to make contact after all this time. Most thought that waiting until the beginning of the season of greening would be the best, but it was decided that if we were to be able to establish the old trade routes that the way through would need to be tested for use for all of the seasons – so only two small teams of travelers and healers were sent." J'far stopped and was silent waiting for a response from the three who were in the shelter other than him and T'soh.

Looking at the two travelers were K'jor, T'som, and R'san. All were standing and there was a feeling of tension in the air, of static, of fire barely contained. When Saige had entered the shelter he had leaned against the entrance frame and had placed a bug that would give the teams back at the facility the ability to monitor what went on in this leader's residence. With the two groups facing each other the silence dragged on and on. Finally K'jor said, "I am very curious as to why now?"

With a look that a parent would give a child who had done something wrong and had been caught J'far asked, "Why now, what? Have you brought us here under false needs, and have decided that we are common criminals and are to be interrogated? That the reason that we detoured and came here was to fulfill and answer some suspicion on your part? I'm afraid if that is all it is, then we will be leaving. There are other tribes and clans who are eager for our goods and services that we can provide. Apparently you and yours are not." He turned to leave with indignation showing in every step. "Come T'soh, we will be sure to place in the writings that this clan is not to be visited in the future by us."

They got almost to the flaps that led back outside and away when T'som spoke. "I'm sorry, about this, but you see we have been fighting a hidden enemy, and our leader is just very suspicious of events that just seem too good to be true, and I have to admit that your arrival in the grasslands does fill those thoughts."

Turning with a questioning look on his face J'far asked, "Hidden enemy, what hidden enemy? I know that in the many skirmishes that are common among all that one is hidden to either surprise or to protect. So why would this arrival bring such suspicion? After all fighting is the way it is."

Through all of this R'san had been silent, just observing. He could see that this J'far was made of the same stuff that K'jor was, and there was no give in either of them. Inwardly he shook his head. For once he was just going to continue to observe and watch the battle. He had to admit it was a strange place for him, since he was usually in the middle of these *discussions*, but sensed he needed to remain aloof as was the one who was with this J'far. At this point T'som continued speaking. "No, we did not get you here on false words. We have one who is very close to the spirit world and do want you to see if there is anything that you and, ah, T'soh can do to bring this one back."

"If this is true, where might we see this one who is so close to passing into the spirit world?"

"First, with the permission of our leader, let us sit a moment, and we can discuss this. With the two of you this close to being out of the shelter, I'd feel better to know that you are going to stay and hear us out."

Still with doubt showing in his posture, J'far turned, shrugged and said, "Why not. This will only cost us a little time, and in the end we can still leave."

"That is very true. Now please sit and hear us out." Turning towards K'jor, T'som swept his arms towards the beckoning roaring fire and all of them proceeded to the chairs that had been arranged close to the heat. Whispering to K'jor as they headed that way he said, "Look, you just about destroyed any chance of us being able to use whatever healing they can do. It's going to be tough enough to convince them to stay once they learn that the one we want them to look at is a female. So don't stir things up too much. This J'far seems to be one of little patience and does not deal with ones he considers fools. So let's not show him that we can be one of them."

Grunting a reply, K'jor remained quiet for the moment. At this point he still hadn't come to any conclusions about these travelers. And the one who seemed to be in charge had a strength that showed he had to be a leader. But if he was, why was he here? He was finding that he was ending up with more questions, and getting no answers from his original suspicions. So for now he would let T'som do the talking. What he said was very valid. By the way the need had been presented he was sure that these travelers would be of the impression that one of the important males would be the one who needed the care. While healers looked in on the females, they did not get the same care as the warriors, or the priests, for that matter. And with the way this J'far had reacted to his question, there was just as good of chance that once he learned that they wanted him to heal a female, he could still turn and leave, leaving them without a solution, and practically guaranteeing this female would pass into the spirit world. So for now he would allow his suspicions to wait and observe these two travelers and see what he could learn. Once they were seated, there was an uneasy silence as the travelers waited to hear what the clan truly wanted of them.

"Look, if our old words are correct, then part of what you do is trade, and the old words stated that your offerings were superior to what we could produce. Is this true?" T'som was watching J'far, but was surprised when T'soh responded.

"I'm the one in charge of our trading materials, and yes our old words spoke of the same thing. But much time has passed, so we, our clan, have no idea if this still holds true. If you will allow me, I will go to the samples that we have on our pack beast and bring inside what we are offering this time around." Without waiting, T'soh stood and headed out the doorway and was gone. The three of the clan looked at each other and then at J'far, who remained sitting, giving the appearance that this could be just another boring day, patiently waiting for an explanation of the needs that the runner had relayed to them, but letting them explain in their own way and time. *I've really got to be careful. I think that who we have here is probably the leader of not only this clan, but I suspect he easily could be the leader of this alliance. Still I have to put forth what I am as J'far, from a position of strength, and one that is not willing to give in to the simple demands of a clan. After all, we, as the travelers, are supposed to be neutral, favoring no one.* Watching the entrance expectantly, all in the shelter shifted in their chairs showing that they were uncomfortable with the situation as it now stood. There was a draft of cold air as T'soh re-entered the shelter carrying a small bag that was made of leather, headed for the area in the center of the circle of chairs, sat the bag down on the dirt floor, and proceeded to open it with a flourish.

"We've only brought a couple of items this trip, again because we have no idea of the needs. After all with the generations that have passed since we last traded much could have changed. But we do know one thing; there is always a need for bow strings and long knives. So I have here samples of what we can provide. After this foray we may know better what the needs truly are, and be able to provide other items." He reached into the bag and pulled out one long knife, and one bow string and looked at the one he figured was the leader, and the older one who he assumed was an advisor of some kind. To the leader he handed the bowstring and the advisor the long knife. "Please inspect these, and give me your honest opinion. If you like what I'm showing you then we can discuss amounts and costs. We have higher quality strings and knives, than what I am showing you presently. But as one should expect the value of the better items is much greater." At this point T'soh shut up, and let the two inspect the merchandise. He could see the surprised look on both as they realized that these items were indeed better than anything they presently used.

K'jor, looking at R'san said, "This string is very interesting; here let me look at that blade." At this point R'san and K'jor traded items, and again inspecting them minutely. Both looked up, and T'soh could see that first they been impressed, but now they were trying to make it appear that while these items may have been better, that they really weren't that much better. Smiling inwardly, T'soh thought. *Yup, here comes the attempt to make these appear to be less than what they are, so that they can try and talk us down. It's an old game, and one from our records, as well as observing these people, have been used for almost as long as there have been items to bargain for – time to drop the hammer, and surprise them.* "These two items are for you to use and test. We will not be bargaining on these this trip. After all they are untested in your eyes, and I cannot set a value on something that you've not tried. So when we return on our next trading journey you will then know whether or not you want more of these things, and like I said, we may have other items to present."

R'san and K'jor looked at each other and then at the travelers. So far even with his suspicions, these two travelers appeared to be no more than what they said they were. Maybe it was just coincidence that they showed up now. And their story to this point was consistent with what T'som suspected had happened. And they did not seem to be aware of what had been transpiring here in the grasslands. Still, he would hold judgment until such time as it could be proved one way or the other. "So you are going to leave this with us are you? If so why not give us another set, that way we have proof if both hold up under the work we would use them for."

Smiling at them T'soh said, "Trying to get something for nothing are we?" He paused for effect, tipped his head to the side and then continued. "Actually we always, in the beginning, give you two of each item, for that very reason. But do not ask for more as anything beyond this will cost you." He then handed them a second long knife and bowstring, closed the leather bag, got up and headed back outside to return the bag to the pack beast.

"So, now that you have examples of our goods, who is this one that you want us to look in on, this one who is close to the spirit world?" J'far asked.

K'jor remained silent and looked to T'som to be the spokesperson for this. He felt that the head priest would do a better job of putting into words in such a way as not to cause these travelers to just pack up and leave. T'som, seeing the look he received from K'jor, knew that it would be his responsibility to get these travelers to look at the female, and also explain why it was necessary.

Not sure how to begin, since the request would be an unusual one, as they rarely used to healers for treating the females. It was something that was the responsibility of the herd. And usually the breeding herd was larger than the warriors, and priests, so it was expected that there would be losses with the herd. It was that way with the wild beasts of the grasslands, and it was no different for them. T'som got up and put his back to the fire and said, "Now on a cold day like today this feels very good." He looked down at the floor before looking over at J'far. "This is an unusual request, and it is because the circumstance is so very different."

Intrigued J'far looked at T'som questioningly, "Please continue. There must be a reason for this, ah, long winded explanation. I personally would think that if this one you want me to see is as close to the spirit world as you have been saying, that you wouldn't want to delay."

"True and this one is so very close, but as I was saying, this request is unusual as it is a *female* that we want you to see."

"A female? Really! Why would that be so? Why would I waste my time on a female? Is your breeding herd so small that even a loss of one going to affect you in such a way that it will have a negative effect on your tribe's future?"

Shaking his head and shocked somewhat at the strength of the reaction from J'far on even the thought of treating a female was a surprise. But, in a way, he should have expected it. After all if R'san hadn't initiated it with this female when he first discovered the ugly wound, then she would have passed into the spirit world a long time ago. Then he required the healer to look in on her, which even for them was unusual. "No, our breeding herd is strong, and we have added many, and this particular one is almost past the time of breeding so that is not the issue."

"If she is almost past the time of breeding, why bother? It is the purpose of the female to bring forth offspring from the union of the warrior class, to make sure the clans and tribes have future warriors, to be sure that after the dropping that these new lives are taken care of, until they can join and become part of this world. So again why bother with this female? Everything you have told me says that she is past the time of her worth. So why not let her pass from the world of the living?"

Now what? Everything he has said is true, and normally that is exactly what would be allowed. But . . . oh, I don't know, somehow he has to understand the importance of trying to save this particular female. "Yes, yes, everything you've said is true. And normally we would allow just that to happen, since passing into the spirit world is just as much of what life is, as our arriving through the dropping. But you see we believe that this one may be a priest."

"A priest? A female in such a position is not something I have ever seen in any of my travels."

Taking a moment T'som approached K'jor and whispered, "How much can I tell him? After all his questions are valid, and I have a deep feeling that if we lie, especially to this one, that he will not have the patience to stay and see this female."

Shrugging, K'jor responded, "I don't have an issue. Just do it, but keep the alliance that we've created out of it. He just needs to know enough so that he will do as we want him to, and that's all."

Nodding he turned back to the fire and its warmth. We've discovered and conquered a hidden clan that lived in the desolation. They are strange, different in so many ways to any of the known tribes and clans. They do not speak the tongue of the people. They live where no one could live and survive, yet they do. We've determined that this place had to be a lair of magicians and sorcerers; after all there could be no other way for one to survive where they lived. As is the tradition, once a clan or tribe is destroyed, the females become part of the breeding stock of the clan or tribe that has destroyed their place."

Cocking his head, J'far, stated, "A hidden people, and ones who did not speak the tongue, this is unusual. Are you sure you are not trying to fool me? After all this could be just a story to pull one into a falsehood. But I would not expect something like that from you, T'som, and a head priest at that. So am I supposed to accept what you say, or am I just going to put it to fantasy?"

"Oh you can accept it as fact. We, other than the fact of where they were existing, wouldn't have thought it too strange, other than this other fact, and it simply stated, is that they appeared to have no warriors, and nothing to prevent their demise."

Laughing now J'far said, "Now I know you are passing on a fantasy. A clan with no warriors and no protection, come on, you really expect me to believe such a tale as this?"

Sighing before continuing T'som said, "Yes, yes I know it does sound like a tale, but it is not. The only thing that we can figure is that they depended on the desolation to protect them, and until the accidental discovery by K'jor, we can say that, that's exactly what had happened. Until they were found, no one knew that they even existed. If you do not believe then you may inspect some of our slaves and see for yourself."

"Okay, let me see if I have this right, you found a hidden clan, destroyed it, and added both slaves, and females to your breeding herd, is that just about right?"

Nodding T'som continued, "Yes, that is right up to that point. And if everything continued like it would have normally, then there would've been no worry. Now what I am about to tell you must be considered privileged knowledge, do I have your word that it will remain so?"

"So far anything you've said requires no such thing. I will reserve judgment as to whether what you pass on is worthy of such a request. After all we know very little about each other, so I cannot make promises in such a situation."

"Fair enough. I will let you judge then, and after you see this female you can then make the call. As expected, all the warriors bred with the new females expecting to see the carrying. There was some resistance initially, but when it was understood that there could be no refusal, there was no issue from then on. Yet, many passed from this world. They appeared to be much weaker than our own females, and the laws dealing with females were upheld. That is one of the reasons that this female we would have you visit is not with the herd, and is being cared for by two other females and our healers. Anyway, when none of these additions to the herd carried, it made no sense. After all, we were seeing our own carrying. So, within the law, the pressure was increased to bring these new females to carry, but to this time, none are. This has led to the belief that this clan is a magic one or that they were workers for our gods, but since we cannot speak their tongue we cannot get answers. The worry, obviously, is that we, as warriors, are being defeated by females . . . By females 'by our gods'! So if we are being defeated by these females how long can we remain strong? Their magic must be strong to be able to do this, and it makes us believe that they, yes these females could be warriors, but they fell so easily. And again, as I stated, it has not been from lack of trying to defeat their magic ways.

"This brings us back to the female who is close to the spirit world. She must be a priest, as not only does she speak the tongue of the clan we destroyed, but she speaks ours as well. She is probably the only one who can explain why we are failing as warriors. And to be defeated by females is unthinkable, and until it happened, unbelievable. So it is this reason that we must try and save this female. We feel it will be our only chance to learn what we need."

Hope rose in the heart of Saige as he heard these words. This meant that this woman had to have been a scout at one time. But he was at loss as to who it could be. He knew that there were no older women with them as they fled the city, and as they were whittled down through the numerous skirmishes and contacts with the primitives, he knew that they had left no one alive behind. So she could have been from one of the other fallen cities, who had, at one time, been a part of the scouting unit before it had been disbanded. Now he had to continue to play the role, and not seem too eager to see this mystery woman. "I have to admit that this story is very unusual, and" –, smiling deeply while shaking his head, J'far continued – "this could be a great and fantastic tale if someone else had spoken it. So, with this tall tale should I trust you, head priest, or should I place it where it needs to be, as a great tale?"

"Oh I guess if I was seeing this from your side, it would be almost impossible to believe. And we are the ones living this, and it is very difficult for us. So I've revealed most to you, and have left nothing of importance out. What say you? Are you willing to, at least, look in on this female?"

Taking a deep breath and shaking his head J'far looked as if he was trying to come to some decision. There was a deepening silence as T'som waited patiently for some type of response. Eventually J'far shrugged, looked directly at T'som, and said. "I guess that it wouldn't hurt for me to at least see this female. Once I do I can decide what I will do at that point."

Smiling and rubbing his hands together T'som responded, "Good! Would you like to go now?"

With a questioning look he asked, "Now? Hmmm, well, I guess, why not." Getting up and heading for the doorway he continued, "Lead the way. The sooner I can see and decide the better chance for the two of us to get back to our original destination."

* * *

He and T'soh were led through the camp into the priest's compound, and to a small building that was isolated from the rest. He assumed that this was isolated to prevent the spread of whatever it was that had made someone sick. Even though he knew that the primitives assigned disease and infection to the gods, evil spirits, or poison, they had learned that sometimes isolation would prevent someone else from getting what the sick person had. With no announcement T'som with the two healers from the clan entered the shelter and signaled for the two of them to follow. He knew that the women that were inside had no right to demand anything, but even still he had difficulty overcoming this courtesy, but knew that he had to act just as indifferent or give himself away. Once inside, they had to wait while their eyes adjusted to the semi gloom and slight haze from the smoky fire that warmed the place. The small room smelled of women and illness, and it was overpowering. Again he knew that these three were unable to bathe, to be able to deal with the normal hygiene that helped a woman. And that by itself could easily lead to infections.

When his eyes adjusted, the first thing he noticed was the fear and utter hopelessness that the two women projected as they cowered before them. His heart went out to them, but at this moment he could reveal nothing. It was probably one of the toughest things he faced in his entire life. He wanted to reach out and comfort them, but knew he had to stay aloof, and appear uncaring. After all, they were just females, and part of the breeding herd, and nothing more. Turning towards the corner he saw a sleeping mat and a woman apparently unconscious, covered, and looking very drawn and pale. Turning to T'som he asked, "Is this the one?" He then pointed to the one on the mat, even though he knew that answer had to be her.

Nodding, T'som appeared to be exasperated by the question. After all wasn't obvious? "Of course, of course it is. What did you think that it would be one of these others that are here?"

Smiling and shaking his head J'far stated, "Now don't start that with me. I can still just leave. As far as I know this whole story is still just that. And this female who is covered is just part of this whole charade to see if the stories about us are true. So I will confirm before I continue. And yes, I can see that this one appears to be in bad shape, but again since I'm not of this clan, nor do I live here, can I accept your story? For all I know, this one is a favorite and you are asking me to heal her just so you can have her back." And before you get angry, again look at it from my side, and you can see that there are many different answers to what I am seeing here, and any of them are quite different than the one you presented." While saying this he swung his arm out with the palms up, making his point.

T'som had to grudgingly agree to this one's conclusions. After all what did they know of their clan, or why this female was here, other than what they had been told. And again he was right, there really was no way for them to confirm anything that they had been told, and there easily could be many other reasons for this situation before them. But, what he had told him was the truth, yet he had to admit it would be easy to discount most of what he said. After all, there never had been anything in either the written or oral histories that spoke of this happening. A female defeating a male through the very basic level of breeding, it just did not happen. "Yes, she is the one, and you are so right, there could be many other explanations than the one I gave. But do you not think that if I was attempting to pass a tale by you that it would have been something more believable than what I said?"

"I guess I'll concede that. After all it is a fantastic tale. Okay, I will see what I can do. Uncover the female and let me inspect her body." The two healers then uncovered the woman who was lying on her side and faced towards the wall. When they uncovered her, first he could see that she was shaking with what appeared to be chills, and second the odor that permeated the area after the covers were removed spoke of old sweat, infection and uncleanness, and was quite overpowering. He bent down and turned her on her back, and she was quite naked and emaciated, barely more than skin and bones. He could see that with those chills that she was running a heavy fever, and that she was not far from death. He, not being a doctor, did not know if what he brought could save her or not. Then as he studied the face he was shocked as he realized who he was looking at. It was Sara, Shayne's sister. He had met her once a very long time in the past, and had been surprised how much they both looked like each other. They could have easily been fraternal twins, but there was an annual between them with Shayne being the older. No wonder she could speak the primitive tongue, she had been one of the scouts before leaving the team. Somehow he had to save her, he suspected that she may be the last of her family, but she looked so bad at this point he just didn't know if it would be possible.

He turned and faced the three primitives who were with T'som he said. "You are quite correct. This one is very close to the spirit world. First what she is lying on must be removed and replaced. It has become evil and must be burned. It is the same for what she is covered with. All must be new, and that needs to be completed as soon as it can be done." Looking back at her he could see that she was shaking, and it hurt him to see her so weak and ill. Looking at the healers he stated that they needed to find something to cover her now, otherwise she could pass as they spoke. Turning to T'som, he said, "I must pray to our gods, and see what can be done. I will try and save this one. But as I begin this I will need to be left alone. You or any of your clan can check in at any time that you feel the need. T'soh will be at the entrance so that you will know that I am inside at that time. If either he or I am not there, then we will not be here, but back at our camp. Now let's move on this!" He grabbed T'soh and they left, and headed back to their temporary camp.

T'som, observing all that the traveler had done, shrugged. He could almost see something in J'far's eyes that spoke of concern. *He really didn't do much other than a brief inspection of this female. Yet, hmmm, I just don't know. Guess we'll just have to wait and see if these travelers live up to their past reputation.* Okay, you heard what the traveler requested. Do it, and do it now! We will allow this one to work, but I expect both of you to check in regularly and be sure that these travelers are only doing what they are supposed to be."

At this point, both healers got to work removing the old sleeping mat and coverings. He had to admit that there was a strong bad odor emitting from the stuff. With the healers now doing as requested he left and returned to both K'jor and R'san who remained behind at the leader's shelter to bring them up to date as to what had transpired in this shelter.

* * *

"Look, I'm really worried. Neither Saige or Staven have returned yet . . . you're telling us not to worry?" Stone asked as he sat inside the tent with the others of his team. The other team was at least four days overdue, but there, as of yet, had been no alarm from the ones who were monitoring the teams from the Alpha. Jessi, and Seirra were on duty in the security office, and he knew that if there was a problem that it would surely have been in the voice of Saige's mate. But she appeared to be calm.

"You're about to have to go out again, Stone. We've been in contact with them and he and Staven both have confirmed that everything is okay. But, as it was to be expected, he's had to change the planned schedule, which means that most likely the other tribes he had plans to visit will have to wait. I've been told that to keep it brief, and to just let you know that they are okay." Seirra stopped briefly, and for what seemed like too long from Stone's perspective, she continued. "Believe me, if there was issues I would be a wreck right now. After all I'm close to bringing in another new life into our growing city, and I for one would want my mate to be here, and if not that, to know that he is okay. And from all that I can see in both the reports and watching as a guardian, they are fine at this moment. So do what you need to do and leave the worrying to us."

Stone had to admit that the final comment almost sounded like an admonishment to concentrate on what they needed to do, and he could understand that completely. This foray as travelers overall was going to be short. So instead of being distracted, he and Seve needed to do what they were supposed to do – knowing that the other team would be doing the same. *I just wish, well, I guess I'm just a worrier. After all when we were still in that cave before the Alpha was located, we thought we had lost both Saige and Shellian.* Shaking his head he could see his thoughts going in the same direction as they had back then. "Okay, Seirra, we'll do what we're supposed to, but it's so hard to remember that we are being closely monitored."

"You don't know how closely." There was a silence followed by Seirra laughing.

"And what do you mean by that?" Stone asked perplexed.

"Well, let's say as we get better with this equipment that we can even watch you go out and pee." Again she laughed before continuing, "I really never realized how good this stuff is. Our ancestors could produce some great stuff."

"You can actually watch us relieve ourselves? Now that could be embarrassing."

"Oh don't worry Stone, I said we could. That doesn't mean that we do."

"That's a relief, I guess. But I suspect that the temptation is still there."

"I guess so, but there's so much going on, why would we really be interested in such a thing anyway? With the six of you out of the complex there are just not enough hours in a day to get everything that needs to be done, done. And with me heading deep into my third, I'm anything but comfortable. This one inside of me is making it difficult to do anything."

This brought back to him that Sorrel was also pregnant. It was fascinating in some ways to know that soon he would be a father. But Sorrel's situation was so different than the rest, from being the first of the women to become pregnant, and the subsequently losing that child, to now being the last of the women to become pregnant. Of course the ones that they had recently rescued were not included in his thinking at this moment. Turning to the other two in the tent, he said, "I guess we will be heading out in the morning, and then if we can hold to the planned schedule, will return in two days."

* * *

As they headed to their encampment just outside the clan walls, Saige whispered to Staven and said, "I know that woman, but don't acknowledge me until we are back in our camp and it has been confirmed that we can't be overheard." It took a few more moments before they exited the permanent encampment and headed for their separate camp. Both remained silent, and both took their time to reach the tent and enter. Saige waited as he wanted a confirmation from the ones who were monitoring them, that it was all clear. In what seemed too long he finally was cleared. With the tent flap closed so that they couldn't be observed he faced Staven and said. "I'm almost completely positive that the woman who is close to death in that encampment is Sara, Shayne's sister. Somehow we've got to save her, but as you saw she is really in a very bad way. It looks like the infection has invaded most of her body and she's barely hanging on. We really need her to survive if for no other reason, than the fact that as a slave to these primitives she can keep us up updated. I don't know about you, but it got a little dicey in there as we butted heads with that leader."

"Yes, it did. I can't deny that at all. I thought there for a moment that you had pushed him too far, and when you got up to leave that first time I thought, okay how's this going to play out? But you guessed right. Sara, who'd of thought that. That means she's been here for a very long time", he looked down while shaking his head, "No, not a good thing at all. How'd she survive until now? Did you see those graves off to the one side when we entered this place? Way, way too many. I have a feeling that too many of them are our people. After all, living in the cities has gotten most of us soft, and unable to actually survive in the wilds. And yes, she looked like hell. I know with me standing by the entrance I didn't have the view you did, but what I saw was shocking enough. And the odor in that place was very overpowering. And when she was uncovered it became infinitely worse. You could smell the infection. Do you think that what we've brought is actually going to help?"

"I don't know, and we need to contact Saar, and see what he says. I planted a bug, actually a couple while we were in there. That way he can see her, and while he can't actually physically check her out, at least visually he should be able to give us some suggestions." He stopped a moment and with a faraway look he asked. "You guys get that? Get the doc or the nurse to contact us as soon as you can, make sure they see the recording so that one of them can give us a direction. And we need it now; I can't say how much longer Sara is going to live if we don't get her something very soon." Looking back at Staven Saige continued, "I can only hope that one of them has an answer. I know that we have everything that we brought, since we never made our first stop. And I think that this time out this will be our only one . . . what's that?" He could see that Staven had also gotten the warning. Someone was approaching their camp. Signaling Staven to sit on the opposite side of their small fire, he sat down on took on the pose of one praying to the gods for the answer to the saving the female, speaking words that a priest would have used.

"J'far, T'soh, I've been sent by T'som. He said that the sleeping mat and coverings have been replaced, and the ones removed are being burned as I speak to you. He wanted to know if there was anything else for he, or the healers to do." The runner remained outside of the closed portable shelter not wanting to disturb the travelers, and yet having been ordered to relay the message.

J'far paused in his prayers and addressed the runner saying, "You may relay back to your priest that he has interrupted our prayers to our gods, and that it may bid an ill wind for doing so. But I feel that the gods will understand, since what your priest has asked is from concern. If he has accomplished this, then this female must be kept warm. The changing of her sleeping mat and coverings will have strained her even further, and even this could be enough to push her into the spirit world. So go and tell T'som that we are praying to the gods to spare this female." Once he finished he could hear the runner leaving, and he waited until the sound of the steps disappeared into the distance, and once again the one monitoring them said that it was all clear. Before he could say anything he heard Saar's voice, and confirmed that he was now listening.

"Are you sure of who she is? Of course you are, I shouldn't have asked that. But from the recordings of her and the live feed that I'm getting now, I just don't know if we can save her or not. She's that bad. Actually worse than Sorrel, and you know how close Sorrel came to death. Look, most of what I sent with you is antibiotics, and enough to treat at least a dozen people. And it's a little stronger than the ones we'd normally use, since they are a little different than us. There's that one small bottle that is in with the rest, it's to be mixed with anything you would give our people. From what I can discern from here, you will need most of what you've brought with you to give her a fighting chance. And you will need to inject the first three over a day so that it goes directly into her system, and doesn't have to pass through the stomach. After that then the ones who are helping can get her to drink the concoction four times a day. So that means that you will have to remain there for at least another day to give her the injections, and then leave the instructions on the rest. I assume that you'll be leaving a complete package for her to use once and if she recovers."

"Yeah, that's the plan doc. It really bothers me to see the abuse our people are living through, and to turn a deaf shoulder and appear unconcerned is very difficult." Sighing deeply before continuing Saige said, "But, we must stay in our roles no matter what we are witnessing. We just are too few to be able to do much as of yet, and the surviving cities cannot do very much either."

It was silent for a moment, and then Saar answered, "I know, and it troubles me to see what's happening, and at the same time feeling so helpless at not being able to help. It makes me feel guilty that I can be here safe, and comfortable, with my family, and it is a family now, and yet see the suffering, see our people dying . . ." He kind of trailed off and didn't finish his thoughts. "I guess we can only do what we can and hope for the best. Bug the heck out of that place so that I can monitor her if you would please. So you now know the order in which to use the antibiotics, and let's pray it works."

"You're not going to get me to disagree with you doc. Okay then, we'll start the process right now, that way we can be out of here the same time tomorrow, and head back to our base camp."

CHAPTER FOURTEEN

It had now been a few days since the travelers had disappeared. And true to their word this first visit in generations was very short. Even though their base camp had been under constant observation by the alliance, it was as if their portable shelters, and all of the equipment that were visible was there one moment, and the within the blink of an eye, all of it was gone, as if it had never been there. Immediately on the discovery they ran to the camping area, and could find nothing. Nothing at all, no tracks, no signs of there ever having been anyone here let alone a base camp. No dropping from the beasts, no ashes or fire pit, not even a single track. It was like the earth had just swallowed them whole leaving no sign or proof that they had ever existed, let alone had been in this place – it was exactly as the stories said. While it was an oral history and in the case of the clans written, most believed that what had been spoken or written was myth. Just as they had thought the travelers were, but they were real, and now they knew that what they had thought was myth had just transpired before their very selves.

Little did the primitives know that it was advanced technology that had been responsible for this little bit of magic. Where the ones that they knew as travelers had been camping and working from wasn't where it appeared. Instead they were located in a hidden valley close by, and with both transmitters and receivers a 3D hologram of their camp had been projected from the actual location of their base camp to where the primitives believed it was located. And since they were not allowed anywhere close to the traveler's camp, the illusion would pass. It was another reason for the power being available in that cave at the base of the mountains. The receiving emitters were well hidden, and only the digging up of the surrounding hillsides would eventually expose them. But there would be no reason to do that, and their small size would, even then, make it nearly impossible to locate.

"I'd of liked to see their faces when we turned off the images." Saige said, as they made their way back up through the trails and tunnels to the Alpha. "I have to admit that our ancestors had set up a pretty elaborate system. I myself wouldn't know where even to begin to do something like this. It's very obvious that they had planned very well with the idea of protection for any who went into the field. I never realized how much we've lost over time, since we've only been sitting on our bottoms awaiting rescue, and not really trying to advance. I guess this undeclared war with the primitives has forced us to face the truth that we really have stagnated, and actually have regressed a bit from where we were when we were a science group. And that makes it all the worse because we were originally ones who supposedly were making the advances."

The other five that were with him as they headed back couldn't disagree. With Judd working the replicators, and he finding something new almost every day, they could deny it, but if they did, it would be as if they were putting their heads in the sand, ignoring the facts as each was presented. "Not to change the subject, but to change the subject, when the two of you *J'far, and T'soh*, didn't show back up our camp, you really had me worried. It reminded me of when you and Shellian didn't return on schedule back at the cave. It was hard to know that you were being monitored, and that everything was in control. I went so far as to contact the ones who were monitoring us, since nothing was being said, and I was told that everything was going well, although a change of plans had taken place. I more or less was told to do what I was supposed to be doing and to let them do their job, and of course they were right. But I couldn't stop worrying until they let me know." Stone paused, took a deep breath before continuing. "So you found more of our people at that clan's headquarters, and to find, of all people, Sara. That is a shock. I didn't know if any of our people had survived the fall of Sequoyah."

"Yeah, we found her, but she might be dead by now. She was so very close when we arrived. And even if she survives, there's nothing but hell in what is left of her life if we cannot come up with some way to end this now. Believe me; it was very difficult, almost impossible really, to put on the air of unconcern that permeates the primitive culture as far as their women are concerned. And while they are treated very poorly, our men fare no better, although their situation is still better than our women. I'm just happy that none of women can get pregnant by these, these primitives. With the appalling conditions, it's no wonder so many of the women die in childbirth. And infant mortality is very high also. If nothing else this trip into the camps have pushed me to a higher level of commitment to save our people."

"If it makes you feel any better, not that it should, the tribes that we visited were probably worse than where you went. There were some of our people with them, but none of them looked well, and I suspect that what was left was just a small remnant of what started out with these tribes. Our people are dying, and here we are. So I agree whole heartedly with you. We've got to end this." Seve looking around at the rest of the group could see the same feelings in their faces. What they had witnessed, and really what the people they had rescued who were from the city of Jade knew from personal experience, that they needed to find a solution, and it was something that couldn't wait.

* * *

Sara came out of the fog of a very deep sleep, close to unconsciousness really, slowly. She felt like she had been ran over by a stampede of, oh she didn't know what, but whatever it was she felt that there wasn't anything that didn't hurt. For the first time in well, she didn't know how long, she was coherent, and she was so weak that any movement made her shake. She felt warm and comfortable besides the pain she was experiencing. She looked around the space she was in and saw that the other two women were asleep. She took a deep breath and carefully turned on her side, and was asleep again. As she drifted off she had a few thoughts flit across her mind, but they seemed so unimportant at the moment, and then she was sleeping once more.

A few hours later she was once again awake, and found that she was very hungry, starving really. Glancing at her arms that were exposed from under the covering she could see that they were almost skin-and-bone. No wonder she was so weak. She could see that both of the women were now awake and were doing things around the area to tidy it up. Finally one noticed her and came over smiling. "You're finally awake. We've been really worried, so very worried. You almost died on us, so close that we thought that you had at least twice. Our captors were very worried about your condition, and they've been here continually. And I suspect that one of them will be here any time."

"How long?" Sara asked. "How long have I been here? I don't even remember coming to wherever this is?"

"Well, the trip to here almost killed you, so I'm not surprised that you don't remember, and it has been somewhere in the neighborhood of a month and a half, give or take a few, around forty five days that we've been here. Look we need to get some nourishment into you to help you recover. While you look really bad, there's definitely a change. This is the first time that you've been back to us in all of that time." Turning towards the other woman Barb' said, "Beth, bring something over so we can feed this starving woman."

Turning her head so she could watch Beth, Sara realized that she had a small pot that sat on a small open fire, and was ladling a broth of some kind in an earthen bowl. While she was watching this, Beth lifted her to a sitting position and propped her against the wall. At this point she realized that she was naked, and asked, "How long have I been this way?"

"Since you've been here," was the simple answer. "There was one point where your sleeping mat and coverings were removed, burned and replaced with new. And throughout that whole time you never moved or gave the appearance of knowing what was going on. I really thought that you were so very close to dying right then and there. And if those other two hadn't showed up, I think you would have."

"Other two? What other two?"

Barbara approached, and asked, "Do you want us to feed you, or are you strong enough to do it on your own?"

Lifting her arms she found that she was immediately shaking, and overall she could see that she had little strength to even do that much. Smiling, even though that was an effort she said. "I think that you had better do it. I just don't have it yet."

"I don't know who they were, since we don't know the language," Barbara said, "but it was obvious to us that they were unhappy with the conditions when they came in here to look in on you. There seemed to be a heated discussion, and immediately after that discussion all of your stuff was replaced. The one who seemed to be in charge had inspected you, I don't know how else to call it, and then gave some type of instructions to the ones we are used to seeing in here. Then for the next day the one returned and did something to you, and continued to look over your body. And from what I could see, it wasn't in the way these primitives do when they want to mate with you. It was more like a doctor would. Then they were gone. We then were given something that needed to be put in your broth, and given to you whenever it could. And I know that when you look at yourself; you know that it wasn't a lot. Yet whatever this one did, it seemed to start you on road back to us. But it's going to a while before you'll even be able to get off this sleeping mat."

Puzzled, Sara couldn't remember any of this. She must have been unconscious. She knew that she would have been removed from the mat, and to lie there in front of the world for all to see that way was something she would normally had not done. "Well, I guess I'm glad that I was oblivious to that impropriety."

"Yeah, we know," Beth said, "we were embarrassed for you. None of us like to expose our bodies that way. But there was nothing that could be done. At least through all of this none of these males have attempted to mate with any of us. I guess as long as we are here to help you all of us are safe from that problem until you heal."

Sara had to admit that the broth that she was eating tasted really good. But even for this short awakening she found that she was tiring rapidly. It was going to take a long time to get her strength back. She wondered idly who these two strangers were. It would have been nice if she had been conscious at that time so she could have understood what was going on, but she wasn't and she couldn't change that if she wanted. "I'm afraid that I'm on my way to falling back to sleep. I can't believe that just this little activity has wiped me out." She found that even saying that much had taken a lot of effort. So with help from Beth, she was lying back down on her mat and was almost instantly out.

* * *

"Saige! Shellian! Where are the two of you?" The voice over the PA system asked. Both of them rushed to the security office with Shellian reaching it just ahead of Saige and with both of the standing in the doorway Shellian asked, "What's going on?" Sam' was napping and was with the other children in the converted daycare center, which had been the classroom for the children of their ancestors.

Jessi turned and faced them and then said. "Look, I'm sorry if I sort of demanded that you get here, but both of you said that if there was any change in Sara, that you wanted to be informed immediately, and there has been."

Saige and Shellian looked at each other and then at Jessi, and Shellian asked, "Okay, so what has changed?"

Shaking her head Jessi said, "Oh, I'm sorry. It looks like she's going to get better. She just woke up for the first time that I can remember, and then with help sat up and ate a little, and is now back to sleep."

"That's very good news, Jessi, very good news indeed." Saige said. "Please keep us informed, and when you go off shift let the others know this, and let's continue to monitor her closely, and thank you very much for letting us know. And I guess what the doc gave us has saved her. That's really wonderful news. As bad as she was when I saw her I really didn't think there was anything short of being here in the medical section that would save her life. The images on the cameras really do not give justice to what she really looked like."

"Shell', your daughter just woke up, and I think that she's looking for a meal. Can you report back to the daycare?" Joci stated over the PA system.

Smiling, with a deep love in her eyes Shellian said to all of them there. "A mother's work is never done, and to have to be part of the leadership of this place too really does keep me quite busy." She then left and headed out to take care of her daughter's needs.

Smiling as his sister retreated Saige thought. *And it won't be long before Seirra and I are parents ourselves. She's due at any time now. But I won't have quite the responsibility that Shell' does since the feeding and such is something I will do, but I don't have the equipment to do it all the time. So it is easier for me to play the leader than Shell'. Yes I know that there will be breast milk set aside for me to feed our child, but most of it will fall to Seirra.* "See you later Shell' and you're right a mother's work is never done."

* * *

Another storm rolled in off the grasslands and K'jor once again could feel the cold clawing at the shelters. It was a time to sit by the warm roaring fire and refrain from going outside. There had been no updates on the female, and as close to the spirit world as she had been, he wasn't surprised. He suspected that if she passed he would be informed as soon as it became known. Right now they were about half way through the season of cold, and the brief meeting that he had with R'san left him wondering if they would have enough to get through this one. So far the storms and cold hadn't let up, and had remained the worst he could ever remember. Well, there was little he could do about it. Their time had been short when the alliance broke for the season of cold, and while they had packed much away, and with R'san working everyone here, there should have been plenty. Still none of them had planned for a season of cold like this one, so it was a great possibility that there would be shortages. Again only time would tell if that would be happening.

His mind drifted once again to that first discovery and when he turned that final corner in that wash. Before him were shelters just like the ones his clan or any for that matter, used. There were a few trees, and dead grasses all around. There was a still heavy silence, one that spoke of abandonment, but at the same time a sense of a deep vibration that could be more felt than heard. The area sloped slightly away from him towards the shelters. There was a soft warm breeze blowing raising a little dust into a spirit spiral. Was this where he would come after he passed to the spirit world? It was a valid question. Yet, something didn't feel right. *As if anything in the spirit world would feel right. Come on if I'm really here then nothing would be as I expect. Even this, these shelters would not be expected.* Taking a deep breath and with some trepidation, he approached the shelters and upon closer inspection appeared to be weathered, ancient and showing no signs that they had been occupied for a very long time. He could see that there was a small ravine that split the shelters, and again just past them he saw the portable shelters that the tribes used. *What is this place?*

He began to search one of the larger shelters, and found just like in his own, sleeping mats, and coverings. There was old abandoned clothing that when touched began to fall apart. *If this is a place of the spirits, why would they have need of clothing?* It was another valid question, and one for which again he had no answer. With no sign of life, he became less fearful, and began a thorough search and with each shelter he searched he became more and more puzzled. Everything that a clan home would need was here, except for the clan. It really looked like whoever had been here just left one day, and never took anything with them. If there had been an attack or the evil spirits had destroyed them, then there should be remains here, something. But there was nothing, but the silence and the ever warming breeze. He moved on through this encampment to the tribe shelters and found the very same puzzling answers. And why would there be both so close to each other? It was a rare thing in the grasslands for any two to be this close. One could not protect like this.

Then he noticed, more subconsciously, than consciously, that as he approached the tribe's shelters that the deep vibration had gotten stronger. *Now what is causing that?* Curious, he began to walk in a number of circles trying to judge where the vibrations got stronger, and where they started to wane. In the direction where it got stronger and in the distance he saw what appeared to be more trees and some type of brush between them forming what appeared to be a wall of vegetation. And as he walked towards this feature, the strength of the vibration increased to the point that he could almost hear it, but it seemed to be so low that it was just below what he could truly hear. Then as he pushed through the brush he found a solid wall that disappeared in the distance along this brush and tree line. He turned to the left and followed it until it ended against one of the hills, which could not be climbed. So he turned around and went in the other direction. And just past the point where he had entered and to the right the wall changed direction slightly as it headed for another hillside. He could see that like the other direction that this hill would make it impassible also. *Just what is this all about? Maybe, just maybe, the area beyond this wall is where the spirits actually reside. That this place where I am is a temporary location where we, once we become spirits, learn to adjust to this new way. Then when we are ready, a spirit or maybe one of our gods, admits us.*

He had to admit that it was one of the many conclusions, but if that were so, why no spirits now? He decided to continue down the wall even though he could see it turn back in the distance to meet that hillside. But not all of it was visible, and before returning he wanted to be able to say that he did all he could. As he continued, the wall turned inward to avoid an obstruction and just past this obstruction there was a closed entrance. He stood there and stared at it. It had to be an entrance or an exit, but it was blocked by something just as solid as the wall. No matter how he pushed or pried it did not move. Even his knife left no mark. Frustrated by being so close to maybe solving this mystery, he sat on the ground cross legged and stared at this obstruction trying to figure out its secret. While sitting there thinking, he realized that the deep vibration was stronger here. There just had to be a way beyond, but he was running out of time. He knew that he was to meet with the hunting party today, and today was leaving rapidly. It was time to leave, but he would remember, yes he would remember. Of course this would only matter if he could cross back into his own world.

* * *

"We've made about half way through the winter, and our time is short." Saige knew that he kept repeating this, but it was true. With each city that had been lost to the primitives their small population was shrinking. And the ones who had been captured and either turned into slaves, for the men, or to become part of the primitive's breeding herds for the women, the life had become a living hell. And with most not knowing the first thing about living, let alone surviving in the wilds, too many had died. He looked around the table and except for the few who were manning the security office, or watching the children everybody was here. "We're going to be having more of these as we brainstorm to both break this alliance, and to completely end these searches and attacks on our cities. We do not have any way, because of the distance between our cities, to be able to defend and support each other. We all know that when our ancestors set these cities up originally it was not supposed to be for the time that has passed, so defense wasn't something that they had even considered, other than hiding the cities in the most desolate places that they could, restrict travel, and just basically hide.

And when you look at it, this is something that has worked for a very long time. But if we want to be completely honest, what has happened to us eventually would have. One cannot remain hidden forever – although this facility has done a pretty good job of it. So good in fact that its location was unknown even to us. Oh it was always mentioned, but no one knew of its location. So, we still have a technological advantage over the primitives. But if you look at some of the history from our home world you will find that such a thing doesn't automatically guarantee anything. There are many examples of a primitive culture defeating one that was technologically ahead of them, and again we are seeing it play out once again right here. So to prevent becoming one of the defeated, we need to find a way to end this now. I know, as you, that the remaining cities are working hard on trying to strengthen their own defenses, and will be able to offer little to no help to us. The only advantage, if you want to call it that, is the fact that we no longer have cities to protect. In this I mean our own. Of course since we are all one people, our ultimate goal is to be sure that all are protected. But by not having to put forth our efforts and resources to protect an existing city, we can concentrate totally on how to stop this undeclared war.

"As all of you know, we have just returned from emulating our ancestors and the way they did their fieldwork. And I think that while it was a very dangerous thing to do, we needed information, and the 'eyes-in-the-sky' couldn't give it to us. I have to admit that with us now knowing what these things are capable of; we have vastly improved our surveillance, and understanding. But to really get what we need meant that we had to actually enter their camps, listen, and converse. And again, thanks to our ancestors, what they had left us was the very solution to be able to accomplish that. The fears, of course, were; would the primitives remember these travelers, and accept them now after all this time. Apparently, and again thank you ancestors, the answer is yes. Every place that we stopped welcomed us. Although where Staven and I went, the leader wasn't just going to accept our story. This one, this K'jor is highly intelligent, and while it was never directly mentioned, I suspect that not only is he the leader of that clan, but there's a good chance that he's also the leader of alliance. Throughout our time with his clan, he remained highly suspicious of us. Yet, again thanks to our ancestors, we knew how to defeat those suspicions, and while he still never fully accepted us, he allowed the two of us to look in on this female who as they stated it, was close to the spirit world. All of you know that the woman in question is Sara, one from our own city. First off let me say it was a shock to find one of our own. Again as you know, she was very close to death. Whatever the infection was it had almost claimed her. Thanks to Saar and the antibiotics that he sent with us, she is now recovering."

He could see the smiles on the faces that this news brought to all of them. He let everything that he had spoken to this point soak in before continuing. He took a sip of water, leaned on the table and continued. "Once she has recovered enough, we hope to use the two-way that we planted in the shelter to learn more. I would guess that she will be safe from any additional abuse until sometime in the spring. It's going to take that long for her to recover, which means that the other two will be safe also. Before you, in the papers that have been handed out, are the translations of the conversations, which were recorded, we had with the primitives that we interacted with. Simply stated, all of us must read this material, and again thanks to these satellites for allowing us to record absolutely everything, so that what you have is accurate. From this and what the videos show us we must come up with a strategy, and put it into effect before the end of winter, or as soon as we can. As you all know, the beginning of spring is a time that the primitives replenish diminished supplies, and until they have, they will not meet back at what we guess is the alliance gathering grounds in that hidden valley. With so few of us we have way too much work ahead of us, but the rest of our people are counting on us to stop this before we are no more than a memory. We truly do not know what has transpired on our home world, and for all we know, we could easily be the last of our kind. So we must, and I must emphasize that word, we've got to end these incursions now. We will be meeting again after the morning meal tomorrow. We won't be discussing any of this here at this meeting today. So take this, read it, study it, put down notes and ideas, we need anything and everything you can come up with. I know that what I've said here this morning places a heavy burden on all of us, but try and have a great day, and let those thoughts and ideas flow. And with that the meeting is done for now. Don't hesitate to ask questions of each other, discuss this, and in the morning let's find the answers, thank you." With that final comment Saige dismissed the assembly and stood and watched as a very silent group left the meeting area. Inwardly he shook his head. He knew what was in those papers, and at this moment he had no answers or solutions to the many unknowns and questions that lay before them. But a solution had to be found.

Everything that was in the paperwork that was disseminated among the people here at the Alpha had also been sent to the surviving cities, with hope that someone somewhere would be able to give them at least some suggestions. Once Sara became well enough to be able to help, albeit quietly and in the background, it would provide more data, and at least some relief for their women, when they learn that they cannot become pregnant under the continual assault of the primitives and their attempt to make it so. Once the meeting area had cleared, he stood and stared out the windows into the small hidden valley where the Alpha lay hidden. Snow lay on the ground and added a white frosting to the evergreens painting a scene of peace, something that was so far from the truth. Sighing and shaking his head, he grabbed the other stacks of paper to disseminate to the ones who were unable to actually attend. Of course they could and did watch it on the monitors that were located in all of the work areas. He felt older than the annuals said, but the weight of leadership, even shared, seemed to age anyone who took the job seriously. Just what were they going to do? With only eighteen members here at the Alpha they were supposed to bring down the whole alliance. This brought out a laugh, but not of humor as much as disbelief. So few, but their people, all of the remaining cities, were depending on what they did here. Could they, would they come up with a solution in time, or would each city fall one at a time until they were no more?

When their ancestors had originally set up the cities it had never been from the idea of defense and support. The planned defense was the isolation and the hiding of the cities in the desolation where the primitives would not go. After all there was no reason. Again originally they had expected to be rescued in short order, and so the type of defenses that they now needed were never considered, and until the discovery of the cities by the primitives, never an issue. Looking through the large databases at the Alpha showed just how much they had lost or forgotten over time. And with little to no travel between the cities, again to reduce the chance of being discovered, this had isolated them even further. In some ways Saige was surprised that the communications circuits had remained, but now was quite thankful that they had. In many ways it was funny how life was. Here in the midst of loss, destruction, and death, life continued to flourish. By not including the eight that they had recently rescued, their small group of ten had increased by three with two more to be added in the near future. Shaking his head all he could say was that life went on no matter what was happening.

* * *

T'som entered K'jor's shelter and said, "It looks like whatever those two travelers did saved the life of the female. It looks like she's turned for the better, but she is so weak that it's going to take a very long time before she's able to do anything more than eat and sleep."

Shaking his head K'jor said, "They continue to bother me. I can't get it out of my mind that there's more to them than what we saw. I still feel that there's just too much coincidence with the timing of their arrival."

"Well, you'll not have to worry anymore about them. They have returned to where they came from."

"Really? Did any attempt to follow them back?"

Shaking his head in answering T'som continued, "Yes, and no. Yes in the fact that we, the alliance, were watching their camp, with the idea that once the camp was broken that they would be trailed from a safe distance. And no because the winds picked up a large cloud of what was called dust, and when it cleared the camp was gone."

"Gone? Do you mean that they packed up that quickly and then left?"

"It's an unknown. Before the dust cloud they were there, and after they were just gone. The ones who were watching went to the camp location and searched it completely. They found nothing."

"Nothing? What do you mean nothing? There had to be something – ashes from the fire, pack beast droppings, tracks, marks where the portable shelters were located, anything."

"I agree with you, but the word is there was nothing. It was like they never were there at all. But we know that not to be true as our scouts witnessed their location and watched from a safe distance. No, it's like they never were."

Taking a deep breath, and sighing K'jor stated. "I've got to go and see this. It is not possible to disappear that way. There is always something left – always."

"Normally I would agree with you, but these who watched were not ones who were out on their first scout or their first raid, they were some of the most experienced. After all from what we know of the travelers it would have to be that way. But in the end these travelers just disappeared, and left nothing behind to say that they were ever here. Yet you have the long knife and the bow string as proof. If you did not have these, and the healing of the female, I would say that all would have been a dream, wishful thinking, but we have the hard evidence right here. And once this storm breaks, even though the distance is great, I say go ahead and check it out yourself. But by then this storm would have wiped out anything the scouts would have missed anyway. So in my opinion it would be a waste of time, and you know it."

He had to admit that what the priest just stated was fact. With another storm raging with the high winds, and blowing snow, anything that could have still been at the camp site would have been wiped out, and it would prove useless and a waste resources that they didn't have. So grudgingly he would have to accept what was being passed on to him. Sighing he said, "You're right, it would be a waste of my time. But nobody just disappears like that. And while what you've said is true, even the best can overlook something, make mistakes, or miss the obvious when they expect it to be different."

"I cannot deny anything that you've said, but there were more than one who were observing the travelers camp, and they were spread out and while it was close to dusk at the time of the large dust cloud or maybe blowing snow, it hadn't been the first one, so there was no reason to suspect that this one would be any different. It was a shock when the air finally cleared and the camp was gone."

* * *

Sara awoke once again and this time didn't quite feel like she had fallen off a cliff and lived to regret it. She found that she was lying on her side facing the wall. As usual the one room shelter that she and the other two women were in was bathed in shadows and gloom. With the only light coming from the fire, and then some light from the outside coming through the many cracks and crevices that allowed the winds into their space. As her eyes focused she could tell that it had to be daytime, and that another storm was raging, as bits of snow would pass through these openings in the walls periodically, and she could feel the breezes slightly at those times. While their situation was hopeless she felt thankful to be alive, well, at least she thought so at the moment. She really couldn't recall much of her time when she had been close to death. She was sure that it was locked somewhere in her mind, but thankfully at this moment in time she was blank.

She really wasn't looking at anything, being in that twilight where one is neither awake nor asleep – a point where one is deciding if they want to awake or just go back to sleep. Suddenly at her eye level she saw something that piqued her interest, but it had to be an illusion, just the way the light played with the eyes. She closed her eyes for a few moments and opened them again expecting it to be gone, but it wasn't.

How'd it get there? Was the question that flashed through her mind. She slid closer to the wall and was expecting it to disappear knowing that the mind could create images from nothing but random lines and curves. But it did not. She took a deep breath, and let it out slowly, then reached out with her hand and traced it with her fingers. And hope flashed briefly in her soul. *It's real, it really is real.* But before she could do more than confirm what she had found, she drifted off once more into a deep healing sleep.

A few hours later she awoke once again, and for the first time that she could remember needed to go. She looked across the small room and saw that Beth and Barbara were awake and seemed to be talking quietly. She tried to grab their attention, but they, at the moment, were not looking in her direction. She cleared her throat to try and speak and found that her voice cracked as she tried. Seeing Beth face her she could see that it was a surprise to Beth to see that she was moving. Beth arose and came over to her and asked. "What do you need dear one?"

"I need to relieve myself; can the two of you help?"

"Oh my yes," turning back to Barbara, Beth could see that she was joining them. They helped her over to the opposite corner where a pot had been set up for that purpose. Once out from under the coverings she felt very cold. The two women placed some clothing on her and she found that she was shaking. *Isn't this ever going to end?* It took all of her strength to perform what she needed to do and to get back into bed, with the image she had seen earlier temporarily forgotten. They propped her up once again and she had some additional broth. With the warmth hitting her belly she could almost feel it go throughout her body. She found that this time she could eat more, but once again she found that as she finished what she could she was drifting off to sleep, and could do nothing to prevent it. She knew that she had a long way to go for her to heal, and that the time of being awake would slowly increase, but for now when she slept her body was repairing itself.

* * *

It had been Saige's shift when he had been going through the many feeds that had been added with their visits to the tribes and clans as the travelers, that he saw Sara stare at the wall, and hope sprung up inside of him. He had placed that symbol where only she would find it, and it was something that would be ignored by the primitives, but known to any who had been part of the scouting unit. To any who were outside of the unit, it would appear to be no more than a series of lines and curves, which easily could be just a random jumble of nothing. But when looked at it in the right way would appear to be one of the birds of prey that this world held. It was chosen as their symbol long before any of them had become members, and all were required to memorize its vague shape. They used it to mark areas when in the field. The bird had been chosen for its ability to see great distances and to be able to locate its prey with this method. The birds could ride the thermals all day, barely moving and would study the surrounding lands for its next meal. The scouting unit had been told that while they were not looking for prey, they needed to emulate what these birds could accomplish with their abilities, and to be able to scout out their intended tribes and clans and to remain invisible and yet gather the intelligence that they needed. Smiling as he saw the recording of Sara finding the sign, watching as she traced the image with her fingers, he knew that soon she would be healthy enough for them to be able to move onto the next phase.

It wouldn't be long until his shift would be over, and then it would be time to eat, followed by their next meeting. He hoped that soon this would be ending for all of them. But for now he had a shift to finish, and the circuits never were quiet, and he was glad that on this shift he had the monitoring shift and not the communications shift that Jed was presently stuck with. But next time around it would be his turn. After all no matter what the rank or position everybody shared in all of the duties. Later as more were to become part of the Alpha that would change, but for now with there being so few, all shared.

With his shift ending, Saige headed to the cafeteria to grab a quick meal before meeting with his mate Seirra at the infirmary. She was in her last third of her pregnancy and had suddenly gotten bigger than they had expected. So today Saar, with the help of Jas would be giving her and her unborn child a checkup, and he had been told that it was important that he be there. He knew that Seirra would probably arrive there just ahead of him. But with his shift ending when it did, there really was little he could do about it. Looking up, he saw Stone and Sorrel come into the cafeteria, both laughing at some inside joke between them. He couldn't remember the last time that the two of them were down at all. While it never had been planned that the two of them become a couple, it was obvious to any that they thrived together. And to see the growing stomach on her brought a smile. It really had been such a worry to her that she could never again become pregnant after the loss of her first child. And that incident now seemed to have been a life time ago. "You two look great this morning."

Smiling at him with that smile of devilment that Sorrel had, the one that could drive a man crazy, she just nodded her head. Stone, smiling himself said, "Yes, you could say that. Understand that you and Seirra have an appointment with the doc this morning. Is there a problem?"

"No, not that I know of – but, Seirra has gotten bigger than the doc thought, so he wanted to make sure everything's okay. In fact I'm just about to head over there now, once I finish this coffee. See you at the meeting later. We'll pass on anything we learn, of course. Besides I know how it works. If we tried to keep the results a secret everyone would know anyway."

Smiling, Sorrel replied, "Funny thing about that. Even with the size of this place and the very few people that are here, everyone seems to know. What is it about that?"

Shaking his head and thinking, *yes, what is it about that anyway?* "I guess it's the way things have always been." Shrugging before continuing, Saige said, "When Shellian and I were working as a team back in the compound, it appeared that she knew things ahead of the release to all of us. I just chalked it up to her ability. But I've learned that it was just something I was unaware of. Oh well, like to continue our conversation, but I'm already late. Catch both of you later." He got up, placed his dishes in the recycler, and headed out the double doors, and down the hallway to the infirmary, entered the doorway, and then into the examination area. He could see Seirra lying on one of the exam tables with the curtain pulled partially back to protect her privacy. He could see two pairs of legs under the curtains and knew that both the doc and nurse were in the middle of their exam.

Seirra was watching and listening to them, so did not see Saige enter. Whatever the conversation, it had her full attention. He waited and watched from a distance, not wanting to interrupt. When it appeared that whatever they had been discussing ended he moved and tried to get her attention, but was frustrated as she wasn't looking his way. So he moved up to the curtain, and said. "Good morning, my lovely lady!"

"Saige!" She said as she saw him. She beckoned him over to join her.

He could see that she was covered in a sheet as he entered the space, and saw that Saar was on one side of the table with Jas on the other. Jas, looking over at Saar asked. "Do you want to tell them, or should I?"

Seirra and Saige looked at each other and then at the nurse and doctor, and Seirra asked with a slight alarm in her voice. "Tell us what? Is there a problem?"

Saar, laughing lightly said, "No, not a problem really." He turned back to Jas and said, "Go ahead, you can tell them."

"Saige, why don't you grab that chair, and sit beside your mate," She pointed to one that was just outside of the curtained area, which he grabbed, and set it next to Seirra. Once she saw that Saige was now seated she continued. "With this increase in the size of you, Seirra, it made us, well me more than Saar, since I've worked gynecology in my past, but I suspected that either you were going to have a large baby, or maybe twins."

Saige and Seirra looked at each other and then back at Jas, and together asked, "Twins?"

Again smiling at the two of them she just affirmed it by nodding her head. "It's the reason that we wanted you, Seirra, to come in. Your sudden growth prompted me to think it could be, and now we've confirmed it. You, Seirra, are going to have twins. With the equipment that we have here, we've been able to confirm that you will have fraternal, and not identical twins, since the sex of yours are one of each. You're going to have a boy and a girl. So, this will complicate the delivery somewhat, but I suspect it will also complicate your lives also. Not to say that with everything that is going on that it isn't already."

Stunned, they looked at each other and then back at her. "And you're sure about this?" Saige asked.

"As sure as anybody can be," she smiled encouragingly, "So I think the two of you need to add another baby bed to your apartment and be prepared for what this is going to add in your lives."

Saar then broke in and said. "Here, listen to this, and I think it will prove it to the two of you." He turned on a monitor and they could definitely hear two hearts beating, confirming that indeed she was carrying twins. "Now, I don't know about you, but that is just about as close to proving it, as it is to be actually holding them in your arms."

* * *

"I'm sure, since the rumor mill is much faster than the official channels, that most of you already know that Seirra is carrying twins. It has been a shock to both of us. And until they explained that there could be two kinds of twins I thought there was only one. But with the ultrasound they showed us the unborn children. And one is definitely a boy, and one a girl, so now I know the difference." Looking over at Seirra with deep affection Saige continued. "While, from what I've observed from the members who have added children to their families, adding one seems to make things much more difficult, so I guess adding two will even complicate things more. But, while this is so, and I'm sure that we'll instantly fall in love with these new lives, Seirra and I, we still must find the answers to our problem dealing with the primitives. So after the births of our children, as with the other women, Seirra will be relieved of any duty until the doc says she can return. I know that during this early time, I'll be distracted, tired, and even be impatient, but that doesn't mean that we don't want to see our goals accomplished. At those times when I or Shell' cannot be here, either Stone, or Saar will take over the leadership, just like it was back in the cave where we spent our first winter. Now with that out of the way, let's get to what we are here for."

He glanced briefly at Seirra, and could almost see an end to a shy smile on her face. Inwardly he found that he loved her more with what had been announced. He wanted to reach out, wanted to protect her, and somehow wanted to be able to eliminate the pain that was in her future, but knew that it was something that women had been facing since the beginning of time. Yet, even with that knowledge, he really wished there was a way for her to avoid it. At least here at the Alpha they had the modern medicines to help minimize it. And, again thanks to modern medicine, there was a greater chance that both the mother and babies would survive the birthing. While in the world of the primitives both the infant and mother dying during child birth was very common.

Looking around the table now and making sure all were ready; he followed this up by glancing up at the monitors and confirmed that the ones who were on duty in the security office, and in the daycare areas were also listening. "All of us have had a chance to review both the images and the translations of what transpired while we were in the roles of the travelers. Now we need to know how we can take this information and make it work for us. So with that, do any of you have any impressions, ideas, direction we should go, or even anything that would allow us to end these attacks?" At first all he got was silence, and the ones attending the meeting looking at each other and at him. He knew that he hadn't come up with anything as of yet, but again had to admit that with the worry he had been harboring for his mate it did not surprise him.

"I don't know what to say," Judd responded, "I mean, well, at least for me this is the first time I've been up close and personal, even though I know it's just the recorded images and conversations that the four of you had when you were the travelers, and then the additional images and such with the devices that all of you planted, so it is taking me some time to just absorb the differences. So, until I understand their way, their thinking, just the way they live, it will be very difficult to come up with anything at all – at least for me."

Saige could see from at the least the members they had rescued from the tribes, the ones from the city of Jade, that there seemed to be a consensus. In a way it surprised him since they had been captives. But when he thought about it, it made sense. They were just trying to survive, trying to adjust, trying to come to terms with the unthinkable, and not try and learn about their captors. Taking a deep breath Saige said, "I guess I can understand that. I've found that even though we were watching the primitives, trying to learn anything we could when we were part of the scouting unit, I have to admit that until finding this place and reading the research notes left by our ancestors, we were a long way from understanding them ourselves." He stopped and looked over the entire group before continuing. Then he looked at the ones who had survived the flight from Sequoyah and could see that while they knew more at this moment they had no solutions either. "Look, I know how difficult this is. We're dealing with a culture very foreign to anything we know. I have to admit spending even that brief time in their camps was very eye opening. I probably learned more about them from our brief encounters then all the time we've scouted them in the past. Their society is much more complicated than I ever imagined, and as all of you know, and I keep repeating this, our time is short, so please, please concentrate on coming up with something to get us going in a direction that could lead to ending this. I guess that's all I have, so let's get to it."

Once again Joci had been stuck with daycare. But she didn't mind. She loved dealing with the young children. And she had to admit that her experience in other areas was next to none. Heck, at the time the city fell she hadn't decided what she was going to do with her life, or even the direction of her education. And truthfully she had very little confidence in what she could or couldn't do. Then the city fell and she, like the other women found themselves raped, treated poorly, and then having to submit to the sexual favors of the primitives. It was something that had torn her both physically and mentally, shaking her confidence even more, if that was even possible. She, like the rest, had watched the vids, and read the translations, and an inkling of an idea was forming, but would she be willing to submit it?

After her rescue, everybody had been kind, and absolutely all of them supported each other. Yet, even now her personal self-confidence was shattered. So she listened more than spoke, and still was more subservient, willing to defer to the older, wiser members, or the more outspoken ones. After all, to have come from their peaceful society, and have it destroyed as it was, and then to be treated as all them were, and to be at a point in one's life to where she hadn't really done anything, helped create what she was presently. Being the youngest adult didn't help either, so working with the young ones was for her very comforting. After all their demands were simple, and watching the antics during their time of play could, for a short time, take her away from her personal hell, and bring a smile. She so looked forward to those moments when, even for a brief time, she would forget. And knowing that there were many more sisters still in captivity, still having to live under that abuse, under that terror of not knowing, with no hope, probably would be the very thing that would make her brave enough to at least present it to someone, but no, never in one of those meetings. She'd be so embarrassed, and felt that the pressure would be just too great. But who would be the right one, which of the many who were here could she confide in? After all, that was the dilemma wasn't it?

CHAPTER FIFTEEN

K'jor stared outside as he stood in the entrance to his shelter. The storm had ended, but the suns held no heat, with the breeze that was blowing briskly, cutting one to pieces if touched by it. He needed to get out, get away from the enclosed feeling that the shelter brought him. Shaking his head he could only stare, not truly wanting to face that wind. It was cold enough right here where the winds would only touch him now and then. Looking around the compound there was absolutely no movement. He suspected that any who may have ventured out because of the promise that the suns gave, changed their minds very quickly and headed back in. He knew that he'd be doing the same thing shortly. Going back to the warmth of the roaring fire, he knew that his supply of firewood would have to be replenished. Sighing, and shrugging he turned and went back inside. Maybe later it would warm a little, and it would be a better time to venture out. Sitting once again in his chair his mind drifted back once again to the beginnings of all of this.

K'jor worked his way back to the point where he had fallen through the veil and could see the ashes of his cold fire pit. Standing around it were the others he was to meet. It had surprised him that so much time had passed. But it must have since the proof was right there in front of him. Knowing that they couldn't see him, he first smiled, and then called out to them. He saw them jump in surprise, and S'lon asked. "K'jor, is that you? Are you now a spirit? Has this land claimed you also?"

So he *was* invisible to them, but as far as he knew he had not passed into the spirit world. Nothing felt different, and even though when he had fallen . . . fallen, maybe that was the answer. Could it be that when he had fallen that he had passed into the spirit world? After all, when one normally did that, they did not come back and report what it was like. It could be that it was just like being alive. But, that didn't make sense to him. He hadn't eaten in a while and his body was beginning to complain. He had taken a couple of nature calls, so he had to be alive. "No S'lon, I'm quite alive and well." Because of the shock and unconsciousness when he had fallen through to where he presently was, he really wasn't sure if he wanted to try it again. But there was nothing to hold him here so gathering the courage he stepped towards the fire expecting to be laid out like he had been, but instead it was an easy passage, and he was before them. The four that had been looking for him jumped when he appeared out of a solid hillside. In fact he could see a little fear in their eyes.

"Is that really you, K'jor?" S'lon's voice quivered a little. "Or are you some spirit here to fool us into believing that you are and are planning to lead us to our deaths, to our passing into the spirit realm?"

Looking over himself, he could see nothing that would make his warriors think this, so he shrugged before speaking. "No, as far as I know I'm exactly as I appear before you."

"If that's so, have you now joined the priests and can touch beyond the veil? Because I, we have never seen anybody just appear out of a solid hillside, or in the air as you just did."

"Well, L'sum, it is me." He trailed off partially distracted. Why was it so easy to pass back to the campsite, while going the other way had knocked him out? Then he remembered what had started this whole investigation and wondered if beyond that wall lay the answers. He thought that the male and female that his warriors had killed here might be from beyond that wall. But why would they have been out where they were found? He was finding that he was developing more questions than answering them. Yet, if these two were out here, then they probably had a way to pass back through this veil and not be harmed.

S'lon could see that K'jor was deep in thought and signaled the rest not to speak, letting K'jor think through whatever it was. He saw him look at him with a smile and so S'lon asked, "What have you figured out?"

"Look, I'll tell you on the way back to camp. We need to mark a trail so that we can get back here, and the trail must be easily followed. I found that out here it, even for one as experienced as we, is easy to get turned around. We need to come back to this exact place. Let's go, and all of you remember this place well."

So, as he requested, they marked a trail well, one that would remain through the changing times. They had need of returning to the hunting, to the preparing of the meat and hides; the cold season was almost upon them.

* * *

Sara found that she finally was able to stay awake longer than just a few minutes, and that she wasn't shaking every time she tried to do anything. She knew that finally she was on the road to recovery, but as close to death, and for the length of time of her illness, her body would take a long time to completely heal, and it would probably be longer before she gained back the weight that she had lost. At least she was coherent, even though through the time of her illness she could really remember very little to none of it. But that marking left where only she would see it, only she would recognize, burned deeply in her soul. Someone from the scouting unit had survived and had escaped, had returned here, and probably was responsible for her recovery. And even though the hope she felt was very small, it was more than she had before this revelation. This meant that there was a possibility that her brother had survived, had escaped with the teams, and that further meant that they would be trying to find a way to defeat the primitives. She didn't know if she would live to see how it would end, but at least she now knew.

She still didn't have the strength to do more than sit, so other than the trips to the pot to take care of nature calls, she remained on her sleeping mat. One time while shifting to a more comfortable position she knocked something loose that fell between her and the wall. It had happened when one of the primitives, one of the healers she thought, had been in the shelter. He had had his back to her at the moment that whatever it was had fallen, so was unaware of the object. She quickly threw the covering over it, although from the brief glance that she had, it probably wouldn't have drawn any attention by the primitive anyway. It appeared to be a small leather pouch, and similar enough in construction to have been made by the primitives, in other words something very common to them, thusly unimportant. She watched and listened, but said nothing, and eventually he left, leaving the three of them alone once again. At this point she didn't want either Beth or Barbara to know anything about what she had discovered. She didn't know if they could be silent about it or not. So she had to keep it to herself for now. Later that might change. So she let the two know that she was going to lie down for a little while, and that they could continue to do whatever it was that they had been, that this visit by the healer had tired her once again.

There was some truth to her final statement, since it really had – but not to the point of needing to sleep again. To tell the truth, that would be happening very soon anyway. She had to admit that it was very frustrating to only last a very short time before she needed to sleep. So she lay down and turned her body towards the wall, slowly brought the bag up to where she could see its contents, and almost gasped when she saw what the items were. What was in here absolutely confirmed to her that someone from the scouting unit indeed had checked in.

* * *

As fate would have it, Shellian was on shift when Sara found the bag. She smiled, but remained silent. She knew that when Sara would have a chance she would check out the contents of that small insignificant ordinary bag and know, absolutely know where it came from. Soon now, very soon, they would be in communications with her, and with her knowledge, and abilities, maybe some additional insight could be found, and they would be able to find a solution that would lead to the end of this reign of terror that the primitives had brought down upon them. And, of course, update Sara on the truth and why the women of the cities that had been captured, could not become pregnant by the warriors. It would be a small consolation to what the women had to endure, but with the knowledge that they wouldn't be carrying the offspring of the warriors, they could at least eliminate one fear.

Saige was taking a break in the meeting room, staring out of the windows; he was so hoping that they would have something by now. Some inkling of an idea, something they could begin to work with, to plan, to be able to not only end this reign of terror and destruction, but to save the remaining captives. He knew that each day they delayed, more of their people died. It was much too cold to go and walk the small hidden valley, and he could see some light snow falling anyway. But watching it and sitting did not relieve his restlessness, his frustration. They were heading for the end of the second winter here in the Sacred Mountains, and he felt guilty that they were well and free when so many of their people were not. Turning when he heard someone enter the room he could see that Shellian must have just finished her shift. She was carrying her daughter who was just content to be in her mother's arms. Smiling a loving smile at the child, that just lit her up, Saige smiled. He knew that very shortly, anytime now, that he would be doing very much the same thing with their twins. Smiling, as he watched the interaction between the two of them he said. "Shell', how are the two of you doing today?"

Looking up at her brother, she said. "We are doing quite well, aren't we little Sam'." She reached down and tickled her daughter and got a giggle from her baby. "You know that conversation we had a long time ago."

"Which one? We've had so many."

"True. But where you were asking why a woman would go through what she does in child birth, and then most of the time repeats it – that one."

Nodding his head he took a deep breath, and let it out slowly. The first time that had come up was back last winter when they were still in the cave just trying to survive, before everything fell even farther apart. "Yes, I do remember, but why bring that up now? Of course I know that other than my mate Seirra, all of you have now gone through labor, and all of you have healthy children, well, except for Sorrel, but she was unconscious through her delivery, so I don't know if that counts. Although she's well on her way to a second child, and I hope this one survives. She at least deserves that."

"Yes, yes she does. We came so close to losing her, and what a double tragedy that would have been. Anyway, if you remember what I said then, it went something about being an observer and not a participant, so I could pass on only what I had observed. Well, I've been through it all now, and even with the drugs it wasn't easy. But I'd do it all over again to hold her and love her like I do. So I think I understand it so much more now. And, I think that's why women have more than one child. We all enjoy the closeness with our men, and the physicality of it all. And then when we get pregnant, it's all wonder and awe, as we feel that child growing inside of us.

Then we begin to want to know who this new person is. How will they look, will they be healthy, what will they be like, and so many other things. So I think that now it all makes so much more sense. Anyway, this really wasn't what I was going to talk to you about. I'm just about ready to head for my apartment for some down time, and to enjoy some time with her before I have to go back and continue on the many projects we have. I just want to let you know that Sara found and opened the leather pouch. So she knows. But from what I can see, she's much too weak to be of any assistance yet. But, at least she is aware, and we are one step closer to finding a solution."

"That's great news sis. I've been restless and a little down thinking about how long we've been here, and thinking about how little we've actually been able to move towards finding a solution to this, and thanks for that other update. With Seirra just about to go into labor, I have been worried sick. Especially when we found out she's carrying twins. So I guess, as you know, when she does, you'll have the leadership until afterwards."

"Yeah, I guess in some ways that's true. But you have to remember that we've actually accomplished a lot. Contacted the cities, rescued those eight from one of the tribes, reestablished the travelers, and learned about our true past. That, in my mind, is quite a lot. And yes I know that we've yet to come up with a solution on stopping the primitives and their alliance, but I'm sure in time we will. Anyway, that's all I have, so I'll catch you later, bro. I need some downtime and some mother time." She smiled at him, turned and left. He watched her leave and once again was alone with his thoughts.

Seirra was sitting in the cafeteria, being quite uncomfortable, and quite nervous. Her time was approaching rapidly, and she'd been having some Braxton-Hicks, false labor, and it seemed like her twins were having a boxing match inside of her. She had dropped recently also, another sign of her impending labor. This was no fun at all, and while she was ready for this to be over, she wasn't ready for this to be over. At this time the cafeteria was empty and she was by herself, and with her mood, not that it was bad, she was happy that it was that way. No, her mood was more introspective and nervous, and she just wasn't in the mood for company at this moment, even Saige's. She looked up when she heard the doors swing open, and watched as Joci entered, who then saw her sitting there, stopped for a moment undecided, and then turned to leave. Smiling Seirra said, "Joci, you don't have to go. If you wanted to get something in here, please do."

Turning around and looking at Seirra, Joci replied, "Are you sure? You looked like you wanted to be alone, and I, ah, I don't want to bother you or anyone really."

"No, no Joci, it's all right." Then waving her arms she continued, "I mean, look at all of this space. We probably could have everybody from the complex in here and all of us still could be alone. So, you won't be bothering me at all." Seirra could tell that Joci had, had a very hard time of it. In some ways she reminded her of herself back in the cave when she wasn't very sure of herself. Although she suspected that it was much worse for Joci, since she had gone through the nightmare, before she had a chance to learn who she was, and the results would be anything but positive.

Joci decided to go ahead and stay. She was both a little hungry and thirsty, and there were some juices here that she really liked. So heading into the kitchen area, she got a roll with some spread, and filled a glass with the juice. Once finished she came back out into the eating area and undecided stopped a moment. She could see that Seirra was having a hard time with her pregnancy at this moment, and she could sense the worry. Coming to a decision, she sat at the same table across from Seirra, but further down at this moment. She still wasn't sure if the idea that had been forming was worth telling anyone. So for a short time she was quiet and just ate the roll and sipped the juice, "Seirra?"

While not looking over at her Seirra answered, "Yes Joci?" She continued to concentrate on the sensations from her own body, and she felt that things were beginning to move rapidly to a conclusion that she couldn't stop.

Joci slid down closer so that she would be across from her before speaking. "You really don't look like this is any fun." She paused not quite knowing how to continue, and then briefly looked away before facing her again. "You know how Saige and Shellian said, that if anybody had an idea about how to get the advantage on the primitives, to let them know. Well, I've had . . ." But before she could say any more she saw a surprised look on Seirra and with slight alarm asked, "What's wrong?" She could see Seirra both staring out in the distance and then looking down.

"Oh no! No, not now! Oh my, I think my water broke."

Looking under the table quickly, Joci could see that the pants that Seirra was wearing appeared to be wet. Alarmed and not sure what to do she made a decision, got up and came around to help her. "Here, let me help you down to the infirmary, I think it's time." She could see the shocked look on her face as well as some fear. It was time and from now until she held the new lives, her body would take over, giving her no choice.

"Saige, Saige, please report to the infirmary, your mate has gone into labor." The intercom then repeated the message. He had still been in the meeting room, and at first because of his thoughts had missed the alert. When it finally penetrated he caught his breath, got up and headed for the infirmary at a rapid pace.

With the message going out over the intercom, everyone in the facility was aware that two new lives were about to enter the world. Sorrel, looking down at her growing abdomen, and being in her late second to early third-third, knew that soon she would be the next. Although, even though she had no memory of it, she had been the first. Sorrel knew that Shellian, with Stone's help, would keep things moving. She suspected that it would be at least eighteen hours before it would be over, and to have your first labor be twins, it had to be scaring Seirra to death.

Joci, after getting Seirra to the infirmary, slowly walked back to the cafeteria. Once there she sat back down, and finished her roll and now warm juice. *Darn, I was just about to tell her my idea. Now what can I do? I felt that she was the only one I could talk to.* She felt miserable and afraid to say anything at all, and her one chance was now gone. *Well, maybe, just maybe, my idea isn't that good anyway.* Sighing, she took her dirty dishes to the recycler, and headed back to the education and daycare area. Again she really enjoyed working here, at least for now.

* * *

K'jor continued his view into the past – "Where were you? And why is it that you want to return?" S'lon asked, as he paced by the campfire. It was evening and the day's hunting had been complete. It had been a very busy day, and the carcasses had been stripped and the meat was drying on racks over the smoky fire. The females were working the hides so that they could be cured and then prepared for the return trip back to the clan home.

"Look, I don't understand all of it yet, but those two had to have come from somewhere, and that somewhere had to be where I was – although I don't understand where I was at all. Like you, I swore that I had crossed over, and what I saw when I entered that canyon seemed to confirm it to me, but it just didn't seem right. If I had crossed over, then where were the ones who had passed before us? Although when seeing a clan home, and the tribe portable shelters, I felt that I had. Yet the place had a silence upon it, a feeling of long abandonment, and a place where there had been no one in a very long time. And if I indeed had passed over, there should have been no way for me to return to this world, yet I stand before you." Smiling as he stood he said, "I guess that even this could be an illusion, something to test me, to find where I truly belong. But I don't think so. There is something deeper going on, and I want to know what it is. I want to know the answers to these questions that are burning in my mind."

"I can understand that K'jor, but that is a place of desolation, there is nothing there for us, no way for any of us to live. We get nothing from it, and it leads us into the spirit world if we go there. So why not just let it lie. We have enough going on with keeping our people fed, and safe from attack."

"I cannot answer that specifically, but there is something that is drawing me there, a strength of purpose that says that there are some important answers hidden there in those desolate lands. And I'm being driven to find out what that is." Turning around and smiling at S'lon, K'jor continued, "Now I'm not going to put our duty behind me to seek this out. We will do what we are supposed to do here, return to our home, and then the next season come here a little earlier to pursue these riddles, and I promise you, old friend, that if there are no answers next time, I will let it go away as the dust disappears with the wind."

K'jor, as he continued to look back, wondered if he'd been wrong. These strangers were definitely not warriors, but there appeared to be something, and he couldn't quite figure it out. T'som had informed him that the one female they were all interested in, was slowly, very slowly mind you, healing. From what could be observed by the healers their best estimate for her recovery could easily fall to the middle of the season of greening. At least these "travelers" seemed to live up to the old records – but why so few? Yes, they had explained why, but ever suspicious, he wasn't sure, and the way they left, leaving no sign behind. It led one to believe that they could be sorcerers themselves. Yet he had spoken with them, and they appeared to be no different. A little smaller in build yes, but even within the clan he could find ones who were built similarly. And as the records stated their skills in healing were superior to their own. But when they were observed, it did not appear to be so. But the results were before their eyes. One who was close, so very close to passing over, was now recovering.

He found that he was going in circles, finding no answers, and actually developing more questions. *Guess I'd better just stay with what I know, and it's becoming obvious that, that's not a lot.* It had been an unbelievable three cycles of the seasons and with the season of cold ending soon, and the preparations for a new greening season he knew it wouldn't be long before they would be searching for more of the hidden lairs. Here in the northeastern foothills they were only a few days travel from the Sacred Mountains, and the point where the travelers had camped. Even though everything would have been wiped out since they had disappeared, supposedly going back to their homes beyond the mountains, he wanted to see for himself exactly where this place was. Again the way they left had made no sense, and the reports had stated that the only way into and out of the area of the campsite had been towards the ones who were watching. There was supposed to be no other way out of that area. And that bothered him also.

As a warrior you never camped where you had only one exit. It was dangerous to not leave yourself more than one way of escape – since one never knew when they would be attacked by a rival tribe or clan, and if the forces attacking could overwhelm their camp – so additional exits could easily be the difference between surviving or dying. Restless, and not just because of having to remain inside because of the severity of the season of cold, he paced his shelter, and every once in a while would stand just outside until the cold winds would force him back inside. This one, even with it being one of the worst, had been tough for him because of the events that seemed to be taking place, unseen, behind, and invisible, leading to a complete and unknown outcome. It was as if the gods were now playing games of chance, and they were the ones in the prize pot to be used as they pleased. Again had he done right to attack and destroy these lairs, these magicians and sorcerers? And why now, yes why had these travelers who had been gone for generations arrive while the united clans and tribes were seeking out and destroying these lairs? Was it all coincidence, or was there a greater plan? And if these lairs were of the gods, why did these not speak their tongue? Ah, but then that wasn't necessarily true, now was it. After all this female – a female of all things – spoke their tongue. So she had to have been someone of high importance . . . But a female?

All of it was becoming more complicated, and as time continued to move, the less he understood. At the beginning it had appeared to be so simple, locate the lairs, bring about their fall, and take slaves, and add to the breeding herds. And all of it was very easy to accomplish. These lairs fell easily, the people within were captured and spread among the alliance, as tradition, well, there never had been an alliance before, but even though that was so, they still abided by the traditions, and laws, and had not deviated. All felt good about their successes, and all felt that with the increase in both slaves, and the breeding herds that their strength and size would increase. Then these strange ones, these magicians began to die, and most did, and what followed could not be believed, let alone understood. In fact if any had suggested such a thing he would have been laughed at and told to go and create other fantasies for their pleasure. And the proof that this was true lay before him right here. Absolutely none of the females from these lairs were carrying. It was noted that they bled as their own females proving that they could carry, but any and all warriors who bred with these females, and he knew that all had tried, never were successful in getting any of these females to carry. They were being defeated by females. Were they that weak, or were these females that strong?

At first it was considered a fluke, and the attempts increased. Many of these new females, like the males perished, showing them that these were not a strong people. Again not a surprise, considering how easily they had been conquered, and their lairs destroyed, but to have the power to prevent the carrying showed a power and strength that was completely unknown, and beyond their comprehension.

He'd been standing at his entrance when the suns were briefly obscured by clouds. Looking up he could see that another storm was rolling in, and the winds had picked up considerably, and the temperatures were dropping rapidly. Shaking his head he thought, *another storm, when will they end? Already this season seems to be intolerable, too long, and much too cold.* He turned a reentered his shelter, and went over to the fire, and added another log. It was going to be another very long day.

* * *

"The last word that we've received from the infirmary is that Seirra is still in labor." It had been eighteen hours ago when it had started, and no recent word had come forth to update them. Shellian, who was the last to go through labor felt for her, but she knew that it was a part of life. She looked around the table and with Stone sitting on her right, was there as the second, "We'll be continuing these early day meetings, even if they are short, until either we come up with a viable plan, or we get something useful from the cities, and as you all know, so far that hasn't happened." She turned towards Joci, and said, "You usually don't get a chance to come to these too often. We seem to have you taking care of the children, and honestly that's not fair to you."

Embarrassed by being singled out, at first she mumbled something, kind of ducking her head. When she realized that she hadn't been understood she said quietly, "Thank you, but I really love taking care of the children, and being so young in comparison to all of you, what could I add?"

Smiling, Shellian said, "Now don't feel like you have nothing to contribute. You have seen, and experienced, and not all of it fun or nice, much of what the rest of your city experienced. You've suffered at the hands of the primitives as the other women did. And I'm sure for one as young as you are, a teenager, that to be treated that way had to be devastating, to say the least. But you're smart, and I've seen that you observe what is happening around you. So, no matter what you think, your opinion, your input is just as important as anybody else here. So if you have something to say, something to contribute, please do. Since you've monitored these meetings, and I'm sure with the children, that you were distracted many times, you know what we've got to accomplish. So if you do come up with something, please let one of us know."

Shellian, seems so strong, so in charge, how can I even say anything to her, I'd be so embarrassed. She's one of the leaders, and I'm nobody, just a kid taking care of their children. I thought about, so many times, how it would be to be a part of the grownup world, and I knew that I'd be there soon. I liked to pretend that I was. What can I say? She looked up at Shellian who was waiting patiently for a response, and could feel the pressure building, and felt her face flush, which just made things worse. Then nodding her head she said, "Okay, if I think of something, I'll pass it on." The rest of the meeting was a blur, and she barely remembered any of it. All of them were heading for the kitchen for the morning meal, and she had dragged her feet so that she would be the last to arrive. *Why didn't I say something?* She didn't have an answer for that. But why would anyone consider her idea worth anything at all?

As she entered the cafeteria, she could hear the chatter of the many voices, but felt that while the chatter sounded happy, how could it be that way? All of them had suffered so much, and others were still suffering. It just didn't seem right. With her head down she pushed through the double swinging doors, and tried to put on a smile, even if in her soul she didn't feel that way. Then over the PA system came the announcement that two new lives had entered the world, and that the mother and father were doing okay as were the babies. This brought a cheer from the ones there. It was always good news when the birthings were successful. There were so many things that could go wrong, and every one that avoided those complications was great news. Plus, with their numbers being so small, to lose any was unthinkable. Joci had to admit that this lifted her mood a little. She had been there at the beginning when labor was just starting, and had helped Seirra down the hall to the infirmary. So maybe she was worth something after all. She could hear the chatter now turning towards babies and motherhood, and the joys and challenges that this brings. Again all she could do was smile, even though the smile was a sad one. Once again she felt that she was on the outside, not part of what was going on. She almost turned around and left, and if her stomach hadn't complained she probably would have. She felt that at this moment, especially after that embarrassment in the meeting, that she wanted to be by herself, but knew that it would be impossible. So after pausing, and being unsure, she reached a decision and went on in, grabbed some food, sat down, and listened to the happy banter that filled the room.

Saige, looking down at a sleeping Seirra, smiled. It was a tired smile, as he hadn't slept through the time of her labor and the delivery of their son and daughter. The girl had been born first so was technically the older one, but that was only by a few minutes. But he could see that there would be a point where the daughter would be pointedly telling her brother that she was the oldest, and definitely the one in charge. They were beautiful, these wrinkled, small lives that were now sleeping contentedly in their small beds, wrapped tightly in the birthing blankets. He had to admit that it was almost impossible to take his eyes off of them. "I wonder what the future has in store for the two of you." He whispered softly. With the work that Seirra had done, and labor was a very good term for it, she needed to sleep as much as she could right now. Again he looked down on her with a deep love in his heart only wanting to protect her, and the two new lives with his entire being.

Saar and Jas, smiled at the scene. Both were tired even though they had worked shifts through Seirra's labor. It was always great when the outcome was positive. *Two new healthy lives, with the mother surviving, and no complications, not that Seirra isn't going to hurt for a while, because she is, it's always a great outcome*, Saar thought. "Saige," Saar said. "Look, there's an exam table right there. So if you want to go ahead and use it to catch some sleep yourself, please do. I can tell by looking at you that you're about ready to drop, you're dead on your feet." He could see that Saige was about to say, that he was alright, but interrupted him before he could say anything. "Look I'm the doctor here, and while you and your sister may be in charge of everything else, I'm the one who's responsible for everybody's well-being, and health, so what I say overrides anything you might want to say here. Look, this place was built to handle more than all that we have here at this moment, so just take advantage of it, pull over that table, and get some rest. We'll pull the curtain and no one will be the wiser that the two of you are here."

Shrugging, Saige could find no arguments to counter, and he really hadn't wanted to leave Seirra here by herself. He knew from what his sister had told him that soon the new lives would be waking hungry looking for a meal, and he wanted to be there to help as much as he could. Taking a deep tired breath he said, "Okay doc, you've convinced me." The two of them rolled the exam table into the same space that Seirra occupied, and they made a bed, he climbed in, and with one last look closed his eyes, and was shortly out.

Turning to Jas, Saar said, "Look, you pulled that last shift, go get some sleep yourself. I was here at the end to help with the deliveries, so am in a little better shape that you. Besides, even here, we've got paperwork to keep up on." Then smiling he looked over at the two babies and said, "Welcome to this world Saharra and Seth."

* * *

"What's that sound?" Shellian asked. She was in the security office with Seve on their shift, and none of the rotating images included the long hallway at this moment. So she got up and headed out into the corridor to look. She froze for a moment, turned and motioned for Seve to join her. Perplexed, he got up and joined her and saw Judd going up and down the hallway on some type of two wheeled contraption. He came up to them and stopped. "What's this thing?" she asked.

Smiling at the two of them Judd stated, "It's what is called a personal glider, at least that's what it says it is. I have to admit that it's fun and it makes it so much easier to get from one place to another in this facility." Stepping off and letting go of the handle, it just stood there.

"How does it do that? I mean with just the two wheels, you'd expect it to fall over." Seve exclaimed.

"True, but it's in its construction, and before any of you ask, the plans for this were in the replicator computer. Thought I would try and make one and see how it worked. I can produce enough for all of the adults that are here. None of the children are old enough or big enough to use one anyway. And they're easy to use, and not much of a learning curve. It's almost natural. Of course, they can only be used on solid surfaces such as these hallways, and if there were roadways or sidewalks they'd be good there also. But it sure speeds up moving around."

Smiling and shaking her head, Shellian asked, "Okay Judd, what else is in that computer that we don't know about? I mean, you used to deal with these computers back in your city, are you sure these plans weren't there?"

"No, and that's surprising. I mean, something like this would've been great to move about the city. Yet, there was no mention of these, and some of that other stuff that we've begun to use. I really wonder why so much of this was excluded from the city computers. They must have had some reason for doing it." Tipping his head to one side before continuing, "Oh well, I guess we'll really never know why. These things will fit through the doors and can be charged right then and there. I'm trying to determine right now, how long a charge will last. So I'll be running up and down the hallways and different sections until this thing dies and needs a recharge." He climbed back up on the glider, grabbed the handle, flipped or pushed a switch, leaned forward a little, and off he went.

Seve and Shellian looked at each other, and went back into the security office. "You know that's a good question." Seve said.

"Good question? What do you mean Seve?"

"Oh the one that Judd just presented us with. The one about what wasn't in the computers at the cities. Why hold back information?"

"You're right, why hold back the information? I guess we could speculate, but so far there's been nothing in these computers on that subject, and maybe it's because we've not been looking. Hmmm, it's something to think about." She sighed and said, "I guess our fun is over, now back to monitoring everything."

* * *

"What's that?" Staven asked.

Laughing Sabryn replied, "That's music silly."

"Oh, I know its music, but we've had none of that since we were back in our own city. And it seems to be coming over the PA system. That's what I meant."

"I guess that's quite true, and I guess I wasn't quite thinking about it that way. I just thought it was nice to hear it again. And until it started playing, I hadn't realized how much I've missed it." She sighed as she watched the monitors, and listened to the chatter over the circuits. Fortunately today there had been very little traffic directed at the Alpha, so it was more just watching the monitors and recordings being made from the many sensors that had been planted by the two teams, plus continuing to search with the "eyes-in-the-skies", to watch for any new movement of the primitives. So it was enough to keep one very busy when they were on shift at the security office. "Now that I think about it, you're right. How come we hear it this way?"

"Ah, I bet Judd has something to do with it. We've had all sorts of gadgets and things we never knew existed until he discovered them in that replicator computer. Not that this music came from there. But none of us had been trained in that way. So I guess in many ways it really is nice that he happened to be with that tribe we raided. Think of the difficulty it would have been to move around like we did. Now I can't see how we can live without this stuff. Yet, the irony is, that we were doing just that, and doing just fine." Shaking his head and smiling, Staven continued, "I'll never understand us let alone the primitives. It seems like every new thing he discovers becomes something we can't do without. And now I think he figured this out, so I suspect that it will just be one more thing that we would miss if he shuts it down. Although, I have to admit that it's something like I've never heard" Hearing someone at the door, he turned around and said, "And speak of the devil, so Judd, are you responsible for our entertainment?"

Smiling, as he leaned in the doorway, he said, "Yes, rather nice isn't it? I was doing a check on the system for the whole facility, and came across this routine, and decided to see what it would do. The neat thing about it is that it will play different music styles each day. I guess they knew that not everybody likes all kinds of music, so it's set to vary the music it plays, and if someone uses the intercom, then it will mute. Plus it has the ability to allow any specific room or area to change or mute it exclusive to them." He came further into the office, went over to the system computer, and said, "Here, let me show you. I think that the way it is set, that at night it plays soft slow moving music, but if one was on shift here, it proba- bly would put you to sleep, thusly the variability built in so that you here could put on something more upbeat." With the two watching he demonstrated exactly how to do it. Staven and Sabryn looked at each other and then back at Judd.

Then together they said, "Wow! That's easy," they both laughed and Staven said, "I wonder why we didn't figure this out. When you just showed us, there is nothing to it."

"True, but until I activated it from the main, it wasn't available. Okay, I know it's over 2000 annuals old, but enjoy, and have fun with it. I've still a lot to figure out, and this is fun." With that he was back out the door and heading down the hallway out of sight.

Again they looked at each other and then back at the screen, "What a find," was all that Staven said. Sabryn just nodded her head in agreement. It really was nice to hear music again even if it was a bit ancient.

* * *

Sara could feel her strength slowing coming back. But it was so frustrating to be this weak. She was lucky if she remained awake and moving for more than an hour. She continued to hoard and hide that small leather bag, and in a sense was thankful for the illness that had almost taken her life. At least she and the two, who were with her, had avoided having sex with the primitive males. The treatment was rough and painful, and uncaring. But she regretted her condition when the scouts had shown up. *But how?* When she had been with the unit they had never approached a tribe or clan, let alone enter one. Yes, she had been away from it for quite a few annuals, but had, from time to time, checked in on her brother, and as far as she could see, their methods had changed very little. At least, she hoped that maybe her brother had been one of the lucky ones. Although from the way their city was attacked, she was very surprised by the little gift, and the placing of the symbol, that any had escaped.

At this point she wasn't sure if she really wanted to bring Beth and Barbara into the loop. Even though they couldn't speak the language of the primitives, there could always be some way that they could give up the information. So now she tried to come up with some method to begin to make contact and find out what had been happening – from no hope, to at least a glimmer. Anytime she felt the overwhelming depression and hopelessness strike her, she would lie down and stare at that symbol, knowing that it was real, and that it had been placed there for her eyes only. To let her know, and she knew that this knowledge was precious to her, and even though she wasn't letting it go beyond her, there was a good chance that it would be critical to the rest who were now spread among the primitives having to submit to their wills and whims. So how was she going to go about it? With it as quiet as it was in this shelter, anything she might say would be overheard. In the end, she might not have any choice, she, no matter what the possible outcome, may have to inform these two women. Were they strong enough? Inwardly she shuddered with the thought of informing them, only to have it revealed to their captors, and abusers. It was a dilemma she'd have to solve soon. But for now she'd bide her time, really study these two women, and hope that the answer would present itself to her soon.

* * *

Joci sat by herself in the cafeteria. She didn't want to go back to the dorm where she could possibly run into one of the other women, not that any of them would bother her. After all, they all respected the privacy of the others. It had been something that had become stronger after their capture and rescue. But at this moment the quiet and loneliness here was what she wanted, and felt that she needed. Taking a deep breath, she folded her arms on the table and placed her head down on them. She found that she was having real difficulty coming to terms with what had happened to her, and as each day passed, it weighed heavily on her. She felt helpless against this internal struggle, and the shame she felt for having to submit that way to the primitives. She realized logically, that she shouldn't feel this way, and she was far from alone from this abuse. But knowing that still didn't prevent what she was feeling. She truly felt worthless, and if the children hadn't cheered her, a number of times, she thought that she would have reached the point of total withdrawal into herself – not a good thing at all.

In a sense she could sense that she wanted revenge against all of the ones who had abused her, and maybe if she could get brave enough to, at least, confide in someone her idea, that it might actually help her heal, and she wanted so desperately to heal, to feel normal again. But at this moment she felt that this was something that was close to impossible. Yet, when she looked and listened to these other women who had suffered in exactly the same way, they seemed to be moving on, why couldn't she? Well, if she had an answer, then she probably would be healing, would be moving on. It could be that one of the reasons was her age. She was the youngest by many annuals, and truly had no peers to speak to, to confide in, and talk things out, and so far, other than Seirra, she felt no draw to any of them. Seirra, so close that day, to being able to pass along her idea, so close to finding someone to confide in and she went into labor, and hadn't been around since. She felt like crying, and could feel the tightness in her throat and chest as she fought back the tears just waiting to flow.

She felt someone lay a hand on her shoulder. It was a gentle touch and completely unexpected. At first because it was a surprise she tightened up and felt the reaction from the one who had touched her. She was almost afraid to look up for fear of the tears that lay just below the surface. So carefully she lifted her head and looked up to see Judd standing over her with a very concerned look on his face. He didn't say anything, just beckoned her to stand, which she slowly did. Again without a word he signaled her to come to him, and when she did he hugged her. At first she resisted, but as the moments passed relaxed, put her head on his shoulder and let the tears flow. With great sobs she just cried it out; with him remaining silent until he could tell that the tears were subsiding. Still he continued to hold her, and she knew that honestly, it was the right thing to do. Finally drained emotionally she pulled back slightly and wiped her red rimmed eyes. She now felt exhausted and completely drained, and again without a word he helped her down the hallway to the entrance of the women's dorm, saying, "I think that getting some rest right now will help tremendously, so please try. And if you need to talk about anything, I'm here. And while I'm not your grandfather, I'm old enough to be, so consider me as a substitute."

She was about to say something, but he put his fingers to her lips, and just shook his head. He pointed to the closed door, reached down, and opened it, and with a gentle push sent her in the direction that she needed to go.

As the door closed he stood there silently for a few moments, and headed back to the cafeteria to get that coffee, *yes, that coffee, probably the greatest discovery of this place.* He'd been watching Joci for quite a while, even back when they were still under the control of the primitives, and he had worried about her then. Heck, he had to admit that he had worried about all of them at that time. And he had to admit that what he felt and saw left him hopeless. After all they had been hidden from the primitives for such a long time, so long in fact that none of them ever considered the primitives a threat. Yet, with what had been transpiring it was very obvious that they had been wrong, very wrong. So for their over confidence and their under estimating of the primitives, they, all of them, were paying a heavy price. And it could see in Joci that it was something that she did not know how to handle, how to cope or deal with what had happened to her. He could tell that it was tearing her up inside, but she continued to put forth a front that everything was okay. But he knew better. But how to reach her, how to get beyond those barriers that she was throwing up?

He was a male, a man, and right now this could be a very real problem. So when he had entered that cafeteria, like he was doing now, and saw her there, he knew that he had to reach out to her, or she might just break down. So he had touched her, and invited her into his arms so that she could, as what had transpired, cry it out. And with this first break in her armor, could he continue to build from there? When he stated that he could substitute as her grandfather, he'd meant it. In a way it would be something that would help him also. He had had young grandchildren, three actually, and all of them had been boys, which he had to admit that he was grateful for at this moment. If they had been granddaughters he didn't know what he would have done, knowing what happened to the women once the primitives got them. His family had always produced more boys and girls, so he had to admit that while he loved his grandchildren, he had longed for a granddaughter. So maybe they could help each other.

Grabbing a cup of coffee, he sat at one of the tables and continued to think. *I've got to keep this going. What is it that young girls, well young in comparison to me anyway, like?* It was a good question. He knew that as they reached the age that Joci was at, they were trying to put childhood behind them. He knew that girls seemed to push leaving home much quicker than boys did. Why this was so, he really didn't know. But he did know that whatever was their favorite thing, that many times this would continue into adulthood, and for some all of their lives. Looking back in his mind's eye he tried to remember what he witnessed when he had been around little girls, and ones who were a bit older. He continued to sit and think, and realized that as he tried to drink his coffee, that the cup was empty, so he got up to refill it, stopped a moment, smiled, and then refilled his cup. He knew what he needed to do. It had come out of nowhere, but as he had looked back, he began to see one consistent thing in his mind. Taking the cup and as quickly as he could move and not spill the precious brown liquid, he headed down to what he considered his office and workspace. He had some work ahead of him.

* * *

Sara finally came to a decision. She realized that she would soon be able to communicate with their mysterious visitors by using sign language. So with care, and being sure that the primitives were not around, she joined the two by the small smoky fire, sat down cross legged, and leaned forward. She could see that the two were watching her intently and just waiting. She also knew that with the weakness that was in her body she had a very long way to go before she could even remain awake for more than a couple of hours, let alone recover. And when those couple of hours ended she could barely think, let alone move. *Well, this isn't solving anything.* Taking a deep breath, she still wasn't sure how to present what she knew, she looked at both of them and said, "I've got to get both of you to promise not to say anything if you see me doing something unusual, just ignore it as if nothing is happening. Because if the primitives even get any piece of this we will be in even more serious trouble than we are now, so when you see me do something out of the ordinary, just chalk it up to me being sick." She paused and looked closely at both of them. She knew that if this information, even as sketchy as it was, was passed on to the other captives that the primitives would eventually figure out what was happening and that would compromise not only her, but the teams that had entered the camps. "It is so important that if I don't get your promises, I can't help us survive. It will bring death down on all of us, not that this isn't a problem already, if the primitives even get a hint of this." Then shaking her head she thought, *not that there's been any way to avoid that since we've become captives to these people. Of course one could be closer than the other, but it can only happen once.* There had been way too much death as it was, and she was proof that this aspect was far from over. She suspected that others probably had died and had been added to the growing grave yard during the time of her illness.

She waited and said nothing, but watched the two. She'd rather remain silent if there was a chance that she wouldn't be able to trust either one or both. In a way she could tell that these women were frightened, and that while they had appreciated the respite from the breeding herds, and all by accident, it was obvious to Sara that they were beat down, defeated, and without hope. So could she trust them at all, but what choice did she have? After all, what did she have to offer other than a little hope, and little was better than none. It could be something they could grab onto, and maybe change their view of the future from none, being black without form, to maybe a little gray with a slight definition. She also knew that soon she would begin conversations with their head priest. Although what it could be about, she had no real idea. So she would, at least in the beginning, remain silent as is demanded of their females, and maybe slightly aloof, but not so much to bring discipline down upon her. Maybe she'd finally begin to understand some things, and again with as much sex that was going on with the primitives, why were none of the city women pregnant?

CHAPTER SIXTEEN

Even though he was drug out from too little sleep, and the constant demands of the twins, it was his shift in the security office. Seirra would be excused from any assignments for at least a month. He had to admit that when the two entered this world he was in awe of what he had witnessed. He hated to see his mate go through this, but knew that it is the way of life. He found that his love had deepened for her and had expanded to include their new children, ones that they now could put a face and personality to, which up to that time could only be anticipated and guessed. Yes, even though they were just babies, he had to admit that his daughter already had him wrapped around her little finger. He knew that he had heard that it was something common, but until he experienced himself, he truly did not believe it. Smiling, he had to admit that now he was one, a believer that is. If his shift remained quiet, it was going to be very hard to stay awake. As time had passed, and the Alpha was no longer new to the rest of the cities, the traffic had lessened considerably, and while they still maintained two in the security office, it was much simpler now. In fact at times it was almost leisurely.

His fellow companion on this shift was Jessi. They tried to rotate everybody through, continually mixing all of the members, so that all would have worked with each other. Jessi was lithe in build, and had naturally darker skin, with light brown to blonde hair that she kept in a ponytail which hung down past her shoulders. In many ways she reminded him of his sister, both being athletic, and both truly beautiful women. Yet, that was where the comparison ended. He figured some of what she was dealing with at this time had to do with what had happened to her during her time with the primitives. But, it could be that she was naturally quiet and reserved. It wasn't that she put herself above anyone, it just appeared that way. In fact, once one was around her for any length of time, they found that it was quite the opposite. He knew that the women they had rescued had not revealed much as of yet, and he understood that completely. After such a lengthy and traumatic experience, it would be only time that would help. She was only a little younger than he, and probably close to the same age as Seirra.

On this shift she ended up with the communications duty, with him monitoring the many cameras, and feeds, that were in place. This included the many small bugs that they had planted during their time as the travelers. Fortunately, for all of them, the cities included, it was still winter, and that meant that they were still safe from the primitives. Glancing briefly over he could see Jessi staring intently at the monitors that were on her side. "I just can't get over these views from above this world," she said to no one in particular.

"Yeah, know what you mean. We were quite shocked when we accidently discovered it. We had no idea at all that our ancestors could do this. And, as you know, that was only one of the many shocks and revelations this place had in store for us."

She turned towards him and asked, "Is it true that you fell into this valley and that's the way it was discovered?"

Laughing, and shaking his head in memory he replied, "Yup, it wasn't the best of ways to find something, but that's exactly what happened. I was fortunate that I lived to be able to tell the tale." One of the monitors caught his eye, and he caught his breath. It was the feed from inside that building where Sara was. And while he was the one who had planted a number of them throughout that clan, and a few within that particular building or shelter as the primitives called them, he had almost been embarrassed to realize that his placement was such that it allowed none of the women any privacy at all. Something that he had learned was very important to women. But there was no way to go back and change the positioning of the bugs. Sara was lying back down, but had opened the pouch and had placed the small transmitter-receiver in her ear. He knew, from an earlier recording that she had confronted the two women, but at this time had yet to get any answers or promises from them. So he knew that she would not be talking at this time, but instead be signing. He was sure that she was rusty, since it had been a very long time since she had need of it.

Taking a deep breath, he waited a moment, picked up the mic, and pressed the switch that would only activate that feed. He turned to Jessi, and said, "I'm about to talk with Sara, I need you to monitor all of this from your side. All of this is automatically recorded, but it's important to monitor it in real time." He keyed the mic and said, "Sara, if you can hear me, just nod your head. We've bugged the shelter, and are aware of what is transpiring." He waited and watched, and saw her nod slightly to confirm she had heard him. He could see that hope was beginning to show in her eyes, but she was trying to keep it from showing too much. "There's much we'd like to tell you, but there is much we need from you also. The images that we receive are sharp and clear, so if you don't get a positive answer from the two who are with you, then we'll deal with the use of signing from your part." He waited, and watched as she signed that she understood. It was done slowly, and with slight movements so as to not let them others know that she was in contact with anyone.

He could see as she did this that she did not appear to be rusty at all, and he asked why this was so. She signed back that it was a game that they had played in her household. It was something that her boys enjoyed doing, so it had become a household tradition that everybody would practice, and be very good at it, with games where one would try and fool another by subtle use of the signing. She then asked about her brother. Saige knew that eventually that question would arise, and he hoped it would have been later. Pausing, and not sure how to answer, he finally just gave up, and told her that he had died during their escape. He could see that this had hit her hard, but what else could he say? So before she asked the next obvious question he told her, that as far as her immediate family went, they knew nothing. He also passed on to her that the scouting unit had been decimated by the primitives, and only a small remnant survived. He could tell that as each of these facts were revealed to her, that it was as if she was being struck physically, and he could understand that reaction completely. He could tell that she was tiring rapidly, and said to her that until later after she had slept that they would talk again, saw the understanding in her eyes, and broke the connection. He watched her as she closed her eyes, and then saw as the tears began to flow as she wept for the knowledge that her brother had not survived.

She awoke with T'som standing over her. He squatted down, and said, "I have much that needs to be said. The travelers who saved your life said that it would be the middle of the season of greening before you would fully recover. But K'jor grows impatient, and is in need of answers that we suspect that only you can give us. Soon, these two females that are with you will be returned to the herd, but not yet. I will be outside of this shelter and expect you to meet me as soon as you've taken care of your needs." He got up and with a quick glance at the other two who were cowering in the corner as far away as they could get, left.

She was still groggy from being very deep in sleep when he had awakened her, and it alarmed her that they would be taking Beth and Barbara from her. She still depended on them heavily. Now what? She slowly got off of the sleeping mat, and carefully worked her way over to the pot to take care of her needs, finding that she was still unbelievably weak. She took a bowl of the soup that had been simmering on the small, smoky, open fire, and carefully ate. The food was really hot, and could have easily burned her tongue. But she needed this nourishment to help her keep her wits about her as she faced this primitive. Not wanting to tell the two women what had been related to her, she made sure that the ear piece was in place, and the tiny, almost invisible bug that would provide the visuals was placed on the clothing she wore, placed just above her breasts. Again the sorrow hit her, as she remembered what this Saige had told her. He, her brother, had not survived, and as far as she knew, she was the last of her family. She knew of no others – and what of her children? She already knew her mate was dead but her two sons were an unknown, and so she had to assume that they were no more also.

As she followed this T'som, she could feel that dreaded weakness returning with full force, making her shake, and feel like she was about to collapse. T'som turning and seeing this, went back and then supported her for the rest of the distance to the shelter of their gods, and helped her sit. Looking her over closely, he could see that she still was in very bad shape, and even though he had told her that they would be removing the other two, it was now obvious to him, that this order would have to be delayed. The distance from where this female was living to where they were presently, was only a very short walk, but before they were even close to half way here, she had almost collapsed. It was again obvious to him that they were moving too fast on this. He doubted that he would get much from her at this point. In fact as he watched her, he could see that she was barely awake, and that the trip here had exhausted her completely. Sometimes he felt that K'jor, through his impatience, pushed things much too quick, and this was one of those times. He understood why, but sometimes one had to wait, no matter what one tried to do, and he knew again, that this was one of those times.

There was going to be difficulties on both sides of this. Females were not allowed to speak around the males since their true purpose was to bring new lives into the clan. Yet, from all indications this female was equal to him, a priest. So they should be speaking as equals, if not for who she was. This was shocking, yet he had listened to the comments from the warriors who had attacked these lairs, and saw for himself that what they said was true. The females from these lairs were equal to the males, and in some places above them. Just how could this be? Looking down at her as he paced, he finally stood in front of her and said. "There are many things that we are not understanding, and one of these major points has to do with the females from your lairs. But before we even move in that direction, I must make you aware that you will be given some opportunities that have never been granted a female. This is being allowed so that we may begin to make sense of what makes no sense to us at all. From what I can see, this will not happen today, since you can barely keep your eyes open, and so I will speak and you will listen."

Even through the fog of exhaustion from the short trip she thought, *I can't believe these primitives. I'm just supposed to listen to your speech, and thank you because you allowed me this privilege?* She concentrated once again on what this one was saying.

"Much of what I'm saying you are aware of, but it is necessary so that there is a starting place. In our world when a tribe or clan is conquered and their place of living is destroyed, then the females must become part of that conquering clan or tribe, to become part of the breeding herds that allows us to strengthen through the new blood and future lives."

He paused a moment, and looked at her closely to make sure that she was paying attention. He could see that she was attempting to do so, and was fighting hard to stay awake. At least that was a good sign. "So, with the discovery of the lairs, our victory over you, and the destruction of your lairs, this made you and the other females bound to join our clan, and the others involved, to further our growth. Even though there was some resistance . . ." *Ha, resistance, that's putting it mildly,* she thought. He could see that what he had just said had brought a brief fire to her eyes, but it was only short lived, so he continued. "All of you were added. At this point it was as it should be." *As it should be? In who's book? Not mine or any of the other women that you have enslaved.*

"And it appeared that all was proceeding, but then with the breeding, nothing happened, no carrying, nothing. It was as if the females from your lairs, those lairs I might add, that fell easily to us, were greater warriors than our own warriors – somehow preventing the carrying and the strengthening of our clan. At first we thought it was just a fluke. After all, the females from the lairs had the bleeding as ours, showing us that you are fertile, so there was an increase in the attempt to overcome whatever magic, totem, or hidden strength, that all of you used to prevent the carrying. But we are still being defeated, and this is something that is unacceptable. If females are able to defeat us, how long will it be before we are defeated in battle?"

So this is what this is all about. But priest or whatever you call yourself, I haven't a clue. With as many times as we've been forced to have sex with your warriors, some of us should have become pregnant. I'm quite happy that it hasn't happened. Because the last thing I want to do as a woman is to bring another one of you bastards into this world. So, for whatever is the reason, may it just continue . . .

"So with this happening, that is why you are here, and as I stated earlier, you will be allowed something that is forbidden to the rest of the females. We will begin, soon, to talk, allowing you to speak. Enough for now, I will assist you back to your shelter, and let you recover additionally. We will talk on this later." With that he assisted her back to the shelter, and to her sleeping mat. She lay down gratefully, and was out almost as soon as she relaxed.

* * *

When Joci had been led back to the dorm by Judd, and with his gentle nudging, she did lie down, and found to her surprise, that she had slept – and when waking felt guilty about it. Still she had to admit that at this moment, even though she was still a bit out of it, and numb from waking from a deep sleep, some of the demons that had been haunting her were strangely silent. She had been so afraid to open up to anyone, let alone a man. Yet, he had been so gentle, so under-standing, and it just seemed natural to cry it out on his shoulder. She could sense no judgment there, only compas-sion. And he said so little, but his eyes had spoken volumes, and she knew that she had found a friend, and maybe like her own grandfather, who she was sure had perished, he would listen to her, and help her, and she knew that she really needed that right now.

She had come so close to being destroyed by what had happened, and she had seen other women who had been, and were no longer alive. She wondered if some of them commit-ted suicide, something she had contemplated a number of times, even after the rescue from the primitives. Looking around, once outside of her personal area, she found that the dorm was quite empty at the moment and she had it all to her-self. Looking at the clock, that was hanging on the wall; she found that she had a few hours before she needed to report to the daycare center to help there. At first she thought that she would just go read something in the area that was set up like a living room, with comfortable chairs, couches, tables, and lamps that projected a soft comfortable light. The floor in the area was covered with rugs, making the area feel homey and comfortable. She had some serious thinking to do. Then her tummy rumbled and she realized that before that incident that she had gone to the cafeteria to get something to eat, and had become overwhelmed. So she changed her mind and instead opened the door only to find a large box sitting next to the doorway with her name on it. *What's this?* Now curious, she picked it up, and found that it wasn't very heavy for its size. She shook it slowly, in case there was something inside that could be broken, and something moved inside, but it didn't have that solid feel. Now, undecided, she didn't know if she wanted to take it to the cafeteria with her, or return to her area and open it there.

After another moment of indecision, she decided to take it back inside to the privacy of her space. She was really curious. There was nothing on the box to identify who it was from, let alone what the contents could be. And the movement and slight shaking didn't give her a hint. Well, she had to admit that this had taken her mind, even temporarily, off her problems. So she entered her space, placed the box on the bed, cut the tape and opened the box, and found a beautiful large stuffed toy bear with a smile on its face, and its arms opened wide. She laughed slightly at the sight. It was as if this stuffed bear wanted to be hugged by her, and she just couldn't resist. *Wow, what a great gift!* When she picked it up and hugged it, she found it to be very soft, and she felt like she didn't want to let it go. *Who?* Yes she wondered who had thought of this wonderful gift. Then looking at the bear she smiled and asked,

"So mister bear, who are you, and where did you come from?" She laughed in delight, someone to confide in, someone who would never judge her, someone who would listen, and someone to comfort her in her nights of terror. He was perfect. Why did she decide that he was a he? That was a very good question, and looking the bear over there was nothing that identified it as either sex. So she looked closely at the face, and thought that it was more masculine, than feminine, so she had made him a male.

As she thought about this, she thought it was strange that she should do that, with all the horror she had faced at the hands of those primitive males. Because of her youth, she had become one of the ones most demanded by the primitives as they tried to get her pregnant. It had been nasty, humiliating, and a very painful experience. One she knew that she would never want to repeat any time in her short life. Well, all of that was behind her. She just didn't know now after all of that abuse and pain, whether she would ever be able to make love with whoever would be her mate some day in the future. She really worried that she would have a real fear, have those hidden scars that just wouldn't go away, and ruin her life even more than it had been already. At least with her new friend here she wouldn't have to face that. She knew that her experiences that she had would always color her life, and she knew that it was that way for all of them. Oh well, that was for the future, once again her tummy complained and she knew that she needed to finish that interrupted trip to the cafeteria and get some food. Looking at the bear she asked, "What do I do with you? Do I leave you here to warm my bed, and be my secret friend, or do I take you with me and if the cafeteria is empty you can sit next to me and we can talk." In the end, at least for now, she decided that she would leave him here, and told him that she'd be back shortly and headed out to get something to eat. As she headed down the hallway, she again wondered, *who is the person that gave me such a wonderful gift?*

* * *

Saige and Shellian studied the video and conversation, if one could call it such, that this priest had with Sara. Of course the conversation was more he talk, she listen, but that was the way the primitive culture lived. Both of them had to admit that giving Sara the right to speak, even though it wasn't this day, was something that never had happened. Women were just not allowed that privilege at all, and could be punished for speaking around the males. From the bugs that had been planted it was quite obvious that when the females were back with the herd, as it was called, they chattered all the time. No different than with theirs when women got together. Both of them wondered when the change would come where women would be considered more than property, and only there to bring both pleasure and new lives. Saige could see the anger in his sister's eyes, but she remained under control. "This is the fourth time we've looked at this, and while it has helped with understanding some of what they do, all this priest is do-ing is speculating about why our women haven't become pregnant by their men." Saige said. "There's really nothing here that can help us,"

Letting out a deep breath in frustration, Shellian couldn't disagree with what her brother had just said. In fact she was just about to say the very same thing. "We've got to be overlooking something. The clock keeps ticking, and our time is very rapidly running out. If we don't come up with something soon, then the alliance will be getting back together, and once again seek out another of our cities. And while there has been much work on the fortifying of the cities, and trying to come up with better fields, and holograms, there's just no guarantee that any of it will work. After all, somehow they've figured out that the belts and clothes that all of us wear allow us to pass through those fields unharmed. So with the amount of people that they've captured and killed, there are plenty of those to go around." She got up and paced the meeting room where the two of them were presently.

Looking down at the floor, he had to agree with her assessment. He had asked the ones in charge of the cities why they couldn't just change the code or something so that the belts and clothes wouldn't work anymore. They had said that they didn't know why, and had asked that very question themselves. And the answer they got back from their engineers made them somewhat angry with their ancestors. They had been told that it was something that had been hardwired into the defensive equipment, and no one knew where it was located within the complicated circuits, or what it was that activated the devices. So it would take time, and research to be able to figure out what it was within these units that were responsible, and then develop a change. And maybe since they were at the Alpha that there could be something there that would give them the answers they needed.

Well, there were no engineers here, and while Judd was good at what he was doing, he wasn't close to being an engineer. So the weaknesses in the system remained. They had placed a high priority for the teams here to search the records for any hint, and again because none of them had the training, it was like trying to find that proverbial needle in a pile of grass, which meant that in the end, the protection would have to come from them, and their small contingent. Shaking his head, he looked at her stating, "Somewhere we're really overlooking something. I know that it's right in front of us, but we're just not seeing it. And it's just as obvious that the rest of the people here haven't come up with anything either. All the morning meetings we've had and are continuing to have, have given us nothing but wasted time." He looked up at the monitor, and saw that Seirra was beckoning him, so getting up he said, "The boss is calling. I suspect she needs help with the twins. I'm sure you'd love to check in on Sam' anyway. So let's break for an hour and then meet back here and see if something has just magically appeared to help us."

Both of them headed out the door, with Shellian heading for the daycare area where her daughter was presently staying, and Saige for their apartment where Seirra and the twins were, with plans to meet later. The time of Seirra returning to help them was still a couple of weeks away. And Saige knew that one baby was a handful, but two could be overwhelming. So he made sure he was available to help as she needed it. He entered the apartment to two crying babies and a harrowed look on Seirra's face. "Okay, which one do you want me to take?" He asked.

Over the crying children she said, "Oh that's easy. It doesn't matter. I think that we have two hungry babies here, and both of them needs their pants changed. So whichever one you take to change, I'll feed the other, and then trade off. Once fed and changed, we can see if we can't rock them to sleep. One of them has that tired type of crying, and I suspect that once both of them have full bellies they will want to sleep anyway. So let's get started, shall we?"

He went in and picked up the first one he came to, and it happened to be Saharra, and took her over to the changing table, while Seirra grabbed Seth and began to breast feed him. Saige commenting more to himself than to Saharra said, "Boy you girls have lots of places to have stuff go when you mess your pants." Yet, he couldn't help but smile, as his daughter had quit crying and was looking up at him and seemed to be smiling at him. It made his heart melt when he saw such things from her, and once again he knew that he was in trouble with this one. "There, all clean and fresh." He tossed the soiled one into the recycler and picked up his daughter and brought her over to Seirra who was just finishing the nursing of her son. He was almost asleep. So carefully they traded babies, and he went over and repeated the process with Seth, who had only wet pants. Although, as he had learned, with boys there were other dangers that one had to avoid when changing their diapers. Eventually with both fed and changed, and with some holding and rocking, they fell sound asleep. He was about to leave when smiling, Seirra pointed out that he'd better change his outfit as there was baby spit up on his shoulder. So before heading in to change, he hugged Seirra, gave her a lingering kiss, that from her side held promises for later, changed clothes, and headed back out to the meeting room.

He was the last to arrive, with his sister getting there ahead of him. Smiling at him she said, "Parenthood is a full time job, isn't it. And with us being in charge, we now have two full time jobs. Hey, when I went to the daycare center to see how Sam' was doing, and of course she was fine, she's such a happy baby, and so far has been easy to take care of, but I was surprised that all the children now have stuffed animals and some small blankets with a silky border that the children are just loving." Pausing for a moment and then smiling once again, "I guess that while it was a great thing to be able to save some of our people from the primitives, I think that we've benefited more than they. That Judd is just unbelievable. He keeps finding things in those replicator computers, and we find uses for them. Now he's come up with another miracle, not for us so much, but for the children. I ran into him briefly, on the way back here, and asked him about it. He said that there had been a reason for him to research part of the system and to find something for the children. He said that the items he created are called teddy bears. He doesn't know why, but whatever the reason, he said that in the notes that these 'teddy bears' had always been a favorite of children, so he replicated a batch, with the accompanying small blankets, and brought them to the daycare center. He said that the toddlers just went nuts over them, and I have to agree. They've latched on to these things and won't let go."

She was leaning against the table, turned around and grabbed something that was behind her, and handed it to him. It kind of looked like an animal, and sort of like the pictures that they had seen on the computers of the creatures from their own world. He could sort of see why it had been called a bear, but the "teddy" part eluded him. "You say that all the kids just love these things?" He felt it and found it soft, and probably the word that came to his mind was of all things "cuddly". She then handed him a second one which was a different color, which he asked, "What's this for?"

She laughed and said, "These two are for your and Seirra's children. He suggested that you read up on childhood history of our people and what they used these things for. So, I'll let you figure that part out. I kind of find them enduring myself. I wonder what he'll come up with next?"

Shaking his head he stated, "Yeah, I wonder." Looking up at the clock, he put the two bears down, and continued, "We're running out of time here. We've got a meeting shortly, and while I know that so far, we've not figured out much, we still have to try. Do you have any new ideas on how to tackle this? I know that I've run out of ideas, and the conversations that we've had with Sara, as short as they've had to be, hasn't produced anything that we can use. And even watching the vids of all the planted bugs haven't given us a clue. I'm afraid that if we don't have some kind of breakthrough shortly that there will be another season of raids from that alliance, and we'll lose more cities, more lives, and more of our people will suffer."

"Unfortunately, nothing at all – I've seen what this has done to our people, and even in the eight that we rescued, I see lingering problems. It's more obvious in the women, but I can see it in the men also. And the one that has shown most of the damage has been Joci. She's tried to hide it, but with the way she's withdrawn, been more subservient, and wants to be alone or just with the children, all point to one having a very difficult time adjusting to what has happened to her. And no, before you ask, she is no trouble, causing no trouble, and has been very good at helping. What I'm seeing is subtle, and it is something that took me a while to realize. I'm sure part of the problem is her age, and the fact that there's no one else around that is that close. I'd guess that she's very early in her late teens, and that's a tough time if everything is normal. Anyway I've kind of been keeping an eye on her," she then laughed a little before continuing, "in my spare time."

Spare time, right, as if any of us have much of that. He knew that the two of them had even less. But what could they do, nothing really, nothing at all. "I guess, I'll take these, ah, teddy bears over to our apartment, and be right back." He grabbed the two stuffed animals and went out the door. Shellian turned around and once again went through the notes that she had studying, trying to find anything that they may have missed.

* * *

When Joci entered the daycare area it was a complete surprise to see all the children carrying much smaller versions of the gift she had found at the door. She laughed at the sight, and thought that it had been a very long time since she had done that twice in one day. These things surely had lifted her spirit. When she turned around she saw Judd standing there and smiling at her. So it had to have been him. With a great big smile on her face she turned around and went to him and gave him a big hug saying, "Thank you, thank you, thank you."

He looked down at this young woman that he was holding, smiling inwardly himself. The gift obviously had the effect that he hoped that it would. He put his finger under her chin and tipped her head up gently so that he could look her in the eyes and said, "It was the least I can do for you, who I consider my granddaughter. I can tell that this has been good for you. So please let's continue in this way." He kissed her lightly on the forehead before continuing, "Now, I know we're just starting out, but I think if both of us try we can make this grandfather-granddaughter thing work." He gently released her, and pushed her towards her assignment. "I think that the children are staring at us."

She turned around and blushed a little, because, as he had stated, the toddlers all were staring at the two of them, and were quiet. When she turned back around to Judd, he had already left, so looking back at the children she began to help. In a short time, she would be relieved as today she was to be at the meeting. Maybe with the way she was feeling that she could actually say something. Especially since that idea she had wouldn't go away, but continued to nag at her. And since there had been nothing else presented that could help; maybe hers was a good one after all.

But later after the meeting, she sat frustrated. While she thought that she could present her idea, she found that she was so nervous, scared really, that she just froze up and couldn't say anything. Why was she having so much a problem with this? After all, she had just as much right to add her thoughts as any of the others, and so far there had been nothing forthcoming from any of the others – so why not her? Before the end of the meeting, the new schedule for working the security office had been handed out, and for the first time she would be taking a shift, and the other person would be Jas. Jas was nice, showing some gray in her hair, but younger than Judd. In a sense she was just about the same age as her mother. Maybe she could open up to her, but then again, maybe not. She'd been locking things up inside of her for so long, that even with this new friendship with Judd, and the fact that he had made her feel better about herself, she just didn't know how to get beyond the barriers that she had hidden behind. Her second shift would be with Stone, and he seemed so strong, so able to accomplish anything, and his mate Sorrel, what a beautiful woman. She had to admit that they seemed perfect for each other. At least with the first shift she would have a chance to learn what they did there.

Judd came past the daycare center where Joci had gone after the meeting and saw her sitting down deep in thought. At the meeting he could tell that she had wanted to say something, but was too scared. Looking around he could see that the center was being taken care of by Jed and Sabryn, so at the moment was in good hands. He went over to Sabryn and asked, "Mind if I borrow Joci for a short time?"

Looking up from the changing table she shook her head. "No, she hasn't actually started back on her shift. The meeting broke a little early, and I'm not to be anywhere but here today. Jed will be returning to the hydroponics after she's officially back."

"Okay, we'll only be gone for a very short time. I'm taking her down to the cafeteria, and on that subject, would you like me to bring you something from there?"

"Yeah, honestly, we had a bad night with Shayne. He had some type of nightmare and it scared him, and as a result was up half the night. He ended up sleeping with us, and kept kicking both of us in his sleep, making what little we got not quality. So lots and lots of coffee, please. Oh, and I like sugar in mine, about a spoonful."

Smiling he said, "Your wish is my command, oh princess!" This brought out a laugh from Sabryn as he bowed to her. He turned around and headed over to where Joci was sitting deep in thought, and not seeing him approach until he grabbed her gently by the arm and said, "Come with me, we're going to the cafeteria, just for a short time." He could see that she was about to protest, and at that moment pointed over to Sabryn and stated, "Oh it's alright, besides we're getting her some coffee while we're there. Since I suspected that she's the one in charge today, I'd get permission from her, and she said go for it. So shall we?" Again he bowed down and with a sweep of his arms in the direction of the cafeteria and asked once again, "Shall we?"

Again she laughed a little. What could she do? He seemed so genuine, and caring, and right now she admitted, even if it was only to herself, this was something she really needed right now. She reached out her hands to him, and he assisted her up, and they proceeded to the cafeteria. Once there, they found a couple of others taking breaks and getting some snacks or drinks. He had her sit down, and he waited on her, bringing some of that fruit juice she loved, and he a cup of coffee. Again something she hadn't started drinking herself. She had tasted it, and found it not to her liking.

He made himself comfortable, sitting across from her and said, "I'm not sure quite how to ask or state this, but I could see in the meeting that you had something on your mind, and that you really wanted to say something – do I have it just about right?"

How'd he do that? Yes she did, but how'd he know? As far as she knew, she had kept her feelings hidden, but now could see that it wasn't so. And if he could figure it out, how many others had? This bothered her even more and almost drove her back into the depression that she had been fighting for so long. Was she an open book?

He could see the emotions playing across her face and in her eyes. He reached across and gently picked up her hands in his and said, "Look, nobody is judging you. All of us are trying to come to terms with what happened to us. That's including our two leaders. We all have our demons, all have our ghosts, and we will always have them. What matters is what we do about it. Everything that happens in life colors who we are. My mate, bless her soul, told me that I was always sensitive to her and her needs, and I'm finding that I can sense things in you in much the same way. You're young, and yes I know when one is, they hate hearing it, but it's true. You don't know who you are, or what you will be, and then in the middle of trying to discover this, well we all know what happened next. Right now nobody has come up with an idea, let alone a solution to the primitives. So if you have something, I'm willing to listen, and then together in the next meeting *we* can present it, and I'll give credit where credit's due. I know with the insecurities that one has at this time in your life that it is difficult to believe you have something to contribute, but you do."

"But . . ."

He interrupted her, and shook his head, smiling. "No, no ifs, ands, or buts, and so on from you – look I know how it is. So let's work on this together. If your idea is a good one I'll let you know. And if it isn't, well then, we can laugh about it. Remember this, and I know it's hard to believe, but I was your age once upon a time, and had all, well not all, since my mate told me that men don't have the insecurities of women, the same insecurities that you have right now. So what do you say, are you willing to confide in me?"

She was quiet for a moment as she absorbed all that he had told her, and asked of her. And she had to admit that she had never considered that Judd had been her age once. Again, if she had honestly thought about it, of course he had been. Otherwise he wouldn't be here now at his present age. Taking a deep breath and with a small voice she said, "Okay, but . . ."

Smiling he said, as he shook his head, "I said, no 'buts'."

Laughing now, because he had said that, she knew that she was just about to protest, and protect herself from embarrassment. "Look, I just don't want to be laughed at, because what I might say, that's all."

"I said that if there were to be laughter from this that it would be both of us, and I promise that it will not be directed at you personally, unless," and he paused a moment and had a look of devilment on his face, "you do something that deserves such a thing. Fair?"

Looking down at the table she noticed that she hadn't touched her drink, and his cup was empty. Sighing she looked up and into his eyes and said, "Okay, I guess so." He prompted her, at this point, to pass on her idea, and that he would give her an honest opinion, and together they could work on it. So she related, tentatively at first, what had come to her. And as she saw the enthusiasm show in Judd she finally got over her fear and told him the whole idea.

* * *

K'jor, looking at the dwindling supply of wood, cursed as another storm rolled in on them. There just seemed to be little or no respite between them this season of cold. It was enough to drive one crazy. But what could one do? It was much too cold and miserable to be out in these things. T'som had visited him a number of times, keeping him updated on the recovery of the female. And he had cautioned him that she was a very long way away from being healthy once again, and to take care of his impatience. They would not be able to move faster than what the gods were allowing. He couldn't argue with that, but he so desperately wanted answers. At least with this severe season of cold time really wouldn't be an issue. He could wait.

With time on his hands once again his mind drifted back to the destruction of the first of the lairs. At that time it was only their clan. When they had returned the following season of greening they had the clothing from the strange ones, and they found that with those clothes they were able to pass through the veil unharmed. They didn't know what was special about the clothing, but whatever it was it allowed them safe passage beyond. He showed the rest of the warriors what he had found on his previous unplanned visit. And it still was as it had been then. He led them to the hidden wall, and to the closed door-way. They waited out the daylight, and then late in the evening with ropes they scaled the barrier, and briefly stood on top. All of them were in awe to what they were seeing. There appeared to be a large clan hidden here – but none like they had ever seen before. They dropped down into the lair that lay before them and worked their way through a silent strange world. As they worked their way deeper they felt that deep vibration getting stronger, but the sounds that were creating it were just below the threshold of hearing.

Eventually they came upon a shelter where the vibrations appeared to be coming out of, and three of them found an entrance, and with stealth entered. They encountered no one as they went deeper into this magic place. Here they could hear and see lights that shouldn't be there. Fear permeated the air that they breathed. What they were seeing was beyond their experience and understanding. But all of them felt that this had to be evil. So they worked on destroying whatever it was. To kill this hidden being that pushed out the vibrations they were feeling and now hearing. Taking a couple of large stone hammers they began to break everything that they could. Eventually a soft high pitched sound assaulted their senses, and then everything went silent and stopped. The sounds, the vibrations were gone. They left quickly, and because they felt that this was a lair of magicians and sorcerers they needed to destroy and kill everybody. So they went to the far side and worked their way back, breaking into every shelter and slaughtering all they found. This lair had to be inhabited by ones who had to be against their gods. And by the morning light not a soul was left alive other than the clan.

It had been a good thing that this evil had been wiped out. So much of what they saw during their attack was unknown, was beyond their understanding. As they left that bloody morning they found that the blocked door was now open, and as they continued down the pathway, the veil that had hidden the entrance had disappeared. Behind them they left a silent dead world. It was later, when they returned to collect clothing and to allow the priests a chance to see the lair, that the idea entered his mind that there was a good chance there were others. And the idea of other lairs, all hidden in the areas of desolation worried him. It was from this he began to approach the other clans and tribes, showing them what they had found, and with this discovery had asked them to form an alliance – one that would hunt down and destroy each lair as they were discovered. In the three seasons of existence, the alliance had discovered many lairs. They had taken many slaves, and many females to add to their herds. All seemed as it should be. These lairs fell easily, who in the end would have thought that it would be the females, after their inclusion into the breeding herds that would defeat the warriors. If any had suggested such a thing, he would have scoffed at for bringing forth such a fantasy. Yet, before him at this very moment, it was exactly what was transpiring. And this brought him full circle, back to his impatience, back to waiting for this one female to become healthy enough to answer those burning questions. With the alliance he commanded a few thousand warriors, and they had been successful on bringing down every lair they had discovered. Yet, not one of the females taken from those lairs were carrying, no not one.

He found that while he thought through all of this he was pacing back and forth in his shelter. He truly was on edge. He needed to get out, but the winds were howling, throwing the snow around and striking the shelters. Even the two skins that covered the entrance were whipping, allowing the cold to penetrate deeply within. And when the skins whipped aside new snow would blow inside and pile by the entrance. No he would have to endure this additional time here inside, out of that storm, even though his nerves were definitely on edge. He shivered when one of the blasts of air hit him and he retreated deeper into the shelter, getting close to the fire, sat down, and stared. The gods were definitely showing their power this season of cold, and it again showed him how weak he was when comparing himself to them. He grabbed another layer of clothing, and wondered how it could be so cold inside the shelter. He shivered a little, and pulled his chair a little closer to the fire, and for a short time stared at the dancing flames as they consumed the wood stacked within its hungry grasp.

While staring his mind took him back once more –

They continued to be successful in rooting out these lairs, and destroying them, allowing no one to escape so that any warning could go out to any that continued to exist – at least until that one. They never did figure out where this small group had found a way past the attacking forces, the many patrols, and lookouts that had been posted. With the amount of warriors that he had at his disposal, it had been easy to cover any and all routes out of the lair, yet this one group had – further proof of their skills as sorcerers. It had taken some time, but eventually they had been located, and through a number of skirmishes, and attacks he had driven them towards the Sacred Mountains, and the trap he had waiting for them. But it had failed and they had escaped into the Sacred Mountains. It had been a complete surprise when word had come back that the patrol, which was guarding the only route was found dead, with no mark upon them, no sign that any had been in their camp. It spoke of deep sorcery.

The following season of greening, hunters who braved the lower areas of the Sacred Mountains reported on finding three bodies, two males and a female. One of the priests and a healer went to check on these reports, and like the patrol that had been guarding the only route into the mountains, these three had no marks upon them to even know why they had passed into the spirit world. The conclusion, simply stated, was that it had been the gods who had gotten revenge on these three. The female had been carrying and was late in that carrying. On closer inspection of the bodies, even though their dress was similar to the tribes, they came to the conclusion that these were the missing ones from the one lair that a small group had escaped. And there had been no way for such a small group to have wiped out that patrol, leaving it once again to sorcery. At least he knew that with this discovery that none had escaped, and his attacks would remain unknown to any lairs that still existed, and he felt that there were many more out there.

CHAPTER SEVENTEEN

"Look", Judd stated, "there won't be another meeting until tomorrow. I know that you've got to go and help with the children, and you love just doing that. I've got a couple of things that I need to do also. So continue to think on what you've told me. I think it's a great idea, and truthfully I'm surprised that someone else didn't see it. I mean it's been staring us right in the face all this time and none of us saw it, but you."

"But Judd . . ."

Again smiling, he interrupted her and said, "Now remember I did say no buts."

Laughing now because once again he had reminded her that was exactly what he had said, and once again she had tried. "Okay, okay. It's just that . . . well, I just thought that since it was something that was there, that it had been looked at and ignored as not important. Are you sure that you're not just being nice?"

"Oh I don't have a problem being nice, and no, that isn't what I'm doing. I really think your idea has merit, and with a direction to work towards, we can probably come up with a way to end this, even with such a small group. But," he paused and smiled, "there I just used it."

With a questioning look on her face, Joci asked, "Did what?"

Laughing he said, "I just used the word I told you that you couldn't"

"Oh." Then she saw the small joke and began laughing herself.

Once both of them had finally settled back down he said, "We're probably going to need some help from one of the cities. After you passed on your idea, some thoughts have been flowing through my mind, and if the rest are up for it then we may be able to finally see an end to these attacks."

"Really?" She asked, not truly believing that her idea was something that any of them would have considered valuable.

Again smiling Judd said, "Yes, really." Looking up at the clock on the wall he got up and said, "Oh my time does just fly. Look I'll talk with you again tonight at our final meal, but I have to go and work on something for the leaders." He gave her one last encouraging smile and went out through the double swinging doors and was gone. But very shortly he returned through the double doors, looked at her and shrugged. "I forgot that I promised Sabryn coffee, and I can't just head off and forget. I've found that there's too much of that as I get older." He went over to the kitchen area grabbed a thermos of coffee, and the condiments that she had requested and once again was out the door.

She took her half-filled glass, got up, and headed back to the daycare center where she had just been before this conversation with Judd. Deep in thought as she headed back, she looked up in surprise when she found herself back, and hadn't even realized that she had walked the halls to get back to the center. Looking up she saw that Sorrel had joined the others in the center, and was looking quite happy that her pregnancy was continuing without any complications. Joci had to admit that Sorrel was still a beautiful woman, even if she was somewhere in her second, third.

"Hi Joci," Sorrel said lightly, "how's everything going with you?"

She had to admit that since she had allowed Judd in her life as a surrogate grandfather that everything seemed to be looking up. Now she would have at least two people to talk to, and maybe she could even begin to develop a friendship with Sorrel. She really hadn't had much contact with her, but there just seemed to be a slight draw towards this woman. Where she felt that Seirra was like an older sister, she sensed that Sorrel could be a girlfriend, something that she had desperately needed, but since the capture hadn't been available. Still a little shy she looked down and said, "Okay, I guess. This has been so hard." Suddenly she felt arms around her and looked up to find that Sorrel had come over and hugged her.

Sorrel laughed and said, I'd get closer but I seem to have something sticking out in front of me that prevent that."

Considering what she knew of what had happened to Sorrel, it really was surprising to her that Sorrel could be happy, and appear to be unconcerned, if only . . . yes if only she could learn, but the nightmares were there almost every night, and the fears that would continue to surface unbidden, how long would it take before she was finally able to get past them? Because she really wanted to be able to move on and just be herself once more. She looked up into Sorrel's eyes and asked, "Can we talk, you know, as we girls like to do? I really could use a friend to confide in now and then." She was quickly embarrassed by what she had just asked, and actually could feel her face heat up, telling her that she had just blushed.

Putting her hands on Joci's shoulders she replied, "Look, there's no reason to feel embarrassed by asking such a thing. Of course, I'd love to be your friend. I'm sure while our experiences are somewhat different, I'm sure that at the same time we have a lot in common." She smiled, patted Joci's shoulder and said, "I've got to go as I have the security office duty, but please come and see me any time."

"Oh, thank you. I've had no one to talk to, girl to girl, since Seirra went into labor, and I've missed those times, and all of the times my friends, back in the city, and I would get together and just talk." She'd heard from the other women what had happened to Sorrel. And while she knew that she could never be as free with her body as Sorrel had, what had happened to her later really showed Joci what a strong woman Sorrel was. So in some ways she really looked up to her. She had survived, had lost a daughter, and while, at times, she could see the sadness in her eyes, she'd appeared to have moved on in her life, and was very much looking forward to this new child that was growing inside of her. Maybe she could fit in after all.

* * *

She was sitting in one of those meetings once again. But this time she was as nervous as one could get. She was truly worried that once Judd presented her idea that she would be scoffed, and laughed at. And even with her growing circle of support, she really didn't know if she could handle it or not. It would just be so much easier not to be here at all, but Judd had insisted, and told her not to worry. She had given him a brave smile, but honestly even that had been hard. So here she sat not really listening to what was being said as the meeting was brought to order. It would have been so much easier to be watching this from the daycare center instead.

". . . Judd had informed me that a very good idea had been presented to him, and one he feels is our salvation. He told me about it, and once he did, it was obvious that he was right. So I'll let him pass on what was told, and if you react the same way that we, Shellian and I, did, then you'll hit yourself for missing the obvious. I mean it was right there all the time, but all of us overlooked it as trivial, and unimportant."

Judd stood up and then presented her idea to the group, and as he did, she shuddered inside just waiting for the proverbial hammer to fall, but it didn't. There was silence as the people around the table thought about what he presented, and she could see the light go on in their eyes as they saw it too. Judd looked over at her and smiled. He'd been right all along. He looked back at the group and said, "As you can see we have much ahead of us to make this work, and like we've been told all along, we will only get one chance at this. And even though she doesn't want to be mentioned, the person responsible for this is Joci."

At this point when he had mentioned her name she flushed hot, very embarrassed for having been singled out. She looked down for a moment to try and get her emotions back in control, looked up, and saw everyone smiling at her. They spontaneously gave her a round of applause, embarrassing her further. Judd came over and stood next to her, looked down at her, and then placed his arms around her and whispered. "See, I told you it's a great idea."

Shellian tapped the table for attention, and Judd returned to his seat. She looked directly at Joci and said, "Thank you. We were getting very desperate with no one coming up with anything at all." She turned to the rest and said, "The winter will be ending soon, and with spring we will be running out of time, since we know that for most of the spring the primitives are trying to recover from the winter months. It has been shown that they begin their campaigns, and while I'm sure they do not call them that it's what they are, late in the spring, and generally run through the summer, and into early fall, where once again they must prepare for the winter. With winter almost gone, as I said earlier, we are very short on time. Judd has suggested that we get the cities involved where we can, and I have to agree. The three of us, Judd, Saige, and myself, have been discussing this a lot, and we're going to put forth some of what we discussed, and expect all of you to contribute. We need *all* input", at which point she looked directly at Joci, "any and all ideas to make this work is welcome." Turning to Jarid, and while she didn't know if Jeanna had worked in the entertainment field as Jarid had, she had noticed that they worked well together. "You and Jeanna will need to team up and come up with a plan and a layout, and the roles that we must play to pull this off. Again we're very short on time, and the pressure is on. To prevent any more suffering and the attack of another of our cities this must work, and work perfectly the first time. So other than the work in the security office and obviously, the taking care of the children, our time will be involved with this project. Saige and Judd will be giving out assignments to everyone. Now if there are no questions let's get to it." She looked around the table, smiling, as she saw that there were many very lively conversations going on – so much different than most of the meetings where there would just be silence as they broke up – a good sign, a very good sign.

She walked down the side of the table to where Joci was sitting, still in silence, and obviously still in shock that her idea could have had such an impact. Looking down at her once she had gotten Joci's attention, she said, "See, we all have things to contribute, and I know that being so young, and again I know how you hate to hear that, but it's true, we feel that many times that what we have, ideas that may have come to us, things we see, aren't important. But as you just saw that's not even close to the truth. Look, why don't you come with me, I'm just about to make contact with Sara, and see if she agrees with this. After all, like you were, she's presently a captive, and in this case the sister to Shayne who was our leader, and as you know died on our flight to here. But she speaks the primitive tongue and has more insight into their lives right now than any of us. So while I feel that what you've stated is correct, and that's why we're running with it, she'll confirm it for us, and if you're right, we may be able to get our people back and end their suffering, all because of you."

Joci, once again could feel the heat in her face as she was praised once again. This was beyond anything she'd expected. So instead of speaking, she just nodded her head, got up and stood beside Shellian, Shellian for heaven's sake, one of the leaders who were responsible for everything, including their rescue. She just didn't feel worthy. She followed Shellian into the security office, which had also become the operations office since they were in constant contact with the many cities, and where they were monitoring all of the bugs that they had planted. With all this additional responsibility they now had three people in here constantly, only reducing it to two at the late night hours. Seve was monitoring the bugs and the views from the above, and Shellian signaled him that she needed his place. Seve exchanged locations and stood by Joci watching, as she, to see what Shellian planned.

With practiced ease, something that would have been foreign just a short time ago, she brought up the images of the shelter where Sara and the two women were residing, and waited as she could see that the primitive T'som was talking to Sara. From the one sided conversation it dealt more with how much she had recovered, and soon they would begin their discussions. From the body language of the two women, who did not understand the primitive language, she could see that there was a lot of fear as they more cowered in the corner, than observed. The two hid as much in the shadows as they could, being as far away from the primitive as the shelter allowed. All of them felt for these women, but at this moment there was very little that could be done other than observing. If this idea worked, it could very well be that soon theirs, and all the others who were suffering at the hands of the primitives, would end, and they would be released. At least that was the hope. Since nothing like this had ever been tried, the outcome was unknown. Seve, who spoke the language, followed the conversation closely, while Joci, who had been studying the language as well as the others who had been rescued, could only pick up a word or two. She suspected that if this primitive spoke much slower that she might catch more.

Eventually, it was obvious that this one was finished speaking as he looked over the three women and left the shelter.

They could see that Sara still had little strength, and once again, even this short session with the primitive had exhausted her. Sara turned to the other women in the shelter and told them that everything was still okay, and that she needed to rest once again. At this point Shellian spoke, knowing that Sara was wearing the almost invisible ear piece that provided both send and receive capabilities. From the hidden bugs she could tell that she had received the voice transmission, signaled slightly that she would continue once she was lying down, did so, faced the wall and signaled Shellian to continue. In a quick precise way she passed on what their conclusions were, and the three of them in the security office saw her eyes fly wide open, and then there was a pause as she considered what she had been told. Then slowly a smile came across her face, even though it was fleeting. They all could see a flare of hope in her eyes as she considered the facts as presented. She followed by carefully signing a very big confirmation. This had presented to her a number of times with different primitives, from R'san to T'som. One way or the other in the words spoken to her, they had specifically presented their suspicions. And like the rest of them it was something that hadn't even occurred to her. They could see her shake her head slightly as she considered the ramifications. She signed simply a question that stated, "How could I have missed something so obvious?"

Shellian replied, saying, "You're not alone on that one. We all did. It took someone who was young and unsure of herself to point it out to us." She smiled, even though she knew that Sara couldn't see them. With the small kit that Saige had left there had been no contacts so the visual was missing. Contacts had to be made for each individual, and without knowing who they might come across it was decided to leave the contacts out. "Okay, you've given us what we needed. Now all we can hope is that we can bring all of this to an end soon. How soon we're really not sure, but as we get closer to what we will try to do, then we'll keep you up to date." She paused a moment as emotion choked her up. It was obvious to Joci that Shellian cared for Sara, and she could understand it. Before signing off Shellian said, "It is hoped that before the end of summer that this will be over one way or the other. Good luck Sara, and get better please." When Shellian turned around both Seve and Joci could see tears in her eyes. Shellian just shook her head and didn't say anything for a short time. "Okay Seve, it's yours again, Joci let's go, we've a lot of work ahead of us, and thank you so very much."

"Why are you thanking me?" Joci asked, quite perplexed.

'Because, my young lady, nobody here had a clue as to what to do, and the clock was ticking. We flat were running out of time, and if nothing happened then other of our cities would have fallen to the primitives, and more of our people would die, become slaves, or have to join those dreaded herds of theirs, suffer, and die at their hands, and now we have something, a chance to prevent it from happening. A chance to rescue the remaining ones, like Sara, who are still alive and suffering, and it's all because of you and your idea, that's why."

A voice came over the PA, "Shellian, your daughter needs you."

Smiling, Shellian continued, "And because of such things as this. I've a family now, that if I lost, it would come close to destroying me. I love Saar and Sam' with all of me, and to lose them would be devastating to say the least, and all of those cities that have fallen have so many of those tragedies, let alone what has transpired since our people have become slaves. I guess in some ways we can say that all of this happened is truly our fault. We grew complacent, and allowed our pride to reach the point where we never considered the consequences for our inattention or lack of diligence. And as usually happens, a leader arose among the primitives that brought them together, and now we are the ones on the run, the ones *desperate to survive*. Now all we can hope is that we can end it, and have our survival assured." She looked up at the monitor and said, "I'm on my way." She turned back to Joci and said, "Guess I'd better go, the boss is demanding my time. Just one last thing, remember everyone here is just as important as any single member and that includes you. So if you have any more brilliant ideas, let someone know please. Now don't take this wrong, but from what Judd told us, you've had this one for a while but was afraid to say anything, and I can understand that completely, but by you delaying, we've lost precious time, and that's all I'm going to say on that subject. Okay then, catch you later, or sooner since I suspect that you're heading for the daycare center, eventually." At this point the two women separated, with Shellian going to her daughter, and Joci heading back to the dorms for a short time before she worked with the children in the daycare center.

Joci had been chastised by Shellian for not saying anything until now, and in a way the dressing down had been mild, reminding her that she was part of this small community and her input was just as important as either Shellian's or Saige's. Part of her was elated that her idea had sparked the response that it had, but she still truly couldn't believe it. Sighing she shrugged and headed for the dorm to change before getting some food. For some reason she was always hungry, and wondered why she just didn't seem to change, weight wise, with everything she ate. She knew that the rest of the women here were always being careful as to what they ate – always talking about watching their weight or something.

* * *

"Judd said that he could get someone who he used to talk with all the time at the city of Catskill. Funny thing, from the images the city sits just outside of that valley where the primitives gather before they begin their campaigns. It's a wonder that it hasn't been discovered." As Saige leaned against one of the walls looking out through the large windows on their hidden valley, he paused a moment. "I only hope that this works. We've got Judd doing the heavy lifting here, and with the help of, ah, who'd he say that was, oh yeah, Charley. With the help of Charley, who appears to do much the same thing as Judd, he figures that they can have everything put together that we'll need."

Shellian, leaning on the table and with arms crossed, thought briefly before saying anything. "I can only hope that they're able to pull it off. I know that we have Jarid, and Jeanna trying to come up with a script, and that means that as Judd and this Charley works on things, there will be changes and they will have to be able to get those changes produced. I know that we've formed teams to work with both Judd, and Jarid, and any of the members of our scouting team will be there to translate what they come up with, and also let them know if what they are working on will fly with the primitives. After all, something that we think might work because of our society would make no sense to other societies. And thanks to Sara, we've learned so much more. Between what we've gathered from those planted bugs, and her carrying that camera, plus what she's been able to sign to us is irreplaceable. Without that knowledge and what is in these computers, we could have tried this and would have failed because we would have been so far off the mark."

"True, it's so surprising that after all that time of spying on the primitives, doing everything we did when we were still in the city, feeling that we really had a handle on how they lived, just how far off the mark we truly were." Looking at his sister, he had to smile inwardly. It was surprising to him to find that now she was a sister, a mate, and a mother, and yet she appeared to be no different to him. *So many roles we play in life. I'm her brother, mate to Seirra, and father to our twins, and other than feeling older because of the burden of leadership, I really don't feel any different – well that's not quite true but close.* "It just goes to show that from a distance things can be interpreted so wrong. I suspect that anytime anybody does research on a different society, or group, or anything that is different, that we must be careful to exclude our own prejudices, views and such when we make conclusions. But how does one do that? I suspect that it's got to be close to impossible." Stopping for a moment and looking down, he said, "It's so hard to believe what has happened to us, and that we are here. In many ways it still seems more a dream than reality. And time is just flying by so fast now I hardly remember what day it is or even what month. I used to think that our time in training, in the many exercises that we did, in our life in the compound, things were complicated, and the days just seemed to go by quick, but in comparison to now, those times were slow and idyllic, restful, and simple – funny how the perspective changes. Heck, it's the annual 3029, or at least I think it is. Although now that I know what we've learned since we've found the Alpha, I wonder what that date applies to."

What do you mean by that?" Shellian asked.

Looking into her eyes he stated, "Look, we know now that we're the interlopers here. That we came to this place to study this culture and to remain hidden, which until recently had been quite successful. And we know that we've been here a couple of thousand annuals, so it becomes obvious that this number doesn't compute. So was it something that our ancestors developed by approximating the time of the rise of a civilization here, or does it apply to when our people began space flight, or is it tied to something else? I know it's something that, in the end, really doesn't matter. But we've been surprised by so much from the discoveries of this place, and the relearning of our true past, it's just another one of those mysteries that we've yet to solve."

"You know, this is something I really never thought about. You know like how we track the day, by the hours, minutes, and seconds." She laughed and then continued, "Hey we have our hands full with the primitive issue. We don't need any more on our plate, thank you, and besides that's off the subject – something to solve later on, if there is to be a later on that is." Pushing herself off the table now that she was standing, she said, "Look I've got to look in on Sam', and I'm sure that Seirra could use some help with Saharra, and Seth. So let's get back together just before the midday meal and go check out how's things are progressing. We've only got a month or so left of winter, and we are going to need to be on site and have most of what we need to accomplish by the end of winter, leaving only the minor details to wrap up after that. I've a feeling, that between children and this crushing schedule that there's not going to be much sleep for any of us until this is over, one way or the other. See you back here shortly, brother." She headed out the door and down the hallway out of his sight.

He had to admit that she was right. Sleep would be a precious commodity for all of them until this was over. And he knew that when one did not get enough sleep that tempers could be short, and frustration high. But, whatever the feelings, whatever the pressures, they could not let up, nor fall behind on the very tight schedules, and the too many things that still had to be accomplished. When they moved out to do the actual ground work, it would leave the Alpha with only enough to operate the security office, since the rest would be needed on site, and they would remain there no matter what the weather threw their way, until they had accomplished what they set out to do. And he hoped that there would be time to run through it and test the many parts to insure that there would be no failures. Murphy seemed to always raise his head at the most inopportune times, and this was one of those times where they could not afford interference from Murphy.

* * *

Looking over the script that was being put together Staven stated, "No, no, you don't understand. If we did it that way they'd know immediately that we aren't who we are saying we are." He pulled up some images on the screen and continued, as he pointed at the screen. "Look here and watch the priest. I'll translate so that you can understand. Remember, they haven't reached the point in their advancements yet to where they know any science at all. So we cannot reference anything that suggests such a thing. You have to look at it as if none of this exists. If nothing else, look back on the early history of our own people, and I'm not speaking of when we came to this planet but back when we were primitives. Study that and see how we reacted." Staven could see the frustration in Jarid's eyes, but if they had tried what he and Jeanna had put together it would have failed, and failed miserably. Looking at the two of them he smiled and said, "Look we're all under both a heavy time constraint and a lot of pressure, but if we do it wrong it won't matter in the end. Do you need someone to come in and help research this so that we can get it close to right?"

The two looked at each other, with Jeanna shaking her head and he doing the same, both giving the negative. Sighing Jarid said, "I've been doing this kind of stuff for as long as I've been in the business, and I have to admit that this is, by far, the toughest thing I've ever attempted. I truly thought that this one would have worked, but again what you just showed us, and translated for us, once again, proves that it isn't right. Okay, we'll take a break, and then the two of us will start over."

At this point Staven left and headed over to help Judd. While Jarid and Jeanna had the burden of providing the direction and words that they would use, Judd would be responsible, along with his counterpart in Catskill, in producing everything that they would need. And most of this was being designed and built at the base of the mountains, at the secondary area where the ancestors had worked during their field work. Stone was already down there, and he was heading down to replace him. But first he needed to inform Saige of the progress or lack thereof, on the script. Again this was something that needed to be complete ahead of almost everything else. Since the actors in this fiction would need to practice their individual parts. He headed down the hallway to the security office where Saige, with Shellian were studying the small valley where the primitives would gather. He heard Saige say, as he reached it, "Look, there's the waterfall, and it does look like it puts out a lot of water. That's favorable, hmmm, three entrances or exits, we've got to reduce that to just one, and look this one leads directly back into the grasslands, so this is the one we need to keep open."

When Staven touched his shoulder Saige turned and asked, "Yes? What is it Staven?"

With both Shellian and Saige looking at him he said, "I've had to reject the latest offering from our script writers. I suggested that they look back on our own time when we were primitives. I also ran a segment that we recorded when Sara was with the priest and translated it for them. And yes, I know that this is critical, but if it is wrong it won't matter. Anyway, heading on down to replace Stone, so he can come back here and help where he can. Unfortunately we have no one who can replace Judd. He's the only one who understands this stuff, and the list keeps getting longer. I'm glad that he's got a counterpart in one of the cities that is close to where we will be working."

Shellian took a deep breath, "Okay, I was hoping that there would have been more progress on the script. Maybe we picked the wrong people to do it. I know that this was his business, and Jeanna had acted some, so she was a good fit to help, but now I don't know. Did you ask if they needed help?"

Shaking his head he said, "Yes, exactly, but both of them declined. Oh well, I'm off, see both of you later."

Looking at her brother she said, "That's really not good news. It's something that we need now." Then looking back at her screen, she said, "Guess we'd better get back at it. Look here", as she pointed at the screen, "it looks like the entrance from the grasslands is just a narrow passage with cliffs that overlook the path. This looks like an excellent place to set up part of our play. So have you thought about the time of day that you want this to take place?"

"Actually, yes. At first I thought anytime during the day would work, but as I thought about it, I think pulling this off at night would have a greater effect on them. And it would make it easier to hide anything that could accidently be seen. Darkness can hide a lot, and with our narrow window of opportunity I'm sure that we'll not remember, or be able to check that everything is hidden from sight. The one factor in our favor at this moment is that the primitives don't have a clue that we know their gathering place, and at no time has anyone from the cities put their noses outside of one other than us, so I think that they will go there with no expectations of discovery at all – and I'm counting on it. Look while these images are nice, with the next major storm we need to take a trip and be on the ground in this valley so that we can get a true feel for the place. Images are nice, but they don't always give one a true perspective. We've even attempted to set up a holos in the meadow area, and while it gave us a rough idea, we just didn't have to power to drive the units so the image was a bit ghostly.

"The other problem that we face is that there will be a couple thousand warriors in there, so this is going to be a nightmare as far as monitoring the situation. We are going to be spread quite thin with constant monitoring from here, and the communications and coordination on the ground. I'm glad that the systems that ancestors have in place allow night vision. All of us on the ground and everybody who will be monitoring this will be using it. But it would be so easy to be distracted because of everything that will be going on. Once we have an overall workable plan we'll begin to practice and test things out with that holos, and some props. Then we'll know if an idea will really work or whether we need to change it. We'll set up in that side canyon where Sorrel and Stone located the pathway down the mountainside. While it's not close to the same size as the valley we'll be working, it has much of the same things so that we, at least, can see if this will work at all."

Nodding her head in agreement she said, "I guess then we had better do our part, and that this had better work. Look, I've got to go feed a hungry daughter, but we've so much more to accomplish than just this. I guess it has been decided that if this works that we will have the primitives deliver their captives back to the same valley. I know originally we thought about using the camping area of the travelers, but that would be just too much of a coincidence to use that site – kind of giving ourselves away."

"True, Seve and I will be heading out to test those emitters to see if they are waterproof, and if they will receive a signal once they're immersed in water. We have Jaiden and with

Starr and Sabryn, they are looking through the archives and research that our ancestors did to make sure that what we are attempting is accurate. They will need to continually check in with Jarid and Jeanna to be sure that we remain true. These people are not stupid; in fact they are quite intelligent and adapt quickly. So everything we do must ring true." Looking at his sister all he could think was that they were moving in the right direction, now if time would only cooperate.

"That leaves Seirra and Joci. They seem to get along well. So as time is available to Seirra because of the demand of the twins, the two of them are looking at accommodations for those that we will be able to absorb into the Alpha, and others that will need to be placed into the remaining cities. Then we still must man the security, slash, operations office." She sighed before continuing, "Just not enough bodies and that ole clock keeps on a ticking. Oh yeah, Jed has been working to get the full hydroponic system up and operating so that if we do end up with a very large number of refugees that we will have enough food to feed them. And while Judd is just too busy with the demands of this project, he'll eventually need to break from that work and divert some of the resources to additional supplies, so that we can fill all the lockers and supply rooms. We really have no idea what we'll need or how much, but I'd rather have too much than too little."

"I guess that's it. Shall we get our part going, now that we're up to date on what has, is, and needs to be done?" They both headed out of the meeting room, down the hallway in opposite directions with a promise to meet again after the evening meal. Shellian had an appointment to go and talk with Sara. The recovery was very slow, baby steps really. Had she been in the facility with the medical care available she probably would have made a full recovery by now. But such things did not exist within the primitive world. Sara was still fragile, and could still succumb in her weakened state, and it had been a miracle that she had survived long enough to receive the antibiotics. Only the fact that she, and the other two women were left alone had probably kept her alive.

"Look Sara, I know that it's something that's hard to understand, but they've come to the conclusion that you must be a priest, well priestess, and that's why they want so desperately to talk to you. To find out what you and the rest of the women are doing to beat their warriors. I know that you haven't a clue, and I'm just going to let it remain there for now. Just be comfortable with this fact, and we've confirmed it here, you and the rest of our women cannot get pregnant from any of them, it's quite impossible. So while we cannot do anything as of yet to prevent having to submit to them, at least you can be comforted from the fact that they cannot get any of you pregnant. And this is why they have concluded that you and the rest of the women are warriors. But because you speak their tongue, and they don't understand ours you have been placed in the same class as their priests. It, from what we can discern from both the bugs, the conversations that we had, and the attitudes presented, has led us to a very difficult conclusion. Since, as you know, we women only have two purposes in life. Bringing into the world the next generation, and the raising of the same to an age where they begin to fulfill their roles.

"So as you are brought before that head priest, you must begin to put on the air of an equal, and that is as you can. I know that the infection that almost took your life has left you without strength and endurance, but all of us are running out of time, and the leader of that clan is running out of patience. This problem has him very worried. I really wish that we'd been able to get you the contacts so that we could pass on the images that we have to be able to let you see the whole situation where you are, not that you aren't aware anyway. We'll try and give you as much data as we can as you go into those meetings with T'som. We need to begin to make it look like that you can see beyond just your small room, to give the appearance that you have the sight, and can see beyond your small boundaries, to begin to build some awe and some fear into them. And if they confront you, you have the very reason that you cannot but on a limited basis show your true power. We have an operation now going that we hope will get all of you safely away from them. It is still months away, and I know that this has to be a disappointment, but where there was no hope before, at least now there might be an end to this suffering and death in sight."

She could see Sara absorbing everything she had just passed on to her and had nodded just enough to confirm that she had heard all of it. It was obvious to Shellian that she was still very weak, and even listening to this long winded explanation had tired her. It was also obvious that she had questions, and was thinking about everything that had been passed. Even though it was obvious that she could barely stay awake, Sara signed a question. "How can you be so sure about this, that none of us can become pregnant? As often as we have to submit, it just seems to be impossible to prevent, although none of have."

"I can understand your concern," Shellian responded, and paused a moment to be sure and word it right, "but from the research that we've done we can guarantee that it's quite impossible. I don't want to give you the reasons that we know this, because if this became known to the primitives I believe that it would increase their attempts at destroying us, and I don't know about you, but for me and the rest, and yes I know you too, we're all *desperate to survive* this, and hope to find a peaceful solution to this. But if not peaceful, even an uneasy truce right now would be better than nothing. When we were there, we planted bugs everywhere, so we know just about everything that can be known about the clan that you're part of. And we will absolutely let you know all of it. Since we have no idea what will be important or what you will be able to use to fulfill your new role. Good luck with it, and get as much rest as you can. And I really, truly hope that very soon that I can see you in the flesh instead of this way." At this point she saw the acknowledgment from Sara, broke the connection, took a deep breath, shuddered a little, left the security office and headed for the daycare center. She needed to spend some time with her daughter. Seeing Sara like that, and watching the other two women cower in fear, shook her to her very soul, and right now she felt somewhat down. She needed this time with her child to temporarily forget about this and just be a mother for a short time.

Sara wondered why Shellian knew that none of them could get pregnant by the primitives. But she had to admit that so far none had. Again why wouldn't she tell her why? Was Shellian afraid that she would somehow let it slip? Well, as sick as she was, she guessed it could be something that might happen. But what was the secret that Shellian couldn't reveal? It must have been something huge, if they felt that by revealing it could increase the primitives' animosity against them. But weren't they the same people? After all that is what they all had been taught. But what if it wasn't so, no, that truly didn't make any sense. Oh well, she found that once again that she was falling asleep and couldn't do anything about it.

* * *

Saige, shaking his hands trying to get some circulation going said, "Damn, this water is icy." He and Seve were at the pond outside of the complex, feeling the cold, very cold really, spray coming off the waterfall. Even though they had sunshine from the two suns this day, there was very little warmth. Snow lay thinly all around them. Again this was something they had yet to figure out. Outside of this small hidden valley the snow was piled high. In some places they could stand on each other's shoulders and still not reach the top. It was a tough strong winter. Had it been that way the first season they had spent on the mountains, none of them would be here today, and all would have been lost. Saige looked down in the cold clear water to see if the casing around the emitter leaked. So far it looked okay. Between Seve and himself they laid ten of them across the length of the pond, just off the shoreline. Both of them had wet clothes now, both from the falling mist from the falls, and from immersing the emitters into that icy water. Turning to Seve Saige said, "I don't know about you, but I'm now thoroughly cold. And these wet clothes aren't helping. Let's go change, get something hot to drink in the cafeteria, and then see if we can make these things work."

Nodding in agreement Seve said, "You'll get no argument out of me. I'm freezing, and that water is just unbelievably cold. It seems cold enough to freeze, so why isn't it?"

"You got me. Along with the lack of snow here, it's one of those mysteries that we have yet to solve. It's obvious that our ancestors knew what they were doing, and that over time we've forgotten much of what they took for granted. It's frustrating to know that we've lost so much, and what makes it even more troubling is that we really have no idea. We only find out as we rediscover something else that we knew nothing about."

They returned about an hour later, warm, and now carrying a thermos of coffee to help keep it that way. "Okay, let's check and see if they've stayed dry. No, we're not going to pull them back out and check, but just see if we can see if any water has seeped in while we were away." A breeze had picked up while they were gone, and had a familiar bite to it that promised that there was an approaching storm. Saige started at one end, while Seve started at the other and they met in the middle. "The five I saw seem water tight, how about yours?" The emitters were in clear plastic containers that had spikes on the bottom to anchor them to the bottom, and none had broken free to float to the surface, so at least that part appeared to be working.

Seve replied, "So far so good. Let's get out of this wind; it just cuts through everything we're wearing."

"No fools in my family, I agree." Looking around Saige could see that the greenhouse area would allow them to see the pond and with the portable unit, from there, they should still be in range to test and see if this would work. So leading off he and Seve headed there, stepped inside briefly to get warm, and the returned to the outside. "Here goes nothing." Saige said, as he pressed the switch. They were to get a 3D test signal if the emitters worked, but instead got nothing. Looking perplexed Saige mused, "I wonder what happened?" He walked a little closer to the pond and tried again, and once again, nothing.

"I wonder if maybe it could be the water blocking the signal." Seve suggested, "And if it is, how do we get a signal to them?"

"I don't know, but I know that they were tested before we placed them in the water and they functioned as they were supposed to do. Well, I guess we can just leave them there, at least by doing so we will see if those cases will remain watertight. We'll need to go talk with Judd and see what he thinks. But for now let's get out of this weather. Heck, in the short time we've been out here we've gone from a sunny day to one where the clouds are starting to build. It looks like that storm is getting here faster than we thought."

* * *

Several days later Saige was walking one of the many hall ways within the complex when he heard children screaming. Very concerned he picked up his pace, and actually began to run as he headed towards the daycare center. Turning the last corner he stopped in his tracks and stared. At this time of day the door into the center was kept open, and on the floor in the hallway was a layer of heavy fog, not much more than ankle high, but what was something like this doing in here? He could see that it had filtered into the open doorway, and was slowly drifting towards where he was standing. He saw Judd approaching from the opposite side walking through this stuff seemingly unconcerned. He had a smile on his face and as he came closer he asked, "Well, what do ya' think?" Seeing the concerned look on Saige's face, he continued, "Oh don't worry about it, this is completely harmless. But you have to admit it's quite an effect, don't you think?"

"You created this?" Saige asked.

"Of course, I was looking over some of the theatrical equipment that could be created, considering what we are trying to do is put on a show, I thought it would be a good place to look for special effects. After all we're going to need everything that we can find to pull this off."

It wasn't long until everyone who was in the facility had come because of the screaming of the children, only to find them now laughing as they ran through this ground fog. They were as perplexed as Saige when they had turned the corner to find a ground fog hugging the floors and drifting through doorways. Turning and facing them Saige said, "Quite an effect, and of course, Judd is responsible. He's assured me that it's harmless, and while at first it terrorized our children, at least the toddlers, you can now see that they are having a blast." Turning back to Judd he asked, "What's your plans for this stuff? Plus we are inside, so it would be easier to make it do this, can it work in a large area?"

"A good question, a very good question. I think it comes down to the size and number. But by looking at the history of these things they have been used in large areas. When we finally set up our mock-up, then we can try it and see. I'm counting on the fact that at night there is little wind, and that this stuff will hug the ground just like you are seeing it now. Remember that there's a full air recirculating system in here, and it still has remained on the floor, although you can see it being drawn into the floor vents. I was curious to see what the stuff looked like. The images I saw in the archives looked pretty spectacular, and as you could see, the initial effect was fear. And before you ask, no I didn't think it would get this far down the hallway, and drift into the daycare center, but no harm done, as you can see, the kids love it now."

"That may be so, but it surely panicked all the rest of us when we heard the children scream, so please warn us in the future if you are trying something that could put us on edge."

Laughing a little Judd said, "Ah, where's the fun in that? Yeah I know what you're saying, but look, at times it is better to surprise someone to get an honest reaction. If it surprises us, or for a brief time scares us, then we know that it could have a more devastating effect on the primitives who have no knowledge of this."

Saige had to admit that what he stated made sense, but at the same time with the pressure, and time restraints everybody was on edge. "Okay, I can see that, but just be careful. Look I know that at one time we were going to be setting up out in the meadows, but changed our minds since the small attaching valley, where the entrance to the trail to the secondary facility is located, has much the same structure as the valley where we will be doing this, so, as you know, we'll be using it. It has the waterfall, the cliffs, the narrow trail into the area and the steep walls. Yes, it's much smaller, but if we can get things to work there on the smaller scale, all we will have to do is scale it up to work in the larger space. So any time that you want to get started on placing everything into position for testing, grab who you need and do it. We need to begin testing all of this and see what we need to change, what works, what doesn't, and what fails miserably. You know like our initial attempts to make the emitters work underwater. That took some work to finally solve that issue, but I have to admit that the effects that can be created are unbelievable. If I didn't know that they were just created images, I'd swear that they were real."

"Yeah, once the problem was solved the results were rather nice." Judd stopped a moment and then said, "Look, I'm sorry about the interruption here, but now that I've seen this, I think that if we can make this work that I have a great idea of how to enhance this to make it even more frightening to the primitives."

"That's great, Judd, but just don't test it here. We really don't need a repeat thank you."

Laughing once again, Judd replied, "Oh, you don't need to worry about that. Did you know that back on our home world that there was a tradition that they did once an annual? It was where they celebrated the dark side of things. From what I could ascertain it originally had come about as a way to appease the dead spirits when we were primitives, but evolved over time as a celebration, more for kids, and that much of what we are attempting to create was common in households. Look come by when you have time and I'll bring up the information and you can watch some of the footage on it, in fact it probably would be a good idea that in the next meeting that we have that all of us watch it. After all, as you've reminded all of us, we need all the ideas we can get to pull this off, and this could get the mind going in the right direction."

"Okay, look we have our normal daily meetings every morning, so do you think you could bring it up on the monitors in the morning? I'll come by later this day and you can show me."

"Yes to both. Look Saige, if you have a moment now, it will only cost you about thirty minutes, so let me show you now. Then if you want everybody to see it then it will be a simple thing to do, and why not have your sister come along, so that we have both sides. I'll be down in what has become my work area, so when the two of you can get over there, soon, please do. I'll be waiting."

After about twenty minutes both Saige and Shellian showed up at the work area of Judd, with Shellian stating, "Okay, Judd we're here, and I must admit that I could use the break, this schedule is really tough. But you won't hear me complain, since we have it so much better than others."

Judd signaled them over to one of the larger monitors where he had some large rectangular boxes set up. When he saw the questioning looks he pointed at them and said, "Oh these things are speakers. It was kind of a hobby of mine back in Jade. These are a very old design, but the sound quality out of them I just love. Anyway, have a seat and enjoy the show."

What they saw, as the archives played, were children laughing and having fun, it was nighttime and they all were dressed in some sorts of costumes. As they approached the houses there were decorations that reflected the dark, and some had those fog generators, others had what looked to be grave yards in the front area. They could hear those children through those speakers, and the quality was unbelievable. When the children would get to the doors they would knock or push a button and the ones inside would then open their doors, at which point the children would yell "trick or treat", hold out a bag, and something would be placed into those bags, and the children would move on to the next one.

"What I want you to see is all the different ideas that were used to give the feeling of the dark. And you can see that our ancient ancestors had many ideas. And you can also see that the very young who are apparently going on this trek for the first time are a bit tentative, but it doesn't take them long to figure out what's going on. And it looks like, even for the adults, that all of them are having a good time. I think they called this Halloween."

The two of them were fascinated by what they saw. So many of the homes decorated in the macabre, so many ideas, who would have thought? They looked at each other and then Shellian asked, "Are you sure about this? I mean I never realized that we did this kind of thing, and made it fun?"

Smiling Judd replied, "Yeah really. Maybe it was one of the reasons for coming here in the first place. While I'm sure that there's going to be major differences, there's probably going to be things that are similar. And let's admit it; death is something that we all face. There's no way to avoid it. Although again if you look through history, many tried, but as far as I know nobody ever succeeded in cheating death. So what do you think? Should everybody see this?"

Together Shellian and Saige replied, "Yes.", and then laughed. Saige said, "Go ahead sis, I'll bow to your will on this one."

"Why thank you brother, Judd, yes I think you're quite right, everyone needs to see this. And on another subject, I know that my brother has let you know about the thoughts on the test area, but looking at the time, the major moon will be in the sky in another five days, and from what we can see it should be a cold clear night. Do you think that we can at least see some of your magic then, so that we can get an idea of its effects? Now we know that nothing is truly ready, but as you so amply proved today, seeing is believing."

Thinking for a moment before answering Judd replied, "I guess so. But don't expect much. There's so much that is untested, and we've really nothing set up as of yet, but I guess we can at least try."

"Good, tap whoever you need. We need to at least see something if for no other reason than to show everyone that we actually are accomplishing something."

* * *

It was late at night and everybody was chilled to the bone. After all, while it had been clear, it was still winter in the mountains. The major moon had lit the countryside in a soft eerie glow, and as they had waited for the show to begin, the cold began to work its way through the many layers of clothing, but now that the short show was over and they were sitting around the tables in the cafeteria, drinking lots of coffee and trying to get warm, there was a cautious euphoria that had permeated all of them that were present. The test, which only had very little of the total planned operations worked, and that was all they could hope. Now with the script almost finished and the translation in the process, it wouldn't be long before they began to film the people who would be in this play.

From this point on until they did this for real, there would be practice, practice, practice, followed by more of the same. Judd, with Stone as his assistant, continued to test and work out the problems as they used the small valley as a test bed, slowly bringing in the different elements, and solving the many unexpected or unknown problems that continued to rise. Winter was almost at an end, and soon they would need to be in the valley where the primitive alliance would gather. It would take time to get everything in place, followed by the hiding of anything that they had worked in the valley. There could be no sign left to make the primitives suspicious that other than another tribe or clan, which wasn't a part of the alliance, had been anywhere close to this area.

CHAPTER EIGHTEEN

"Charley, look you've got to provide that stuff. There's no way that we will want to transport it from here. It's just too far, and there are too many things that could happen. Again it must be ready. Storms about to end, or at least switch to rain, and we have to have everything on site before they end, and the primitives begin their annual foraging after the winter. Plus most of the heavy lifting needs to be complete before then also. We need that rain to help hide what we're doing." Judd looked down at the monitor where he saw his buddy Charley.

"Yeah, I know," Charley said, "But look, this stuff isn't something that's that easy to produce, let alone handle. And with everything else that you've requested, well let's just say, that while we have the cooperation of the council and every-body here, since we've learned how close the primitive headquarters is to us, it still has taxed our capacity. And since much of this was never in our replicators, it has taken time to get the software integrated, tested, and operating. We've found that back when these cities were set up, that for what-ever reason, it was deemed that none of the replicators would have this stuff, and they added software to block its addition if someone, oh you know, like me tried to integrate it back into the system. Even with the help of the software engineers here at Catskill, it's been a nightmare, and as you once again so aptly pointed out, time is not our friend. So we are very far behind on the requests, the needs that you have laid out to us, and, to be honest, even the needs of the city.

"Heck, since we've learned that all the cities are vulnerable, and even changing the frequency to our protections has failed, most of the time and resources has gone into coming up with some solution. It is another one of those unanticipated problems from our ancestors. It seems that they wanted to be sure that at any time that it was necessary, any of the citizens would be able to pass through the veils, and not have to worry about them. So there is woven into every stitch of clothing "IR" tags that automatically adjust to the changes. And we now know that is what the primitives are using to pass unharmed through our protections. It makes it very simple for them, and it is obvious that it didn't take them very long to figure this one out. And on that subject are you sure this show that all of you are planning won't be figured out also?"

It was a question all of them had been asking, and as complicated as the plan was, the whole thing was more a timing thing, than anything else, and that was one of the many reasons all of them were practicing so hard. Most of the operations would be handled by the computers that they would have hidden on site, with redundancy in every system, including the many machines and equipment that would be playing a direct part in the play. After thinking about this Judd answered, "All we can hope is that they won't. We have one hole card at this moment, even though I haven't had a chance to talk with her, but in a sense she is our front person. It turns out she is known by the people who rescued us. She is a captive of the clan whose leader is the leader of the alliance."

"A woman? Charley exclaimed, "I understand that women are no more than baby generators, and have no rights, or even are allowed to speak in the presence of any male. At least that is what all of you have passed on to us."

"And that's very true. I know it from first-hand experience having to watch our captive women submit to their males, and not be able to do anything about it, other than vow that somehow we could end it, and now we have that chance."

"Okay, I guess you just confirmed it then, but how is this particular woman going to help?"

"I'm really not allowed to say a lot on that subject, but let's just say that she has left an impression on the clan that she is more than just a woman, or in their case, a female. Anyway, this is off the subject, how much time are we looking at? With this next approaching storm, which is going to be another strong one, we'll be hauling everything we have from here to the site, and after we cache it there, will be coming to pick up whatever you have ready, plus anybody that you have, that is going to do the grunt work, which is necessary to get this set up. Every male here will be on site, leaving the women to operate the Alpha, and to monitor everything. We're quite short here normally, but by cutting the staff literally in half, it will be a critical shortage, and the ones left here at the Alpha will be pushed to the very limit on monitoring the situation as things develops and at the same time keeping us informed as to what is transpiring. As you know we've been testing all of this stuff, but the area where we were working is very much smaller than that valley, so while we've scaled up everything, there's no guarantee that it will be enough. That's why we need it in place well before the time of need, so that we can test everything when it is in place, and modify or add as necessary. Remember this valley or rift is huge, and lies just outside of the desolation, making it a very convenient jumping off point for their attacks, since all of our cities are located in that desolation."

Taking a deep breath and exhaling it slowly, Charley shook his head, "I just wish that we had more time, but I guess if wishes came true we'd see a rescue shuttle from our home world." He paused a moment and then almost whispered, "Who'd of thought that we weren't from here but somewhere out there in the vast unknown. I've had a chance to look over what was sent from the Alpha, and it sure makes one yearn to see it. I mean the images of this world from space are spectacular, and the images of our world make this one pale in comparison." Sighing Charley said, "Okay, I know that the storm will hit us first and that I've got to have as much as we can ready for you. So, one way or the other, I guess we'll actually be seeing each other face to face for the very first time, instead of just over the circuits."

"Yeah, I guess that's very true. You know maybe the isolation between the cities isn't a good thing. I mean I understand why they did this, our ancestors, but nobody can support anybody, and right now that is something that is very necessary. We're being lucky that you're as close as you are to that valley. Okay then, see you very soon." At this point Judd signed off, stood a moment staring at nothing, shuddered a little, as another dark thought went briefly through his mind, left and headed back to his shop.

* * *

It was moving day, well, that's what they decided to call it anyway. It was the day that all the men would be leaving the facility and with the storm raging, head for the valley of the primitives, as they had begun to call it. Once there they would cache the materials out of the weather with some of the portable shelters they were carrying. They were more than just tents, and could for a while be temporary living quarters, workshops, or whatever they needed. These units used air bladders to form ribs that supported them; being double-walled they did a fair job insulating any from the outside elements. They had enough vehicles that everybody was driving and no one was a passenger. Once they were set up, and the equipment unloaded they would then head over to the City of Catskill, meet Charley and his crew, and return. Then no matter what the weather presented, they would be working from dawn to dusk, and Saige was sure, as was Judd, that at times they would be working deep into the night.

The night before all had bid their goodbyes and they had proceeded down the trail to the secondary site, checked all the equipment one last time, and had "batched" it, before heading out just before dawn. Even with the vehicles it was a couple days travel to reach the valley of the primitives. At least with the storm there would be no sign of their passing. Again like their surveillance vehicles that they used when they scouted, these had the capability to either hover, or move on wheels, all according to the terrain that they were traversing at that particular moment. And when they finally reached their destination, it was with gale force winds and snow blowing and dropping from the sky causing white out conditions. At least there truly would be nothing left of the trail they had made coming here.

All of them got out of the vehicles and went to the lee side of the biggest one to get out of the wind. Even still it was almost impossible to hear over the gale. "I don't know if these shelters are supposed to stand in conditions like this. Did anybody see the specs on these things?" Saige asked. All he got was blank stares as the wind whipped his words away. It was freezing, and even with the heavy protection the cold was penetrating making all of them shake from the cold. "Look, this reminds me of our first winter on the mountain. Our research suggests that this valley is a result of ancient volcanic action as it was part of what created those mountains. So let's spread out in teams of two and see if we can find a cave or caves for us to spend the night. At least with our portable heaters we won't be lacking for heat, but this is absolutely miserable. So let's do it. Use the vehicles to get close to the walls, and then use the headlights to illuminate the area to make it easier to see. Use your headsets to keep in contact, and if anybody finds one that is big enough to hold our team, and then let us know and then we can use it for tonight. If necessary, tomorrow we can attempt to find something better if we need to. "

It had taken a full two days to reach the valley, and even though it was difficult to tell, they had arrived just before dusk. The only way they could judge, other than by the time, was the slowly darkening sky and the subtle deepening of the shadows in the surrounding area. With care, and half the vehicles now circled close to the area where the leader of the alliance stayed when the alliance was in the valley, they headed out in teams of two in the remaining vehicles towards the perimeter of valley. The storm was even interfering with the headsets, setting up a continual static making it harder to hear anything at all. So between the sounds of the storm, the vehicles, and the static, it took them a while to recognize that there had been a cave found, smaller than the one that they had lived in that first winter, but big enough to hold the team, but it had taken until full darkness had fallen for it to be located. Eventually they moved just enough equipment inside so that they could heat the small space, have some hot food and lots of coffee, and have a place to bed down. Once inside and out of the wind it was like a pressure being lifted off of all of them, and the silence in comparison to the howling storm left their ears ringing. Nobody felt like talking as they were beat. So one by one they grabbed their food, ate it quietly and then turned in. Tomorrow would be soon enough to begin the set-up. And with this storm raging there was little to no chance that any of the primitives would be out scouting. It was just too nasty. The last thing that Saige did before he retired was to contact the Alpha letting them know that they were here and safe, although with the fierceness of the storm they would be spending the night in a cave.

* * *

For the next three weeks, with the help of the team from Catskill, they worked putting together and testing the equipment. They found, about three quarters of the way up one of the cliff faces, a hidden cave that was invisible from below. It was from this cave that they put their control room, placing a hologram over the entrance to hide it completely from the eyes of the primitives. Again this was set up to allow them to peer out and monitor with their own eyes if one of the many cameras and monitors failed. They placed a robust solar power system that was installed on a couple of the inaccessible cliff tops, placing them in such a way to avoid detection. Again the cave that they chose for their control room confirmed that this area at one time had been volcanic. Here, because of the size, they were able to put the storage batteries, and once all the equipment was installed, the one very large cave seemed a bit cramped. Yet with everything planned they couldn't reduce the size or amount of equipment.

The storms were lessening, showing all of them that winter were running out of energy and spring wasn't far off. Time was very short, and it just seemed like there was just too much that still needed to be done, and not enough accomplished. All would be up before dawn, and work late into the night, and at times they would break into shifts and with the great beacons would work throughout the night. As each piece and section was completed, they would test it, and test it again. And in areas where it was critical, not that most of these weren't, redundancy was the order of the day. Pressure was on, and with each short test and failure, replacements had to be installed. Soon it would be time to return the team to Catskill and they would be on their own, continuing to test, and run through the timings.

Standing in the early morning light Judd said to Charley, "Well, this has been a lot of very hard work, but we surely couldn't have done this without you and your people. I can really say that now, looking back on what we did here. Now for the rest of us before we return to the Alpha it's just test, replace where necessary, clean up and get out of here ourselves until that time when we see the movements of the clans and tribes heading in this direction warning us that it will be show time. Remember the frequencies, not that it's important that you do that since they will be given to every city that still exists." He reached out and shook Charley's hand, at which point Charley just nodded, climbed into the crew section of the vehicle with his crew and the vehicle pulled away heading off into the direction of Catskill. Judd watched it until they were out of sight sighed, turned around and headed back to the base camp. He glanced back at the cliff face where the hidden cave was located. It surely looked different with the scaffolding removed, and just the rope ladders hanging down. These ladders would allow them access to the many areas that they would have to reach before pulling them up and hiding them. Once the primitives were here in this valley they would be staying within that upper cavern out of sight and out of harm's way. They still had much to do, and they hadn't tried running everything completely through the program to see if the system would hold up.

He had to admit that a very hot cup of coffee this morning would be just the thing he needed. He was finding that he just didn't have the reserves that he had in the past, and that his recovery from being tired took longer. His mind said let's go do this and finish it, and his body would argue back starting with the question, "You want me to do what?" Just where were those reserves he had in his youth? It seemed as the long days had passed that it had been more and more difficult to get moving in the mornings, and his mind remained in a fog much longer than he could remember. He was finding it was easier to make mistakes, and mistakes he would have never made if he had been fresh. It frustrated him to no end – admonishing himself continually to concentrate, to get with the program. *Oh well, we'll be done soon, and once done rest will be there.* As he entered back into the camp area it appeared to be so empty now. With him there were only nine of them now. Breathing out deeply he stared at their small fire went over to it and warmed his hands.

Saige looking up from where he was sitting said, "I guess we're back to just us now. I'm glad that you had that contact; I can tell that we really wouldn't have been able to do this on our own with this small of a crew. Thank you for this, and of course before they left I personally thanked each one of them." Looking around the campsite he said, "I must admit that this place looks a lot lonelier at this moment with only us. But it is a lot quieter now, and I admit that right now the quiet is very nice. With all the work going on at times it seemed like we were building a city right here in this valley instead of setting up a show. I must admit that this gives me a much better appreciation for the work that goes on behind the scenes of some of those stage shows we used to go see now and then when we still had a city."

"You did that? I was under the impression that the scouting unit never left your compound and came into the cities."

Laughing Saige replied, "Well for the most part you are quite correct. But as rewards for teams we would be able to go get something special in the city or most of the time go see some stage entertainment. There were competitions four times an annual and the winners were allowed half a day to do what they pleased, and were given passes to the plays, and to go to the markets to get some trinket or the like. It was fun, and it gave us something to look forward to now and then. And the competitions were always fun, even though there was always a serious side to them." He paused a moment with a serious faraway look in his eyes, "But I guess in the end, it was proven that we weren't as good as we thought we were. Had we, then so many more of us would have survived that flight from our city."

Judd thought a moment before saying anything. He hadn't been there, but from his time at the Alpha he could see that this was something that continued to weigh heavily on both of the leaders, and he could understand it. Nobody had seen what had transpired coming. "I don't know how to answer that Saige, but none of us were prepared for what happened. And how could you and your scouts know that your team was the last? If the rest had kept the program, then there's a slight possibility that we would have had some warning, but would it had made any difference? I have no answers, and I know that you and Shellian keep beating yourself over the past, something we cannot change. Yes I admit that like some of those games that are available on the systems and boards, it would be nice if we could either start a level over, or take a move back on a board. Life, unfortunately doesn't allow second chances that way. So we have to live with what happened to us, and learn from it or be doomed to repeat. I would say that the two of you, and yes the rest of the scout team there at the Alpha has definitely learned from it."

Waving his arms around in the direction of the whole valley he continued. "Look here's your proof. If you and yours hadn't gained something from that nightmare I really don't think we would be here doing what we are. I don't think that I and the rest from Jade would be there at the Alpha either, and the knowledge that has been passed on to the other cities would have been either. Yes I know that it's in our nature to keep bashing ourselves for some oversight or mistake that we made, but it's part of life and if you think about it, we make small mistakes all of our lives. It's what we learn from those mistakes that makes the difference. And from my humble point of view, you and the rest here and back at the Alpha have learned quite a bit. And none of you have sat back and just watched the grass grow. We are here just about, hopefully, to correct a very big mistake made by our leadership, by our people, and save many lives, much misery, and destruction. And why is this happening? Because you learned, and were then willing to apply what you learned."

Looking around the valley once more before looking back at Saige, Judd continued, "Look, none of us can predict the outcome from this little adventure. All of us are hoping that it works. But what if it doesn't? Does this mean that you'll give up and throw in the towel? From what I've seen the answer is obvious, out in the open, it's there for any to see. No, you and the rest will continue to try to come up with something else, and continue to press on until either all of us are dead, or you have succeeded. I can see why this Shayne passed on the leadership to the two of you. Your abilities have been proven in fire, and because of this the two of you have, if nothing else, gotten stronger, you've been tempered to a strength and resolution of a high quality stainless steel of unbelievable flexibility and strength. And if you cannot see this, the rest of us can, and that's why we follow you and Shellian. You've proven your right to lead us." Looking around he could see he now had an audience. He smiled briefly and to all of them he said, "Sorry about that. I didn't mean to get up on the box and say all of this – although I won't take any of it back." He could see that the rest completely agreed with him.

A final test and everything appeared to work. They spent the next week wiping out any trace of their work and occupation of the valley, and hoped that the early spring rains would bring new growth furthering the illusion that the valley lay untouched. Through much of their time snow lay on the ground, and they had set up camp in the areas where the tribes of the alliance had, so that any paths and such that they created would blend in with the existing ones. It was time to head back and let the lands recover and finish hiding what they may have missed.

* * *

The rains had come and gone in the grasslands and the new growth and lush grasses had pushed up through the soils that were being warmed by the twin suns providing food for the herds as the migrations from the warmer areas to these areas that were normally under snow. The primitives were out, knowing that the meat from these beasts would be thin, yet it still was needed. This last season of cold had been the worst that any could remember, and while there had been enough fuels for the fires, and food, what they had been eating towards the end barely fulfilled their physical needs. All needed to get out and begin the renewing so that they would be able to prepare for the next unknown season of cold. And once this was accomplished, then and only then, would it be time for the alliance to meet in the valley, send out scouting parties, and find more of those hidden lairs.

K'jor remained somewhat frustrated as the female had yet to recover enough to be able to answer the burning questions that he wanted to ask. Yet as this one healed it was becoming more obvious to both himself and T'som that this female was a priest. Yet what tribe or clan would place a female in such an important position? Still he had to admit that as they attacked these hidden lairs, it appeared that these females held important positions, and were not a part of a breeding herd. This was something that he couldn't understand. It made no sense at all. Females and their position within the clans and tribes were for producing young, to insure the next generation. And as in the herds, only the strong would breed with them insuring strength for the future. Yet what he had observed in these lairs was nothing like this at all. It was beyond his comprehension and understanding. This had to be an aberration, what he saw was not normal, and another reason to see the end to these lairs.

Sara was frustrated with her slow recovery, but at the same time was thankful. Because had she made a full recovery, she knew that she would be warming some warrior's sleeping mat, completely against her will, but that wouldn't change or prevent it from happening. So with the brief meetings that she had with the priest she began to build her character as one who was equal to him. With the help of the bugs and the team back at the Alpha she knew what was happening within the clan, and of course most of what was happening out in the wilds. This information she used to present herself as not only a priest but a seer, one who had visions and could see even the intimate details. She could see at first surprise and disbelief from T'som as she met him as an equal. This was unheard of and at first she could see that he was indignant wanting to put her, as a female, in her place. But at that very moment she used her inside knowledge and told him exactly what he had been doing, and who he had bred with in the last day. She smiled inwardly as she saw the shock on his face, confirming the information that the team had passed on to her. Maybe she could get a small amount of revenge and begin to make them fear her a little. But she knew that this was too much to hope for. But the thought was nice.

The best part of this whole episode was the hope she now felt – something that hadn't existed for so long. She only wished she could bring the other two inside with her and let them know, but she had realized long ago that with the fear these two had, it would have been too easy for them to become traitors and try and protect themselves by giving her away. Now instead of knowing in her heart that she would die here under the thumb of this clan, she had hope that soon this could be over and she would be free of them. The ones at the Alpha wouldn't let her know what was planned, but only that her role as a priest would help. She had been told that the reason for not informing her was the chance of what they were planning could get back to the primitives. At first she was hurt by this, but realized that the less that knew of these plans the better the chance at success. So she had to be comfortable with what they were asking of her and know this imprisonment could be over very soon.

* * *

Seirra was back in the rotation for the security office and she saw that the tribes and clans appeared to be preparing to move. It was time to get the team into place. Her mate Saige, Stone, Judd, and Staven would be the ones on the ground. It was almost show time, and they needed to be there well ahead of any early arrivals. Seve would drive them there and then return. She announced over the PA that it was time to get the next phase of the operation into motion. She could feel the electricity go throughout the facility. Shorty they would know if all this planning and work was worth it. In the cafeteria they had set up monitors that would allow all who remained at the facility to watch the many hidden cameras that had been placed in the valley. Joci would be given a front row seat to this, since it was her idea. But would it bring an end to the attacks? This was a question that was on everybody's mind. Not only the ones at the Alpha, but all the remaining cities. The pressure and fear that had permeated the cities was substantial. With no one knowing who would be next, and with the failure of finding a way around the system that their ancestors had put into place, there would be no defense against the primitives. What had seemed to be a good idea at the time of implementation had come back and left the cities wide open to attack. With the cities that had fallen, the primitive warriors had enough clothing to outfit twice the attacking force's size – allowing them to pass unharmed through the fields and into the unprotected cities. At this moment the only protection was the illusions created by the holograms, and the shock fields, this had worked in the past, but not now. Somehow, somewhere these primitives had figured out the difference. Now it was only the distance between them and their locations within the desolation that had given them any respite.

* * *

K'jor looked on with satisfaction. While it had been a tough season of cold, looking around he could see that most of the tribes and clans had returned to this meeting place of the alliance. Soon, very soon he would be leading the greatest force of warriors that had ever gathered in the history of this place. Instead of fighting each other they had found a common enemy to unite against, and somehow through this he was leading. Yet he knew that if they didn't find any more of the lairs that this alliance would fall apart, and the old ways would return. In the next few days the scouts would be sent to locate more of those hidden lairs, and once located they would continue as they had in the past, attacking, destroying, gathering more slaves, and adding to the breeding herds. While many of the ones who had been taken in the past had passed into the spirit world, it was of no consequence. There were others out there to replace them, this he felt deeply inside of him. And soon, the one female who was still recovering from being at the brink of the spirit world would be able to provide answers. Yes, answers to the questions that burned deep in his soul.

This night there would be a meeting of the tribe and clan leaders just outside of his shelter as they renewed vows to stay and be strong within the alliance, to find how all had fared over this last brutal season of cold. He felt that the clans with their permanent settlements probably fared better than the nomadic tribes. Still what the tribes gained from the alliance was a strength they never had individually. And even though there were fewer warriors in these tribes, they benefited from the slaves and increases to their herds in proportion to their size. As he walked the camp areas he could see the smoke rising from many fires that marked the center of the camps of the combined alliance. He couldn't help but smile, and feel pride rise up inside of him. He led this combined might. With it just maybe, after they had accomplished what they were trying to do, this alliance could be used to bring other troublesome tribes and clans in line, and if they would not cooperate then, with this force they could be removed as if they never had existed. Shaking his head in disbelief, what he was seeing before him was something that had never been accomplished before, and this would be at least the fourth season of fighting, or maybe it was five, he truly couldn't remember. But what he had accomplished was unheard of. Looking at both the oral and written history, the records spoke of only a couple of tribes or clans ever alliancing and for only a short time. Here and over the time of its existence, he had thousands of warriors to command. Turning around to his second he asked, "What do you think? I really held out little hope back after our first season that we could hold this alliance together, but now after all of this time it is still here and still strong."

S'lon looked around at the many fires, and back at K'jor nodded his head in agreement. Like K'jor he'd had doubts that this alliance could be held together, but so far there appeared to be no weakness in it, and he thought that as long as this one common enemy existed that it would remain that way. He could see the pride in K'jor, and why not? He had been the one who had the vision to approach these many tribes and clans to convince them to join together. He really had held out little hope that K'jor would be successful, yet here before his eyes was the very proof that he had been. "I must admit that at the beginning I held out little hope of success, but you proved me wrong, and the proof is right here. I have to admit that this is a very impressive sight. And to see that most are still with you speaks much for your leadership." So many of the ones who were within the alliance had been bitter enemies at one time, and to prevent a renewing of the hostilities, the camps were set on opposite sides of the valley. Sometimes old hatreds died a hard death.

The suns had set and as dusk turned to darkness with stars shining brightly and the many fires rivaling those stars for attention, soon the major moon would rise, changing the landscape to a ghostly, shadowy image. It was a time for the spirits to walk, but K'jor knew that the priests had asked that this valley be protected. For both the major and minor moons provided the lesser light where the spirits dwelled. He could see the leaders approaching the meeting place and anticipated this first gathering of war. His faith was strong and his strength could be no better, he felt deep within that these other hidden lairs would be his soon enough, and then all could return as it was before, secure in their minds that they were in control of their destinies. No hidden lairs to threaten who they were or the directions that they may want to travel. *Yes soon we will have destroyed all of these lairs, and who knows, maybe we can move on and use this hammer to bring the troublesome tribes and clans in line and maybe keep us united.* These thoughts brought a smile to his face as he saw the future that this alliance could bring to this world.

As the major moon began to rise above the cliffs shining its soft dim light into the valley shadows and illusions of movement began to manifest all around them. And with this rising a slight breeze more sensed than felt moved the small grasses, and then a deathly silence fell that was unusual. So unusual that even the noises from the camps stopped. Looking around for a cause K'jor could find nothing. He could see that the other leaders had stopped in their tracks and were doing the very same thing. There was electricity in the air, one of anticipation, but of what none of them knew. This was very strange indeed. He turned to make a comment to his second, but before he could even state anything the sounds of drums assailed him, and all who were in this valley. But these were like none they had ever heard. The very volume shook them. The drums seemed to be emanating from the cliffs where the waterfall fell into the valley. As one they all turned and faced the cliffs, and before them sitting on the ground cross-legged were giants, except they had never seen any giants this big. In front of them were the drums and they were beating out a constant rhythm with high points and softer measures leading them to anticipation of something else happening.

They didn't have long to wait because across the ground heading towards them at a rapid pace was a ground fog that began to take on a life of its own. Dancing and rippling, moving around all barriers and leaving nothing untouched. This brought a ripple of fear as at points it began to glow as if it was a living thing. Then the campfires in the all of the camps changed color, going completely blue, dancing higher and stronger. When one looked into these changed fires they could see sprites dancing among the flames, adding more fear. What was happening and what was this they were witnessing? Had the very gods decided to visit them? A very valid question to be sure. Then in the middle of these blue flames that continued to increase in size, beings took form and began to point at the tribe and clan members bringing them close to panic. Never had any faced demons but before them now were such. Even though at this moment these demons appeared to be part of the fire, the primitives had no idea if these would remain so. Fear continued to build, but the worst was yet to come. K'jor stood there transfixed with what he was seeing and hearing. Maybe he was about to get his answers to those so many questions, but at this moment he wasn't quite sure that he would like these answers. Turning towards the priests that had accompanied him he asked harshly, "What is this? I was under the belief that this valley is protected. Does this look like it is to you?"

All the priests could do was shrug. One responded, "We have laid down our prayers and protections, and it has worked in the past."

Waving his arms around wildly and with some anger K'jor asked, "Does this look like your protection is working?" He could see from the fear in their eyes and that they had no answers. He decided to head towards these cliffs and face what was there. He wanted some answers as to why, and while he knew that he was mortal, as far as what he was facing at this moment could be no different. With a fast pace he headed towards these distance cliffs finding that he was able to only go a short distance and the fog suddenly jumped away and strong winds struck him pushing him back. When he stopped and retreated a little, the winds ceased and the fog returned boiling at his feet. Suddenly he jumped back. It had felt like something had grabbed at his feet, but with the fog could see nothing. Stomping, and striking the ground beneath this fog he found nothing to make contact with, and retreated further until he was back at the edge of the camp. It appeared that he or any of the ones gathered here would not be allowed to approach those cliffs. Looking over at others he could see that some others had tried exactly what he had and were now at the edge of their camps staring at the cliffs with others watching the demons that remained in the many fires.

Whatever was happening, or was going to happen, the line had been drawn and whatever it was definitely had their attention. Most of the warriors in the camps were now staring at the cliffs remaining quiet, waiting to see what would be shown to them next. The moving ground fog took on an eerie glow with shadows moving within it making it appear that there were creatures living within that fog. And as the shadows would approach a warrior, the warrior would feel something touch him and he would jump. Yes there was something there, something that could attack them, but how could they retaliate? All there were was shadows and nothing of substance. How did you fight something that wasn't there? All of them had considered themselves warriors, and had no real fear of fighting others, but this was different, so very different. They were being attacked, but could not return in favor. And the fires continued to dance with the demons still controlling them, the fog and its many shadow creatures continued to flow around them, and all they could do was watch and wait.

The drum beat changed and in one abrupt roll stopped, and silence once again reigned. Instead of lessening of the fear it only heightened it. These giants remained silent and motionless. For what seemed like forever the silence continued. Suddenly the waterfall began to glow in a soft light which continued to get stronger. As its strength grew the giants bowed and touched their mighty heads to the drums, lying prostrate across the drums swaying to the motion of the waterfall, rising back up and began to beat the drums once again, but this time it was a softer and slower beat. The warriors' attention was now directed completely on the waterfall which now glowed in a strong light, and in that light they could see a being forming, forming out of nothing but the mists, and as this was happening the skies above them lit with mighty fires and explosions, erupting in many colors, and in those eruptions another being was forming out of nothingness. If there had been fear before in the camps it was nothing to what they were feeling at this moment. It was obvious to all of them that the very gods that they worshiped were showing themselves to each and every warrior that was here. And if this was indeed what was transpiring how did one survive? After all a mortal could not fight and win against an immortal – a god.

But the gods weren't finished with them as the very ground, close to those cliffs, there began to form another being. The demons had been enough, the addition of this ground fog and the shadow creatures that dwelled within had made it worse, but now at least three of their gods were making an actual appearance, would there be more, and why were they doing this? Was it to show them their power over all things living and those who had passed into the world of the spirits? K'jor was at loss to explain any of this, and he knew that the priests, from their earlier reaction couldn't. So he would have to wait as the others. Yes he had to admit that he feared what he was seeing, but so far he wasn't frozen to inaction. He knew that a line had been drawn by whatever or whoever these beings were, and the warriors had been warned that they could be hurt or killed if they crossed that line. So he continued to wait, as they all did.

The god of the waters was now visible and had been looking down. He looked up and directly at them pointing with his mighty finger right at them, this was followed by the god that hung in the sky and he too pointed directly at them. Both had a stern disapproving, reproachful look on their mighty faces. The third had yet to form, the one of the earth. Then this one came into sharp focus, and they were shocked to learn that this god was female. The god of the earth was female, how could that be? Of the three she appeared to be the one whose look alone could send one to the spirit world. She, like the other two pointed at them. Absolutely all the primitives now stood in complete shock and fear frozen to their very cores by what they were witnessing. The three gods turned as one and pointed to the cliff top, a place completely inaccessible to any other than the gods. As they pointed the cliff top lit up as if it was daylight and where the light shown stood a single individual dressed in a hooded robe, looking a little like their own priests, but at the same time not.

This priest was looking down and his face completely hidden in shadow. He turned to the three gods and bowed to them each individually, and as he did each god acknowledged this homage. The god of the earth turned and faced the primitives and spoke directly to them. The voice was deep and full, and when she spoke it filled the valley with power. "I see that you are shocked that I am female. Yet it should not be so. After all as your mortal female bring forth your new generation it is I who brought forth all that live on this world. It is I who gave your first people their lives, it is I who produced the herd beasts, the grasses that they eat, the plants, all that is living is because of my creation." At this point she ceased and was quiet.

The god of the sky took up the next statements. "I am of the sky. I am responsible for the rain, the snow, the winds, the clouds. It is I who will give and withhold the rains, make them light, make them heavy, allow your foods to prosper or to wither, to chase the beasts away with the winds or storms, I provide this." He fell silent.

The third picked up from there, "I am the god of the flowing waters, of the lakes and oceans, I change the rivers, bringing it close or taking it away, building great lakes where the fish dwell, move it close to the beasts so that they may fatten and provide meat, take away when I am unhappy." He fell silent.

Then to the warriors' surprise the demons that were dancing in the flames began to speak in unison. "We are of fire. We can create fire from the sky, burn off great areas of the grasslands, forests, we will not be controlled by such as you, but allow the use of fire to cook your food, to keep you warm in the season of cold, and we watch always."

All of these gods, once again turned towards the priest that stood on the cliff top, pointed and as they pointed the drummers chanted something that could not be translated. This single priest was raised into the air standing on nothing with his arms outstretched they could see blue sparks emitting from his fingertips. The god of the sky turned back to the shaking warriors and asked, "K'jor, why have you attacked and destroyed our servants, our priests? They were hidden from you in the desolation. They were intermediaries between us, the spirit world and were tasked with the responsibility to watch, from a distance, you and yours. Yet you have come into the very place that you are not to be, a place of the spirits, a place where you can only visit with no way to survive if you remain. Why have you done these things?"

The god of the waters picked up from there and said, "We have been watching and have been greatly troubled by your actions. We sent warnings, which you ignored, we sent a harsh season of cold, which you ignored, we have been patient waiting for your understanding that this was to stop. Yet, here you are, as are all these warriors, getting set to start another campaign against our servants, against us. How are we to interpret this, to see your actions? And finally how are we to respond? These were things that we have discussed among ourselves. In the end it was felt that we should reveal ourselves, not all obviously, but we three were chosen. It is here that we draw the line in the sand. We have passed on to our servant who now is before you some of our power, although it will be only here and only now. This ends here, and if you and your alliance of warriors continues in this vein, we will bring forth all the power that we have and destroy all of you, all of the clans, all of the tribes, and the god of the earth will begin again, creating new life to replace you and yours if necessary. We require that you return all that you have made slaves, all that you have added to your breeding herds, return them here or feel the wrath that we can bring down upon you. The time is short and we who are over you will now have our servant demonstrate."

Again the three gods turned and pointed at the priest who was suspended in the air. At the moment they pointed he glowed absorbing the power from the gods. This priest then spoke, "The time is short, by the end of the season of greening all that have survived your abuse will be placed here in the valley of the gods. They must be returned unharmed; we know that many have passed into the spirit world, for they have told us of the abuse they received from you. The females were protected and because of this protection could not carry any of your offspring. It would have been an affront for such to happen." At this point this priest swept his left arm out from his body and as he did lines of explosions traveled rapidly across the valley in front of the warriors, and everywhere these explosions took place warriors from the spirit world appeared standing in ranks looking both at the warriors and back to the priest who seemed to be commanding them. They stood in ranks keeping beat with the drums that had picked up the tempo once again. These warriors who had passed into the spirit world were now shouting in unison, tapping the spears that many carried in time with the drum beat.

Then this priest swept his right arm from his body and great explosions followed closing off the two exits into the desolation, forever blocking access from this valley. He spoke saying, "Let this be known, that with the closing of the routes to the desolation that this is a symbol, a warning that as the Sacred Mountains are only available to the priests, and yes we allow the hunters to hunt in the low areas, so shall the desolation become sacred. For it is there that we priests and servants of the gods live by their request. Return the priests and servants, and understand this – this will be your one and only warning. If these attacks continue then in short order all who will have participated will join the ones in the spirit world." At this point he brought his hands together in a single clap, and out of the sky fell a large fireball that struck in the middle of the warriors from the spirit world setting the area on fire, this was followed by a spectacular explosion and numerous smaller explosions in the night sky, drawing all of the warriors attention to the display. When the light had faded they looked back to the cliff top, but it was dark and empty, and as they looked around all was as it was before. The ground fog was gone, the drummers were gone, the gods and spirit warriors were gone, and all that remained was a deathly silence. The gods had spoken, and had put forth their displeasure, and demonstrated what would happen if they did not comply. For once K'jor, who had been singled out by the gods, was silent. He now had his answers, and felt fortunate that he was still among the living. It was obvious to him that the gods saw each and every individual and what they did with their lives. He had worried all of the season of cold if he had been wrong; he wondered why these females didn't carry, and why a female would be a priest. Now he had all his answers, and much more.

The gods had said that this was the valley of the gods, and so it would always be known. For it was here that they revealed themselves to mere mortals. No wonder the servants to the gods had female priests, since the god of the earth turned out to be female. That was a shock, but once explained made perfect sense. New life came from the female, so all life had come to be in the same way. He could deny it if he wanted, but the power demonstrated tonight was so beyond any he and all the others had ever witnessed, that he did not want it brought down upon them. He, and the rest, would comply with the demands of the gods, and the desolation would thusly become sacred as the mountains, and with the appearance of the gods here in this valley he knew that there would be a demand that this valley also become sacred and he wouldn't argue that at all. In the morning they would break camp, head back, and bring those slaves and additions to the herd back here unharmed, and then, other than the priests, leave this valley and the desolation to the gods.

* * *

Joci sat in awe of what she had just witnessed. If she hadn't known that all of this had been created by them she could have easily believed that it was all magic and sorcery, and that the gods had actually made an appearance, vented their displeasure, demonstrated their power, warned their creations, and returned to wherever they went. It was a spectacular display – just unbelievable. She felt the emotions rising in her and she began to cry, but through her tears she could hear cheering behind her. With tears running down her cheeks she turned and saw the rest of the Alpha crew cheering for the success of her idea. She was completely overwhelmed. At no point did she feel that her idea had any merit, but here was the proof that she had been wrong. Was it finally over? Had they succeeded in bringing an end to the threat? It would be known in the morning, but from what they could see the answer was yes.

Saige made his way silently in the dark back from the cliff top and with the assistance of the night goggles reached the entrance to the cave and entered. Seeing Judd leaning against one of the dimly lit walls he asked, "What happened? Got that message from you in the middle of the performance that we had to jump ahead and skip part of what we had planned and jump to the end."

"We were almost out of power. We tested each element of this darn thing a number of times to be sure it would all work. But we didn't run the thing clear through to see if we had enough battery storage to make it happen – we didn't. In fact I was worried that we wouldn't get that finale complete before everything just died, it was that close."

Shortly they were joined by the other two who had worked other operations, and other than the reduction of the one part they all felt good. So they waited out the night monitoring the camps with the remote cameras, through the portable unit that had a self-contained power supply, and as the dawn began to break they could see movement from the camped tribes and clans as they prepared to leave. Joci's idea, and the subsequent work, and planning had brought about the results that they had hoped. The attacks should now cease and the remaining cities be untouched. They still had much work ahead of them, but at least now it would be from a place of safety instead of war.

Yes they'd return back to Point Alpha and have a quiet celebration of a job well done. And with the returning of their people to this valley they knew it would take time. Then came the hard work of placing them, but all of that was for the future. Now for the first time since the first city fell they could feel safe. Safe with the knowledge of their true past, and be able to look to a real future.

F. D. Brant

E P I L O G U E

Winter was upon them and with the primitives once again locked inside their homes it had been a time to travel. Saige with Seirra stood on top of a small rise inside the compound that had been their home since they had joined the scouting unit. It was a bittersweet moment. He was holding his daughter Saharra, and Seirra their son Seth. Time had flown as their twins were close to walking, and with this being a strange place to both they could see both the excitement and fear in the children. Saharra clung to him, and he hugged her smiling, although it was a sad smile, and introspection had set in. It seemed almost like another lifetime that they had been here, living, unconcerned, practicing and learning. The clouds above them were gray and sullen, full of moisture and a light rare mist was falling, chilling them as the soft breeze would caress them. He could see the rest of the original team with their children, yes Sorrel had successfully carried and delivered a daughter, and with the healthy baby, one could see the additional worry and fear melt from her, and she was very happy. And to break from tradition she named her daughter

April, but was it really, after all her daughter was born in the Alpha.

They were exploring the many buildings that stood vacant and broken, the places that had been home to all of them. Here they could sense the ghosts of the past, in this once thriving city which was dead, that had fallen to the primitives so very long ago. Towards the entrance to the city they could see Sara, she still was weak, but Saar had given her a clean bill of health, and with the care at the Alpha, she had recovered. Saige couldn't help but smile when he saw her kneeling down and straightening something on one of her sons. She had been through hell, and fortunate that when it ended that she was reunited with her sons. So few had been returned when compared to the numbers that had been captured. So many had suffered at the hands of the primitives, and had died. How many families were no more? It was a question for which he knew that he would have no answer. This was now a lonely silent world, this city, and a world that was not truly home. Maybe someday, their ancestors would look upon their birth world, if it still existed, and return home from a world that was to be a temporary assignment, a temporary stop in their lives. But time had shown that one can never predict or plan for the outcome that hides in the future, and while it was unknown to them, as to any who existed in this universe, at least they knew that with what their past had presented to them, they could face whatever the future handed them.

Turning to Seirra Saige asked, "What do you think, should we go join the rest of them? I feel that this is the last time we'll ever see Sequoyah, and now the Alpha is home, at least for now."

Like Saige, Seirra smiled, but it too was a sad one. So much had happened, so much had changed, so much tragedy, and yet here they were. Looking down and then into his eyes she said, "Yeah, lets."

F. D. Brant

A Taste Of History Past, Or That's Another Fine Myth You've Gotten Me Into

The satellite remained in geosynchronous orbit above an unnamed planet located in a distant binary star system. It was one of the many that had been placed here thousands of cycles around the suns in the past. At the beginning the activity had been high and the AI that was part of who he was had been kept quite busy. It had been a time of discovery and time of communication between all of them and the ones who had created them. There had been much traffic from the shuttles that brought messages and needed supplies from the great galactic ships that roamed the vastness of space bringing news from their homeworld. It was enough to keep all the AI's busy and content. After all they were fulfilling their functions. And there were trips from some of these same shuttles to repair the satellites to keep them functioning and in tip top order. There had been upgrades and while they could never claim to be truly conscious or sentient as the ones who had created them, still with their memory cores and abilities to see, to hear, to communicate with one another and with the ones who had created them, it had been enough.

Then the shuttles came no more. The communications traffic from the Alpha had continued as it was for a while, and then it slowly dwindled, and disappeared. It seemed that they were on their own, forgotten, unwanted, unneeded, but this was something that was beyond their comprehension, their understanding, so they continued to do as they had been programmed. But without the periodic trips from the creators to replace broken and worn parts they began to fail. And one by one they went dark, falling towards the planet as they lost their ability to hold their positions, and as this ability failed they were pulled slowly towards the planet and then in a streak of fiery light and death disintegrate in the atmosphere as any meteor would.

Yet before this became the known reality, and after 2346 turns around this binary system, they were needed once again. The Alpha once again was filled with the creators. But to their disappointment it appeared that these new ones knew not of them and what they were capable of performing for them. Still as they watched, the Alpha became more and more active as systems that had been placed into the "down and maintenance" mode came back to life, back on line. And then the joy, when, once again, part of what they were designed to do, had been rediscovered and used by these new ones. Yet, they had used only a very small part of what they, the satellites, were capable of performing. And he was the Alpha among the satellites, and all of others answered to him as he answered to the creators. But as the messages of needing repairs piled and as he sent the requests on to the creators they never responded, no shuttles answered their calls for help. And finally as would be expected, the first went dark. Dumping all the information it had collected, ejecting its memory core as it had been programed, to save what was there, followed by the silent plunge into the atmosphere and the streaking fiery death.

Another 513 cycles passed and their pleas for help continued to go unanswered, unheard, and were unknown by the creators. At this time the shuttles arrived once again from deep space and there was once again a major flurry of activity, but this time they were completely forgotten as the many hidden cities emptied out and became vacant . . . ghosts. And once empty great plumes of smoke from what was known as the desolation climbed into the skies, marking the end of these hidden cities. And then finally the Alpha Complex too went silent – leaving only the satellites, the abandoned shells that had once been the cities, and the Alpha, as the reminders that another people had been here at one time. *Soon, yes very soon he too would be joining his brothers in that fiery death.* His systems were failing, his pleas for help falling on abandoned facilities, with no ears to hear, no voices to respond, no hands to help. He was completely alone, forgotten, and well beyond what these primitive people that he observed, the ones who lived on this unknown planet could do. And soon he like the others would be gone, leaving the ones ignorant that such as he had ever existed, had been watching them from their skies.

Only one last function left to perform. A burst transmission to the Alpha with all the accumulated data, the ejection of his memory core and he too would cease to exist . . .

F. D. Brant

C H A P T E R   O N E

Kal stood on a slight rise. It was either late in the Season of Green or early in the Season of Pre-harvest or Heat, as his ancestors would have said. He really wasn't quite sure since he had lived all his life in one of the many large villages. He had only met his mate a few turns in the past and right now she was back at the shelter taking care of whatever it was that she did. These open spaces here in the grassland plains bothered him. He was used to the more closed areas as one who had spent all of remembered life working with his family at their business of providing baked goods to the residents. So there had been little time for such things as going out and just staring at the wide open spaces. Yet here he was. There was a wind blowing and the grasses gave the appearance of waves as the winds moved among them. He could hear the roar of the wind as it rose and fell, hitting him with a warmth that dried the sweat on his forehead. It promised to be a warm day. Sighing and shaking his head, he was quite undecided as to what to do. If he hadn't been given that gift on the celebration of his twentieth by an old family member he would have been quite happy to live in his ignorance. But he had, and so here he stood, staring at nothing. *Why me? Why was it me, the one chosen within the family to receive this?*

At first he was excited, especially when he had learned that this record, this archive that he had been given, went all the way back to one of the clan leaders who had played a major role in what had become of this world. Then, even though he was sure that he probably had been told before, he learned that he was a direct descendent of this particular clan leader and why their last name was Kaygor. Although from the records that were put together by the clan scribes and religious leaders, all from that time, he – the clan leader – had only one name and his was K'jor. *So how did we get Kaygor from K'jor – and why that apostrophe in the name? Oh, that's right, I was told that at this time in our history we were a warrior race, and there was fighting all the time between the many clans and tribes that existed, and that only could be added to a name once rank had been received, whatever that rank might have been.* He had to admit that as a child, the idea of fighting in battles as warriors sounded, well, sounded romantic. Save the female and such. But as he had read the translation, since the language had changed much in the 1500 turns or so, he was shocked to learn how the females had been treated. Thinking about his mate, he could never imagine, in his wildest nightmare, of such a thing. And once his mate had read it he could see anger in her eyes that such a thing had been the way of the past.

He remembered her angry retort, "If any male tried something like that today, we'd put him in his place immediately!" He could see from her stance that he had better just agree and let it go at that. He could understand, as what this appeared to be was no more than slavery for the females, and giving them very little worth, other than producing the next generation. Smiling he remembered thinking about that and wondered how it must have been to be able to have any female at any time – but knew that it was just a young male's fantasy for such a thing. Yet as he had continued to read and study the rather large document he ended up with more questions than answers. Well, again, no surprise there, after all he was a student of history, and what had been taught, as he had gone through the learning centers, was very boring and something he felt that he would never need anyway. But with this close and intimate view he began to search the archives and records, and as he did he began to feel a hunger in his soul to find out the answers to the riddles that were now before him, and this was the reason he was now standing here in the open grasslands.

As time had passed by, and the true understanding of the natural world was discovered, the many gods died a natural death. Yet, there appeared to be an incident recorded in this record, from his ancestor, of a meeting between them and these gods. But from what they knew now, this was impossible. But as he researched it further, in his spare time of course, it was consistent. Whatever tribe or clan that had become a part of that first alliance, the same story existed. Of course there were slight variations between the records, but that was to be expected, since people would see things differently. And, of course, what records that still existed too many were incomplete. But one thing that was consistent between all of them was the statement that they were confronted by their gods. It had appeared that this alliance was brought together to destroy an unknown people who had lived in the desolation. But even now in his time this desolation was avoided, so it had been assumed that this part was probably not true, and was just misdirection from where they were really traveling. But wherever this had been, this valley where this incident was supposed to have happened, became off limits and had been renamed the Valley of the Gods. And these supposed gods had put this valley, the desolation, and the Sacred Mountains; yes they were still called that, off limits – not that the Sacred Mountains hadn't been anyway – although later an altar had been placed in the valley.

So if it was consistent throughout all of the records that he had researched, why was this incident considered myth? It made no sense to him at all. And as time had passed leading up to now, this valley had become myth like this supposed confrontation with the gods. No one knew if it had really existed, and if it did, where its location would be. He felt that if that valley could be located, then he would be able to solve these many questions, and answer the riddles of the gods. And were these other people real, as it was suggested in the written word, or imagined as the views of today believed? And once again that was why he stood here staring. He needed to be heading back, since there was much work awaiting his strong hands. At least as he worked the dough it allowed him plenty of time to think. And this he must do because the final decision would change his life forever, and who knew maybe the race of people that he came from.

He kept going back to the many visits that he had had with the higher learned ones, both during his time of learning, and before studying the ancient manuscripts that had been passed on to him. The learned had stated, "These gods that had been created by our ancient ancestors were just that, created from their primitive minds trying to put some understanding to what they were witnessing". In a way it did make sense. They knew that the Sacred Mountains had been formed both volcanically and by uplifting caused by something they called plates. It was also known that their ancient counterparts believed that the desolation was the home of the spirit world, the place where the dead dwelt, and not a place for the living. Again it was easy to understand how that conclusion had come about. But now it was just the badlands, and desert, a place where little moisture reached, not allowing much to live and survive in that harsh environment. And the idea that some hidden people, who in the end, had supposedly been the servants of these gods, and lived permanently in the desolation, was ridiculous. If any tribe or clan had lived there, it would have been only for a very short time. After all there was nothing to support life. And as far as he knew, and he had to admit his ignorance on the subject, water was nonexistent.

And this most outrageous of all was this supposed Valley of the Gods. The only reason that it was mentioned at all was because it seemed to be a turning point in their history. Up until the supposed incident in that fictitious valley, females' roles were well established, and had not changed for as long as there had been a written or oral history. But after this mythological encounter with their gods, slowly females began to take on more important roles within the societies. This was something that did not happen overnight, but over hundreds of turns. And no matter whom he talked to, or asked, once again, the general consensus was quote, "The Valley of the Gods, real . . . I think not. It is just a myth, a legend, with no hard facts to back it at all. It simply was a turning point in our culture and nothing more." What could one say to counter this belief? And after reading, with much difficulty, the inheritance he had received, the descriptions were too graphic, too real to have been imagined. And at the same time he didn't want to show these learned ones his source knowing that they would probably take it from him and he would never see it again. And if he pressed them to return it, he was sure that they would deny that such a thing was handed over to them and that it never existed. Because what was in this document would counter everything they thought that they knew about that time in their history, and "my, we couldn't have *that* could we".

This document, when it had been dropped into his lap, was unbelievably huge. And with the time that had passed, some of the earliest parts were fading to illegibility. It was very important, in his mind, that this be copied so that none of what was here would be lost. So painstakingly he and his mate had been making copies, and by doing so was becoming intimate with the content. It was she who pointed out this one female that had supposedly, by today's view of their history, come from one of those destroyed lairs in the desolation. And while females of the time were not allowed names, this one had one, a strange one to their way of thinking. And it was written in the notes that she was a priest of the gods. How could that be? No female was allowed such a place of importance. He hadn't really been listening that closely since he had been concentrating on his own section, but slowly it penetrated his thick skull, as she liked to tell him, and he looked up and asked, "Name? . . . A female with a name, and not only that, but rank? Are you sure?" She had given him that look and shook her head, and had brought the pages over so that he could see for himself. And it was right there, and this female's name was Sara, whatever a Sara was. Although, he had to admit, he was beginning to understand why that name was beginning to become popular in their culture.

It stated that she, as well as the people captured from these hidden lairs, spoke a different tongue and it was because this female spoke this strange tongue as well as theirs that she had come into the written word. And what had transpired to bring her into the story at all had to do with the captured females. As was the tradition and law at the time, if a tribe or clan was destroyed in battle then the females that were captured were added to the victor's breeding herds, as they were called. This had a twofold purpose. First it showed the superiority they had over their enemies, and secondly strengthened the clan or tribe, by adding new blood to the next generations that would come from the unions. But these strange females never carried, never conceived, and many died through the early turns of captivity. These warrior races feared that somehow that while these females appeared to be weak on the outside, they were defeating the warriors by not allowing any to be successful when breeding with them. Supposedly in this Valley of the Gods, the tribes and clans got their answer as to why, and all of these strange ones were taken to this valley, and were never heard from again. All of this had a ring of truth to it. It was just too fantastic to have been made up.

Then there was mention of these travelers who used to visit the many tribes and clans, and that they were regular visitors who provided services and traded, their goods being superior to any that could be made at the time. That for the longest time they had quit their trading, and suddenly, when all of this was taking place, they appeared once again. These travelers stated that their homes were beyond the mountains. But in the recent past there had been treks to that area, and it was found to be a barren hostile world with no sign of habitation. So were these travelers myth also? It really didn't make much sense to him. Everything that the two of them had read had a consistency of fact to it, and all of it fit together very well, too well as far as he could see. All of this had to be real, all of it had to have happened, but how could it be proven?

As they continued to work their way through this massive work, at what they guessed was approximately five hundred turns after these events, there was an obscure notation that only covered a few pages talking about the gods becoming active in the Sacred Mountains once again. Something about late in the Season of Falling that a deep rumbling of sound came from the mountains, and even though the gods had been silent for such a long time it appeared that now they were unhappy about something. This roaring continued off and on, throughout the following Season of Cold, and ended somewhere in the beginning of the Season of Greening. This had taken place at a time when the gods were beginning to fall out of favor with the people, but this incident brought them back into favor for a while. *Just what could this incident have been?* He wondered. He knew from asking that the extinct volcanoes had remained so, and even the storms that were common in those mountains had never produced such a sound. There had been no earth shakes to signal something was about to happen, just the deep sounds and that was all — so many mysteries and no answers. Was all of this just a story, a figment of someone's overactive imagination, or was it the truth as his ancestors saw it?

In his mind and with the discussions that he had with Jura, his mate, there just seemed to be a consistency that went beyond just primitive fears and imaginations. Yet how did one prove it? As he had thought about it before, in his past, there was no way that he wanted the learned ones to get this family treasure, and truly that was exactly what it was. Not in the sense of wealth, but it provided a consistent history of his family line back to the original leader of the alliance. As he kneaded the dough and prepared it for the second rising his thoughts continued to return to what he had read, studied and copied. With so much effort going into it he had almost memorized what was there. And at times it appeared that he, in his mind's eye, was there right next to the unknown writer, observing, thinking, and writing those words down. At times it would distract him enough that he would come close to burning some of the breads or missing an ingredient. And as time continued to flow he found that the stories were beginning to possess him.

In the mornings, as he would look into the reflecting glass, he kept telling himself that he was a baker, not a warrior or explorer, and there was no way that he could ever be one. Yet, his family history, for which he now had in his possession, said that he came from warrior stock. Although how that could be determined was beyond him. Since the carryings were random, and the sire of the child could have been any of the warrior class, so what was it that determined that he had descended from this K'jor? Besides, from what he had read, he wouldn't have had the opportunity to "breed" with the females, as it was called back then, because he wasn't a warrior. Only they had the right. He thought that in some twisted way this made sense. The time of this K'jor was a very violent time, and there were tribes and clans that were being destroyed, wiped out all the time. So if one was to survive then strength, cunning, and great leadership all were necessary. And like the wild herds that they emulated, it was the strong that bred with the females producing the next generation.

"You seem distracted this morn," Jura commented, "I know you've become more so since you inherited that history of your family's past. I have to admit that it is something to study and try and understand. But we've got our work to do, and it needs to remain in its place." She smiled, reached out and grabbed his hands. "I'm quite happy to be living now instead of back then, especially since I'm a female. And the idea of being in one of those breeding herds and not even allowed a name – how horrible. And I suspect, since no one really bathed, it had to stink pretty badly. And since a female wasn't allowed to clean up after being physical with a male, it had to be pretty ripe in the places where they lived." She shuddered from some inner thought, shook it off before continuing. "Honestly, I'm surprised that any survived at all. But obviously some did because we're here. And while it doesn't say so directly, my guess would be that infant mortality and even female mortality had to be pretty high."

Silent as he absorbed what she had said Kal thought about it and smiled before speaking, "Leave it to a female to think about such things. But now that you mention it, you're right it had to stink, let alone be unhealthy."

Laughing she said, "Of course I'm right. I'm female and we're always right. Or haven't you figured that out yet?"

With a slight laugh he pointed over to where they kept that historical record and said, "Oh I don't know about that. Maybe our ancestors had it right and you females needed to be put into herds just to keep you separate and wanting to control everything. I think, if I remember right, that when in the presence of a warrior you females were to remain silent." He paused a moment with a devilish grin, "Maybe just maybe they had found a solution." He could see that he had gotten the response he wanted and just laughed. "Look, in their time it was how both wanted it, and it must have worked, but I would never trade what we have for such a thing."

Somewhat mollified she responded, "Well, I hope not. And I don't think any of you males could ever push us back into that type of life style. I want more out of life than just being a baby maker, with no hope of being anything else but a place for some male to leave his seed."

He could feel the humor rising in him again but decided not to throw another barb, even in fun, her way. Instead he said, "I can see that. And I guess that's the way it really was. Females producing the next generation, taking care of them until a certain age where the males were separated and the females remained. I have to admit that it's so much better this way. Look it's almost time for me to head out, and soon you'll have to also, we seemed to have drifted from what started this. Yes, this is beginning to consume me. I think it's because of the way it's stated in the narratives and the words of the different scribes over time. It is matter of fact, with little embellishments at all. Yes we can dismiss anything they wrote about the gods, but from their time and perspective these gods were as real as you or me. And yet our learned ones state that everything that we've read is fiction – myth. I don't know about you, but this doesn't read like fiction to me. I have the feeling that we didn't get this by accident. And I'm beginning to feel a strong urge to prove what we've been studying. And before you ask, no I have no idea how. So much has changed since that time in our history. Most of the grasslands that they knew in their time are now farmland. We have villages, and townships everywhere, and land has been modified to make all of this work. So even the crude maps would be next to useless, yet . . ." He trailed off as once again he had that faraway look, shaking his head he said, "Darn, time to go – catch you at the mid-meal." He got up went around the table hugged and kissed Jura with the response showing much promise for that mid-meal. "Darn! You make it hard to leave."

Laughing she said, "That's not all that's hard. Now get out of here and I'll see you a little later."

* * *

Kal could hear the rich deep voice of his mother as he worked in the bakery. She was in charge of the business and was very good at it. His father Pehel worked the other side of the business. He, with his helpers, would contact the farmers, contract for the grains they required, and then would pick up the harvest making a judgment call at the time to be sure that the grains met with the quality that they demanded. He had confided in him that it was one of the secrets to the quality of their goods. He remembered the excitement, in his youth, when he had been allowed to go with his father on one of those journeys. While exciting, yes, it had been hard work. And he found that at night, on this trip, he had no problem falling asleep, but had much difficulty in coming back to life in the mornings before the sunrise. He remembered huddling around the fires trying to shake off the morning chill that made him shiver. That hot drink both warmed his cold hands and his insides. It was his first introduction to the business side of his father. Kal learned that his father was well respected, and would drive a hard bargain, but would be fair in his practices with any he dealt with. Kal remembered his father saying, "Kal, it is very important that you treat everybody with respect – especially if you want to have it reciprocated." He would pause and then point out the fields of ripening grains stating, "Look at all of this. For this farmer it is what supports this land, himself, and his family, just as the bakery supports ours, and the many who work for us. We are not a big business, but it has supported many generations of the Kaygor family. And it is only by being respectful of the many that we can continue to survive, to grow, to be able to provide for ours.

"It is easy for one to become too big for their britches, so to speak. And what I mean here is not when one eats too much, or as a child outgrows what they are wearing, but one who in their mind begins to believe that they are so much better than any around them. At that very moment they have doomed themselves. Yes, I know you've seen some of them go on that way all the way to the grave, but at what cost?" He reached into his pocket and pulled out a large coin and showed it to him, "Look these individuals with that mindset begin to pursue this and everything that once was important – oh like family and friends, and even trust and such – go by the wayside, and this is all they love and all they consider important. Everything is based on how they can get more, and nothing else has any interest unless it increases their coffers. Can this keep you warm at night in your bed, and before you answer, yes it can rent love for the night, but that's all it is.

"They can't see the others who are shaking their heads behind their back, or the hate he's created because he's cheated someone out of something. And while he will have many who proclaim to be his friend, in the end, it is his coins, his coffers that they really are only interested in." Again he stopped and pointed out the ones who worked for him, "It would be easy to cheat these, the ones who work for us, but what would that produce but ill will and grudging effort from them. They would only then be working for me for what I pay them, and there would be no loyalty, and I wouldn't be able to trust them at all. Because they need the work they would stay, but if someone else offered them something better, they'd be gone before a syllable could escape my mouth." Again he paused, stood up and swept his arms out saying, "Look its 1543TOG and there's much happening in our world. It won't be long and treks like I'm taking will be a thing of the past. I have seen machines that are just now arriving that will replace much of our beasts. I can see a time when these new machines will do most of the work for us allowing us to do much more with less. But that is in your future more than mine. But underlying all of this is that respect, that trust." Sighing and taking a deep breath he continued, "Without that we'll return to the ways of our distant ancestors and become a warring race once again, with all the suffering and death that goes with such a thing."

That conversation, well not really a conversation since he listened as his father spoke, had stayed with him had opened his eyes to much that he had never seen before. And with these new eyes he began to see the respect that not only the workers had for both of his parents, but it was the same with the suppliers, and even the community. And he began to see the others and that his father had spoken the truth, and at that point he had vowed to never be like them, even though again as a child, he had thought that having what these seemingly important members of the community had would have been a really great thing. Studying them he began to see how empty and hollow they and their lives really were, and could hear the horrible things being said about them behind their backs.

He was a middle child with four older brothers, and three younger sisters, all working somewhere in the family business. But unlike other such enterprises, his parents did not expect any of their children to remain with the business if it was not something they were good at. They had pushed learning, and to find what each of them were good at, but at this moment he was quite satisfied working in the bakery. He already knew that one of his younger sisters was being trained to take over as she had shown a strong talent towards all aspects of the bakery. In a way it was truly funny that it should be this way – females running a business, when their ancestors had put so little value on them in the past. All he could do was shake his head at their unbelief in the value that a female could add to the community with their many skills and abilities. Enough of this dealing with past subjects, he could hear his mother calling him to some chore that needed to be done, and he knew that even though he was family, here it bought him nothing. When you worked here, there was always much to be done, and everybody including his mother worked at all aspects of the work, none were privileged because they just happened to have been born into the family of the owners of this business.

Later when his time at the bakery was finished he headed over to the higher learning center. He wanted to talk with one of his favorite learned who happened to teach history. Sabohl had taken special interest in him when the learned one could see that Kal had a strong interest in the subject. And as the turns had passed by their friendship had grown. Now, carefully he would approach asking questions, and trying to start discussions that would hint at what he had learned from this ancient document that was both a secret and a personal history of their family. But so far Sabohl stayed with what he had taught. The history was exactly as he and the rest of the learned, the leaders in their field, said. He would say, quote, "From what has been found, what has been discovered, and the research that has been done on the fragments from that time of our past the conclusions that we, as a group, have made are accurate. Yes, yes, there have been some very small disagreements from ones who are not as we, and we laugh quietly and with a knowing smile, because they have no proof that would stand up. And besides we've been down that path before. We know that what we have within our group is as accurate as we can make it. These dissenting few aren't worth our time. After all we know what we know, and so far there's been nothing presented to change that."

It was one of the main reasons that he had never shown his learned friend this document. It would have blown large holes in much of what they were teaching, and what they believed of their ancient ancestors. So with the statements made he was sure that they and probably even his friend, to protect their high position and views, would make this document disappear. So carefully and quietly he would suggest something that he had learned from the text, or ask a general question, but so far he had gotten nowhere at all. But at this moment Sabohl was his only source to try, albeit on the sly, by asking if such and such a thing was possible, or if maybe this particular location had been discovered, or if there had been a digging on an ancient clan home. Unfortunately he had been frustrated by having to be so general. But at one point he got permission to visit one of those sites where they were uncovering the past. It was something that he had always wanted to do, but now had further reasons for doing so.

With his mate and the rewriting and studying of the document he finally had decided that he was going to, at least, locate the clan's home. It was a starting point, a place where these writings had originated. From there with the crude maps, ones that had been created towards the end of this ancient society, he was hoping to be able to search the areas with those ancient creations to follow the stories as they unfolded and to see with his own eyes the actual locations where it all had happened. And who knew, maybe find out the truth. Yet, he was beginning to understand, as he aged a bit, that the truth was not just the "black and white" of his childhood, but began to take on other shades, showing him that the truth could be many things, say different things, and be interpreted in so many ways. And a partial truth could really be a lie because all wasn't presented, allowing the ones who presented this partial truth to say that it was the full truth, and not actually perpetuate a lie. Smiling inwardly, as they knew that by doing this they were manipulating the ones that this was directed at, and getting the results they expected. It had been so much simpler as a child. In the world of the adult nothing said was exactly as presented. There were always hidden meanings and innuendoes hidden within.

So with these thoughts he was very, very careful on how he presented or asked anything. He had to think things out, and be careful of the questions that would be directed back to him. He must present to this learned one, that what he was asking or suggesting was only speculation on his part. And still being young and learning the ways of this world it was doubly difficult. He had been almost caught a couple of times, and only quick thinking or luck had saved him. And, if he truly thought about it, the ego of the learned one, who probably just considered it rubbish from someone who had the passion but not the discipline or turns of experience. But at this moment it was the only place that was close enough that he could ask. And eventually he got permission from Sabohl and his equals to visit a site that they were excavating, although most of the work had already been done. He being told, "It can be allowed, only because most of what we can find out from this site has been found out. So grudgingly they've allowed you permission to go, but with the admonition that you just observe and touch nothing. And yes, before you ask, you can ask them questions. I've already informed them that you pester me all the time with questions. Just understand that they do not have the patience that I do, so don't weary them with too many."

So with a leave of absence from the bakery, and his mate at his side they had taken the journey to this hidden site – hidden because there were still ones who would loot such places, or would plant things to strengthen their point of view. Of course the learned one had to go with them otherwise they would not be allowed on site, and for the last part of the journey they would be placed inside an enclosed cart so that they could not locate the site once they had returned. And once they had arrived it was anticlimactic to say the least. He was disappointed that there appeared to have been so little that had survived the ravages of time. He even wondered how they had determined that this had been a place of clan occupation. But eventually he began to discern the small hints, depressions, and regular formations that were not from the natural world that surrounded them. It was hard to believe that an ancient people had lived here. But by having visited the site and learning what was allowed it gave him a way to ask questions that related directly to the document, but could be applied to the visited site. "Sir", he always addressed Sabohl that way, "I've been wondering something."

Smiling at Kal, Sabohl stated, "That's not unusual for you. It seems that ever since you and your mate visited that site that all you have is questions, but one doesn't learn if one doesn't ask, so I have a few moments before I must get back to those student papers, so ask away." Sabohl leaned back and put his hands behind his head and took on an air of patience, and waited.

"Okay, going back to that site, I see that the place was divided into different areas. The area for the warriors, with the leader within this area, the area for the females, and within this one an area for the offspring, but it's this third area that I question."

"Ah, the one where the priests lived and performed the ceremonies to the gods, is that right?"

"Yes, yes that's right. If I can remember what we saw there," and here he needed to be careful since what he was asking had not been directly answered, but again it had been a while since their visit and he was hoping that it would be a natural pathway, "it appears that these priests had their own breeding herd, why? From what we were taught only the warriors had the right to breed, as the term was used back then. Yet here seems to be a contradiction to that."

Laughing a little Sabohl couldn't help but get a little dig in, "Ah youth and always hung up on breeding. But I know what you mean." He paused for effect, "Okay how do I word this? Priests were their own class then. They had power equal to the warriors, and the lead priest was equal to the clan leader. In a way they together ruled the clan. The warrior leader, and it always was a warrior who led the clan, and the head priest were on the opposite sides so to speak – the warrior leader dealing with the physical world, and the head priest dealing with the gods and spiritual world. It was one of the reasons for the separation that we saw at that site. That separation represented the division from the physical and spirit, and both ruled each. Allowing the priest caste to be as the warrior caste, allowing both to have their own breeding herd, and the offspring from those unions remained in each realm. In a sense, from what we have been able to learn, priests were considered warriors against the ones who had passed into the spirit world. We've found enough evidence to be pretty sure that this is accurate. I know that it had been consistent to all the permanent sites we've worked. And along with the few records we've found this is how we believe it was. Does that answer your youthful question, Kal?"

Nodding his head Kal said, "Yes, quite well, thank you. I really never thought about it in that way. But now that you've explained it, it makes perfect sense, thank you. I've got to head back, but you've left me much to think about." Once again he thanked him, and took his leave. He really had much to think about, and it strengthened his determination to find out who this Sara was, and why a female in that time period would have a name, and why would she claim to be a priest of the gods, it was something that was so inconsistent that it rang on myth. Yet, what made it more fantastic was the fact that it appeared that the head priest had accepted this as fact, and how could that be? He hoped that Sabohl didn't suspect anything; after all it was a dangerous question. Still he may have considered it a privilege that one of his students would want more information than just what was taught in the learning centers. But, if he knew the truth as to why he had asked . . . well he had no way of knowing, so at this point and time it would be better to leave well enough alone. And not to go back, no matter the temptation, and ask a pointed question once again for some time.

The seasons were approximately 135 days long, given their path around their suns, a total of 540 days, and their cycles were broken into those four parts, and within these four parts they further broke their time down to fifteen parts of 9 days each. They began each turn on the official first day of the Season of Green, and ended it on the last official "day of cold" with celebrations marking the passing of each season, and one that marked the *time of the gods* (TOG), that supposed day when they had revealed themselves in what had become the mythological Valley of the Gods. As he had read over the events of that day, or truly dusk to dark, it must have been something to have witnessed. Smiling inwardly he thought, *yup, if this thing ever did happen. I can see, in my mind's eye, joining that large contingent of warriors, preparing for a campaign, the excitement and the anticipation that had to be going through every one of them. And to have been the leader of all of this, looking over the assembled might that was there, knowing that they were yours to control, and feeling the pride, and yes I'm sure the power, must have been quite a rush. And knowing in your heart that you were the first to bring the warring clans and tribes together, to fight a common enemy, ones hidden in the places of the spirits, and that on past campaigns that you had been victorious, and that was why all of these warriors were still with you. Yes, to have been at your height of strength and with your confidence soaring as high as the fliers, and with the conferences with other leaders as the strategies were laid out, all going as planned, only to have it end. End when the gods appeared to you and the tribes and clans in that valley, ordering you to end this war against their servants, and to be told it had been the gods who had protected the females, and to learn that the god of the earth was female had to be such a shock. This ran counter to everything in their culture, but explained much.*

Yes, I wonder what it would have been like, to be a primitive, with the superstitions and fears I would be living with, and to have the actual gods appear? I might just up and die right there from fear, or at least pee my pants from fear. Yet, my ancestors were warriors, ones used to going into battle against one another, and while I'm sure that fear was a normal part of their life – heck it had to be – after all every part of that culture had something to fear in it. So whatever happened on that fateful day that we celebrate every turn it had to have been pretty spectacular to leave the impression that it obviously did. So why does the learned ones of today feel that all of this did not happen and was only a myth? It just doesn't add up at all. He found that he was outside his shelter and had no knowledge that he had traveled that distance between the learned centers of his village to his home. Taking a deep breath he opened the door and went inside still deep in thought and realized that Jura had said something, "What, sorry was thinking about what I learned today, can you say again?"

Shaking her head with a knowing smile she said, "All I said was welcome home, and did you get the information that you wanted from Sabohl? But I can see that you're kind of out there right now."

"Okay, you're right, I am. And that's kind of why I am. He more or less confirmed what we had wondered." He then went on and explained the conversations and answers he had gotten, "And that makes what we've read here in this so out of place." He picked up the huge document with both hands, since it was quite heavy, shook it slightly before setting it back on the working table. "It's an anomaly just like their description of the disappearance of those travelers. You know, one minute they were there, and a large dust cloud blows across their camp, and when it clears it was as if they were never there. And of all that we've worked, this disappearance of the travelers would be the one I would put to myth, or at least to an overactive imagination. But if we are to accept that this confrontation of the mythological gods happened, and that a female actually had a name and not only that was of the priestly caste, then we must accept this also. Either all is as they saw it, or all of it is myth. I just wish I knew which it was."

Placing her hands on her hips Jura thought a moment before answering, "We weren't there, nor were we privy to what our ancestors believed, or their true culture, so who knows, maybe all of it was imagined. In many ways it just seems to be a big fantastic story, a fantasy, and there's no way such a thing could have happened. I can see why all of those learned ones would go in that direction. I can hear them saying, "Look, it's impossible for such a thing to have happened, so it has to be one of those things that happened in their minds, a product of their lives and superstitions, so it is myth. After all there is no proof other than what our ancestors said, so why should we believe them?"

She did such a great imitation of one of the learned that he couldn't help but laugh. "You should have gone into acting – that was great. And you're probably quite right. Yet I was told once that if you throw out everything that you know is false and then what is left has to be the answer – the truth, no matter how fantastic it may appear, and I'm coming to that conclusion now. Yeah I know we don't have access to all that the learned ones have, but they don't have this either. So I guess both sides don't have all the facts. Look, I've got some time coming to me, and I know that you will have some free time also, so, I was thinking . . ."

She quickly interrupted him, "Stop right there – when you begin to think, if I remember right, that was when you used to get yourself into trouble in your youth."

He couldn't help but smile, because what she said was the truth. "Okay, you're right, but what I was going to say is that we are really not very far from what I'm guessing is the location of that clan I'm supposed to have descended from. Of course this is just a guess. I know you enjoy the outdoors much more than I ever claimed. So this would allow us time to ourselves, and give us a chance to do a little exploring, included in that exploring is each other, of course. And it would give me a chance to begin to learn more about this, what was it you called it, oh yeah camping. I know it was something you and your family did a lot. The only thing I can relate it to was the caravan trips I took with my father, but then we had many people around us, and I suspect if I compared it to what we've read, we were more like a tribe from that time period. Not really roughing it like you did."

"You males always are thinking about that. But you're right, we used to do that all the time, and it was fun."

Smiling now he asked innocently, "Doing what, getting physical or camping?"

Now laughing she pushed him away, "You know the answer to that one, so don't put something into what I said that wasn't there."

Again laughing he said, "Why not, after all you females do it all the time to we males." And this got them both laughing.

She raised her right hand and through the tears from laughing so hard she said, "Guilty as charged sir." Then giving time to get the laughing back in control she said, "Look, I think it's a great idea but not now. If we begin to do this then you need to be a lot more prepared than you are. And what I mean is this; there are still dangerous beasts out there. And if you really think about it you would remember that in your father's camps they posted guards. Now I know part of the reason for those guards was the possibility that some bad individuals would try and steal what your camp had, but part of it was to protect both the pack and cart beasts. So I suggest that first we go and take a couple of days in one of the local wilderness areas that have been set aside for that. They have what they call rangers who patrol these places and make it safe for villagers and such who really just want to experience the wild without the danger or experience to protect themselves. Then you need to practice with the sling, throwing knife, and staff. And if you get reasonably good with those we'll add the bow. But right now neither you nor I have bows, nor do we have the funds to add any – so for now it will be those other items.

"After all where this crude map shows the location of that ancient clan site, while possibly close, is pretty isolated, meaning that we would have to do the protecting. And right now that would be me. I know that's not very female of me, or very male of you, since our culture was originally built on the males doing the protecting and with the females returning the favor with, as they called it, breeding. But so much over the time since then has changed, and we are no longer truly warlike, not that there's no fighting or battles happening. We both know better than that. And with our populations rising as they have, we have tamed much of the land to our use. This has allowed us the ability to specialize, and so many of the skills that were necessary for survival back then have been lost. I really think that the reason we go camping is to try and capture a little of what it must have been like for the tribes who were always moving, and even the clans would camp through the times they hunted the wild herd beasts. But, of course, I don't need to tell you this since history was one of your favorite subjects, and with this ancient document literally falling into our laps, we've seen even more, up close and personal.

"Besides, we have nothing to camp with. No portable shelter, no cooking pots, no clothing, and no portable sleep sacks, let alone the necessary packing equipment." She paused a moment to catch her breath and continued, "Look we don't even have the funds to get most of what we need, and I'm the one who shouldn't be telling you this, normally it's the other way around. Still, as you so aptly said, I'm the one with the experience here. So if this is what you really want to do we need to start getting this stuff together as we can afford to do so. I'm sure that for a couple day getaways into one of the reserves that I can borrow from my family. But this is something I don't want to make a habit of. So if this is the beginning of many trips, and I suspect that it is, we need our own stuff, and it will have to be quality, which means not cheap."

He sat quietly as he listened and realized that everything thing she had said was true. Here in his excitement he was ready to just go out and do, but now knew that this was a foolish thing. "Okay, I get it, and once again you're right," he laughed again.

She asked with a half questioning look on her face, "What?"

With a smile as she sat across from him he stated, "I was just imagining that if a warrior back in those times had heard what I just said, and then had to take instruction from a female as to how to protect one's self that he'd been laughed out of the clan or tribe." And once again this set them both to laughing as she saw the image in her own mind. "Okay, you've convinced me," he said, "so when do we begin the training with that stuff, you know the staff and such. So, do you think it's a good idea to borrow your family's camp gear? And when do you think it would be a good time to try this camping out?"

"I probably can get the gear anytime I want it, and as you said, you have some time coming to you. So let's see if I can get what we need from them, and then get the foodstuff that works best for that kind of living, so maybe at the end of this nine day, which we still have seven left. Yeah I think with your help that we can go away for a couple at that time. We'll make it for two nights, that way you can see how it is to sleep on the hard ground, and how little sleep you get when you're not in your own bed. But I have to admit that being in the fresh air, the smell of the morning meal being cooked over a campfire is wonderful. Still there are downsides also, and the only way to learn about them is to experience them. So I guess we can make it three days and two nights, with travel there on the first, and travel back on the third."

"Okay, let me know when you have the camp stuff, and I'll let the bakery know that we'll be gone for three days. Of course you'll do the same for where you are working."

CHAPTER TWO

"Hey, look a letter from Sabohl, I wonder what he wants to discuss? He rarely writes, prefers to remain aloof in his place as the leader of history." Looking around the table there were four or five who were considered, next to Sabohl, as the experts on their culture's history and sociology. It was one of the meetings that they had scheduled at the change of seasons. Sabohl rarely attended these things, leaving the sentiment that he was above these meetings and wouldn't lower himself to their level feeling that he was so far above them that talking and discussing anything with them would be a waste of his time and intellect.

"What does that ole stuffed beast want to pass on to us mortals anyway?" Jaie asked. This brought out a chuckle from the others.

Still standing Tesam looked over the group with a smile, "Okay, I'll read it to you and then we all can have a good laugh." He shook the letter importantly and read out loud. *"Fellow learned ones"*, laughing at the opening Tesam said, "Look he's actually admitting that others might have learned something." Again this brought out laughter. But as he perused the writing deeper into the letter his demeanor changed and the rest at the table could sense that change. There was a silence for a few moments that appeared to fill the air with apprehension. Tesam then continued, *"We may have a problem developing that could threaten our very positions as experts in our history and our views and understandings of the sociology of our ancient ancestors. I'm watching, with concern, one past student of mine who has shown a strong interest in our history. It may be of no consequence in the end, but the questions that he is asking are very pointed and direct, and I fear where they may lead. From the way these questions have been presented I would suspect that he knows more that he is telling, and the questions are to either confirm or deny what he already knows. The last question he asked more or less gave him away to me, since the subject that he was questioning has never been taught in any of my classes, let alone any that all of you have presented.*

"It may be that he or maybe someone he knows has located a piece of our past that has been unavailable to any of us, but this, of course, is all speculation as he has been careful to give away nothing, and to appear to be just another student wanting to learn more. I plan, discreetly of course, to have their, he and his mate's shelter searched to find out if they have something in their possession that could be the source of this interest. And if so will have it removed so that he will have nothing to support whatever theories and truths that may exist. Without that said proof, he will come off as any other crackpot, and allow us to remain in the seat of leadership within our fields. I have learned, since I as all who are in this village, frequent the bakery, that he and his mate will be away for a few days providing us the opportunity and time to do a

complete search and after leaving, to leave the shelter as it was before we entered, so other than this missing document, if indeed that is what it is, there will be no sign that any has entered. They will not be able to claim theft, and with this item gone, they will not be able to prove that it ever existed.

"What I need from you, but really to maintain what we have and who we are, is surveillance, and this must discreet, and remain unknown to the ones we need to watch. After all if they actually do discover something we need to know and know immediately, so that we can put our own spin on this discovery, or discoveries. So I will leave that portion in your capable hands, and since I happen to live here, I, with my team will monitor his activities while he is here. Once he and probably his mate head out from this place, then it will be you and your team's responsibility to follow, record, and be prepared to beat him in the announcements of whatever discoveries he might make. In fellowship of one learned to another – Sabohl."

After reading the letter and the implications that it presented, the room was silent. "Do you think that he has the right of it?" Tesam asked.

"Well, the old herd beast has always found some way to protect his position, and seems to have been able to see things that could lead to trouble for himself and his position, and if he feels that this threat is real," Jaie paused for effect, bent his head sideways and shrugged, "who knows really. But if this threat is real, and I suspect that it must be if he wanted to stoop down to our level, which as you know, is something that would be very hard for him to do. He's always rubbed our faces in the fact that he was superior to us in all ways, so he must feel threatened and believe that it will threaten our positions too."

"So," Jaie asked, "what are we to do about it? Do as he asks, or just ignore it. And you notice that he never named who this individual is. I think that by doing this he again was protecting himself."

"How so?"

"Look if we go along with this and one of our staff is caught, then he can deny that he not only knew nothing about this, but had no involvement at all – leaving us to take the full brunt of the retaliation that would come from this."

Jaie thought a moment, then leaned on the table, "Which means that he, once again, has protected himself, and at the same time leaving us vulnerable and open to, the very least, the loss of our prestige and positions. Yes, we'll need to think about this, and tender our response as carefully as this letter he has sent to us."

Shahe had been quiet throughout the reading of the letter and the discussion that was now following, he interrupted and said, "What all of you, well at the least the two of you have stated is fact. Once again he's covering what he sits on, and many times seems to use to think with, and yes I agree that if we go along with this preposterous scheme of his, because of the way of this letter, we are the ones who would be out in the open. But at the same time if indeed what he states is accurate, and who knows really, then all of our hard work, all of our political maneuvering, all of the enemies that we've made along the way, to get where we are will have the necessary, ah what was that stuff, oh yes, ammunition to attack us. So tell me do we have a choice in this? I think that sending back a very neutral letter neither offering help, nor promising anything at this moment would be the best we can do. Then we need to begin our own independent investigation. One that would include watching this old windbag and maybe we can catch him in something, and actually bring him down. It could be that he will do something that will be his own downfall and allow us to usurp him and get rid of him." He leaned back in his chair with his hand on his chin, but remained silent, turning the control back to Jaie.

* * *

Kal was black and blue from the beating he was taking from Jura as she taught him the use of the staff. And what hurt more was the fact that she seemed to be enjoying it. He had to admit that she was very good with it, and that there was much more to its use as both a defensive weapon, and one that could be used to attack. Every time he figured that he had it down and was about to best her, she came up with some other subtle move and he found himself on the ground and many times in an embarrassing pose as she would place the point of the staff on his chest, showing once again that he had been bested. Shaking his head he said, "I never realized that there was so much to this thing. I thought that this was only going to be an after-midday practice and I'd have it down. You know it looked so easy when you started making those moves, and showing me. But you warned me that it was going to take a lot of time to master, and I have to admit that I thought you were very wrong about that, but it's very obvious that I'm a long way from your skill." Again shaking his head before continuing, "And you say that your brother and sister are better than you? That's really hard to believe. So I guess the question is this, how long, oh mighty learned one, will it be that I'm at

least capable of using this simple tool?" He, although carefully, bowed towards her, which brought laughter to her lips.

Returning his bow with one of her own, she said, "Oh
you're progressing. I'd place you in the advanced beginners.
As I've told you, I've been doing this most of my life. And
once my parents finished their training with us, we, my brothers and sisters and myself, would play games where we would
form teams, and as you would expect most of the time these
teams were females against males, although there would be a
game of chase that we played where all of the rest would
chase one of us, and we had to use the staff against the rest. I
must admit that those were very intense games, but it forced
us, even though we weren't realizing it, to become much better. Especially when one of us would come up with something
new to try, sometimes this something new would work, and
sometimes it would fail miserably. And even though we didn't
know it at the time, our mother would monitor our progress,
and if we really felt like we were good and as she called it, too
big for our britches, she'd come out with that smile of hers
and have all of us come at her, and she'd promptly beat all of
us. It wasn't until later that we learned that she had been the
champion of her area, and that's how she and father met. Both
had been the best at this in their respective townships, and he,
my father, couldn't believe that a female could beat him,
when there hadn't been a male that could challenge him that
was anywhere close by.

Sighing and with a distant smile she continued, "I'd really
would've liked to have been there to see that match. Both of
them talk about it now and then, and there are smiles on both
of their faces as they'd recall it. We'd sit and listen as they
would recount the encounter from their side. I'm sure like

most stories that it has grown over time, but it still was quite a tale. They were very good at describing their battle, and we all could see it in our minds, and since we'd been using the staffs ourselves we could see the moves and countermoves that both had made. And after a long time and many matches that ended in draws, she beat him with a move he had never seen before. And even to this day when they talk about it you can see that smile of triumph on her face as she had beaten a male in a battle. Something that our distant ancestors would have thought was quite impossible. But she did it, and after that they developed a strong friendship and now they have been mates for what seems like a life time." Again she paused, and then laughed, "You know what, it has been a lifetime, and they're just as much in love with each other now as they were before any of we children were around. Dad really adores her and says that if she hadn't defeated him in that contest that they may have never become what they are today. So I guess even though this is a long statement to get to this point, don't feel too bad by being defeated by me, I grew up using this thing, and have had champions training me, besides the competition that one's siblings add to the mix."

"Well, I admit that makes me feel a little better, but only a little. I'd seen others work the staff and it looked so easy, so I never considered it something I'd be interested in, but you've shown me that it's far from easy, and that I've only begun to understand the very basics, including the choosing of a good staff." He smiled inwardly, only because it probably would have hurt to smile outwardly. Still as he looked at his mate he, at times, found it hard to believe that she would have accepted him when he asked if she would become his mate and he hers. After all she was lithe and had a hunter's flow to her movements, smooth and graceful, and in his eyes a beauty that rivaled any that he had ever seen. And who was he, just a lowly village bound baker who had done nothing specular. Not the type that would attract someone like Jura who had lived in the outback, and was never really comfortable within the confines of the villages and townships. Someone who could probably have had any single male as a mate and to his surprise she had chosen him. And with their time together he was learning so much more that this beautiful, complicated, and intelligent female had to offer. And of course, being a male her physical side, and her naked beauty, drove him crazy.

As time had passed, and both their love and strength in the relationship grew, he couldn't see any time in his life where he would not want her around. They just worked well together, and even though he had heard about couples who had been mates for many turns completing each other's sentences or thinking in the very same way, coming up with the same conclusions at the same time, he had just shoved this off as myth within those special relationships that some have. Yet, he could see that it was beginning to happen inside theirs, and so with personal experience he now believed. Again, as far as he was concerned, it was another one of those signs that said that they were just right for each other. Yet, at times like these where her experience far exceeded his own he could feel his wounded male ego trying to get in the way. After all he was supposed to be better at such things. "Okay, I can accept that, but are you sure that you aren't just humoring me by saying that I'm probably an advanced beginner? Watching you work that staff makes me feel clumsy, awkward, and completely uncoordinated. Absolutely anything I tried you countered it and countered it in such a way that you made it appear to be of no consequence or no effort at all, almost like you were bored."

She laughed, and then teased him a little, "Ah has my little male had his ego hurt because his mate, a female no less, can easily beat him?" This got him going for a moment and she laughed again. "See, I know what buttons to push to get your pride showing. Now why not just go run a bath, both of us did a lot of sweating and kicked up a lot of dust while you practiced out here, and then I'll join you in the tub and really show you how much I care."

Again she was right, she did know what to say or do to get him going, and he had to admit that with his sore muscles that a hot bath would be great, but with her with him he knew that he would forget about those sore muscles. "Sounds great! Just one question though, when do you feel it would be a good time to take that camp trip? I've got to give them plenty of notice at the bakery so that they can cover in my absence."

"Oh, I'd guess, at least another couple of nines to both get everything together, and to get you better prepared. We still have to go over the throwing knives, and how most of the stuff works, so we're still quite a way away from going." She then smiled a smile that showed promise of what was coming.

He returned one of his own and stated, "You're the boss on this one, and I'll head on in and get that tub filled."

* * *

"I think that we'll send a letter back to Sabohl, and tell him that we aren't interested in his little games, since the only time he seems to want our cooperation is when there's something that might threaten his mighty position on high. Then, we can do two things; first use our own people to watch Sabohl, and from there maybe find out who this individual is that seems to be threatening him, and secondly, once we find out we can then, in our own way and time, do our own watching and learning. Maybe finally one of us can get that old windbag to budge and at least, if not grudgingly, admit that there are others, such as us, which have the knowledge and understanding, to be his equal in this field of study. And who knows, maybe he'll trip up and we can catch him in something and depose him, and allow some new blood to take over the field. He's been dominating this for much too long. But with the allies that he has cultivated over the turns, and powerful ones at that, he's been untouchable." Tesam sat down at this point and turned the table back over to Jaie.

"Can we do this and be successful, is probably the best question I can present. Maybe the alternative to this would be to give a very neutral response, neither promising support nor holding support from him. So that it could appear that we have promised nothing, but at the same time left the door open for possible support. With him we have to be so careful because of those powerful allies of his. And, as you stated, it is because of them that he remains aloof and where he is. Let's remember he is not stupid, couldn't be really, to have been able to hold on to his position for as long as he has, and while we all have our own powerful friends and allies, we cannot defeat him openly, so our letter to him, if this is what we decide to do, must be well written and subtle, and in all ways we must cover our behinds." Jaie could see the agreement from the others at the table as what had been both read to them, and what they had discussed so far. It was going to be a very difficult road to walk, full of obstacles, traps, blind turns, and unexpected outcomes, and it would all begin with this letter for all of them. They all knew that however this went that in the very end it would be affecting not only their careers, but their very lives.

* * *

Sabohl left his home early. It was to be a busy day since there were tests for his students, and the anticipation of a response from, well he'd guess that he'd give them a grudging nod as being near the top in their area of teaching, but in his heart he knew that they just did not match up to both his intellect, and his ties that he held that allowed him to remain as the only one on top. *Let the rest fight, scratch, and crawl for those few positions that are below.* No one could touch him, and with his spy network, and the power that he welded he made sure that it would remain that way. It had galled him that he had to stoop down to those underlings. But even with the size of his network, there was only so much he could do, and he suspected that this time he would need their help, and their networks to be successful and keep things status quo.

He lived on the grounds of the higher learning center but had other shelters in many of the villages, and while the breezes this morning were somewhat chilly, they held a promise of a warm day ahead of him. At times he wondered how it was that one could come to that conclusion, yet time and time it had been proven to be accurate. There must be some inborn sense that could predict this, but he had never figured it out, and in reality never truly cared anyway. History was his passion, and the weather could do what it wanted. After all, nobody had figured out how to control the weather, but with his iron grip he controlled the view and understanding of their history. Part of his persona he had developed was one of tolerance and acceptance to new ideas in his field, but behind this façade it was far from the reality of who he was. Walking through the doors into the learning center he smiled at the underworker who took care of the many small tasks that kept the center operating. Today Nacy, a female sat at the desk working whatever it was that she did. He really didn't know, and he really didn't care. He smiled and said as he bowed, "Ah good morn to you, Nacy. I would guess that it will be a warm day today, and is all well with you?"

Smiling back, although there was no feeling in it, as she understood where she and any of the other workers stood with this one she responded, "Yes, you're probably right, and it is a busy time for all of us. I see that you've arrived early today. I've just finished the sorting of the incoming letters for the staff here, and there's one for you that just arrived from that other learning center that you told me to be on the lookout for." She got up turned around to a sorting cabinet, and grabbed a handful of sealed letters and papers, turned around and handed them to him. "I do hope that whatever it was you were looking for is there." At this point after he had taken the pile she had handed him, she sat back down and returned to her work ignoring any further contact, which was fine with him.

Trying to keep an air of unconcern and normality he headed for his small office, just off the space where he did his teaching, entering the office, he closed and locked the door. He didn't need anyone walking in on him at this moment. Putting the stack aside he took the one letter that held the seal that this group used and opened it, reading it quickly, and when finished, felt anger rising, but with his iron control quickly squashed it. He then sat down and reread the letter once again.

"Sabohl, it has been so long since you've even acknowledged that we exist. It really must have been difficult for you in your high station to reach down to us commoners, the ones that you've always held in contempt. And how, time after time, you've let us know exactly what our place is in your world. Yet now you are reaching to us for help. We must admit that this has come as a complete surprise, and we will take into consideration what you are asking, but at this moment that is all we will do. You have provided this group with very little facts, and since this can be taken in any direction, again since we only have your word for it, we will await further proof from other than you. Yet, if what you have stated in your letter to us is proven to be fact, we indeed will be able to possibly assist. But, as you must be well aware since you seem to know all, we have many projects operating at this moment and have no one we can spare.

"Still if what you are intimating is true, there is still plenty of time to end whatever imagined threat that you are seeing here. After all our history wasn't written in a day, nor have the discoveries and the writing of our history, as we now know it, written in a day. So with this in mind we feel that there is time on our side, and we can continue with those stated projects. It is something, from your letter and the tone it implies, that may at some time require our attention, but that time is not now. If you have more information that you would like to pass on, we eagerly await your response. And please, if you do respond, please provide more than just your word. Since it is easy to twist words to say only what you want someone to hear and see, hiding the true meaning and truth from all. As always, your fellow learned, we are eager to hear back with

such proof. Signed Jaie, temporary overseer of the historical learned."

Sabohl sat silently for a while staring out at nothing. He was furious, how dare they ignore his summons to action? He was sure that they would jump at the chance to assist in this endeavor; one that he was sure would keep them exactly where they were – the leaders of their field. But obviously he had been mistaken. Rereading the letter once again, it again set off his anger, and looking for something to take it out on, he found a hapless drinking glass sitting empty on his desk, which he then grabbed and flung it against one of the walls, shattering it in small pieces from the energy of the throw. *So they'll wait until I can provide more proof will they. They had their chance, now it will be me, and only me who will do this and take the credit in the end, putting out another of the many fires that have threatened our positions over the cycle of seasons. We'll see who will win this in the end.*

He suddenly realized that he could hear movement outside of his office, and some time must have passed since he had entered. And from the sounds and voices it appeared that the students were arriving for classes. So getting his anger under control, and putting on the air of a concerned learned, he exited his office, went down the hallway to the staff that kept the center clean and stated that he had accidently broken a glass, could they please clean it up for him while he was teaching. Getting the response that he expected he left to meet his students.

* * *

"Look you're better with the throwing knives than you are with the staff, but that still doesn't make you very good yet." Jura walked across the dirt area where the targets had been set up, grabbed the throwing knives and brought them back. "These that we are using are for training only. No reason to destroy a good knife when one is learning." She suddenly smiled and snuffed a laugh that was about to surface.

Looking at her with a questioning look he asked, "What?"

"Oh, I don't know where it came from, but with all the reading, writing, and studying of that history of your family, well let's just say that it brought up an image in my mind of a female back in that time doing what I'm doing for you, and how it would have been for both of us."

He thought a moment, and began to get an image in his mind of what she had just suggested, shook his head before speaking, "Yeah, I can kind of see it, and we both probably would have been disowned by the clan or tribe or whatever that's for sure. I can see it now, a female knowing how to use weapons and a male that doesn't. So what is this? Is what I'm seeing correct that we have a female that wants to be a warrior, and a male who can't seem to be one. Next thing we're going to see here is she'll want her own name. Her own name, imagine that." Standing there like he thought an unbelieving warrior of that time would stand, he continued. "Next thing we'd see is this female wanting to be the clan leader. Clan leader, imagine that. A female with a name and one that is a better warrior than this male, and what's to happen next, she refusing to carry?" This brought laughter to both of them.

With tears running down her face from the laughter she finally said once she could, "Not bad, and unfortunately probably much too accurate. Okay warrior want-to-be, let's do this again, and then before we go back inside to clean up, we'll work with the staff again. You're getting better, I think that you could defend yourself successfully against a child right now, but would be defeated by anybody with any experience."

Smiling he said, "Thanks for the confidence. Come on I'm not that bad, am I? I really thought I was getting it down."

Again she laughed, "And getting up off the ground too many times to count. Anyway this isn't getting any of this done, and we've so much to do before that trip."

Yeah you're right, and I've talked to the one who passed on that family document to me, and he said that he would take it and all of the notes and writings we've done, and keep it safe at his shelter while we were gone. I'm glad he agreed to do that, if no, I don't know who'd I'd fallen back on, maybe the bakery itself. I just didn't feel comfortable leaving it in an empty shelter, and the thought of taking it with us where it could become more damaged, didn't appeal to me either. Okay let's go through it again. Dusk is approaching and it won't be long until we can't see out here anyway. And again I know that you want to work with me with the staff in the twilight so I can begin to sense with my ears as well as my eyes what's happening."

Later as they were sitting around the table Kal said, "Come on Jura, I have to be improving. I mean I actually got you on the ground once."

"You mean when I stepped on that rock that rolled under my foot? I guess you can count that, but yes, in very small steps you are improving. It's just that you need to get past thinking about what you're going to do and just do it. I know, it takes time, and it takes practice, and I've had a lifetime of both. Still we both know the importance of this."

"Yeah we do. It's just that here in this village I never needed to learn this stuff, so I have to start from scratch, from nothing. Plus working mostly in the bakery, and not on the road with my father, who had his workers who were versed in defense it was something I had no need of knowing. But if we are to do what I want to do, then it must be learned. I know that once you get into the wilds, the outback, that life changes, and the ones who can defend themselves are the ones who survive. Look I've a full day at the bakery tomorrow and it will be dusk before I get here. I know that you have an earlier day, so if you would, can you drop off all of this work that we've been doing on this thing to my uncle, that way it will be one more thing out of the way. If you agree with my progress, I think that in another 9-day we can begin on setting the date for this first camp attempt."

"I don't see why not. We've everything we need, and I think, as far as the camp skills go, you've come far enough along that you won't burn down the camp area."

What could he say? It was true that he really hadn't done anything like this in his life. Even the few trips with his father, all the camp setup and work were handled by the workers, so he really hadn't learned from them. The rest of his time had been in the village and working at the bakery – so no experience at all. "Come on, I'm not that bad, am I? While it has been very obvious to me that this is your area of expertise, and I'm just a poor kid from the villages, I think I've picked up most of what you've been showing me."

"Yes, yes you have. But part of what I have planned for us when we are there camping is a day of nothing but hiking. There's some nice trails that climb through the foothills, and with some of the maps that I have, you can get some real experience comparing the area to those maps, and learn to read them better. While the copies that we've made of those primitive maps aren't equal to any we make today, we still have to try and follow them to the areas depicted in them."

The next 9-day truly moved by them was some speed. With work during the day, practice sessions at dusk, and the lessons on map reading, and skills for the outback, there was little time for more than a quick meal, a bath together, and falling into the bed exhausted. But the day finally arrived, and with the borrowing of one of the pack beasts, and this was something that he was better at than she, they headed out. He had to admit that he was somewhat excited about this. He was going to see first hand, if he could actually do any of this and enjoy this different world. Growing up, other than the brief times of play that all children find time to do, it had been learning the business of the family and assisting and learning responsibility related to his age at the time. So to take a few days off was a new experience, and to be able to do this with his mate made it even better. The two of them and only them was a rare thing even now, and there were no children in the picture as of yet. They both knew that when that time came that even those few precious moments of intimacy would be much harder to come by. And by knowing this that sometime in the future there would be a good chance that they would look back on this nostalgically, with smiles on their faces, as they recalled this small respite from their daily lives.

It took three quarters of a travel day to reach the camp area. It was relatively close, by travel standards, and actually sat between a number of small villages. They had stopped at one of these and had their zenith meal, and probably would stop here again when they returned. The food was actually quite good, and what surprised him was the fact that the products from their bakery were available here. This raised the respect he had for his father, knowing that not only he contracted for the supplies they needed to keep the operation going, but sold the products to many of the outlying villages and townships. Yes he knew that others had been responsible for the beginnings of the business, and because of the quality, it had grown, but when his father had mated with his mother and she joined the family it was then that business began to grow. Between his hard work and mother's business sense they had grown to be the largest in the surrounding area. In fact, if he had heard it right, his parents were planning on possibly purchasing other smaller bakeries, and begin selling directly in the villages and townships, making the product fresher, and thusly better. So to even get this time off was a privilege.

When they finally arrived Jura eyed the areas that were available with a critical eye before selecting one site that was close to a small hillside. "Here, I think this one will do. It will have some shade during the day, and by being here against this small hillside we will be safe from any major winds, and we're far enough back that we are somewhat isolated, but not really."

At first he couldn't see why this site, but as she explained it, it became obvious as to why. Another lesson learned, picking a site where to set up your camp is critical. "After you pointed out your reasons, I could see it, but I have to admit that I thought that maybe another area would have been better." Smiling he said, "Wrong again. Even with everything that we covered back at the shelter I still didn't see it. I can see why you wanted to take this trip. And as you've said time and time again, nothing like experience."

"Good, because now comes the fun. If one has never really set up one of these portable shelters then it can take much time to figure out. Even if you've done it a number of times, and then a great period of time has passed, you find it hard to do." She stopped a moment and swept her arms around to include their chosen campsite, "Then when you think you've got it right, one of the stakes that the ropes are tied to pulls out and the darn thing, if it's the right stake, falls down on you. Look once we get this set up we'll pick a place for the campfire, clear it down to just the soil, and while you wondered why I wanted to bring our own wood, if you look you'll see the area had been picked clean. And that's because the ones who come here either don't bring their own, or didn't bring enough. So anything that could be used has been."

Again she had been right. In what he thought would be a simple operation took many trial and errors before they had the portable shelter up and to her satisfaction. They finished the unloading of the pack beast, and she said, "I've been here before so I know a little about this place. If you take the beast around the hill just over there, there's a small area they've provided that has fodder and water for them. Plus it's protected from any of the wild beasts that might be interested in having our pack beast for a meal. And that's one of the reason it costs us to stay here. Oh and before we put down the sleep sacks, and I know we've brought a little padding, make sure that all of those rocks and small pebbles are removed, it makes it so uncomfortable trying to sleep on them."

* * *

"I don't know 'bout you but now that we're back a bath would be a great thing." They had returned the pack beast to the pens after dropping off the packs in their supply shelter.

The suns were setting and dusk was upon them. Both were tired and he had to admit that he had learned quite a bit. And presently he had to admit it would have been stupid of him to go off tramping through the outback with as little experience as he had. In fact from what he'd been learning he knew that if he had survived at all, he'd probably would have been back, giving up on those wild ideas of his. Jura was leading as they headed for the door.

She stopped puzzled, turned and said, "Something's not right here. I don't know what it is at this moment but let's be careful. I can't put my finger on it, but even before we enter our shelter I feel that something's different." She'd taken the key out of her pocket to unlock the door, and when she had placed the key into the slot it didn't feel right. When she turned it, it just spun as if there were no guts in the lock. "This lock's broken. I think that someone may have broken into our place while we were gone." That stopped both of them as they looked at each other.

"I wonder why someone would do that? I mean, it's not like we have anything of value, really." Kal looked at Jura and shrugged, "Now what? Do we just go in, or do we wait?"

Breathing out deeply he said, "No, I guess with it getting dark we really aren't going to see anything, so I guess we go in being careful to not disturb anything and see if we can find anything missing." He replaced his mate and taking over the lead, quietly opened the door, just in case anyone was still there, and even though the door creaked a little, it wouldn't have been enough to alert anybody that could still be inside. But the shelter was empty. Lighting the lantern that hung inside the doorway, and then the candle that sat on the table to the right where they prepared their food, they did a quiet, slow, careful search and found the shelter empty. Whoever it had been was no longer here.

"Well, that's a relief." Jura turned and once again faced Kal and shrugged, "I don't get it. We didn't broadcast it to the world that we would be gone these past three days, and certainly there would be other shelters with much more valuable stuff to steal than our place, so why ours?"

Shaking his head in response Kal said, "I really don't know. It doesn't make sense to me at all. And when we looked around, again if that lock hadn't been broken showing us that someone broke in here, then it wouldn't have been obvious." This caused him a brief pause as a thought crossed his mind. "But if it was just some thieves that broke in here, why leave it like they weren't here?"

"I don't know, maybe to give them more time before we reported the crime, or maybe if it was something they wanted that we wouldn't miss for a while and maybe in the end think that we misplaced it. Who knows? But, that's a very valid question. In some homes of friends that had been broken into their stuff was scattered everywhere as the thieves went through the shelter as fast as they could, grabbing anything they could find of value, and getting out as quick as they could." She waved her arms around and said, "This, this appears to have been a careful, slow search, and an attempt to make it appear like they weren't here at all, and first off, if that lock hadn't been broken, the subtle items that were out of place might not have alerted us at all. No this was a careful well planned operation. Whoever this was took their time, tried to hide everything that they did, and tried very hard to leave everything as we left it."

"I don't know about you, but we're not going to solve it right this moment, and I'm itching from being so dirty. I did not realize that one got this dirty just camping out. Then once we're finished with a bath, and have eaten a little, we can write down what is out of place, and where it was. Maybe that will give us some hint as to what it was they were after. At this point I can't find anything missing, so we truly can't even report a break-in. And because both of us are really just starting out on our own, other than what we got as gifts at the mating ceremony, we have very little to interest any thief, and nothing that would be valuable enough to risk being caught."

She laughed lightly saying, "Yeah, you're quite right. I'll go draw us a bath. You get the water going so that it will be a hot one. Right now I think that would be much nicer than cold water. Besides hot water helps relax those sore spots one always gets when one does something different."

"You're not going to get me to argue. I do have to admit that I do have a few sore muscles. I never realized that sleeping on the ground or doing things around a camp could create so many sore muscles and spots. And a hot bath would ease all of that. I have to admit that I'm glad you suggested it, and then we were able to go and do it – camping that is. Okay I'll get a fire going in the stove and get the water heating. Maybe one day we'll be well off enough to have some of that new stuff that coming out, that only the rich can afford right now – indoor plumbing."

"Yes! How wonderful something like that would be. Then we'd no longer have to go outside to the privy, or to have our bath in that small attached room. Although I guess we're lucky with the bath. Most are still in their own small shelter a little away from the main one. And who knows, someday there might even be something to wash one's clothes other than by hand. I know right now that when we take the time at the end of the 9-day to do that chore, it's an all day job and that's when we're both working at it."

With a faraway look in his eyes he smiled, "Right, like that's going to ever happen. But I guess we can dream. And I have to admit something like that to help with those chores that never seem to end would be really nice. Yet, I guess, if we were to compare how we do it now, verses how it used to be done, then our ancestors would probably be jealous of us."

She laughed as, in her mind, she could see the females of the past standing, staring at her with help, first from a male, that alone would be a shock, and then to be able to bath in hot water instead of the cold river if at all. Then to take care of those daily chores and needs as they now did. Yes, they'd stand there with the hands on their hips just shaking their heads in disbelief. "I see what you mean. I guess each genera-tion has its conveniences that the previous one would love to have had. But that still doesn't mean that I'll avoid dreaming about such things."

"I can understand that, hey better get that water moving, I'll help you haul it inside. I can see the water that's on the stove is beginning to steam, and I'll need to dump it into the ol' wooden tub and get more heating. Shouldn't be too long and we can jump in and soak off this grime."

* * *

Sabohl sat in his office dealing with student papers, one of the things he both hated and loved. Hated because it was something that involved so much of his time and effort, and so many were really bad. But, every once in a while, like his past student Kal, there would be papers that showed promise, and some were brilliant. In this Kal's case though, it was obvious that his direction would be the family business, and he felt that it was such a waste of talent. But one did what one must to survive. He shrugged as these thoughts ran through his mind. There came a soft knock on the door, and he looked up. He couldn't remember any appointments that he had with any of the students, and unless this was one of the staff, who knew better than to bother him as he worked the papers, there shouldn't have been anybody. "Enter", he said gruffly, and waited until the door opened, "What are you doing here?" He asked rather sharply. "We were never to meet, especially here."

The person at the door, dressed as a student bowed slightly with a smile on his face, came inside and closed the door. "That is true, but I felt that this chance could be taken, especially if I appeared to be just another student of yours. With so many running around this place, who would look at another such one anyway?"

Sabohl had to admit that he was probably right, but this irritated him to no end. There could be no known connection between himself and this individual or the others he was part of. "Okay, you've made your point, and again you're probably quite right. Still there is too great of a chance that someone could recognize who you are and my association with you must remain unknown. Why take this chance? This is something that can hurt both of our reputations."

"Let's just say I felt the risk was something that I could take, and as you can see, you have no choice, so accept that in what you are requiring of me and my own that there will be some risk to you. After all, it is unavoidable. Besides I will only be here briefly and be away. Then we can continue to communicate through notes and such at the designated drop points, and have no physical contact at all – protecting both of our reputations."

Sabohl leaned back in his chair put his arms behind his head, stretched, then leaned forward. "Okay, your point is well taken," he said rather gruffly, "so what is so important that it was worth this encounter?"

Smiling, although there was no humor in that smile the guest said, "I'm just reporting on that excursion that we agreed upon. I felt that it was important since you would not be at the exchange for a few days, and again I felt that you should be brought up to speed in person." Here he paused, leaned forward placing his hands on the small desk and said, "First off, as requested we searched, but found nothing out of the ordinary. It was just a shelter, and there really wasn't anything in it worth stealing. The couple is just above poor. I think, from what I've learned that the shelter that they are living in belongs to the family and bakery. From what I've learned and what is common knowledge, this family business provides shelters for their workers, and that includes family. And since this one is family, one would assume that the shelter that was provided would have been a cut above the ones they hire to work for them. But it is not so. We found nothing at all as to what your request stated should be there. So while it's not my place to say anything on this subject, I think you may be wrong."

"You came by to tell me this? This information could have waited until I picked up the letter. And you're right, it is not your place to tell me what I can and cannot do or assume."

Still leaning forward, and now with a look of hardness in his eyes, the guest continued, "Do not push that attitude towards me. I'm not one of your students that you can intimidate, and it will never work with me, so stop before you get yourself into something that you have no way out of. Yes, this information could have been left, but that is not the main reason for this visit. If you remember the specific orders given, stated that once we left there could be no evidence that we or anybody was there. Unfortunately they have their evidence."

"What? What do you mean by that? Evidence – what evidence would that be? I was very specific on that account. I cannot have this one suspicious that someone is trying to find something."

"It couldn't be helped, and it was unexpected. The one who was picking the lock to get inside cursed, and I asked, now what? He said that the lock was old and with his manipulation it simply broke. So when they returned they would know that someone jimmied the lock. And like I said, it couldn't be helped, and once it broke we couldn't replace it since we had no idea of what their key looked like, and besides any work would have been obvious."

Anger began to rise in Sabohl, but with effort he gained control as he stated, "As if the broken lock wasn't. You told me he was the best at this kind of thing, and now this?"

With no apology in his voice the guest said, "He is, and that's as much as I will say. Now that we are up to date I'll say good day to you." At which point not even waiting a dismissal he turned and left, closing the door behind him, disappearing among the many students walking up and down the halls. Sabohl sat at his desk looking at nothing still attempting to get his anger under control, taking a few deep breaths he thought. *This operation was supposed to leave no evidence that anybody had broken in. But that's not what happened, and now they know. But what do they know? After all it could appear that when the thieves broke the lock that they just panicked and left.* Sighing deeply and giving himself a shake he finally got back into control. *I've still a couple of classes to teach.* He got up went around the desk, opened the door, and headed down the hallway to his classroom.

* * *

"Jaie, Temporary Leader of the Historical Learned:

"Good day sir, it has been wise that I've been planted here at the higher learning center. As I have been instructed I have been monitoring the learned of interest. He had a visitor to-day, and while dressed as one of the students, one could see immediately that he was not. While I was not in position to overhear what was discussed, what I did hear suggested that whatever had been planned did not produce the expected re-sults, and that there had been evidence left behind to give them away. As to what this endeavor could have been, I, un-fortunately, have no hint. But suspect that it probably relates to the subject that had been broached in the correspondence to your people. I took the liberty of having this visitor fol-lowed, albeit discreetly. After all it would do us harm if either the subject we are watching, and the ones who made contact with him become aware of our interest. As new information becomes available it will be passed on. I know that this is be-yond the normal reporting times, but felt that it was something that needed to be brought to the learned of the board immedi-ately. May our endeavors be successful."

CHAPTER THREE

It had been 3 9-days since they had returned and discovered the break-in. Yet with a careful search and discussion between the two of them, they found nothing amiss or missing. So whoever the thief or thieves had been they obviously were looking for something specific. They had reported the incident to both family and the local law, but with nothing to report other than the broken lock, there wasn't anything anybody could do, other than increase their individual alertness. But neither of them, Kal or Jura, could watch the shelter all of the time, so it was vulnerable to additional break-ins. Plus its location didn't help at all – since it was partially hidden making it easy for the incident to be repeated. After discussing things for a while, Kal realized that the only thing that wasn't in their home at the time was that family history. So as to keep it safe, they decided that it should remain with the uncle who had passed it on to him in the first place. At least there in that shelter someone was always present, making it almost impossible to repeat what had happened at their shelter. Besides, with the work that he had to do, he was quite busy. It was close to celebration time once again, and all of them were working especially hard to get the extra product out that would sell well. And when he would go home at night, and it was night, since they used all the daylight hours to work, he would be exhausted, and found that sleep was almost more important than anything else. As he sat at the table with his mate at the end of another difficult day he said as he breathed out deeply, "Jura, I smell of bread and sweetbreads, and am covered in flour. Need a quick bath, a quick meal, and much sleep. But I have to admit that this break-in still weighs heavily on me."

"Well, you're not the only one. It's something that's never happened to me before, and I suspect not you either. Here for the longest time you feel safe, and then this happens, shattering all those illusions that one has about being safe in one's shelter. I mean when we are on the trails or roads we could expect that there would be a slight chance of being attacked, but usually it's something that doesn't happen very often. Like you, this has bothered me a great deal. I'm just thankful that we weren't here." Jura shuddered at that thought and briefly closed her eyes.

"Yeah, I have to agree, but it also makes me wonder. While we didn't try and keep it a secret that we would be away for those few days, it seems that someone had been listening closely. And I hate to admit it, but maybe I wasn't as smart as I thought I was when I asked those questions of that learned."

She looked at him questioningly, "Are you accusing your old mentor of arranging this?"

Shaking his head he said, "No, not really. But you have to admit that this is a possibility. When you look at the way this was done, I mean that if there hadn't been that broken lock we probably wouldn't have looked that closely when we came back, and they would have gotten away with this. And the reason my mind keeps going back to him is this; he's considered top in his field, and with what we've learned from that family historical record would refute much of his ideas. So if that document should disappear, what proof would we ever have to present? We'd have nothing, nothing at all. So he could look at us, smile a sad smile, and ask us to show the world the proof, knowing that we couldn't do it. Thusly leaving he and his theories as the dominant ones."

Looking down at the table and thinking Jura said, "I see what you mean. And those questions you've been asking might have tipped him off. So, to protect himself and his position, he'd want to know what you really had, and if it was a threat to him or his theories, and if so, eliminate it. When you begin to think about it that way I can see why you'd come to those conclusions. But is it accurate?"

Shaking his head once again he answered, "I don't know, I really don't. And it is a worrisome thing. Because I've always trusted him, and his knowledge, plus he always seemed to be willing to take the time to listen and answer the questions I had. Of course putting it in this new light I can see it would be a great way to stay ahead of anybody who might be able to usurp him or his position – to appear to be friendly, knowledgeable, and willing to be there for his students. Again I might just be blowing smoke into the air, but if I was a thief breaking into a shelter, because of the risk, I'd steal whatever I felt was valuable and not traceable back to me, and that's not what happened here."

"Yeah, that makes perfect sense, so I guess I'm happy that we decided not to leave that family history here or it would have been gone, and we'd have no way of proving it ever existed. Hey it's getting late, go take your bath, and I'll have a bite for us when you get out, then we can head off to the sleeping space, tomorrow comes much too quick as it is." What they had been discussing made a lot of sense, but there was no hard proof. She turned and headed in to fix a quick meal. She heard him sigh, get up and leave to take that bath.

* * *

It was another 9-day since the celebration, and he had to admit that all the work had been worth it. With other family members and workers they had staffed their booth, and by the time the three day celebration was over they had sold everything, plus some as they had rushed to add to their supplies. That didn't mean that he and Jura didn't end up with some time of their own to enjoy the crowds, the music, and the festivities, to go to the dances, to enjoy the reenactments that were always performed. But now all of that was behind them and everything was returning to normal. His father was out on another supply run since the increase in uses for the celebration had depleted much of their on-hand stock. It was just after the midday break when his mother called him into her office and suggested that he sit down, which he did.

Once he was seated she leaned forward placing her arms on the desk in front of her. As usual the desk had its piles of work, but even though to the untrained eye it appeared to be a complete mess, he knew that this was far from the truth. She could find anything at any time she needed it. "Kal, as you know, your father and I have been looking to expand what we are doing. He recently came up with a very good suggestion and we've been pursuing it. And from the responsibility that you've shown, and the efforts that you've been willing to put forth, we felt that you should have the chance to help make this work." At this point she paused looking at him to see how he was reacting. What she saw was a questioning, and while it was subtle, a mother could always see what was happening with her children.

Now what? "What is it that the two of you have been discussing? I know that like the rest here that I work for the business, and family has no privileges. And we must earn our positions, and it is something that makes sense. Other than that and the fact that I've been required to learn the business from all aspects how does this discussion apply to me?" Then he had a thought but at first dismissed it, yet it persisted as he remembered when the business had been turned over to his parents a very long time ago. Was it time for that to happen for him?

She could see the thoughts, questions, and conclusions flit across his face as he remained open. Of course, in her mind, she doubted that others could read him like she could, well maybe Jura, but other that she, no one else. She smiled, "What we've been looking at is this; expanding this business."

"But we've already used up all the land and space available to this bakery. How'd it be something that could be done? Did you and father purchase the lands next to the bakery?"

"No, and I can see how that would make sense. No that would require too much of an investment, and the cost of building and converting is still beyond our money."

"So if that isn't something you can do, have the two of you decided to buy a mercantile instead, expanding beyond the bakery?"

Again she smiled, "That, by the way, is probably a pretty good suggestion – something that the two of us hadn't thought about, but no. Still it's surely something to think about in the future. No, what we've come up with is something that allows us to expand but at the same time to keep the investments within our means. Plus we've both seen how passionate both you and Jura are on following up on our family's history. Especially since that record dropped in your hands. In fact we, your father and I, suggested that he pass it on to you. We could see that history was something that held a serious interest with you. So who better? Now we felt that there needed to be a way that would allow you to pursue that, and at the same time help the family and the business that we operate, and to allow us to continue to grow, and what we've come up with allows all of that to happen."

How could all of what she had just related to him happen? He was definitely puzzled. "Okay, I may be a little dense here, but I can't see how all of that can be fulfilled."

"Simple really . . . In many ways I'm really surprised that nobody has done this. But from what we know, nobody has. And once I present it to you, you'll see it also. Instead of buying the land around here, doing all the required work and cost of adding what would be necessary, why not buy another bakery in a different village or township, and expand into a new place. Still using all the techniques and innovations that we've come up with and kept secret, and that's just what we did. We want you to go and be in charge of this new bakery that we purchased over close to where your mate is from. That will get her closer to her own family, and with the supply runs and such you'll still be in contact with us. And once it's up and operational, and all the workers have been trained, and you've found someone who can be an underboss, then this will allow you the freedom to search the family history and try and locate the places spoken in the writings. So how does that sound?"

At first he was stunned, and for the longest time silent. "Let me get this straight, you're saying that instead of just expanding here that you two went out and bought another bakery, and you want me to run it? Not that I don't appreciate it, but do I really qualify? There has to be at least one or two who have worked with you for turns that are better than I am."

"That could be, but we've been working hard on grooming you for taking over the business sometime in the future. But at the same time with what we've been doing the business has been growing and we needed some way of taking advantage of it. And yes there are a couple that have been with us for a very long time. In fact for a short period of time you'll have one of them with you to help get the new bakery operating to our quality. And believe me you will not be left on your own. Both of us will visit periodically to see how it's going. We know that for the first few cycles of seasons that we probably will be lucky to break even at the new operation, but that is expected. I suggest you talk with Jura and be ready in the very near future to make the move. At first you will be living in the back of the bakery, but eventually as the operation begins to show a profit we will purchase dwellings for the ones who work for us. Now get back to work, discuss this with your mate, and then be prepared to make this move. It has many benefits for all of us." With that she waved him out of the office and back to work.

The rest of that day as he worked his mind continued to go over the conversation, well more listening than talking, but it meant that he would be leaving the village that he had always known as home. Unlike his mate who had left her home to join his, he had never faced such a thing. At first it excited him, and then he became nervous. After all, all of his contacts, all of his friends, and most of his relatives lived either in this village or very close by. And before he knew it he was heading home, and still being deep in thought over the implications of this revelation found himself opening the door and not remembering the walk from the bakery to their shelter. Jura had arrived earlier. She worked part time helping out some of the older members of the community. She could see that faraway look in his eyes and wondered what was going on. "Kal, is there something wrong?" She asked cautiously.

"What? Ah, no, nothing's wrong."

"Okay, I know something's going on, so are we going to play twenty questions, or are you going to fill me in?" At this point she pushed him towards the table and then sat across from him waiting expectantly for an answer. As she sat down she crossed her arms, placed them on the table and leaned forward.

Not quite sure how to start he gathered his thoughts, and inwardly laughed. He then asked himself, wasn't this what he had been doing since he had received the news from his mother? Looking down and then briefly up, he cleared his throat and began. "I've been informed that there are changes coming and those changes will involve me directly, and truthfully both of us." Again not sure how to continue he paused. After all this had come as a complete surprise to him leaving him to wonder as to how would this affect Jura? "I've just learned, today in fact, that the family business will be expanding."

She smiled, "Ah, and that's the news! Great news if it is true." Again she paused because that comment he'd made did not match the look on Kal's face. With a look of consternation on her own face she realized that there had to be much more to it than just that. "Okay. I can see that there's more to it than what you just told me . . . oh, this change will somehow affect us, do I have it right?"

Smiling back at her, even though it was a nervous one, "Yes, as always you've figured it out before I could say anything." He then went over the conversation that he had with his mother and how everything would change for both of them.

It was her turn to be silent as she absorbed everything he had just told her. "So when is this to take place? I mean it will be wonderful to be closer to my own family and my old stomping grounds, so to speak, but I have to admit that I've established strong roots and ties here. It will be hard to give them up. So how long do we have?"

"I really don't know. Mother didn't go into a time line, but I suspect that it will be soon. So I guess we should be planning on making the move in the not too distance future. I know that we've been in this place for a while, so I suspect that as all of us do, we've been accumulating stuff." He laughed before continuing, "Look, if I remember it right, when we became mates and first moved into this place we barely had enough of anything to fill one room, let alone the whole place. Now look at it, every room is full and comfortable for us."

She had to admit that the shelter had filled up over time, but how else could one make a shelter their own? Yes, it would be difficult to decide what went with them, what they got rid of, and what they stored. From his description the space they were initially to live in would be much smaller than this. "Knowing your parents as I do now, I'm sure that they've planned this for a long time, worked towards it, and are just about ready to make it work. So I'm sure that in that planning they had you in mind all of the time, which means that they'll give us the necessary time to prepare and make the move. I suspect that we'll be using the pack and cart beasts that they use for the caravans that your father operates." Again she paused as another thought came to mind. "Oh my, that means that I'll have to leave what I'm doing and try and find something in that other place."

"Yes, that's probably true, but I suspect that there'll be plenty to do at this new, well new to us, bakery so that there will be no lack of work for either of us. And I suspect that we'll be using some of the earnings to support ourselves. She, ah mother, said that they didn't expect the operation to be profitable immediately, and while she didn't say so, I suspect that is because that part of what this place earns will have to support us."

* * *

It was now 1513TOG, and they had been at this new bakery for two cycles of the seasons. And all that they had speculated back in their old shelter now had answers. Both had worked hard and full time in the bakery. And as the bakery was named, back where the original one was, this one was also called, Bakery of Kaygor. With the skills that he had obtained from all of the time working in the family business, much of what he did not realize that he had learned, this new location began to grow almost immediately. And the time that was necessary for it to earn a profit turned out to be shorter than his parents had projected. But the work had been hard and both of them found no problem falling asleep at the end of another busy day. In truth that first turn of seasons found them working from dawn to dusk with no break, and all the 9-days were also worked with no time off. So now with the operation showing a profit, and workers trained, the two of them felt that finally they would take one 9-day off and be able to spend some time away from the bakery, and quality time with each other.

But before the opportunity to actually take that time off, fate once again intervened, and they received word that his uncle had passed away. His uncle had lost his mate a few turns earlier to some disease that slowly wasted her away until there was very little left. He hadn't fared well after her passing, and had withdrawn. The family had been quite worried, but there was very little they could do. So instead of joy and time with Jura they returned to the village where he had been raised, and where most of his family lived. In those two turns, two cycles of the seasons, he had all but forgotten about the family historical record, and his thoughts of finding the locations mentioned within. But now after the funeral, with the family gathered, all remembering the good of the dead, and of other family members, who had passed on, brought back what he had received from that uncle, and the fact that he had returned the family history to him to protect it. Now it would be back in his hands, and again it brought it back to the forefront, all that he had planned on doing with the knowledge that was contained therein. He remembered that conversation that he had with his mother about making this move working in this new bakery, and making it thrive. And that eventually once all was functioning as it should that he would be free to pursue the answers to the riddles this document provided.

While it had been a sad time for him since this uncle had always been a favorite, but with the work that the two of them had been involved with, there had been no time to stay abreast of family. The only contact that they had had with either of the families, hers and his, was by letter and by contact when his father would come by with the supplies. And even here, he did not visit every time. So he wasn't even aware of what had been transpiring with his uncle until he learned of his death. And now with the will having been read and the personal belongings passed to who they were bequeathed, the families returned to their own homes, sad in the fact that another member of the older generation was gone, and with the knowledge that slowly they were moving towards being that older generation. "I remember as I was growing up," Kal related, "he'd show me some things, and was always funny. Coming up with these little jokes and stunts to pull on others – I really wish I had known." But he hadn't, and no one had figured out how to go back in the past and correct mistakes. They'd been so busy that at times it seemed hard to breathe let alone get away.

Looking down at the letter that his uncle had addressed to him and only him, he stared at it unopened, not really wanting to open it and read the last words from him. After all if he put it off then he would still be with him with some wisdom or insight to pass on. It made him realize that his parents were not getting any younger. And while this uncle had been the oldest of the siblings he had died somewhat young. What made this sadder still lie in the fact that there had been no offspring from him and his mate. Kal suspected that was one of the reasons that they got along so well. He had become like a son to him. "Well," Jura asked, "aren't you even going to open it and read what he wanted to say to you?" They had finally returned to their shelter, which fortunately was no longer the back of the bakery, but a real separate shelter. They both sat at the table where they ate, discussed things, and worked the books.

Shaking his head and looking down he said, "I'm not sure. I know that once I do that he will be truly gone – not that he isn't. But this is the last of anything that is personal from him, and once I've read it then whatever I had of him will be gone. I mean, well I'm not sure what I mean." Sighing and taking a deep breath, "I'm saying this really bad, but as a child I looked up to him, and from there we begin to develop our views of someone else. I guess, even though there was no real reason to do so, I kind of looked at him as my hero. No, he never did anything hero like, but was there when my parents were tied up with some problem with the business. It seemed that he was always available if I needed someone to talk to or confide in. I'm sure that being brothers, my father and him, that if he felt it was important that he would pass on whatever it was we talked about. As a kid you don't think about such things. He'd take me on small outings and such. We'd have these great adventures, at least in my eyes, and we were close. So by not reading this I'm kind of trying to hold on to some of that, some of the mystery. This is the last of that and once I've read it then there will be nothing more ever."

Taking a deep breath herself before replying Jura said. "For someone who couldn't explain it very well, I think you did a great job. So I'll not push you to read this until you're ready, even though as a female I'm very curious as to what your uncle wanted to pass on to you. Okay different subject, but we have that family history again, what are your feelings on that? I know back when we were working on it all the time that you wanted to pursue what we had discovered. To find out if any of what is written there, and what we've been taught in the learning centers is accurate.

"I don't know at this moment, haven't even thought about it, let alone consider it. I guess for now until we've gotten everything where it needs to be it will just have to wait. I guess if time allows we can start working on it again to make sure it is preserved for others down the trails of time. I suspect that once we start that we'll become passionate once again."

"True, and while on the subject of family, mine contacted me recently and suggested that all of us get together for a couple of days, and I thought it was a great idea. And with us originally planning on taking some time off, for which we still have a couple of those days available, I agreed. Besides, this will be fun, and help you get over that loss that you just suffered. So we'll be heading over there the day after tomorrow." She smiled pausing a moment, "Besides I've been bragging about how much you've improved with the staff."

This brought his head up since he had been looking down at the table. "What? You've told them about me practicing with you? I admit that I've improved, but you can still beat me most of the time."

"Oh come on. You've come very far. Now I actually have to work at defeating you. Besides you've only had one person to work against. I want you to go against my siblings and if you feel up to it, mom and dad." Here she laughed when she saw the panicked look in his eyes. "Oh come on, it won't be that bad. In fact I think you'll have a great time, and if it isn't more than listening as all of us recall our good times."

"Right and me having trouble sitting because your family beat the crap out of me with the staff, what fun would there be in that?"

Laughing again from his comment Jura said, "Ah is my little male worried that he could be bested by my sisters, let alone my brothers or parents?"

From the tone of her voice he could tell that she was teasing and all he could do was smile and shake his head, "No, not really. I know they will beat me. While, as you've pointed out I'm so much better now I'm not good enough to beat champions, or in this case former champions. And working with you I've dealt with too many bruises and tender spots. So I can imagine how I would fare against the rest of your family." Sighing he continued, "Still, I have to admit that seeing your family would be nice and would take my mind off of my uncle's death. So what do we do with this family history, now that we have it back? I don't want to take a chance that it will disappear like it almost did."

"Good point." She stopped and thought a moment, "I don't know, how about the bakery? There's usually someone there all of the time."

"True, but there's that back entrance, the one we get supplies, and that area where we lived is just off of the hallway. It would be so easy for someone to sneak in there during the busy parts of the day. Heck you wouldn't have to sneak. It's so noisy that a crying babe couldn't be heard. It is a problem. When he was alive it was a great place for it to stay, but now . . ." Both were silent. Nothing had ever come of the original investigation from the past break-in, since all they had to go on was the broken lock. So whoever had been responsible was still free. And even though it had been two cycles of the seasons they had tried to keep vigilant, but had seen nothing to even raise their suspicions. He still believed that Sabohl was responsible, and because of this had never gone back to ask any more questions. Plus it was soon after that that they had made the move and had been heavily involved with making this new bakery work. And since that initial attempt there had been no others.

Breathing out and leaning back in her chair she said, "Well I really have no answers. And right now the fewer who know about this the better. But we do need to come up with something. I don't want to leave it here when we aren't. We still only have partially copied it, and if it disappeared we'd have nothing."

"Agreed, so I think that we'll take it with us when we visit your family, at least we'll have it with us, and maybe we can come up with some type of answer or solution."

* * *

He'd been right, while indeed he had improved, through practice; it had only been against the same individual. So as he went against other members of her family they found weaknesses in both his attack and defense, and had taken advantage. And for the first time he became involved in one of those free-for-alls Jura had talked about. While it had been desperate, since he was the least experienced, it forced him to react instead of think, and he found that he could make some of the moves quicker than he ever had. And while it would be time before the bruises disappeared he had to admit that it had been a lot of fun – rough fun, tough and brutal, especially since all of them were now adults, with no quarter taken or given. Even her parents would join and show the youngsters how it was done. And they still could whip any member of the family, and make it appear easy.

Breathing quite hard after the last free-for-all, he asked, "All of you did this kind of thing all of the time?"

Laughing, Fara the youngest sister of Jura's family stated, "Why of course. But we'd only be allowed to do such a thing after all the chores and such were done. And here there are always a lot of chores. I guess, in a way, this stuff was important too, but we looked at it as a game, as something fun to do. And as all kids have a tendency to do now and then, it could get out of control, and then mom and dad would come out and put all of us in our place." This brought a laugh from the rest of the family.

He could imagine, in his mind's eye, what that must have been like. The parents had been much younger then, and even now they could still whip any of them. Their skill was unbelievable. And he could understand why her parents had wanted them to become proficient with the staff. It gave them piece of mind knowing that any of their children could defend themselves if the situation warranted. Yet, when he had first witnessed one of their free-for-all's, before getting brave enough to join one of them, he couldn't believe the frenzied attacks and movements as they pushed to win the match. And while there were bruises that resulted there almost seemed to be a dance within the chaos he was witnessing, and as each one was eliminated until there would only be one winner, the dance would become almost beautiful. Then they would all laugh and do it again. Finally they convinced him to join, and the one thing that turned out to be consistent was he became the first to be eliminated. All of them were just too good, and that included Fara who was younger by many cycles of the seasons than he.

Finally, as in all things, it was time to return to the bakery and work. It was always there, and there was always work. They said their goodbyes and added promises of returning when they could. With the pack beast they headed away from the farm out to the main trail, and then to the major road that would bring them back to High Trail, the village where they were working and living at this time. Many of the villages were named far into the past as this one had been. The main road that they now traveled had originally be a trail out of the foothills and had picked up the name High Trail. Since this particular village had served the many travelers it had become known as High Trail, just as the one he had grown up in had been known as Cross Trails because it was where two major trails, which were now roads, had crossed. It had been a location that was perfect for a village. While Cross Trails was much larger than High Trail, neither had grown large enough to become townships. Both had farmlands that supported the communities. Cross Trails sat within the great grasslands, while High Trail nestled in the foothills on the edge of the great grasslands.

It was the beginning of the Season of Falling and when they had left it was early in the morning. They could see their breath in the cold crisp air, and coming out of a warm shelter had sent both of them to shivering as they adjusted to the cold air. With the feel in the air they didn't need to look at anything written to know the season. This got Kal to wondering, since they had just gotten back the family history, and had brought it along for protection, if that clan home could be somewhere close to where they were. After all they were in the foothills away from the Sacred Mountains, and if he re-membered right, this clan home wasn't that close to those mountains, and as far as the village of High Trail, and the family farm they were not very close either. But as soon as that had entered his mind he shrugged it off, since there were many areas that existed in the many foothills that were around, and much of them were a very long way away from the Sacred Mountains. What this began to do for him is to raise his curiosity and desire to delve back into that history and try and solve what was presented in those many words from the past.

Eventually as the suns climbed in the sky it warmed, and between their exercise and the warming of the air the chill left, and it became a comfortable day to be out and about. Breathing in and out deeply Kal said, "This is becoming a really beautiful day, and a good one to be doing exactly what we are. But it also brought to my mind my ancestors. They'd lived in an area something like this. I wonder what they were thinking when this weather hit. They had to be more knowl-edgeable than I, after all their very lives depended on knowing the seasons. They'd know that it would only be a short time until they would be locked up inside because of the winds, snows, and such. And at that point they would need to have enough of everything to get through that time, and if not, death would come knocking – not that death wasn't a constant companion. Between the fighting, diseases, poor health, and who knows what it's surprising that any of them survived. And the line I come from was a clan, and when you compare the clans to the tribes, well the clans, because of their settle-ments, were so much better off."

As they continued down the road, Jura listening to the clopping sound of the pack beast's steps, and the gentle creaking of the leather bindings used to tie the packs to the frames that the beasts carried, was quiet. She was enjoying the walk very much, and like him thought the day was a great one. Not only that, but the feel of the air, the smells of the land, the odors of the grasses as they had cured giving off a sweet smell, made her appreciate and remind her of the home where she had grown. The mornings were a little cold when they started, but from the feel of it now, the rest of the day, up until they reached the village at about dusk, should remain very nice. "As, I said in the past, I'm glad I'm living now and not then. And yes, at times one could easily wonder how anybody survived that time in our past. But it is obvious somebody did since we are here." Smiling and with a faraway look in her eyes she said, "I wonder how future generations will look back on ours. I mean that while we find what we have, and what we can do is good, and proper, and we live comfortably, even though we work hard to achieve it, but it really isn't an issue or a problem for us. Still they may look back at us and wonder how anybody would survive in this time just like we're doing when we're looking back."

Laughing Kal said, "You know I've never looked at it that way, and you're probably quite right. So I guess when we are directly in our time that it seems okay. I mean there are good times and bad times, and with the day-to-day stuff happening we rarely have a chance to look at the big picture, just trying to keep everything going. So I guess that it probably was the same for them. Still I suspect that with that lifestyle they really never looked back at earlier generations except as spirits. So I guess we should be happy with where we are and know that most likely our future generations are going to see us as primitive in comparison to where they are at that time."

She laughed and shook her head. "Now that's funny, I mean really funny. We don't consider ourselves anything close to that way. We see new things coming along all the time to make things better and easier, and while we can't necessarily afford this stuff right now, there's a great possibility that sometime in the future that we can. And when we have it we'll appreciate it so much more because we've done without all this time. Then to think that someone in the future will look back and feel pity for us because we didn't have something that they do. And they would wonder how those, you know ones like you and me, primitives could ever survive?" Again she laughed as the images flashed once again through her mind. "I guess it's all perspective. When one is in the midst of life it is what it is, and when one looks at another's life whether it is in the near past, or distant past we compare where we are to them, and probably while it's something that would be natural to do, is really unfair."

"You know taking these trips with you is really a wonderful experience. You bring up thoughts and ideas that I have myself, and it helps me make sense of what I'm trying to understand. I guess in many ways it is always great to have someone to discuss things. And I have to agree with everything you've just said. It makes perfect sense, but sometimes things that appear to make sense at the moment fall apart later when other facts are presented. But somehow I don't feel that's going to happen this time. Being a village kid I've never had the opportunity to experience this life style much. And I'm finding that I really love it. I guess with what we're planning on doing very shortly I'd better. Since I know that we will be out here much of the time, and again I know how we are, and I'm not just referring to the two of us here, never satisfied. If we are cooped up in the village we long to get away, once we are away, we cannot wait until we are back home, and when we are working we cannot wait until the day is finished so we can relax, and so on."

Jura cocked her head to the side, and smiled, "Very true. I can see much of that when I visit with my female friends. Some have children and some, like me don't. Now I'm not pushing for a child at this time in our life, especially with all that we're about to do, but I see that very thing in our conversations. Some of them are saying how wonderful it must be to have a child, and they have that romantic faraway look as they imagine how it will be. Then the ones with children comment something to the effect, *be careful what you wish for*, and so on. And I can see much of what you've just said in how I view things. And here I thought I was the only one."

"I guess it's more common than I thought. But it only makes sense when you think about it. If we were really satisfied with where we are, then there would be nothing happening to change anything, and there's a good possibility that we'd still be like our primitive ancestors and still have that dreaded lifestyle that led to short hard lives. This brings me back to this; what are we going to do with that history? I know that I've been given custody of it, and must somehow protect it. I know that we've continued to work on making legible copies of this thing, and we've almost completed that part of it. But we, I need someplace that is safe to store that thing. Since that attempt, at what we figured, to steal this document, I've been racking my brain trying to come up with a safe haven for it, and really haven't. I feel that someone wants this desperately, and we both know who that someone is. I know that we just got it back, but when I looked it over, I never realized that we were that close to finishing it.

"I thought about my side of the family, and all of them are quite busy with their lives, and while yes, this is about my side of the family, can I put them at risk? And at the same time, your side lives in the outback on a farm, making them an easy target if someone wanted to steal something from them." He paused a moment and actually laughed, "Now that would be funny really."

With a questioning look she asked, "What would be funny?"

"I was just imagining what a surprise a bunch of thieves would get if they tried to steal or break into your family's farm. Here these thieves would feel that they'd have it all under control and to meet your family with the matriarch and patriarch of the family staff champions and all of the children trained by them. I think the bad guys in this case would be in for a real surprise, let alone a good beating. I could see the surprise on their faces when they realized that they didn't have the upper hand, and that they had better leave or get beat up."

She was silent for the longest time, which made him wonder if he'd said something wrong. She stopped and faced him, "Well, it's not as funny as you make it sound. You see, that very thing did happen. Remember we are somewhat isolated, and as you can see, at this leisurely pace that we are taking, it will be dusk before we enter High Trail." She did smile as she recalled the incident in her mind, "And I think that you probably had it about right. We did beat them up pretty badly, in fact after that we were never bothered again. I guess the word got around that we weren't worth the trouble."

"Really? I was only thinking about something like that happening. And it actually did, wow, why'd you never mention it? After all it had to be a pretty traumatic time."

Again she paused before answering, "Actually the being scared part didn't happen until it was over and the thieves ran away. When they approached appearing to be innocent, we knew something was wrong, and when one of them reached out to grab both my mother, and one of us girls to get their way, we knew what was happening, and once we did it was just sort of reaction. It was touch and go there for a little while since they were spread out trying to cover all of us. And that probably was their undoing also. They expected just a normal farm family not us. They figured they could intimidate us into submission, and instead it was they who were put down. It was very intense and there seemed to be nothing but chaos for a few moments, but suddenly it was over, and the bad guys were running for their lives. It was then once we were all back together and found that other than scrapes and bruises, which we got when we practiced with the staffs anyway, we were okay. At that point we realized what could have happened and that's when we all felt it emotionally."

He realized that both of them had been standing there along the roadway with the pack beast patiently standing there waiting for them to continue, swishing its tail at some irritating bug. They both began walking again. "I never realized that something like that happened. And you say you or the family was never bothered again? How long ago was this?"

Shaking her head she said, "I really don't know, quite a while ago. I was still a kid. After all I'm one of the middle children, and I think Fara the youngest was just walking, so a very long time ago."

"And you and your family have never been bothered since. That must have been quite an impression you left on those thieves." Taking a deep breath Kal looked around, "I have to admit that I'm quite happy that it went the way that it did. I know that many times in those situations that the ones who try this have their way with the families and in the end just kill them to keep any from identifying them, allowing them to go do it again to some other unsuspecting isolated family. And if it had been that way, you and I would have never met, and fall in love and become a couple." This brought a smile to his face, "So I'm very glad for the way things turned out, and if you don't want it mentioned, I'll let it lie and just keep it between us."

Looking at Kal, Jura replied, "Oh we never tried to keep it a secret, but we also felt it wasn't important to announce it to the world. Doing such a thing might be considered bragging, and if someone thought it was such they might decide that we were a challenge and they would come by and try and see if they could succeed where that other gang of thugs failed. So we never made anything of it. Yes we passed it on to the other farms so that they would be alert to the fact that we had some bad ones working our area, but other than that we kept it low and quiet."

"Just had a thought, and then I'll just drop it. When these thieves first attacked, none of you had your staffs, right?" She shook her head, "Okay that means all of you were unarmed at that moment, so how'd that work out? I mean obviously well since you are here and your family is all okay."

She smiled as once again she remembered back to that moment in time. "If you think about it, one has to learn moves that allow one to defend themselves if they've become disassociated with their staff. So there are unarmed methods of attacks that allow one to recover their staff and resume the match. We've not practiced any of them, and back there at the family farm we all held on to the staffs during those few free-for-all sessions that you were invited to join. Obviously, well maybe not to you, but to the rest of us, we kept it toned down a bit for the rookie that joined us. And it was a couple of those unarmed moves we used that allowed a couple of us to get free, get the staffs, and toss them to the others. After that it was a rout pure and simple."

He smiled at her, "You're right, I couldn't tell that all of you went easy on me. From my point of view I was barely holding may own, and it was fast and frenzied. And I suspect that with this revelation that since all of you went easy on me, that the few times that I thought I had the upper hand, so to speak, truly wasn't the way of it at all."

"Before I answer that, let's just say that you've improved tremendously from where you started back a couple of cycles of the seasons ago. But honestly you're not in the same class as even my youngest sister, so yeah we went easy on you. But you have to admit that you learned some new things."

"Well that means I took a hit to that old male ego thing. Especially if the youngest female took pity on this male, but you're right I did learn a few things going against the rest of you."

"If it's any consolation to your male ego, as you know, we were trained by the best, and I think honestly that right now there'd be few out there that you couldn't defend yourself against if it came down to it. But I wouldn't go out and start challenging anybody as of yet. As time and practice continues and we have a few more visits to my home it will change. And to give you another hit to that male ego of yours, remember that I'm with you and if need be I can defend you."

"Gee thanks." And this brought laughter from both of them. "Hey where'd the time go? Look we're almost back and the suns are beginning to set. Oh well, back to reality on the morrow."

CHAPTER FOUR

It had taken longer than he had expected to finish the re-writing of the family history. Once complete, they used only the copies, spreading the original among the family members, so that if any single part was either stolen or lost, it overall would be just a small portion, and with copies available they would be able to fill in the missing parts to present a complete history. With the help of her siblings there was now available more than one copy which, once again, was spread among her family. With the suspected attempt to steal it in the past it was the only way they could come up with to protect this precious history.

Sabohl continued to have them watched, albeit discreetly. He still felt that they, Kal and Jura, were a threat. And even though he had no proof that a document existed, he felt strongly that it did. Still two cycles of the seasons had come and gone and presently there had been nothing to show for all of this work. Yet he could not relax until this was confirmed one way or the other. He had thought that a second attempt to break into their shelter would be a good idea, but the only op-portunity had been when a family member had passed away.

It really hadn't been that long since they had moved from the premises of the bakery to the shelter they were living in presently. And while they lived at the bakery there was absolutely no chance to sneak into their quarters and do a thorough search. There was always one or the other going in and out of their place any time throughout the day, and with no specific schedule, there was no opportunity. When they had finally moved into the shelter, she had remained there and put it together like she wanted it to look. Again with no schedule to allow a quick and thorough search it had to wait.

It wasn't long after that that they had left to attend the funeral, but while they were gone the workers watched the shelter continuously not allowing any stranger access. It, in his mind, was the proof that he needed that said they were protecting something. After all why go to all the trouble if there wasn't anything of real value? So with impatience he watched from a distance waiting for the opportunity to present itself.

"To the members of the Historical Learned, and Historical Society: I pass on my humble offerings as a fellow learned. As you are well aware, we of like thought have continued our monitoring of Sabohl. If nothing else, his resolve has strengthened, as has his contacts with his people, and you know of whom I speak, continue. He is more determined to find this mythological document, since at this moment he has no proof that such exists. But it is obvious to any who know him that he is consumed with this. In truth we are in no way positive that such exists. Yet if it does, it would be an important find and possibly shed light on our past. All of us who study the past know that we are making conclusions from very incomplete records and discoveries. And since no one is

around from that time we have no way of confirming any of what we've either found or conjectured. As you are aware, Sabohl has reached his high position through intimidation, politics, and pure guile. While much of what he presents could be a true history of our past, it isn't the only theory that is out there.

"So far we haven't been able to catch him doing something illegal. Although we know that he uses members of the thieves' guild, which by the way, doesn't exist, to accomplish much. After all if there is no hard evidence then he can continue to be the authority. And one of the easiest ways for there not to be hard evidence it to have it conveniently disappear. Again because of the way he operates, he is nearly untouchable. It was only because of that one visitor that we knew to tie him to this guild. And we've had to be very careful when we've followed him to his drops, for which there are many. But we've never been able to reach what it is that he leaves at these drops. Our best have seen that these are in such places that they are watched all the time. So if any of ours approached and attempted to gather this information they would know immediately that it had been compromised. This is as much as we can tell you at this point and we must continue our predator-prey game, and hope that he slips up at some point.

"As requested, we have continued to monitor the ones who may have that very important document, but if indeed they have it, they have also been very careful to both hide it from view, and give the appearance that it doesn't exist. We may know much more soon, as it appears that there is about to be a change. It appears that very soon the operation at the bakery will be turned over to the underboss, and the two of them,

Kal, and Jura, will be heading out – as to where, and as to why we haven't a clue. Yet if it has something to do with this document it should become obvious. We can see that we are not the only ones who are aware of this change, and there has been an increase of his agents here in High Trail. Will keep all of you informed as we can. With the increase in the presence of these it has become more difficult to remain hidden ourselves. So do not become worried if more time passes than expected – as always, your fellow learned."

* * *

"Sara, we really have no idea how long we will be gone. You've proved your worth and because of this have been handed the operation while we are gone. I'm sure that both Idala and Pehel will check in on you periodically which only make sense. After all they own the business, and want to see it grow. Jura and I have to go north for a family matter and the questions and problems left for us to solve will take an unknown amount of time." Looking down and trying to think if he had forgotten anything he felt Jura poke him in the ribs. He turned and faced her and asked, "What?"

Smiling she said, "I know that you are worrying over every little thing, heck I do it too. But she is more than capable to doing this. So let her do her job, okay? We've still a couple of things that need to be packed, and the daylight is waning fast enough."

"You're right." He turned back to Sara shaking his head, "Okay then, it's yours. I guess we'll see you when we do, and good luck with this."

Sara had remained silent throughout the final conversation that she was having with her boss. She remembered back when her mate had suggested that she apply at the bakery.

While the income he was bringing in was adequate, barely would probably be more accurate, additional income would be nice. And as things happened there never was enough to cover those extras. But never in her wildest imagination and dreams did she ever see herself in this position. But at the same time, knew that she had earned it. And with the rise to this position there had been an increase in earnings which had allowed them to live better than they ever had. Plus a shelter had been provided so that they no longer had the cost of paying someone else to have a place to live. "Yes, sir, and ma'am, I will not fail either of you. Now get out of here and do what you must, and know that this business is in the hands that both of you trained, and one that you've told a number of times that she was very good at this. Plus, as you have stated, I will not be on my own. Good luck with this venture, whatever it is."

And with nothing left to say Jura and Kal turned and headed back to their shelter. Kal saying, "Sara, such an unusual name, it's one that is rarely heard or used. In fact the only place I've ever seen it is in those papers. If I remember right it was the name of that female that came from those mythological lairs that our ancestors were destroying."

"Yeah, that's right. I knew that recently I had come across the name, but couldn't remember where. I thought when she was hired that it was a very unusual name. And she said that it had been one used in her family every couple of generations, and that they were proud of it, but really never knew when it had shown up in the family. When we go back to that time in the history we didn't have, weren't allowed names, so maybe because of this female who had one, one of the females picked her as a hero or something. After all she stood up against the males of that time and gave the appearance of being their equal. That would be a very good reason for someone to choose that for her name when we were finally allowed to have them.

"Of course when I start thinking about that time it always makes me angry. To think that we were thought so little of. I guess if I had lived then, and saw a female standing against the status quo I probably would have considered her someone to look up to. Although I'm looking at this from this time back to their time, and I suspect that I have it all wrong."

With a questioning look Kal asked, "Wrong, how wrong?"

"Well, my guess would be that when one lives in a society and the world at a particular time, one is what the society is. After all, from birth to death we are immersed in that life. So our world, our beliefs, and way of seeing the world around us is colored by that society that we live in. So if this Sara came into it from a different culture, then it would have been very difficult to adjust to this new situation, and the females that lived in our culture at the time would not have liked the new stock, so to speak, to come in and upset the hierarchy, that they enjoyed. With new females in the herds, these new females would have demanded the attention of the warriors, because they were new, taking away from they who were a part of the clan or tribe, making life for the new ones hell from both sides. Having to submit to the warriors, and then being put in place by the females, who has always been a part of the tribe or clan. Because we live in a different time, and different circumstance, we have a tendency to project our views and ideals to our past. This, many times, removes the truth and hardship that all of them lived at the time, and cleans it up, and makes it appear black and white. I guess because

I'm female, and I wouldn't change that for the world, I'm a little more sensitive to our past than you would be."

"I must admit that everything you've just stated makes absolute sense. I know that we've discussed this in the past, and I can see why you would have such strong feelings on this, especially since we are planning to search for this location in the northern foothills – the place where this supposedly took place. Not that we will be able to experience that time of our history if we do find it. But by finding it and comparing what we have with what was written it should make it more real, and by finding it we will be able to, and I know it's not going to be that simple, find those other mythological places that were talked about. From what I can gather from the records this clan home was occupied past the time of the revival of the gods, and then when or soon after the wars between the clans and tribes ended this place was abandoned. So it will have changed much over the time that it existed. This, of course, will make it difficult to pin down the right time period. But I suspect that there would have to be trails and such leading to and from this place giving us further help and following up on the rest. Well, I guess we can keep talking the rest of the day if we wanted, but this is not getting those final preparations completed."

The morning came quick, and as planned they had a small meal, headed out and packed the two beasts that they would be using, and before the suns crested the distant grasses and foothills, and with the gray of dawn, headed north on the high trail road towards where he had grown up at Cross Trails. Their plan was simple, throughout this day to travel, and then spend the night in one of the many points along the way for travelers. Then somewhere close to the end of the second day to be back at Cross Trails. High Trail was located far south, although there was much of the continent that continued in the southerly direction. To travel from High Trail to the Sacred Mountains would take two 9-days to accomplish, and to travel the full length of the grasslands, even though most was now broken up with the many farms, and beasts husbandries, would take so much longer.

No longer being the wild open area that it had in the past, it could take a full season or fifteen 9-days. This of course was north to south. Past the Sacred Mountains the area soon became another place of desolation, but unlike the great desolation that ran down the coast of the continent; this was one of ice and snow. The few hardy adventurers who had traveled there found no evidence that any people had ever lived and thrived there. But as harsh as it was, it was impossible to stay long, and to do a really good and thorough job of searching the area out. There was a long range of mountains – although not very high when comparing them to the Sacred Mountain range – that ran the length of the continent. From what they had learned, it was this range that helped create the area of desolation by blocking the moisture that came off of the one large ocean. As the ones who studied the lands and weather stated, "These mountains push up the clouds and rob them of their moisture, and when they get to the other side there is nothing left to nourish the desolation – simple and easy." Although it had been harder to explain how the rains and yes the snows reached the grasslands. And finally when an explanation did arrive it had been too technical for most.

If they had a way to view their world from above it probably would have made it much easier to explain the weather patterns since all of the land mass and the clouds would be observed. But there was no way to do that presently. Although the far thinkers believed that one day they would be able to do just that. Most just laughed it off as something that couldn't – wouldn't happen. It really hadn't been that long ago when they had finally began to travel to many of the islands, and now many had growing populations on them. Others, of course, were still unexplored. On the east side of the grass-lands laid a couple of changes, one being the badlands. Rough harsh lands of canyons, and little growth of vegetation, with loose soils and falling rocks, seemingly hot all of the time, and the second, a series of steppes that had become known as the foothills. Her parents and family farm existed in one of these, as had the clan home in a different set. While not as rough as the badlands, there were similarities to both areas. Whereas the hills or mountains on the west were soft and roll-ing, covered heavily in trees and plants, these were covered in tough vegetation, the soils rocky with large boulders every-where. Trees did exist here, but were more spread out. There were many places to hide from an enemy, and many places a large clan could live protected by what the land provided. If one traveled coast to coast, east to west it would take half the time, when compared to the north – south, even with the tougher terrain that one had to travel.

The desolation itself actually was broken up in a series of deserts with small oases between most of them. Very few of these deserts had any vegetation at all, and the ones that did, this vegetation barely hung on. Because of the mud hills and mud flats that existed in many of them, even though they had ceased being mud a very long time in the past, demonstrated that these areas weren't always dry. So with these facts in their minds, and knowing with such a large world around them, to find even one of these mythologies would be close to impossible. Many in the present and their past had attempted it, but so far none had been successful, and thusly the belief that all of this had to be mythology. But they felt that their chances were much greater on finding and solving this unknown past. They had something nobody else had. They had the direct record, the actual words written, had rough maps, had approximate distances. And even though those distances were more marked by days of travel than actual distance, it was more than the rest ever had. So as they began this adventure, they felt good about their chances. But doesn't everyone when they begin a new quest?

"Chill in the air this morn," Kal commented, "guess we should expect that. We are heading towards the end of the Season of Heat, and there's a taste of the Season of Falling in the morning air."

She shivered briefly; they had just left the warmth of their shelter into this cold morning air. She looked back as they had finished packing and had started down the road, knowing that it would be a very long time before she saw their home again. Sighing she said, "True. But shortly we'll appreciate it. Once the suns rise and start warming things we'll wish for just this coolness." Nodding her head as if in agreement with what she had said and looking at him, she stopped briefly and once again looked back.

"What are you doing?" He asked.

Smiling she said, "Look it's going to be a very long time before I see our place again. So I'm taking one last look, and putting this image in my memory."

He stopped at turned and did the very same thing, "Good idea. I probably would have kicked myself later when I thought about it. Guess we can do the same thing with the village as we leave. After all we've spent a lot of time here, and you of course, much more than I. We've got to know most of the people here, and it is hard to leave such a friendly place." They walked through a silent village that was on the verge of waking up to face a new day and the routines that made it normal and comfortable for those who lived and worked here.

In the shadows, for which there were many this time of the morning, two watched patiently as they watched the pack beasts and the ones leading them, head through a very silent village. They hung back so as to not raise any suspicion. Turning to one the other stated, "Go get word to our boss that they're on the move, and with this pace they'll be easy to follow. My guess would be that as they head north they will be going towards Cross Trails where he is from. It is time to alert all of the ones along this road from here to there. Catch up with me at the first marker outside of the village. I'll wait for you there, and we can continue to follow them and keep a safe distance until we hand it off."

The one he was talking to just nodded and silently disappeared. This other continued to wait with a smile. From what he could see this baker and his mate were unaware that anybody was behind them and held serious interest in them. *Well, let them continue to think like that. It'll make my job easier.* He continued to lean against one of the shelters in the shadows between two of the shelters until they were out of sight. He slowly entered the main way through the village and casually headed in their direction giving the appearance that it was just a random direction that he was heading. And unknown to these thieves, they were also under the watchful eye of others, others who were there to help protect whatever it was that Kal and Jura possessed.

Trehe turned to the others that were with him and quietly gave orders for these two to be watched, followed, and to find out whom they made contact with so that they could continue to find all the hidden ties, links, and directions that Sabohl had himself tied to. Soon they hoped to be able to topple his stranglehold within the learned community. But, as in history, time would tell, and nothing had been written as of yet to make what was transpiring history. After this one minor incident entered the history books it could be that nothing would have changed, or all would have. Would they look back and smile at their success, and the gains that they learned, or would Sabohl be the one smiling with another success at maintaining his position, running the present board into hiding and shame? A lot was on the line, and the two main players in this game hadn't a clue.

"Funny how it seems to chill," Jura said as she shivered from the morning breeze that had just reached her, "actually feels colder just before the suns crest and shine their daylight on us. It's like the night says I won't give up right up until the light wins out."

"True, and," as he smiled at her and she could see that from that smile he was going to make some smart remark, " You're not going superstitious on me are you – bringing back those many gods of our ancestors who controlled every aspect of their lives, by making a comment that gives the night life, and making the night alive."

She turned and faced him and gave him a loving shove and said, "No silly, and you know better than that, and besides I can tell when you're serious and when you're joking and you gave yourself away on this one."

Looking down and with that smile, the one that had attracted her to him in the first place he said, "I guess after all the time that we've been together it's just hard to pull something over on you, but I have to agree with you it always seems to chill just before those suns approach the horizon. I guess I can see how it could appear to someone that this had to be a fight between two gods – one that ruled the night and one that ruled the day. With both dawn and dusk being a battleground as one fought to gain control. You know it's kind of strange when one actually reads the words in such a document as we have. While we may laugh, at times, because of how they viewed something, at the same time when one gets the mindset that they must have had, then it becomes easy to see it from their point of view. Well, maybe not easy, because, as you've said, we don't live in their world, but, it becomes easier to see it from their side." Since both of them had stopped briefly he turned around and looked back. Shaking his head he commented, "I guess we can say its official – can't see High Trail at all, now. For us it won't exist for a long time."

She turned around and looked, took a deep breath, "Yeah, and I already miss it. After all it's been part of my life for most of it." They both headed back down the road, soon, in the overall scheme of things, they would arrive at Cross Trails, spend a couple of days, and then continue north to what they would guess would be three days from the Sacred Mountains. In a way it was a surprise that these ancient mountains had never been renamed after the fall of the gods. This, of course was an unimportant point. Still, if they could find his ancestors' home, it would be from there that all of the rest of the locations that were considered part of mythology should be located.

* * *

"Look we've tried this from a number of directions, and so far none of it has worked. So let's think about this for a moment." Jura was frustrated with the results so far. Both of them felt that it would have been relatively easy to find this place, but as the 9-days had passed and no success she was just about ready to give up.

Taking a deep breath as he looked around, both of them were sitting in their camp that they had located just about three days from the Sacred Mountains. It was from here that they had been scouring the surrounding areas for some sign of that ancient site. "I know that both of us felt that this would be easier than it has turned out to be, but I guess if it'd have been easy someone else probably would have found it by now. We're having trouble and we have a rough, although I have to admit it now, a very rough idea of its location. I think I know why the exact location was never mentioned in the text. Well, at least I think I do. What comes to my mind is this; first off it would have been unwise during that time to reveal your location, and secondly they knew where it was so why state something that was obvious?"

Staring into the fire that they had built and then looking out towards the grasslands, their camp was located in area that hid them from the surrounding open country. They had located the camp at the base of the foothills knowing that somewhere in those foothills that clan home existed. Sighing she said, "Yeah, I guess that would make sense. But I have forgotten how tough 'roughing it' can be. As a kid I loved doing this, but now find it's not quite the same. I feel dirty, I itch all the time, and I have to admit it, to have a privy would be nice. Funny how important something becomes when you don't have it. I just figured that by going to the base of the Sacred Mountains and backtracking those three days, give or take, since I would guess that their three days of travel would cover a greater distance than ours . . . But I forgot how large an area we are talking about here. These mountains cover great distances to the east and to the west, and the foothills themselves while not as big seem to cover vast distances also. And from the descriptions of the area where they were located it could be a thousand different places. So much of the area looks the same when it is described in general terms as this is. I guess I was a little, well maybe a lot, optimistic about finding this place. I guess for both of us you could throw in naïve, which would make sense, since neither you nor I have ever done anything like this before. It makes one appreciate the ones who do this all the time. I guess we only see the results and not the work that went into the finding of these ancient sites."

"Hmm, sounds like the pot's boiling, would you like me to dish you up some of this stew?"

Nodding and smiling she replied, "I guess so. But I have to admit that I'm getting tired of this too. I guess the excitement has just left and for some reason I'm wanting some of the comfort that we had in our shelter."

"Okay, point taken. I know that you've done this because of me, and my passion to find out the truth. Yeah, and I know that the truth can be interpreted in so many ways and still be the truth, but you really didn't have to join me on this adventure. Oh don't get me wrong, I love having you with me, and sometime in the future we probably will look back and think that these were the best of times. You know times where we were free to do as we please, and not be tied down with whatever responsibilities that we will have then. We'll forget the bad and just remember the good – but point taken. Tell you what, tomorrow let's head into that village, you know the one that probably has been here at the time of these ancestors of mine. It's on the road that leads into the Sacred Mountains. We can take a couple of days, rent a room, and act like we are visitors on vacation. It will give us time to recharge, and buy what we need to continue this, how does that sound?" He had to admit that looking at her here at the camp, that she was still a beautiful female in his mind. Even with her brown hair somewhat disheveled and clothes that were loose fitting but couldn't hide her body, but he knew that right now a break would be welcome to both of them.

"Mother raised no fools, of course. I suspect that if it was possible that I'd soak all day in a bath and maybe even then not feel like I got all the grime off of me. I've never gone this long without a bath even as a kid when they were something to avoid."

"Okay then, we'll pack up in the morning and do it. Besides maybe we'll get lucky and something there might help us, I doubt it but one never knows." He stood up and headed around the fire and asked her to stand, he then gave her a loving hug for which she returned. They clung together for the longest of time, and then she began to laugh. "I think we better take that stew off the fire, I believe it's beginning to burn."

"He started laughing also and stated, "Are you sure it isn't us? After all that hug and the way we were close surely got me interested."

"Oh you males always are thinking that way." Then in a teasing voice she said, "I bet even as dirty and smelly as I am, you'd still think that way and if I offered you'd take me up on it immediately."

Smiling he threw his arms out with the palms up inviting her back into his arms. "Why of course. I find you attractive no matter what you look like, or how dirty or odorous you become. Besides if we do become involved tonight, we can always repeat it once we've cleaned up back in that village and having a room for a few days in the inn."

Coming back into his arms and putting her head on his shoulders she whispered, "Then, how can I refuse such an offer. After all you're not so clean or fresh yourself. And if you can stand me, I guess I can stand you. Just understand this though, we may be trying to find where your, and I guess if I really think about it, our ancestors and where they lived, but I'm not going to do what those females at that time did."

With a questioning look he asked, "Did?" Then as he thought about it he simply said, "Oh." Nodding his head before continuing, "Of course not. After all we are a very long way away from that time and place, and much has changed for the better since then, and you don't have to prove anything to me. Besides", he decided to tease her a little, "I'm the only male in this relationship and I don't require that kind of proof that you did your duty to the clan."

Then laughing and teasing back she asked, "Are you sure? After all with the way it was back then I would be dealing with many of you males." She saw the look of surprise in his eyes and just laughed harder. "Now come on, you are the only male in my life, other than, let's see, hmm, there are my brothers, and my father and then there's . . ."

Interrupting her he said, "Okay, okay I get the point. But I had to admit there for a moment you had me going." Then pointing to their portable shelter he asked, "Shall we?"

* * *

"Sabohl, this is an update to let you know what is transpiring with the two that you have an interest. They traveled to the Sacred Mountains in the north, and have backtracked just about three days from them and have been scouring the foothills. Whatever it is that they are looking for must be somewhere there. Although considering the very size of this minor range one could be searching their whole life and never find anything. They recently pulled camp and headed for one of the local villages. At this time we feel that we've remained hidden from their sight, and neither is aware of our presence. Because they have been somewhat stationary, we've added others to make it easier to watch. If there is a change we will pass it on immediately."

After reading the note he had to admit that whoever wrote this one was better educated than most of these he dealt with. *So they are searching for something in the northern foothills are they?* This confirmed in his mind that they had to have a source, something ancient that had sent them to this location, but so far nobody had seen it, and even with people eavesdropping on their conversations, nothing was discovered. Yet there had to be a reason for them to be there, and not only there, but searching all over those foothills. He'd need to get a note right back to those who watched. But even if he sent it out today to one of the many drops it would probably take at least one 9-day for it to reach them. Well that was something that couldn't be helped. There was no way presently to move something like this any faster. He couldn't use the signaling system that moved important messages, so he had to depend on the hand carried method, and dealing with these people who were less than trustworthy could actually add time to its arrival.

Still, he had to be careful to leave names and such out of these notes so that if they fell into the wrong hands that they could not come back and incriminate him. He could answer saying that whoever was accusing him of something couldn't prove anything. After all it was just a note and nothing more, and could mean any number of things. He was still angry with that one visit that happened a few cycles of the seasons in the past. It came close to exposing him and his many less than honest contacts that he used. But at this point in time it appeared that no one noticed, which meant that he was still in charge, and still safe. Leaning back in his chair with his hands behind his head he stretched, shaking his head, and sighing slightly he thought. *Still got more papers to read through and grade before I can get that response out to one of the drops so that it can be on its way.*

* * *

"Now that was a wonderful break, and to be clean for the last 9-days is wonderful." Jura stared into the fire at their new basecamp and actually felt relaxed and refreshed. It had been a nice diversion, which sounded funny to her. Since normally their diversions had to do with leaving the village and maybe go camping. Now it was just the opposite. They had found a place where a small stream ran. Upstream and just a short distance from their location there was a waterfall and at the base the water pooled in a small pond before continuing on its way. Surrounding this pond was a number of large boulders making access somewhat difficult, but accessible. Plus it provided privacy and while the water wasn't heated it still allowed both of them to bathe and not feel so dirty. The way the stream twisted and turned their campsite was completely hidden, making them feel a little safer than they did in their last campsite.

It had been an accidental discovery since small and large streams were a common sight here in the north. The plan had been to head back to their original site, but had detoured briefly because of a wild beast, and came across this stream. Pushing through some of the vegetation that grew because of all this water they found this place, a little oasis of clear ground surrounded by boulders and small hills with the only entrance and exit being through that vegetation. Smiling Kal said, "Yes, that was rather nice wasn't it? And you're right this is quite the opposite of what we're used to. And to find this place, for what we are doing I cannot ask for better. We have privacy, we have our own pond, to both bathe and fish, and plenty of boulders to take care of our nature calls, and all of this is invisible from the outside. Heck, even where that small falls comes in here you can't see in. It's like this is our own little world. Of course when we build a fire, the smell of smoke would draw someone to us. But there doesn't seem to be anybody out here but us, although there probably is."

"Yes there probably are others around; still I'm happy with this. Now if we had a permanent shelter built here it would be almost perfect, but since we can't this is just about as good as it gets."

"Yes, and this allows us to search a different portion of these foothills, and we double checked when we came back and we are still just about three days from the Sacred Mountains, so this could be the area."

For the next 9-days they searched the areas close to their new campsite and came up empty. Sitting by the fire that last night, with frustration showing in both of them, it just hadn't occurred to them that it would be this difficult. At least they were learning, and finding that slowly a map of the area was developing in their minds. And in those mental maps there were still a number of blank areas but slowly the large area was beginning to make sense, and as each blank area was filled in, the map shrunk in size. Warming his hands over their small fire, and then leaning back against a convenient boulder Kal said, "So far, from any of the descriptions and the rough map that we have none of this looks right. What is it that we're missing? I know that when maps were made during this era that there was never a specific orientation like all of them do now. It was more based on a key landmark, something that was familiar or commonly known at the time."

"Yeah, and that's the problem, we don't know what that common thing is. It would have been nice if it was orientated like all of today's maps with South on top, but I guess if that was the case then all of these ancient sites would have been located by now, and maybe the way we view our history would be different, but who knows that may not be true either. I wonder why it was decided to make south as the top of all the modern maps?"

"Could be because most of us live in the south, and because the weather gets a little nasty up here, that there are less of us here, it would make sense to base it on where most of us live. Of course this is just a guess, mapmaking wasn't something I studied."

"Well, being that I'm from the outback so to speak, we've used maps and been comparing them to the lands for as long as I can remember, and so far there's nothing at all that is similar to this map. Of course I know that if one approaches an area, one that they are familiar with, but from a different direction that that known area looks strange and unfamiliar until we change our position and then it just clicks. I suspect that this is what we are facing here. With no way to orientate the map, and not knowing what they used as their landmark, and who knows how much has changed since this place was abandoned, we've missed it. And let's face it; the land does change, even if it seems unchangeable. So something major on this crude map may no longer exist as it did in the days when this was created."

"True, so very true. I guess all we can hope for since this was made towards the end of their time at this place that the changes aren't great." Kal sighed, "I really did believe that this would be so much easier than it turning out." Looking around and then up at the night sky he continued, "That's really beautiful. Until we started doing this kind of stuff, you know camping and spending time away from the villages, I never appreciated the night skies or so many other things truly. Being one from the villages I was used to having noise and people around me all the time. So getting used to the quiet and the night sounds, feeling the soft breezes, feeling the changes that this world tells you have been a learning experience. I guess by being from where I am, and now doing this I can appreciate your life so much more and I'm finding that I prefer it over the life in the villages."

Smiling Jura said, "I told you it would be this way. But words can never, and I mean never adequately explain the differences. You really have to experience them for yourself. And in that I mean not just two or three days, but like now where you live it for a long time. It is only then when you shed your village ways and you begin to listen to what this natural world is trying to say to you, that you begin to understand the differences. Of course," she stopped and smiled with a faraway look before continuing, "there's many who try and before too many 9-days are over, are running, screaming and heading back to the protection of the village." She shrugged, "It's just something I'll never understand, but I guess some can only live that way. I know that while I've been living with you and we've been living in the villages it still isn't an easy thing for me to do. It's like there is a constant invisible pressure which places a restlessness on me, making me yearn for the outback. But don't take me wrong here, you're my mate and I'll be with you wherever we end up. Although I have to admit it, other than some of the necessities that a village can provide a female, I'm loving every day that we are out here." She looked up at the stars, looked down and was deep in thought and in her own world for a short time. He waited knowing that she still had something to say. "I don't know how to put into words, but being here in the natural world where we came from seems almost healing. Yes I know that it can be a dangerous unforgiving place, but at the same time when this soaks into you, you almost feel healed, whole, and feel like you've returned home. You feel more alive, oh I don't know, but it's the way I feel."

For a while both of them were silent allowing the night to surround them, the slight breezes to whisper to them, the small beasts scurrying along their way, the sounds of a night flyer passing overhead, and just the silence that almost seemed deafening. After what seemed a long time both looked at the fire and saw that it had burned down to just coals. Still neither felt like moving both lost in their own thoughts and the night. Finally Kal said, "I guess we could stay out here all night, and probably it wouldn't matter, but I think it's time to retire, snuggle a little bit, enjoy our closeness, and get some rest."

It was late morning with Kal sitting close to their fire. He looked around their private oasis, although this probably wasn't quite the right word for it. As far as he could remember it had to do with an area in the wastelands where there was water. Well, at least they were surrounded with water. Jura had commented that she needed a bath and had headed for the pond that was just out of sight of the camp. He heard something from that direction and figured it was her returning and got up and began to head in that direction only to be faced by Jura who was wearing only the moisture from her dip. Immediately he could feel the desire rise, and was sure that she could see it also. Shaking his head he stated, "Seeing you like this makes me want you right now."

Yeah, I'm sure, but I forgot to bring a drying cloth and a change of clothing. I had decided to wash the ones I was wearing as they were almost as dirty as I was. And on that other subject," there was a look of what he couldn't quite figure out in her eyes, "oh yes me female, you male. I must as a female submit to you since you are the male. No wait, that's not quite true. It is this way me female, you warrior, only then must I submit." She stopped and laughed before continuing. He wasn't sure where this was going, "No you are not warrior and as such I am not required to submit to your needs, but I am a better warrior than you, so you must submit to me!" She then walked over to him, they hugged, and he complained saying, "Hey, now you've got me wet."

She laughed again and said, "Well then, we better get you out of those wet clothes, don't cha' think?" After a rather passionate session, both retired back to the pond, this time with the proper changes and drying cloths and helped each other with their baths.

Later as both sat around their small fire both feeling comfortable they began to go over the rough map and notes that they had brought. "Look something we did consider is that the land does change. I bet even these small streams like this one moves its channels as things happen over time. Even though there are few trees in the grasslands, many of these streams have quite a few, so if, oh say because of a storm some of them would fall into the stream, then these fallen trees could force the stream to change direction. And who knows, while most of the time it would be a slight change, other times it could dam it in such a way that the flow has completely changed – never going past the blockage where it used to go but now in a new direction." Kal paused as he thought this through. "I know we are looking at around a thousand cycles of the seasons, and usually things don't change that rapidly, other than what we do to it. So, maybe one of the ravines that led from the grasslands to the somewhat hidden trail, which led towards that clan home, is no more, or so many other things. Who knows they could have deliberately misrepresented something on their map so that if it fell into the wrong hands that the ones who acquired this couldn't find their way there to be able to attack it."

Leaning back against a rock she contemplated what he had suggested. "Yes, any of those could be fact. Yet we have no way to prove any of it. So far we've been unable to orientate this thing with any of the land that we've searched. It's a very frustrating thing, it really is. Look we've kind of shot this day by getting such a late start. Let's just go out to some of the high points and look over the areas. Then as the suns begin to set we can watch the shadows to get a better idea for how the land really is. Maybe from that we can get some ideas of where to search next."

"Sounds good to me, I'm so glad that you showed me that. Being from the villages it is something you just don't think about. After all you have the streets through the villages and shelters of different kinds that are your landmarks so something like that wouldn't cross my mind. Besides not only is it educational as far as learning how the land lays, but it is also beautiful. You can feel the beginning of the evening cooling, and sense the increase in moisture and the shadows are beautiful as they stretch across the landscape." Kal paused in thought, "I think we should pack something to snack on, so how about we leave after the midday meal. That way we won't have to take too much and have half a day to explore."

"Works for me, let's do it." Jura got up went inside their portable shelter grabbed their carrying packs a brought them outside, tossing his to him. "I guess we should put these in order then."

* * *

There had been a rather stiff breeze off the grasslands upslope to where they stood on top of one of the higher foothills. Looking south they could see the foothills running up to the edge of the great grasslands, and in the vast distance to the west a slight haze that probably marked the edge of the desolation where it was not uncommon for dust to being stirred constantly by the winds. To the north stood the great ranges of what they had known as the Sacred Mountains, making the foothills a minor inconvenience in comparison, and to the east the vast foothills and somewhere lost within these was that hidden home of his past. It wouldn't be long before the shadows would show how rugged an area this truly was. Both had found a large flat rock to sit as they waited just a little longer. Soon they would have to head back, since they had no desire to work their way back to their camp in the dark.

Between them they studied a copy of the crude map that had been made towards the end of the occupation of the clan home. As the shadows lengthened revealing more of the hidden canyons smaller peaks, and ravines they turned and twisted the document in many different directions trying to establish some type of orientation that would line up what they saw on the map with the real world that they were observing. "I don't get it. There doesn't seem to be anything on this that compares to what we are looking at." He couldn't keep the frustration out of his voice as he looked once again on the scene before him and looking at the map.

"I know what you mean. I really thought that it would be a very simple thing. After all we had a map." She laughed, "I guess we set our expectations too high – very naïve of us if I do say myself." Taking a deep breath she continued, "Oh well I guess we can try this again in the morning. We really need to head back."

Sighing he said, "Yeah, I guess you're right. If we don't find something shortly that shows up on this map I guess we'll be moving our camp again – although it's going to be hard to give up this one. Okay, let's head back." They rolled the map back up and placed in her carrying pack got up and headed back for camp.

From a different hill and unknown to Kal and Jura, two watched them as they got up and headed back to camp. One turning to the other said, "From what I could see it looks like they were trying to compare something they had to this area. I wonder if they have a map or something. Look we need to follow them, because the last time they relocated their camp we never did figure out where it was. Who knows, maybe if we can locate the camp we can sneak in after they're asleep and steal it – but, on second thought maybe not. We'd be giving ourselves away and could come away with nothing. Besides we're being paid to do this and this is much easier than some of the other things we've had to do." The other one remained quiet and nodded in agreement saying only, "We'll watch."

And another team looked at each other with both smiling, since they were close enough to catch the conversation of the observers as they waited, until the two who had been observing Kal and Jura moved on down towards their hidden camp. "Seems for such an empty land it's getting kind of crowded out here. This brought a chuckle from his partner.

"Yes, isn't it? At least we won't have to reveal ourselves to protect them. Had these two decided to raid their camp we may have had to show ourselves. Guess we'd better be heading to our camp."

CHAPTER FIVE

OTHERS

Another 9-day had passed with nothing to show for their hard work other than covering more of the foothills. They had moved their camp, not wanting to leave such a perfect campsite, but nothing in the area had produced any results. So they moved two days hike to the east and while it wasn't as nice or as hidden as their previous site it would have to work. "I don't know how long we've still available to us. I've never been this far north and I don't know if the seasons are shorter, longer, harsher, or anything really." It was early morning and he and Jura were heading out to try and orientate the map once again, wanting to use the morning shadows created by the rising suns. There was hope that finally after all the time that they had been traipsing through these hills that something would finally go their way.

Jura shivered a little, "Yeah agreed. These mornings are becoming quite chilly. Definitely reminds me of the Season of Falling. So there's a good chance if we don't find something soon that we'll have to call it for this time and head back."

Breathing out heavily and watching his breath create clouds and then dissipate in the cool air Kal said, "It will be very frustrating to have spent all this time out here and have to return with nothing but our tans to show for it. At least we don't have to worry about those predators, you know the Skaiths. I think the last one was seen a very long time ago. I think that they were from a very early time in this world. And from what I've heard about them we would never know they were around until it was too late. With their speed of attack and strength, there'd be a blur and it would be the only warning we'd get. I know they sent fear through any who might have caught a glimpse of these solitary hunters. It was another reason to stay out of the Sacred Mountains, since they seemed to be mostly there. Although there had been reports that they hunted the herd beasts in the grasslands and foothills close to those mountains. And, of course, that's where we are. While, it's been frustrating enough to have this rough map and come up empty, still this is so much better than becoming a meal for one of those beasts."

"Agreed. I understand that just their cry was enough to send chills and fear in any who happened to be close. Should have worn something warmer, it's really cold this morning." As they had reached another of the many small peaks the morning winds touched them with a chill that penetrated to the bone. "Brrr, let's see if we can find a place out of this breeze. If I'm this cold I might be concentrating on being cold instead of looking over the countryside." They walked a little to the west and partially down and found a warm pocket of air, and by experimenting found that just a little way in any direction they were immediately back into the cold air. "I don't understand this, and probably never will, yet I ran into this very often back on the farm. There seems to be places that were either colder or warmer than the surrounding air and no reason that I could see for it to be that way, and here it is again right at this spot."

They got close together for each other's warmth and waited for the shadows to form. It appeared to take forever for the suns to rise high enough so that the morning shadows could form. At this moment the suns held no warmth as their breaths still came out in great clouds, and when the slight breezes touched them it sent chills through their bodies. Unfortunately, where they had retreated, their views in the direction that they wanted to observe were hidden, while the areas towards the grasslands were plain to see. Shrugging Kal said, "I guess if we want to see what we came here today to see, we can't stay here. Although right now being warm and being this close to you is a reason to stay here . . . but can't, so let's go see what we can see."

All she did was smile, stood up and together they braved the cold morning air and headed back to the top of the hill. Once they arrived both of them immediately forgot their chilled condition because what they were seeing, in the distance, in those morning shadows, matched the crude map that they had been using. Pointing Jura stated, "Look! I've stared at this map so often that I have it memorized, and truly thought that we wouldn't ever see something on the ground that would match it but look." She stopped briefly and turned to Kal and asked, "You see it don't you?"

He had been in awe when he had seen what she had. It had driven him to silence. He had reached a point that he had almost given up. It wouldn't have been much longer and they would have had to head back and wait through another Season of Cold before they could try again. But here before them, after all that time spent in useless searching, finally – finally it was before them. "Yes, I see it. But, how do we get to the path that goes there? From here I can't see it, and I think once we get back down into those small canyons and ravines that it will be easy to miss. From what I remember when reading my history, the pathway wasn't easy to find when it was traveled, and now it's been a very long time since anybody has traveled that way, and there's a very good chance that the entrance could easily be overgrown and hidden."

As he spoke these things she thought and had to admit that he was right. Up here it was plain to see, but once one dropped down and didn't have this view then everything changed. And because there had been no travel they could easily miss the entrance to the trail or path that led to the abandoned clan site. Plus he was again correct by saying that the entrance could be easily overgrown. So with the sudden elation from finding the landmarks noted on the map and thinking that finally they had found it, she realized that it might take days to find their way to what they had been searching. Trying to point out the positive, she said, "Well, at least we know we're in the right area. Look, I think we need to move our camp a little closer to what we've just discovered so that we can search this out. With all the failures that we've had up to this point, to be finally in the right place is a relief. It, in a way, simplifies things. Instead of all these foothills three days out of the Sacred Mountains, and even I was surprised as to how big an area it is, to finally have narrowed it down to this . . . well, I don't know, this area? I know to be this close, but at the same time still not there, and we've only got three or four 9-days left before we will be facing the Season of Cold." Taking a deep breath she said, "Okay, I know what we have ahead of us is still daunting, but standing here and reveling in the fact that we finally found it isn't going to get us there."

"You're right, so shall we go break the camp and move it then?" She nodded and both of them headed back down towards their camp to begin the preparation of breaking it down, packing the two pack beasts, but before all of this they would eat.

* * *

The two who were monitoring them had risen late that morning and were sullenly sitting close to their campfire. Every morning it was becoming colder, and this was getting old. At first it seemed like a nice break from what they normally were involved with. Besides, they had been almost caught the last time they had broken into a shelter to steal something, so this was a welcome diversion, and a cooling off time, a time to disappear. But now, both were missing their booze, and the companionship of a female, now and then. "Look, I'm just about done with this. They can't be out here much longer anyway. We can't be too far from the Season of Cold, and I don't want to be anywhere out here exposed during those storms."

The one he was talking to sat across the fire from him only nodded his head in agreement. At first he had been happy to be away, but now he would be very happy to be away *from this*. "Guess we better see what our two little fliers are up to." The other only grunted. So leaving their fire burning they got up climbed the hill that their camp was located behind and carefully peered into Kal and Jura's camp. "Crap! They're breaking camp, and we're not even ready to follow them." They turned rapidly around and headed back to their own camp and began hastily to break it down, not bothering to extinguish their small fire, as there was no time. All they did was to kick some dirt over it. Grabbing their dirty pots the one that had spoken earlier yelped, "That's hot!", and immediately threw it back on the ground where the liquid that was inside sloshed out and spilled out onto the ground. There was no portable shelter to pack as they were too lazy to put up such a convenience, threw whatever gear they had into their carrying packs, and rapidly climbed the hill where they had hidden behind to watch the two, and follow remaining out of sight.

"I wonder what prompted this move?" The other thief asked quietly. The only response he got from the other, who had made himself the unofficial leader, was a shrug of the shoulders. Well, he hadn't expected an answer anyway, and he was quite content to let him lead – meant less for him to do and be responsible for. Besides, if this went wrong he could blame it on him because of the other's choice and be free from any retaliation. Soon they were out of sight of their old camp and were concentrating completely their prey.

After they were out of sight three walked into their abandoned camp with the leader looking around and shaking his head. It was apparent to the three that the ones who had camped here were lazy, slovenly, and careless. Turning to the other two he said, "Better put out that fire we don't need it to escape. I've seen what fires do to the grasslands, and it isn't pretty." He watched as the other two carefully extinguished the campfire. While they did this he did a careful search of the camp finding nothing of importance. Turning back to the two who had completed their assignment he said, "Guess we better see what these two are up to, and soon one of us will have to return and update our contacts." The three left the camp, and with care, began tracking the two thieves, although a child from a village could have followed it.

* * *

As they hauled the pack beasts along Kal stopped a moment followed by Jura who had a questioning look on her face. He seeing this answered, "Look, I just realized from reading all of that in the document that there is a main path or entrance to the route from the grasslands. I know that it doesn't show it on this map, but I suspect that was to prevent someone using it, if, for some reason it fell into enemy's hands, at the time. Even close to the end of the time that they lived there, there was fighting, battles, and such all the time, even though things were beginning to change. It would only make sense to keep something like that out of this thing."

"I hadn't thought about it, but you're right. So what do you want to do? We're not too far from the grasslands, do you want to head back to them and see if we can find the entrance?"

"Jura, I just don't know. I suspect that the beginning of the trail was well hidden so that it couldn't be seen, allowing any enemy just to follow and attack. But at the same time, I don't know if we can come across the trail here in these foothills. It is a problem, what do you think?"

"You're asking me? That's a tough one. If the beginning of the trail was hidden in their day, it could be completely gone now, with no travel for all this time and no use, and there could be no possibility of finding it by cutting across the hills like we are doing now. Hmmm, okay look you have a good point saying that the entrance is from the grasslands so let's stop a moment and think about it."

"Yeah, let's see if we can put ourselves in the place of our ancestors, and before you say it I'm not meaning the place where you females were at that time, I know better."

Smiling at him although there was no humor in it she replied, "Better not, you know it's a sore subject to me." Taking a deep breath before continuing, "Okay, let's see . . . it would have to be easily recognizable, but at the same time defendable."

"Not only that, but there would have to be something close by that would place them higher, so that they could observe, in the distance, to prevent another tribe or scouting party to stay hidden and far enough away preventing someone approaching the trail to see them, but close enough to so they could mark the location."

She just shook her head as she thought about it, "Yes, all of the above. The problem is this, there's probably hundreds if not thousands of such places that all of this would fit when approaching the foothills from the grasslands."

The two herd beasts, unconcerned with what their masters were discussing, grazed contentedly; they knew that once this respite was over that they would be required to move again. "Okay," Kal said, "what if we work the edge of the foothills stopping periodically, climbing one of the hills and align the landmarks with the map. We should be able to make it line up and maybe the combination of that would lead us to it."

Nodding she said, "Yes, that might just work, although I wonder if there's something on this map that might give us a hint. After all the map wasn't made for those who lived at the clan home, it had been put together for the ones in the growing alliance. So there should be something there on the map, a meeting place that would have been in the grasslands. Something close, but not so close, as to give its location away. I'd suspect that they would have blindfolded the ones that they would bring into the clan home at least part of the way so that it wouldn't be revealed. Although from the description it would have been a difficult place to attack."

"That's probably true of leaders who were not members of that alliance. From what I remember reading, runners approached all the time, so its location had to be known. Still the less that knew meant less chance of attack."

By midmorning they had set up their next campsite and then, more by luck than design, they thought that there was a good chance they had found what they were looking for. It was an ancient trail, more sensed than seen, and it led in direction that would provide defenders the ability to aggressively attack an approaching hostile clan or tribe thinning their numbers as they approached. "If this is the right place," Kal stated, "then maybe we should have brought the supplies with us. I've the feeling that we're going to need to break camp once again."

"Yeah, you're probably right, but what if we hadn't found this trail, then what? I don't like trying to set up a camp at the end of a day. What's this?" She asked. It appeared that at this point the trail split going in opposite directions and not a hint as to where either direction would lead them. Before them was a cliff rising above them, again giving defenders a point to attack enemies. As they stood there looking in both directions undecided Jura talking as she thought about what was before them said more to herself than to him. "Hmmm, I wonder . . ."

With a questioning look Kal asked, "Wonder? Wonder what?"

Pointing in both directions of the trail where it had split she said. "Look, this is only a guess, but I suspect that both trails will meet and become one again on top. I know it's hard to tell right now because both sides run along the base of this cliff and then turn away from us and we cannot see where they go after that. Look I'll take the left branch and you take the right. We'll follow the splits as they go for a little while, and if either side seems to lead away, then we can backtrack to here and choose one that seems more promising. How does that sound to you?"

"Jura, you've had way more experience than I have on this, and really what do we have to lose other than time? And if I am honest here we've lost a lot of that with our fruitless searching, so what's a little more? Okay so how long?"

"Oh I don't know, we need to give it long enough that we can be sure what's happening. Okay let's use our shadows. When they have doubled in length from what they are now and we haven't met then we'll come back and meet here and discuss what we've discovered."

"Okay, works for me." He bowed and swept his arms out and asked, "Shall we?"

She laughed and curtsied and responded, "Why thank you sir!" Then on a more serious note said, "Okay if we don't meet higher up see you back here soon." She headed off on the left branch and he stood for a brief period of time until she turned the corner and was out of sight. He then turned and headed down the right branch and once he made the turn, in his case to the left, the trail immediately began to climb. It was a steep climb and it had a couple of switch-backs, fol- lowed by heading away from the area where they had split winding among large boulders, again a great place for defense, before turning around as he approached the top of the rise and headed back in the original direction.

* * *

"Hey, look they've split. It would be easy to kill them now and then we could get out here and just blame it on some predator that is out here. I'm tired of all of this and I long for a village and some wine and a little female companionship."

The other, the one who had unofficially taken charge looked hard at his partner, "What are you suggesting? We weren't sent here to kill these two, but to find out what they were looking for. So get any of those thoughts out of your mind. Who knows, maybe they'll return to this spot, and anyway, we can't take a chance of being seen, so we're going to wait right here." Both of them settled into as comfortable position as they could and still watch the trail, or trails since it appeared to have split. They would be paid for this work, and it was easy, so why sweat it?

* * *

Jura after making the right turn found that the trail continued up a canyon for a short distance and then started climbing out. Here the rise was gentle and the trail straight. The trail was sort of heading in the original direction that they had been going when they had reached that split, but as she neared the top coming out of the canyon it turned back towards the top of the cliff where the trail had split at the base. It dove back down into a large ravine again giving any defenders the upper hand in a fight. It remained this way for a distance and because of the depth of the ravine there were more shadow than sunlight, hiding any and all landmarks. Eventually it climbed out where there were a huge amount of boulders. She stopped and caught her breath. She was literally at the point on that cliff that they had looked up at. The view from here was over-powering in its beauty. And while hiking the ravine there was little air movement, once out the cool breeze chilled her as it dried her damp sweat soaked clothes. As she looked out over the trail that they had hiked earlier that day she heard a noise off to her left and turned to see Kal approaching with a smile on his face. He said, "Guess you were quite right. Although with you here ahead of me I'd guess your way is shorter." He paused and looked in the direction that she had saying, "Wow, what a view." He was about to turn and face her when a movement caught his eye. At that moment she had been look-ing at him so had not seen it, still he asked. "Did you see that?"

She turned in the direction that he had been looking puz-zled by his question. "No, see what?"

"I don't know for sure, but I saw movement out of the cor-ner of my eye, but by the time I tried to locate it, whatever it was quit moving." He studied the back trail as she joined him and from her silent question he pointed where he thought he had caught that flash of movement. Shaking his head he commented, "I don't know but I'd have sworn that I saw a person on that trail, or at least that's what my mind is telling me. But I don't see anything at all now, so maybe it was my imagination."

Quietly as she studied the area from their high point she shook her head. "No, I suspect that what your mind told you is accurate. You've got to remember that we are wired to catch movement. As my parents told me time and time again, it is a survival thing. And it would have held true for protection against those wild predators and when we became tribes and clans and were warring with each other it would have become even more critical." She paused thinking, and more to herself than him, said, "I wonder why there'd be someone on a trail that is no longer traveled unless we are the reason. Yes, that's the only thing that makes sense."

Listening to her conversation with herself he realized that what she said had to be correct. They were being followed, and it was only because of this accidental high point that that allowed them to look back over the trail they had just hiked. He suspected that his ancestors had used this point for just this purpose. "Okay, that makes sense, so now what? And why would anybody be interested in following us? I mean we have no treasure, our camp gear is anything but new, and pack beasts are cheap and available to the poorest of our villages. So that only leaves us, and it makes me wonder if we've been watched all the time we've been out here."

"A possibility," Jura said, "but we have no proof, and really at this moment we can't be sure that's what you saw, still I suspect it was, so like you, what can we do about it? We can't even know how many may be out there or what their agenda is." Both were leaning on their staffs, which meant that if it came down to close combat both were armed, trained and ready. "I think we better get back from being so exposed. If they wanted to attack us from a distance we have left ourselves pretty visible here." Both of them, at this point, looked at each other and carefully backed away from the cliff edge to the boulders that would provide protection yet allow them to monitor the trail.

"I wonder how long we've been watched?" Kal looked down at the bare ground and back to the trail, took a deep breath, "I bet that this could be from Sabohl, after all, it's the only thing that makes sense. We really, as I said, have nothing of value to attract thieves and such, and we aren't searching for some hidden treasure, and for most, what we are looking for isn't even worth their time to read it in a local paper. And we've surmised that he was behind that break-in a few cycles of the seasons ago. So it would only make sense that he hasn't given up. And what have we just done? We've led him right to what we think is the clan home. I know we haven't found it yet, but both of us are almost positive that we aren't very far away from it now."

"If what you're saying is right, then this is very frustrating. We're doing all the hard work and he has his cronies following to make it easy for him, and we've kind of just gave it to him. Like you, I thought that he had given up, but if what you saw, again, is accurate the obvious answer is, no he hasn't."

Sitting there and staring out at nothing Kal continued to be silent. How could they lose whoever was following them? And it was very important to locate the clan home since all the other locations that he wanted to find and rediscover would be based from there. "Of course I might not have seen anything and it was just my imagination, but I know I did, so wishing it away isn't going to change anything. So what do you want to do? The obvious problem is that we are on the trail and I suspect we will be close to the clan site soon. And whether we delay or not will change nothing."

Shrugging she said, "I guess we just go on. As you so aptly pointed out everything that we are trying to locate is based on this location." Both of them got up from where they had been sitting and with a sense of foreboding continued up the ancient untraveled trail and away from the cliff top.

* * *

"I thought we had waited long enough before starting to follow them again. Then as we moved they showed up on top of the cliff and looked right at us."

"Yeah, and both of us froze in position. I have to admit I was beginning to cramp from being in such an awkward position, and then they stayed there for a very long time talking about something before disappearing out of our sight."

The one who had taken the leadership role cursed, and kicked a loose rock that lay in the trail. "All we can hope is that they didn't see us. I guess let that be a lesson to both of us. We kind of got impatient there and almost blew the whole thing and gave ourselves away – although I have no way of knowing whether they saw us or not. Let's get off the trail and wait for a while longer. It's obvious to me they are going to stay on whatever this is. Let's go find some shade; it's hot out under the suns." Both of them left the trail and found a straggly tree that at least got them out of the direct suns' heat. "We'll give it a little longer and then we'll head up the trail and try and see ahead. But that's the problem. It seems that this faint trail is climbing so they will stay above us."

* * *

"Let's stop here." Kal had a thought cross his mind, "We need to look at that map again. From what we've found so far this trail has a number of overlooks and places where they could safely attack an enemy."

"True, so what's your point? Oh . . . hmmm, I don't know if these places would be marked on this crude map because had this had fallen into a rival's hands then they would know where to look or how to work around the ambush points. Also from looking at the position of the suns and our location I think that we'll be having a dry camp tonight. If everything pans out as it appears at this moment we can move our camp to the abandoned site on the morrow."

"I didn't think about that, but you're right. I suspect if we headed back now we would make our camp by nightfall. So what do you want to do, continue or return? It doesn't matter now since we've located the trail. One day or another isn't going to change anything. I know that if we dry camp it all of our gear in our regular camp will be okay. It's well hidden, at least I think so. And we've had to do this a couple of times." Kal stood up and paced for a moment as he continued to think this through.

"Going back isn't a bad idea, but if we are being followed then we probably would run into whoever it is, and we don't even know how many of them there are. And who knows, maybe it's just a coincidence and it was someone hiking through the area. Although, the chances of that happening, considering how remote an area this is, and with no isolated farms and such out here, I'd guess it's near impossible." Jura stood up also and walked back down the trail. Although from this point she couldn't see their back trail at all. "Hard decision, hard decision that's for sure. So what do you want to do?"

He laughed and said, "I asked you first. I must admit after all the failures we've had I kind of want to see what's at the end of this trail, but also know that if we are being watched that we're not going to be the only ones who know this. So if we go back to the camp and return tomorrow, will whoever is following us continue on and then claim they discovered this, and we have no right to be there? Or are they just some hired thugs who were sent to watch us and then report back to whoever it was that sent them here? Without more information I just don't know. Maybe we should go ahead a little further and see if we can find one of those ambush points and wait. Then if a small group shows up we can confront them and see if we can find out."

"Are you sure that you want to do that? If there are a lot of them we won't be able to defend ourselves at all and will be at their mercy. And if they are riffraff, I, as a female, do not want to be in their control. Since we are quite isolated, who's to say what happened to us if we never return."

Looking down at the ground with his hands behind his back as he thought about it, "I have to admit I didn't consider that. And you are quite right. We are by ourselves and it would be easy for us to disappear, victims of the outback, the wilderness. And as vast an area as we've come to know it, it would be easy to hide our bodies and we would never be found, leaving only the mystery of what happened. So now we've gone full circle here once again, I guess we better just continue on with the knowledge that someone is behind us and watch for them."

"Yeah, I think that's probably best." She came back from where she had been studying the trail behind them and asked, "Shall we?" They both had taken off their travel packs and now picked them up and put them on and headed back up the unknown trail with the knowledge that they were being followed, leaving them with an unknown future as well.

The trail wound and twisted through the foothills giving the defenders many opportunities to harass an attacking enemy. In fact they could see a number of places where there had been work performed to strengthen defenses along the way. There were a couple of areas where the trail wound through narrow canyons giving the high ground to the defenders. From the direction they had come there had been no way to climb to these defense points. It was only after leaving these narrow confines that the way to the top presented itself. Even here access wasn't easy. As the suns were beginning to set they turned the corner around a huge rock wall and before them was a plateau that sloped uphill gently. Ahead of them was a large grove of trees that blocked their view of anything beyond. Stopping and taking in the beauty and catching their breath, since the last portion of the trail had been a steep uphill climb, they studied the area.

Pointing Jura said, "Look, doesn't that look like stumps of some of the trees?"

"Yeah, it really does, but now the question is, is it because they simply fell and this is what's left, or is it because they were cut down."

She smiled and said, "We're not going to know just standing here so let's go look." They headed over to the stumps and inspected them, looking closely at the remains.

"I'd guess that either one of those small beasts that uses its teeth to cut down trees that they then use to dam streams, or crude axes. It doesn't look like the winds were responsible – besides there's not trunk on the ground." Looking around carefully Kal couldn't even see any branches that may have been part of the tree. "No, I'd guess that this was done by a person, you agree?"

"Yup. Let's head on in and see what's beyond these trees, shall we?"

He bowed and swept his arms outwards stating, "After you oh mighty one, I bow to your demands, and your expertise."

She laughed at his antics and took on the air of the rich and walked casually in the direction they both were going, which got both of them laughing. He caught up with her and they pushed their way through the stand of trees, dead branches, and debris, and stopped. Before them a rock wall rose and disappeared behind trees to the north and south. This rock wall faced west and at this time of day reflected the setting suns light. Towards the north end there was a split in this wall and they could see that at one time there had been work to reinforce this split. Both headed towards this point. As they did they noticed that south of this area there appeared to have been worked fields although long abandoned. And off of this south wall a small waterfall and a stream ran down through these fields and disappeared into the trees.

As they approached this split they found some of the tree trunks that had been placed here and a broken gateway. Again, as they entered the path that led through the split it continued uphill, again giving defenders the better position. This ran for a short distance, this narrow gap in the wall, and then it opened up into the compound which sat on a higher plateau and was relatively flat. *They found it!* And as the suns began to set in the west behind them, they were shocked at the size of this upper plateau. There had been nothing to suggest that the area they were presently in was anything but a small rise. Instead a village could have nested here comfortably. They could see where there had been shelters but with the passing of time most were just piles of rubble marking the locations of where the shelters had once set. Although the paths that had developed over the time from the many genera-tion who had lived here, as they had moved from place to place within this clan home, were very apparent.

For a moment in the elation of discovery, after so many failures, they had forgotten about the ones who had been following. And the two had lagged far behind, once that incident on the back trail had almost compromised them. But since then, the two that they were following had remained ahead and out of sight. But their trail was obvious on this little used trail. Shortly they climbed the last portion and entered the stand of trees that Jura and Kal had been in just a short time earlier. The one in charge looked at the other and said quietly, "Who'd have guessed that these would be here. Look we're out of daylight, so I guess we better set up a cold camp here tonight. It's quite obvious that they'll not be returning to their new camp tonight and had probably planned on staying over."

"Yeah, it does look like doesn't it? I'll get us some wood, there's no lack of dead branches here, and we can at least have a small fire to heat something up, and from the feel of the air it's going to get cold up here tonight, so the fire will help keep us warm."

"I don't know if that's such a good idea. After all if they're close by they probably could see it."

"Hey, we don't know if they saw us back there or not, and I'm not going to give up the comfort of a small fire. Look, we can head back down the trail and find a place that's hidden if you like, but I don't like being cold."

Shrugging, he had to admit they didn't know if they had been discovered or not, but he didn't like being cold either, and with the lengthening shadows he didn't think they could head far enough back down the trail to find a place the stay. "Okay, you've convinced me. We'll just stay on this side of these trees and away from this trail and that should keep us hidden from them." Both of them worked to the north of the trail, found a small pile of boulders that had flat ground inside and decided that this would work. There was barely room for the two of them plus their small fire, but at least with the rocks they could build a fire next to one and get heat reflected back at them and hopefully with this makeshift shelter keep most of the evening breezes from chilling them too much.

Kal and Jura carefully walked the huge area in the failing light both silent as they walked the grounds of his ancestors. "I guess," Kal said quietly, "we better find a place to set up camp before it gets too dark. I don't think we'll lack for fuel for our fire." He stopped and looked around and just to the south of the entrance the land fell away into a natural bowl. Looking inside this bowl they could see that at one time it had held a rather large shelter. Pointing he said, "That might a good place, out of the cold night winds, but the cold air might settle in there, what do you think?"

"Don't know really, but there's a good chance for the air to settle there. Hmmm," she mumbled as she looked around in the dimming light. "I don't see anything that would be better so why not?" Both of them headed back to this natural bowl and when they descended they found that at this moment the air in the bowl was still and a bit warmer than the surrounding air. Smiling, she said, "I think I like it already – hadn't realized that it had cooled that much already." Looking around at the openness of this plateau she commented, "Bet the winds just whip across this place. There's absolutely nothing to stop them. It has to be a miserable place in the Season of Cold."

They worked quickly with practiced ease as they set up their dry camp at the bottom of the bowl close to the ruins of what had to be a large shelter. Once set up both headed out and working through the compound where a number of trees had grown since the place had been abandoned they found plenty of wood to feed their fire. As both of them got back together with their armloads of wood Kal asked, "Thought I smelled smoke from a campfire when I got close to the entrance to this place. But it was only so brief that I wasn't sure. Did you by any chance smell such a thing?"

"Now that you mention it I think so, but it was so subtle that I almost immediately dismissed it. Well, if both of us smelled it then it has to be real. I guess the only question is; where is it coming from?" Thinking for a moment and climbing up the slight rise out of the bowl she sensed the direction of the breeze, stood there for a few moments to be sure and said, "With the time of day, we have an up canyon wind, which means that it would be flowing naturally from that tree stand and lower plateau up through that split that leads into here. So that fire has to be where we came from, probably the ones who are following us, I would suspect."

"I guess that this would confirm it then", Kal paused, "but we probably should sneak down the slash and see if the smell gets stronger. If it does then we know that they are behind us, and then maybe if we are careful we can try and locate their camp and find out how many are following us."

"I concur with the first part of your idea, but if there are many of them, they'll probably have guards out and neither of us is good enough to sneak up on a camp. So let's just head down and see if the strength of the smell gets stronger, if so, then we can be pretty sure that it's them. Besides, we need to stay on this side of those trees, because there's a lot of debris, dead branches fallen leaves and such, and in the dark we won't be able to see any of it." Careful, because it would be much later when one of the minor moons rose, and even with their eyes having adjusted to the darkness, it was still very difficult to see anything, they worked their way back to the split in the wall that gave them access to the lower plateau.

With a rock rolling out from under his foot Kal went down on his backside. He fought down a curse and tried to slow his slide as he slid down the steep slope that they had just tackled. After finally being able to stop and stand back up he whispered to Jura, "really hope that wasn't too noisy, and that hurt." He could feel a burning on his hands and arms making him realize that he had lost some skin as he had slid down the path.

"Yeah, I bet it did, but I don't think we have to go any further, the smell of the smoke is definitely stronger here and I suspect that there's a camp close by – probably on the other side of those trees."

"Yeah you're right, it's really strong here, and I think if you look over there to the north end there seems to be a small amount of haze hugging the ground – could be the smoke laying in there in a pocket of slow moving air." She nodded in agreement, at this point both turned around and headed back to their camp inside the ancient compound.

* * *

"Do you think that the two we are following continued up the trail that they found?"

The one who had taken charge just shook his head and said, "Nah, don't think so. They know nothing about what's ahead of them any more than we do. So I suspect that they are camping just as we are. After all they did have their carrying packs on so that means that they were prepared to camp overnight somewhere if they needed to, and again who knows how long this trail goes, I don't. And once it started to get dark they would have to stop, and before you ask, no I don't think there's another way around and they have headed back to their other camp. I believe that they would have to go past us and we would know."

Both were staring into their small hidden fire, making them night blind. Once they had picked the area they were going to build their fire they walked away to see if the camp was hidden from any who would walk the trail and as far as they could see it was. The only factor they didn't take into consideration was the three that were following them. These three were on a lower level looking up and as it darkened they could discern two glows that marked the two campsites.

"I guess this Jura and Kal are safe for now. There seems to be a little distance between the two sites so they haven't been bothered yet. Although, I don't know what we'll do, if these two who are following them, decides to attack them. I guess that we will have to stay out of it because we cannot be found out." They were staying in their own camp, a dry camp with no fire and cold travel rations.

One of the underlings with him smiled, "I really don't think that will be an issue. If you remember, Jura is an expert with the staff, and I suspect that she's been training Kal. So if those two decide to attack them, up close and personal, I believe it is they that will be in for a surprise. They'll go in thinking because there's a female that it will be easy pickings. In a sense I'd like to be there, you know a Loki in the grass, as those two low life's get what's coming to them if they are stupid enough to think that they can bully the two of them." This brought a chuckle out of the three as they pictured the surprise on the two who would have thought they had the upper hand only to find that they didn't.

* * *

With morning Kal and Jura were up and exploring the discovered site. He stood in awe and felt more like whispering than saying anything out loud – in a way this was a sacred site for his family. This was the place where the alliance had begun, and it was from here that all of the rest that was written in the journals could be located. He realized that even with the size of this small plateau, in the Season of Cold where you would be isolated to your shelter, that it must have closed in on everybody. While this would have been a place that would be easy to defend in time of attacks, the area was exposed enough to allow the winds to whip through the area sparing no one. It truly had to have been brutal. Clearing his throat Kal said, "It's hard for me to believe that we've actually found it. If I remember right in the reading of the journals that area where we camped last night is the location of the female shelter, and if that's so, to the north of this would have been the leader's shelter. Then further to the east we should find where the compound was divided between the warriors and the priests. Plus on this side of the compound there would have been shelters for the rest, the ones who kept this place going – you know, like the slaves and young males in training, and the ones who just did all the other mundane things that it takes to make it work. I think that we should probably spend all day here sketching everything we can figure out, and mark its location on one of the better maps that we've brought with us. Maybe spend another night before heading back and getting our gear and setting up a camp right here. How does that sound to you?"

"Okay I guess, but I don't know if we have enough food and such for another night. It might be better if we just went back and got our stuff and moved it here. After all, this place isn't going anywhere."

"True, but I worry about what the agenda of those who are following us may be. If we leave will they move in and claim that they found it and that we had better leave?"

"Darn! I forgot about them," Jura exclaimed, "I was wrapped up in looking this over and in the excitement they slipped my mind. Maybe with full daylight we should go see what we are facing, and if it's only a couple maybe suggest that they leave?"

"Yeah, but would they? This is a problem, I don't want us to be separated but maybe it's a way of doing it. Look you're better at sneaking than I am just because of where you grew up, and I'd feel better if I knew that you were away and safe. And, before you point out that you're much better with the staff and defending than I am, I think that if we do it this way they are less likely to come after me as a male than you as a female. They might think that you'd be an easy mark and make it difficult. As it is, if you were to leave now you wouldn't be back here until dusk."

He could see the attempt in her eyes and her face of trying to counter what he had just said, and was remaining silent for a moment. Finally she took a deep breath and shook her head and said, "I can't argue against that logic, you're right even with my skill, by myself, I'd be a target even if there's only a couple. Out here a female alone, against who knows who, could make for a very bad outcome. But I'd be alone heading back to our camp, packing it, and then coming back, so I don't know which is worse, do you? Tell you what, let's go down there and see what we are facing. The drift of the smoke from their fire put them on the north end of that lower plateau, probably on the other side of the stand of trees that is there. If we sneak around from the south we can do two things. First we can locate their camp, and second if we get lucky we can see how many are following us. Hmmm, I just had a thought . . ."

Trying to lighten the mood a little he asked, "You had a thought, really?" He then he smiled showing that he wasn't serious. She went ahead and hit him on his shoulder anyway which did hurt, "Ouch! What was that for? You know I was only kidding."

"Yeah, but so am I. If I'd been serious you'd be picking yourself off the ground just about now. Anyway there may be a way that both of us can chance it and go. I really don't like the idea of separating. We become much easier targets then even if there's not many of them. We know that both of us, I'm speaking of those unknowns behind us and you and me here. All of us had to stop because of darkness and camp for the night."

"I'm with you so far, please continue."

"Well, who's to say that we found anything at all? I mean that these unknowns have probably been following us since we've been up here and we've hit nothing but dead ends and returned to our camp to start over, so what if we head back down the trail talking like we were very disappointed but this promising lead turned out to be nothing but another dead end and we need to get back to camp, pack it up once again and then head further east and see if we can find something else."

"Yeah, that would be consistent with what's happened so far, but would they go and look where we spent the night . . . Because, if they did that they would know the truth."

"Yeah, that is a problem. Hmmm, what if we do it this way then – we both leave and we show our disappointment that this trail was a dead end, possibly a hunter's camp at one time and we discuss this just as I suggested, and we both are mad because we just wasted all this time on another dead end. We both slowly head down the trail, and then pick one of the points where we can watch our back trail, soon after we leave and go past where we suspect that they are camping, to see if they follow us. If they do that immediately then we'll know our discovery will be safe, and if they don't, we can turn around and come back. The only problem with coming back is that we'll be giving ourselves away and they would know that something's up."

Kal was silent for a moment, thinking. *What a dilemma, should we go or should we stay? Either way there could be problems.* "I don't know, because really, if they don't see us, then they'll assume we've just continued along the trail, not knowing that it ends here, and when they came along to continue following us they would walk right into our discovery. So I guess we'll have to chance it and make an appearance and do as you suggest. That way we can see if we can make them follow us back and head back to our camp and break it down and maybe figure another way to get to the trail head."

"Then we'd better do it," Jura stated with some urgency in her voice. "We really don't have anything to pack other than rolling up our sleeping sacks. I think that shortly the suns will be cresting that rock face that sits on the east end of this place. We can still make a quick sketch of the area, with two of us working the sketch, so that we can say that we really were here, and maybe help protect our rights to discovery."

With the decision made and while it hadn't been spoken they had decided to leave together, once the quick sketch had been created, and to announce to the world that this was another dead end and they needed to head back to their camp."

* * *

The two that were following had had a bad night and when the dawn came both were deep in sleep unworried that their quarry would escape them. Even though there had been a close call the day before, it appeared that they had gotten lucky and had not been viewed or discovered, and that was very good news. This meant that they could continue to do little to nothing, other than follow them, and with a little care, remain an unknown. As it got closer to the time of the suns showing above the foothills both of them still in the twilight of just waking up heard voices which immediately brought them fully awake. They looked at each other and then at their dead fire and then froze in position as the voices became stronger. Listening, all they could hear was disappointment in the voices, as they lamented another failure and another dead end. Peering around the rocks where they were hidden they saw the two talking about the fact that all they found was a dead end and an old hunter's camp, and what at first held promise led to another wasted day, and there were so few of the days left before the Season of Cold would be upon them and they would have to give up until the next cycle of seasons. The voices faded as the two headed down the trail and out of sight.

Grabbing their gear, and not taking the time to make sure that their fire was truly dead they hurriedly threw their gear together and took off after them, not bothering to check the camp where Kal and Jura had spent the night. As in so many other attempts, it was obvious that this wasn't what they had been searching for either, so why bother searching the area where they had spent the night? The two who were following, hung back just far enough so that they would remain unseen, and shook off the dregs of waking from a deep sleep and felt once again that luck was with them. Now they had to be careful, and trail a little further behind and make sure that the ones they were following didn't take off on some side trail, thusly losing them.

The three who were following the two who were following Jura and Kal had remained further down the trail with one scouting ahead, when the one who had been doing the scouting ran back to them. He stopped to catch his breath before being able to say anything. "All of them are heading back down the trail towards us, and we only have a very short time to disappear." Looking around, there wasn't any place to go so they headed rapidly back down the trail to where there was a ravine that cut into the side of the trail and curved around out of sight. Unfortunately it wasn't very deep but with the concentration of the four coming back down the trail they hoped that they wouldn't be looking too hard. The only advantage they had was twofold, first this wouldn't be some place that one would normally conceal oneself, and secondly they were not visible from a higher point on the descending trail. They had to lie flat, barely hidden, with only the grasses providing anything to block one's view.

They heard, more than saw, the first two pass their location and continue on, none the wiser that they were here. Their positions were uncomfortable but they had to wait what seemed like forever before the heard the second pair approach their position, quietly talking as they slowly continued down the trail. The three waited until they were sure that enough time had passed to safely come out of hiding. The one who had been scouting simply said, "That was too close."

* * *

Jura, as they headed back down the trail at a rapid pace to force the ones following no time to check out their camp commented, "Look I have a feeling that whoever the ones are they aren't very good in the outback. I guess in some ways yes they are since we didn't even know that we had someone following us from the beginning. But look," as she pointed to the trail, "their tracks are as plain as daylight. If any of my family had been doing this we'd eliminated our tracks so that they couldn't accidently be found later like this."

"At least by them doing it this way," Kal replied, "we can see that we're probably only looking at a few of them, which means if we did have to face them it would be a little more equal." He stopped, and it took a second before she stopped, as it had been unexpected. Shaking his head, she could see that there was a little bit of anger in his stance. Breathing out a deep cleansing breath Kal said, "This just sucks. And to think I trusted that learned, that Sabohl, and now he has been watching us ever since. I know I don't have any real proof, but who else could it be? It makes me want to confront these few that are following us and get the truth out of them. Although I suspect that they aren't tied directly to Sabohl but someone else. Look we have another issue, and I know we briefly talked about it before heading out this morning, but I've been thinking about it as we led them away. And it's not only the fact that when we return that we'll give ourselves away. We can only stay there so long and we have to head back. We'll be the only ones who know that we were the first, and there's no quick way for us to get back. Plus, I wouldn't know who to report our find to anyway.

"Originally I just figured it would be you and me and the families who would know about what we've found. Then when we would have had the chance to search out the different locations and have an understanding of what we've found find the right people to report it to and go from there. By us being followed like we have been, none of this is going to happen. At least we now know that what the journals say is accurate, and that they weren't some forgeries that had been planted in the family in the past. What they say is true and real, which means that the other places talked about are real also. Meaning that the way we are viewing our past is not right. These places are not myths or creations of our ancestors, they are very real.

"I guess, like so many things that we do, we go into it with an unreal expectation of how it will go. And if we both think about it, finding or trying to find this site is a good example. Both of us figured that with the crude map that it would be easy to just use the map and walk right up to the clan home. Well, we both know how well that worked. Here it is almost the Season of Cold and after working through the end of the Season of Heat and most of the Season of Falling we've finally located it only to find that we have been under observation the whole time and none the wiser for it. And teaching the ones who are behind us a lesson will not change anything. They'll still know and we can't change that. And I can't just kill them, although I suspect they probably deserve it. So I guess after this long winded talk it comes down to, now what?"

Jura listened quietly with her hands on her hips as he spoke. After finishing, she remained quiet, cocked her head to the side, and said, "Here's a thought, and like leaving this morning it has risk, not that everything we've been doing doesn't. Instead of heading back to our discovery we could just pack up, look dejected and defeated and call it a season of failure, even though we know better. We might be able to give them enough of a misdirection that this will remain safe until we can find someone who could help us. And it's becoming obvious that we're going to need help. Although who to ask, I really don't know either."

"It's something to think about, and I know that we have some time before we reach our camp. In fact it will probably be between the zenith and dusk before we get there. So we'll be spending at least one more night in our more permanent camp. Maybe we can come up with something, and I think your suggestion is a good one. But anything we do is a problem at this point. Well this isn't getting us back to camp, shall we continue?"

C H A P T E R   S I X

INTRIGUE

It had been a hard decision since they had actually been, even if so brief of a time, in the clan's ancient home, the home of his and hers by becoming the mate of Kal, ancestors. But now they were back in High Trail checking on the bakery and all the paperwork that seems to always multiply. One would swear that it could reproduce itself. While they had been away the business had grown under the care of Sara and she had suggested that they pick up a second site as they were now outgrowing the one that they were in. So for the Season of Cold they would work through all that they had to do, touch bases with his parents, and bring the family up to date with what they had discovered. For now it would have to remain within the confines of the family. And they hoped that it would be enough, and the ones who had followed them through their season of searching hadn't returned to that last place where they had made their discovery.

Then the word got out that in the near future that Sabohl would be making a major announcement about a discovery in the far northeastern foothills and one of importance. And at this point they knew that he had stolen their discovery, but even if they tried to counter this *up and coming* announcement that Sabohl would be sure to silence them. If they hadn't been sure of Sabohl's position, they now had personal proof of the way he worked. Again, while there had never been proof that the break-in had been requested by Sabohl, this reinforced this thought that he had a strong role in it. Too many coincidences, too short of time between knowledge that Sabohl had gained to the actions, and here was another. Breathing out deeply and feeling somewhat defeated, Kal said. "We were so hoping that when we left like we did that whoever this was that was following us would just ignore what we found and we could safely go back in the Season of Greening. But I guess we were wrong. Probably should have moved our camp and at least tried to check out a couple of additional areas to, as you call it, lay a false trail. Something made them curious enough to go back and find what we had found, and now it's lost to us. Who knows what mess he'll make of the place, and how he'll bend it to fit his own interpretations. This is so wrong!"

Feeling helpless Jura could only be silent as she listened. She felt betrayed also, but who were they but just a couple of bakers? How could they go against one of the most important people in their world? She knew that he wasn't really expecting any answers from her, but it seemed so unfair. *Yes but life is unfair.* She heard her parents telling her that in her mind. Sometimes you saw someone who never deserved what they had, continue to receive undeserved rewards, acknowledgements, and the ones who actually should have remain unknown. It was that way of the world now, and as far as she knew, it had always been that way, and probably always would be. "I know you don't expect me to answer those questions since I have no answers and you know it, but there's got to be some way, or someone out there that can help us. There's just got to be." Again she was silent. Then in a much softer voice, one that held no confidence she said, "Although I have no idea who that would be or where to even look."

She leaned forward on the table that both of them were sitting around. It was the end of another busy day with not enough time to accomplish all that had been set before them, and she had to admit that she was tired. Yet the next few 9-days were going to be no different, and once everything had been brought up to date with the bakery, they needed to start their planning for the next season of searching. Yet, before any of that could be accomplished they had to find someone who could help, pure and simple. If they continued like they were doing, then as they made their discoveries, Sabohl, who seemed to have them watched all the time, would just claim it as his own, as he had on their first major discovery. It almost made one want to forget the whole thing. But now that they had located the first she was finding that she had a desire to continue, she felt that she was catching fire like Kal, and wanted to go find those mythological places and prove that they were real. Shaking her head she said, "I just don't know, there has to be someone out there who knows about how this Sabohl works, and is trying to end his reign. I'm sure that we aren't the first that he's stolen from, and if he continues in his place of power, we won't be the last."

"True, but I don't have any ideas as to where to even begin to look. And I'm sure if we had a way to see in the dark we'd find that there are people out there watching us. I mean it took us almost all the time we were out there searching to discover that we were watched. It was a shock to say the least. Now if . . ." His thought and statement uncompleted, as out of nowhere there was a single knock on their door, this being a complete surprise since it was dark, and rarely would any come by this time of night. They looked at each other and then the door, "Now who could that be?" Carefully he got up and peered out the window that allowed them to see the entrance, but there was nobody there. Now curious he went to the door and opened it and confirmed that there was no one there. Puzzled he stepped out and almost tripped over a small bag that was all but invisible. It was something that hadn't been there earlier. So instead of bending down to pick it up he kicked it inside, closed the door, walked to the window and looked once again trying to see if anyone was there, anyone at all. But the roads were empty, and all that was visible were the lights from the other shelters in the area.

He was now more in the dark than he was before opening the door. Once outside he had searched carefully, with his eyes, every place he could see, which truthfully, wasn't much. It was one of those rare nights that none of the moons would be visible, so it was as close to pitch black as one could have. So after seeing nothing with his eyes after giving them time to adjust to the night, he listened very hard for any sounds that would have been unusual, but again it was silent, other than the normal night sounds. Once back inside he looked at Jura shrugged and shook his head when he saw her questioning look. "I don't know, there was nothing, no sounds and it was too dark to really see anything. And whoever tossed this," he pushed the small bag with his booted foot, "made sure that they couldn't be seen or heard." He breathed heavily undecided, but eventually bent over and picked up the small leather bag which was tied shut with a leather string. From the feel he could tell that there was a rock to give it weight and what felt like paper inside. He brought over to the table and sat back down across from Jura tossing the small bag on the table, where both stared at it.

After what seemed much too long of a time Jura finally broke the silence and said, "Well, I guess we better see what's inside, don't you think?"

"I guess so, and we really aren't going to learn about what's here just looking at that sealed bag." He reached for it and with some work was finally able to untie the knots. He examined the bag as he did this and found that it could have been any of the thousands that were made and sold so there was no clue as to the owner from the bag itself. The string was threaded through the top of the bag and took some work to get the bag fully opened. The rock that had been placed inside was large enough that it took some real work to remove it, and in the bottom was a tightly folded paper. After removing the paper he examined it and saw that once again that the paper was just that – ordinary cheap paper. Looking up he could see that Jura was burning with impatience and curiosity, so he handed the folded paper to her and signaled her to go ahead unfold it and read it, which she did. He waited patiently and really couldn't read what she was reading but shortly she passed it to him and he then read:

"You've now learned the extent that Sabohl will go. Just know that there are others who are just as aware. We cannot reveal ourselves to you at this time, but know that we truly know who discovered the site that Sabohl is claiming as his own discovery. There will come a time when all of this will come back and haunt Sabohl, but as you have so learned, he has much power and control. Remember you are not alone in this."

It was short and sweet, but left neither closer to an answer of the owner or owners of this unorthodox delivery. And while the note promised an accounting sometime in the future, and that there were others aware, it didn't improve their present situation at all, and truly left a bigger mystery. Like how could they know that the two of them had discovered that site? "I don't know how to take this? I mean this could just as easily be coming from Sabohl as well as someone else. So we could be fooled into thinking that there's help out there, well maybe help out there since there are no promises, and in the end it being Sabohl manipulating us to do his bidding. But if it is someone else, that means that there had to be a lot of people out there following us around while we searched. And if that's so, how many, and how does that reflect on us? I mean we weren't looking for people out there watching us, and as a result we didn't know until it was too late. Would we have been able to see them earlier than we did, or were we just too wrapped up in what we were trying to find to notice?"

"Yeah", Jura responded, "everything you've asked are valid questions, and this is getting much more complicated than I ever imagined. And when we started this I just figured that we would be out in the outback, the wilderness, by ourselves, trying to find that ancient site. Instead we seemed to have led an army around those northern foothills and never saw them at all. Like you, I figured that once we moved to High Trail and had worked all that time before starting this that we were free of Sabohl and his minions, but I was obviously very wrong. And now, if we are to believe what is in this, this unusually delivered note, then there are others who are just as aware and are working against Sabohl."

"Yeah, but can we believe it? I know that the delivery was dramatic, if one wants to think about it, but if, well not if, since we know that we're being watched, that means that this other shadowy group is also staying out of sight, staying in the background and trying not only to remain hidden from us, but from Sabohl and his organization also. Hey, I'm just a lowly baker, who like everybody has a family history, and I know that I'm not the only one who can claim to have come from the clan that K'jor was the leader of, and part of our historical past. After all there were lots of leaders over the time that clan existed. Yes we can trace the beginnings of change from him and his time, but we also know that there are other influences and it was a very long time past his time that the changes truly began – so why the interest? What is really happening in the shadows, in the depth of the night, and how'd we get mixed up in all of this?"

"I don't know, and I don't like it. After all while you, and I guess me now, we are bakers, but in the beginning I was just a female from the farm. One who only visited the villages now and then, and dreamed of someday doing something other than farming. But this – this is nothing I want to get involved with. No I don't mean chasing your family history, but this *intrigue* that involves ones in power. Like you I thought it would be nice to actually find those places that are talked about in those documents, those journals from your family, and whole heartedly wanted to search for this as much as you did. I guess in some ways it was being romantic. In those cheap stories that one can buy, while the hero and the heroine go through tough times they always triumph in the end. And even there they leave out much of the hard boring stuff. So when one tackles something like this it is easy to forget that there's lots of hard boring stuff. And I have to admit that there was or is." She paused for a moment and smiled, "But I suspect that after much time has passed both of us by that we'll personally forget the hard boring stuff and create a romantic story of our own."

He laughed which turned contagious and she joined him. Once they could catch his breath once again he said, "You know I never thought about it that way, but I suspect you're right. I know that when I was still young, very young really, we'd go see family and there'd always be stories going around. And I have to admit that many of them left me in awe to what they were talking about. In my mind I would create adventures from those stories. But like you just stated, all the boring stuff probably had been left out, and the stuff where they got hurt or failed, and only passed on the good stuff. Do you really think we'll be like that when we get old?"

She shrugged, "That's hard to say, but I suspect that it will be the way of it. I've seen the same thing in my family gatherings and there are oldsters who are living around this village always willing to pass on some gem of wisdom, or tell a tale from their past. So maybe as we get older and begin to lose much of the vigor of youth, the strength, and mind begins to fade that one only has their past to live for." She stopped a moment took a deep breath and let it out slowly. "I guess when you look at it that way it's tragic. We work and try and accomplish things in our lives, some work, some fail, but suddenly what you are no longer matters and the young ones have taken over and you are now the one looking in and wondering what happened. It really has to be hard."

With the swift change he hesitated as he thought about what Jura had just stated. "That's very true and really has to be hard. It seems that time robs us of our strength, our ability to think and act, and it happens so subtly that one never notices it until one day it hits you in the face and you're old and, well maybe not useless, but one probably feels that way. I know that with my sires that I'm beginning to see much grey in their hair, and while they still seem strong and virile, it's obvious that in a few cycles of the seasons that they will be moving over as their parents did before them. And it seems to happen so fast." He got up and paced for a few moments with his hands behind his back. The direction that their conversation had taken was off the mark to where it had started, but that seemed to happen often. It was as if the mind was unruly and needed to be disciplined to keep it on track. "Look we kind of gotten off the subject where this all started, and like we said, we're nothing more than simple bakers, and this stuff that's happening behind our backs, unknown to us, is so far beyond that I would never have guessed such a thing exists. So now we're in the middle, and if the rumors that we've read are correct, then our hard work, or discovery, will become someone else's, and that sucks. I suspect that this is common, but until it happens to you, you just don't realize that it's this way."

"Yeah, I surely didn't. But what can we do about it? I know that we wanted to go back and map the area better than the quick sketches that we did before we left . . ." She paused deep in thought for a moment.

Curious as to what she was thinking he waited before asking, "What?"

She shushed him and continued to think. "Look we need to find out who these people are who contacted us tonight."

"Why? We don't even have a hint to as who they are, let alone know a way to contact them."

"Yeah that's true, but look we need to find out because if they are part of the search for our history, maybe, just maybe we can beat Sabohl at his game and get credit for the discovery."

"How? Really?"

"Yes, really. Look we've worked hard on finding the clan home, and I would just hate to have Sabohl grab all the glory from it, so if we can contact this other group, if indeed there is another group, then with the rough drawings we did, and the marking of the location on our maps we could get this out ahead of him and claim it as our own, which it is."

"Okay, I agree with you, but now we have two mysteries to solve. First who is this group and where are they? And secondly, how many does Sabohl have watching us, and if it is a lot can we make contact with this other group and not give them away, and will they be willing to help? I know that they, in their note said that they are here, but that's a long way from coming out in the open."

Jura then added, "But there's a third also, and that is this; do we have enough time to prove it was our discovery before Sabohl and his release the details, undermining our facts, and truths? Hmm, let's look at that note again, maybe there's something there that we missed. I'm sure that there wouldn't be much on it in case it fell into Sabohl's hands, but it probably wouldn't matter, because even this much would be enough for Sabohl to probably figure out who this was. So they were taking a very big chance getting this into our hands." They spread the crumpled, folded note out and studied it closer, but could find nothing, until they turned it over, and there on the back was a small mark. But neither had ever seen such a mark, and really if they were truthful, it could have just as easily been just part of another correspondence, and this scrap of paper could be just that – scrap.

* * *

Sabohl felt satisfaction with the results that had come out of his feelings that that upstart had been hiding something from him. To have kept the surveillance up for as long as had been required had cost him much in both time and finances. Now, because of them, he sat upon one of the largest discoveries in his field in two lifetimes. He laughed quietly and asked himself just what could they do about it? Answering himself he said quite smugly, "Why nothing, nothing at all." There was no one who could challenge him or his position and it was going to remain that way. He was very good on putting up the front of being the helpful friendly learned, but if any knew him as he really was they would've realized that this was only to gain possible information that he could use later, and he had a great memory. Soon, with this discovery, he would be able to cement his position and leadership to the point that absolutely no one would be able to challenge him, and that damned board would just vanish as all did in time.

He lived alone and preferred it that way. And if he had need of a female, and what male didn't, he'd have some of his female students who looked up to him until he grew tired of them, or maybe a female or two from the society that he frequented, and if all else failed there were always those of the lower caste, or the shelters of females for that purpose. So he had no need of a companion, and friendships were a way of learning something he needed and nothing more. Besides he was enough company, and by being this way there could be no accidental slip up because he let his guard down at home.

After it had become obvious that the two, Kal and Jura, headed back at what seemed to be an unsuccessful search in the northeastern foothills, he had become frustrated. He knew in his heart that they weren't there just to be away from the business. And by the way they were up and down those hills it was further proof that they were looking for something. So as the sparse reports came back he encouraged his contacts to keep following them. And in the end these two were never the wiser that they had been followed, being watched. And when that last report had come back saying that the two were done for this cycle of the seasons he thought it a little strange. Yes it would only be a short time before the Season of Cold would be upon them, but there was still a few 9-days left before it would strike – much too early in his mind to be quitting. So he sent word back to have the ones that were close to that final area to contact the two that had been following and with the four of them to retrace that last place that Jura and Kal had been before they quit. Soon word got back to him that indeed the two had located an unknown ancient site, and what did he want them to do?

With the flush of both excitement and confirmation that he had been right, he moved quickly to secure the location and to claim another discovery. But before he could officially make that claim he personally would have to make the journey to give credence to the fact that he actually found this site. And he had to make sure that the higher learned center was aware that he was out searching, and the reason was some old document that he had discovered, which of course, led him straight to this unknown location and unknown ancient site. He would be gone three 9-days to give the illusion that he was out attempting to nail down the exact location, but really had just spent it in the closest village under an assumed name remaining comfortable. Yes he had taken a single trip out to the location so that he could officially say that he had actually been there. And once the time had passed he returned and announced his discovery with maps and rough drawings. Now let any try and take it away from him. *Yes, I need to continue to watch these two. I really suspect that this isn't the only place that they will discover in the end, and it all will be my discoveries when it's all said and done.* Again he laughed as he drank his liquor. All was going well and all was going to be a part of his long ranged plans.

* * *

Jaie, standing as he faced the historical society said, "I really didn't expect him to move that fast. But I guess it makes sense. He didn't get where he is by sitting on his rear end. What we need to do now is find out if we want to make ourselves known, more than that note that was left at their door. Are we ready to come out in the open, and with what Sabohl has done to them, would they be willing to accept our help? I think that with the results of their hard work and the subsequent loss to Sabohl of that same hard work, they just might. Although we will be walking a very fine line if we do. There's a good chance that Sabohl will figure out that we are more openly opposing him, and with the speed that seems to surprise us, do something unexpected that could be a major problem for us." He sat down and for a while it was silent.

Tesam stood and voiced their dilemma, "True, absolutely everything that you just stated is fact. Yet, if we do nothing he'll continue to build his power, and nobody, and I mean nobody will be able to challenge him until like that old male in the herds who is the one servicing the females, some young one comes along who is stronger and takes his place. He could easily destroy us, and with his claim that he located this site, unless we can inject some doubt on that claim, it may be enough that he will be that old male, that old bull who is wily, and even though the young males are stronger and probably faster, it is his experience that allows him to continue to rule over the females. We cannot allow this to continue, but honestly I have no answers on how to prevent it. So maybe it will be in our best interest to actually contact these two, the ones who actually made the discovery and see what they may have that can counter Sabohl's claim of being the first." He sat down.

Shahe then stood and was quiet for a moment as he thought through what had been presented, "Okay, I think we're all coming to the conclusion that we will need to make contact with Kal and Jura and find out what they have to counter Sabohl's claim to this site, and we must do it quickly or he can claim that they only copied what he put out there, and that what they are saying is false, trying to take his discovery from him, and after all, everyone knows that he, Sabohl is the greatest in his field, and there are always upstarts trying to take it away from him, so why not now? So I guess the question is this; how do we contact them, and still keep it a secret from Sabohl's minions?" At this time he sat down and the hall where they were meeting was silent.

* * *

It was an unbelievably busy day at the secondary bakery. With the innovations that his parents added, and the varieties of breads and such, it seemed that soon, even considering the small size of High Trail that they would have to expand again. They were getting well known in the area and were drawing people in from well outside of the small village. And there had been a rather large order from a private learning center slash religious shelter. Yes they still existed, but no longer did any worship the old gods. Instead they now considered that there was only one God who ruled not only the creation of this world but of all that they could see. And because this order had not been given to them in advance it had put them far behind and their normal on-hand amounts dwindled rapidly. Turning to Jura Kal said, "Look I'm going to make a quick trip across the village to our main bakery and see if I can get some stuff from them. We've run out of the sweetbreads that are in such high demand. When we got that order from the learning center it included almost all of our fresh supply. I just hope that they're good for it." At this point he took off his apron and turned the selling counter over to her; he smiled and said, "Be back as quick as I can."

Stepping outside he shivered involuntarily as the cooler air struck him. But it was only momentary. As always it was warm in the bakery, and even though the smells of fresh breads were pleasant, he found the fresh air sweet smelling and invigorating. Taking a deep breath and throwing the large empty sack over his shoulder he headed out at a rapid pace. About half way to his destination someone tripped in front of him and stumbled into him. The stranger apologized profusely for being so clumsy. All he could do was shake his head and smile. If he wanted to be honest he had to admit that he could be that way himself. The interruption only delayed him a moment and finally he reached his destination, and found that the main bakery was doing a lively business also. Taking out the large key that opened the back door and with the rattle of the small chain that the keys were attached, he entered the maelstrom of organized chaos. He heard orders for the different breads being yelled out and the staff was in a frenzy trying to keep up with the demand. One would have thought that they were close to one of the holidays. Catching Sara as she flashed by him he yelled to be heard over the noise and asked if she could see him for a few moments after she finished helping the customer that she was filling an order for. She nodded and pointed to the small office for which he returned the nod and watched her as she headed out to the front and was gone from his sight.

He headed inside and closed the thin door and was rewarded with a reduction of the din that had assailed his ears. Taking a deep breath he let out a sigh of relief. Who'd have thought that a bakery could be so noisy? He reached in his pocket to pull out the list and found something else in his pocket along with the list. *How'd that get there?* He thought. *I distinctly remember putting the list there, but the pocket was empty.* At that moment Sara entered the office completely out of breath, and taking a deep cleansing breath herself said, "It's crazy out there! I know on the first of the 9-days we are busy but nothing like this. I mean I'll take it over being bored with nothing to do, but this was a real surprise. Okay boss, what can I do for you?"

Looking at her he smiled as there was flour in her hair and a smug or two on her face, "Well if it's anything to you we're running crazy over there also. So much so that we've run out of some of the breads. I'm hoping that you can give us some of what we need, and to keep the books straight I have the money to cover the stuff." He handed her the list and waited as she looked it over with a look of concentration on her face. "Hmm, I think we can fill most of this. Look I'll be right back. Better give me that sack also then I won't have to make two trips." And with that she was back out the door.

Shaking his head the thought, *who'd have thought that it would be this way? After all most make their own, and while a bakery would provide some stuff, it was never a lot. Now we can't keep up with the demand, and when a special order, like what we got over there, comes in, it can push us beyond what we have on hand. Hmmm, I wonder if we should make it a requirement that special orders be given to us in advance, that way we can be prepared – something to think about.* He leaned against the small desk that was piled high with unfinished paperwork and unfiled reports. If things continued like this for both locations they would need that third location very soon.

In what seemed to be a very fast time she came back into the office like a whirlwind with not only the filled list but the detailed billing. She was breathing hard from the effort that she'd put forth. "Look, I grabbed a couple of the workers and we were able to get this together much quicker, and we did have enough to cover what you need over there, plus while they were getting the product I ran a cost on it." At this point she handed the totals over to him and set the heavy sack on the floor.

He glanced at the figures and agreed, pulled out the money, paid her, thanked her for the speed, and she smiled back and was back out the door to continue the supervision and work. All he could do, once she had left, was to shake his head. Such efficiency, they all could learn from her. He took the receipt and lifted the now heavy sack and left, heading out the side door, the unknown note completely forgotten. He needed to get back since what he had in the sack was needed now, not later.

It wasn't until that night and the chaos of the day had vanished, with the quiet of home both sighed and let out a slow breath, finally this day was over. Both of them smelled of the bakery, the breads, the yeast, and their clothes covered in flour dust. It was time to change out of these work clothes and get into something more comfortable, something that they could relax in. As he went through his pockets to clean them out that he found that folded note once again. Unfolding it he found that it was too dark in the room that he was presently to be able to read what it said. So he headed out to the table where they had a lamp sitting that cast a brighter light. Jura was already sitting there snacking on some crackers from the bakery while she studied the books, looking over the lists of supplies and what they were short and what would be in need of replacing. Looking up as he sat down she commented, "We're going through this stuff faster than we projected. I'm going to need to get an order out to your father's caravan so that we can get the shortages in, and Sara stopped by briefly at the second bakery to pass on her needs list. She's in just about as bad as shape. Who'd have thought that we'd become so popular here and in the surrounding areas. Not me." Spying the folded paper in his hand she asked jokingly, "What's that, something from a secret admirer?"

He smiled, "Ha ha, very funny. Actually I don't know whose it's from. Somewhere along the way from the second bakery to the primary this ended up in my pocket. I know for a fact that I didn't have it when I headed over there, and when

I reached in for the list that we had put together it was there. The roads were pretty crowded, especially for a small village like this. You'd have thought that we were heading into a holiday or something important, but it was just another day. So it could have been anybody, anybody at all." He paused as he thought about his trip and remembered that someone had stumbled into him and had fallen. He had assisted the individual back up before continuing. "Hmm, that must have been it. Someone fell and I helped them back up. It would have been the perfect opportunity to slip something into one of my pockets." He looked down at the small folded piece of paper and noticed that it was similar to that other note that had been left on their doorstep.

Curious now, Jura asked, "Well, are you just going to stare at it, or are you going to open it up and read what it has to say?"

Again smiling he said, "I thought I would just stare at it." He could see that she was just about ready to hit him, and it was obvious she was burning up with curiosity. "Okay, okay, I was just thinking that this paper looks much like that other scrap we got the other night. So there's a good possibility that this is from whoever passed on that other one." He carefully unfolded the note and was silent was he read it. After reading he was quiet and she asked, "What?" He passed it over to her and here she read the words on the note.

"It is important that we begin to work together. We know that with what has transpired with Sabohl that trust is not an easy thing, and we could easily be working for him. We will be contacting you further, but must remain in the background so that Sabohl doesn't get wind of our involvement. We are aware of your discovery, and can help you beat Sabohl at his

own game, but we must do this before he has a chance to publish and thusly establish your find as his. We will be in contact with you in the next few days so be prepared with whatever notes and such that you have. Our options and time are very limited."

Like he she was silent. Looking up and then at Kal she asked, "What do we do? We were both discussing the fact that we needed help, and suddenly it's being offered. But can we trust this offer, or is it like it so stated that they could be working for Sabohl, I don't know, I just don't know. But I will say this, if there's a way to beat him I'm all for it. We did all the hard work, did all the searching, and to have him claim that he was the one and that no one other than he is responsible for this find just burns me up."

At this point trying to keep it light although he felt much the same as she, he touched her and said, "Ouch!"

Questioning that comment she asked, "Ouch, what do you mean ouch?"

Laughing now he said, "Look I know it's a very serious situation, but your comment about burning up made me do it. I know you are a hot female and I just wanted to see if your body agreed with your statement." Again he could see that she did see the humor but didn't feel it was the right time. "Look, I know, and what we have to decide is whether to trust whoever this is, or continue on our own, and the one thing both of us have already concluded is we cannot continue on our own. So now the question becomes, what can we reveal to this mystery group and what do we want to keep away from everybody? This is a very fine line that we are walking here. But at the same time I don't want us to get so wrapped up in this *intrigue* that we aren't we. That could be a bigger disaster for the two of us."

As she thought about it, what he just said made sense. With so much more going on and with everything becoming very complicated, with no clear answers, it would be so easy to slowly let their relationship slip away, and not be the wiser that it was happening. And if that did happen, and both were at that point in time, would they be looking back, questioning what had happened to bring them to the breakup? "You know I would say that what you just stated would be something that a female would figure out before you males. So I'll give it to you this time, you're right. As we've been discussing, this has gotten far beyond what we thought it would be when we, with your family's blessings, started our research and searching." She sighed, "I guess in the end it's never as simple as any of us think it will be. And I never figured that there would be outside influences and all of this happening just because you wanted to discover your, and I guess because I joined your family, and my past. Why has it gotten so complicated?"

In a soft voice Kal said, "I don't know, I just don't have any idea." At this time both were quiet with their own thoughts, Kal thinking – *We just don't have much to make a decision here, so what's the answer? If I really admit it, I haven't a clue, not one. When I had asked those questions, innocently of course, who'd have guessed that that old learned would be one who stole from his students –not I.*

Jura, leaning on the table and staring at the lantern that sat in the middle of the table, was completely at loss as to which way to go, or even to know how to come up with a decision on this one. As the note stated this could be a ruse to bring them further out into the open and then steal the rest of the valuable information that they had in their possession. And if this other group was legitimate, who could say that they wouldn't do the same thing as Sabohl? They – she and Kal – knew nothing of them either, and it could mean that they would be stepping deeper in the quagmire with a heavy fog rolling in obscuring everything – leaving them no direction, and no way out at the end of all of this.

"Look," Kal said, "We're going to have to trust someone, and right now if this note is from someone inside of Sabohl's organization, then there's little we can do about it. Still if it is someone else, then they may be our only way to keep this. I feel that we've no choice here, and if you think about it, which I know that both of us have been doing, then we've got to do something. So I think we'll need to trust this group, at least initially, and say yes. But at the same time reveal nothing about what we have as far as the family history that revealed this location to us, and if at a later time they've proven themselves then maybe at that point we can let them in on more of what we truly have."

"I guess that makes sense." Jura leaned back in her chair put her arms behind her head and stretched. "All I can say is that for me, as I've been thinking about it, I've only gone in circles with no answers at all. I know that we need help; I know we need to trust somebody, but whom? And because we know that we've been backstabbed by Sabohl, someone you trusted, then who's to say that it will be any different with these guys? We don't know them at all. For all we know they may be laughing at us right now knowing that we have no real choice in this, and in the end they'll get what they want, and we will be the ones who do the work and get nothing." She shrugged, and threw her arms out in surrender, "I just don't know. We know so little, just so little. After all, like you said, we're just bakers, business people trying to earn a living, and learn about your family's past. Is that so much to ask? Is it so much to ask people to just leave us alone and let us learn the truth?"

Again, in a quiet voice Kal said, "I guess it is, I guess it really is."

* * *

It was the middle of the present 9-day and the bakeries remained extremely busy, again as to why they had no answers, but appreciated it. Still it meant that there was too much to do and too little time to accomplish all that needed to be done. So the notes were temporarily forgotten until in a transaction another note was exchanged. When he realized that was what had happened he could only see the back of the individual who had passed the note to him as he left the bakery. With the crowds of people still waiting to be served, he couldn't stop and follow, and there was nothing out of the ordinary for Kal to be able to identify this individual. Shaking his head, he put the note away and promptly helped the next customer in line. It wasn't until he broke for the midday meal that he remembered the note. And as he and Jura sat in the office he looked up at her and said, "We had another note passed to us."

"Really?" She was sitting on the opposite side of the small desk with a sandwich in her hand and water sitting on the table. She placed the sandwich down and asked, "Did you see who it was?"

All he could do was shake his head. "By the time I realized what had happened, whoever it was was almost out the door and all I saw was his back. His clothes were nondescript, average build, nothing to identify, and no, before you ask, it's been way too busy to even find time to read it. So we can read it together." Taking a bite of his sandwich he could hear the din from the floor of the bakery. Even though many took the time to eat at the midday, it was still chaos out on that floor. He unfolded the small note, noticing that once again it was written on the same paper as the others. He read aloud these words:

"Time is very short. Sabohl is putting together his report. If we do not have something before the end of this present 9-day then he will have won this round. We will stop by every-day around the time you received this note. If you are with us then it must be now. Place your response inside the sack. The contact will be wearing a dark shirt with a torn pocket, and will comment that he had just caught this pocket on a nail, and it was his best shirt too. He will then purchase one loaf of your heavy grains bread, and be flustered as he can't find his coin purse. At which point he will look down and comment, "Ah there it is". According to the response that we receive will determine how we will proceed."

"Pressure's on that's for sure, so what do you think?"

"Too little time, too little knowledge, and still we have to make a decision – this sucks."

He laughed a little and commented, "I don't think we can put that in the return note."

"And why not? After all that's exactly the truth.

"You know you're right, but I think we need a little more than, 'it sucks', don't you think?"

CHAPTER SEVEN

THE ANCIENT CLAN SITE

It was cold, and it was snowing intermittently. Again he asked himself, why the heck was he, and especially Jura, here? While they had beaten Sabohl on both the announcement and the location, it did not matter because at this moment his minions controlled the site. Although there wasn't anybody here that could be tied directly back to him – he wasn't stupid. Kal, Jura, and the field members of the Historical Society or board, and again these members couldn't be traced back either, were looking at the entrance to the ancient clan home. They could see the smoke rising from a couple of fires, but other than that there was no movement. Not that the movement could be seen from their location. It had always been one of the advantages of this location that any attacking force would have to attack uphill and the only entrance was through a choke point giving all the advantage to the defenders. When he had finally viewed the location for the first time he really wondered how his ancestors had conquered this place. Whoever had occupied this location before his ancient ancestors would have become extremely careless to have lost it.

Well, it didn't matter now, since this place had been abandoned for a very long time, and now a descendant from that clan had come back to claim it. Not really, but in a sense this was exactly what was happening – although what was here belonged to all, not just he and his family. So here they stood in the snow and winds, remaining within the small forest out of sight.

Trehe, facing him asked, "What do you want to do? It would be nice if we could have a fire since it's so very cold right now, but I know that's not an option. We have no idea how many, or if they've just hunkered down or they have guards up and watching. There's just no way to look into that place at all to get that information."

"Yeah, and it's no wonder my clan kept this until they abandoned it. Besides I'm just a baker. I never knew anything about making attacks or searching out some place to see how many might be defending a place. So this is something you're much better at than I am."

Trehe shrugged, "Not really. I've been assigned, well the group that I'm a part of, is assigned on keeping track of everything that Sabohl is involved with. And believe me, that's a full time job all by itself. He's smart, and he keeps his ties hidden as much as possible. And, as you've learned, much of his ties are to less than reputable members of our society. After all, as we explained to you, it was this group who were responsible for the break-in of your shelter when you were gone. Look I'm freezing out here. We need to come up with some way to get inside there and expel the ones who are there, some ruse or something. I really don't think there are that many, but I could be wrong. Oh, by the way can you use that staff?"

"I'm okay with it, but I'll never be as good as Jura."

"Jura? Your mate? A female who is good with a staff, really . . . Now this I've got to see."

Kal smiled, "I wouldn't challenge her, it might damage your male ego."

Trehe laughed, "Then this I've really got to see. You must be just fair if a female could beat you."

Shaking his head, Kal said, "Don't say I didn't warn you." He turned around and signaled Jura to join him and once she did he said, "Jura, Trehe wants to challenge you to a round with the staff. I warned him but he can't believe that such a small female, or any female, could defeat such a big male as he. So let's head to the other side of these trees – besides the exercise will warm us up." They headed out the backside of the trees close to the area where the original two that had followed them had camped. The others followed not knowing what was transpiring. Turning to the rest Kal said, "Your leader has challenged Jura to a round with the staff. He said that he would go easy, after all there's no female out there that can defeat a male. Not my words but his." He looked over at Jura who had an evil smile, and he knew that from being with her as long as he had that Trehe was just about to learn an important lesson."

As they entered the area where the boulders were Trehe stated, "Look I'll go easy on you. After all you are a female and aren't very big."

"She smiled back saying, "Two falls is standard for a round. Is that okay with you?"

"No, I said I'd go easy so one is fine, unless you want it the other way."

"I think two is better. That way if you fall both times it can't be the result of you tripping or something, leading you to believe that this was just a fluke."

"Okay, shall we?"

A line was drawn in the dirt, although because of the cold and the light snow it was more a scratch than a line. Both toed the line to signal they were ready and she at first appeared to handle the staff a bit clumsy. Trehe seeing an advantage immediately attacked but to his surprise she easily blocked his attack followed by a quick counter that swept his feet out from under him and he landed heavily on the ground at which time she placed the end on his chest marking a fall. She turned demurely and casually toed the line allowing him to see her very feminine posterior, turned around and leaned back on her staff. She smiled and simply waited until he stood up and carefully approached the toe line. "That had to be an accident young one, but you won't be able to do that again."

Again she smiled and didn't say a thing. She stepped back casually again inviting him to attack which this time he refused. He was noticing that there appeared too much efficiency and fluidity to her movements. So with heavier concentration and care he came at her with his staff at the ready position. No, he wasn't going to allow some slip of a female beat him at this. Attacking with a feint, followed by a sweep at the knees meant to bring a person down she easily dodged the move and then blocked the follow-through. Again she smiled at him and at all times didn't appear to handle the staff well at all. Yet, everything he had tried, to this point had failed. It was time to just finish this and put her down. So he attacked with the idea of coming down on her head followed by a strike with the lower portion of the staff aimed at her hips followed by an upper cut directed at her chest and neck. To his surprise she easily blocked every one of those moves. *Who is this female anyway?* She teased him with what looked like an unskilled move, but with what he had experienced he didn't take the offer.

Again she looked at him and smiled. The ones who were witnessing this were silent. Their boss had bested every one of them a number of times, both in practice, and in some of the rounds they had worked to keep in shape. Here was a female who had already put him on the ground, and so far he hadn't been able to get past her defenses – unheard of. Both came to the ready signaling that they were ready to continue. Using what he considered his size, weight and strength he feinted with an attack low using his left hand to bring the lower end of the staff at speed to her legs followed by an immediate swing through to bring the upper end of the staff to the top of her head. While this move looked awkward, he had practiced it much and it had been one of the moves that he used to successfully defeat the ones who worked with him. Inwardly he was smiling because it seemed that the move was going to work as it always had in the past. With speed and precision he made his follow through expecting to make contact, only to find that she had immediately blocked the move and had followed through with one of her own using the left end of her staff to hit him in the stomach.

The move was completely unexpected and had pushed him back and off balance, and instead of following through, and putting him on the ground a second time, she deliberately placed the left end of the staff on the ground and held it at the ready giving him a chance to recover. *Again, who is this female?* Now cautious, he approached studying his opponent.

Yet there seemed to be nothing special about her or the way she held her staff. He was at loss as to how she had been able to block his attacks and feints, let alone turn the tables on him. He decided that he would use a flurry of combinations to overwhelm her, starting with an attack at the legs with the bottom of the staff, bringing it around at her head with the upper end followed by a thrust and then an attack to her mid-section, but she blocked every one. She smiled at him and said quietly, "If you want to stop now and save your male ego we can, and I'll even allow you to call it a draw and that you just had a bad day."

Here was a way out. He suspected that with the ease that she'd defeated all of his favorite moves that most likely she could have put him on the ground a second time and won the round. "Okay, I'll accept that, but I don't want you to go around bragging that a mere slip of a female defeated me."

Again she smiled, "I said that we could call it a draw. I'm not looking to brag about anything like that. After all it would mean that there would be many out there that would want to challenge me just to prove I was lying. Besides, whether you want to accept it or not, I'm better than you, and it has nothing to do with your abilities, which I have to admit, are pretty good. But you see my sires are regional champions with the staff, and I, with my siblings, have been trained since we learned to walk on how to use the staff. Then we used to have free-for-alls involving all of us children and then every once in a while my sires would join the fray. We'd all end up with our share of hurts and bruises, but it was fun. So instead of proving that I can beat you, which I think you now know that I can do, I thought it would be just as wise to test your skill and just give you a taste of mine. Kal did warn you not to do this. He's had a taste of our wide open staff sessions where all of us attacked each other."

Shaking his head and smiling looking briefly over in the direction of Kal and then back at her he said, "At least you could have warned me, then I wouldn't have made a fool of myself."

Again she smiled, "Would you have believed me if I suggested that I was better than you?"

Shrugging he said, "Probably not. I've never met a female who was interested in the use of the staff, let alone be good at it. I guess the joke's on me." Turning and facing Kal he asked, "So I guess you did warn me. And you being her mate how have you fared against her?"

Kal laughed, "I have more bruises, bumps, and hurts to count and that's not including the many to my ego as she easily bested me and still does. But you see because of where I come from and do I never really needed to learn to use the staff. So I was clumsy and awkward, slow, and she was patient to bring me along to where I am. But I don't come close to her competence, or ability. Then I visited her family on the farm and witnessed one of their free-for-alls, and then got involved with them. To be honest I got beat up pretty good. And even her youngest sister bested me without even raising a sweat. Look they told me a story and after watching them in action I know that they didn't exaggerate anything at all. Let's just say that the ones who attacked them got a surprise and quickly left."

Laughing now Trehe said, "At least you could've reinforced that warning to me."

"Well, if you think about it," Kal replied, "I did warn you, but for some reason you didn't believe me."

"I guess that I have to admit that's a true statement. I figured that she was just putting me on and that I needed to put her in her place." He then laughed harder, "Guess it was me who got put in his place." He stood quietly for a moment deep in thought. "This gives me an idea, since I now know that I won't have to worry about you, Jura, and it's this . . ." He went on to explain and the two of them could see the logic in it. It would be a way to get inside the site and with the two of them, Kal and Jura drawing attention to themselves the others could sneak in and then drive out whoever was occupying the site.

Even though it was difficult to tell through the lightly blowing snow that was falling, dusk was on its way, and the dropping temperatures were reflecting that change. "Hey Kal," Jura said, "There's a chance that we can get out of this up above." It was hoped that the ones who were occupying the site presently didn't know that it was the two of them that had located this place back in the Season of Falling.

"Are you sure? I mean we've somehow got ourselves all turned around and we need to find a place for the night." He was trailing a little behind giving the appearance of reluctance for passing up the shelter that the trees may have offered.

She stopped and turned around. "Look I know that the trees could have provided some protection. But both of us know that when we were standing in there trying to decide whether to continue or stay that the winds just cut, so there's a chance that just a little ahead there might be someplace better. Besides if we don't then we can always return to those trees." Not waiting for a response she headed up through the gap in the rock face and he followed.

Both of them had spoken loudly making it appear that they were trying to be heard over the growing winds, but were actually putting on a show for the ones that were just a little ahead of them. They were hoping by being so obvious that any attention would be drawn their way, and as they passed through that gap, the others hid behind that rock face so that they could listen for the expected challenge. "Hey Kal, I smell smoke. I think someone has the same idea." Jura stopped and waited for Kal to join her, and both took a deep breath as they were nervous at this point, since shortly they would be challenged, and they would know how many were here. They didn't have to wait long as from the direction where the leader's shelter had originally stood they were approached by four individuals. "Whew, are we glad to see you," Kal said. "We made a wrong turn somewhere down below and it wasn't until we got up here that we realized it and then the winds picked up and it got colder and the snows started blowing and we knew that we needed to find some place to wait out the night. I wanted to stay down in the trees, but my mate here," he pointed at Jura, "wanted to look a little further before it got dark. And I guess she was right. Since it appears that the four of you have already established a camp which means that it has to be a better place than where I wanted to camp. You know down in those trees."

The one who appeared to be the leader looked at the other three knowingly and then at Jura and Kal. He smiled and said, "That's true. This is a better place for a camp. What are you doing out here in this remote place? There's nothing around for a very long way from here."

Jura looked disgusted and pointed her finger at him saying, "He thought he knew a quicker way through this area. We were heading for that small village that sits close to the Sacred Mountains. We are to meet some of his distant family members who wanted to meet me, but I guess they'll just have to wait. Hey maybe you guys know the right trail." She smiled and then with the encouragement of the leader the two began to retreat towards the hidden fire. Jura then asked, "By the way, what are the four of you doing out here? Did you get lost too?"

This brought laughter from the four. Since they were from the underworld, thieves and such, they felt that luck had just turned in their direction. After all they had been complaining about being stuck here in the cold, with no female companionship or any ale to drink and what shows up at their proverbial doorstep but a female, and accompanied by a single male. And with the remoteness of this location, if the two disappeared and were never heard from again then it would be chalked up as the outback taking two more. Yes it would be an enjoyable night, at least for the four of them. The other two, well that was their problem wasn't it? So concentrating on the two of them, the four surrounded them and casually led them back to the fire with all sorts of imaginings in their minds of what would be happening this night. But when they headed around the small obstruction that hid their fire both from sight and the winds to their surprise six unknown males were standing there warming themselves.

Looking over at them Trehe said, "Nice fire you've going here and such a nice location. Oh I suspect all those plans you had wanting to take advantage of the two poor lost travelers isn't going to happen. Instead the four of you are simply going to pack up what you have and leave. Now before you say anything you have two choices in this, you can go without putting up a fight or you can, but in the end the results will be the same. Besides knowing the type I'm looking at here I suspect that what you had planned wouldn't have happened anyway. You see that female that looks like such an easy target would have whipped all of you and probably not even raised a sweat doing it." He could see the disbelief in their eyes and he smiled. "You know I'm almost tempted to let you try. But that would be a waste of effort and energy and you'll need that energy to get back down before this storm moves in with full force. So be good little ones, grab your gear and just leave, and let your bosses know that this site is no longer yours."

* * *

Sabohl was furious. He wasn't used to the idea that someone would do to him what he had been doing to others for many cycles of the seasons. He figured that even though the two, Kal and Jura, had gotten the information and announcement that specifically identified the site that they had discovered, in the public view ahead of him, that in the end he would still win. He had control of the site after all, and later he could claim that they were the usurpers claiming something that he had discovered with his team and they had ridden his coattails so to speak. Then came the word that not only had they beaten him to the specific announcement, but now had ejected his people from the site and they now were sitting on it. *Well, one thing for sure, this cannot stand. I've got to get them out of there and immediately begin to undermine this whole thing. Just because they did the legwork means nothing, the site is mine. They have no right to it. I'm on top because I know better how to treat the site, how to let others know what is there, and most of all, how to interpret what is found.*

The blowing storm outside rattled his door and with the air that escaped into the room where he was sitting caused the lights to flicker dangerously, coming close to being blown out. None of this helped his mood. He stood and paced a bit and went over to his rather large roaring fire and warmed his hands. At least he had this one consolation; he was here where it was warm, while they were on that site of his in this storm. This brought a chuckle to his lips and an evil smile. *They weren't going to be there long.* He'd be sure of that – although at this moment he really had no plans of how he was going to remove them. The only satisfaction he had, even though the news had been bleak, was the cowering reaction from the ones who had reported the failure to him. He remembered yelling at them and literally throwing them out of his shelter. He really needed to learn to control his temper. *Let them freeze, in the end I'll still have the site, and I'll still be in charge.* He paused a second in his thoughts as another crossed his mind. *Who's behind this? It can't be just those two. Even with family help they wouldn't have the understanding or wherewithal to pull this off. But from what I've gathered nobody recognized the ones who were with the two of them. Is there someone else working in the shadows?*

He looked around his shelter in that particular room. It all appeared to be too ordinary, too normal, *why is this happening, why is this particular operation falling apart*? Hadn't he planned well, and hadn't he kept on top of all of the developments, hadn't he kept the two under constant surveillance, yes, so why were things going so wrong? Well, this had to change and change now. With a decision he sat back down, wrote a quick note, shrugged into his heavy coat and exited the shelter. It was night, and nobody was here to notice that he had left, and nobody would think it strange if he went out at night. It was another one of the many ruses that he had developed over time. This going out at odd times so that it would appear to be something that he normally did. He stuffed the completed and folded note into his pocket and headed out the door only to be hit was a very strong and cold wind that snatched the door out of his hands and slammed against the side of the shelter, blowing loose papers off the tables inside, scattering them everywhere. He cursed, grabbed the door, and slammed it shut. *Damn, now I've another mess to straighten out, and damn my temper.*

Unknown to Sabohl, like he, and his many minions who kept watch on the ones that he deemed important, he too was under observation. And as long as they remained unknown to him, they would be able to track and document his night time travels, which in the end could, and probably would become critical in finally destroying the power that he held . . . Finally eliminating his narrow minded views, and the refusal to accept any others however compelling – other than his own. "I wonder where the great Sabohl could be heading out on such a night as this?" One of the unknown watchers asked.

"Don't know, but I suspect that when he got that news earlier today that it didn't bode well for the ones who had reported it to him." This brought a quiet laugh from the three of them who had the duty tonight. "I guess", the first one said, "that we had better see what he's up to." He stood up in the shadows and asked, "Shall we?" Knowing most of the routes that Sabohl took, the three of them spread out and covered them while remaining hidden and in the shadows. They suspected that he was heading for one of his many drops, and because it was as nasty as the weather was, maybe for the first time they might get a chance to see what was actually written there, but they really doubted it. Besides it wasn't worth the chance of discovery. It had taken too many cycles of the seasons to establish their network and to have him discover them now, well that could end their chance of toppling him and getting someone in there who was more conducive to the ideas and facts that were being presented and uncovered.

* * *

The storm had rolled in with its full fury – winds, blowing snow, and so much of the white stuff falling that it was almost impossible to see. Jura wondered how their ancestors survived in this stuff. And while the location was such that it was an easy place to defend, it surely didn't protect one from the elements. The eight of them had moved their camp back against one of the rock faces that was located on the east end of the site. She suspected, from the reading of the journals, that this was where the priest compound had been located. And when she saw the layout of this area it made complete sense. The priests were the warriors of their ancient gods and not warriors against other tribes and clans. So to have the whole clan of warriors between the entrance and the location of the where the priests lived meant that if an attacking force reached the priests' compound, then all was lost anyway. Still that didn't help keep one warm when facing one of these storms this far to the north.

If anybody had any sense at all, and that includes me, none of us would be out in this. I'm an outback female and used to nasty weather, but this is so much worse than anything we face down from where we are from. I thought those storms were bad, but now I've been proven to be quite wrong. And it would now make sense that the ones they were supposedly chasing, that remnant from one of those lairs, the ones who died in the Sacred Mountains would have to face even harsher storms than this. With them having to fight for every step and not prepared for any of this, plus to have been with child and from the words this female was late in her carrying, it's no surprise that they died. Although that doesn't explain the death of that patrol, who knows maybe they had some bad food or something. Anyway with only three surviving to that point it would have been easy for them to sneak around that encampment and disappear into the Sacred Mountains only to succumb to the weather. Now that sucks, it really does. To have been so close to safety, and away from the attackers, only to die in one of the storms. I wonder who these people were and whether we needed to bring destruction down on them like we did.

Well, maybe, since we did find this site, this could mean that the rest that are mentioned in the journals are real. Even though they are dead and gone now, and not just from destruction and death, but almost from memory, and who would have thought it would be that way? Actually so close to being forgotten completely, and then their whole lives were being turned into myth instead of being real. Yet being here right now and being cold was very real. She wondered how her ancestors could live like this. At least the clans had permanent shelters, but the tribes moved all the time with those temporary shelters, and they had to be so much worse than the clan homes. But all of this was unknown, conjecture on her part. Shrugging, she didn't have any answers, and she snuggled deeper down under the coverings to keep warm. While the rock faces kept most of the winds away, every once in a while a gust would find its way in and chill them more than they already were. Finally she moved closer to Kal and snuggled up close to share their body heat. The fire that the group had burning was more for cheer. The storm seemed to steal the heat right from it, although if one got up very close they could feel some heat. Smiling and trying to keep it light Kal whispered, "Careful there Jura, I might think that you're interested in getting physical as close as you're getting."

She forced a smile and shook her head. "Yeah I can see that, but I'm not the type that will perform in front of an audience, and you have to admit we have one. Plus, even though I know you're joking, you'd not get me to undress in this kind of weather. So we'll just have to share each other's body heat and try and keep warm that way."

He put his arms around her and pulled her closer saying, "That's fine with me, at least we're together. And I don't think we'll have to worry about anyone moving in this weather – although I doubt that Sabohl will take this well. I suspect that we're going to have to face something after this storm clears. After facing this one, and knowing that there are probably others on their way, storms that is, I think I'm quite happy not to have lived here back in the distant past. This would have been just pure misery. No wonder there were so many deaths recorded during the Season of Cold. Our shelters we have now are so much better built than they were in the days of the journals; at least I think so from the descriptions. Although I have to admit that having you this close is so tempting – something about being male with a female this close to me, especially you – oh well, so be it."

She smiled back at him even though it was a weak one. *Yes getting physical would have been nice.* It would have taken her mind off of being so cold, even if it was for a very brief period of time. And the physical activity, while not vigorous, would warm one, followed by the afterglow and the closeness, sharing everything they had. *Yes, such a nice thought.* This brought her full circle as she thought about the life style of their ancient ancestors. The idea that a female, when requested from the herd for breeding would be required to be ready, which meant that she'd be without her clothes – in weather like this, right. There had to be something that wasn't written in those journals that covered weather like this. Well, she'd have to search them out and see. One thing for sure being a female and having to live that life style was beyond her comprehension. So what did the females do? There was some distance between the shelters where the female herd lived and where the warriors' shelters were located. And a warrior would have to first go to the herd's location, make his request, and return to the warrior's shelter where the female would make an appearance. *Guess our ancestors were much hardier than we are today. Because there's nothing mentioned it probably was considered unimportant. Wow, unimportant? For one to have to move through this stuff, not fully clothed, and consider it nothing – almost impossible to believe. I guess that would make one appreciate the warm body on the other end though, but afterwards to immediately return – still beyond me, that's for sure.* Still, she had to admit that right now that warm body next to her was very nice and comforting.

Kal had to admit that having Jura this close to him made it almost impossible to think of anything else other than mating. It was the nature of the male, at least from what he had gathered in his short life, to be physical with a female whenever she'd allow it. And even though many males felt that they controlled such encounters, it really wasn't true. Of course if the encounter was forced, that would be different. But in a normal relationship, since the female received the male, it was her decision if and when it would happen. And, of course, there had to be included in this, the fact their fertile cycle led to the bleeding at which time mating was not allowed. Although here and now, while they were under the large cover they would be out of sight of any here, but it would be obvious to any who looked their way what was happening. Then they faced the problem of how to handle cleaning up afterwards. So he knew from a practical point of view he would have to leave it at the thinking part, and leave the physical part out. Even though he had fun teasing her, and at the same time he had to admit that she returned it in like. Taking a deep breath and letting it out slowly he said. "Yeah I know that we'd enjoy it, but it's just something that we'd probably regret later. I mean I know that we'd both enjoy the closeness and the heat, but there's no place to take care of what we'd need to afterwards, and there's always that particular odor that tells anybody who's close by what one was doing." Shaking his head he continued, "Although . . . Although with you this close . . ." He hugged her tighter which she returned and the clung to each other for a while listening to the howling winds, the whipping of the small portable shelter flap where the supplies were kept, and the crackling of the blazing fire. Soon they would retire to their own cold portable shelter.

* * *

It was two days later when the storm finally blew itself out. When they all emerged from the portable shelters it was to a transformed white world. Yes there had been a little snow around before this, but just enough to say that it had snowed. Now it appeared to be closer to the middle of the Season of

Cold, although it truly was only beginning. Trehe turned to all of them as they stood there and stated, "If this amount fell from this first major storm, then this place will get buried pretty deep in this stuff." Turning to his group he continued as he pointed to four of them saying, "As you know there's a village close, a couple of days away from here. I need you to go and pick up additional supplies. Plus we'll need to get something that will allow us to build some better lean-tos. I can see that these portable shelters are just not going to work by themselves. So go and there's an account set up there so place these items on that account. The ones that we work for will be sure that what we get is paid for. Now go and be back as quick as you can. Yes I know that knocks us down to just four of us here, but I think if we do this now that we will beat any retaliation that Sabohl will be sending. And we all know that somewhere and somehow he will not take this lying down."

As the four left he turned to Kal and Jura and asked, "What were your plans for this place once you discovered it?"

Looking at each other and then back at him Kal said. "I, we really never thought that far ahead. I mean while I have enjoyed history and excelled in it really, that was in the learned centers – I really have no practical experience in this at all."

Laughing, even though there was no humor in the laugh Trehe said, "You really didn't consider what this would mean to our people? That finding this place would start the change of how we view our past and could change what had been conjectured about that time?"

"Well, yes, actually that part did come to mind. But once we found this place," he paused trying to find the words, "hmmm, what I mean is that we really never knew if we could find it. Yes we had this rough map, but it had never been made with the idea or the way maps are made today with south being on top and north being on the bottom. So as large, as we learned, an area as these northern foothills are we could have spent a lifetime looking and never find the proper orientation, let alone the proper place, in these foothills to match the map. We were lucky that it only took a season, but even still we had some hints that helped. But we hadn't really thought much beyond just finding it."

"I guess that makes sense. Well, now that you have found it, now comes the problem of keeping it. Because soon we will be receiving guests, guests from Sabohl – he won't give up this easily. Especially since this is a very, very important abandoned site, critical really. And I can guarantee that if he fails in his next move that this won't end it either. The Season of Cold is long and we are in a very remote area. Even with the advances that have been made, since this place was active, people are lost to be never found out here. So if for some reason you were to disappear and your bodies never located it would be just be a case of someone else falling victim to the outback. While I cannot begin to know what is happening back where Sabohl lives and who he has contacted, I know that he has something in the works and that will bode bad for us. It will mean that there will be little or no chance, other than maybe mapping this place, to work or research it. Instead, once we have the tools, we'll have to do as your ancestors did and make this into a fortress once again. So we have much work ahead of us."

Shaking his head Kal said, "I really didn't expect any of this to happen. I mean when I got this information," thinking as he was passing on this he thought. *So how much do I dare tell them? I know that they are risking their lives to be here and to help. But what is their agenda, why have they gotten involved? And I really haven't even begun to know who they represent. This still could be an elaborate ruse by Sabohl and we are the ones that it's being played against.* "There was a great possibility that what I had wouldn't be worth the paper it was written on. It could have been something that was added to my family long after this place had been abandoned, and since my family claims to be from this clan, the clan of K'jor, then there was always a possibility that someone in my line decided to create a map to give credence to the family history. So, in the end, it easily could have been a chase after those twirling dust spirals that we all like to chase when we are young. It was another reason why neither of us had thought beyond just finding this place."

Throughout this conversation Jura remained quiet, but what Kal was saying wasn't quite the truth. Later she would confront him as to why the deception, but for now, because she didn't understand, she remained silent. *Just what is he doing? Doesn't he trust these people? Well, I guess I can understand that. This adventure has turned out to be so much more complicated than either of us thought it would be. With the blessings of his family of course, we went out looking for his, well ours, since I'm now part of his family also, past. And while, yes, he's supposedly from an important clan, and again supposedly a direct descendant of K'jor, the first leader to unite the tribes and clans, it was still kind of a private thing.* Sighing quietly as she continued to watch and listen to the exchange her thoughts continued. *But here we are just after one of the storms in the north inside the abandoned clan home and who'd have thought that, not me. At first I had held out little hope of finding this place, and then when we did that that would be it. Great! We did it! But instead here we are in the middle of something that's so much bigger than the two of us and this truly beyond our understanding.*

She found that she had been staring out at nothing and had actually quit listening and was caught off guard when she heard her name. "Yes?" She turned towards the one who had mentioned her name and it was Kal who signaled her to come away with him to a different part of the site. She followed as he headed back towards the rock face that they were using as a windbreak and sheltered area during the storm. She waited until they had reached the area where they were staying and asked, "So why the misdirection? The ones who are here are helping us, and as far as I know, they don't have to."

"Now I can't say for sure if that's true or not. I just don't know enough about them to really know who they are and what organization they're a part of. They've been pretty secretive on that aspect. So I don't know anything really, and because of this I still don't trust them. They could be laughing behind our backs with the secret knowledge that they actually work for Sabohl, and all of this is to get us into their confidence and when we fully trust them we then become their victims. This has gotten so much more complicated than I ever expected. Yeah, I knew that this site could be important, but I didn't expect all the trouble finding this place has caused and from what I can see, will continue to cause. In a sense, even though we are the discoverers here, we are the ones on the outside. And as we continue, it just seems that things are becoming as clear as mud and we know less and less. I'm almost sorry that we started all of this and sometimes wish we could just go back to before this started, before we made a decision to pursue this, change our minds and let someone in one of the future generations do the discovering. But we can't change any of this and so here we are. And because of this I'm not going to reveal any more than I have too."

She paused thinking about what he had just said and could see the logic in it. Truthfully what did they really know, and like he said, the two of them were the ones on the outside. From her observations of this team that was helping them, and especially Trehe, it appeared to be an old game – one that they had played too many times. Who'd have thought that all of this was going on all of the time and ones like the two of them being completely unaware? And if it was like this for the learned, how was it for others vying for power? She had to admit that this was a very scary thought. That there was always someone in the background trying to get on top and stay there and others just as determined to topple them. Taking a deep cleansing breath she let it out slowly, "Yeah, I guess now that my eyes are being opened it would be nice to just go back to when I was ignorant of all of this. But, as you've said, we can't undo any of this and we are very stuck – and unfortunately, as you just pointed out, at the mercy of Trehe and his group. In a way I wish I hadn't tipped my hand back there and shown them my skill with the staff. If they are working for Sabohl then we would have a chance to get away because of their ignorance."

"True, in a way this is like one of those really bad books or bad dreams where you know what's coming but can do nothing to stop it. And what has been aptly pointed out is our isolation, and we are really isolated here." Kal began to pace just a little, realized that was what he was doing, and stopped.

Shaking his head he said, "Don't want to it to appear that we may be doubting them." He was silent, shrugged, saying, "I'm out of ideas of how to get us out of this mess, and I have to apologize to you for putting you in the middle of this."

Quietly Jura replied, "Not your fault. I walked into this with my eyes open. I just hope that Trehe and his are here to really help. And yes, we stupidly walked into this and have completely isolated ourselves – not a good thing, that's for sure."

CHAPTER EIGHT

DEFENSE

It took a 9-day for the ones who had gone for the supplies to return. In that time another storm had blown through and for now it was clear and very cold. So other than when they went down to the tree line to gather firewood and look to building up the fortifications, they all stayed close to the fires. Nothing throughout this time had led either Kal or Jura to completely trust the group that they were staying with at this time. While they were not prisoners by any means, with the weather as it was, they were going nowhere. So other than trips to take care of nature they remained together. But at the same time were attempting to make it appear that they had no suspicions or fears. It was a difficult road to walk. For all they knew, they had enemies within, and enemies without. Still both had to admit that at this point, other than the suspicions that they harbored, Trehe and his seemed only to want to help protect this important site and the two of them.

Now with the full crew back, and with the tools that the ones brought with them, they began to build a gate across the open path into the ancient clan home. To put up a similar defense that the ones who had lived here so long ago had done, successfully defending it until it had finally been abandoned. While weapons had improved over time, as is usually the case, this location still had the advantage that to enter and attack required the attackers to go through a bottle neck with the defenders being on higher ground, leaving the advantage to the defenders. Still with such a small group and their constant need for firewood, they had to leave the protection and work the trees and haul the dead wood up to where it would be available. At this time it was the weak point in their defense. So once they had finished their rough gate all of them proceeded to drag as much of the wood and scrap up to their camp within the compound.

"You know," Trehe said, "that moving this wood warms you twice."

"Twice?" How could that be?" Jura asked.

Smiling he replied, "It's quite simple really. As we work to move this stuff up to our camp, the exercise warms us, so that's the first time. Then we burn it and feel the heat and it keeps us warm, and that's the second time. So it warms us twice."

"Okay smarty, I guess that's true. I must admit that I hadn't thought about it that way, but you're right." She stopped and rested a moment as the piece of dead wood she was dragging up was heavier than she thought and she needed a break to get her strength back. Looking around she could see most of the ones there was doing the very same thing – moving the large limbs, stopping, catching their breath, which was coming out in clouds of steam, and then continuing the trek up the hill. Eventually she was ready once again and began dragging her piece up into the area where they were stockpiling the wood. She stopped suddenly as an idea crossed her mind.

Grabbing Trehe she said, "Look I just realized that we may be making a mistake."

"Mistake? How so? Do you mean moving wood up by the camp?"

"No, no, we need to do that. But we are putting all the wood in one pile. I think we need to put it into a number of piles because it is the one thing we have no way of replacing. If those others that you suspect are coming find a way to set it on fire, then we would have to abandon our defense because it would be too cold for us to be able to hold it."

"You know you're absolutely right, and I didn't even consider it. Hey, I'm the one with the experience here, and I missed that one completely. Okay we'll do that immediately."

That night they rested since it had been a full day of hauling the wood up to their camp, and both Jura and Kal were finding muscles that they didn't know that they had. The skies were unbelievably clear and the stars were so bright that it seemed one could reach up and touch them. As they stared up at the night sky it suddenly lit up with a bright fire as a fireball streaked across the sky briefly lighting the area. It had begun it's streaking above the sacred mountains in the north and appeared to be traveling completely across the visible sky until it disappeared in the distance slowly growing dim as it traveled away from them. "Wow! That was spectacular!" Jura exclaimed. "I know that I've seen a few of these things back on the farm but nothing quite as bright or as large as that one. I always wondered what those things were, but I probably will really never know."

"Know what you mean. Although from the village and the light that comes from it you never see many of them. It's only after you've gotten away from those lights that one can see more of them. And I always liked the lightshow anyway, didn't think anything about them. I guess I can see how our distant ancestors would have considered them something from the gods." Both of them moved closer together because of the bitter cold. With the clear skies it appeared that any of the heat, not that there had been much, had been sucked away from the earth leaving only the cold. This made the warming fire so much more inviting as well as each other.

* * *

For the next several days it remained clear and cold. While it was necessary to continue to work on their defense, one couldn't remain too long from the heat of the fires. Kal thought, *what a miserable place to have to spend the Season of Cold.* The area was exposed to the winds coming from above off the higher peaks in the northern foothills. He began to understand why his ancestors had finally abandoned this place. With the exposure they had on this small plateau, once the need for defense was ending, there were many other locations that would provide a better place to live. Yet, he had to agree that it was a place that would have been hard to conquer. Making him again wonder how it had first been done. Looking at his hands he could see blisters forming. While no stranger to hard work, the life as a baker created other calluses and these did not come into play with the cutting and moving of timber as they worked to create a new stronger wall and gate to block the single way into and out of this area.

Inside the site they were careful to only walk and travel along one path so as to not disturb what history might still be locked here. And even though most of what had been here was constructed of wood and had long disappeared over the interval of time that had passed, there would be other such things that would remain. But these thoughts at this time were the furthest thing from his mind. Sabohl would be doing something to take back this site so that he could claim it as his own. It had become obvious to Kal that this one was very smart to have been able to maintain his position of the learned and leader in his field and at the same time be ruthless in the background to maintain his leadership. So he really had no idea what would transpire and had to depend on Trehe who appeared to be experienced in dealing with Sabohl. His thoughts were interrupted when he heard one of Trehe's team yell out that someone was approaching. Looking up from the log that he was dressing, removing the limbs and smoothing so that it would fit into the hole that had been dug, as it was to be the support for the gate, the one that the rest attached, he paused.

Leaning back and stretching his back and twisting his neck to relieve the pain from bending over so much, he looked towards the trail where any that came here would have to approach, and watched as Trehe and the rest headed down to the tree line and disappeared. He turned at the sound of approaching footsteps and saw that Jura was approaching with a questioning look. Shaking his head he said, "I don't know."

She came up and stood beside him shaking from the cold a little. "Getting away from the fires makes one appreciate them," she said. For now she had taken over the cooking duties, not that she couldn't have assisted with the building of the gate, but someone needed to do this chore, and right now to build this thing required brute strength and she hadn't been blessed with that. So together the two of them stood looking over the tree line waiting to see what would happen. Turning once again and facing Kal she said, "I barely heard the yell, couldn't make out the words really. But the others took off quick. You didn't go with them?"

With his arms folded and continuing to look out over the lower area he said, "No, Trehe signaled me to stay here, so that's what I'm doing. They didn't look worried so I don't know if there was only a couple of whoever it was or maybe something else. I guess we'll just have to wait and see." Looking at her he could see that she was shaking so he put his arm around her. At this moment from the work he had been doing he wasn't cold, but suspected that if they stood around too long that he would join her. "Why not head back to the fires. You can at least look over at me and I can either yell to you or signal to you what's going on. Truthfully it's no fun being cold and I have to say this makes me appreciate my ancestors much more if they faced this every Season of the Cold. Suspect that they probably spent most of it inside their shelters anyway. I know that I would."

"Okay, I have to admit that I'm very cold just standing here. But, well, if you keep me informed I guess I'll head back." She gently pulled away from his embrace and reluctantly headed back to the fires. She had to admit that this place was so much colder than where she had grown up.

As he waited he found that he was beginning to cool down and soon he would have to join her by the fires if there was no sign of what was transpiring soon. Turning so that she could see him he smiled, although from this distance he didn't know if she could see that or not, then signaled that nothing had changed. He turned back around to see Trehe emerging from the trees and with him there were now at least nine others that he had never seen before. Alarmed now, he turned and signaled Jura that he wanted to meet her and hurried in her direction as she did his. "I don't know what's happening but we have at least twice the number that we did just a short time ago. I truly hope that they are really here to help, because if we've been fooled there will be no way out for either of us." This raised the tension level on both of them, but there was nothing that they could do to change it now. "It would be so easy for us to disappear and never be heard from again, and with all of this open land our bodies would never be found, and we'd just become what so many others have. Darn! I know I've said it before, but I almost wish we were back just working the bakery and ignorant of this, being warm and safe, maybe looking to the day when we became a family. Yet, here we are." Shrugging and shaking his head he was silent. *Why us? Why has things just gone this way? Am I so naïve that I couldn't see this coming? Well stupid, obviously the answer is yes.*

Jura remained silent she was at loss as to what to do. While Trehe had appeared to be just who he said he was, there really had never been any proof one way or the other, leaving both of them unsure. Sure everything seemed to be in order all the way back to when they began to contact them through the notes and bakery, but all of this had been beyond her and so subtle that it was well beyond her grasp. Were they now to be at their mercy, and especially she since she was the only female here, to be played with as these wanted? It was a scary thought, and one she wanted nothing to do with. But she was learning that one could easily walk into something completely ignorant and then pay the price for that ignorance. She looked at Kal and asked, "What do you want to do? It's not like we can just get up and walk out of here. In fact with the ones who are here we were never really alone. There was always some-one with one or the other of us. And now there are more." Closing her eyes and grimacing, she quietly said, "I can only hope that what we've been told is true. Otherwise I believe that we are in a very big mess and there's no way out." *I thought that at the beginning of all of this we would be having fun, well in a sense fun. We'd be having an adventure that in our old time we could look back, tell stories about that time, and smile as we made the adventure seem so much more than it truly was. But now is there even going to be an old time for us? Are we going to leave a next generation to learn, to grow, and to discover things that we've never dreamed of? Or, is this where it will end for us? Well, I guess we'll know shortly.* "Let's go back to the fire, I'm getting cold."

Together with arms around each other's shoulders they strolled back to the fires and sat down on one of the logs that had been dragged here for just that purpose and waited. After all, what else could they do? In moments they would have their questions answered, one way or the other, and in the end it probably didn't matter since they had no control on either the answers or the outcome. They didn't have long to wait as the much larger group approached the campsite and both of them could hear the pleasant conversation and some laughter that was being spread among the group. Jura's ears perked up as she thought she heard some higher voices. *Did that mean that they brought children with them? Now Jura that doesn't make any sense,* she admonished herself. *Well, if not young ones maybe a couple of more females?* She wondered why she had come to the conclusion that there was more than one. Since she only had heard the voices. *The voices that's it. There is more than one. Hmmm, this could change that fore-*

boding feeling I'm having. If they have brought other females then maybe it's just as Trehe has said. She laughed inwardly at this conclusion. *Now that really is stupid. Not all females have mates, or are nice. They could as easily be here just to service these males and make something for themselves out of this.*

Jura and Kal didn't have to wait very much longer as the combined group reached the fire. Along with the group came a couple of pack beasts fully loaded with supplies, and now counting all the new faces there were a total of eleven, making the group that was part of Trehe seventeen. They definitely were outnumbered, very easily could end up being prisoners, but as he looked over the group saw that there were three females with them. Okay what were they doing here?

Trehe looking at the two of them could see a little fear and a very questioning look. He smiled and said, "I know that this is unexpected, and I wasn't sure that we'd be able to get them to come. That's why I didn't say anything to the two of you. But now that they are here and obviously made it I can bring you up to date. When the four left to get those additional supplies, part of what they needed to do was to send out a call for help, but again as I just stated I didn't know if we would get any help and would be left on our own. Again we'll go over the introductions later, but let's just say that the ones who joined us will help in the protection of this place, and begin the real research here. We need to do both if we are to establish this as an official ancient site." He could see that Kal was about to say something and he held up his hand and shook his head. "Kal just let me finish please. I know it appears that we are trying to take over your discovery, but you did discover it, and all the records will reflect that. And we know, unofficially, that this is an important site. But until we can prove it by doing digs here, it is only conjecture. And to keep Sabohl from claiming that we took this away from him we need the proof as soon as we can get it. So this is why it was important to get these people in here."

He looked at Jura, and continued. "Look I knew that once this group arrived that it would look very bad to you. After all you're the only female here, so along with the request for this help I stated that you were here and because of this any who wanted could bring their mates along. I felt that it was important for you not to feel either so isolated or threatened by there only being males here, and having other like-minded females would help put your mind at ease. We really are who we said we are. I know that with some of what's been happening, it's hard to remember that. I hope that this helps put your mind, both of your minds at ease, and what we've said all along is the truth." Trehe waited with patience knowing personally that having this go the way that it had that he would feel much the same way, have the same doubts, and of course, fears. While he wasn't a female so couldn't know exactly her feelings, still it had to have been real fear and worry. Had they been bad ones then she would be paying a horrible price for making the mistake of being here. In truth, no matter how careful one was, it was still too easy to step into something unexpected, and find one in serious trouble.

Jura and Kal looked at each other, and then Kal took a deep breath, again paused before speaking. "I know you keep reassuring us that you and the ones who are here are on the up and up, but it surely is difficult to believe. Every time we turn around you're surprising us with something else, some new revelation. Of course we're on edge. What did you expect?"

Jura thought, *I really am worried. What other surprises are they going on spring on us?* "I really don't understand this. Is the threat that Sabohl presents that great? After all he is only a male, and yes one of the learned, but only one person."

Pausing before replying Trehe said, "One male, one person yes. But he fought his way to the position that he's in. He is smart, and has no allegiance except to himself. He uses whoever he can, and when he has what he wants then he dumps whoever it was that helped him get that piece of whatever it was. And, not that you don't already know this, he can and does put on a front of a learned that is willing to help any who want to learn, to find out things, to research to help unlock our past. Then he pounces, takes whatever work and effort that these did and claims it as he own. And he's always looking for ways to cement his power and to remain the one who is the only information that will be accepted for the way our past is. A very narrow view of the world, don't you think? But that is unimportant to Sabohl. Just as long as he has the power to shape things in the way he sees it that's all that matters to him.

"Have you ever wondered why he has no mate, or companion?" Trehe looked directly at Jura when he asked the question. He knew that it was something that she had noticed, and had actually pointed out at one time. "Because, first off, no female could stand his selfish ways, his air of superiority, and secondly if he needs to take care of his physical desires he takes it from some adoring female in one of his classes, or delves into the underside of the villages and townships and gets a female that sells her services. From his point of view, that's what a female is for, and that's all she's worth. He could have easily survived back at the time in our history where we only had the clans and tribes. In some ways he's a throwback, someone out of time. And he fights to win, no rules but his own. Yet none of this can be seen from the outside, by his students, by our society. He appears to be friendly, always willing to lend a hand to help, one who only wants the truth about our past to be learned so we can truly understand where we came from and where we can go. Always willing to listen to a student, answer their questions, and direct them where they might find the answers.

"Yet, in the end, one only has to look up those he stepped on, and continues to step on to learn the truth. But even here he's very careful to make sure that any of these victims are placed in such a way that they become ineffective and thusly not a threat to him, or if he sees that they can and will be a threat, well then through some accident or other situation they die or disappear, very conveniently and in such a way that it can never come back to him. We've followed his ties to the underworld, but he is so very careful. While we and our network are quite aware of his movements, his contacts, and his life, he has yet to slip up allowing us to catch him. And since he has isolated himself as he has it makes it easier for him to keep those slipups from happening. And while I know that this has been a long winded explanation, it's necessary so that you can understand why it is necessary to bring these others in here.

"If anything, Sabohl is consistent – predictable really. You see this isn't the first site that has been found by someone else. But are they around, are they still alive – probably not. Once he has confirmed this or that discovery, and he has his ways of keeping track of what's happening in the field as we call it, he has his underworld contacts come into the site, take it over, hold it, and then moves his own teams in, announcing to the world of this new discovery that he's made. And you've had personal experience, so you know that what I'm saying here is the truth. You were watched the whole time you were searching for this site – the whole time. How do I know this – simple really, we have teams whose job it is to keep tabs on his contacts from the underworld. They follow them wherever they might go. And there were two constantly dogging your searches, and it was only through accident that you discovered this when you found the trail to this place. Again, how do we know this, because one of our teams was there when it happened. So in some ways it was you two out searching being spied on by Sabohl's people, while we followed them." At this point Trehe laughed, "Look, in a way while this area usually has none of us around here since it's so isolated, for a while there it was actually crowded, and unfortunately before this is over it's going to get even more so. In fact it may look much like it did when this site was occupied with an attacking force trying to get inside to claim it as theirs. And remember we are very isolated here. So whatever happens and the results from the actions that happen here will never get out. And the only information that the world will hear will be what this site is and what it represents, nothing more."

Looking again at the two of them Trehe looked as if he was about to go and join the newly arrived members, but instead stopped and began to speak again. "Look what we play here – although play is probably not the best of words – is a very old game, one that has been played out here from the very beginning of time. And what I mean is this, there was a time, and not one of us knows when that was, we became conscious thinking creatures. I suspect that at the beginning we only survived because we could think and outsmart the other predators that were looking for a meal. But eventually we started to get together to form what eventually became our clans and such. And at this point we had become the top predator out there and began to fight with each other. Probably the competition was one of the reasons we continued to grow, to improve in our abilities to think, to act. I guess the pressures of the times kind of forced this growth on us.

"I know this is getting a little long winded again, but I think once you hear me out that you will see that while the times have changed, we really haven't. Maybe it just dressed up and a little more sophisticated than it was in the past. But if you strip away everything that it hides behind, then it's really no different than what we were when this site or any of our other people during that time were here. The only difference now is that it happens more with words than with the long knives and bows. This is not to say that those are no longer used. All of us know better than that. And I suspect sometime in our future because we've descended from warlike people that this is still in our blood and as such we may find ourselves in wars of unimaginable size compared to what it was, again when this site was occupied, or even what we can imagine today. And because we can see that we've advanced one can only assume that our weapons will do the very same thing – which means that our ability to cause misery and death will increase.

"I suspect that the ones who will live during those stressful times in our future will wonder why we do this and why it is so, and this is why the past is so important. So important that one person shouldn't control what is put out there, to make sure it is only his ideas that control. Because it is our past that leads us to our future, and to interpret it correctly requires many disciplines and much thought and study at the very ancient sites such as this one. Then this information, as it is gathered, must be passed out to as many of the learned as we possibly can get it to. Because we never know who will find that one key that will unlock a mystery that no one else had been able to solve. So in a sense we are fighting just as our ancient ancestors did. Only here the battle is for knowledge, and who knows, it still may be survival, but again knowledge. Since having the knowledge and the understanding that sites like this can provide, allows us to understand who we are, where we came from, and possibly where, in the end, we will go. But when one like Sabohl is controlling all of it then none of this is happening and as long as he can control this, we, as a people, as a society, will be the losers.

"Sorry about this, but I cannot help but be passionate about this. No one person should control this. It's just too important, and it's the reason that I'm in this fight right up to my ears. I've watched as Sabohl has changed and twisted the facts to fit his ideas and theories, and he is so closed minded that he refuses to allow any competing idea or theory, and crushes any unmercifully. You see I was one of those he crushed. And no, before you ask, it is not the reason that I am doing this. I'm not looking for revenge." He smiled before continuing. "Although I suspect that at the beginning of this it was that. And if we look at our past I'm sure many of the battles that we fought had revenge as the motive. Now it's more to do with the restriction of knowledge and what this knowledge could do for us if we could get it out there. I know with life as it is, not many have time to do other than what is necessary to survive, and so much of this may seem unimportant. Yet, if we are to better ourselves, we really must know who we are, who we were, and what has changed, why we've gone the way we have, and so many other things. Without this knowledge and it must be as accurate as we can make it, we will find ourselves repeating things that at best should be left alone and never repeated.

"Okay, again, sorry about this. It's just when I have an audience, and in your case a captive one at that, I kind of preach. Anyway, I'd better head over and join the others, and you can join shortly and we'll make the introductions and then begin to decide how we'll tackle this project as well as the protection of this site from not only Sabohl and his minions, but once word goes out, there will be looters and others who just want to see our past. We have to try to work this in a way that anything that we recover can be authenticated and not messed up because we have someone here who just wants to dig everywhere because they think that there might be some treasure here. In truth the only treasure that truly is here is the knowledge about our past, but we of the learned would only see it that way." At this point Trehe turned and left heading over to join the others leaving Jura and Kal alone.

Both were quiet and then they looked at each other. "Wow," Jura exclaimed, "passionate about this isn't he? I guess if we both think about it we won't have to worry about them being secretly part of Sabohl's team. At least I don't think so."

"I think I have to agree. And unless he's that good of an actor you could really see, as you said, his passion for this work, and his dislike for Sabohl and what he is doing." Kal took a deep breath, and looked over at the other group who were in a separate camp. "I guess we'll see some others set up in their own portable shelters since, if I heard right, there are other mated couples in that group. At least I'm happy that there will be other females here now, but the only downside is that we don't know them. Still if I've learned anything since we've been together, it won't take too long before all of you will be chatting like old friends." Again he looked up and across to the other gathering and saw that Trehe was signaling the two to come and join them. He breathed out heavily before continuing. "I guess we'd better go and join them then."

Arm in arm they headed over to the others with no expectations of how this would go. After all the rest knew each other, and even though this site was their discovery, they were still the outsiders. As they approached they could hear the voices of the many as they talked among themselves, but as they got close it became silent with an air of anticipation. Smiling first at them and then turning to the rest Trehe said, "And here are our discoverers. As you know this place has, in many ways, been our special and probably one of the most important sites that had never been located. It is here that the leader was able to create the first alliance that eventually led to what we are now. But with so much time that had passed since his time as leader, this place, and its location has passed into the realm of myth. And in many ways the history that we study reflects that. Well, now with the location known maybe we'll be able to find if other parts of our history that is marked as this was, myth, may in fact be real. Not that you don't know but these two are Kal, and Jura. Kal's family history says that he's a direct descendent of K'jor, and this clan. Again, with the way things were done back then, and he agrees by the way, it would seem to be impossible to know who one's sire was. Still if that cannot be determined, at least it can be said that he is from this clan." Trehe then introduced all the new members that had just joined them here at the site, and they all seemed to be friendly, and just about as passionate about the past as he had assumed Sabohl had been.

Later when both of them were back inside their portable shelter Jura said, "Well that was a spirit-spiral introduction and evening. With all these new names it's going to take me a while just to put the faces with the names, but I suspect that we'll not be having a lot of contact with them anyway. I'll, most likely have more contact with the other females since with me there are only four of us, but there are now thirteen males including you. And from what I could gather from the conversations, most of them will be setting up areas to begin to learn about this place with all of us taking our turns at guarding this place from Sabohl and his cronies. But this is only the first night, so who knows, things might and probably will change." Smiling she looked deep into his eyes and said. "Not to change the subject, but to change the subject, I would really love to have you very close tonight,"

What could he say about that? He had to admit that he just loved to get as close as he could. He smiled back and said, "For me that's never a problem. I love getting as close as we can, and enjoy each other's bodies."

* * *

The following few 9-days just flew by as they continued the reconstruction of the gates, bringing in the additional wood for their fires and began the tedious work of working this site. And, of course, the weather refused to cooperate with storm after storm hitting them with a fury that none of them were comfortable with. And as another storm raged pushing all of them back into their shelters Kal looked out stating, "If I had a choice, and from what I've learned so far, this would not have been a place that I would have chosen to live. Yeah, because of the lay of the land it is one of the most defendable areas that we've seen. But that is just about the only good you can say about it. This is surely a miserable place to live during the Season of Cold. And if our history says anything, nobody moved in that season. So why not find different Season of Cold headquarters and avoid all of this."

"I'm sure that it crossed their minds a few times." Jura replied, "But I suspect that if they abandoned this place for a warmer location that when they returned they would have found someone else occupying it. And from what I can see it would have been nearly impossible to take it back. So they would have just stayed and suffered." Jura could understand, since she had to admit that it wasn't a very nice place to live this time in the cycle of seasons. As of yet she or Kal for that matter, had no opportunity to experience it in any of the other seasons. It had been close to the Season of Cold when they had discovered it, and had returned back to their home in High Trail almost immediately.

Both of them heard the crunching of the snow as someone approached their shelter. While they were still living in the portable shelter that they had brought with them, it had been reinforced with other materials to keep it from being torn and destroyed by the winds. Trehe then called out, "Are both of you decent?"

They looked at each other and then at the portable shelter flap and Jura replied saying, "Yes, just trying to keep warm and out of those wicked winds, and why wouldn't we be?"

Trehe laughed as he replied, "Oh I don't know, let me see . . . very cold, by yourselves, mates, trying to keep warm – you know, things like that. Conditions like this have led to new lives."

She laughed and said, "I guess that's very true, and it does seem like when you get close together to keep warm that it does go further than that. Yeah, we're decent, so come in, come in."

They could hear the stomping of feet and then the flap was pulled back and Trehe crouched down to get through the opening, entered, and sat down next to the entrance. With him came a blast of cold air that immediately sent a chill through the two of them. Seeing their reaction Trehe said, "Sorry about that, but there's just no way to keep that cold air out when you enter a place. In a way wish we could build some more permanent shelters, but until we know more about the layout of this place we can't afford to mess something up."

Looking at the two of them Trehe leaned forward placing his hands over the small fire. He noticed that the fire was close to smokeless and what smoke was produced curled up towards the roof and out through a small opening that was there for that very purpose. The materials that the portable shelter was constructed from made it somewhat stiff, but with these winds it still flexed and snapped giving the illusion that it could fall at any time. "Look, first off now that we have close to a full team here, you truthfully don't have to stay here. Once the Season of Green arrives it would be a great time to be here, but now it is just miserable. As you know we've been more involved with making this place defensible once more than actually doing any research. And the way these storms are rolling in here I suspect that we won't be do-ing much research until this season is over. Now I'm not telling you to leave, but I want you to know that it is as option

– not that traveling in this kind of weather would be easy. And if you decide to go nobody will feel that you just cut and ran. In fact some of the others suggested it. In a way we'd love to just leave a very small crew here, someone to just occupy this place to keep it under our care. But with what may show up here at any time we really don't have much of a choice, but you do." He could see that they were about to protest so he held up his hands to cut them off and continued. "Look, we don't need an answer right now. Discuss it between the two of you, come to us and ask questions, anything. Just be sure if you decide to ask any of the other mated couples here that you announce your arrival. That way nobody gets embarrassed when one walks in on a compromising situation." Here he laughed again and said, "After all like we both agreed it is quite cold and such situations does lead to other things."

He paused a moment cleared his throat and said, "Not to change the subject, but enough on that. I understand that the two of you have a general map of the layout to this place, is that right?" He waited as again Jura and Kal looked at each other before looking back at him. "Look, we know at least this much, and while we never discussed it directly, you had information that led you to this site. It was obvious from our field operations, as the two of you searched all the areas that you did. There was nothing random about it at all. So if you do have something that would help us when we are finally able to actually work this site it would be much appreciated."

Kal looked at Jura who just shrugged. "Look, I know that you know that I'm supposed to have been from this clan. A little had been passed down through the generations, and I guess either because I have an interest in history, or maybe because this is the first time in history that it would be safe, well not truly safe, but maybe the first chance to actually go out and search I was sort of elected. So, yes, I had something to go on. But what surprised me, and I know Jura, is just how large an area this is. So I, we feel very lucky to have located this in our first season of searching. And yes I do have a very rough drawing of what this place was supposed to look like when there were people living here. I know that we've tried to be very careful, all of us that are here right now, of avoiding any obvious areas of past occupation, and from what I can see we have. I know that *note taking* is a very big part of such an operation. Besides all the digging and sifting, and so many more tedious things, so if you could give us some paper I could probably transfer the rough drawing I have, which I want to keep since it is part of my family, and then you would have exactly what I have. Look, it still worries both of us, even with the assurances, that we could lose this site. So we are trying to be so very careful."

"That's a very understandable position," Trehe shrugged, "and even now there's no way that there can be real trust between us. Too much has happened. And in that I mean this has all transpired rather quickly, and the two of you have had to react more than having the time to really think it through." Again he paused and took a deep breath. "Look, I don't know why but life just seems to be that way. So much that happens is unplanned, unforeseen, and all we can do is adjust as it happens and hope that what we decide is the right decision. Yet, as you well know, many times those decisions are made with too little information and, usually, too little time to make those decisions. It's no wonder that so many times what we decided, once we have the time and a chance to look back makes us think that if we only had better information, or more

time, then what we decided would have been so much different.

"In the games that we play when we are young we find
that we can always start over and do it again, but life doesn't
give us that opportunity. So we muddle along from one decision to the next, never knowing what our future or the
outcome of those decisions will be. And many times we sit
there and curse ourselves for being so stupid or reacting in a
certain way, wishing that we could go back and change it. But
I guess the real question would be, would we? Even if we
knew all the facts, and knew what the possible outcomes
would be, would we truly make a different decision or go in a
different direction? But since we cannot go back and try, all
this is no more than an exercise in futility. So all we can do is
go on with our lives, and hope that we've learned something
from our past, and this is the whole past – you as an individual, the two of you as a couple, the places that you live, our
society, and even all of us – if we don't, then its shame on us,
and rightfully so. And I guess that's one of the reasons why I
do this, and go against Sabohl. What he does is to maintain his
position of power and appear to the rest as the one in the
know. But what he really is doing is quite wrong, since his
version of the past isn't necessarily the correct one. And as
you have seen he is ruthless in his pursuit of maintaining that
position. It leaves the rest of us searching for ways to defeat
him. And it's sad, in some ways, because if he would be willing to accept what there is out there, work with the ideas and
such that have been presented, then we'd know so much more,
maybe understand much more. But alas, it's not to be. So here
we are fighting our own little war. And like in any war there

are casualties, but most of these casualties are the destruction of knowledge instead of individuals, but the tragedy is no less.

"By narrowing and restricting what we know of our past and why we are where we are is truly a dangerous stance to take. It means that somewhere in the future, because of what we think is the way we were in the past, the decisions could be completely wrong and lead us to our own destruction. If you think about it, not that you haven't, what we did in our past put us here where we are today. Sometimes the changes took a very long time to happen, other times very quickly. I guess a good example of this would be how some tribes over time established more permanent homes and became the clans. Yes we still had the nomadic people, and in some ways we still do. But this change continued until we now have our villages and such – a very slow change for sure. Then we have the forming of the alliance, no not the small ones, but this re-ally major one that was brought about by your ancestor. This was a rather rapid change, and from what little we can under-stand about it, it was outside influences that brought about. Yet at this very moment, we have no idea what those outside influences are. This was followed almost as quickly with the disillusion of the same alliance by the mythological meeting of the gods in the mythological valley. Still when one looks at the brief time it existed this was the real beginnings of change. But we know so little and with Sabohl using his power to keep the history as he sees it, there's a great chance it will remain that way.

"Look again I didn't mean to spout off to you like this, but whatever your decision, to stay or to leave, it's up to you. Again I know that there's no way if what we, the group I rep-resent, are being honest with you or not. I know I can stand here, well it's really not that easy to stand in these shelters, but you know what I mean, and tell you that we are here to learn, to help you establish this site, and still be lying. In fact everything I've just said could be a lie. So again with too little information, and too little time, both of you are left with making a life changing decision." He shook his head and smiled, "But as both of you know too well, that's life." He turned to leave stopped a moment before exiting and said, "I don't need an answer now, so think about it and when the two of you are sure come to us and let us know. Either way, stay or go, we'll back you." Taking a deep breath he steeled himself for the cold harsh weather outside of the shelter and exited leaving a fresh blast of frigid air behind as the flaps opened and closed.

Again both looked at each other and remained silent. Trehe had been quite passionate in what he had relayed to them, and what he said was very true of life. "Wow!" Was all that Kal could say.

CHAPTER NINE

SABOHL RETALIATES

Sabohl sat inside his study. It was warm and comfortable, but he didn't feel the comfort. Whoever this was that was attacking him they had beaten him at every move. He was not used to losing, and soon with his spies in place he would learn who was behind this, and when he did they would pay. He'd been too long on top not to know how to play the game, to find out who was behind this. Obviously it couldn't be those two naïve ones who, unknown to themselves, had located this most important site for him. All had gone just as everything in the past had up to a point in time. It appeared that once again he had won, and soon the accolades would be coming forth praising him and his efforts to advance their knowledge of the past. He had to admit that it had felt great to be back in the game, of taking advantage of those minor players. It had been a long time since such as this site had been found. And he had heard rumors that he was starting to lose his place, his position because he hadn't found anything new, hadn't advanced any new ideas, and appeared to be set in his ways, like that old bull herd beast who was beyond his prime still fighting off the younger to keep the right of breeding with the females that he ruled.

So when Kal had approached him with those questions he knew that here was a chance to prove his detractors wrong. Once again one of his students would provide a new site, new research, and conclusions – his conclusions of course. He knew, because of his experience that his conclusions were the only ones that mattered. No matter how logical, or how much the facts might have supported others out there, he ruthlessly suppressed both their theories and the ones presenting them. He had immediately put this Kal and his mate Jura under observation. Knowing that eventually they would slip up and reveal what he wanted to know. And if not then he would use his underworld connections to steal it. It didn't matter, as long, and in the end that he had the information and received due credit for the hard work, even if this hard work wasn't his own.

It was night and the soft glow from the candles created a room that was both cast in shadows where the light didn't reach, and yet at the same time comfortably lit, giving the feeling of warmth. He could hear the fire snapping and popping, and every once in a while the sound of water sizzling as a drop found its way down the chimney. There was a rain storm raging out in the night, but as well as his shelter was built he barely noticed. Again his anger seethed. *I'd better get myself under control. I know about my temper and if I release it, which has happened much too often lately, I could get careless, and that's something I cannot and will not do. Someone out there is beating me at what I do best. Well, so be it. But once I find out who this is, then we will see who wins in the end. This is only a skirmish in a small battle, and it's a battle I intend to win. So whoever you are, enjoy it for now. Because in the end I will have my victory, you can count on it.* He started to sip the wine that he had in the glass that was in his hand but noticed that the glass was empty. Sighing he got up went over to his supply and refilled the glass returned to his chair and sat heavily staring out at nothing, not even hearing the winds that were buffeting his shelter.

Tomorrow would be another day, and it was a day full of classes, so he wouldn't be able to devote any time to the problem before him. Besides, he had to maintain this front of the learned, the one who wanted to teach, to assist. It had worked well for most of his life, and he saw no reason to change now. It had given him all that he needed. He was the leader in his field, he could have female companionship whenever he needed it, but not the attachments that lesser males seemed to need. With his place of power it had brought him wealth, and with his contacts he controlled so much more than any realized. *Yes, so why change now?* Yet he felt restless, unsure, as for the first time in for as long as he could remember, it hadn't gone his way. Was he losing his touch, his ability to move, to outthink his opponents? He snorted at such a thought. Again this was only a minor setback, and soon he would counterattack and be on top once again.

After refilling his glass a second time he sat back down and again stared into the fire. He could feel his anger once again trying to control him, and he fought desperately to bring it under his iron control. If he didn't come up with something shortly, maybe this very night, then that thin veneer that marked him as one of the betters might just be destroyed – but, what to do? Yes, there had to be something that he could do to retaliate even if it was against his former student. He knew from his network that they were presently on that site that they had discovered, proving that they indeed were the discoverers and not he. Again from that same network he knew that there were others with them, so making a direct attack and blaming it on the many criminals that lived on the edges of society would prove to be impossible. And, from the ones who were monitoring the site, there were too many there, and the original place where there had been protection through that gap had been replaced making the site virtually untouchable. Even the archives spoke of this location being impregnable, and continually occupied, until abandoned when such places were no longer required. But there were other ways to defeat any enemy. This thought brought a smile to his face. Yes, definitely, there were other ways.

At this very moment a heavy blast of wind struck the shelter shaking it to its very foundation, snapping him briefly out of his thoughts, but at the same time a glimmer of an idea was forming. *Yes, yes, there are so many other ways of attacking while leaving no evidence behind that I am responsible.* He laughed, even though it was dark and the laughter had no humor in it. *This storm is perfect.* It would cover what he would do, and so very few would be out in such nasty weather, and with the rain falling as hard as it was, it would wash away any tracks that might be left making this appear to be an accident. Then once he had accomplished this he would head for the down side of the village pay for a female, and afterwards head back here, show up at the higher learned center and feign surprise that such a tragedy happened. After all, with all this wind and rain how could such a thing happen? With his mind made up and the anger still boiling just below the surface, again threatening to erupt, he got up from his chair, dressed in dark clothing appropriate for both the night, and the weather, gathered the materials he needed, and prepared to leave. This time he would do this himself, something that he hadn't done in a very long time – actually since he had attained his position as the leader in his area of study.

* * *

The two who were watching the shelter shivered when the last gust of cold wind struck. There just wasn't any place they could go to get completely out of this miserable storm. It would have been easy to abandon their post, since Sabohl rarely went out in such weather. Yet, from time to time he did, and because of this they stubbornly remained watching and waiting. Soon, others would relieve them and they could, at the time, get out of their wet clothing into something dry, and get warm before finding something a little strong to drink and head off to get some sleep. But until that time here they were. The one in charge turned to the other and said, "This is bad, and it just sucks. It would be so easy just to go and just say that we were here, but I know better. The moment we would do something like that would be the time he would decide to leave."

The other smiled, although it was a smile of misery, and just nodded in agreement. *Who'd be stupid enough to be out on a night like this?* He asked himself. Then he laughed quietly when he realized that he and the other was out on a night like this. "Yeah, it would be so much nicer if we could be out of this looking out instead of being in it." He shrugged before continuing, "But what can we do? He has beaten us time and time again over the cycle of the seasons. And as time has passed he's gotten only stronger and more cunning, holding on to his position with the tenacity of one of the old clan leaders. I guess what they say is true . . ."

"True?"

"Yeah", he laughed, even though it was a bitter one, "theories and ideas change within academia and science, one death at a time."

The leader thought about the statement and had to admit that it was very true. It seemed that even when something was presented with all the proper research and data to back it up, that if it went counter to the thinking of the time, this person would be belittled, black listed, and ostracized, and could even be destroyed. And, if later, much later usually, what he had originally presented had proven to be accurate, vindicating the person who had presented it originally, it was much too late. "I can't disagree with you. Not at all, I've seen it happen . . . hey, he's leaving, and dressed in really dark clothing. With the night like this, he's really going to be hard to follow. I wonder where the ole anarchism is heading now." With the cold and dampness that had become a part of them, all of this was forgotten as they set to follow Sabohl, and remain hidden.

Sabohl didn't head for the main thoroughfare through the village but immediately headed for the back trails to remain hidden from sight. That he was up to something was quite obvious, but what, was the question. With the lateness of the hour and the miserable storm there was little chance that any would be out and about, so why go this round-about way? All they could do was speculate, and follow. That he had a destination it was obvious, but from other times of following, this was not a common direction for him. Sabohl was keeping up a very fast pace making it more difficult for the ones who were following to remain hidden. Thank the gods for the storm and darkness. Without such they would have been discovered. Eventually Sabohl turned a corner around one of the many shelters and headed out into an open area. It became obvious that he was heading to the storage shelters.

With the winds blowing as hard as they were, driving the rain before it, so when it struck the raindrops felt like spikes, it hurt. Both of them stopped and watched as he disappeared into the storage shelters before moving across the open area between the shelters where business was carried on, and the shelters that were used for storage. The one looked over at the leader and asked, "What do we do? We can't follow him too far into this area, there's really no place that we can be out of sight."

Shaking his head the leader replied, "I don't know, I really don't know. Somehow we've got to figure what he's up to, and why he decided to come here." The leader looked around, even though there was little to see with it being as dark as it was. "Look let's slip in a little closer and get out of this wind. At least between a couple of the shelters we'll be out of most of it and maybe something will come to either of us as to how we can cover this." The other with him affirmed the thought and they carefully moved deeper into the storage shelters, trying to peer around them and locate Sabohl.

Even though he had been told the location by his spies, Sabohl, with the deep black of this stormy night, had problems in locating the one he wanted. And with the frustration of the failures of the near past his anger threated to break free once again and become a furious rage, uncontrollable until it burned itself out – taking its revenge on anything or anyone who happened to be near. He fought hard to maintain control, and stood there motionless as he fought this inner battle. Finally after who knew how much time, he had the anger under control once again, although he could tell that it would be easy to give in to it. Looking around the many shelters he finally located the one he was searching for, and with his strength and tools he brought with him, broke the hasp that kept other than the owners out. Once inside and out of the weather it was as if a weight had been lifted. By being out of the storm it was almost deafly silent. Well, it wouldn't matter as he was only going to be here for a short time and be gone.

From under his clothing he pulled a small candle and using the striker lit it. Then surveying the surrounding floors he began to spread lamp oil on many of the items within. Near a stack of flammable items he placed a small saucer filled with the lamp oil. And on this he floated another small, short candle. Then into this saucer he placed paper that would absorb most of the oil and trailed this paper over the sides. So with what he spread throughout the shelter and this timer, it would give him time to be away, but not too far because he wanted to see his handiwork. He repeated this in a couple of other locations, lighted the short candles, and exited, heading now in a different direction and not back to his personal shelter. When this succeeded he would celebrate. He smiled. *So you think you can beat me do you? Well, we will see about that.*

The two remained hidden behind one of the supply shelters watching for Sabohl when suddenly he reappeared and headed off in a different direction. There was a small open field that he was heading across, completely open, and even in this darkness the two would have to wait until he finished crossing or take a chance on being discovered. *Just what was he doing here?* They moved towards the last row so that they could continue to observe when the heard what sounded like a "whoomp". Turning towards the source of the sound they saw a fire's glow in one of the shelters. "Of the gods", exclaimed the leader. "The fool has set one of the shelters on fire. You continue to follow; I've got to get some help. If this fire gets out of hand, and with these winds we could easily lose all of these shelters. The only good thing out of this is that they aren't very close to the village. The bad is much of what the merchants own is here – now go!"

The other took off to continue to follow while the leader ran back to the center of the village and sounded the fire alarm, a bar of metal hanging from a chain with a striker. By the time, since it was the middle of the night, people began showing up the fire was quite visible and raging among the storage shelters. Quickly a fire team was organized and they began to attack the fire. But it had gotten a strong foothold and was now beginning to ignite the other shelters around the one that was burning. The winds were roaring and rain coming down in sheets, but the rain had little or no influence on the intensity of the raging fire. As the villagers fought desperately to put out the fire they found that either they were soaked by the pouring rain, or scorched by the heat from the fire. "We've got to knock some of the shelters down!" Someone yelled. "We've got to create a break or we're going to lose them all." There must have been close to a hundred shelters here, for which at least one third were presently either burning or about to burn. And as each new shelter exploded into flame, the heat and intensity of the fire increased to the point that no one could approach the flames. No one needed any light to see as the fire with its great yellow flames leaping high in the air lit the surrounding area in its yellow light turning the black of this stormy night into day. Soon shelters that were rows away from the head of the fire began to smoke and then burn. Even destroying rows of the shelters wouldn't work now as the sparks and coals being thrown into the air by the massive fire storm began to rain down on other shelters, and since all were constructed of wood, began to smolder and burn. It soon became obvious to the desperate villagers that there would be nothing they could do but watch as the roaring ever increasing beast of flames spread beyond anything they could do.

How'd it start? What and maybe who was responsible? In the chaos from the first alarm to the present no one knew who had rung the alarm, but it hadn't been soon enough. And standing there in awe as they were watching the power of the flames continued to destroy. It was no surprise to them that their ancient ancestors had assigned a god to this force of nature. From the intensity of the fire and the heat being generated they were forced back away from the destruction, and with trepidation watched as, for some, their life work was disappearing before their eyes. Many would be wiped out by this, others would recover, but it would be many cycles of the seasons before the village could be as strong as it had been before this devastating fire. With shoulders slumped and depression setting in they watched helplessly as shelter upon shelter collapsed into flaming ashes.

* * *

Once away from his handiwork Sabohl turned and watched for a short time before heading deeper into poorer side of the village. He needed a female to finish out this evening; one he felt was going to be quite successful in his revenge against Kal and Jura, and the unknown ones that seemed to be behind them. He heard the fire alarm and was surprised that it was discovered this quickly. *Oh well, probably some passer byer.* So he turned once again and looked towards the storage shelters and even though he couldn't directly see them, he could see the yellow glow reflecting off the low cloud cover. He laughed quietly. *Success! Let them try and stop me. Let them try and topple me from my position!* He then continued his interrupted journey and headed down towards one of the smaller rivers that flowed on the edge of the village. Here was where the females who sold their bodies to any male were located. And for either a short time or for the night a male could have a female companion. It came down to what one was willing to pay. Yet when he reached the entrance he was barred from entering. "What's this?" He demanded.

"Sorry about this sir, but you have been banned from this establishment, and are not to be allowed inside or to be with any of the females who work here."

Sabohl could feel the anger rising again. With the fire he had just set some of it had abated, but now with this new aggravation it threatened to engulf him once again. "What do you mean barred?" He bellowed.

Without batting an eye the guard, bouncer really, stated, "It seems that you were overly rough with one of the females last time you were here, and she was unable to work for almost a full season. And while your coinage is good your behavior is not. None of these females who work here will have anything to do with you or your ways. So I suggest that you leave and not return."

"And if I decide that I don't want to leave, what can you do about it?" Sabohl asked angrily.

"Then we will make you find reasons to leave. There are more here than just me, and if necessary all of us will be sure that you leave, and, I might add, we will not be gentle. Consider it a reminder that roughing up can work both ways. Plus it would be easy to get word out about your activities down here. And while this is something that is known about, this place here, it really is never mentioned in polite conversation, nor is the males who use our services ever identified, *unless there are problems* – if you get my drift. So please just move along and nothing need to be said, or acted upon."

Taking a deep breath and barely able to keep his rage under control Sabohl smiled, although it was quite forced. "Okay, you're point is taken. I'll quietly take my leave." He turned and with the blind rage filling him, headed in a direction that he had never been, deeper into the poorer and bad side that all villages seemed to have.

From the shadows the second watched and listened to all that had transpired, and all he could do was shake his head and continue to follow. But where Sabohl was heading wasn't safe for anyone. Especially one of his rank. But he couldn't do anything about it other than follow, keep his notes, and eventually tie in with the leader of his team, who at this moment, was quite involved with that conflagration that Sabohl had caused. And if Sabohl got into trouble what could he do about it? Nothing, nothing at all. Heck, he would be putting his own life in danger by following him into this area. So with all the stealth he could manage he continued to follow and remain hidden from all. And shortly what he feared began to develop as he lengthened his distance. He could see a small group begin to gather and follow Sabohl, who appeared to be completely unaware of the danger he was in or even that he had gone in the wrong direction.

* * *

With this refusal to be allowed inside Sabohl's anger began to get the best of him. Yet, through this fog he realized that he needed to leave before he really did something stupid and forever get banned from this place. So he stomped off not looking at all as to where he was going or the danger he was putting himself into. Because he had strong contacts with the underworld, and as far as he was concerned, was safe anywhere he wanted to go, he headed out. Although in saner moments he knew better. If he wanted to be honest the group he dealt with was only one of the many who lived in the shadows of society. But with his anger in control he really was being careless. He didn't notice when he had turned in the wrong direction and now was heading into a part of the village that even the group he contacted would stay away. He just needed to push through and let his anger burn out and get back in control. At least he had been successful in extracting revenge earlier this evening. Suddenly he realized that his surroundings were strange to him, and he looked around and could see shadowy figures converging on him as if he was prey and they were the carnivores.

His mind flashed danger, danger, danger, but it was too late. With the fires he had set all the village would be there, and here where he presently was, would be no help. He was completely on his own. Could he talk his way out of it, or would he have to fight? In a sense the latter part of this question brought a grim smile to his face. With his mood tonight fighting might be the very thing. Again, reason pushed its way into his mind as he knew that there was no way that he by himself would be able to overcome the size of this gang. He stopped and searched his surroundings for a place that he could better defend himself and allow these to only approach from the front making it more difficult for them to attack. Yet, at the same time, he needed a direction available that would allow him to escape if the opportunity presented itself. He realized that he was still close to the river, and there was an old dock, rotting, unused, and falling apart making it an ideal place to protect himself. If it became too hard to defend then he had the river to jump into, and with the darkness of the area he would be unseen once he was in the water. Yes with this storm raging it would be dangerously cold, a raging torrent, but the danger just about to approach him was greater. Quickly he picked up his pace and feinted away from his planned point and then picked up his pace even more and cut to the old dock, and headed out towards the end being careful to keep his balance as it swayed under his feet making him realize that the dock was in worse shape than he first thought. Looking around in the dim reflected light he could see that there was debris and trash scattered all over the place. There seemed to be a few stacked empty shipping containers which further narrowed the approach. He hoped that because of the instability of this old dock, the stacks of trash, debris, and old containers that it would further his advantage making this gang have to approach much more carefully than they had planned.

* * *

The one who was following looked at the movements that Sabohl was making and at first it didn't make any sense to him. It was obvious that he was now aware that there was a gang of thugs closing in on him, but it had been too late to avoid a confrontation. As he watched he saw Sabohl appear to head in one direction to suddenly dodge and head out on the old dock. *Why'd he do that?* It didn't make sense, but it must to Sabohl. He saw the old dock sway a little, and knew that it was in very bad shape – but what to do, what to do? He, by himself couldn't help, there were just too many of them. And besides his orders were clear – Sabohl could never learn that he was under constant observation, and was followed every-where he went, and if he revealed himself, then as smart as Sabohl was it wouldn't take him long to figure it out. So, with a helplessness of events beyond his control, he remained hid-den and watched as everything slowly unfolded before his eyes.

* * *

As the villagers watched, the final shelters that were on the edge were consumed by the roaring conflagration. And slowly with nothing left to burn the flames began to slow in their rage, and now the storm with the winds and rain became, once again, the dominant force, slowly overcoming the flames. Now instead of the roar of the fire, there was a replacing sound of hissing as the rains finished what the fires had be-gun. With most of the village turned out to attempt to suppress the fire they stood there numb and in silence at the destruction that lay before them. Too much in shock to even think, or con-template how such a thing had started, or the results of that fire, or what the true loss had been, at this moment. Then, slowly, since there was nothing left to do, they broke up and headed back to their personal shelters, defeated by what they had just witnessed. Tomorrow they would return and see if anything, anything at all could be recovered. Although from what they had witnessed, and how they were feeling at this very moment, it was very doubtful.

At least they could be thankful that these particular shelters were not very close to where they actually lived. Had it been, then there could have been many deaths, as the fire tore through their places of work and personal shelters, leaving nothing but the ashes of the village. If that had happened would they rebuild on top of the ashes of their previous shelters, or would they have moved? That was an unknown. It would have been something that would have been a hard choice for any of them to make – something that none of them had ever contemplated. It probably would have come down to how many would have died and who had survived. By the fire starting when it did, it easily could have caught the whole village sleeping, and with no warning or no time, the deaths could have been very high. So with these thoughts they quietly returned, smelling of smoke, and covered in soot. Eventually leaving only one or two who continued to stare unbelieving at what they had witnessed.

One of these slowly withdrew and was out of sight. He had been the one who had sounded the alarm, and now needed to find the one who had continued to follow Sabohl. But with the storm still raging, and only a general idea as to direction, he really had no idea. At least he could head to one of the planned rendezvous points that had been set up for this side of the village. There were a number of these marked for the teams throughout the village and surrounding area, and since he had seen them head in the direction he was presently going, he decided to head to the closest one. It was a cold depressing night. With what had transpired, and what he had witnessed, it made it so much more so – but what to do? It was obvious that they knew who had started the fire. Well, sort of. Since they never really witnessed him setting the fire, it could have been coincidence after all. But he suspected that there was a connection between Sabohl and what had happened here. Yet, one didn't just go and accuse one of the most important learned of such crimes. Shaking his head, he realized that there was no proof, and if they came forward, they could be accused of starting the fire also. And how could they explain it away? It angered him that Sabohl was going to get away with another one.

He finally reached one of the meeting places and began to pace. The other hadn't arrived yet. He wondered what was transpiring, but there was no way to know. If truth be told he could be waiting at the wrong place, since it was likely that Sabohl had just circled around and headed back to his personal shelter. And with that thought he wondered if maybe he should head back there, but decided against it and wait a little longer. If he didn't show up soon he'd head out over that way and see if that had happened. And with that decision the time continued to drag by slowly without any change. So he decided to head over to Sabohl's shelter and see if indeed the other was there. Unfortunately it was completely on the other side of the village and would take him some time to reach there. So before leaving in the dim light he left a brief, very wet note that stated for him to wait here if he came to this meeting point. Taking a deep breath and shaking off a shiver he headed out rapidly to see if they had returned. Yet, when he arrived back at the place where they would observe Sabohl's shelter no one was there and the shelter was dark. *So they hadn't returned. Where'd they go? And where are they?* He laughed a bitter laugh, if he knew that he wouldn't be running around like this on this stormy, cold, very wet night.

He waited what he considered was a reasonable amount of time and when no one showed, he headed back to the other rendezvous point, taking his time to check on other locations as he headed back across the village. Soon he and his assistant would be relieved and the dawn couldn't be far away. But with this storm he suspected that it would require the suns rising to lighten the area well enough to know that it was dawn. At each point he checked he came up empty and eventually returned to his starting point after leaving the devastation left by the fire. Again back, he was alone. With no idea of what to do or where to go, he was becoming alarmed. Normally they were to stay together, but tonight there were extraordinary circumstances that had required them to split up. Now he was here with not a clue as to what had transpired after they became separated. Shrugging inwardly, at this moment there was very little he could do but wait.

The only advantage to this location lay in the fact that it was out of the way, and there was very little chance that one of the villagers would come by and start asking questions. So he waited, hoping that his partner would show, and in what seemed much too long he could finally see someone approaching his location, and once he was close enough in the uncertain light, he recognized his partner by his walk and waited as he slowly, cautiously approached this meeting place. He wanted to shout out, "What has happened?" But held this in check, and when the one who had followed Sabohl had joined him, he found that this one had an odd look about him. So he waited, and found that he didn't have to wait long as his assistant took a very deep breath, shuddered a little, leaned back against one of the stacks of unused lumber and shook his head.

"I think Sabohl is dead." He whispered.

Shocked at what he had just said, the leader asked, "What? Are you sure? What happened?"

"Look, when I left you and followed Sabohl he headed for that shelter down by the river where females sell their favors. It seems that once he had accomplished what he had set out to do he was going to celebrate by taking a female. But he was denied access. From what I could gather, in a previous visit he had roughed up one of the females, and now is barred. This set him off and it was obvious that he was furious, because he took off in the wrong direction. I think if he had been in control of himself at this point he would have just headed back to his shelter and leave it at what he had already done.

"I've heard word that the whole storage complex was destroyed, is that right?"

In a subdued voice the leader answered, saying, "Yes, the whole thing. Once that first shelter's roof collapsed the winds drove the fire into the rest of them. By the time anybody could get there, even though we tried, there really wasn't much that we could do but watch as it burned."

"Then this has become a very bad night." He paused, as he absorbed this information, and sighed a bit. "This is going to destroy many of the businesses here. I guess we can be considered lucky that it didn't get into the living shelters."

Nodding in agreement, the leader said, "Very lucky indeed. Anyway continue on if you would."

"Oh, yeah, I guess that would be a good idea." He looked out over the leader's shoulder and paused as he stared out into the distance. While this wasn't the meeting point where they would change shifts it was the secondary location. "I think that our replacements are arriving."

Turning around and looking in the direction that the other had been looking he saw two figures materializing out of the darkness – dawn must be close. They waited until the two arrived and the leader of the night shift then signaled him to continue.

"Okay. Anyway, like I said, he must have been angry because instead of heading back in a safe direction he went deeper into part of the village where it is very dangerous. There are a number of gangs, much theft and murder, and who knows what else, since good people just stay away – especially if they want to come out alive. And you know, the deeper you go the worse it gets, and he continued to go deeper. I became worried not only for him, but for myself. Then, I really had hoped because of the time of the night, but it was a lost hope, one of those roaming gangs found him . . ."

"And they killed him right there before your eyes?" The leader asked.

"If it only had been that simple, no, and that's why I can only say I think he's dead."

The two that had just joined them had very questioning looks on their faces and the leader of this team asked, "Killed, who was killed?"

The one who had been following Sabohl said, "The one we have been assigned to follow and report on, you know Sabohl."

"He's dead?"

"I, think so, but let me finish, and I think you'll understand. When the gang showed up I didn't know what to do. Should I go in and help, should I stay and watch – that kind of thing. I realized that even with two of us there'd be no chance, and our orders are very clear. There must never be any contact between us and Sabohl. So I watched from a hidden place, deep in the shadows. I could see that Sabohl was still furious, but he seemed to realize his situation and began to look for a place that he could defend himself against a group this size. Personally I wouldn't have picked where he did, but when there is no time to really look one takes what seems to be convenient, and for him it was an old rotting dock. In a way it was a good choice forcing the attackers to come at him with the maximum of two at a time giving him some advantage in the fight.

"The leader of this gang yelled at him saying, 'Just give us your valuables and we might let you live.' At this point the rest of the gang laughed, immediately letting anyone who happened to be around that living past the next few moments was quite unlikely. Sabohl bellowed something back at them, and while I couldn't hear the words it incited the leader and the gang to go after him immediately. But with the restrictions only a couple could attack at a time and for a while Sabohl held his own. The problem was the dock. With all the bodies that was on it, and its poor condition it began to sway, throwing the ones fighting off balance. And during one of the shifts of the dock I saw Sabohl lose his balance and one of the attackers was able to stab him once. But at this point all this action was too much for the dock and it collapsed into the river taking half the gang with it and, of course, Sabohl.

"At this point the rest of the gang left quickly and began to head downstream to see if anybody had survived. But with this storm raging the river was a maelstrom of boiling water, tearing downstream at a terrific rate. In fact from what little I could see it wouldn't be long before the river would go beyond its banks and begin to flood the lower areas." He shuddered for a moment before continuing. "I just don't know how anybody could survive that even if they were strong swimmers and were in great shape. While Sabohl is big and strong, he had been stabbed just before the dock went into the water. No, I don't know how bad, and because of the bad light, I don't know if he was able to grab some of the flotsam or other debris that was both from the disintegrating dock and what was already in the river or whether he was able to get back ashore. So I can only assume, at this point that he drowned. But, I have no proof, none at all. And with the speed of that water his body wouldn't even wash up on the banks until a very long way away from here, if ever."

The other three were silent for a while, and the leader of the relief asked, "What should we do now? I mean there's no one to know what happened, or where Sabohl is, or even if he's alive."

The leader of the night team thought a moment, taking a deep tired breath since this last night had been very stressful and very eventful. "Look, if he survived then somehow he'll return to his shelter, so I guess the best thing would be for the two of you to stake out his place and see if he does return. After we get some sleep we'll put together a report and get it off to the history board or society leaders and after that it's in their hands as to what happens." Again pausing because he could feel the weariness pressing in on him now, and it was becoming harder to concentrate let alone think, "Look, I think that this is out of our hands and all we can do is watch his old haunts and see what happens. I don't know what else we can do."

F. D. Brant

FROM SITE TO HOME

Storm after storm rolled in on the site and it was another 9-day before they finally broke, and with the morning light it was clear, calm, and very cold. Jura and Kal were thankful to finally be able to leave their portable shelter into the cold crisp air. With their breathing producing great clouds of steam, it had become obvious to all that this was a horrible place to spend the Season of Cold, and probably one of the main reasons for its abandonment once the skirmishes and fighting among the tribes and clans became a thing of the past. There were so many other places to live that could provide more comfort. Still as they stood outside in the frigid air it wasn't long before they were shivering and retreated briefly back inside where the fire kept it warm. "I must admit", Jura said, "that I was looking forward to getting out of this shelter and into some fresh air. But after doing just that, well, here we are back inside." She laughed and just shook her head. I don't know which is worse, the raging storms that we've just experienced, or seeing the suns shining and finding that it's so cold that we can't even stay out and enjoy it."

"Yeah, I have to agree. Maybe as the day moves a little it will get a little warmer, and if we stay out of that icy wind and find a sheltered area maybe we can soak up a little of that sunlight, and I'm all for soaking up lots of that right now." They heard the crunching of the snow which meant that someone was heading their way. So both of them opened the flap and headed back out to see who it was and found Trehe approaching. "Good day to the two of you. It's so nice to see that there are still two suns in the sky. After this last series of storms I began to wonder."

The two smiled and Jura said, "Yeah, you and me both. But once the suns did come out I didn't think it would be this cold." She was stomping her feet as the cold from the frozen ground began to penetrate her footwear. Then that icy breeze reached out of them and they involuntarily shivered. "Boy that wind is cold!"

"So what brings you our way this day?" Kal asked.

"First off to make sure you were okay. With those storms raging as they were nobody was out and about to check on each other, and secondly to let you know that we will be expecting someone to show up today and bring us up to date on what has been happening away from this isolated site. I think when these last storms arrived that whatever resistance that may have been camping outside this place probably gave up and headed for warmer grounds. I know I would have if I could. This place is just miserable this time in the cycle of seasons. All I have to say is that our ancestors, and of course yours, since they were the ones who occupied this site, had to be hardy people. Between the fighting, and health issues that would have existed because of improper things like hygiene and such, creating disease, and then with these storms brewing as often and as hard as they seem, it would force them to remain inside giving a chance for clans to be wiped out with some disease, and if I remember right that almost happened here. And now I can more appreciate and understand why they left once they could. Great place to defend, almost impossible to attack, but a really really bad place to live for almost everything else. Look, both of you are shivering, not that I'm not very far from it myself. We have a bonfire going and some hot drinks let's get over there and enjoy the heat of both the fire, some nice conversation, and grab one of the cups so that it will warm our hands as well as our insides."

Jura smiled, and said, "You don't have to ask twice, lead on please as that just sounds wonderful." Together the three of them went across the site heading towards another part of the rock face that was the back defense for the site when people had lived here, and as they approached, Jura and Kal could see all the rest standing around the fire taking advantage of the heat. It also became obvious that the location of this fire was out of the winds which helped. They could see the welcoming smiles as they joined the rest of the team that was here. One of the members, she didn't remember what his name was said, "Ah to actually see sunlight, and enjoy the warmth, even if it is this fire, and to be able to actually get out, what a relief."

She couldn't disagree with that statement. She had to admit that with all the time that they had spent inside their portable shelter with the storms raging one after another and with little or no break between them she, and she knew that

Kal also, had been going crazy. She had heard it called shelter sickness, but until now had never experienced it personally. Well, now she had and wanted no part of it. She smiled as she faced the roaring fire putting out her hands and feeling the heat as the clothing she was wearing began to warm and transfer heat to her body. The only problem with these fires was that one could only warm one side at a time, leaving the other side cold and miserable. So, one played the game of continually rotating different sides to the fire, hoping that eventually one would get comfortable and warm. "So how did all of you fare? I mean we are all living in small places and those storms just wouldn't end. I was going stir crazy and time seemed to drag. And the continual winds, the howling it set up as it came roaring out of the lower places was deafening. Then it seemed to always be gray and at times hard to see the difference between night and day it was so dark out. Being from a farm I felt that none of this would be an issue, but I was wrong."

This brought a bit of laughter from the others gathered around the fire. And she could see a lot of nodding showing agreement in her assessment of situation. One of the other females who were here with her mate said, "You surely have that right. I've been on a few of these sites with my mate and figured that this one would be no different, but . . . but most of the time we've only worked the sites during the Season of Green, or Season of Heat, wrapping up during the Season of Falling and not being around when the storms really begin to roll in. I have to admit I was ready to run outside in those storms screaming bloody murder. That shelter where we're staying seemed to be closing in on me and kept getting smaller and smaller." Again this comment brought a chuckle from the rest as similar sentiments seemed to be the way.

Trehe then commented, "If things go well we should have supplies arriving later today. And on a side note, I wonder how our watchers have fared? Guess we'll know later once our supplies arrive. I was beginning to worry that we'd run out with the way these storms had continued unabated. I have to admit that it will be nice to get both the supplies, since we are running out of just about everything, and updates." Here he paused for a moment let out a deep breath and said, "With the size of this group we go through a lot of food, and, of course, the second and probably more important part, to find out what has been happening in the rest of the world. That's always the problem when we work these sites, we have no idea what's happening at all, and when we do get updated it's already old news – of course not as old as what we are working on at the time." This elicited additional laughter since most of the ones here had worked together a number of times in the past on other ancient sites.

* * *

It was working towards evening and the needed supplies had yet to arrive. But then again because of the severe weather that had just passed it was no surprise. They had briefly checked the camp of their watchers and had found it abandoned. So, for now, they were alone. They figured that the storms had driven them out. And here again there was no surprise since the watchers were in the open with little to protect them from the storms. So a couple of the team stood watch where they could see down into the valley that led into the grasslands. Eventually, as dusk approached they signaled that the supplies would be arriving at dark as they could see them approaching, but with the distance still to go it could easily be very dark. At least tonight the major moon would be casting light making it easier to see. The ones watching then built a large fire to signal the approaching supply train that they had been sighted and expected.

As the night approached the rest of the team joined the two and all began to watch the progress as the supply train was climbing the last portion and then arrive at the flat area. At this point Trehe approached the leader and they embraced. "It is well that you have made it." Trehe stated.

"I cannot agree more. The storms were delaying us much too long, and I, we were worried that things would have been bad here. I know that there's always an emergency cache of food, but that can only last so long, and we are already a 9-day behind because of the weather. So with what we normally bring we've added additional to resupply that emergency cache. Hey, it's cold out here, so shall we continue on in to your camp, or are we going to just stay here all night?"

Laughing Trehe said, "Oh I thought we could just stay here. Of course, of course, let's get into the camp. The ones who have the cooking chores have been busy, although what we have will be pretty bland, since we have run out of any variety and were getting pretty deep into those emergency supplies. And as you know what is there is stuff that is hardy and keeps one going, but has never been the best tasting stuff around." He swept his arms in a welcoming way, and asked, "Shall we go then?"

* * *

The two of them had packed hurriedly since the news that had been brought by the suppliers had relayed the incidents in High Trail. Their supply shelter would have been one of those that had been destroyed, and with no word directly to them they really had no idea what kind of loss they faced. At least the bakery was part of a larger operation, so recovering would be easier for them. But with the total loss of everything that had been in those shelters others had not been so lucky, and this would have an effect on their business for some time to come. And once down and away from the dig site and back on the main trails it would take them at least another couple of 9-days to return to their home in High Trail. The Season of Cold was still raging but the Season of Green would be arriving soon, even though from the ferocity of the storms it would be hard to believe.

At least, as they dropped down in altitude and headed south, the snow and icy winds were changing to rain making the main trail and road a muddy mess, but still better than the icy cold. Yes, where the road was more traveled it had been graveled, but not much more than that. So it was subject to the soils that lay underneath. And much of that was a red sticky clay that the gravel sank into and it then stuck to one's foot-wear causing one to have to stop periodically and scrap it off. Two days earlier they had split with the supply team as it headed north towards that same village that the two had stayed in when they were searching for the old clan home. Now night was approaching and they were not close to any of the villages that existed along the road. So looking for a place to spend the night they left the road and headed east towards a small grove of trees that at least promised some protection from the winds that were chilling them.

The clouds hung low and a heavy cold mist was falling obscuring the distance, covering them with a wet gloomy depressing landscape. Both were wet and miserable and quite happy to call it a day, but again had wished they could have made it to a village and find a place to stay for the night that was out of the weather. But the gods hadn't favored them that way so here they were searching for a campsite as dusk approached. Kal turning to Jura said, "I had hoped, but I guess because we are still so far out that the villages are more than a day apart. If the farms and such aren't around there'd be very little to support a village, since travelers in either direction are light, and certainly not enough to keep a small village going." Taking a deep breath and looking around he could see that the trees were further away than they had expected, but at this moment they were finally approaching them.

Jura, shivering a little when the winds struck her, just nodded her head. She was more than ready to call it a day. When they had started, the skies had promised this mist, and after they had started, it had begun and refused to let up, and from the look of the clouds would be continuing through at least this night. As they got closer to the trees she saw that they had grown close to a small hill and off of that hill ran a very small stream. Still by not really knowing the area she had no idea if it ran all the time or was dry during the Season of Heat. Yet the way the area was put together it appeared to form a small bowl with the exit for both them and the stream facing towards the road. "I'm ready for a fire, some real heat, and some hot food. Originally I was thinking that we could forgo the temporary shelter, but now I want to get out of this, dry my wet clothes and get into something that is dry. I'm tired of being drenched to the skin."

He nodded in agreement as they arrived at the trees. And once there could see that others in the past had used the area for the same purpose, as there were a couple of fire rings and ashes from long dead fires. The trees provided plenty of dead wood, so fuels to maintain their fire wouldn't be a problem.

Looking over the area they decided to build the fire in one of the pits that hid the fire's reflection from the trail. While they were armed with their long knives and staffs, and felt safe, it was better not to advertise their location. They were still isolated enough that they could depend on help from no one, and after spending so much time with the size of the team they had left; they had become comfortable with all those additional bodies around. They quickly set up camp and staked out their pack beast so that he could get both graze and reach water, with the two of them between the entrance and where the pack beast was located. After the portable shelter had been erected she unpacked the cooking gear, and began to put their sleeping sacks together while he went out and gathered wood for the fire. After the fourth trip he felt he had enough for their needs and to maintain a small fire all night to help keep away any of the wild beasts who might be curious.

He then built a fire, even though it was a bit difficult with nothing but wet wood to work with. Fortunately, from all the time that they had spent in the outback, they always carried dry tinder and small materials to get a small fire going. Still even with this help the dampness of the wood made it a very slow process with much smoke, hissing, popping, and spitting, as the small fire fought to overcome the moisture trapped in the wood. Looking out from inside of the portable shelter Jura said, "Lots of smoke and steam, no heat, and barely a fire."

"Yeah, ain't it true, and I've got to stay on top of it or this wet wood could put it out. This heavy mist isn't helping either. I guess once I get it going we'll stack the wood I brought over here close by so that the heat can dry it out and make this easier." As he continued to work on the fire a large gust of wind entered the bowl, swirling around and spreading the burning tinder for a few moments, and briefly extinguished the fire. And while they were just outside the trees great drops of very cold water still fell on him, making him shiver. "I guess the wind and storm doesn't like the idea of us building a fire here," he commented as he went back to the chore once again. Fortunately there was a very small bed of coals forming from his fire starting materials and soon had a weak fire going once again. In what seemed like forever he finally had a roaring fire going and for both of them steam was now coming off their wet clothes, slowly overcoming the additional moisture that the mist provided. "Oh, does that ever feel good," Kal commented.

She smiled although it was forced. "Yeah it really does. The way this day has gone I felt that I would never be warm or dry again, and the way that fire refused to burn I was beginning to think that we'd have a cold wet camp tonight."

"Well, I guess we could have gotten real close and let our body heat warm us," he said half in jest. Seeing no humor in her eyes he shrugged. "I guess we better get to cooking a meal so that we can get something to eat other than cold trail rations."

"Again, you're not going to get me to argue. Right now anything hot, this fire, the food, and even you dear one is welcome." She smiled at him even though it was a tired one. She would be happy when they finally were back in their own bed, and shelter.

It was almost full dark and they huddled close to their fire trying to keep warm in the heavy mist. The heat at least kept them semi dry, but if the storm decided to change its mind and go to full rain then cold or not they would have to retreat inside of their portable shelter. As they stared into the fire, which for any who lived in the wilds knew was wrong, since it destroyed your night vision, they were half asleep. But, at this point, both were weary from the cold nights on the site and the time on the road. Unfortunately they were still quite a few days away home. It was then when both jumped when someone out in the darkness hailed them, "Yo' fire!" They looked at each other and then out in the darkness and Jura moved into the portable shelter and both withdrew their long knives not knowing who could be out there. Then in the way of their time Kal answered, "Come and set", then he added, "But come friendly."

This brought a chuckle from the unknown individual who within a few moments approached their fire, and to their surprise was riding a pack beast. Once in the light of the fire he climbed down. Again he chuckled when he saw their disbelief. "Get that a lot when others see me do this. I'm really surprised that others hadn't thought about it. After all we've trained our pack beasts to carry our supplies, why not us also? Anyway, you'll not have to worry about any others I always travel alone." He looked at their camp with a practiced eye and smiled. "Well set up, defendable, and not visible from the trail – good, good."

"If what you just said is true, how'd you find our camp?" Kal asked.

"Oh, I've spent a night or two here, and because of a delay I got here later than planned, and was actually surprised to find this place being used. Not many are around here this time of the seasons – too miserable." He squatted down put his hands to the fire and smiled once again. "I really wasn't looking forward to getting my camp set up in the dark, and with it as wet as it is, to get a fire going. But imagine my surprise when I found one already burning – can make one right curious." He leaned back and sat cross-legged and continued. "Yeah, yeah, I know it goes both ways."

They looked at him and guessed that he had to be twice their age, and was dressed in rough handmade clothing. He looked as if he belonged to the hills and grasslands, as if he was as much a part of them as they were of him. "Ah, I thought the two of you looked familiar."

"Familiar, have you seen us before?" Jura asked from just inside of the portable shelter. "I know that we've never seen you."

He then laughed a full deep laugh and said, "I'm never seen unless I want to be." He then leaned forward before continuing. "You're the two that has been traipsing out here in the wild lands, the outback. Lookin' for something say I, and unknown to you others who were watching what you were doing and where you were goin', with not a hint that you had that they were there. Well, I said to myself, this place is gettin' crowded so maybe it's time to head somewhere else. But I was curious. After all there hadn't been anybody in those foothills that I could remember, other than a traveler now and then. And you were lookin' for something – it was obvious. So I decided that since there wasn't much happening anyway I'd stay and watch, and see what this was all about. Had to admit with everybody that seemed to be there it was almost too much for me. You see I'm a loner and prefer it that way. Don't like people. Oh I can take them now and then, but eventually I have to get back and away, live off the land, and enjoy the solitude. Villages and such are just too noisy for me. So I'm happy with just my beast and this world around us here." At this point he took a deep breath and shut up.

Jura and Kal looked once again at each other and then at this stranger, with Kal stating. "You say you were watching us, and those others, and nobody saw you at all – that's hard to believe."

Again he laughed. "Did ya' see the ones who were following you all the time you were searching? And to think that not only were they watching you but another group were watching both you and this other. All I could do was shake my head, and you were none the wiser about any of this. And both of those groups were clumsy, thinking that they were good at what they were doing. By the gods I could have come into both of their camps and stole them blind and they'd been none the wiser. Thought about going in and shifting things around a bit, just to mess with their minds, but it was more fun to watch all of you stumble about thinking that you were alone and were good at living out here." He again leaned forward and said, "Look, I don't know about you, but my stomach thinks my throat has been cut and I have a few items I can add to the meal so let's continue our conversation after we eat something. Besides I need to take care of her, my beast. Mind of I stake her over by yours. That way they'll have a little companionship. After all they originally were from those wild herd beasts and are used to company, other than you and me."

Silent for a moment after this one relayed to them what they had been doing for the last cycle of the seasons, Kal had to admit that they had thought the two of them were alone, but it had proven otherwise, and here was someone who thought it was a joke watching all three groups move through the wilderness. "Sure," Kal said, "It's okay, and what you just said is true. I know our beasts originally were of the wild herds, but that was a very long time ago. And . . . yes I guess you can join us, since you've almost invited yourself anyway. Besides it is a very miserable night and some additional company can't hurt."

Again this stranger laughed, "Okay then, it's settled. I'll go take care of the ol' female and be back before you can get the pot on the coals." At this point he jumped up and was out of sight into the darkness almost instantly.

Jura turned to Kal and whispered, "He really moves fast and is very quiet. I've the feeling that if he had wanted to do us harm that it would have been very easy, and we'd be none the wiser."

What could he say, she stated it so well. "Yeah, but maybe this is a good thing. At least with another in camp it would be less likely that we'd be attacked by bandits or such."

With a large smile on his face the stranger reentered their camp saying, "Ah talking about me are we. Not that I can blame you. But you have nothing to worry about me. In fact before you move out in the morning I'll be gone and you'll wonder if I was ever here. Mark my words, I rarely reveal myself to anyone, but I have to admit you've left me curious, and I felt that this was a good chance to maybe get that curiosity answered."

"Why would you be curious? We were just out and about searching for some ancient site, that's all, and we aren't the only ones to have done that." Kal paused, looked over at Jura and then back at the stranger, "Nothing unusual about that."

"True, true, and if it had continued to be just the two of you I probably would have watched a while, and got bored and then moved on. But when these others were out there too and everybody following everybody it becomes more of a puzzle. Now I like puzzles and solving them. This wild world is full of them and they change all the time keeping me on my toes. Make a mistake out here and you're dead, just that simple."

"That's probably true. And I guarantee that we were quite unaware of the others until we saw them following us when we were higher than they were and we caught them in the open." Here Kal paused again wondering if he should say more, and decided while he was beginning to like this stranger he really didn't know anything about him and it was still important to keep it quiet. Even though there was a possibility that Sabohl was dead, knowing him, there was just as much of a chance that he was still alive and biding his time. And, who knew, this stranger could easily be an agent of Sabohl's who used different tactics to get information. "I really don't know why. I just know that after we discovered them that they became more of a problem, and then that other one showed up and offered to help, and that's really it."

Waving an index finger at them the stranger again smiled and said, "Say what you want, but just from what I observed I know better. But stick to your story if you want. Besides what was so important about that place anyway? I've been there a few times – found some old pottery and places where fires had been built. Felt that this had been a place where some of our oldsters had lived temporarily. Nothing important though. Found other places with much the same stuff. Although, different stuff in the desolation. Tough dangerous area – no water, no game, no nothing but heat, dust and a land that looks the same no matter which way you enter; easy to get lost, easy to die, and none the wiser."

Suddenly interested both Kal and Jura leaned forward with Kal asking, "You've been to the desolation? It's a place that is shunned even today."

"Yeah, it's one of those puzzles. Yah see I haven't always been the wonderer that I've become. I went to the learning centers; I know our history, and the myths surrounding the desolation. And it was a puzzle . . ."

"And you like puzzles!" Jura blurted out.

Laughing and slapping his leg with his hand the stranger said, "Yup, you're learning, you're learning. So I've been working the edges, been deep into the Sacred Mountains too – mighty strange stuff up there, mighty strange. Did you know that there are caves everywhere, and that there are a few where no beasts will enter? Not only that but they seem to have their own heat, and once you're inside they seem both to glow with a soft light, and remain warm. Strange. Now I would have considered it something that didn't need second thoughts if there had been only one of them. If we want to be honest we have no idea what this place can create and it could just have been a freak, some peculiar combination that created it, but I found many of them. Still there was nothing, no other sign, so maybe they are from some of our ancient ancestors." He shrugged, "Who knows, not me. After all it's another . . ."

Again Jura interrupted saying, "Yes we know, it's another puzzle and you like puzzles."

Taking the plate of food that she handed to him he laughed again. "Yeah, and this one is probably one of the many I'll never solve – too cold up there for me. So those caves were welcome. But they are located high, nowhere close to the bottom. Nobody goes there – no reason really – just rock and trees and water and such. Nothing to keep one alive other than the herd beasts, but even most of them keeps to the lower areas. Did you know that there are places where there's boilin' water, and at times this hot water is blown high into the air – quite a sight, but dangerous so very dangerous." He leaned forward and pointed to a massive scar on his left arm. "Learned the hard way, I did. That's from that hot water. Hurt like the dickens it did. So now I stay away from any of those things I find. My mom didn't raise any fools, and I learn quick. Of course, if one doesn't out here they aren't around very long – become food for the beasts."

Kal and Jura looked at each other and both thought what a strange person he was, but he had been to many of the places that they wanted to travel, but it was obvious that while he liked to talk that there was very little chance of getting his help, but would it be wrong not to ask? Kal taking a deep breath as they ate; actually needed to finish eating before the food got cold as it did in such weather. "Look you really seem to know a lot about the outback and we could use help. We are trying to locate a number of places that our ancestors frequented, and we only have vague clues."

Shaking his head the stranger said, "No, no not interested at all. Can't abide by people very long before I go crazy and have to be out on my own. And on that note, did you know that the Valley of the Gods is real and not a myth like they taught us in the learning centers?"

This got both of their attention immediately. "It's real?" Jura asked.

"Quite, but don't ask me where it is because I don't know."

"But you just said that it's a real place and the only way you could know that would be if you had gone there." Kal looked at him questioningly. "So which is it? Myth or real?"

"Oh it's real, but I found it accidental like. I was following my supper, trailing it and had gotten a shot off with my bow – thought I had hit it, but off it went so I continued to follow." Staring out in the distance as if remembering he continued, "A very remote place, close to the desolation, very hilly, very rough, and again like the mountains a lot of caves in the hillsides. I seen it duck into this crack and wasn't sure if I wanted to follow or not, but I don't leave no wounded beast so I followed it into that crack and to my surprise there was a trail that twisted and turned through a very narrow canyon with the mountains, or foothills probably is more accurate, holding tight. Looking up I could see no way one could get atop these things other than the fliers, so didn't worry about something coming after me. After a while I finally emerged in what could be called a hidden oasis. Meadows, herd beasts, even a small lake and a waterfall. Many trees and from that lake a stream ran all the way across the area. It was shallow and easy to cross. I was frozen in awe for a few as I drank in what was here.

"Then things began to click in my mind. I mean I'm pretty good a remembering my learning. First off even though it is a peaceful place, it felt haunted. I felt like I was watched and continued to look around, but really there was very few places one could face danger. So carefully I explored, and like outside this place there were caves everywhere in the faces of the cliffs. And then I found it." He stopped to grab more food from his plate.

"Found what?" Jura asked.

After taking a few more bites and wiping his mouth with his sleeve he smiled and gave the look of conspiracy, lowering his voice he said, "The altar to the gods that is described in the myth. It's right there exactly where it said it was, and at the moment I knew I had to leave. I know that we don't believe in those gods anymore, but it explained the strangeness I was feeling and I got out there as fast as I could, and no I never saw that beast that I had targeted. It was like it just disappeared once it got inside that valley. Anyway, later, much later really, I decided that maybe I should go back and make sure I was right. But was never able to find that entrance, and I tried a number of times. Suspect that the valley keeps its secrets and knows who is close and who isn't. So if it doesn't want anybody to find it, the valley confuses the mind, changes the trails, makes one go in circles. After a while and too many attempts I gave up and haven't gone back, and I don't plan on it. After all the valley allowed me to see that it wasn't myth, but decided not to allow me back, and as such I decided that it could be dangerous if I continued to search.

"Look, like I said, I'll be gone before you are moving in the morning, but if you plan on pursuing these places then I might drop in on yah now and then, maybe point you in a particular direction, and don't ask me my name, I feel that when I'm out here that I have none as the beasts that live here. So when I'm here I'm nameless and prefer it that way. But don't you worry if you are out here, somewhere along the line, I'll know it, and be watchin'." He stood up handed his empty plate to Kal, stretched, and said, "Haven't done so much jawin' in a very long time, and I'm jawed out. So I'll be sayin' good night to the two of you. I'll be with my beast. We kind of protect each other, and thanks for the eatin' it was good, but I'm already feelin' a little crowded. Thanks for everything." And with that he faded into the darkness and was gone – leaving only the dirty plate as a sign that he had even been in their camp.

In the short time that he had been here he had passed on more information than they had before, and sat in awe and silence as they absorbed it all. "What do you think?" Kal asked.

"I really don't know. Almost feel he's kind of crazy. But there surely is a ring of truth to what he said. So maybe it's a smart kind of crazy. Guess we better clean up our camp and head for the sack. With all the time we've been on the road and trails I'm exhausted and could use a good night's sleep before we head out again.' She paused a moment and stared out into the night in the direction that the stranger had disappeared. "I wonder . . . I wonder if we'll see him again."

"It's obvious that he goes where he wants and is good at this life he has chosen, so I suspect that if he wants us to see him we will. He did say that he'd show up at our fires now and then, and I believe he will."

As he had so stated, when they rose in the morning he was gone, and no sign that he had ever been there. Both wondered it maybe they had dreamed him up. The night before had been miserable, wet, cold, and they had been very tired. Maybe the fire had hypnotized them, or they had drifted off to that twilight place where you're neither awake nor asleep but somewhere in-between. But when they looked they found their fire had been built back up and was burning brightly and a fresh pile of wood was stacked nearby. "How'd he pull that off without us hearing him?" Kal asked. He felt, while not the best of being outback, that the time that they had been doing this, his skills had sharpened, and even Jura had mentioned that he was much better at living in the outback. But this stranger had entered their camp while they were sleeping, brought new firewood in and stoked their campfire with them being none the wiser.

"Well, I guess we aren't as good as we thought, or we were so tired last night that we just didn't hear anything." Jura paused as she thought a little, "And that isn't a good thing." She took a deep breath and said, "I guess we might as well get something to eat, break our camp, and get down the trail. We still are a very long way away from where we need to go."

* * *

They had been back at least one 9-day and were still catching up on the news of what had happened. They found that the business had been lucky, far luckier than others who had lost everything in that conflagration. They had gone out to where the storage and supply shelters were located, and while much cleanup had been done it was still quite obvious from the complete destruction how hot this fire had been. One would have thought with the rain falling as hard as it was that the fire wouldn't have been able to do this, but it had. And the information they had received stated that the area remained hot for at least two 9-days, and it had rained most of that time. It had turned out that their supply shelter had been almost empty. The load of new supplies was late in arriving because of the rains. Had the supplies arrived on time then the shelter would have been filled to the top. Since, under the guidance and hard work of their foreman, Sara, the bakery continued to grow, and thusly why the use of one of these isolated shelters instead of the one that they had used in the past. That one was still being used but only to keep what they needed daily on hand and close by.

They had asked, of the group who had been keeping tabs on Sabohl, "how'd he get up here", since he had been living and working in the learning center back in Cross Trails. It was then relayed to them that after a cycle of the seasons Sabohl took a leave of absence stating he needed some time to refresh and had moved up here to High Trail, and maybe teach as a guest learned in High Trail. Because he did have a shelter here it would be no issue. And after he had refreshed his mind and spirit he would return. One of them stated, "We knew that the real reason was to be closer to the action, to be able to watch the two of you, and to be able to get his underground moving much faster . . . since it would take quite a while for a message from here to reach him down in Cross Trails, with the returning message doubling the time; much too much time as far as he was concerned. And we figured that had to be the reason, since immediately upon arriving he made contact with his network."

They then learned of that tragic night when the shelters burned, and how this team had followed him and once the fire had started, had to divide up with one staying with the fire to alert the village, and the other following Sabohl, the rejection, the bad choice of direction, the subsequent fight, the collapse of that old dock, and the disappearance of all who had been on that dock at the time it entered the swollen river. "So we have no proof as to whether Sabohl survived that plunge or not. With the waters flowing as strongly as they were, his body would have been carried far downstream and maybe all the way out to the ocean, since this one empties into it. Plus the one who had watched it all transpire swore that Sabohl had been stabbed at least once. But in that uncertain light he couldn't be sure."

"And there's been no sign of him?" Kal asked.

The others just shook their heads with one saying, "No, none at all. A few of the bodies washed up on the banks much further down, but none were Sabohl. So what happened is truly a mystery."

* * *

They remained throughout the remainder of the Season of Cold, and helped the village wherever they could. Nobody knew how it had happened, and again the secret team that had been keeping track of Sabohl had no direct proof that he was responsible so couldn't say anything. Because that storm that had been pummeling them at the time of the start of the fire, it was the reason for the lack of on-hand supplies. The storm had come out of the north, and the same storm had been responsible for the supply caravan delaying and finding shelter to wait it out. So the bakery was almost completely out of the necessities when the fire began. Yes there had been a number of sacks of different flours and grains, but most of what was there had been unusable, giving the appearance to any who happened to be inside that there was more there than there truthfully was.

Contacting the rest of the family, who by now had a number of bakeries throughout the region, being operated by his siblings and overseen by their parents, much information was available. Available simply because the supply caravans, the contracts with the farmers, and the many bakeries provided a continual flow of what was happening. And because of this the forward thinking of his parents the whole family was becoming quite wealthy. Yet, it was hard work, diligence, and the many hours of planning that made this possible. Also because of their growing importance and having such a great source of information, the family became sellers of information. This wasn't known to the general population, and was never to be revealed to the same, for obvious reasons. So when word was put out to be watching for Sabohl, there was confidence that if he had survived his ordeal that this would be known. Yet, all inquiries came back negative. So with no body, and no proof, everything hung in limbo. Still the general feeling was that he had died and his body washed out to sea.

When the word went out of the fire and loss, the Kaygor family and their many workers descended upon the village and offered assistance wherever they could. They cleaned up the burned shelters, helped the many families that had lost everything to the fires, and had only their personal shelter and little else to live in. Kal remembered his mother and father saying, "There's enough evil in this world, and as we continue to grow and become more successful, when something like this happens it is important that we help, that we provide what has been lost – all within our ability, of course. You see, a little charity now, can benefit not only the ones in desperate need, but can provide a favorable image of us and our business. It is easy to be greedy and turn one's back on others who have not been so blessed, to let one's ego get in the way of helping where it is needed, all because one is above such things, such suffering. Yet, were these same ones not customers, the same ones who were buying our products? Yes, we do provide a good product, and with care we've done well, and built our business. But, if we are not willing to give back, then, no matter how good we are, the quality of what we sell, in the end it will leave a bitter taste in the people's mouths and they will look elsewhere, and then we will be no more. No more because of our indifference, of our failure to show compassion to those who through no fault of their own need help. Yes, some will never recover from such as this, but others will. And all of them will remember, and remember who helped and who turned their backs. And while they may say nothing, those feelings will be there deep inside. And while it may not show immediately, eventually these who observed will use their abilities to move away from those who turned their backs.

"And if they, the ones who ignored the plight of their fellow villagers then run into dire straits, it will be then that they learn, the hard way, the cost. Most are willing to help where they can. But most do not have the means in which to do too much. Most of the time it comes down to their physical selves, and of this they give freely, and when it is over, whatever the emergency or loss, they will return to their lives, and go about the day-to-day thing never looking for rewards or even recognition for what they did. It takes families like ours who have prospered to be able to help beyond just the physical, and as long as we are in charge of this family it will always be that way. And, in the end, we hope that once we have left this world that it is the same with all of you."

It was a good philosophy to live by, and once the work had been done they all returned to their interrupted duties and lives, not looking for any personal reward, and it was time, since the seasons had moved forward, as they always do, to prepare for the next search. Word reaching them from the ancient site that they had discovered was promising, as the different areas of habitation had been mapped out, a burial site discovered, which was strange – not that there was a burial site discovered, but the method and markings used were so different. When they had inquired how so, the response simply stated, was, "These burials were vastly different from any that have been uncovered in the past, and most appeared to have been female skeletons, although there were some males. And because of the type of landscape, and weather all that remained were the skeletons. So no further answers could be drawn."

Both Jura and Kal discussed this, but by not being on the site they personally hadn't seen these burial sites, and the drawings really held no clue. Was it the beginning of another change in how their ancestors viewed life, or was it something else? "I don't know about you, but when we both started this search because of your family archives that were given to you, I thought this would be easy. Well," Jura paused a moment, "well, easier than it turned out to be. And who'd have thought that we'd become part of some larger intrigue, so naïve that's what we were."

"Yeah, really. Here I thought that I could get help from Sabohl, not realizing that it was one of the methods he used to increase his reputation, and to steal discoveries from his students and others in the field. May the gods look well upon him." He smiled and said, "Yeah I know, we don't believe in those gods anymore, but the saying has been with us for who knows how long."

CHAPTER ELEVEN

THE SEARCH

They decided that this time since they had a starting point, the old clan home, that they would attempt to discover the location where the warriors hunted every Season of the Green to replenish their meat and skins after the tough Season of Cold. Because it was here that the story in that archive really began. For generations they had traveled to the same general area, and while, at times there had been rare confrontations with other clans and tribes, this was the norm. If that one wounded herd beast hadn't darted into the desolation at that very moment when K'jor was the clan leader, then their history and how they lived presently could be far different.

Buoyed by the success of finding the original clan home, well the one mentioned in the records, they felt that it would take no more than a season to locate the clan's hunting grounds. But they were wrong. They worked the areas to the south of the clan home covering every space from the clan site to a number of the smaller villages and farms that existed in the great grasslands. While the location of the clan home was mapped out, and had assisted them in finding its location, there was no such thing for the hunting grounds. Only brief descriptions, and because it was common knowledge among all of the clan – the hunting grounds – nothing was written, other than it was a few days travel to the south, by a small stream, with trees, and close to the desolation to the west. While the description of the actual camp was very specific, time would have changed even that. Trees die; streams change direction or dry up, even the land itself changes. And with the description, by being as vague as to the actual location, it could have been thousands of places that all had similar lay-outs. If one wanted to be honest, the desolation ran the full length of the continent from the north at the Sacred Mountains to the southern foothills before meeting the seas to the west.

And the final direction, south, didn't help at all other than point them in the right direction. The warriors could have just as easily headed directly west until they made contact with the edge of the desolation using it as a barrier against attack from rivals, and then proceeded south. And if this had been their route, their final location would have been vastly different than if they had gone directly south or had stayed in the foot-hills weaving their way through protected trails and valleys before emerging into the grasslands and heading for their camp. Sitting by their campfire during the middle of their second season in searching Kal said, "This is so very frustrating. Here we are in the middle of another season, and on the verge of the Season of Falling and we've found nothing, no hints, and are no further along than when we decided to look for their hunting camp. I know, I know, this camp was just a tem-porary place that was convenient, and there were no permanent shelters built, but one would think that with the generations that used the same place that there would be something. And to think that there had been a meeting with one of the tribes during the time of the alliance meant that others knew of its location also. So why can't we find it?"

She shook her head, "You know why, and while the location was known at that time and in that world, so much has passed by, so much has happened since that time that what was once known by all is now known by none." She sighed and took a deep breath, "I know that we've gone over the notes at least a hundred times, but we must be overlooking something. There's got to be some kind of hint that we've missed and are continuing to miss."

"Yeah, you're right, and I think part of the problem is our way of thinking has changed."

"Changed, I don't understand."

"Okay, look we are no longer a warlike people. Yes there's still fighting, and there's a lot of bad people out there, but it is so different from that time where anyone away from their clan or tribe was fair game. If the person was a male, they'd be killed, and if a female she'd be bred. The clans and tribes fought all the time, and until that first true alliance had been formed it remained the way of life and death. Yes disease and childbirth took many also, but if one was a male, the most likely form of death was battle against any of the rivals out there. So this camp had to be such that it would have been easily defended, and while known by others, it was such that they wouldn't attempt to attack it. So we probably need to look at factors that make a location good for defense as well as for the required hunting." He took a deep breath, paused, and shook his head, dropping his voice to almost a whisper. "The only problem with this is what would fill all those requirements? I mean it could have been a small ravine, or depression where the water ran close by, or it could have been wide open not allowing any to approach unseen."

She laughed, "Oh yes, that really narrows it down. I think you just described just about any place and area out here. I'm glad you thought it out. Now I'm sure we'll just go out and find it in the morning." This brought laughter from both of them. As they settled back down she said, "You're right you know. We have no need to be continually on watch for a rival clan or tribe looking to attack us, so in some ways we've grown less watchful, and aren't always looking for the best trail, the best direction that would give us the advantage during a fight. This will take some thinking. Maybe we should stay here for a couple and start trying to put ourselves in their situation. Maybe, by starting in the daylight, we can study where we camped, and see if we can find out how badly we did in choosing our camp, from their point of view."

"You know, that might be a great way of trying to get our minds going in the right direction. But, in the end, I'm sure that we'll only appear to be babes when comparing what we will come up with, compared to them who lived this life for as long as they remained alive."

"Very true, but at least we'll begin thinking like they did, and I'm sure that will eliminate many areas that we would have searched."

With the rising of the suns in the morning and after the first meal of the day, taking care of what nature did to everybody, they looked at their present camp with different eyes — finding both good and bad in their choice of a campsite. First, the good; water close by, camp located against a small hill that hooked around in such a way that it was partially hidden, and very defendable from at least one of the approaches. But both had to admit that the bad far outweighed the good. Their choice of camp allowed too many approaches, so that an enemy could be almost in their camp before being seen, the hill they were camped at the base of allowed easy access to an enemy approaching from the back, giving them the higher ground, and most of the approaches from that direction were protected. So all an enemy would have to do would be to keep their attention drawn forward and then make the attack from the top of the hill, and that would have been that. "You know, at first I thought we had done pretty good job of picking our campsite. We're close to water, partially hidden, plenty of dead wood for our fire since there are many trees close to that stream, and we are far enough back not to keep any of the beasts who might get their water from this point. But I can see how poor a job we did from the defense part of it, and as you said last night we are just babes at this." As Kal continued to look around he was seeing more that made their choice a bad one. Taking a deep breath he said, "If we had been here back then we wouldn't be here now, and I can see that quite clearly."

"Yeah, I see it also. Of course there would have been more than just the two of us. Nobody during those times went out alone, let alone with two. And if it was just two it was usually the warriors who used their skills to remain hidden and out of sight as they moved. And while we've improved since we've been out here for so long, I'm sure that we again are poor at doing just that. This means that even when they hunted they worried about being hunted, so all their concentration couldn't be just on the hunt. They must have always had other members of the hunt being lookouts for rival tribes and such." She paused a moment as another thought entered her mind. "So how did they determine the lay of the land? I mean we get up on top of a high point and look it over and plan how we are going to travel, but to do that would expose you to being seen, and seen from a very long way off. So they must have had other ways."

As she asked those questions he realized that they really knew so very little. What is common knowledge is rarely recorded or written down since everyone knows. So when such is lost there are no records to recover that lost common knowledge. And it would only be through similar circumstances that that knowledge would be rediscovered. "Yes, very good question. How would one go about figuring all that out and not reveal their position?"

". . . Nothing in those pages about that that I can remember . . ." Jura walked over to a log and sat down with Kal joining her, actually standing behind her and massaging her shoulders and neck. "You're so good at that," she whispered

He hadn't realized that he was doing that, but knew that he enjoyed it and that she did also. "It's one of those joys, and I'm glad that you like it. But like you, back on that original subject here, I don't remember anything on those pages about this either. So here we are so many cycle of seasons later, and we don't have a clue. Maybe if that character that came into our camp that rainy night showed up we could ask him. He seems to know how to disappear into the lands. I know it was dark when he showed up, and it rained most of the night, and once we were up that next day he was gone, yet he moved with a grace that made it seem like he and these wilds were one and the same. He probably does much of what our ancestors did with little or no effort, and probably doesn't even think about it. It's as much a part of who he is as is breathing."

"I almost forgot about him. But you're right. He seemed to just flow, to move in such a way that it appeared each and every move he took was planned, but at the same time you could tell it wasn't a conscious effort, and it was just a part of who he is. Yes, but I suspect that if we asked he probably couldn't tell us – probably doesn't even think about it or how he does it. He just does it and it's become part of his nature – who he is. Just like you're a male and I'm a female."

He laughed at that and said, "Amen!"

She looked at him questioningly and asked, "What?"

He smiled, "Oh what you just said. I'm quite happy that I'm a male and you're a female. It works out well for both of us." He then got this wicked grin on his face and said, "Shall we go and prove it?"

"Oh you males, always have that on your minds." She smiled and just shook her head.

"Can I help it if you bring the male out in me? After all I love all of you, and that definitely includes your body." He began to teasingly touch her in places that would get her interested, and she put up a token fight but he could see that she was beginning to respond to his touches. At first he was only going to tease her, but he could sense the passion rising in both of them, and they, hand in hand headed for their portable shelter.

Later, after both of them had bathed in the stream and were absorbing the warmth from the suns, he reached out lovingly and touched her hand, and she returned the touch. "I love times like this. I guess one of the advantages of being out here trying to find those places from the past, that we can explore each other and learn more about each other, and get even closer."

At this she laughed, and said, "Now I don't think we could have gotten any closer than what we were, but I know what you mean. And yes being out here like this allows us a little more freedom on our loving each other." She sighed, took a deep breath, grabbed her clothes, since both of them were lying on the grass naked, allowing the suns and the heat to dry them, got up and began to head back to camp. "I know we could spend all day doing what we did, and I'm sure that we'd enjoy every moment of it, but we've got to get our journal up to date, and then begin again."

When she got up and he could see her in her full naked glory he could feel the passion rising in him again, and reached up and pulled her down to him for which she giggled, and said, "Never satisfied are you."

He smiled lovingly up at her and asked, "Can I help it if you do that to me? After all you looked so inviting I just couldn't resist a second chance."

With a look of devilment in her eyes she said, "Okay, but after this we really have to get something done."

He laughed and said, "I thought that is what we are doing."

All she could say was, "You!" And she then laid a very passionate kiss on him which excited him even more, not that her naked body didn't.

Later as the suns were setting and they were back in camp both looking over the journal Kal asked, "So how do you want to word our discoveries?"

She looked up innocently and asked, "Discoveries, which ones – the ones where we decided to attack this problem by trying to think like our ancestors, or the one where we discovered our bodies?"

At first he didn't catch what she was saying since he was deep in thought, but then what she had asked penetrated and he began to laugh. "I would think, since somewhere in a future time that these journals will be read, by other than you or I, the former would be what is important. From what I've learned about you females – such a discussion between mates is fine, but it is not for public consumption."

"While you males like to talk about your conquests," She shot back.

"Now, now, now that's not always true. In fact, yes there are a number of males that brag all the time about such things. But I suspect that quite the opposite is true."

"Opposite, how so?"

"In my humble opinion, the ones that are bragging are probably not getting any. It seems to be an axiom that if one is physically involved that one doesn't hear much about it, but if they aren't, then the mouth runs over."

"Well, I wouldn't know. It's not that way with us females, I can say that for sure."

"It could be, since I really only know one female intimately . . ."

She looked up at him once again with that innocent look, and asked. "And who would that be?"

* * *

With frustration in his voice Kal said, "These maps are next to useless. Yeah they show many of the villages, but the lay of the land is only general at the best, and even this isn't very good. Heck it's almost impossible to even pinpoint exactly where we are on these things. I really thought that they would help. I'm no cartographer or artist so I can't add a darn thing to them." They were standing on the rise that was behind their camp as they watched the suns rise out of the east. Even the stream that they had camped close by wasn't accurately represented. In fact it was depicted as having ended further east than their present location. "I wonder how much of what is here is as inaccurate as what we are seeing now."

She couldn't disagree with him. She was becoming as frustrated with these things as he was. When they had brought them along forsaking something else, it was with the understanding that these things would help. Well, they hadn't. "I guess if someone isn't living in the area then it might as well say, 'here the land belongs to our mythological gods, and we will only mark it as such'. Yeah, I was really hoping that they would help. But probably the best use we could find for these things is kindling to start our fire. What a waste of finances to have even purchased them. Well, I guess if this is the only disappointment we have in life, then we can count ourselves lucky."

Breathing out heavily he replied, "Yeah, I guess so. Still it would have been nice . . ." Both of them jumped when another asked, "Nice, what would have been nice?" Both sort of recognized the voice, but couldn't immediately place it. Turning around rapidly they both saw that individual who had stopped by their camp that cold rainy night.

"Where'd you come from?" They asked in unison.

He gave them a funny look and said, "From right down there, isn't it obvious?" He looked at them and said, "Oh, it's you two . . . Been a while. So you out looking for those ancient places again?"

Answering back in the same way Kal said, "Yes, isn't it obvious?"

"Well, one never knows what one will find out here. So from where I was I seen your camp, not very well hidden. In the old days would have been a target, that's for sure. So again I was curious."

They smiled and Jura said, "Yes, and it was a puzzle as to who was out and about, and you like puzzles."

This brought laughter from him. "Remember she does, yup, remembered. True, true, and there was something familiar about the camp, but I couldn't figure it out, so decided I would come closer. Now I know why. It is your camp. While most camps are put together much the same, there is always differences." He tapped his forehead and said, "An' I remember differences." He saw the large paper in their hands and asked, "So what's that?"

Kal replied saying, "Something worthless. It's supposed to be a map of the area out here, but it's next to useless. Nothing on it is right." Pointing over at the stream that they could plainly see below them he said, "See even that is wrong. By this thing it ended quite a distance to the east of here, yet here it is."

He glanced at it and said, "Don't use those things, have no need, already know what's there and what's not. Waste of space, waste of time." Then looking at the two of them he asked, "So what puzzle you solving this time, what place are you looking to find?" Again he laughed a little. "I may have been there, might give you a hint, but not give it away. Let you solve the puzzle –it's so much more fun that way – makes one think, makes one grow."

The two of them again looked at each other and back at him. With what little they knew of this person he could have been to where they were searching, but how far could they trust him? Yet, they had been unsuccessful all of last season, and this one was getting late. So any help, any help at all would be appreciated. So with a silent agreement between them Kal said, "We are looking for the hunting camp that K'jor and his clan used. From what we could discern, they used the same camp every hunting season. And while locating the clan home was important, it is what happed after that that changed us, changed our history. So we want to find that place where it truly began."

He was silent for a while. It was obvious that he was thinking. "Hmmm, good puzzle, interesting, out in the open, but at the same time hidden. Not like you – easy to see, easy to find. I'll think about this, but you must remember that there were so many others who also had their camps, who also returned season after season. So to find only one . . . yes, a good puzzle . . ." It was obvious that he was deep in thought and actually appeared to have forgotten that the two of them were there. Looking up he seemed surprised to see them, and then he smiled. "Will let you know, but not today. But will say this, while the herds are no longer large and they originally ranged all the way to the Sacred Mountains, most of the tribes and clans hunted to the south of here. In places where it became green earlier in the season to give the beasts time to put on meat. Others waited until the migrations took the beasts north, but most did not." Then apparently tired of company, and of talking he just walked off the hill down to his beast and then disappeared behind a small hill and again like when he had left their previous camp it was like he had never been there.

"There's one quiet, sneaky person. We never heard him approach and we just watched him disappear in broad daylight. If I believed in sorcerers and magicians I'd swear he is one." Kal turned back to her and shrugged. "I guess we can guarantee one thing."

"And what would that be?"

"Oh, now that he's found us again that he'll be showing up now and again and asking more questions."

"Yeah, that's probably very true. At least he gave us a direction to look. By what he told us we are still too far north. I guess it's still early enough in this day that we can break camp and head further south, and set up again before dark."

"Guess so. It's obvious that he knows more than he's saying, but at least he pointed us in a new direction. I really didn't think that they could have gone any further south. We are a few days out of the clan home. But that is the way we reckon it. We really have no idea how much ground they could cover in a day, and from the records they were three days away from the clan."

"The land is quite open here," Jura said as she looked around again, "and we have had it proved that we definitely set our camp in a place where it was easily spotted, as he just showed us. Darn he makes me jumpy when he does that." She paused a moment before continuing, "Yeah, I didn't think that they could have gone too much further south, but he could be right. Still the only way we're going to know is to head that way, and standing here isn't getting us moving, so shall we?"

It was mid-morning by the time they were packed and heading south, leaning a little west. Using the suns to mark their direction, with the surrounding landscape being similar there was nothing to mark, as a distant point, to keep them on the line that they planned. In truth, since there was not true destination, in the end, it probably didn't matter. They were searching for signs of ancient occupation, and not a particular place. Water wouldn't necessarily be an issue as small streams crossed these grasslands creating islands of trees that hugged the banks or at times grew in the shallow waters redirecting the water around them, and eventually changing the course of the water's flow and direction. As the day progressed the winds picked up and it grew warm. They knew that as they continued their general and slow movement to the west that the grasses would become sparse and the heat would increase as the desolation became a stronger influence. Since this was something that never had been studied that they knew of, it was unknown as to whether the desolation was growing or remaining the same.

There were some theories as to why the desolation existed at all, since the storms that provided the moisture for the grasslands, came up from the south where the grasslands bordered the sea. It was just north of that point that the hills on the west began to influence and to funnel the storms away from the coast and up through those grasslands, denying rain and water to that strip. As the storms would move north, the lands slowly rose in altitude until they struck the Sacred Mountains, which pushed the storms higher into the air changing it from heavy rain to snow and ice. And now that there had been some exploration beyond those mountains here was a place of permanent ice and snow – very inhospitable to life in general. It had created another one of those historical mysteries that someday they hoped to solve, as they were attempting to unravel the surviving ancient writings they were using as a guide. That other mystery had to do with a clan only known as the travelers who consistently, over the generations talked about their home being north of the Sacred Mountains, but nothing had been found to indicate that such a clan had ever existed, further strengthening the myth theory.

They broke for a midday meal and watched as thunderheads began to develop over the eastern foothills. It was travel rations since they wanted to be moving as quickly as possible. "He said that many of those hunting camps were set up further south, but that doesn't mean that any of those can be tied to our clan. It'd put us at least five days out of where they lived, and the writings specifically state that this camp was only three days out." Kal just shook his head, it didn't make sense. But where they had been searching further north there was nothing.

"True", Jura said, "but we are looking at this from what we can cover. We still don't have a clue as to how far warriors could travel in a day. I suspect that physically all of them were in better shape than we are now. Even though I suspect that our health is better . . ." She paused and shuddered as she thought about this. "So dirty and unhealthy the way they lived . . . I'm really surprised that any survived long enough so that we can now look back on that time."

"Yeah, but it must have worked because we are here, and you're right we really have no idea. To cover this much distance in three days would have meant that they probably jogged the whole distance, and that would have included the females that went with them. Those were some tough people. If that idea is true I probably would have been beat up by any of those females and they wouldn't have raised a sweat, and the warriors would have probably just shrugged it off as they would a crawler."

She smiled and said, "I beat you, and not once but several times, and I suspect that I still can."

"Well, true. But you know what I mean. That had to be such a hard life no matter which sex you were. I think I prefer now to then."

"Yeah, me too. But I wonder . . ."

"Wonder? Wonder what?"

". . . What you would have been, oh mighty baker that you are. Would you have become a warrior, a priest, or just one of the workers who remained with the clan to handle the slaves and other such stuff?"

"I really don't know, but we know where you'd been stuck, and you've already given me your opinion on that." Standing up and stretching he said, "I guess we better continue on. We have half a day to travel yet, and still need to find a campsite for tonight."

* * *

It was dusk when they found their next camp, and this time they had studied it from their new found way of looking for a campsite. One that offered defense, provided water, and fuel for their fires, and still allowed them the ability to observe what was happening around them. Here, as they had approached this area, they began to see the first signs of ancient campsites and ancient fires. So that, well, they still didn't know what to call him, since he refused to give them a name, still insisting that when he was in the wilds that he as the beasts required none. Anyway the information that he had passed on to them seemed to be accurate. What else did he know and wasn't willing to pass on, or maybe didn't know he knew, and it was only when they met and they passed on what they were trying to do that it would remind him. He surely didn't appear to be hiding anything and had been forthwith the information that they received from him so far.

As night closed in around them it gave the appearance that they were the only two that existed in this whole world. There were the sounds of night, and the coolness that slowly increased as the time moved by them. "I wonder", Jura asked, "how it was before the clans and tribes, when there were only small groups of us around. How lonely it must have been. How scary knowing that the creatures out there could be your meal or you could be theirs. Now slowly we are taming this world, but there are still a lot of dangers. Yet, to do what we are doing without a large group around us would have been unheard of – not that people don't just disappear out here, because they do. Still, to be here back at the beginning of our people when it could have gone either way . . ."

"Yeah, that would have been an interesting time . . . time before any history that we know. And no, I wouldn't have been interested in living then either. Death had to be very high, and I'm sure that there were many groups that were wiped out, from who knows what. Disease, attacks by the beasts or rival groups, floods, landslides, and so many other traps that I can't think of right this moment. Not a time to relax at all, no time to think about what might be, just a struggle to make sure you lived to face another day, and with no guarantee that when you made it to that day that you would be around to finish it." He laughed, "Enough on that depressing subject. It's part of our distant past and as far as I'm concerned it can stay there. We have enough mystery with what we are trying to solve, thank you."

They both lay back and stared up into the night sky watching the stars, and then every once in a while something would streak across the sky in a blaze of light and be gone. "I wonder what those things are?" Jura asked.

"Don't really know, but that reminds me of that really large one we saw back at that ancient site. The one that came out of the north appeared to be right over the Sacred Mountains – never seen something so big or bright like that at night, other than our moons."

"Yeah, that was pretty spectacular, that's for sure. Well, whatever they are, they can stay up there. Think I'll turn in, lying here I'm finding that I'm falling to sleep anyway . . . New areas to look at tomorrow . . . g'night." With that she slowly got up and headed inside the portable shelter leaving Kal alone. He felt tired himself, but at this moment couldn't get up the energy to move from his comfortable position, and continued to stare at the night sky, only waking later realizing that he had fallen asleep. The fire had burned down to just glowing coals, so he threw a large piece of wood on the coals figuring that it would last until morning, and headed to his sleep sack, morning couldn't be too far off.

* * *

Through the next couple of 9-days they searched and continued moving south until just before the zenith they came upon an ancient isolated camp. Looking at their notes and at the surrounding landscape this came close to matching. They were approximately six days away from the clan home – six days! Yet the words within the text spoke of the distances being only an easy three days away. Was it deliberately misrepresented, or could their ancestors actually cover this much distance in the time stated? Yet, everything that had been confirmed within that text has proven to be accurate, so why would they misrepresent the distance here? Still the texts never mentioned the return times only what it took to reach this location.

Yes the site showed changes since the time that the clan used this as their hunting camp. The stream was no more and the trees that had provided shade during the heat were just snags. Sometime in the past the stream either dried up or changed course isolating this location, leaving the trees without a ready source of water. And if they were to stay here they too would have to find a new source of water. Still when looking over the descriptions given, the directions given to any who sought this camp and comparing this to the actual lay of the land there could be no doubt. Highly defendable, easy to see any enemies approaching, and close to where the vast herds once roamed, with the desolation not too far to the west of them – in sight really, but probably at least a half day away. And they began to really appreciate the location as it was virtually invisible until you almost walked into the camp. In fact that is exactly what had happened to them as they continued their searching. When looking from the outside of this location it could have been any of the thousands of ravines, or small depressions, never giving a hint to the large area that was here or how uninviting it appeared from the outside.

As they had noticed once inside, it was easy to defend. Any place an enemy would approach they would have to expose themselves to the sky, to highlight themselves, making them an easy target. While the ones inside of this location would be difficult to locate, and with water readily available, plus and since this was a hunting camp, food would be of no issue, so the idea of a siege became no option either. It would take an overwhelming force to rout and kill the ones within this camp, and since the main purpose was to hunt for all, there truly would be no reason to attack. Again, from the writings, it stated that attacks did happen, but of these, most were from opportunities presented or a particular tribe or clan had become troublesome to all. And this would be those rare times when a couple of the tribes or clans would ally and attack. Yet all of this during this time of the cycle of seasons happened very rarely – so much so that it happened less than once a generation.

In quiet reverence Kal walked the camp where his ancestors had used for generations of hunting. It was here that the whole story truly began. It was here that was the beginning of the change of direction for this whole world. Even though at the time that it had happened, no such thoughts were in any of their minds. The leader, K'jor, had been left with a puzzle, and it was one that he, for who knew why, needed to solve. Yes, this camp continued to be used long after K'jor was no more. Yet . . . yet it had been here that what they were as a people today could be traced back to this very location, this very spot of earth. While the finding of the clan home held importance, in his own mind it was this place, a camp that was used once a season that held a much greater importance, a greater value, to all of them. While it had been important to find the clan home, it had been necessary so that the rest of the story could be located and told.

Jura watched as he walked quietly around the site. She didn't say anything, knowing or at least guessing what must be going through his mind. Now, with the writings that they had, they had been able to locate two places that had been placed in the myth status by the historians. Those writings that his family had held on generation after generation were finally bearing fruit, and slowly uncovering their true past. What was still ahead of them, what was still to be discovered? She really didn't know, but the writings had been accurate, so all she could assume was that the rest of what was written there probably was accurate from their ancestors' point of view. She looked and could see that they'd been here for a while and the suns were beginning to head towards the hills that were located in the desolation and quite visible from here. "Kal, we need to setup camp, and while we have water enough for now, we'll have to find more."

Kal barely heard her as his mind was drifting to images of what must have transpired here, cycles of the seasons after cycle of the seasons. He could almost see the ghosts of the warriors and the females who would prepare the skins and meat for the trip back. See them bring in the large herd beasts that required at least three warriors to bring down, and twice that many to bring the carcass back to camp to be efficiently processed and packed. It was like he was being allowed to look through the veils of time and see those ghosts going about their lives, unknown to them that one of their future ancestors was watching. He could see the almost smokeless fires, the numbers of warriors and females here. There must have been a least fifty warriors, with a minimum of ten females if not twice that number. It was like a small village with all the activity going on. Yet there was a quiet the defied the size of the group. They moved with a grace and seemed more to flow than walk. As if they were part of the land, part of the wild places. He knew that there was no way he could ever be that graceful, obtain that way of moving. It was completely unconscious on their part, and he knew if he tried that he would have to think about it all the time, taking away that awareness of the surrounding areas that also seemed to be a part of them.

They were never still, their eyes were forever moving, never staying on one point at any one time. Yet, when they did remain still, it was as if they were the land, it was as if they became invisible, disappearing from sight only to reappear when they moved once again. In that movement, and those times of stillness nothing was wasted. It seemed that each move, each pause, had a purpose. In some ways he envied what he was seeing. Still, he realized because of their lifestyle, the continual fighting and hunting that this was a very necessary part of who they were. If they made a mistake or hadn't learned their lessons well when they were children they wouldn't be here now, but dead. As he remained on the edge of this ancient campsite he could also see the seriousness of what they were doing. The clan depended on them for their meat, and all the work that he was witnessing reflected that goal. He noticed that the portion of the camp where the females resided was the center where they were protected by the warriors who surrounded them. He became alarmed when one of them looked directly at him and he flinched, but then shook his head and smiled. There was no way that this warrior from the past could see him, or if he did, there was no way he could touch him, since the veils of time stood between the two. Then as it appeared the scene faded and he was alone with Jura and they were standing in this long abandoned camp of their ancestors. Quietly he said, "Yes, you're right . . . we do need to set up our camp." Yet, he continued to stare, trying to understand what he had been shown; but no answers came.

THE DESOLATION

"That was quite a vision you had a 9-day ago. I wonder what brought it on and why you were allowed to see the past that way?" They were standing on the edge of the desolation, knowing that shortly they would make their first foray into that inhospitable place. Jura looked carefully at what they were planning and since neither had ever been this close, they really didn't know if their plans covered everything, nor did she like what she was seeing.

Kal shrugged and said, "I really don't know if what I saw was real or not, or whether it was just my mind playing tricks on me. But there had to be something to it, because we found proof that the camp was laid out just about the way I saw it in that vision. Who really knows what exists in the natural world. Maybe there was a brief rift that allowed both the ones from the past and me to look across that veil, even for a moment and see, for them, that there would be a future, and for me, proof of our past and how they lived. I just don't know. I do know that after the vision was over I began to doubt it. Still as we worked the site and we found evidence that it was as I saw, it left me more puzzled, and I guess if I admit it, still doubting, even though the proof was being uncovered each day." He looked into the desolation and honestly didn't want to set foot in there. It had a reputation and that reputation was very bad.

"Now that we are here it makes me wonder what was going on here. I mean from the writings it speaks of many smokes coming out of the desolation at the time there was renewed belief in the gods. You know when the rumbling began again in the Sacred Mountains. It wasn't very long after that, that the smokes, up and down the length of the desolation, are recorded. But look, there just doesn't appear to be anything that can burn here. It's barren, there are no grasses, except here on the edge, and it's still early in the day and I can already feel the heat building, reflecting off that bare land." He stared into the desolation once more and could see that on the edges that the grasses attempted to invade but was largely unsuccessful.

"Look, if I remember right, those writings stated that the priests were brought out at a later time to get their take on what was found – you know right after they had destroyed the lair. Also from the descriptions made by the warriors, and by K'jor himself, it was almost impossible to find your way around in there. So my thoughts are this; they probably marked a trail into the area they wanted to go. So let's hike the edge, and see if we can find some type of marker that would lead us in. Remember they were hunting when they trailed that wounded beast into the desolation. That means that they were not a very long way away from camp – far enough to hunt, but not so far as to make it difficult to bring in their kills. So, I'd guess no further than a half day out, and then, only if it required that distance. If you think about it, traveling a half day, taking down a few of the beasts and then having to haul them all the way back to camp would be a waste of time and effort considering the amount of meat they would need."

"Makes sense to me, besides the longer we can remain on the edge, at least until we have a better idea about this place, the better I feel about it. And that idea about leaving a marked trail is probably true. I'm sure that for the first few times in they tracked. But looking at what we are seeing here, tracks wouldn't last long. There's already a dusty haze as the breeze is picking up. I think that tracks would be wiped out rather quick leaving no sign of one passing through. In fact, if I remember right, it said that in the writings."

Taking a deep breath and shaking her head Jura continued saying, "I guess we're just stalling a little here. So let's work the edge." They were just outside of the camp carrying enough supplies to last for a couple of days, if need be. But both of them suspected that where the ancestors had entered the desolation chasing that wounded beast couldn't be very far away. Still what they considered not far away and what their ancestors would have, had proved to be vastly different.

It was pushing the zenith when they came upon a rock cairn. And until they found it there had been no sign of any entering, leaving, or the placing of markers of any kind. Looking further to the south, still on the edge of the desolation, they could see nothing else that resembled this. So using this point they stopped and had their travel rations. They had brought their pack beast with them, not wanting to leave it alone. Also the beast was now carrying all their water and knowing what had been told about the desolation, they knew that there would be no water. It had been another reason for the present belief that the *priests and servants of the gods* couldn't have lived here, and as such was just a part of the larger myth surrounding this time in their history.

As they sat there staring into that foreboding place Jura asked, "What do you want to do? How do you want to tackle this? I can't see anything, at least from here that shows us any other markers. Yet, there has to be, especially if this is the right place. Distance was a little further than I thought it should be, be that's me not them. We already know that they could travel over greater distances in a day than we do, heck almost twice the distance. So it could be the same about their hunting range."

"I think what we should do is just work inside this area to see if we can find any other rock markers or cairns. Half of this day is already gone, and I'm not of the mind to be inside the desolation in the dark. Again from those writings, wherever it is that we need to go is probably at least a half day inside. So let's just do a cursory look, and then move our camp. There's a stream close by so we won't have to keep going out like we are at our present camp to get our water skins refilled."

"Okay, it works for me. I have to admit that the idea of getting stuck in there in the dark isn't something I want to do either."

The next morning as the suns touched the horizon they were ready to make their first trip into the desolation. The plan was simple really, just work in far enough to be able to see their camp and to see if this cairn that was positioned on the edge of the desolation, was the starting point they were looking for, or that it was just another dead end, left by a later or earlier group representing something long forgotten. Yet there was also a worry about those mud hills, well they weren't mud now, but there was nothing on them but the exposed earth flashing back colors of red and yellow, with large boulders exposed half buried in those hills and they appeared to be close to the edge. Meaning that it would be easy to lose one's way almost immediately. And if the writings said anything at all, it was a warning that even for an experienced warrior these lands looked the same no matter where one was, and tracks disappeared almost as soon as one made them, leaving only the suns as a marker as to the direction one traveled. It definitely was a land for the spirits, not the living.

And as the cycle of the seasons had passed with hundreds passing, the feeling hadn't changed. Many had tried to search the desolation, and many never returned. The ones that had sworn that they would never go back to that place, as it was only a place of confusion, dust, and heat. Cooking one's body and mind, confusing even the most experienced – yet it was here where K'jor and the clan had gone, discovering the servants of the gods, those mythological gods that they now knew never existed. So what was it that they had found, and what had caused all that smoke when it was quite obvious there was nothing here to burn? So with this knowledge and with some trepidation they began their journey into the unknown. Looking into the desolation they could see that there was already a haze as the morning breezes began to pick up, causing the light powdery soils to begin their daily ride in the currents, and to once again settle at night when it calmed, leaving the ground without a mark, without a track, leaving no trace that any had passed here.

Had anybody been standing there as they made this first exploration, it would have appeared that they were slowly turning transparent as the dusts swallowed them, making them disappear from sight as if they were no more. Kal coughed and sneezed before reaching into the pack he was carrying. Looking over at Jura he could see that she was doing the same thing. They stopped as they dug in their packs for something to cover their faces so that it would be easier to breath. The fine particles of dust were too easy to breathe in. Even though they had seen the dust clouds forming, they hadn't considered the consequences. At least the herd beasts had a natural defense against this, and wouldn't be having the issues they were. Both turned and looked back to where they had entered and found that it was already obscured to the point that they couldn't be sure of its location. "How'd they do it?" Kal asked, "I mean they supposedly followed a wounded beast in here to finish it off, and then found that male and female here. They then returned to the camp with not only the slain beast, but the clothing of the two, and from the writings made it sound like it was no big deal."

"Yeah, big difference between reading it and living it." Jura looked back once again. "Look, I think we're going to have to come up with a better method of doing this. We're really not that far into this area and already we've come close to losing sight of where we need to return. And looking at this, this dust and such, how would the ones who entered mark a path? From what little I can see, and I really mean what little I can see, there are no paths, nothing that one can latch onto to know where you are or how you can backtrack. And if the winds really start blowing hard I have a feeling that it will be almost impossible to see anything at all. Yeah, this is making me respect our ancestors even more. Like you said, from their writings it was just another day."

With an unspoken agreement they turned around and headed back to the cairn that they were using as a landmark. After reaching it they looked at each other and both of them were covered in a fine dust with the footwear full of silt, changing the color of their clothing to that of the desolation. "No wonder there's never been any bodies recovered from here. We've only been in there a short time and look at us. If someone died in there it wouldn't take long to bury the body or make it invisible just from this dirt. Besides I don't think many would have spent too long looking anyway. We're already learning, personally, what the dangers of this place are." Kal looked back over his shoulder into the desolation and could only shake his head.

Jura began to brush herself off raising clouds of dust as she did. "Well, one thing for sure, if there were people or clans that lived in there, they would be safe from anybody out here. And that's a very big 'if'. If it hadn't been for that accident they would not have been discovered and our history would probably be very different. You know it's kind of funny how just one small incident like this ended up bringing major change to us. Makes one wonder, what other inconsequential incident that happened in our past may have led to some other major change for us, and this world. I guess we'll really never know, since such things aren't considered important at the time, and it's only after much time has passed and one can look back to that point in time that it becomes apparent."

They hiked up and down the edge of the desolation to see if there might be an area where the powdery dust wasn't being stirred by the winds producing that haze that obscured everything. "We're going to have to rethink this. I felt that we could just hike in there keeping that cairn in sight and mark something so we'd have a direction to both go into that place and find our way back out. I really didn't think that the dust would be that big of deal. Boy was I wrong. How'd our ancestors do this anyway?" Kal stopped and stared knowing that while the desolation was so close, it was still beyond them at this moment.

"Yeah, I just figured it would be easy too, at least take a small excursion into the area – kind of learn a little about it and then come back out. We spent less than the morning time in there and learned nothing – exasperating to say the least." Jura stood there next to him with her hands on her hips coming up with no solutions. Both hiked back to the cairn and began searching around it to see if there was something that identified why it had been built here, but after a long period of time had passed and they came away with nothing, it just added to a very frustrating day. "There's got to be a time when that dust isn't so bad, and maybe back when our ancestors entered here it wasn't this bad. Things change and I'm sure it's the same for the desolation." With nothing found and no solutions, they returned to their camp somewhat depressed.

Once they arrived back at camp they unpacked the pack beast and staked him out on some of the grasses where it began eating, unconcerned about what its owners were thinking about. As long as he had food and water and was treated well he could care less. "Well, this has been a successful day." Kal said sarcastically. "I surely have a puzzle to solve, and speaking of puzzles didn't our friend say that he had been in the desolation?"

"Yeah, I think he did, but he didn't say how far or whether it was just along the edge like we ended up doing today. That's a very dangerous place, and a tough one to crack. No wonder people get lost and die in there. And I didn't see many rocks and such when we went in there either. That's not to say that there isn't any, but that means if we are to mark a trail by using stones then we'll need to bring our own, and from those clouds of dust today we'd have to plan on marking our trail at least twice as often as we would normally. That's a lot of stones."

All Kal could do was nod his head in agreement. They really didn't have any idea what the interior of that place held. There could be plenty of rocks for them to use, or like the edges have none. Stones added up to much weight, and that would mean that something else would have to be left behind. The beast could only carry so much, and even with their packs they were limited to what they could carry. "At least there are plenty of stones here by this stream but with that dust how large of stack would it take to remain visible, or not get buried?" It was a very good question, and another for which they had no answer.

Jura took a deep breath and let it out slowly, saying, "I guess we can finish out this day here, sleep on it and try again tomorrow. With the after-zenith still ahead of us we can begin to pack some of these river stones and at least try setting up a few inside the desolation to see how many we will need, and what the maximum distance will be to allow us to see them. I think for the next couple of days we should experiment and see what works and what doesn't."

"Good idea and I think we probably should do that away from where we plan to finally go in and explore. That way we won't get confused by some of our experiments if we tripped across them. Of course if we did, and we had set them up somewhere else, then we'd know that what we finally settled on didn't really work since we would have come out in a different area than where we went in."

* * *

For the next several days they tried a series of methods and found that on some days the dust wasn't as bad, but others it was worse. They finally settled a method that would use the smallest amount of stones, and yet point them in either the direction they headed going in, and the direction necessary to head back out, and finally after a 9-day, they were ready to attempt it once again. They were hoping that as they headed deeper into the desolation that they would come upon markers left by their ancestors, especially if this cairn represented the entrance that they had used. Their strange visitor never entered their camp during all of this time. But that didn't mean that he wasn't watching them. He had already shown them his ability to stay hidden. So there was no way to know if he was around or not. So with hopefully enough stones, and enough supplies and water packed, and with the rising suns, they began their trek back into the unknown.

Once again inside the desolation the cairn disappeared from sight and the mud hills became more visible and were closer than they thought. The clouds of dust made it appear that they were further away than they really were. Upon examination they were of a crumbly type soil that once wet probably made clay of some kind, but once dried out would break apart killing any plants that might try and grow. Here the land was very broken, with the hills and the small depressions all looking similar, making it easy to become lost. So far the supply of rocks that they had brought with them was holding out, and that was a good thing since they had yet to locate any within the areas that there were traversing. The dust was less of a problem the deeper they got in. It seemed that these mud hills provided a partial wind block, which was nice, but the downside came as the suns rose higher in the sky. With no vegetation, and little wind the ground began to heat up and shortly it was almost unbearable – it was downright hot.

Taking a break in what little shade they could find, they could see that their clothes were becoming soaked from their sweat, and this wetness was picking up the dust, creating a mud layer on their clothes making the situation even more uncomfortable. "Why would anybody want to live here?" Jura complained. She was uncomfortable, hot, and felt dirty from her head to her toes. And while working on a farm, such work could get one dirty – this was far worse. She itched, felt like she was in that oven that they used in the bakery. And there was no place to get relief. What made it worse still was the fact that they hadn't reached the time of day yet for the maximum heat. They were still short of the zenith when it would become the warmest, hold that way until late after-zenith, and then begin to cool. Now the worry was did they bring enough water? Oh they had plenty, but they were sweating it out almost as fast as they drank it. Looking around where they were they could see their last marker, which was a good thing because no matter what direction they looked, it all looked the same. All the hills were rounded, the depressions slight, and only the shadows gave a hint to direction. Once the zenith had been reached, even that would be taken from them.

"I'd say we need to find a place out of the direct suns, find shade and wait until it cools a little before continuing, but there's no place to do that. This just sucks. Why would anybody want to live here?" Kal swept him arms around to emphasize his question. After all there were so many other places to live than this. Still, at this time, they stopped to take a break.

"I don't know, and I don't know if we'll find proof one way or the other. But maybe, whoever they were, they had little or no choice. I know, there are always choices, but we really have no idea who these people were, if they were, so I don't know."

"I know, I was just spouting off. This place is unbelievable, miserable and whatever other words I can come up with to describe it. I know one thing for sure; I wouldn't want to live here. The grasslands during the Season of Heat gets warm enough for me. This, this is so much worse than I ever imagined it could be, and we're in the Season of the Falling."

"Point taken, and to add to that is the fact that we are only a few 9-days out of the Season of Cold, which means that it's not nearly as hot as it would be at the beginning of this season." Breathing out heavily and standing back up, she asked, "Shall we? Sitting here or hiking and being uncomfortable isn't going to make much of a difference, and we can't find anything sitting here."

They began moving off in a southwesterly direction, now being surrounded by these dry mud hills, small valleys, ravines, depressions, and nowhere water or vegetation of any kind. It was a very dead world. No wonder their ancestors had considered it the land of the spirits. Nothing living could survive here and this only deepened the mystery. How would anyone survive in this, let alone a clan or tribe? There was absolutely nothing to support life. Since entering these hills they had been forced into the direction they were taking as any of the other directions were blocked, and the trails, if that is what you could call them, were narrow and went through the small breaks in those hills. Eventually they came upon another cairn and from that picked up a trail marked in stones. Most of these markers were half buried in the fine powdery soil that they were hiking through. Each step they took created a small cloud of dust at their feet, and their clothes from their knees to their feet were heavily caked with it.

With the stones that they had brought with them, they added to these old markers to make them easier to find when they left. And because they couldn't be sure that this old trail would lead them back out, the made sure to heavily mark where their markers joined this one. They knew from the writings that the hunters had trailed the wounded beast deep into the desolation, although it was still on the edge when compared to the actual size of these lands. It had taken the hunters about half a day to do what they did here and to return with their tale that they had passed on to K'jor. Then once they had returned to the hunter camp the following hunting season, K'jor had explored some of this area trying to get answers to his nagging questions, finding , in the end, that hidden lair of "magicians and sorcerers", as they had called them. It meant that they were presently walking the same grounds that their distant ancestor walked. And all who had followed him, to destroy that hidden lair in the distant past.

And one of the lessons that they were still learning had to deal with distances traveled in a day by their ancestors' verses what they could travel in a day. Their ancestors could go double the distance as they flowed over the landscape, moving with stealth and grace, covering vast distances with little or no effort. So, taking that in consideration, they felt that it would take them at least a day to get to where their ancestors had found the beast they had wounded, and of course, those two strangers. At least for now, with the existing stone markers they were traveling much faster than they had when they blazed and marked their own trail – eventually, as the suns were setting only to enter another bowl like area, where they found another cairn. It was too late in the day to do any more exploring so they set up camp here, and once set up began to look this area over. There were a couple of small caves, and from the descriptions in the writings this had to be the place where this encounter had happened. Although how they determined it was an unknown, since once again, those writings spoke of confusion and the similarities of the landscape, which they could now personally attest.

They had packed fodder for the pack beast and water for all of them. Their plan was simple, be here for no more than two or three nights and leave on the third or fourth day to be back at their camp they had set by that cairn that marked the division between the two areas – the grasslands to the east, and the desolation to the west. Yet as the shadows began to grow and the suns set, there became a chill to the air that was unexpected. Still if they had thought about it they would have realized that with nothing to hold the heat of the day it would just evaporate as their sweat did. And once the suns did set it became a very cold and uncomfortable night. With their fire burning, again from the wood that they had packed with them, it was silent – a too silent world – making them feel that they were being watched by unseen eyes. But there was no one other than the two of them and their beast. But the feeling was overwhelming and they became jumpy. No wonder their ancestors felt that the spirits roamed here – it was a dead haunted land, and once they were done with their exploring they would be glad to leave, to be gone. And if they found nothing, there would be no reason to return, which was fine with both of them.

Eventually both them fell asleep, although they awoke often thinking that they heard something approaching their camp. They would listen hard but hear nothing, only to fall back into a troubled sleep, and with the first gray in the sky found both of them shivering and building a warming fire. Both were blurry eyed and exhausted as if they hadn't slept at all. No word was spoken as it would have taken effort and energy which both felt that at this moment there was none. Sighing Jura finally said, "Bad night, hate them."

He nodded in agreement, not having the energy at this moment to put it into words. In a way he thought it was funny that right now as both of them sat shaking from the morning chill trying to get this fire burning hot enough to get some heat out of it, and that he, and he was sure she, looked forward to the rising of the suns and the heat they would provide them, only to curse them later in the day.

Eventually as the suns touched the horizon they began to move a little. Anyway they looked at it; this would be a tough day. With as little sleep as they had, even thinking clearly would be hard if not impossible, and they would have, also, to be careful with their tempers. Both knew that they would be short today and it would be easy to find faults that could set either of them off. Again, with the lack of concentration, it would be easy for their minds to drift off the task, and here, especially, it was very dangerous. While they were still close to the edge of the desolation and the grasslands, they were far enough inside that if they got themselves turned around it could mean failure and their very lives.

So with these thoughts, they picked up the trail and followed the old stones with care. And as the previous day they added their own to be sure to keep this pathway visible to them. The trail wound through many of the mud hills, small depressions, shallow valleys and ravines giving one no idea where it was leading. Soon they were longing for the cold morning as the heat became oppressing, closing in on them, and with the small breezes giving only temporary relief as they dried their sweat soaked clothes, leaving them worse off as the heat sucked the life right out of them. In the distance through the heat waves there appeared to be another cairn which lifted their spirits a little. At least they knew that they were still on the marked trail even if there was no true trail there. When they reached the cairn they found themselves in an enclosed bowl which concentrated the heat even more, making it almost unbearable. It appeared to be a dead end. Had they come all this way only to find nothing? It surely appeared to have been a waste of time. Jura looked at Kal and asked in a tired frustrated voice, "Now what?" She was exhausted and quite done with this, and finding this apparent dead end caused her flagging energy and spirits to collapse.

He was at loss for words as he looked around this sun baked landscape. Why place a cairn here of all things? There seemed to be no reason, none at all. In the unbearable heat and the waves of heat, causing the lands around them to shimmer, he walked further into this bowl and began to walk the perimeter, and hidden in a fold that was invisible from where they had been standing, he found an opening. Turning around and facing Jura, who hadn't moved, and to his eyes, appeared to be on the verge of collapse, pointed and said, "Looks like it might continue here. This is kind of hidden unless you get in the right place." He signaled her to follow and found himself in a narrow ravine or small canyon, the floor covered in loose sand. It wound and twisted through a number of turns and then the hills that formed the sides began to drop away with the path he was following change and began to widen and open up. As he made the final turn he stopped and his jaw dropped. He was at a complete loss for words. It was as if the words in those writings had come alive and he was now standing as his ancestor had described the scene.

Jura was trailing a little behind and when she saw him stop, even though he was still partially hidden by the twists of this trail she wondered what happened. Only to stop as she came up beside him and see the very same thing he was staring at. Both were silent for a while and in silent reverence entered into this hidden area that his ancestor K'jor had first set eyes upon. The very thing that had set their world on the path it was presently on. Before them sat those same shelters that he had seen. Only time had not been kind. Still because of the dryness of the area these shelters were still somewhat intact. Although the roofs have collapsed a very long time in the past, and many of the walls had collapsed together forming piles. Yet enough remained so that they could be identified for what they had been – shelters. As they approached these long empty and abandoned shelters they could see that original strip of vegetation, now long dead that had blocked the view of that wall, and below and ahead of them the other shelters constructed as the tribes had, again showing the wear of time. "It's just as described in the writings," Jura whispered.

It was almost like they had entered sacred ground. For this had been one of the strongest myths, and one, that any in their world thought would always remain as such. Yes, in the past others had tried, and many had died in their attempts. Making most believe it wasn't worth the cost to prove it one way or the other. Yet here they stood as K'jor had. Only in their case they wouldn't be facing the same issues, the same problems or puzzles, since these had been solved so long in the past. The present puzzle was; why did someone live here in the first place? Now, from personal experience, it made no sense. It was a land of the dead not the living; unbelievably hot during the day, and very cold during the night – making this land un-inhabitable for all. They had yet to find any living thing be it plant or beast, in the torn ragged land. "I really don't believe what I'm seeing. It's got to be a mirage. But we can reach out and touch this so I know it isn't." Kal was almost as quiet in his response back to her as his eyes took in the sights. The heat forgotten, they quietly walked the area where the two places were located – the clan home and the tribe home. In a way it was a learning experience since there hadn't been any-thing like this in at least a thousand cycles of the seasons so no one really knew what these shelters truly looked like or how their ancestors arranged them.

After spending some time among these ruins of their past, they headed towards the wall that was visible beyond the dead vegetation that had originally blocked the view of any who had entered this small hidden valley, and began to follow in the footsteps of their ancient ancestors. For them it was just as it was for their ancestors. From this point on it was into the unknown. What was it that lay just beyond that wall? That wall that was still too high to climb, too high to see over, leaving everything that existed beyond to speculation. Yet the writings had described what had transpired back at that time, and the killing of the ones who had lived in this place. As they approached, their appreciation for the ones who had constructed it increased. Its sheer size dwarfed them, and while much of whatever had covered it had been blasted by the winds over time, there was still a slight hint of the color that it had originally been. Sort of an off white that rivaled the colors of the surrounding hills leaving just enough of a contrast to make the wall stand out from the barren land.

Again silence was upon them. How was something like this constructed? There had never been found in any of the discoveries anything like this. And, as far as they knew, they had no ability to do this today. Kal reached out and touched the wall and found that it had the feel of a rough rock surface, and of course was warm from the heat. As he ran his hand over the rough surface he could see small grains of something falling off. Both stood there in awe of this massive construction, so simple, and yet so beyond anything they could do themselves. "It's no wonder that our ancestors thought that whoever built this was magicians and sorcerers. It had to be shocking to find this kind of barrier and know that it isn't natural. By the gods, I almost feel that way. This is just unbelievable." Looking up he felt that it had to be at least twice his height and maybe more.

Jura remained silent as she stared at it. *Who could have done such a thing?* With what they had discovered so far, she was expecting something completely different than what was here. Even now, like Kal, it would have been easy to pass this off to the supernatural. Quietly and with reverence she said, "Shall we walk along it and see what we can find? But if this is what these people were capable of, I'm almost afraid of what might be on the other side of this wall. I mean look at this! Really look at this. It's so simple, but at the same time demands our attention. It reflects strength and power without being obvious. And why is it here and why did these people do this? From what we can tell there's nothing in the desolation that could require such a thing. Yet, here it is. And if I remember, in those writings, every lair that they attacked and destroyed had one of these surrounding it where there were openings in the land. So what we are seeing here isn't isolated, it was common."

"Yeah, but that brings up another question."

"Another one? I thought we were finding too many already. But what would that be?"

"Well, think about it Jura. I mean really think about it. It's obvious that we couldn't do this when this was discovered, and we still cannot today, so who are these people? I mean who were they that they could do all of this, and live here where no one could or should live, and from the size of this it was more than one or two families. Plus, in those writings that we are using, they said that this was one of the smallest that they discovered and destroyed. We already know that we can't live here, and that's why this place is largely unexplored. As experience has shown, most that go into the desolation don't come back out. And now that we've had firsthand experience, we know why. So again, who were these people and how'd they do it? And I guess that leads to another one. I know that we've been trying to find the hunter camp and then this place, but from what we've seen so far, and I know this is just the beginning, do we announce our discovery or do we say nothing about it? I mean, look at this, really look at this. What does this say about us, and then comparing what we are seeing here, and I know we aren't even inside of this yet, are we really ready for what this both reveals and says about our world?"

They began walking along this wall before he continued. "Look, this flies in the face of logic and in what we truly know about our past. There is no record anywhere that supports what this represents. This changes everything. It raises questions such as; were we more advanced than now at some time in our past? And if that's the way of it, what is it that caused this world to lose what it had and became the clans and tribes of our past? There's just so much that something like this makes me want to question, and of course, I have no answers."

Jura remained silent once again as she absorbed what he was saying. It was a dilemma that's for sure. They had been eager to search and find this place – the place where their history began to change and lead them to where they were presently. But this was so beyond expectations, so beyond anything she had imagined. She honestly had thought that the writings had exaggerated this wall, but found in fact, that it understated it. *I really don't understand any of this.* She thought. *And Kal has raised some very valid questions. I know that I'm overwhelmed with just this wall. What is it that we will find beyond this? I'm almost afraid to find out. In a way I guess that I feel that we are so far above our ancient ancestors with what we are able to do. But here, right here is this. And it's old, so very old, and so far beyond us. What does this truly say? What does it say about us?* They came upon the jog in the wall, the very one mentioned in the writings, and before them was that doorway into that unknown world that K'jor and the clan destroyed so very long ago in the past. What would they find when they passed through that door leaving this world behind and entering into the lairs, as they had been called at the time of their destruction. She paused not sure if she really wanted to, and at that moment shadows started to build. She, looking around, realized that the day was just about over and they would have to wait as night was approaching and they'd need to set up camp. Thinking about what they had brought with them, tomorrow would be their only chance as they would be running out of what they had packed. In a way she was glad for the respite, since she wasn't sure if she really was ready for what was through that doorway. This wall had been shock enough for one day.

As it seemed to be in the desolation, the suns rose early. There was no trees, no mountains, nothing to block their early rise. So with a quick morning meal out of the way they made their way back to that wall, following it down towards that single entrance. They had camped by the ruins of the shelters that were like the clan shelters of the past. Something familiar, and at the same time there was additional wood so they could avoid using their meager supply. Now with the shadows stretched deeply from what shelters remained standing and that wall both could feel that morning chill that penetrated deep making both of them cold. Both looked back towards their campsite which wasn't visible here. Since there had been a warming fire there, and as of yet the suns hadn't begun their job of warming the area, and what surprised them was their breath coming out in clouds of steam – that fire was beckoning. There was reluctance in both of them. The wall had been a shock and was enough to make them feel inferior to whoever had been the ones who had constructed this thing. The writings had said that this doorway had been sealed at the time of discovery and after stopping whatever monster was responsible for that deep vibration that was more felt than heard; the doorway opened and had remained so since that time.

And that became the next mystery. They had expected a swinging door, the same that was on every shelter that ever had been built, yet this was not that way. Instead it appeared to have withdrawn into the wall. How could that be, and how, if they were seeing it right, did it do that? Again, this was something that they couldn't duplicate even now. In a subdued voice Kal said, "I guess we'd better go inside. You know I just can't get over the feeling that we're being watched. But, other than us, I haven't seen a living thing, and all I can feel is this very cold morning breeze, and hear nothing but silence. It really does feel like a haunted land. But, again, I don't know about you but that breeze is cutting, and I'm thinking that on the other side of this wall we'd be out of it. So shall we?"

Jura just nodded her head. She really wasn't sure she was ready but had to agree that getting out of the cold wind would be nice. She hated being cold. She signaled him to lead. He shrugged and took a tentative step through that opening in the wall. He really couldn't see much as the light from the suns was directly in his eyes, but once inside it cut that wind and it immediately felt warmer. They stood side by side looking to either side of them seeing a large avenue that followed the base of the wall in both directions. And while broken and cracked it appeared to have been some type of hard surface now gray with time, but giving the appearance of having been originally a much darker color. Picking up a small fragment Jura asked, "What is this stuff?" Handing it over to Kal all he could do once he had it and had inspected it was shake his head in the negative.

Where the suns light were striking them they could see another avenue that moved directly towards the suns. Soon they would be high enough that what the bright sunlight was blocking would become visible. Kal pointed to their left and said, "Let's go that way for now. At least we'll be heading back in the direction that we came from." So quietly, as to not disturb any of the dead, they walked along the wall on the inside passing a number of shelters and avenues. All of the shelters that faced the wall were nothing but walls. There were no windows or doors at all. Yet when they passed the avenues between these shelters they could see small porches, doors, and windows. As they continued their circuit of this strange place they found that it was laid out in a circle with the avenues acting like lines heading to the center. Making it easy for anyone who had business towards the center to head back out to where they may have lived. These shelters appeared to be made of the same materials as the wall. Yet here they could see that many were damaged and that there had been fire in others. All that they were seeing, as far as the damage, had been reported in those writings. It was uncanny – the accuracy. It was like they arrived days later to find this place, and then describing what was found to a scribe so that it could be there for future generations. The clan of K'jor had done their job well.

Finally, with the suns to their backs, and both had to admit that it felt good; they were more clearly able to see the layout and the size. This place had to be as large as Cross Trails if not larger, and Cross Trails was one of the larger villages. So far they were only searching the outer areas of this dead silent world, and there was plenty to see. As they worked their way towards the center they found other avenues that ringed this place so that any could go to any portion within that they desired. They realized that they probably could easily spend a few 9-days and not see everything that was here. And they only had today in which to explore. They finally decided to choose the large shelter that was in the center of the, well what would they call it? So going back to the writings they learned that the ones who were called sorcerers had called them cities, whatever that was? So using that unfamiliar term they found themselves at the shelter in the very center of the city. It was larger than most that they had passed and this one had no windows, and the doorway was twice the size of the others that they had seen. Like the entrance into this place through that wall, the opening into this shelter was also open, and it appeared that the doors retracted in the same way. As they studied the doorway they could find no hinges that a door would have hung on, and there were grooves in the floor and wall showing where doors would have been.

As they entered it became darker and they had to wait until their eyes adjusted. Looking up they found that there had been openings created in the roof to let light in. Dust lay on everything, and there were no tracks of any kind here. So they would be the first to disturb the sleep of the dead, and the silence that permeated everything. As they crept across the floor they found that it wasn't just dirt, crushed stone or rough wood planking. There appeared to be something on it that formed patterns. Both of them crouched down and with their hands pushed away some of the dust to get a better view of what this was. It appeared to be large squares of some material that made the floor shine, and whatever these thing were, they formed an understated checkerboard pattern. "What is this stuff?" Jura asked.

Again this was something that was beyond them and Kal replied saying, "I don't know. And with this dust and dim light we're really not seeing it very well."

"Yeah, that's very true, but I sure would love to have something like this on my floor. It'd be so much easier to take care of and so much more pleasing than what we have."

As they crossed the room there seemed to be some type of equipment that lined one of the walls, but what this was and what it did was completely unknown. Afraid to touch any of it they stared in awe. There were chairs for people to sit, but again these were unlike any they had ever seen. Kal accidently bumped one as he was trying to get a closer look at what appeared to be a smoked glass panel and the chair moved away easily and actually the seat spun slightly. "Did you see that?" He asked

This place was making her nervous, almost frightened. There were things here she didn't understand and felt that she would never understand. It was another one of those moments that brought understanding to her as she realized that their ancestors probably had felt the same way. And for them it was a different situation. The writings stated that what was here seemed alive. But how could that be? What she was seeing didn't – couldn't have been alive, yet that is how they felt. This place almost made her believe in magicians. How else to explain this? "Yes, Kal, but I don't like the feel of this place at all. Can we go look somewhere else please?"

He could see that she was shaken so he nodded and they walked quietly to a railing that was on the far side and across from where they had entered. But once they reached the railing they were disappointed as there were no skylights to reveal what was below. The light barely penetrated and what could be seen were just the very edges of a floor further below and past those shadows nothing but darkness. Looking to the left both could see a set of stairs leading down in that darkness. Both were reluctant to use them and enter that dark area. They looked at each other and they could see that they were more than willing to leave things as they were. Kal walked over to the walkway and found what appeared to be a chain hung across the entrance and a small sign attached that simple stated "POWER UNIT # 1". These words meant nothing, and the script was foreign to their method of writing, so they couldn't even be sure that there was a meaning attached to what they were seeing.

They headed back outside and had to admit that it was great to be back out in the sunlight. Just what was it in that strange room inside that windowless shelter? "You know, like the bakery, this place could have been used for business or such, But, that's only a guess. I didn't recognize anything in there. Even the familiar things, like chairs, are very different." Kal looked around and the shelters he saw more or less reminded him of the village center. The place where business was handled, and when he thought about it the shelters they had first passed as they came here looked to be places where one would live. "I think we should look in some of these others that are close to this one, and then finish by looking in a couple that is further away from this center. What do you think?"

She didn't know what she thought other than she didn't want to go back into that one they had left. Still curiosity drove her on and she looked around seeing if any drew her attention. Looking across from where they were standing she spied one that seemed a little different. There appeared to be a curved area in front and a large round, well she wasn't sure what to call it, but in a way it looked a little like a bowl that they would serve soups and stews in. But this was huge. Pointing she said, "Let's go over there. I want to see what that thing is, and the whole front of that shelter appears to be made of glass or something like it. Look how it reflects everything. And I think if you look closely we can see us in it, and all the other shelters around."

Both headed over and inspected that large bowl like construction, and when they looked inside as they approached, there was nothing to indicate what it may have been used for. They found that the edges were large enough to sit and was of a height that invited one to do just that, so they sat down. At this point Kal looked at the sides that curved down and away from them and noticed some type of material sticking to the sides. He scraped a small piece off and studied it for a moment. "I think I know what was in this thing. I think it was water."

"Water? Really?" She leaned over and looked at what was sticking to the sides and realized that he was probably right. But this would mean there was a lot of water, and here, in the desolation? Where'd it come from? Looking at the center of this – what would she call it – an artificial pond, there appeared to be some type of sculpture, but again, what it represented or what it did was beyond them. Kal climbed in and carefully walked to the center where the sculpture was, walked around it and then joined her. "Well," she asked, "figure anything out?"

He shook his head and said, "No." At this point he climbed out. Shaking his head he thought, *another question to add to so many others. I really thought that this place was myth, and yet here it is. Then I thought that my ancestors had it wrong considering the people who lived and died here were sorcerers and magicians, and yet here we are this many cycle of the seasons later and I feel the same way. Can I blame them when I have the very same reaction?* This place was strange, foreign, beyond anything they could have imagined. That it was old was quite obvious. And yet, except for the dust of the ages that lay upon everything, one could imagine people living out their lives here today. But why in the desolation, and where did they get their water? They had to get it somewhere, and this thing that held all this water was proof. But again, where, and how? "Okay, another mystery. Shall we go inside this shelter then?"

She agreed and they once again entered through what appeared to be a double doorway with those mysterious doors that had retracted into the walls. Light streamed through those open doors and what appeared to be glass walls at least making the interior space brighter and more inviting. One of the first things they noticed was that it was cooler inside even with the open doorway. Although, as they moved back and forth, passing that entrance, they could feel the heat as it invaded this space. Just past the entrance was what appeared to be a large desk – one who was standing could comfortably approach and lean on. It seemed to be made of some polished wood, but where would that come from? Looking over again they saw those strange chairs and more of that equipment.

Looking back behind to the wall they saw normal doorways, a couple behind the desk and more running down the back wall to either side of the desk. On the front of the desk was another sign of that strange script that stated, "ADMINISTRATION".

Leaving the desk area, they walked up to a number of the doors, and each had a sign on them. All these doors were closed and appeared to be more along the lines of doors they were familiar with. They also saw a couple of areas where there was seating, and some strange machines marked with that strange script once again – one stating "SNACKS", and the other "BEVERAGES". Again, like their decision to leave the other shelter, they decided to leave without further exploration. Their time was very limited and they really couldn't spend much time on any particular shelter. And, once again outside, the bright light momentarily blinded them. "I think that you're right, this is just like our village center. I think I'd like to see how these people lived, so let's go out a little further and check out their personal shelters." Jura turned around and looked again at shelter they had just vacated and wondered what it was like when the living had been here. And at the same time felt lucky to even have the chance to find and explore this place. The writings spoke of the other lairs found, and their ancestors had destroyed these others with fire. With this being the first, their ancestors had simply attacked and killed the residents.

It was somewhere between the fifth mark and sixth, and their stomachs were reminding them that it was getting past the zenith and they hadn't taken time to eat anything. So once they had left that last shelter they looked around for any shade that they could find, finally settling on a shelter that had a small overhang. Here they leaned back against its wall, taking off their packs and digging out travel rations and a container of water. Their day was divided into ten marks as was the night. They were running out of time for this trip. And on the morrow they would have to make a quick trip back to the base camp in the grasslands. They had entered the desolation heavy, but would be returning light, and since they wouldn't be trying to locate the way to go, the return trip should be faster. They were quiet as they ate, not really tasting what it was that they ate as their eyes roamed these strange silent shelters. What had it been like when there were the living here? Yet, as it had been since they entered the desolation, they still felt as if they were watched, that this dead land, this dead lair was filled with spirits that watched everything that they did. But all that moved in this silent world was the winds, a bit of dust, and debris that the winds picked up. It was like they were the last of the living.

Jura shuddered saying, "I don't know about you but I've not been comfortable since we've entered the desolation, and once we came in here it's been worse. I feel like I want to panic, to run away screaming, from, oh I don't know what, but whatever. This place depresses me greatly, and I can't even tell you why." She fell silent not knowing what to add to what she had just said, yet she felt as there was more that needed to be said. "It's like, again, I don't know if I can even find the words . . ." Here she trailed off and just shrugged.

Quietly Kal responded, "I know. This place feels like death. Yet, when you look at the shelters, what is here, none of it reflects that – none of it at all. Okay, let's go through a couple of the ones we think that people probably lived in, and really our day will be close to over and we can leave this haunted land. And once we're back in our camp in the grasslands we can decide what we want to reveal later. But we will at least need to bring our writings up to date as to what we found here, and update our personal maps – especially if we ever want to come back . . . Although, truthfully, if I want to admit it, I really can't figure out why I would want to do that. Like you, I feel that this place, these lands, seem almost alive in the sense that it doesn't want us here and is letting us know. Making us feel uncomfortable, making us feel like we are being followed, watched. Yet, everywhere we look, every place that we've been, everything that we've touched shows no sign of the living – just us."

What could she say? It was exactly like this, and it made no sense, no sense at all. They got up from their zenith meal and randomly picked one of the larger shelters that appeared to be a place where one would live. One of the signs that they took for this was the doors. These doors were similar to what they were familiar with – none of the type that disappeared into the walls. Most of these shelters had small overhangs to project shade, and many of these areas had chairs made out of an unknown substance, furthering the illusion that the owners were away, and would be soon back. As had been the case of the large central shelters, many of the doors were open and the one that they had chosen was one of these. Before entering, they looked through the dirty windows that were located on either side of the entrance, but couldn't really see anything. So quietly they entered not knowing what they would find. Again, like when they had left that previous shelter, their eyes had to adjust to dim interior. So they waited a moment before continuing. The first thing they noticed was an odor that spoke of age. This room appeared to be a place for whoever had lived here to gather. There appeared to be something soft on the floor, and it covered the whole room. It kind of reminded them of rugs, but there never had been any of this size, or texture. It begged them to take their shoes off and walk barefoot across it. But it was also covered in dirt and sand that had blown in through the open door.

Now that their eyes had adjusted they went from room to room looking at what was here finally reaching what had to be the sleeping areas. Many of the rooms in this shelter had doors, which were a surprise, and one of the biggest surprises was upon opening one they found what they thought had to be the room where one took care of nature calls. This was something that was rarely part of the main shelter, but usually a small shelter close by. Plus there was a place to bathe, and clean up. There was a small frosted window which didn't admit much light, so most of what they saw was in heavy shadows. Yet, they felt that their conclusions had to be right. Thinking about it they didn't remember seeing any of those out-shelters when they had come into this place. Neither spoke as they searched and explored this shelter. It seemed that silence was appropriate. So they moved on to the next closed door.

Upon opening it they both stood shocked at what they saw. This had to be the sleeping area and on, well it wasn't a sleeping mat since it was much taller than that, were two bodies, more skeletal, although there still was skin attached. And it was obvious from the dark stains that surrounded them that they had been killed here and their blood had stained what had covered them. From what they could determine the two remains appeared to be male and female. They closed that door, went to the other side of the one that they had inspected before opening this one and opened another closed door. Here they found another room like the sleeping room, and in it were smaller versions of what the two had slept on, including one that had to be an infant sleeping mat. And like that other room, there were bodies here – obviously children. Both of them entered the room just far enough to be able to see the whole grisly scene. Jura picked up what had to be a child's toy and idly turned in her hands as she looked at the bodies.

Kal turned facing Jura and saw tears forming in her eyes, and a couple beginning to run down her cheeks. He could understand her feelings. Taking her into his arms, he gently led her back out of the room and quietly closed the door. The urge to explore more of this shelter was now gone, and he led her back outside where they sat on the chairs under the overhang feeling the warm breeze. He didn't say anything but let her cry it out. It was so different to have read it in the writings. Now facing the reality of what their ancestors had done shocked him, and he knew her. When the writings said that they had killed all that lived within this evil lair, it never dawned on either of them that this meant literally everyone – males, females, and all the young ones. How could they not have realized that? Breathing out quietly he asked, "Should we look through any of the others, or should we just leave and call it enough?"

Jura had finally quit crying and looking at him through her red rimmed eyes and dirt streaked face from where the tears had run she said, "I'm done. Let's just leave and let this place return to the ones who died here so very long ago." So quietly both of them got out of the chairs and headed back out through the doorway in that wall, back to their camp by the clan like ruins and shelters, packed everything that they were not going to need for this night and watched as the suns set, ending their time here in the desolation, even though they wouldn't exit until the morrow.

VALLEY OR NO VALLEY

They had all of the Season of Cold in which to bring their notes and thoughts up to date. Both had begun to realize the hard work that went into these searches, and to be prepared for anything when they discovered what they were searching for. Who'd thought that once those ruins were located in the desolation, with the passage of this much time, that there would still be evidence of what had transpired there – not either of them, that was for sure. Both learned that experiencing it had a much greater impact on them personally then reading it in the old writings. It seemed so much more impersonal. So much so that it was easy to separate one from the idea that real people had died, and from what evidence they had gathered with their brief time in those ruins, it became obvious to them that these people had no weapons. Yes, they had argued, their ancestors may have taken whatever weapons that these people had, but there was nothing in the writings suggesting such a thing, nor was there any proof on the ground that such existed. This meant, their people had attacked, and wiped out, a clan that had no way of defending themselves, resulting in the slaughter that they had discovered at that site, after all this time.

They had yet to come to any conclusion as to what they were going to reveal about their time in the desolation. After all, their main objective had been to locate the hunter's camp to demonstrate the range that their ancestors roamed. The trip into and the attempt to locate that first, again what was it these people had called it, oh yes, city, was just that. So that portion of their research writings and field notes they kept separately. Instead they wrote detailed notes covering the camp, from its layout and the finding of broken spear points and other artifacts. While all of this was true, it reflected more time than they actually spent, yet it gave the appearance that they had, thusly covering their time in the desolation. Those ruins felt haunted, felt as unseen, unknown eyes were watching them during their whole time there. And the ruins spoke of a difference, and a knowledge that was well beyond them even now. So, they felt that it should remain unknown to the world as it had until it was rediscovered sometime in the future. Later they might change their minds, but for now that place would remain vacant with its ghosts and spirits and be left alone by any from this time and world.

Once all of this had been written, discussed, edited, and finished to their satisfaction, it was time to prepare for the next season. They had plans on locating the mythological place, the Valley of the Gods. Until that incident recorded in the writings of not only K'jor's clan, but of many of the tribes and clans that had become part of the alliance, this valley had simply been the place of meetings and gatherings of the alliance. The place where they planned and carried out their attacks on what they called the sorcerers and magicians and their hidden lairs in the desolation. From their talk with that, well they still didn't know who he was or what to call him, so they settled on the wild one, they knew that the area they needed to search was north of where they lived in High Trail, and south of that hunting camp. And again, it had been located on the west side of the grasslands and had bordered the desolation with at least two ways directly into the desolation from it, but only one entrance from the grasslands itself. The description given in the writings suggested that it was located in an area of much broken land, with many dead end trails and canyons, and among all of this was the valley, a hidden oasis with grass, trees, and water, while much of the area was drier than the grasslands themselves.

Again, with their conversation with the wild one, they had gotten a better idea of what they faced, since he had stated that at one time he had actually been in that valley, but had never been able to find his way back. Suggesting that the entrance was well hidden and even if found could easily be lost again. Also, from the writings they had studied, they learned that the entrances, or at least one of them on the desolation side, was open and was very easy to travel. Although if one was looking at the entrance from the desolation, this one held no promise of going anywhere at all, looking like so many of the other dead ends. So if one didn't know, then with little promise of going anywhere it would be passed up and ignored. But both of them admitted that they had enough of the desolation and decided to try and locate the entrance from the grasslands, leaving the desolation entrance, if it still existed, until later if need be. But, again, it stated that when the gods had made their appearance that the two exits into the desolation had been destroyed, so these probably were not options anyway. Still they wouldn't know until they were actually in that valley.

Both had spent a lot of time in each other's arms after their grisly discoveries, making them realize that there was much on the outside that could influence their lives, and nothing was promised or guaranteed. What they had discovered there had changed both of them forever. Again what had started out as wanting to discover their true past, but not really being too serious, had turned to just that, and with the discovery this further changed their personal views of their world, their lives, and just how fleeting all of it was. Not that they weren't close, because they were, but these discoveries brought them even closer together, trying to live and accept every moment, knowing that they could end up being like those dead. Through the Season of the Cold, they spent time with their families, worked the business, and talked long and many times deep into the night. Family now meant everything to both of them, and both knew that someday they would have children, and raise the next generation who would continue in the ways of their families. This was the way it had always been, at least after the times of the clans and tribes, and should continue long into the future.

* * *

The Season of Green had been well along when they began this cycle of the seasons search. There still had been no word on the fate of Sabohl. His body had never been found, so this was still an unknown. With him out of the picture the others had replaced him in the hierarchy and new ideas were being put forth. With the discovery of the ancient clan site and the discoveries made there, some of what had been considered myth had been shown to be fact, requiring a reexamining of their history. Most of these new discoveries, because of those ancient writings that had remained within Kal's family from the time of the ending of the clans and tribes, were the maps, in words and drawings that led them to these places lost in time. Some of the discoveries included tools, long knives, and to their surprise some ancient bow strings – although, the bows themselves, hadn't survived the passage of time. And that left them with another mystery – who had created these items?

While the condition of these discoveries were poor, it was obvious that even with the abilities that they had now to forge knives and braid bow strings that gave the strings strength and longevity, these were far superior to what they produced. It was suspected that these were trade items from the travelers, who had stated, as quoted from the writings, "They lived in a cold wet place requiring their people to come up with solutions to prevent their bow strings from stretching when wet, and for the knives to hold an edge and not rust." Whoever these travelers were, they had been lost in time. Their home never located, and whatever methods they had used to create these items had been lost with them. So the tribes and clans coveted the few that had remained when the travelers came no more. And as it was the first time they had disappeared it was the last. There was no tapering off but a sudden and instant end, with no explanation or reason as to why, and thusly why these travelers had ended up as myth in the present time.

Still with the travelers being mentioned quite prominently in the writings, to both Kal and Jura, they had to be real. But that was for another time. They were out to locate the Valley of the Gods, again another location placed as myth. Because of what was known it would have been impossible for the incident described by so many of the clans and tribes to actually have happened – it just did not make any sense. Especially now, since they were aware of many of the laws of nature – not all by any means, but discoveries were being made all the time. So what had been witnessed by them, in that time, was tied to something they may have eaten that caused mass hallucinations. Yet with the consistency of what was reported, none could explain it away – so another mystery. And there seemed to be so many more of those mysteries than hard facts. Why was this so? Both of them wondered, since their ancestors had lived during that time, had recorded what they had witnessed. Of course it was interpreted by the way they viewed the world in their time. Still, even looking at it that way, no one could solve this riddle. This led to the theory that what had been witnessed in that valley was something that had changed over time and had become the myth that they now knew – but no one really knew.

So they had two and half seasons this cycle to attempt to locate the hidden valley. Fortunately, that accidental contact with the loner who roamed the outback had given them hints as to where to look. They remembered coming out of the desolation hot and tired, seeing the heat waves move across the landscape and what seemed to be a very large male standing there. He appeared to be twice the height of the normal male and they could see that he was watching them. So they approached cautiously not sure what they were going to face. And to find, as they got closer, his size began to shrink, and once nearly out of the desolation, they could recognize who it was. They didn't know why, but for some reason he had attached himself to them, showing up now and then to see what they had learned or found. It must have been something to do with his curiosity, his liking of puzzles. It was the only explanation that they had. Still that brief time with him, before once again he tired of being around people and disappeared, they had learned the general area where the hidden valley was located. So it was here that they would concentrate their exploring. Who knew, maybe this time it wouldn't take a couple of cycles of the seasons to locate this place.

Yet the word from the ones who had been in that area spoke of a broken land, a smaller version of the Sacred Mountains, some said. That led them to believe that it was probably the same forces that had formed both of these areas – although it was only a guess on their part. He, after all, was just a baker, and she a farmer. They headed out early in the morning on the eighth 9-day of the Season of Green, and headed north and west since High Trail was located on the eastern edge of the grasslands up against a number of low lying foothills. It was in these foothills that Jura and her family had farmed for generations. This trip would probably require at least two 9-days to reach the beginnings of the area that they wanted to search. Then from the description they had been given, they knew that they probably could spend the next several seasons there and not locate all the canyons, valleys, and hidden areas. There didn't appear to be any one person who knew the whole area. So over the time that they had spent back in High Trail, they had gathered what information was available and had a rough, albeit, inaccurate map of the area. Even with this, there were many blank areas and lots of conflicting information. They truly had their work set out before them. Still, with high hopes and copies of those ancient writings, they headed out.

* * *

They had already spent a 9-day in the area more setting up camp and getting a feel for the surrounding terrain. On the edges of this vast area it was hilly, and as they worked their way deeper into what they were now calling badlands they found sharp rises, cliffs, canyons cutting through plateaus, some areas heavy with trees, others with grass, and then like the desolation a few of what they saw was bare of any vegetation at all. It was a tortured broken land that one could easily get lost in. And when they first saw it they understood why their ancient ancestors had chosen this area. If an enemy were to attempt to follow them into these broken lands it was so very easy to spread out and disappear leaving the followers too many directions to go and by doing so weaken their own forces. The area had a raw rugged beauty about it that drew one in wanting to see what the next rise and valley would present. And this was a danger in itself – it would be easy to become lost, with the washes turning and twisting in multiple directions, branching off, and turning in on themselves. Many of these narrow canyons showed signs of heavy flooding, and because of their narrowness they also were in shadow a good part of the day. So using the suns as a way to determine direction, many times was impossible.

The area spoke of a rawness that said don't attempt to tame us, we have always been here and will be long after you are no more. It was a land of many streams, a few rivers, and many waterfalls. Here caves abounded with some hillsides filled with them giving the appearance of villages in the hills. At no time did they find sign of any ever having been here, let alone living here. They found that they could hike all day running through a series of those small narrow canyons only to turn a corner and find themselves looking at a large meadow being fed by one of those many streams and see in the distance another waterfall. And the waterfalls were of infinite variety. Some fell from great heights while others were a series of falls, and still others broke and split and ran off the cliffs in different directions. Never were there two alike, but each unique to itself. In some areas they could find long dead cinder cones, proof of this area's volcanic origin. Then close to a series of these cinder cones they found hot springs, and a series of geysers. Since this was the first time they had personally experienced geysers, even though they had read about them in the learning center, the view took their breath away leaving them in awe of what this world was showing them. Out of those hot springs ran small rivulets that created small streams, and as the water flowed, it left colored deposits on the soil adding further beauty to this hidden world.

Because of the remoteness of the area from any village or farmland, they kept their pack beast with them fearing that there could easily be some predator that would attack and kill it leaving them without a way to move their supplies. As they worked their way through the land they added to their maps, and while the maps in their mind were very incomplete, as the ones they were creating on parchment, slowly they were beginning to see and understand this place. A number of times as they had worked their way west they would find places where a particular canyon or valley that they were exploring would open into the desolation. Showing why this area had been chosen to organize those attacks on the hidden lairs. Yet, the prize eluded them. Time and time again they felt that they had been close, and studying the ancient rough map that they had in their possession, it looked right, or felt right, only to find that it wasn't so.

As the Season of Green moved on into the Season of Heat they were beginning to have doubts that the entrance would ever be revealed to them. Both were sure that they had to have gone by it a number of times. Both remembered the words of that wild one who stated that he had been in the valley once, but when trying to find it again could never relocate it. And knowing what they did about this one, if he couldn't return to it, then the entrance was well hidden and only circumstance and time of day would reveal it. Finally narrowing their search down to a specific area deep inside these badlands, they had set up camp after moving it from the hills just outside of the badlands. They had decided that they needed their working camp to be in the area that they were searching, and they had discovered enough meadowlands within to keep the pack beast fed. With a new site established, both were sitting watching the suns set over the cliffs off to their west, seeing the shadows grow and the light soften towards dusk, it had been another frustrating unsuccessful day. "Look, I don't know about you," Kal stated, "but I feel like we are so very close."

She laughed and asked, "How do you mean that?" She reached out and put her arms around him and asked, "Do you mean like this?" At which point she kissed him, smiled and pulled back, and leaned forward before continuing in a little more serious tone. "Know what you really meant, but I just couldn't help it. You just seemed so serious and your statement could have meant so many different things. But, I don't have any answers. Just like when we were trying to find that old clan home, we've run into obstacles and part of those is the map that our ancestors provided. Again, like we discovered last time, there's nothing consistent in what's up or what's down, or what direction is what. And some of the things they've used for landmarks have disappeared over time. Orientation is also hard to figure. Both of us have decided that if a tribe or clan were newly added that they would be given a map like this to lead them to the meeting place. But at the same time they left something out so that if the map fell into the hands of an enemy they couldn't discover this meeting place and set up an ambush."

"Yeah, and the problem that both of us are facing is that we can't speak to any of them since they've been dead for such a very long time. So without that verbal key we're banging our proverbial head against a wall."

"True, true, at least we can say we've seen some very beautiful country, and seen sights that others haven't. So if nothing else is to come of this we have that."

He couldn't help but smile. She always had a way of bringing out the good side of what they did, even if he hadn't seen it at the time. "You are so right. This whole area is very beautiful, and because of its isolation very few come here. So it's almost like we're the first, even though we know better."

They spent the night in each other's arms. It had been one of those romantic nights with the major moon rising giving the lands a magical feel leading them to being physical a couple of times. Finally satiated from their love making they both fell to sleep with a soft warm breeze coming off the desolation which lay to the west of them. The night was slowly cooling and later before the morning chill made them cover up; they remained on top of their sleep sacks with only a light covering to keep them warm. And with the morning both of them took a quick invigorating dip in pond that they had camped close to. Shivering from the cold water both headed back to the roaring fire that they had built before heading for that morning dip. Wrapping a drying cloth around themselves they absorbed the heat the fire was throwing out.

Finally they grabbed their clothes that had been placed close to the fire, dressed, enjoying the warmth of the clothing on their cool skin. Finally warm and with only their hair now wet, Kal walked out and away from their camp while today Jura had the kitchen duty and was fixing the morning meal. It had been a magical end to the day and a wonderful night last night. Still, they were no closer to solving this puzzle. And when he thought about it that way, it brought a smile to his face, since that wild one liked puzzles and had dropped in on them a number of times since that first visit so long ago. Well they surely had one here. Kal knew that they were close. This area where they were camping matched well an area on that primitive map that marked a gathering place that was close to the hidden entrance into the valley. He stood and watched as the suns began their daily rise above the canyon walls promising the heat that would be arriving soon. Yet right at this time the heat the suns produced felt great. About this time he heard Jura say that the food was on, and if he wanted it hot he'd better get over here. Turning around and smiling, even though, because he was between her and the suns, so she couldn't actually see him well, he said, "Yup, that's how I like my food, and my female – hot." This brought a laugh out of both of them as he came back to the fire and joined her.

Later, after the camp had been cleaned up, and the suns were up high enough to cast some deep shadows, they began to study the canyon walls that surrounded them. Seeing how the lay of the land truly was. Both sat on a small rise arm in arm, enjoying the peace and slight breezes that surrounded them at this very moment. It seemed that all was right with the world, and with them, as they reveled in each other's company, not speaking, but enjoying the closeness, the quiet, and each other. What more could they ask for? Well, other than the shadows revealing the trail into the valley, but there was a warmth, a deep companionship here, and both realized that these forays into the wilds had made them ever so much closer, so much deeper in love with each other, leaving them with a deeper commitment and desire to be with the other. It was one of the important aspects of these searches that hadn't originally been considered. They spent the time this way until midmorning talking about nothing and just holding each other.

Finally Kal said, "I think I could spend all day just doing this, and by the gods, why not. After all a down day now and then is nice and necessary, so let's just take a leisurely stroll around this canyon and just idly look around, take it easy and not push anything today. This day, so far has been very nice. I feel the need just to be close to you today – can't explain it, but it's so."

She smiled, even though it was one of those rare shy smiles. She'd been thinking the same thing actually. The last day or so she found herself being drawn closer to him, and last night had been wonderful, and now today it just seemed right to let it just continue. She looked into his eyes and said, "You're not going to get me to argue. I feel very much the same way. So, I know what you said, but is there something specific?"

He smiled back at her and said, "No, not really. I know originally we were going to do some searches here, but it can wait. Just let the day become what it will. Although with last night being as good as it was, I think that if the day goes as well, I'd like to repeat it if we could."

She laughed. "I thought as much. But you're not going to get me to argue after all I agree with you, it was wonderful last night. Okay, we'll take the day as it comes and then we'll see."

* * *

After a very relaxing day the day before both felt recharged and ready to tackle their task at hand. They really couldn't remember the last time that they had taken a full day to just enjoy each other and block out the world. But time moves on, and it was now in the past. With the primitive map in hand they were comparing the landmarks on the map with the canyon they were presently in, and so far had been unsuccessful in making anything match once they got beyond the area that they had identified as the initial gathering area before heading into the valley. With no distances marked they could still easily be at least a day away or it could be here. But with all the growth of the trees and bushes nothing was easy. Yes there were a few trails through this stuff which allowed them to approach the canyon walls, but all of it was hard going. Where they had their camp was grasslands like where they came from, a rather large meadow, but as they approached the water flowing through this canyon, the trees became thick as did the bushes. And for whatever the reason, it seemed that these bushes were thickest at the canyon walls.

Another 9-day had passed without much success when, as the suns were setting they watched a shadow fall wrong across one of the faces of the cliff. It should have lain straight against the wall but instead dipped and disappeared showing that there had to be a crack or something else here that wasn't normally visible to the eye. So with the fading light they quickly headed towards this illusion before darkness claimed it. And if that happened they weren't sure that they could come back to this place and find it again. The wild one had stated that he had only found the entrance by following his intended target and after leaving had never been able to find his way back. So if one did not mark the entrance, the chances of finding it again were close to zero. Most surprising of all was the fact that the area they were heading to, was out in the open, not blocked by either trees or bushes. It was a spot that they had passed by, who knew how many times, giving it little thought. They had studied this face a number of times but have never seen anything to would lead them to believe that there was a way through. This wall appeared to be solid.

Even as they approached the wall they couldn't see the break in it and once they reached it, it still wasn't obvious. No wonder this trail had never been found and thusly had been placed in the myth category. If there was no way into such a place, then the place probably did not exist, and if it did not exist it had to be myth. And it was now almost too dark to see so one of them stood at the point where the shadow had appeared and the other went quickly to gather what stones they could find to place a small cairn here to mark it so that in the morning when they would have the whole day ahead of them they could come back to the exact location and do a much better search. It would be awhile before the minor moons rose tonight, so with care they stumbled back to their camp full of energy and anticipation for what they would discover on the morrow. In a sense it was frustrating to both of them, but there was little they could do about it. Of course what was there could turn out to be just another dead end. There were breaks and cracks all through the walls of this canyon and most were just that. So the odds were that this would be the same. But, this couldn't be answered at this time.

It was late before they could wind down enough to sleep, and with their expectations high they had a wonderful physical session that left both of them breathless. They lay in each other's arms for quite a while afterwards, and slowly their breathing eased and both fell asleep until later when the chill of the night finally penetrated and they climbed into their sleep sacks, and fell immediately back to sleep. Both surely hoped that, with all the time they had spent in this broken rugged land, with the Season of Heat winding down, and the time of harvest was fast approaching, this was what they had been searching for. They were once again running out of time. One did not remain out here in the Season of Cold. It was obvious to them as they had explored the many canyons and valleys. There were signs of flash floods and high water everywhere. So it was an area to stay away from if one wanted to remain among the living.

The morning broke bright and cold. One of the signs that signaled the Season of Falling was approaching. The morning chill had a bite to it that made them want to stay close to their fire. Their breath was coming out in clouds, being quite visible in the morning light, before evaporating and disappearing completely. Looking over at Jura, Kal thought. *She doesn't look so good this morning – hope she's not getting sick or something.* "Is something wrong? You're looking a little off this morning."

She smiled at him even though it was a weak one. "Don't think so, but my stomach seems a bit queasy this morning and these smells that usually seem to cheer me up almost make me sick just by smelling them."

He saw a surprised look on her face and she got up rapidly and headed back behind their portable shelter and he heard her throw up, not once but several times. Yeah she definitely had caught something. This surely would put a damper on the day and what they had hoped to discover, but her health was so much more important to him than finding that entrance. He watched her as she came back around, appearing to be a little shaky, and sit back down. "That was unpleasant", he said. No sooner had he said that that she was immediately back up and headed once more behind the portable shelter and he heard her heave again. *Wow, whatever it is its nasty.* "Are you all right?" He asked He heard a bit of mumbling but couldn't make out what she said. Finally after a while she finally came back around and sat down once again, looking a bit white under her dark tan. "I guess we'll just stay in camp today and see how this progresses with you. I'm not going to leave you by yourself when you're obviously sick." He could see that she was about to protest, but he put up his hand to silence her, shaking his head he said. "Look, this can wait, you are what is important. Not some old trail or valley that will still be there long after you and I are gone. So don't protest, we still have time . . . I just don't want you getting any worse."

This had come out of nowhere and was completely unexpected. She had felt great last night, and buoyed by their possible success yesterday it had even given her more energy, and she had to admit that last night they'd been as close as they ever had been, actually almost desperate for the need of each other. This had only happened a few times in their relationship and every time that it had happened in the past, they would look forward to those rare times when it would show once again. *So, why now?* What did she catch? Well, whatever it was she didn't want it to be around very long, they had too much to do, and the seasons were winding down once again towards the time when they would have to abandon what they were doing. She watched, as Kal puttered around the camp, watching her as she tried to put on a happy face trying to look better than she felt. Inwardly she had to smile, because the concern that he showed was very genuine, and she had to admit that she appreciated it very much. With their research of the past she had become very knowledgeable of how life had been for females and it wasn't pretty, nice, or anything that she could think that she'd want to live or do.

Yet, as the morning progressed her stomach began to settle down and she wasn't feeling like she'd need to go behind their portable shelter and lose whatever was still there. Truthfully, with all she had done this morning there really couldn't be much left. Sitting there she drank cold water and attempted a little of that bland travel bread that they had with them. She wasn't sure if she wanted to put any food into her system, but felt that she needed to try. The last thing she really wanted to do was repeat her earlier episode. Gingerly she nibbled the bread, and drank a lot of water and found that she could keep it down. Then, to her surprise, she felt fine. *So what is that all about anyway?* "Kal, I think the worst is over, so why don't we go over and at least look. It's really not that far, and if I begin to feel bad again it's a short distance back to here."

He looked her over carefully, and still could see some paleness underneath her tan, but at the same time she didn't appear to be as drawn out as earlier. He breathed out deeply still concerned saying. "I know, but are you sure?" He walked up behind her and gave her one of those shoulder rubs that she loved and heard her respond as she sighed with pleasure. "We can wait, we really can."

Looking over her shoulder and up at him she said, "That really does feel good, but I'm okay. It seems whatever that this was has faded and right now I'm good to go."

Still reluctant he shrugged. "Okay, I'll let you set the pace, and if you feel like you need to come back and lay down or something just say the word and we can come back."

She stood up, looked him in the eyes, smiled, saying, "Works for me." And headed off in the direction where they had discovered that crack in the wall. He paused as he watched her walk away, shook his head, shrugged, and then followed.

It took them the rest of the morning to reach the split in the wall – not that this was the only such place. They had checked out a number of these cracks or splits finding the rest nothing but what they appeared. As they approached, they looked at the ground and could see a subtle trail or path that appeared to be heading directly into that crack, and once they reached and studied what was there, were really surprised by the size of the opening. There was some low lying brush that had grown over the opening and this crack ran parallel to the cliff making it appear to be just a small crack unless one happened to be standing at the right place to see that it went deeper then it appeared. Once they entered into it, they got their second surprise. The actual entrance was narrow but immediately past that point it opened up wide enough that they could walk side-by-side. Still the cliff walls remained tight along this trail making it impossible to go anywhere but along this trail. And because of the steepness of the sides and the overall narrowness, the trail remained in deep shadow furthering its invisibility. Absolutely nothing to show that this trail had existed from the outside, making it easy to overlook.

She shivered briefly because of the change in temperature, leaving the sunny canyon that they had been in to this perpetually shadowed trail. With her shiver she could see once again his concern. She smiled and again confirmed that she was all right and they continued hiking down this hidden twisting trail that literally cut through the mountain. They truly didn't know how long they had been following this trail but suddenly it made a sharp left, and like the entrance from the other canyon, suddenly dumping them into a very beautiful valley – a valley that appeared to be completely enclosed. And the trail – the one that they had used to enter the valley – giving the appearance of being the only access, although a well-hidden one as they had found out, had to be the one used by their ancestors. Since, like the other side, this point appeared to be as well hidden, they quickly built another cairn to insure that they could find their way back out. The suns were well towards late in the day when they exited into this hidden valley, so removing their packs and taking a quick break they decided that they would make the trip back. There was no time left to do any exploring at all. On the morrow they'd pack everything and move into this valley to explore it and see what hidden secrets would be here. At this moment they really didn't know if this hidden valley was the legendary Valley of the Gods or not. As twisted and broken as the land was here, this could just be another of the hundreds. Kal, watching Jura carefully, couldn't see anything that reflected that illness she had earlier in the morn so was at a loss as to what had happened. So with dusk not far off they headed back out the trail, pushing so that it wouldn't be completely dark by the time they reached their camp.

Yet when they awakened next morning she again was ill. Just what was going on with her? It seemed like her stomach couldn't handle anything in the mornings, well at least the last two anyway. And again, like yesterday, after a short period of time and eating of the travel bread, things settled down, and they made their move, packing up everything and moving deeper into the broken land. With their pack beast they reached their destination just a little earlier, set up their camp close to the pathway in and out of this canyon. And in the distance they could see some wild herd beasts grazing, and every once in a while staring at them as if they had never seen the likes of them before. They could hear falls, although, because it was cross canyon from them, it was muted somewhat, and not too far from where they had set up their camp, the stream worked its way across the valley and disappeared somewhere towards the herd beasts. And as the suns set, it was on a beautiful, peaceful, tranquil setting. It would be another day before the true exploring would begin, and with the seasons slipping away as they were this would be close to the end of the search for another cycle of the seasons.

Marking off on their calendar the end of another 9-day, they sat around their campfire enjoying the peace that seemed to permeate this place. Slowly as the heat of the day dissipated and the chill of the night arrived, with its soft down canyon breezes, they moved closer to the fire saying nothing and enjoying what was being offered. Finally Kal spoke saying, "If this place isn't the Valley of the Gods, it surely could be. I can't remember feeling this free of worries or having to think about ways to keep the predators away from our pack beast. It's like we're away from the worries of this world, and such things aren't allowed here. I know that it's just an illusion, but at this moment that's the way it feels to me."

Jura thought a moment, and nodded her head in agreement. Yet there was that nagging worry as to what was causing her to be sick in the mornings, and yet feel okay the rest of the day. Just what was going on anyway? Still, he had a point; this place seemed to emanate a quiet and peace that they hadn't felt anywhere else. She sighed, for some reason she felt that all was right with the world and that didn't make sense. Maybe it had something to do with the atmosphere here in this hidden place – one of so many in this area. "Yes, I feel it too. But I don't know why. And maybe it's not important to know why, but to just accept it and leave it at that."

* * *

This is getting old, she thought as she was again behind their portable shelter heaving her guts out. *What is happening to me? And whatever it is, why is this only happening in the morning, and I feel normal the rest of the day? And why is it that that really bland, travel bread seems to be the only thing that settles this down and I'm fine the rest of the day?* She had no answers to these questions and she knew that Kal didn't. She could see the worry on his face since this was the third day in a row that this was taking place. They were far from anyone who could help if this turned out to be more than a nasty inconvenience. Yet, at the moment that's all it seemed to be. She had never liked throwing up, and hated the taste it left in one's mouth, but just couldn't keep it from happening. Well, maybe it would go away in a few days – although, she had to admit, if today was the day it went away it wasn't soon enough. Once this bout was finished she headed for the fire and the bread that he handed her. There was little else he could do. Again like the other two days once she had gone through the episode, had eaten that bread, her stomach would settle down, even though certain smells would make her queasy, but once past this point she'd be okay.

With the suns rising over the walls that surrounded this valley, they viewed an idyllic scene making both want to sit and watch as the day came alive. It was time to explore the valley and see what was really here. So they started by doing a circuit around by going from right to left as one looked to the center of the valley. As they headed this way they could hear the sounds of the waterfall getting louder, and as they turned a small corner, they could see the full falls in front of them. They could see that as time had passed that it had cut back creating this deeper indentation in the cliff walls. And that's exactly what you would have called them – walls. As they looked around the valley it appeared that all the walls were almost vertical. Climbing them would be next to impossible. As they approached the falls, the mist off them cooled the area and created small rainbows as the sunlight filtered through the mist. The beauty almost took their breath away. Still standing here they began to chill and moved on back into the sunlight to get warm once again.

On this first time around they carried nothing but some water and food for a zenith meal if they were out and away from their camp that long. Later when they began their serious exploration of this valley they'd bring their noting materials so that they could write down their first impressions, and what they discovered here. Once they had warmed, they continued their trek around the perimeter, and soon discovered a number of caves in one of the faces, and what appeared to have been a possible exit that had long been closed from what looked to be a landslide. Guessing at the location of this closed exit they could see that it might have led to the desolation. They knew that they had to be close and this one seemed to point west. And as the suns continued to climb into the sky they found that this place was actually much larger than they first thought. It was nearing the zenith and they guessed that they were less than half way around the perimeter. Soon they'd break eat their midday meal and finish the circuit.

The valley had many areas that formed offshoots from the main area, enlarging its size tremendously, and it was close to dusk by the time they had made the initial circuit getting a feel for the size and shape. This valley seemed to be a world untouched by any. There seemed to be a peace that lay over the area – one that they could more sense than feel. So when they finally reached their basecamp, they were relaxed. It seemed more like an outing than them exploring a hidden valley deep in the badlands. They thought that most likely they had located what could have been originally exits to west out of this valley. Exits that probably emptied into the desolation, but so much time had passed since these routes existed that it was difficult to tell whether it was their imagination or what they surmised was correct. The only way they truly would know would be to locate, from the desolation, the other side where these blocked trails exited. But that would be for a later time, if they felt the need to confirm what they had concluded.

So with night they watched as the major moon rose over the cliffs and lit the area with a soft ghost like light that made the valley even more magical. They could almost see spirits move through the grass and trees, crossing the small stream. But all they truly heard were the night crawlers as they sounded off looking for a mate. And since the sound was unbroken they knew that nothing was out there. If there had been a danger, then they would have fallen silent – silent until that danger or perceived danger had disappeared. So, with this music in their ears they fell asleep in each other's arms, knowing that on the morrow they would begin to search the center of this hidden paradise, and soon, and very soon, be heading back to their home.

* * *

As had become the norm for Jura, she went through her normal bout of throwing up, but instead of grumbling about it came back from behind the shelter smiling. Kal looked at her questioningly as she sat down next to him and put her arms around him and laid a big kiss on his mouth. "What was that for?" He asked, quite surprised by her actions.

"Well, mate of mine I have to say I have been a little slow to recognize what this is all about." Here she laughed

"All about?" He looked around and asked, "Are you meaning what we are doing? I thought we knew all about that."

Again she smiled and just shook her head. "I see you're just about as dense as I've been. Haven't you figured this out yet?"

Still at loss at the point she was trying to make, all he could do was shake his head – again not sure where she was leading him – although, as far as he was concerned, she could lead him wherever she wanted.

"Okay . . . look, and think about it. What would cause a female to be sick in the morning and then get better as the day goes on?"

He got this look in his eyes and suddenly realized what she had been trying to tell him. "Are you saying that you think you are carrying?"

With that she laughed again and threw her arms around him and said, "Yes!"

He sat there stunned. It was the last thing he expected. Although he couldn't deny that they had been quite physical out here. But it was the very last thing he expected. "Wow", was all he could say. He then hugged her back, completely at loss for any words. He whispered once again, "wow."

With that news it changed the atmosphere for both of them but they were close to returning anyway, and this early in the carrying would only mean the morning sickness and very little else. It would be later that problems could develop and that would be under the care of the females that helped other females through this time in their lives.

As they worked their way to the center of the valley, and in an area filled with tall grass they found it. The alter they all had read and studied back in the learning centers. It was facing the section of the cliffs that the waterfall bordered. In front of the altar was a wall, which was built of stone but was only about knee high. They saw that its shape was such that it formed a "V" and the point of that "V" pointed in the direction of the same cliffs where the altar faced. So, it had been here in this very valley, so very long ago in the past that their ancient ancestors had met their gods face to face, changing the name forever to the Valley of the Gods. Although how that truly came about and what had happened here still was an unknown, a mystery that may never have a true answer. They knew that such gods did not exist, and that there were natural laws at play, for which no gods controlled. There was one creator who had created everything, as they saw and understood it, and laid the laws of this world down, and would not have appeared as their ancestors had insisted that their gods had.

So understanding and solving this part would come to others. While they had yet to accomplish everything they had set their sights upon, with the carrying that Jura was now doing, it would have to wait for another time. And who really knew if that other time would arrive? Their desire to search the Sacred Mountains would now be on hold, for who knew how long. And maybe in the end it would fall to one of their ancestors to discover those hidden secrets, those other mysteries that lay deep in those mountains. They had accomplished what they had set out to do – changing myth to fact – proving the family writings to be accurate and it was enough. Now they had their true lives ahead of them and it was very promising – yes, very promising indeed. Much of their past had been what they had searched and discovered, but it was another generation's past. Yet, with the knowledge gained, changing myth to fact, they now knew much of their true past and the influences on their world. Now was the time to create their own history from their present, and with the changes that this had wrought, their future appeared to be truly strong – strong indeed.

EPILOGUE

With the suns rising it promised to be another hot and humid day. He was alone on this island and how he had arrived here was a blur and how he would find a way off an unknown. At least there was fresh water and plenty of food – although his choices were few. He looked to the east once again as he had done every day since arriving here. It had been difficult at the beginning and the passage of time hard to track. There only appeared to be two seasons here – wet and dry. So he guessed that he must have been here for approximately three cycles of the seasons, but he had no way to track the passage of time accurately. The island was large enough to provide support for a small population, at which he laughed bitterly, since at the moment, it was a population of one. His clothes were rags, a remnant of their former selves.

He cursed his lack of control over his anger for what was probably the thousandth time. Had he controlled it that night then he wouldn't be here now. But that was the past, and again he laughed bitterly since the past was his specialty. But no more, no, he was stuck. He couldn't see the mainland that was just over the horizon, so he paced his prison. After all that's what it really was. At least it might as well have been. He knew that there were small boats that worked the large sea, but rarely came to these islands. There was nothing to attract them here. Some day that could change, or maybe some sailor would get brave and want to see what was out here, but for now here he was. He truly missed the game, the fencing between his rivals and himself. He wondered what had happened to those two and if they had been successful in what they were trying to accomplish. But here there were only the winds, the island, the sandy beaches, and the squawking of the feathered fliers.

He remembered that night, when his anger drove him into the wrong part of the village, the fight that had followed – the collapsing of that old dock after he had received that wound. Yet, even as he recounted this he smiled. Before that knife wound he had taken four of the bastards out. He still had it. But then that dock collapsed and into that rain gorged river he went with the rest of them. He had been lucky that he had found a major piece of that dock and had clung to it as it tore down that river trying to shake him off as a beast shook water off its back. Yet somehow he had remained with it. Eventually exhausted he had passed out, only to find that it was broad daylight and he was now in the sea when he had awakened. And at that time panic had risen as there was no land in sight. And in whatever water flow he was in, it continued to push him west. Somewhere during this time he passed out again only to awaken when he found himself beached on this island and that had been a long time ago.

Sabohl paced the eastern shore walking the beaches looking east. *Someday, yes someday I'll get off this island. Then all of you had better watch out – because, when I return, and this will happen, I will reclaim what I have lost.* He smiled as his thoughts reached out for that distant hidden shore. Yes someday he'd leave this prison, this island, and the world better be ready.

F. D. Brant

F. D. Brant

ABOUT THE AUTHOR

F.D. Brant always wanted to write, but life got in the way.
Finally after retiring he got his chance.

Storytelling and writing has always been F.D. Brant's passion,
but responsibilities took preference. And because of those
responsibilities it took retiring to allow those passions to come
to fruition. Since retiring he has written 9 books, and
maintains a weekly eclectic blog, Words in the Wind.

Growing up in the backcountry he learned the appreciation of "doing things for yourself". Because it was impossible to call in someone to repair anything one either did it themselves or went without. This led to the appreciation of the natural world, and the daily struggles that one faced as nature threw problems at the family that had to be overcome, leading to confidence and self-sufficiency. This led to the strong characters that populate his stories and books. And his female protagonists are strong willed and confident – something that he saw in both in his mother and sister.